James Gray Stevens

A digest of the reported and unreported cases

James Gray Stevens

A digest of the reported and unreported cases

ISBN/EAN: 9783741194641

Manufactured in Europe, USA, Canada, Australia, Japa

Cover: Foto ©Andreas Hilbeck / pixelio.de

Manufactured and distributed by brebook publishing software
(www.brebook.com)

James Gray Stevens

A digest of the reported and unreported cases

A DIGEST

OF THE

REPORTED AND UNREPORTED CASES

DETERMINED IN THE

SUPREME COURT OF JUDICATURE

OF THE

PROVINCE OF NEW BRUNSWICK.

FROM THE YEAR 1825 TO EASTER TERM 1873 INCLUSIVE, WITH SEPARATE TABLES OF NAMES OF CASES AND A TABLE OF CONTENTS.

TOGETHER WITH

AN APPENDIX.

CONTAINING

THE RULES OF COURT,

ALPHABETICALLY ARRANGED AND COLLATED FROM THEIR COMMENCEMENT TO THE PRESENT TIME.

BY

JAMES GRAY STEVENS, Esquire,

One of the Judges of the County Courts of New Brunswick.

SAINT JOHN, N. B.:

J. & A. McMILLAN, PRINTERS AND PUBLISHERS, 78 PRINCE WM. STREET.

1874.

To The Honorable

JOHN CAMPBELL ALLEN,

One of the Judges of the Supreme Court of Judicature of the Province of New Brunswick.

Sir,—

In dedicating this Work to you, in grateful acknowledgment of your kindness, I am but returning, in great part, the results of your own labour.

My efforts, in the preparation of the Digest, have been stimulated by your ready co-operation.

In the benefit that the Legal Profession may receive from the Digest, you will seek your reward.

In your approval of the Work, and its use to that Profession, I shall not be wanting in mine.

JAS. G. STEVENS.

PREFACE.

In the following Digest I have endeavored to embody, in a classified form, the various Decisions of the Supreme Court of the Province of New Brunswick, as contained in the Published Reports of Messrs. Berton, Kerr, Allen and Hannay, and the Manuscript Reports of the late Chief Justice Chipman, published in 1849, as edited and prepared by the present Mr. Justice Allen.

The Digest also contains the Principal Cases unpublished in any of the above Reports, embracing a period from the year 1825 to Easter Term 1873 (inclusive), these latter numbering upwards of five hundred Notes, containing Decisions on the most important departments of Common Law and Equity, and Equity Practice.

I have gratefully to acknowledge my great obligation to Mr. Justice Allen in having, with a most willing liberality, not only placed these latter Notes at my disposal, but also in great part prepared them for publication with the utmost care, and at the expenditure of much labour, and by which the value of the Digest has been materially enhanced.

I have likewise further to acknowledge his valued assistance rendered me in epitomizing and condensing in many cases the abstracts of the Judgments contained in the published Reports.

It is to be much regretted that the Cases, of which but a note is given, have not been continuously published in full, and that so many *hiatuses*, so to speak, have been permitted in reporting the Decisions of our Court, marked, as all along they have been, by so much legal ability and learning, and justly claimable as common available property; it is so far well that they are now in some manner and extent preserved,—a circumstance mainly attributable to the attention and labour of Mr. Justice Allen.

As to the mode in which the Digest is prepared, I am alone responsible. I have endeavored to classify the Cases under appropriate titles most likely to occur to the mind of the professional man, and whilst I have endeavoured to avoid unnecessary repetition, the matter has been frequently referred to under different heads, facility of reference being kept always in view.

Appended to the Digest, are the Rules of Court, alphabetically arranged and collated for ready reference.

I have to acknowledge the kind assistance rendered me by I. Allen Jack, Esq., in supervising the proof sheets, thus having relieved me from labour, and greatly forwarded the publication of the Work.

The typographical execution will, I feel confident, meet with approval, and whilst there will be found some errors in names and in cross references, these are attributable to my own oversight, not to any fault in the printer, and are of an immaterial nature, the errors in the cross references chiefly occuring in the letter A. I have in part noticed them in an Errata, and the professional student will understand and rectify the mistakes.

An index of Names of Cases is given separately, distinguishing the published and unpublished Cases.

How far I have succeeded in presenting a creditable Digest, I leave the Profession to judge, conscious, that notwithstanding its many defects and desirable amendments, now apparent, I have spared neither time nor labour in endeavoring to make it acceptable to them to whose generous consideration and use it is now submitted.

JAS. G. STEVENS.

October, 1873.

CHIEF JUSTICES

AND

JUDGES OF THE SUPREME COURT,

FROM THE FIRST SITTING OF THE COURT IN 1785 TO THE PRESENT TIME.

CHIEF JUSTICES.	Appointed.	Resigned.	Died.	
George Duncan Ludlow,	Nov. 25, 1784		Nov. 13, 1808	
Jonathan Bliss,	June 28, 1809		Oct. 1, 1822	
John Saunders,	Oct. 19, 1822		May 24, 1834	
Ward Chipman,	Sept. 29, 1834	Mich. Va. 1850	Nov. 26, 1851	
Sir James Carter,	Jan. 8, 1851	Sept. 1865		
Robert Parker,	Sept. 22, 1865		1865	
William J. Ritchie,	Dec. 6, 1865			
JUDGES.				
James Putnam,	Nov. 25, 1874		1780	
Isaac Allen,	Nov. 25, 1784		Oct. 12, 1806	
Joshua Upham,	Nov. 25, 1784		1808	
John Saunders,	Oct. 20, 1790		May 24, 1834	Chief Justice.
Edward Winslow,	July 2, 1807		July 1815	
Ward Chipman, Sen.,	June 28, 1809		Feb. 9, 1824	
John Murray Bliss,	July 9, 1816		Aug. 22, 1834	
Edward J. Jarvis, (temporary appointment from October 1822 to April 1823.)				
William Botsford,	April 2, 1823	December 1845	May 8, 1864	
Ward Chipman,	March 17, 1825	Mich. Va. 1850	Nov. 26, 1851	Chief Justice.
Sir James Carter,	July 12, 1834	Trin. Va. 1865		Chief Justice.
Robert Parker,	Oct. 6, 1834		1865	Chief Justice.
George Frederick Street,	Dec. 20, 1845		1855	
Lemuel A. Wilmot, (appointed Lieut. Governor of New Brunswick, July 1868.)	Jan. 8, 1851			
Neville Parker, M. R., (Court of Chancery was abolished, and the Master of Rolls was transferred to Supreme Court by Act 17 Vic. c. 67.)	1854		August 1870	
William J. Ritchie,	Aug. 17, 1855	Present		Chief Justice.
John C. Allen,	Sept. 22, 1865			Puisne Judges.
John W. Weldon,	Dec. 6, 1865			
Charles Fisher,	October 1868			
A. Rainsford Wetmore,	May 25, 1870			

TABLE OF CONTENTS.

A.

D.

E.

Q.

R.

ANALYTICAL DIGEST

OF

DECISIONS OF THE SUPREME COURT OF NEW BRUNSWICK,

FROM 1825 TO HILARY TERM 1873, INCLUSIVE.

ABANDONMENT.

Of joint trespass, on trial. See Trespass, 25.

Of right to vote. See Election, 2.

ABATEMENT.

See Pleading, II. Bills and Notes, VI. 9.

Proceedings against Absconding Debtor not abating by death of debtor. See Absconding Debtor, 12.

Items included in previous suit. See Action at Law, VIII.

Husband and Wife. Death. See Husband and Wife, 2.

ABSCONDING DEBTOR.

1—Supersedeas.

The Court has no power under 26 Geo. 3, c. 13, to grant a Supersedeas of a Warrant of Attachment, issued against the goods of a concealed debtor, unless it appears that all the creditors consent thereto. *Ex parte Gove. Ber.* 187.

2—Refusal to grant Prohibition.

The Court refused a rule either for a prohibition or *certiorari*, in regard to proceedings under the Absconding Debtors Act, 26 Geo. 3, c. 13, taken before a Judge of an Inferior Court of Common Pleas, it not appearing, upon the affidavits, that the Judge had acted illegally in any part of the proceedings. Application had been made to the said Inferior Court to stay the proceedings, but it did not appear that such application was in the form prescribed by the seventh section of the Act, and the Court, after hearing the parties, made no order in the case. *Ex parte Waite*, 1 *Kerr*, 175.

3—Right of Trustees to maintain Trover.

The trustees of an absconding debtor, duly appointed under the Act 26 Geo. 3, c. 13, may maintain trover to recover the value of certain goods of the debtor, wrongfully converted by the defendant before any proceedings taken under the Act; such right of action being transferred by the operation of the Act from the debtor to the trustees. *Ritchie* v. *Boyd*, 1 *Kerr* 264.

4—Debtor Administrator—Right of Trustees in Property.

Under the Act of Assembly 26 Geo. 3, c. 13, the Trustees of an absconding debtor do not become entitled to the property and credits held by such debtor as administrator of a deceased person. *Wilson* v. *McBrine*, 2 *Kerr* 535.

5—Right of Trustees to sell Property—Possession.

The trustees of the estate of an absconding debtor appointed under the Act 26 Geo. 3, c. 13, have a right to sell and convey the real estate of the debtor, though they have never taken possession. *Doe* v. *McGuire*, 1 *All.* 612.

Fraudulent Conveyance.

A conveyance from an absconding debtor which is found to be fraudulent and void, cannot defeat the title of the trustees; for being void as against creditors, it is also void as against those who represent them. *Ibid.*

6—Property seized—Liability for rent.

Property seized upon a warrant issued under the Absconding Debtors Act (1 Rev. Stat. c. 125) is not liable to the landlord for a year's rent, though notice of his claim is given to the Sheriff before the delivery of the property to the trustees. *Stanton* v. *Johnston*, 4 *All.* 54.

7—Action against Debtor—Suspension—Bail.

Proceedings under the Absconding Debtors Act do not suspend an action pending against the debtor; nor are the bail discharged by the plaintiff filing with the trustees his claim against the debtor, and having the amount adjusted. *Christie* v. *Lawrence*, 4 *All.* 115.

8—Foreign Residence.
Where a debtor was a resident of the State of Maine but did business in this Province and went away for the purpose of defrauding his creditors. Held, That he might be proceeded against under the Absconding Debtors Act. *Regina* v. *Steadman*, 1 *Han.* 369.

9—A Warrant cannot issue against a person as an absent debtor under 1 Rev. Stat. cap. 125, unless he has been a resident in the Province. *Ex parte Kettle*, *Hil. T.* 1861.

10—Investing of Property—Notice—Publication.
Proceedings were taken against S., a debtor, under the Absconding Debtors Act; a Warrant issued 27th November, and notice as required by the Act, was published in the Royal Gazette, December 2. The warrant was delivered to the Sheriff of York on the 10th February following. On the 5th February, a creditor of S. having obtained judgment against him in the Supreme Court, issued an execution and recorded a memorial of the judgment in the County of York. Held,—Weldon, J., *dissentiente*, That the publication of the notice divested S. of the property, and vested it in the trustees, without the issuing of any warrant to the Sheriff, and so defeated the execution. Per Weldon, J., That the notice in the Gazette could not be imported into the case to prevent the plaintiff from reaping the fruits of his judgment. *Kerr* v. *Scovil*, 2 *Han.* 10.

11—The real estate of an absconding debtor is divested by the publication in the Gazette of the warrant of attachment, and vests in the trustees when appointed, and is not affected by a subsequent conveyance by the debtor. Therefore where proceedings were taken against an absconding debtor in February 1860, and notice of the warrant was published in the Gazette in April 1860—Held, That the estate of the debtor was thereby divested, and that a subsequent deed from him was inoperative, though the trustees were not appointed until several months after such deed. *Robichcau* v. *Black*, *Mich. T.* 1871.

12—Death of Debtor—Effect of Notice.
Proceedings under the Absconding Debtors Act, 1 Rev. Stat. c. 125, do not abate by the death of the debtor within three months after the publication of the notice of the warrant in the Gazette, nor by the debtor being declared bankrupt in England within that period. *Ex parte Archibald*, 2 *Han.* 30.

13—Foreign Corporation.
A foreign corporation having an agency and carrying on business in this Province may be proceeded against as an absent debtor under the 1 Rev. Stat. cap. 125. *Ex parte, The Columbian Insurance Co.*, *Hil. T.* 1871.

14—Jurat—Signature—Want of.
The want of a signature to the jurat of the affidavit of the applying creditor upon which a warrant of attachment is issued under the Act 26 Geo. 3, c. 13, is a fatal defect in the proceedings, and is not waived by an application for a supersedeas by the debtor. *Ex parte Nason*, *Easter T.* 1833.

15—Insolvent Act of 1869. Effect.
The Absconding Debtors Act 1 Rev. Stat. c. 126, is not repealed by "the Insolvent Act of 1869," their provisions not being necessarily inconsistent The former Act applies to persons and cases not provided for by the latter Act. *Ex parte Reynolds*, *Trin. T.* 1872.

16—Property acquired by debtor subsequently to appointment of trustees—Vesting of.
Where proceedings have been taken against a person as an absconding debtor, and trustees have been appointed under 1 Rev. Stat. c. 125, property acquired by the debtor after the appointment of the trustees, does not vest in them.—*Hannington* v. *Harshman*, *H. T.* 1873.

Supervision of Proceedings of Trustees.
See Supreme Court in Equity, 9.

ABUTTAL.

Replevin—generality of description.
See Pleading I. 31.

ACCEPTANCE.

Of Bill by agent—authority.
See Principal and Agent, 10.

Per procuration—authority—agency.
See Bills and Notes, II.

Protest—evidence of acceptance.
See Bills and Notes, III. 3.

Extent of—sale of logs.
See Contract, 12.

Acceptors of Timber Orders—liability—usage. See Contract, 6.

1—Proof.
Action against drawers of foreign bill of exchange payable at so many days after sight, and averred to have been accepted, but afterwards protested for non-payment. Quære, Whether proof of acceptance is necessary beyond the protest for non-payment? If not necessary in ordinary cases, whether it would be, where the acceptance purported to make the bill payable to third persons, and the protest for non-payment is made upon the presentment to such third persons only? See *Pollock* v. *Cunard*, 2 *Kerr*, 201.

2—Statute of Frauds—Acceptance.
A mere delivery of goods by the vendor without an actual acceptance by the vendee of some part thereof, is not sufficient, within the statute of frauds. The receipt of the goods by a common carrier from the vendor, without any specific direction or authority from the vendee, will not amount to an acceptance by the vendee, within the statute. *Daley* v. *Marks*, *Ber.* 346.

ACCOMMODATION BILL.

Indorser receiving property consideration for promise to destroy bill. See Bills and Notes, V. 3.

ACCOMPLICE.

Confession of third person to implicate. See Criminal Law, III. 1.

ACCORD AND SATISFACTION.

See Contract, 13.

Retention of Draft—Presumption.
Plaintiffs, merchants in Boston, had sold goods to defendant in St. John, and he had made payments on account; there was some dispute whether the price of the goods was to be paid in gold or American currency. On the 13th May 1865, defendant sent the plaintiffs a gold draft for $719, stating that he considered that it would balance the account between them. On the 19th May the plaintiffs acknowledged the receipt of the draft, but denied that it balanced the account, and stated that they would hold it subject to the defendant's order; and on the 23rd May he requested them to return the draft to him. They neither answered the letter nor returned the draft, but afterwards sold it in the money market, and claimed a balance. Held, That the draft being of an uncertain value, dependent on the price of gold in the United States, might be accepted as an award and satisfaction of the plaintiffs demand, and that by retaining and disposing of it after the defendant had requested them to return it, it might be presumed that they had accepted it in full. *Nash* v. *Dever*, *Hil. T.* 1866.

ACCOUNT.

Debits and Credits—use of one side. See Evidence, XI. 13.

General account included with bill of costs. See Attorney, VIII. 32.

Reference to Barrister. Non-use of evidence. See Supreme Court in Equity, 4.

ACCOUNT STATED.

See Assumpsit, III. a.

ACCRETION.

Receding of low water mark. Extension of wharf. Covenant binding assignee. See Covenant, 7.

AC ETIAM.

No cause of action in *ac etiam* clause. See Practice, VI. 1.

ACKNOWLEDGMENT.

See Evidence (Admissions). Acquiescence. Of deed. Want of memorandum of due acknowledgment. See Deed.

Official character of person taking. See Deed, 12.

What a sufficient acknowledgment of deed. See Deed, 13, 28.

1—Promise to pay debt barred by bankruptcy.
In an action to recover a debt from which the defendant had been discharged by the Bankrupt Act, the plaintiff relied upon the following promise to a creditor of the defendant since his bankruptcy: "I acknowledge that I owe B. (the plaintiff) and you, as soon as I am able I will pay you." Held: 1. That this was not such a distinct and unequivocal promise to pay the plaintiff as was necessary to entitle him to recover. 2. That the plaintiff

should have declared specially on the conditional promise, and proved the defendant's ability to pay. *Blair* v. *Albee*, 3 *All.* 9.

2—Acknowledgment, no promise to pay.
A mere acknowledgment of a debt by an administrator is not sufficient to take the case out of the Statute of Limitations; there must be an express promise to pay, and if there is more than one administrator, *semble* that the promise should be by all of them. *Gibbs* v. *Sewall*, *Trin. T.* 1833.

When must be made to bar Statute of Limitations. See Limitation of Actions II.

3—Admission of Title—By verbal declarations.
The verbal declaration of the grantee of land that he has sold it to a person under whom the defendant claims, is not sufficient to shew title out of the grantee. *Doe* v. *Todd*, 2 *All.* 261.

4—By written agreement to buy.
L. having been in possession of land upwards of twenty years, made a written agreement to buy it from the lessor of the plaintiff, but, before the time of payment, went away leaving the defendant in possession, and stating that he could not pay for the land. Held, That this agreement was an admission of title in the lessor of the plaintiff, and that he might recover in ejectment without any other proof of title. *Doe* v. *Little*, 2 *All.* 558.

5—Acknowledgment of Title—Petition in Probate Court—Statement—Statute of Limitations.
A statement in a petition by defendant to the Probate Court, for letters of administration, that certain land in his possession belonged to the intestate, on which petition letters of administration were granted to the defendant, is a sufficient acknowledgment of title to the heir of the intestate to prevent the operation of the Statute of Limitations. *Doe* d. *Spence* v. *Welling*, *Trin. T.* 1866.

6—Offer to Lease—Bidding at Sale.
A verbal offer by a person in adverse possession of land to lease it from the owner, or bidding for the land at an auction of it by the owner, is not an acknowledgment of title, within the Statute of Limitations. *Doe* v. *Hasson*, 3 *All.* 451.

7—By Letter.
In ejectment, the lessor of the plaintiff relied on the following letter as an admission of title by the defendant: "If you intend to sell the place, I want you to give me the first offer as soon as possible; write me an answer the first opportunity; don't sell it to nobody till you let me know, and as to the money it shall be ready as soon as you give a good deed." Held, Not a sufficient acknowledgment of title in the lessor to be submitted to the consideration of the jury. *Doe* v. *Brown*, 3 *Kerr* 321.

Declaration on Examination. See Limitations of Actions II. 3.

ACTION AT LAW.

I. Commencement of Action.
II. Condition precedent to bringing Action.
III. Form of Action.
IV. Right of Immediate Action.
V. Right to Determine Contract.
VI. Suspension of Action.
VII. Before Expiration of Credit.
VIII. Former Recovery.
IX. By and against whom Maintainable.
X. For what Maintainable.
XI. Notice of Action.
(Parties entitled to—Service of.)
XII. Joinder of Actions.

I.

1—Commencement of.
The issuing of writ, and not the filing of the declaration, is the commencement of an action. *Stiles* v. *Brewster*, 4 *All.* 414.

2—The day of the issuing a summary writ, and not the day of teste, is considered the commencement of the action. See *Stephenson* v. *McLellan*, 1 *All.* 19.

3—Time—Demand.
A reasonable time must elapse between demand of money held by stakeholder and commencement of suit.

Where the race for which money is deposited as a stake, has not been run, the stakeholder is entitled to retain the money till he has an opportunity of enquiring to whom it belongs; but he has no right to hold it beyond that time, because one of the parties to the race withholds his assent to the payment. The plaintiff deposited £100 with the defendant as a stakeholder, to abide the result of a race to be run on the 5th November between the horses of plaintiff and K.; the race was not decided, and on the 11th November the plaintiff demanded the money, which the defendant refused to pay, stating that K. claimed it as the winner of the race: an action for the money was brought on the 22nd November. Held, That a reasonable time had elapsed between the demand and the commencement of the suit, and that the defendant was liable. *Kinney* v. *Stubbs*, 4 *All.* 126.

II.

Condition Precedent.
In an agreement for the construction of a rail road, it was provided that all damages claimed by either party for non-compliance with the contract, and all other matters in dispute between them, should be decided by arbitrators whose award should be final. Held, In an action for work done under the contract, that it was a condition precedent to bringing the action that the amount of damages should be ascertained by arbitration. *Myers* v. *St. Andrews Railway Co.*, *Trin. T.* 1863.

Quære—Whether, if defendant had prevented the arbitration, the plaintiff could not recover for work and labour? *Ibid.*

III.

1—Form.
Since the Act 21 Vic. c. 20, a declaration may be framed as in an action on the case, though the injury complained of is a trespass. *Brown* v. *Thompson*, 4 *All.* 228.

Quære—Whether, independent of the Act, such a declaration is not sufficient after verdict? *Ibid.*

2—Against Sheriff.
Case, and not trespass, is the proper remedy against Sheriff for refusing to give a confined debtor the benefit of the gaol limits. See *Caldwell* v. *Winslow*, 2 *All.* 203.

SED. See Supra 1. Infra 3.

Against Attorney—Declaration disclosing sufficient cause of action in assumpsit. See *Pleading* I. 60.

3—Trespass—Distress for Rent.
The option granted by the Act 50 Geo. 3, cap. 21, sec. 7. To bring trespass, or case, is to be understood according to the subject matter of the grievance, and not the mere election of the party. See *Trespass* II. 22.

4—Trespass—Continuance of.
After a recovery in trespass, every continuance of the wrong, is a new trespass, the remedy for which is by action of trespass, and not case. *Wallace* v. *Milliken*, *Trin. T.*, 1833.

IV.

RIGHT OF IMMEDIATE ACTION.

Covenant—Action before eviction.
See Covenant, 12.

Master and Servant—entire contract—dismissal without cause. See Damages I. 15.

1—Where a party to a contract disables himself from performing it, the other party's right for the breach immediately attaches. *Gilbert* v. *Campbell*, 1 *Han.* 471.

2—May recover for goods delivered under contract for work, where both parties have disabled themselves from performance. See *McAvley* v. *Geddes*, 4 *All.* 526

V.

RIGHT TO DETERMINE CONTRACT.

Deviation—Seaman's wages.
See Justice of the Peace, II. 3.
Shipping Law.

VI.

SUSPENSION OF ACTION.

Executors.
Actions against Executors and Administrators for recovery of debts, not suspended for eighteen months. See *Executors and Administrators* I. 2.

Agreement—breach of—private account.
See *Assumpsit* I. 1.

VII.

BEFORE EXPIRATION OF CREDIT.

1—Breach of Agreement.
When goods were delivered under an agreement to be paid for by endorsed notes payable in . . . days after delivery, the vendor recovered in assumpsit before the expiration of the time of credit for a breach of the agreement in not giving the said notes. *Brown* v. *Frink*, *Ber.* 363.

2—Special Contract.
Payment to be made after logs driven

into boom. Verdict general on special and common counts. Plaintiff could not recover, as special averments had not been proved, and credit had not expired, and because estimate of damages had been based upon the contract. See *Campbell* v. *Todd*, 3 *Kerr* 171.

VIII.

FORMER RECOVERY.

1—Failure in Proof—Items disallowed.
Where in assumpsit for goods sold and delivered, the plaintiff has recovered the value of part of the goods contained in his bill of particulars, but not the whole, some of the items being disallowed by the jury, under the Judge's direction, as not proved; no new action can be maintained for such items. *Ramsay* v. *Hamilton*, 2 *Kerr* 511.

Quære—Whether the plaintiff could in such a case expressly withdraw part of his demand from the consideration of the jury, in order to bring a new action therefor? *Ibid.*

2—Payment.
A party who has made payment in goods or money on account of articles sold and delivered, and who, in an action brought for the price of such articles, has failed to prove such payments, cannot afterwards maintain an action of *indebitatus assumpsit* against the vendor to recover back the money or the price of the goods. *Wilson* v. *Cameron*, 1 *Kerr* 542.

3—Landlord and Tenant—Former adjudication.
If a tenant defends an action for rent, and a reduction is made on the amount claimed on the ground that he has been evicted by the landlord from part of the premises, he cannot afterwards maintain trespass against the landlord for the same action which he relied on as an eviction in the former action. *Rourke* v. *McCullough*, 4 *All.* 361.

Replevin—evidence of former recovery in. See Evidence III. 17.

4—Pleading—Judgment.
The defendant pleaded that the contract declared on was made by him jointly with W., and that the plaintiff had before impleaded the defendant and W. for not performing the same promises, and issue being joined, the cause was referred to arbitration, the award to be entered as the verdict of a jury—that the arbitrators awarded in favor of the defendant and W., and that judgment was entered up thereon: Held, That the plea was not double, as the real defence was that the matter had been already adjudicated upon, and the joint contract was only alleged as introductory thereto: Held, also for the like reason, that the matter was properly pleaded in bar and not in abatement. *Collins* v. *McDonnell*, 1 *All.* 250.

A judgment in favor of three joint contractors is a bar to a second action by the same plaintiff, against two of them for the same cause of action. *Ibid.*

5—Withdrawal of items from particulars—Confession for remainder.
In an action for goods sold and delivered, brought against a firm, part of the goods included in the plaintiff's particulars had not been accepted by the defendants, in consequence of one of the firm having absconded, and the partnership having been dissolved before the arrival of the goods; the plaintiff withdrew the charges for these goods from the particulars, and the defendants gave a confession for the balance of the account. In a subsequent action for these goods, against two members of the firm, on an alleged sale to them since the former action, they set up as a defence, a recovery in the first action. Held, That there was no evidence of a former recovery. *Ames* v. *Carman*, *East. T.* 1871.

Judgment. Satisfaction for wrong done. See Trespass III. 5.

IX.

BY AND AGAINST WHOM MAINTAINABLE.

1—Judgment Creditor. Not discharging Debtor.
An action on the case will not lie against a judgment creditor for omitting to discharge his debtor from prison upon an equitable satisfaction of the debt, there having been no order for his discharge, and the creditor not being legally bound to discharge him. *McPhelim* v. *Wilson*, *Trin. T.* 1862.

2—Defendant arrested the plaintiff on a covenant for payment of a mortgage debt, and while he was in custody his equity of redemption in the mortgage was sold by the Sheriff under an execution issued on a judgment confessed to the defendant as collateral security for the payment of the mortgage debt, and was purchased by and conveyed to the defendant by the Sheriff. Held, That as the arrest was legal, and the action of covenant was not legally determined, nor the debt actually paid, the defendant was not liable in an action for wrongfully continuing the plaintiff in prison after the purchase of the equity of redemption, though the mortgage debt might thereby in equity be extinguished. *Ibid.*

3—Tenants in common.
A tenant in common is liable in assumpsit to his co-tenant when he sells more than his share of the common property with the consent of his co-tenant. *Shaw* v. *Grant*, *Ber.* 110.

4—Whether any and what acts short of the destruction of joint property will enable one tenant in common to sustain trespass against his co-tenant. See *Wiggins* v. *White*, *Ber.* 97.

5—One tenant in common cannot recover in assumpsit against his co-tenant for the value of his share of common property unless a sale by the co-tenant be actually proved. *Doyle* v. *Taylor*, *Ber.* 201.

6—Parent.
Father of illegitimate child, not liable to third persons for the expense of supporting such child, unless it has been incurred upon his authority, or he has contracted to pay for it. *Forrest* v. *McRae*, 2 *Kerr* 174.

7—Corporation. Chamberlain.
Direction in Act to the collector of money assessed, to pay money collected over to the Chamberlain, the Chamberlain cannot sue the Coll‐tor. Action must be brought by Corporation. See *Corporation* 9.

8—Fence Viewer.
A person employed by a fence viewer to repair a division fence under the Act 1 Wm. 4, c. 9, on failure of the occupier to make the repairs directed, may maintain an action against such occupier for the amount of such repairs. *Stevenson* v. *Stanton*, 2 *Kerr* 670.

9—Public Agents.
The defendants, under the Act 7 Wm. 4, c. 28, were by the General Sessions of the Peace for the county of York appointed a committee of management for the erection of a new gaol; and in that capacity contracted with the plaintiff, binding themselves and their successors as such, on behalf of the said county, and subscribing their names "a committee on behalf of the county." Held, That they were mere agents for the public, and not personally liable on the contract. *Blair* v. *Robinson*, 3 *Kerr* 487.

Public Officer. See Public Officer.

Barrister and Counsel.
No legal remedy to recover remuneration for professional services. See Attorney.

10—Sheriff not liable for neglecting to arrest on mesne process unless plaintiff has sustained damage. See Sheriff 11.

11—Clerk of House of Assembly liable to person employed by him. See Assumpsit III. 47.

12—Joint Occupier of Land—Trespass.
A person working a farm on shares, and occupying part of the house jointly with the owner of the farm, has not such a tenancy as to prevent the owner of the farm from maintaining trespass on the land. See Landlord and Tenant 8.

13—Husband as representative of Wife —Legacy.
If a legacy is bequeathed to a married woman who dies before any act done by husband to reduce it into possession, he can only maintain an action for it as representative of his wife, though he may be beneficially entitled to it. *Collins* v. *Cahir*, 2 *All.* 103.

Legacy—Payment to Executor—Discharge of Party. See Assumpsit III. 19.

Constable—Certified Fees See Criminal Law.

14—Payees of Note—Delivery by one.
Plaintiff and two other persons being payees of a note indorsed it generally, the others giving the plaintiff authority to collect it: plaintiff put the note in the hands of an attorney to collect, who, without authority, compromised with the maker. Held, That the agreement to collect the amount of the note having been made with the plaintiff, he could sue the attorney for negligence without joining the other payees. *Berry* v. *Hutchison*, *Mich. T.* 1865

15—Part Contractors—Rescission of Contract by—Action in name of all.
Where some of a number of joint contractors had settled with the defendant,

undertaking to rescind their contract and to substitute a different one, against the consent of the other contractors, they may sue for a breach of the contract in the name of all the parties. *Palmer* v. *Long*, *Ber.* 122.

16—Legatee—Termination of Trust. A legacy was bequeathed to the plaintiff, to be paid to her father in trust for her, and to be put at interest by him for her use till she attained eighteen years of age, and then the amount of principal and interest to be paid to her. The legacy not having been paid to her father—Held, That the trust was at an end when the plaintiff attained eighteen years of age, and that she had then a vested right, and could sue for the legacy. *Livingston* v. *Powell*, *Ber.* 225.

17—Joint Deposit—Death of one party—Survivor's right. A receipt for money deposited in a bank was given in the following words: "Received from P. C. and H. C., to be drawn by either of them, or the survivor, $1400; for which we are accountable with interest, on receiving 15 days notice." P. C. sent the receipt to the bank and applied for the money, but the Manager not being satisfied that the person who applied had authority to receive the money, declined to pay it. P. C. died three days afterwards. Held, That on his death the right to receive the money vested in H. C., and that P. C.'s administrator could not recover it. *Condon* v. *Bank of B. North America*, *Trin. T.* 1870.

18—Master and Servant — Contract for whole services—defendant working for others. See Assumpsit III. 20.

19—Pond Keeper—not liable for loss by storm. See Pond Keeper.

20—In fraud of third parties—Semble. An action cannot be supported on a contract made between two persons in fraud of third persons. See *Sharp* v. *McKeen*, 2 *Kerr* 524.

21—Parties not in *statu quo*. See Assumpsit III. 34.

22—Obligees of bond payable to A. or B., or either, cannot be sued in name of one unless the other is dead. See *Harris* v. *Drummond*, 4 *All.* 267.

23—Insurance—loss payable to. Assignment of policy. See Insurance.

24—Married woman—Husband insane. The amount due from a boarder under such circumstances, vests in the woman as her separate property, and will not pass to the husband's representatives on his death. *Abell* v. *Light*, 1 *Han.* 97.

25—Widow—Dower. A widow cannot maintain action at law for dower in land in which her husband had only an equity of redemption during coverture. See *Doe* v. *Estabrooks*, 4 *All.* 455.

26—Surveyor of Lumber. Assumpsit lies by a surveyor of lumber to recover his fees against the first purchaser after the survey, under 1 Rev. Stat. c. 96, sec. 10. *Ferguson* v. *Muirhead*, *Hil. T.* 1866.

27—Overseers of Poor. Paupers brought into Parish. The overseers of the poor not having any corporate rights, cannot maintain an action against a person who brings paupers into the parish, who become chargeable thereon, such act being no injury to the overseers individually. *Gillespie* v. *Phillips*, *Mich. T.* 1861.

Infant—Ratification. See Infant.

Rector—Party to maintain trespass. See Trespass I. 8.

Corporation when no Rector. See Trespass I. 9.

Purchaser may recover deposit on failure of title. See Assumpsit III. 24.

Remainderman—Right to maintain ejectment without demand of possession. See Will 8.

Constable. See Constable.

Seaman. See Seaman's Wages.

Registrar—Medical Act. See Action on the Case I. 3.

Infant—Coming of age—Promise to pay note. See Bills and Notes II. 5.

Wrong Doer cutting timber. See Trover II.

Trustees Absconding Debtor—Trover. See Absconding Debtor 3.

Master of Ship—Loss by jettison. See Carrier 1.

Pawnee—Replevin for wrongful taking of goods pledged. See Bailee.

Collector of Customs—Loss by accidental fire. See Action on the Case 1.

Ship Owner against Insurer—Jettison—Contribution. See Insurance 36.

License of Crown Land. See Action on the Case 4.

Exchange of Goods—Promise—Account subsequently rendered. See Assumpsit III. 33.

Officer displaced without cause. See Assumpsit III. 8.

Breach and damage in life time of testator. See Executors and Administrators I. 8.

Magistrate not taking examination legally. See Trespass V. 2.

X.

For what Maintainable.

1—Judgment in Magistrate's Court.
Courts of Justices of the Peace, established under the Act 4 Wm. c. 45, are not Courts of Record; and assumpsit may be maintained on a judgment recovered in such Court. *Young* v. *Woodcock*, 3 *Kerr* 554.

2—Foreign Judgment.
A foreign judgment is not a debt of record, but only evidence of a debt; and the simple contract on which it is founded, is not merged in it. *Fergus* v. *Wardlaw*, 3 *Kerr* 665.

3—No action will lie in this country on a foreign judgment, if the defendants were not resident within the jurisdiction of the foreign Court, and had no property or agent there, and were neither served with process in the foreign country, nor defended the suit; though they were served in this country with notice of the pendency of the suit, and the judgment may have been obtained according to the practice of the foreign Court in similar cases. *Cyr* v. *Sanfacon*, 2 *All.* 641.

Seduction. See Seduction.

4—Serving Processes.
Under the Act of Assembly 6 Wm. 4, c. 1, s. 11, a person serving processes directed to the Sheriff, but without any authority from him, is precluded from maintaining any action for his services. *Herrington* v. *Lugrin*, 1 *Kerr* 109. See General Rules 113.

Second Action—Staying proceedings when vexatious or negligent. See Second Action.

Constable for Services—Certified fees. See Criminal Law.

Quantum Meruit—Contract rescinded by parties disabling themselves from performance. See Assumpsit III. 56.

Fires—Negligently kindling. Action of debt to recover damages will not lie. See Fires.

Damages—Splitting up Claim. Party cannot split up his claim for damages, and proceed for a part of the trespass at one time, and part at another. See Trespass IV. 7.

See Separate Titles of Actions.

XI.

Notice of Action—Parties entitled to.

1—Police.
The Police Act 11 Vic. cap. 13, sec. 23, enacted that in all actions to be commenced against any person for any thing done in pursuance of the Act, notice in writing of such action should be given to the defendant one month before the commencement of the action. Held, per Chipman, C. J., Carter, J. and Street, J., In an action brought for breaking open a house, that the defendants (one of whom was a policeman, and the other acting in his aid and under the orders of the Mayor) were entitled to notice; the policeman, because he acted in the *bona fide* belief that he was in the legal discharge of his duty, and the other defendant, because he acted *bona fide* in aid of the policeman and under the belief that he had authority to do the act complained of. *McNichol* v. *Gray*, 2 *All.* 73.

2—The Police Act 11 Vic. c. 13, s. 22, does not authorize the arrest without warrant, of known residents of the place; nor is a person who acts as a principal in directing a policeman to make an arrest, entitled to notice of action under that Act. *Foley* v. *Tucker*, 1 *Han.* 52.

3—Policeman—Belief, bona fides of—Submission of question to Jury—Counsel's duty—Decision by Judge.
In an action against a policeman, if it appears by the plaintiff's evidence, or it may reasonably be inferred from the facts, that he acted under a *bona fide* belief that he had authority by the Police Act 12 Vic. c. 68, to do the act complained of, and therefore would be entitled to notice of action, the plaintiff's counsel should ask to have that question submitted to the jury, or the defendant's coun-

sel may ask it: if neither counsel ask, and the question is not submitted, the Court may determine whether there is evidence to shew reasonable grounds of belief. *Harvey* v. *Marshall*, *East. T.* 1865.

4—Owner of Property—Dam overflowing.

Where a defendant became the owner of property with a dam on it which overflowed plaintiff's land, he was held to be entitled to notice before action brought. *Belyea* v. *Hamm*, 2 *Han.* 27.

5—Justice of Peace—Requisites of Notice.

A notice of action stated "that you, the said E. P. (defendant), on the 23rd December 1863, at the Parish of K., and County of K., and on divers other days and times, etc., wrongfully and maliciously, and without any reasonable and probable cause, advised and encouraged one H. P. to bring an action in your Court, before you as a Justice of the Peace, against the plaintiff, in a matter of real estate, wherein the title of land was and did come in question, and wherein you had no jurisdiction as a Justice of the Peace, (setting out the proceedings and the award of judgment against plaintiff,) and that you, the said (defendant,) on the day and year last aforesaid, issued in the aforesaid case, wherein you had no jurisdiction, as aforesaid, an execution on the said judgment against the goods and chattels of the plaintiff, and caused his goods and chattels to be seized under such execution to satisfy the same." Held, That the issuing of the execution was a continuation of the previous proceedings in the suit; and, therefore, that the time and place of the issuing was stated with sufficient certainty in the notice. *Pickett* v. *Perkins*, 1 *Han.* 131.

5 a—When special damage is claimed in consequence of an unlawful imprisonment by a Justice of the Peace, *e.g.* the cost of obtaining the plaintiff's discharge from prison, it should be stated in the notice of action, otherwise the plaintiff cannot give evidence of it. See *Sewell* v. *Olive*, 4 *All.* 304.

6—The trial of a civil suit by a Justice of the Peace is an official act, and he is entitled to notice under 1 Rev. Stat. c. 129 before bringing an action against him for wrongfully proceeding in the suit. *Picket* v. *Perkins*, 1 *Han.* 131.

7—Justice of Peace—Reasonable grounds of belief.

Defendant, a Justice of the Peace, commenced a trial, but being required as a witness in the cause, another Justice took up the trial, during the examination; after which, the defendant resumed it, and during the latter stage of the trial, committed an assault on the plaintiff. Held, That though the defendant at the time he committed the assault was acting without jurisdiction, having no right to resume the trial under the Rev. Stat. c. 137, sec. 28, still, if he had reasonable grounds to believe that he had jurisdiction to do so, he was entitled to notice of action; and that this question should have been left to the jury. *Sumner* v. *McMonagle*, *Mich. T.* 1864.

8—Justice of Peace—Second notice after discontinuance—First notice available—Requisites—Tender of amends—Time.

A notice of action for false imprisonment was served on defendant, a Justice of the Peace, on the 19th March, and a writ issued on the 17th April. The plaintiff took out a rule to discontinue that suit, and got an appointment to tax the costs on the 9th July. On the 7th July, a second notice of action was served on the defendant, and a writ issued on Monday the 9th August. Held, 1st. That if the second notice was bad, the plaintiff could avail himself of the first notice, notwithstanding the discontinuance of the suit commenced thereon. 2nd. That the second notice was sufficient, though it did not allege that the defendant had acted maliciously,—he having acted, either entirely without jurisdiction, or in excess of his jurisdiction. 3rd. That though the last day of the month's notice expired on Sunday, the defendant had not the whole of the following day to tender amends; and therefore the action was not commenced too soon. *Hatch* v. *Taylor*, *Hil. T.* 1872.

9—Constable.

A constable appointed by the Sessions under the 1 Rev. Stat, c. 56, and acting under the Justice's Act 1 Rev. Stat. c. 137, is entitled to notice of action. *Rebicheau* v. *Arsineau*, *East. T.* 1864.

10—A constable appointed by the Municipality in an incorporated County is not entitled to notice of action under 1 Rev. Stat. c. 56, in an action for false imprisonment under an execution issued by a

Justice of the Peace. *Hunter* v. *Maddox*, *Trin. T.* 1865. See Act 31 Vic. c. 19.

11—Constable—False imprisonment—Railway Act—Limitation.
The Act for the regulation of Railways, 21 Vic. c. 18, authorized the appointment of constables within a certain district, and gave them all the powers and privileges incident to the office of Police constables by the Portland Police Act, 11 Vic. c. 12. By section 40 of that Act, no action shall be brought against any person for anything done under the authority of the Act, unless it is commenced within three months. The defendant, a constable appointed under the Act 21 Vic. c. 18, arrested the plaintiff on a charge of having committed a breach of the peace within the district. Held, In an action for false imprisonment, that the defendant was entitled to the protection of the Act 11 Vic. c. 12, s. 40, and that the action must be brought within three months. *Boyce* v. *Pitfield*, 4 *All.* 443.

12—A constable who executes a capias in a suit in which he is the plaintiff, is not entitled to notice of action before being sued for the arrest. *Condell* v. *Price*, 1 *Han.* 333.

13—Commissioners of Roads.
By the Act 13 Vic. c. 30, which authorizes the appointment (among others) of commissioners of roads, no action is to be brought against any person for anything done in pursuance of any of the provisions of that Act, without a month's notice. Held, That a commissioner of roads, not appointed under the 13 Vic. c. 30, nor any Act thereby repealed, but acting under a previous Act, was not entitled to notice. *Basterach* v. *Atkinson*, 2 *All.* 439.

14—The Act 13 Vic. c. 4 directs the mode of laying out and altering roads, and the 13 Vic. c. 30 authorizes (*inter alia*,) the appointment of commissioners of highways, and directs that no action shall be brought against any person *for anything done under any of the provisions of that Act*, without a month's notice. Held, In an action against a Commissioner of highways, for laying out a road through the plaintiff's land, that he was acting under the provisions of the Highway Act, (13 Vic. c. 4,) and was therefore not entitled to notice of action. *West* v. *Atherton*, 2 *All.* 653.

15—Replevin—Constables.
The action of replevin is not within the Act 13 Vic. c. 30, s. 15, which requires a month's notice before an action is brought against any person for anything done in pursuance of the Act. *Sterling* v. *Jones*, 2 *All.* 522.

16—Service of.
A notice of action to a Justice of the Peace need not be served by the Attorney of the party who sues. See *Chilton* v. *Powell*, 1 *All.* 578.

17—Any person to whom such a notice is given to serve, is the agent of the party for that purpose. *Ibid.*

18—Place of abode of Plaintiff's Attorney.
The name and place of abode of the plaintiff's Attorney need not be endorsed on the back of the notice: it is sufficient if it appears on any part of it. *Baxter* v. *Hallett*, *Trin. T.* 1863.

19—Commencement of Action.
In an action against a Justice, the plaintiff gave no evidence that the action was not commenced till the expiration of a month after the notice; whereupon the Judge directed a nonsuit, to which the plaintiff did not submit, and obtained a verdict. On motion for a new trial, it appeared by the Nisi Prius record that the declaration was entitled more than a month after the notice. Held, That this was *prima facie* evidence of the time of commencing the action, and that the nonsuit was wrong, but that the plaintiff should have submitted to it; therefore, a new trial was granted. *Ibid.*

20—Signature.
In an action brought by husband and wife, for the imprisonment of the wife, the notice of action was signed "J. G. C., attorney for the said Priscilla Gabbles," (the wife.) Held, Insufficient, and that it ought to have been signed on behalf of the husband. *Gabbles* v. *Douglas*, *Hil. T.* 1864.

21—Policeman—St. Stephen's Police Act—Reasonable ground—Jury.
By the St. Stephen's Police Act, 27 Vic. c. 55, s. 1, policemen appointed under that Act were to have "all such powers, privileges and advantages," as any constable appointed by law has, or may have by virtue of the common law, or any Act of Assembly. Section 3 authorized any policeman on duty to arrest, "without warrant, any idle or disorderly person

whom he shall have just cause to suspect of having committed or being about to commit any felony or misdemeanor."—Defendant, a policeman, arrested the plaintiff without a warrant, on information given by E. that the plaintiff had feloniously set fire to his barn. In trespass for false imprisonment—Held, 1st. That policemen appointed under the Act were entitled to the benefit of the provisions respecting notice of action given to constables by 1 Rev. Stat. c. 56. 2nd. That, in order to determine whether the defendant was entitled to notice of action, it should have been left to the jury to find whether the defendant, at the time of the arrest, honestly believed, and had reasonable ground for believing, that the plaintiff had committed a felony, for which he was liable to be arrested under the Act. *Murphy* v. *Ellis*, *East. T.* 1871.

XII.

Joinder of Actions.

Since the Act 21 Vic. c. 20, s. 5, the plaintiff may join in the same declaration, an action for trespass *quare Cl. fregit*, and slander; each of the counts being in the form of trespass. *Lipsett* v. *McLaggan*, *East. T.* 1863.

ACTION ON THE CASE.

I. By and against whom Maintainable. Liability.

II. Negligence.

III. Nuisance.

IV. Obstructions.

I.

By and against whom Maintainable.—Liability.

See Action at Law.

1—Collector of Customs.—Accidental Fire.

The Collector of Her Majesty's Customs, who has, as such, the charge of the Queen's warehouse, is not liable to an owner of goods deposited therein for a loss to such goods by accidental fire, although he may have refused to open the warehouse and permit their removal during the fire; if in so refusing he has acted under a sense of duty for the general good, and not maliciously with intent to injure the plaintiff, or in a negligent, wanton, or arbitrary manner. *Kirk* v. *Smith*, 2 *Kerr* 187.

2—Landlord and Tenant—Fire.

In an action by a landlord against his tenant for negligently allowing lime to get wet with the tide, in consequence of which the landlord's property was burned, the jury were directed that to render the defendant liable he must be guilty of gross negligence, and that being aware of the danger of getting the lime wet, he negligently stored it without taking ordinary care to protect it from the water; but that if he had taken such ordinary care, and it got wet by an unusually high tide, he would not be liable. Held, That, taking it altogether, the direction was correct. *Upton* v. *Pingree*, 2 *All.* 186.

3—Registrar—Medical Act—Pleading.

By the Act 22 Vic. c. 18, s. 11, every person in the Province possessed of a medical degree or diploma to practice medicine or surgery, from any college in Great Britain, Ireland, Canada, France, or the United States, authorized to grant the same, shall, on payment, etc., be entitled to be registered under the Act, and by s. 12, no qualification shall be entered on the register, unless the Registrar is satisfied by the proper evidence, that the person is entitled to it. Held, in an action against the Registrar for refusing to register the plaintiff, 1. That the defendant was not liable unless he acted maliciously; and that an averment in the declaration that he *wrongfully* and *injuriously* refused to register the plaintiff, was insufficient. 2. That the mere production of a diploma to the Registrar, was not sufficient evidence of the authority of the college to grant it: the declaration should have averred that proper evidence of the plaintiff's title to registry was tendered to the defendant. *Peterson* v. *Harding*, 4 *All.* 583.

Sec. 2 declared, that the Act should commence and take effect from the 1st June 1859; and sect. 6 authorised the Governor to appoint a Registrar as soon as convenient "after the passing of the Act." The Governor's assent was given to the Act on the 12th April 1859. *Semble*, that no appointment could be made under sec. 6 before the 1st June. *Ibid.*

4—Licensee of Crown Lands—Wrong Doer.
A licensee of crown land, with authority to cut and take away timber therefrom, may maintain an action on the case against a person who wrongfully cuts the timber, in consequence of which the licensee sustains damage. *Beckwith* v. *McPhelim*, 2 *All.* 501.

5—Sheriff—Reversionary interest of Plaintiff.
Plaintiff leased cattle to T. for ten years, at the end of which time T. was to give up the cattle, *or others in their stead*, in as good condition as at the date of the lease. Held, That the plaintiff had no absolute reversionary interest in the cattle, and could not maintain an action on the case against the Sheriff for selling them under an execution against T. during the term. *Good* v. *Winslow*, 4 *All.* 241.

6—Judgment Creditor—Refusal to discharge Debtor—Equitable satisfaction—Action on the case not sustainable. See Action at Law IX. 1.

7—Continuance of Trespass.
An action on the case will not lie for the continuance of a trespass; as every continuance of the injury is a new trespass. *Wallace* v. *Milliken*, *Trin. T.* 1833.

8—Vendor—Vendee—Breach of Duty—Third Person.
The defendant became the purchaser of a quantity of timber lying on the close of T. L., and agreed with him to remove the same by a certain day. T. L. sold and conveyed the land to the plaintiff, who called upon the defendant to remove the timber; and the same not having been removed at the time agreed on between T. L. and the defendant, the plaintiff proceeded to remove the same, and incurred expense in so doing, which he required the defendant to pay. Held, That no action could be maintained by the plaintiff against the defendant for any supposed breach of duty in not removing the timber; the only ground of action was on the contract, and did not vest in the plaintiff, so as to be enforced in his name by reason of his purchase of the land. *Rae* v. *Rankin*, 2 *Kerr*, 453.

Declaration—Form—Trespass on Case. See Action at Law III.

9—Tenants in Common—Waste—Damages.
The saws, water wheel, and mill gear, fixed in a saw mill, and the cog-wheel of a grist mill, the property of two or more tenants in common, are a part of the inheritance, the damaging or taking away of which, except with the intent to repair or replace them, is in nature of waste, for which one tenant will be answerable to his co-tenant. *Linton* v. *Wilson*, 1 *Kerr*, 223.

In an action on the case for waste, the damages are confined to the actual injury done to the premises. *Ibid.*

Grantee—Right to make Water Course. See Deed V. 8.

Sheriff—Not arresting. See Action at Law IX. 10.

Landlord and Tenant—Want of Restitution—Title—Defence—Damages—Evidence. See Landlord and Tenant VII. 5.

II.

Negligence.

1—Injuring Nets—Done negligently or not.
In an action for injuring the plaintiff's net with a raft which the defendant was navigating down the river M., the declaration stated that in consequence of the defendant's carelessness and mismanagement, the raft struck against and damaged the plaintiff's net. Plea—not guilty. Held, That the only question for the jury was, whether the act complained of was caused by the negligence of the defendant; not whether it was done wantonly or maliciously. *Wolhaupter* v. *Foley*, 4 *All.* 90.

In the progress of the raft down the river, it became bent, which rendered it more difficult to manage. Held, That though the defendant being only a carrier, might not be liable for the improper construction of the raft, he was bound to use that care in the management of it, which its malformation rendered necessary to avoid injury, and that the jury were properly directed to consider whether he had done so. *Ibid.*

2—Allegation—Injury—Caused by negligence.
In an action for injuring nets set in a public river, by running into them with a raft, it is sufficient to allege in the declaration that the injury was caused by

the negligence of the defendant in navigating the raft. *Wolhaupter* v. *Foley*, 4 *All.* 167.

3—Surgical Practice—Gist of Action—Negligence—Intent immaterial—Pleading—Proof.
The declaration in an action against a surgeon for negligence, stated that the defendant *wrongfully intending to injure the plaintiff*, did not use proper care, etc. Held, That negligence being the gist of the action, the defendant's intent was immaterial, and the averment of the wrongful intent need not be proved. Also—That evidence offered by the defendant to disprove his wrongful intent was not admissible. *Kelly* v. *Dow*, 4 *All.* 435.

Evidence of Negligence in Surgeon. See Evidence III. 10, 11.

4—Towing Vessel—Collision—Indemnity—Presumptive knowledge of unlawful act—Ratification—Implied liability of principal—Damages. See Principal and Agent 22.

III.

NUISANCE.

1—Erection of Dam—Overflowing land.
A., the owner of land, through which a river flows, is entitled to recover damages in an action on the case from B., the owner of the land adjoining, situate lower down the stream, for erecting a mill dam upon his own land, which caused the water to flow back upon A.'s land. *Smith* v. *Scott*, 1 *Kerr* 1.

The circumstance of A.'s being present while the work was going on, and himself assisting as a labourer in the employ of B., is not conclusive evidence of a license so as to estop A. from maintaining such action; but is for the consideration of the jury, in connection with the other circumstances of the case, particularly such as tend to shew that A. could not have been aware of the effect of the dam. The extent of the license, if any, was also a question for the jury. *Ibid.*

Quære.—Whether a license in such a case could be inferred? *Ibid.*

2—Erection of Dam—Mortgagor and Mortgagee.
A mortgagee of land through which a stream flows, is not liable for an injury caused by a mill dam erected by the mortgagor in possession, though the money for which the mortgage was given, was lent by the mortgagee for the purpose of building the dam. *McNaughton* v. *Fraser*, 3 *All.* 247.

3—Erecting Dam—Question left to jury as to erection—Continuance and Injury.
In an action for overflowing land, the plaintiff alleged the injury to have been done by the defendant's raising a mill-dam, and thereby overflowing more land than the dam originally did. It appeared, on cross-examination of one of the defendant's witnesses, that he had worked the mill for a longer time during the summer than the former owner did. The jury were directed, that if, by the original dam, and the way it was used, the land was overflowed only in a particular manner and at particular seasons, and the defendant had within twenty years used the dam differently, and overflowed the land in a different manner, and at different seasons of the year, the plaintiff should recover. The jury having found for the defendant—Held, That the direction was right. *Lawlor* v. *Potter*, 1 *Han.* 328.

4—Damages—Limitation of Action.
In an action on the case for a nuisance in overflowing the plaintiff's land by a dam, which was erected by the defendant more than six years before bringing the action—Held, That the effect of a plea of the statute of limitations was not to bar the action, but only to limit the recovery of damages to the last six years. *Connors* v. *McLaggan*, 2 *Kerr* 446.

The jury were recommended, but not positively directed by the Judge, at the trial, to confine the damages to six years; but the Court refused to grant a new trial on this ground, there being evidence of actual damage during the last six years to the extent of the verdict, and no objection being made at the time to the Judge's charge, or any reason to think that the jury had exceeded the true estimate. *Ibid.*

The plaintiff was in possession of the land in 1830, when the dam was erected, but the grant of the Crown did not actually issue until 1838. Held, That the recovery of damages was not necessarily confined to the date of the grant, although such grant was put in evidence by the plaintiff; the grant might be deemed confirmatory of his possession. *Ibid.*

5—Erection of Steam Mill—Evidence—Damage—Surplusage.
In an action on the case for a nuisance in erecting a steam mill on land adjacent to the plaintiff's dwelling house, the evidence of persons living in other adjoining premises as to the injurious effect of the steam mill upon them, is admissible, in order to show by necessary inference, the damage done to the plaintiff by the erection. No other damage need be shewn than the abridgment of the plaintiff's enjoyment in the occupation of his premises. The judgment will not be arrested because in one or more of the counts annoyance to the plaintiff's tenants, as well as to himself and family, is alleged: it will be deemed a surplusage. *Barlow* v. *Kinnear*, 2 *Kerr* 94.

6—Repairs—not keeping in—Consequential damage—Semble.
If injury to plaintiffs' property was caused by the negligence of defendants in not keeping a dam in repair, the plaintiffs might recover the consequential damages in an action on the case. See *Philps* v. *St. John Water Co.* 4 *All.* 24.

IV.

Obstructions.

1—River Driving.
Held, That Barnaby's River (a branch of of the s. w. river Miramichi), which extends about twenty-eight miles into the country, and had been long used for the navigation of boats and canoes, and for floating down logs and timber, was a common highway above where the tide flowed, and that the plaintiffs might maintain an action against the defendant for obstructing them in the driving down timber, by the erection of a pier and boom in the river, though the river, there, was within the defendant's grant: Such rivers may be private property, and yet subject to public rights. It is not necessary to shew an actual pecuniary loss or damage in order to maintain such an action, but if the plaintiff be obstructed while actually using the navigation, it is sufficient. *Esson* v. *McMaster*, 1 *Kerr* 501.

2—All rivers above the flow of the tide, which may be used for the transportation of property, as for floating rafts and driving timber and logs—and not merely such as will bear boats for the accommodation of travellers—are highways by water, and subject to the public use; and in determining whether a river is public or private, its length and depth at ordinary times, and its capacity for floating rafts, etc., are proper to be considered. *Rowe* v. *Titus*, 1 *All.* 326.

In an action for obstructing a river by erecting a mill dam, it is not a proper question for the jury, whether the benefit derived from the public from the mill, is sufficient to outweigh the inconvenience occasioned by the dam. *Ibid.*

3—Wharf—approach to.
A person in possession of a wharf, built without authority below low water mark in a public navigable river, cannot maintain an action on the case against the owner of a vessel for obstructing the approach to the wharf by occupying the stream in front (but not touching the wharf), in the ordinary course of navigation. *Eagles* v. *Merritt*, 2 *All.* 550.

Quære, If the vessel had lain an unreasonable time in front of the wharf, or there had been a malicious intent to injure the plaintiff in his occupation, whether the action would lie? *Ibid.*

Semble.—That a person in possession of such a wharf might maintain trespass for a direct injury to it, or an action on a contract for the use and occupation of it. *Ibid.*

4—Lights.
The plaintiff being the lessee of land on which there were two houses, assigned the lease to the defendant, excepting one of the houses during the remainder of the term. Held, That the defendant was liable to an action for obstructing windows existing in the plaintiff's house at the time of the assignment, though only recently constructed—the exception being construed as a grant by the defendant, from which he could not derogate. *Longmaid* v. *McNichol*, 3 *All.* 497.

Alley-Way. See Deed V. 4.

Fishery. See Crown Grant 21.

Fishery—Erection of Weir. See Fishery 3.

Erection of Dam in public stream—Injunction to restrain persons not obstructed, from destroying dam. See Water Course.

ACQUIESCENCE.

Contract—Variance in—Defendant's Conduct—Evidence of Assent. See Assumpsit III. 42.

Boundary Lines—conditional assent to running. See Crown Grant 11.

Presence of Plaintiff at erection of Dam. See Action on the Case III. 1.

1—Judgment debtor, in sale of land.
The acquiescence of the judgment debtor in a Sheriff's sale, and subsequent possession of the land by the purchaser short of twenty years, though presumptive evidence that all the necessary proceedings have been taken, will not give a title to the purchaser by estoppel. *Doe dem Hazen, v. Hazen*, 3 *All.* 87.

2—The plaintiff claimed fifty acres of land under a deed in fee from his father J. B. in 1822, of a tract of four hundred acres, of which the fifty acres were part, which deed was subject to a condition that J. B. should receive and enjoy all the profits and emoluments accruing from the land during his life. J. B., in order to pay a debt, about two years after the conveyance to the plaintiff, and with his consent, caused the fifty acres to be sold by the Sheriff; the plaintiff bid at the sale, and afterwards agreed with the purchaser upon a division line between that and the remainder of the land. There was no proof of any judgment or execution against J. B., or of any advertisement by the Sheriff under which the land was sold. Held, That if the plaintiff had a present estate in the land at the time of the Sheriff's sale, his acquiescence in such sale would not divest him of his estate. *Doe v. Baxter*, 3 *All.* 232.

Plaintiff working under defendant's claim of right. See Railway Company.

ACQUITTAL.

Part Defendants—Entry of Judgment. See Costs 97.

Depriving acquitted Defendant of Costs—Application—Time. See Costs 17.

Allocatur, allowance of, to acquitted Defendant. See Costs 98.

ADJUSTMENT.

See Pleading II. 4. See also Insurance.

ADMINISTRATION.

See Executors and Administrators.

ADMINISTRATION BOND.

See Bond D.

ADMINISTRATORS.

See Executors and Administrators.

ADMIRALTY.

1—Jurisdiction.
On motion for a prohibition to the Court of Vice Admiralty. Held, That that Court has jurisdiction under the Statute 8 Geo. 1, c. 12, and 2 Geo. 2, c. 35, to entertain a suit *in rem*, instituted by the Crown against Pinetimber seized as cut on Crown Land without license, and to proceed to adjudge the forfeiture and condemnation thereof, although there has been no prosecution for the pecuniary penalties imposed by the said Acts on persons cutting or carrying away the same. A prohibition was accordingly refused. *The Queen v. 162 pieces of timber, Ber.* 410.

2—Proceedings—proper judge of.
When a prosecution is carried on in the Court of Vice Admiralty, that Court is the proper judge of the mode of proceeding applicable to the case, it being a matter of practice which, if irregular, may be corrected upon appeal, but is not a ground for prohibition, especially after judgment has been given. *Regina v. Beveridge*, 1 *Kerr* 58.

ADMISSIONS.

See Evidence I.

ADVERSE POSSESSION.

See Limitation of Actions.

ADVERTISEMENT.

Sheriff's Sale—Number of Lot left blank—not invalidating sale. See Sheriff's sale 1; places of advertising. See do. 4.

Executors Deed—Affidavit—Evidence of advertising. See Evidence IV. 2, 3.

Notice of Sale of Land—Posting Notices. See License 11.

AFFIDAVIT.

I. AUTHORITY TO TAKE. BEFORE WHOM SWORN.

II. INTITLING.

III. IN PARTICULAR CASES.

IV. PARTICULAR PERSONS.

V. JURAT.

VI. MISCELLANEOUS.

I.

AUTHORITY TO TAKE — BEFORE WHOM SWORN.

1—British Consul.
An affidavit made in a foreign country, and duly authenticated by the certificate of a British Consul, is sufficient to authorize a Judge to make an order for bail. *Drake* v. *Wentworth, Hil. T.* 1834. See Acts 19 Vic. c. 41, s. 7, and 27 Vic. c. 40, s. 7.

2—Attorney of petitioning Creditor.
Affidavit, upon which a warrant under Absconding Debtors Act is issued, may be sworn before the Attorney of petitioning creditor. *Regina* v. *Steadman*, 1 *Han.* 369.

3—Judge—Nova Scotia.
An affidavit sworn before a Judge of the Supreme Court of Nova Scotia, whose signature is verified by an affidavit made in this Province, may be read in this Court. *Kirk* v. *Ansley*, 1 *Kerr* 301.

4—Verification of Signature.
Affidavit of due execution of Power of Attorney to demand costs made in Nova Scotia before a Judge there. Verification of his signature necessary by affidavit made here. See *Fraser* v. *Harding*, 2 *Kerr* 290.

5—Commissioner of Supreme Court—Proceedings in other Courts.
A Commissioner authorized to take affidavits to be read in the Supreme Court, has no authority to take an affidavit of the service of an order for review of the proceedings on a trial before a Justice of the Peace. See *Regina* v. *McIntosh*, 1 *Han.* 372.

6—Commissioner, Court of Bankruptcy—England.
An affidavit sworn in England before a Commissioner of the Court of Bankruptcy, describing himself to be a Judge of the Court, and purporting by the jurat to be a Court of Justice, and to be under the seal of such Court, may be used in this Province under the Act 19 Vic. c. 41, s. 7. *Crane* v. *Cazenove*, 4 *All.* 578.

II.

INTITLING.

1—One of two Defendants.
In an application by one of two defendants for relief under Insolvent Act, 1 Wm. 4, c. 43, the affidavit was intitled in the name only of one of the defendants, the applicant Held, The intitling was sufficient. *Wilmot* v. *Cornwell, Ber.* 31.

2—No Cause in Court.
Where an application was made under the Act of Assembly 6 Wm. 4, c. 11, ss. 11, 12, by a Sheriff against an Attorney, to compel him to pay the Sheriff's fees in certain suits in which the writs had not been served by the Sheriff, and the affidavits were entitled in the name of the Sheriff against the Attorney by name. Held, That the affidavits were improperly entitled, there being no such cause in Court. *Drury* v. *Howe*, 3 *Kerr* 588.

3—Affidavits used in moving for a rule *nisi* for a mandamus are irregular if entitled in a cause, but the rule will be discharged without costs. *Regina* v. *Justices of York*, 1 *All.* 90.

4—Variance in description of Plaintiffs.
Where the title of a cause described the plaintiffs as "trustees for all the creditors of the estate and effects" of an absconding debtor, and the affidavits served on the plaintiff with a view to the discharge of bail, in their titles described the plaintiffs as "trustees for all the creditors, etc.," omitting the words "of the estate and effects," held sufficient. *Allison and others, trustees* v. *Robinson*, 2 *Han.* 161.

5—Several Causes—Same Rule moved for.
Where the same rule is to be moved for in several causes, the motion may be made on a single affidavit, entitled in all the causes. *Brown* v. *Trenholm*, 2 *All.* 515.

6—Abbreviations.
The abbreviations "Pltff' and "Deft" in the entitling of an affidavit are bad, and a rule obtained on such an affidavit will be discharged. *Raymond* v. *Caldwell, Hil. T.* 1864.

III.

IN PARTICULAR CASES.

1—By Sureties on Limit Bond.
Both sureties on limit bond should join in application for relief on equitable grounds, and collusion with principal denied by both. See *Goodwin* v. *Murray*, 3 *All.* 595.

2—Should state that application is made at the expense of bail, and without collusion. See *Bradford* v. *Fenton*, 3 *All.* 407.

3—To hold to bail—Interest Money.
An affidavit of debt, stating the defendant to be indebted in £100 for principal money paid and advanced by the plaintiff for the defendant, "and in £50 for interest upon the said principal sum," is bad as to the interest: but the causes of action being separate, the arrest will stand for the amount properly sworn to. *Simonds* v. *Simonds*, 2 *All.* 468.

4—To set aside Judgment.
An affidavit to set aside a regular judgment and let a party in to defend, must give a clear statement of merits. *Rippey* v. *Austin*, 4 *All.* 77.

Where there are several defendants—*quære*, Whether all should join in the affidavit of merit? Where two out of three defendants made affidavits, and only one swore to merits—Held sufficient. *Ibid.*

5—To set aside arrest—Certainty as to name.
On an application to discharge a defendant, arrested by the name of John Henry Oviatt, his affidavit stated that his "name is John Hilder Oviatt." Held insufficient. An affidavit in such a case should be as certain as a plea in abatement for misnomer. *Thompson* v. *Oviatt*, 2 *All.* 118.

6—Security for Costs.
A demand of particulars is not such a step in the cause as to require defendant applying for security for costs to state in his affidavit that when he demanded particulars he was not aware of the plaintiff's residence abroad. *Johnston* v. *Glazier*, *C. Ms.* 141.

Attachment for non-payment of costs—affidavit should state the place where demand made. See Attachment 19.

Should also state the time when made. See Attachment 20.

IV.

Particular Persons.

1—Jurors.
Affidavits of Jurymen stating that they had received evidence after retiring from the bar, cannot be received to impeach their verdict. *Att'y General* v. *Boyer*, *C. Ms.* 78.

2—On a motion for new trial, an affidavit stating that one of the jurymen had informed the deponent that the verdict was decided by lot, will not be received. See *Hodgson* v. *Carr*, 3 *Kerr* 499.

3—Affidavits of Jurors refused to be received stating that they found the defendant was not in a proper state of mind to understand the deed, and intended to assign that as a reason for their verdict. See *Babbet* v. *Cowperthwaite*, 3 *All.* 373.

Sheriff on Deed—Time of making. See Sheriff's Deed 3. See Deed I. 37.

4—Party—Attendance of Witnesses.
Affidavit should state the belief of deponent that witnesses attended the number of days. See *Taylor* v. *Travis*, 3 *All.* 505.

Administrator on Deed—Evidence of what. See Deed I. 24.

Executor—Deed. See Deed V. 7.

5—Arbitrator—affidavit of
Not admissible to shew that if they had known they had no power over the costs, they would have awarded a different amount to plaintiff. See Arbitrations and Awards V. 3.

V.

Jurat.

1—Omission of Place.
When the jurat omitted to state the place where an affidavit taken before a Commissioner was sworn, the Court would not allow it to be read. *Rankin* v. *Downes*, 1 *Kerr* 88.

2—Signature.
Omission of signature in jurat of affidavit of applying creditor under Absconding Debtors Act, a fatal defect. See Absconding Debtor 14.

3—Description of Commissioner.
If an affidavit is properly entitled in the Court, it is sufficient in the jurat to describe the person before whom it is sworn, "A Commissioner etc., Supreme Court." *Ex parte Morse*, 3 *Kerr* 366.

4—Illiterate Person.
The jurat of an affidavit made by an illiterate person, must state that it was read by the Commissioner to the deponent before swearing, in the terms of the rule of Hil. T. 1848. *Ex parte Irvine*, 2 *All.* 472. See General Rules 2.

5—Omission of words.
If the words "before me" are omitted from the jurat of an affidavit, it is a nullity. *Lyons* v. *Ellison*, *Trin. T.* 1862.

6—Obliterations.
If there is an erasure, obliteration, or alteration in the jurat of an affidavit, it

cannot be read: but where it appeared, on inspection of the affidavit, that the alleged obliteration was a flourish with the pen, forming part of the signature of the Commissioner, the affidavit was held sufficient, though such "flourish" passed through the date of the jurat and partially obliterated it. *Doe dem Trider* v. *McIntosh*, *East. T.* 1871.

7—Objection to jurat—when must be taken.
Where copies of affidavits in support of a motion have been served agreeably to rule 2, Hilary Term, 6 Wm. 4, any objection intended to be made to the jurat of the original affidavit should be taken before the affidavit is read, and cannot be taken afterwards. *Jarvis* v. *Peck*, 3 *Kerr* 507.

Commissioners name omitted—Motion refused for defect. See *Belyea* v. *Hamm*, 2 *Han.* 27.

VI.

Miscellaneous.

1—Shewing Cause.
Where the facts stated in the affidavit, upon which a rule *nisi* is obtained are positively contradicted by the affidavits used on shewing cause, the latter must prevail. *Ellis* v. *Newton*, *Ber.* 77. *Ray* v. *Desbrisay*, *Mich. T.* 1866.

2—If the affidavit in support of a motion, and that in shewing cause are contradictory, greater credence is to be given to the last affidavit, unless there are circumstances in the case to throw discredit on the latter; therefore, on motion of a party for the restitution of certain rooms in a house, supported by affidavits, which were contradicted by affidavits in shewing cause, and the probabilities of the case supported the last statement, the motion was dismissed. *Doe dem Johnston* v. *Roe*, 3 *Kerr* 400.

3—Deponent's Addition—Memorial.
The omission of the deponent's addition in an affidavit of the Clerk's signature to a memorial, does not make it a nullity. *Scott* v. *Garnet*, 2 *All.* 624.

4—Unsuccessful application—Previous Affidavits.
Where an unsuccessful application is made to a Judge, and afterwards renewed before the Court, all the affidavits used before the Judge should be produced. *Riordon* v. *Dunn*, 3 *All.* 124.

5—Irregularity—Waiver.
An irregularity in an affidavit to hold to bail is waived by pleading to the action. See Practice VII. 4.

Exemplification—Proof of. See Evidence VII. 5.

6—Amended Affidavit—Security for Costs.
Where an application to a Judge at chambers for security for costs has failed on the merits, a new application may be made to the Court on amended affidavit. See Costs 6.

Sheriff's Deed—Deputy Sheriff. See Evidence XI. 1.

Casual Ejector—Judgment against—Vacant Premises. See Ejectment VI. 2.

Lost Deed—Secondary Evidence. See Evidence VII. 18.

7—Ejectment—Non-payment of Rent.
Affidavit of service of declaration by fixing a copy to the door of house, should state the name of the tenant from whom the rent is due. See *Doe dem White* v. *Roe*, 2 *Kerr* 360.

8—New Matter—Filing Affidavits—Leave.
There is no arbitrary rule that an application for leave to file affidavits in answer to "new matter," under the Act 19 Vic. c. 41, s. 20, should be made before the argument commences on the affidavits containing the new matter. Wetmore, J., *dissentiente*. [See Swinfen *v.* Swinfen, 1 C. B. 364.] *Mitchell* v. *Sawther*, *Mich. T.* 1871.

9—Leave will not be granted to file affidavits in answer to "new matter" under the Act 19 Vic. c. 41, s. 20, where the facts sought to be answered must have been within the knowledge of the party at the time he made his affidavit, and should have been stated by him at that time. *Ex parte Gilbert*, *Hil. T.* 1873.

10—Perjury—when not assignable on.
Perjury cannot be assigned upon an affidavit taken before a Commissioner who had no authority to take the affidavit. See *Regina* v. *McIntosh*, 1 *Han.* 372.

11—Service—Sufficiency of Affidavit.
When the affidavit stated service of motion to have been on B. W. H., without stating that he was the party's attorney—Held, insufficient. *Brown* v. *Bartlett*, 3 *Kerr* 369.

12—Affidavit should state name of person upon whom process served, when not served personally. See *Sandall* v. *Godsoe*, 1 *All.* 441.

Part Affidavit—Admission on Trial. See Defamation 14.

See Practice in Equity.

See General Rules 5, 109, 120, 96, 32.

AFFINITY.

Sheriff—Coroner. See Jury 6, 7.

AGENT—AGENCY.

See Principal and Agent.

AGREEMENT.

See Contract.

Written Agreement to purchase Land from Owner—Effect. See Tenant at Will 2.

For Sale and Conveyance of Land—Possession under Agreement. See Tenant at Will 4.

Sale of Stranded Vessel—Possession—Agreement passing, no property. See Shipping Law 7.

Agreement in writing for exchange of lands accompanied by possession—Operation of. See Deed V. 1.

To sell Land—Refusal to complete Agreement—Liability for Use and Occupation. See Use and Occupation 1.

To Lease—Payment—Provision for Purchase—Liability of Defendant. See Landlord and Tenant 4

Subsequent Parol Agreement to Deed—Effect of. See Deed V. 8.

1—Liability—Limitation of—Construction.

Defendants, trustees of A., an insolvent debtor, purchased from the plaintiff, lumber sawed by him at a mill which had been occupied by A., and in consideration thereof agreed to release him from all debts due by him to A., and to pay him £120. It was stipulated in the agreement that the defendants were not to be personally chargeable for the payment of the money, but that the lumber alone was to be subject to the payment thereof. Held, That the effect of this clause was not to exonerate the defendants from liability if they improperly appropriated the proceeds of the lumber (as in paying a claim for rent on the mill), but to limit their liability to the true net proceeds of the lumber. *Nisbit* v. *McLean*, 2 *Kerr* 565.

2—Substituted Agreement—Position of parties altered by—Defence in Action.

K., who held a quantity of logs claimed by P., sold them to H., who placed the money in the hands of defendant, both parties agreeing that if not replevied by P. in six days it was to be paid to H.—P. was about to replevy, but before the six days expired, K. agreed with him to submit the matter to arbitration, the money to abide the event; but after the time elapsed, K. refused to arbitrate, and claimed the money under the first agreement. Held, In an action against defendant on the first agreement for the money, that as the substituted agreement altered the position of the parties, it was an answer to the action. *Keith et al., administrators*, v. *Skinner*, 1 *Han.* 584.

3—Compensatory Agreement—Want of consideration—No loss sustained—No right of action—Fraud on Crown.

Plaintiff and defendant being licensed by the Crown to cut timber on adjoining tracts of land, and the defendant having by mistake cut upon the plaintiff's license, they entered into an agreement whereby the defendant, in consideration of the timber cut by him on the plaintiff's license, granted and made over to the plaintiff all his (defendant's) interest in a certain part of the ground described in his license, with the right to cut and carry away the timber therefrom, and agreed that he (defendant) would not cut any more timber on the ground so transferred to the plaintiff. Held, 1st. That as the timber when cut by the defendant on the plaintiff's license remained the property of the Crown, and did not vest in the plaintiff, he had not sustained any loss of property by the defendant's act, and therefore there was no consideration for the agreement. 2nd. That without the assent of the Crown, the agreement did not operate as an assignment of any right to the plaintiff, and therefore the breach of it gave him no right of action. 3rd. That the effect of the agreement being to allow the plaintiff to commit a wrong on the Crown it was illegal. *Sharp* v. *McKeen*, 2 *Kerr* 524.

4—Signing of agreement delayed—Subsequent signing—Retrospective effect.
Where an agreement to perform work has been reduced to writing, but is not actually signed till a future day, there is nothing to prevent the parties from binding themselves and making the agreement effective from the day it was entered into, though prior to the signing of it. *Fenety* v. *Simonds*, *Trin. T.* 1863.

5—Construction—Logs.
A contract to deliver a quantity of logs does not necessarily mean "merchantable logs," according to 1 Rev. Stat. c 96, but may mean such logs as are actually got in the part of the country where the parties live, and in construing the contract, the surrounding circumstances, and the fact that merchantable logs could not be got in that part of the country, may be taken into consideration. *Dollard* v. *Potts*. *Trin. T.* 1866.

6—Personal liability—Company represented to be incorporated—Misrepresentation as to incorporation.
Plaintiff entered into an agreement with a Society by name, to do certain work: the Society was represented by the Committee acting on its behalf to be incorporated, and the contract was under seal, represented to be the corporate seal of the Society, and by a clause in the contract it was provided that the Committee should not be personally or individually liable to the plaintiff. It appeared afterwards that the Society was not incorporated. Held, That, as there was no Company to be held responsible under the contract, the members of the Committee who had received the benefit of the plaintiff's work were personally liable; that the clause in the agreement against their personal liability was only intended to apply where there was an incorporated company liable on the contract, and was repugnant and void where there was no such company to whom the plaintiff could resort for payment. *Hodge* v. *Reid*, *Mich. T.* 1872.

7—Statute of Frauds—Interest in Land.
Where the respective owners of adjoining lands agree by parol to a survey and marking of the division lines, the Court in an action of trespass, *qu. Cl. fregit*, by one against the other, Held, That such agreement was not within the statute of frauds, not being for the transfer of any interest or title to lands. See *Lawrence* v. *McDowall*, *Ber.* 283.

8—Parties entitled to bring action—Interest.
Where the words of an agreement are joint, yet if the interest be several, each party may maintain an action, thus:—Where the defendant guaranteed "that the wages due W. K. and G. N. from J. K. for making timber shall be satisfied when they brought the timber up," and the contract of hiring by W. K. and G. N. was separate and distinct. Held, That each could maintain an action on the guarantee. *Neville* v. *Joseph*, *Hil. T.* 1832.

9—Right to rescind agreement.
Where a number of persons jointly agree with another as to any particular matter, the agreement can only be rescinded by the consent of all. *Palmer* v. *Long*, *Ber.* 122.

BREACH OF AGREEMENT.

Unpaid Instalment—Damages—Cross Action. See Damages.

Action before expiration of credit—See Action at Law VII.

Action for breach. See Assumpsit I.

ALIEN.

1—Liability for Tax.
An alien resident in this Province is liable to the payment of an exempt tax of thirty shillings annually, under the Militia Act 6 Geo. 4, c. 18; and not merely to one payment of that sum. *Watson* v. *Haley*, 1 *Kerr* 124.

2—Tax, when recoverable.
The alien tax imposed by the Act 6 Geo. 4, c. 18, must be recovered by the quarter master in office when it is incurred; therefore, a conviction for £3 for alien tax for the years 1845 and 1846, on the prosecution of a quarter master appointed in 1846, not being severable, is bad. *Brannen* v. *Dunn*, 1 *All.* 218.

3—Officer's Return—Evidence.
The return made by a captain of a company to a quarter master of militia, according to the Act 6 Geo. 4, c. 18, stating a party to be an alien, is not sufficient evidence of that fact. *Brannen* v. *Leavitt*, 1 *All.* 220.

4—Recovery of Judgment against, for tax—Evidence.
The recovery of a judgment against a party for his tax as an alien, on the prosecution of a quarter master of militia, without shewing that it has been paid, is not sufficient evidence of his being an alien, in a prosecution for a subsequent year's tax. *Brannan* v. *Williams*, 1 *All.* 221.

5—Discharge.
An alien cannot discharge himself from the tax imposed by the Act 6 Geo. 4. c. 18, by showing that he had enrolled himself and served in the militia of the Province. *Brannen* v. *Williams*, 1 *Kerr* 222.

ALTERATION.

1—In Deed—Materiality.
Whether an alteration in a deed of conveyance of the number of acres sold is such a material alteration as to require explanatory evidence before deed is admitted in evidence. See *Moran* v. *Laird*, 3 *Kerr* 403.

Of Writ—Statute of Limitations. See Amendment 30. See also Limitation of Actions III. 1, 2.

2—Re-sealing Writ.
An alteration made in, on the return day of a writ, though before it is returnable, vitiates it, unless it is re-sealed. *Andrews* v. *McKenzie*, 1 *All.* 264.

Of Highway—Notice. See Highways 11.

ALBERT MINING COMPANY.

See Joint Stock Company 15.

AMBIGUITY.

Boundary Line. See Crown Grant I. 5, 9.

Policy of Insurance, description of voyage. See Insurance 21.

AMENDMENT.

I. Pleadings.

II. Writs—Returns.

III. Records—Rolls—Bail-piece—Rules.

IV. Miscellaneous.

I.

Pleadings.

Warrant—substituted for Summons. See Malicious Prosecution 5.

Nisi Prius Record—Copy—Variance. See New Trial III. 53.

Amendment at Trial—Description of Mill. See Pleading I. 24.

Replevin Bond—Statutory form. See Bond 18.

After Demurrer Books delivered—Allowed. See Pine *v.* McLauhlan, *Ber.* 81.

1—Variance—Record—Description.
On the trial of an issue on *nul tiel record*, a variance between the record produced and the description of it in the declaration and replication may be amended. See *Roberts* v. *Watson*, 1 *All.* 2.

Declaration.
Promissory Note—doubt whether given to one or both defendants. See Pleading I. 26.

2—After Judgment on Demurrer.
Court granted leave to amend the declaration where the plea, if allowed to stand, might be a bar to the whole cause of action,—the demurrer having likewise arisen out of Acts of Assembly, complex and difficult in construction. *Coy* v. *Barker*, 1 *All.* 29.

3—After second Demurrer.
After judgment on a second demurrer to a declaration on an administration bond, leave was given to make a second amendment; the plaintiff's counsel stating that he had been misled by an expression of the Court in giving judgment on the demurrer. *Sherlock* v. *McGee*, 1 *All.* 436.

4—Declaration—Indorsement of Bill.
In action by Survivors of Firm, the declaration alleged the bill was indorsed to Firm. Held, That the declaration might be amended under Act 7 Wm. 4, c. 14, s. 7. See *Tarratt* v. *Wilmot*, 1 *All.* 353.

5—Trespass—Error in copying Declaration.
Where an attorney's clerk in copying a declaration in trespass, inserted the word "whereas," in consequence of which the defendant demurred, and the plaintiff being unable to discover any error in the draft of declaration, applied to the defendant to be allowed to inspect the copy served, and offered to pay him the costs of amending, if necessary, which the defendant refused to comply with, and on argument of the demurrer, judgment was given for the defendant; the plaintiff was allowed to amend on payment of costs up to the time of the demurrer—it

appearing that the draft and copy of declaration filed were correct. *Wilson* v. *Andrews*, 1 *All.* 670.

6—Trespass—Defendants not all served with process—Striking out of Nisi Prius Record and Declaration, name of defendant not served.

In trespass for assault against three persons, one of them was not served with process, the others appeared and pleaded, and a verdict was found against them. A motion having been made to set aside the verdict and Nisi Prius record on the ground that the cause was not at issue till the other defendant was before the Court, the plaintiff was allowed to amend by striking the name of that defendant out of the Nisi Prius record and declaration, and the defendant's rule was refused. *Ayre* v. *Main*, *Mich. T.* 1866.

7—Adding Counts—Refusal.

In an action against the registered owner of a vessel for negligence of the master, whereby the cargo was detained, and the plaintiff sustained damage, and had to pay a sum of money to get possession of the cargo, a verdict was given for the plaintiff. On motion to enter a non-suit on the ground that the defendant, as registered owner, was not liable, the Court refused to amend the declaration by adding a count charging him with being the agent of the master, and wrongfully advising him to detain the cargo unless plaintiff paid him $496, and alleging that the defendant did detain the cargo till such money was paid,—the object of such amendment being to retain the verdict for the amount so paid to defendant. *Newbury* v. *Young*, *East. T.* 1872.

8—Striking out name of one of defendants—Not shewing prejudice.

An application to amend at Nisi Prius by striking out the name of one of the defendants was opposed on the ground that such defendant was entitled to costs, and that the other defendant was entitled to show by affidavit that he would be prejudiced by the amendment. The Judge offered to receive the *viva voce* evidence of the attorney and the other defendant on those points, which was declined. Held, That the amendment was properly made, without costs to the defendant, whose name was struck out. *Morrow* v. *Hamilton*, *Hil. T.* 1872.

9—Variance in Note—Judge's decision on trial.

In an action on a promissory note alleged to be payable on demand, the note offered in evidence was payable twelve months after date: the plaintiff having applied to amend, the defendant asked for time till the next day to obtain the affidavit of the real defendant. The Judge refused this, but offered to allow the defendant about half an hour for the purpose, which he declined, and the amendment was accordingly made. The Court refused to interfere with the Judge's decision,—it appearing that there was but one note between the parties, that the defendant had seen it in the hands of the plaintiff's attorney after the action was brought, and had promised to pay it, but afterwards refused to do so. *Minas Insurance Co.* v. *Rivers*, *Trin. T.* 1872.

10—Ejectment—Demise expired.

Where the demise stated in a declaration of ejectment had expired, the Court refused after a delay of three years, to allow the plaintiff to amend by extending the demise, though it was suggested the defendant would set up the statute of limitations as a defence to a new action. *Doe* v. *Todd*, 1 *All.* 601.

11—Where an action of ejectment was commenced in 1849, the demise in the declaration being for seven years, and judgment was signed in that year, but no writ of possession was issued, and the tenant had since died; the Court refused to enlarge the demise, though the lessor of the plaintiff swore that he had abstained from issuing execution at the request of the tenant, who had promised to pay the costs and to indemnify the lessor of the plaintiff against a legacy which was charged on the land, and which he had been obliged to pay in 1864. *Doe d. Fauls* v. *Jones*, *Mich. T.* 1865.

12—Description—Abuttals.

In trespass *quare Cl. fregit*, not describing the close by abuttals, defendant pleaded *liberum tenementum*, and proved title to a close within the parish mentioned in the declaration; the plaintiff was allowed to amend, setting out the close by abuttals. *Desbrisay* v. *Livingstone*, *Trin. T.* 1864.

13—Special Entitling—Commencement of Action.

In an action on a promissory note dated 22nd April 1864, payable twelve months after date, the declaration was entitled of Easter Term 1865, (the first day of which was before the note was due,) and the

Judge allowed the record to be amended by entitling the declaration specially of a day subsequent to the note becoming due. Held, (after inspecting the writ in the cause) That the amendment was properly made. *Brown* v. *Foster*, *Hil. T.* 1866.

14—Consideration—Allegation—Proof. It is necessary not only to allege the actual consideration, but the proof must correspond with the allegation. In this case the plaintiff alleged that the consideration consisted of *certain standing trees, goods, wares, and merchandize, and stumpage;* the evidence shewed the consideration to consist of stumpage alone. A verdict having been taken for the plaintiff, subject to a motion for a nonsuit, the Court allowed the plaintiff to amend on payment of all costs, and made the rule absolute for a new trial instead of a nonsuit, on the condition of the payment of such costs. *Whitney* v. *Marks*, 1 *Kerr* 179.

15—Entitling Declaration in the Record—Limitation of Action—Insurance Policy. By one of the conditions of a policy of insurance the non-commencement of an action within a year after the loss was declared to be a defence. In a suit on the policy this objection was taken; it appearing by the Nisi Prius record that the action was commenced after the year. Application to amend the entitling of the declaration in the record was refused, there being nothing to show that such amendment would make the record correspond with the declaration on file. Evidence was also offered to show the time of commencing the action, which the Judge thought insufficient, and the defendant had a verdict. Held, That his decision was right. *Commercial Bank* v. *Ætna Ins. Co.*, *Hil. T.* 1863.

16—If it had appeared that the declaration on file was entitled of a term within the year. *Semble*—That the Court on motion for a new trial would have amended the Nisi Prius record to correspond with it.—*Ibid.*

17—Plea—After Demurrer. After demurrer is argued the Court will allow the plea to be withdrawn upon payment of costs of demurrer. *Strang* v. *Bell*, *Ber.* 287.

Replication—Omission of entry of former proceedings. See Pleading I. 7.

Death—Suggestion of. See Summary Action 4.

18—Bill in Equity Pleadings—Practice. A Court of Equity has an inherent power to amend the pleadings in a cause, and an amendment may be made *ex parte;* though, ordinarily, notice should be given. *Wiggins* v. *Hendricks*, *East. T.* 1872.

In a foreclosure suit, the mortgage was particularly set out in the bill, and the land described as being in the Parish of K. (according to the mortgage): the bill was taken *pro confesso*, and the plaintiff afterwards discovering that part of the land was in the Parish of N., obtained an *ex parte* order to amend the bill in the description of the situation of the land. The property was sold under the decree in February; the defendant knew of the advertisement, and was present at the sale; and in May he applied to set aside the proceedings for irregularity. Held, 1. That the mortgage having been particularly set out in the bill, no amendment was necessary. 2. That if the amendment was necessary, the defendant had not been prejudiced by it. 3. That if an amendment made *ex parte* was irregular, the defendant should have applied before this sale, to set aside the order, and had waived the objection by his delay. *Ibid.*

II.

Writs—Returns.

1—Sheriff—Return on writ. Where the Sheriff had under an execution against B., at the suit of A., levied on the goods of C., and returned the execution satisfied, but C. had since recovered the amount from the Sheriff, who was indemnified by A., the Court allowed the execution to be taken from the files of the Court, in order that the Sheriff might amend his return, A. having lost the fruits of his execution. *Ketchum* v. *Giberson*, 1 *Kerr* 510.

2—Execution and Judgment—Variance. On a motion to set aside a judgment and execution on the ground (*inter alia*) that the execution differed in amount from the judgment, a cross application to amend the execution was granted on payment of costs. *Lynott* v. *Seely*, 1 *All.* 35.

3—Ca. Sa. An application to amend a *ca. s*[illegible] issued sixteen years ago, by inserting [illegible] *testatum* clause, will not be granted unless the writ is found on file, or some record of it is produced. *Quære*, Whether such an amendment would be made after such a lapse of time, and after the defendant had been arrested on a second execution, which was also irregular. *Brown* v. *Partelow*, 3 *Kerr* 324.

4—Summons—Death of one defendant.
Where one of the persons named as defendant in a suit, had died before summons issued, the pleadings were amended by striking out his name, and answer was re-sworn. See *Byers* v. *Harrigan*, 1 *Han.* 231.

Writ of Inquiry.
If necessary to set out whole declaration in writ—May be amended. See Practice X. 5.

III.

RECORDS—ROLLS—BAIL-PIECE—RULE.

1—Nisi Prius Record—Ejectment—No issue.
If after the jury are sworn in an action of ejectment, it be discovered that there is no issue, the trespass and ejectment being charged on the record to have been committed by the casual ejector instead of the defendant; the proper course is to discharge the jury, and amend the record at Chambers. *Doe dem Andrews* v. *Seelye*, 3 *Kerr* 134.

2—Judgment Roll.
On a declaration containing five counts, there was a verdict for the plaintiff on the second, and no notice taken of the others. After the expiration of two terms, while a motion for a new trial was pending, the plaintiff entered up judgment on the verdict without any continuances: the defendant brought a writ of error, assigning as grounds, the absence of any finding by the jury on the four counts, and the want of continuances on the roll. The Court allowed the plaintiff to amend the roll by an entry that the jury were discharged from any finding on the other four counts, and also by entering continuances from the return of the *distringas* to the time of signing judgment. *McMillan* v. *Ritchie*, 2 *All.* 469.

3—Nunc pro tunc.
Where the plaintiff's attorney had accidentally omitted to insert the amount of damages and costs in the judgment roll, but issued execution for the amount, the Court allowed the roll to be amended *nunc pro tunc*; though the defendant (relying upon the omission) had brought an action of trespass against the plaintiff for seizing his property under the execution. *Smith* v. *Sonea*, 4 *All.* 266.

4—Judgment Roll and Execution—Errors.
Semble, That errors in the judgment roll and execution are not sufficient to invalidate a *bona fide* sale made by the sheriff; as they may be amended. *Doe* v. *Donnelly*, 3 *Kerr* 66.

5—Postea.
If a declaration contains several counts, some of which are bad, and a general verdict is entered on all the counts, the postea may afterwards be amended by confining the verdict to the good counts, if the evidence given at the trial was admissible upon them, and it cannot be inferred that any of the evidence or any part of the damages was given distinctly on the bad count. *Milner* v. *Gilbert*, 1 *All.* 51.

6—Bail Piece—Right to amend.
Where the defendants' attorney in preparing a special bail piece by mistake omitted one of the initial letters of the plaintiff's name, but stated the name correctly in the notice of bail, and proceedings were taken against the bail, the Court refused to set aside the recognizance roll on account of the variance between it and the bail piece, and allowed the plaintiff to amend the bail piece by inserting the initial letter, on payment of costs, it appearing that the bail could not have been misled by the mistake, and that no injustice would be done by the amendment. *Estey* v. *Brown*, 2 *All.* 527.

Such a mistake would have been amendable without consent of the bail, before the Act 14 Vic. c. 20. A bail piece is a "legal proceeding," within the meaning of that Act. *Semble*, That the bail would have been liable on the recognizance, without amendment, if the facts had been properly suggested in the recognizance roll. *Ibid.*

7—Consent Rule—Terms of amendment.
The defendant in ejectment entered into a general consent rule; at the trial, the Judge directed a verdict for the defendant for all but a small part of the land described, but the jury did not agree, and

after the trial, the defendant obtained an order to amend the consent rule by striking out that portion of the land, on the ground that it was included by mistake. Held, That as the plaintiff was entitled to a verdict for that part of the land, and consequently to the general costs of the cause, the amendment could only be made on payment of such costs by the defendant. *Doe* v. *Day*, 3 *All.* 440.

IV.

MISCELLANEOUS.

1—Alteration of Writ—Refusal to amend.
Where the plaintiff altered the return day of a writ from the first to the last day of a term, in consequence of which a verdict in his favour was set aside, the Court refused an application to amend the writ by striking out the alteration and restoring it to its original form, though the plaintiff was barred by the statute of limitations from bringing a fresh action. [illegible] v. *O'Donnell*, 1 *All.* 361.

2—Promissory Note—Refusal to amend.
The declaration in the first and second counts stated a promissory note made by the defendant to the plaintiff 31st March 1841, for £104, and in the third and fourth counts a note dated 9th July 1844, of a similar amount; the note proved was a joint note, made by the defendant and one J. F. E., to the plaintiff, dated 28th February 1842, for £104 17s. 1d. Application was made to amend, which was refused. On a rule to set aside the verdict: Held, That the note set out was a separate note, and the note proved was a joint note; that if the note had been truly set out the defendant would have had a right to plead in abatement; and therefore the Judge was right in refusing the amendment, and the variance was fatal. *McKeen* v. *Estabrooks*, 3 *Kerr* 369.

3—Judge refusing amendment.
When a Judge at Nisi Prius refuses an amendment, the Court will not review his decision unless they are satisfied injustice has been done by the refusal. *McAllister* v. *Day*, 4 *All.* 37.

Semble, That an amendment which would introduce a new cause of action, ought not to be allowed. *Ibid.*

4—Name of Parish—Variance.
A variance in the description of the parish in an action of ejectment may be amended under the act 7 Wm. 4, c. 14, after the counsel has addressed the jury, and the Judge is not bound to receive new evidence on the part of the defendant, to shew that the parish was not rightly stated after the amendment. *Doe* v. *Pitt*, 1 *All.* 385.

5—Adding name—Foreclosure suit.
Where an amendment was made in a foreclosure suit, by adding plaintiffs after the filing of the bill, the defendant was allowed a month to answer after service of the order to amend, and of a copy of the amended bill. *Wright* v. *Evanson*, 1 *Han.* 232.

Declaration amendable as to description—Amendment must be made at trial. See Pleading I. 24.

Lateness of Amendment—Consent rule. See New Trial III. 54.

Agreement of reference at Nisi Prius. See Arbitration V. 6.

Amendments in pleadings in Equity. See Practice in Equity.

ANCIENT DEED.

See Deed I. 7.

ANSWER IN EQUITY.

See Equity.

APPEAL.

See Privy Council.

" Supreme Court in Equity.

Entry of. See Practice V. 3.

Insolvent Act of 1869—Summary convictions. See Certiorari I. 5, 6.

1—From Judge in Equity.
The Supreme Court has jurisdiction to hear an appeal from the decision of a Judge in Equity, though notice of the grounds of appeal has not been served on the Judge as directed by the Act 17 Vic. c. 18, s. 33. *McDade* v. *Peters*, *Mich. T.* 1871.

Reviewing Judges order for leave to appeal. See Practice V. 5 a.

2—From Probate Court.
Appeals from the decision of the Probate Courts must be made to the Supreme Court, and not to one Judge sitting in Equity. *Ex parte Roach*, *Mich. T.* 1871.

3—Costs.
When a Judge declines to hear such an appeal for want of jurisdiction, he has no power to give costs to a party appearing to oppose the appeal. *Ibid.*

4—Granting further time.
When in consequence of an appeal having been made to the wrong tribunal, the time for appealing allowed by 1 Rev. Stat. c. 136, s. 46, had expired; the Court granted further time on filing a proper bond for costs, and on paying the opposite party the costs of applying to set aside the appeal. *Exparte Roach, Hil. T.* 1872.

5—Cause depending on credibility of witnesses heard before Judge—Finality.
When a cause was heard viva voce before a Judge in Equity, and defendant, altogether upon the credibility of the respective witnesses, the Court refused to hear an appeal from the Judge's decision. *Smith* v. *Armstrong, East. T.* 1872.

6—Decree—Variation or reversal of—Subsequent proceedings.
If a decree or order of a Judge in Equity is reversed or varied by the Court of Appeal, any subsequent proceedings in the cause take place in the Court below. *McLeod* v. *Thomas, East. T.* 1871.

7—Filing Bond—Leave to appeal—Conditions.
A Judge in Equity refused to hear an appeal from the Probate Court on the ground that he had no jurisdiction, that the appeal should have been made to the Supreme Court. Application was then made to the Supreme Court within six months after the decision in the Probate Court, and leave given to appeal, on which the appellant filed a bond for costs. On application to set aside the order for leave to appeal, on the ground that the affidavits on which it was obtained, were improperly entitled, and that the bond was not in the form required by the 1 Rev. Stat. c. 136, s. 46, the appeal was ordered to be heard on the appellant filing a bond conditioned to pay such costs as the Supreme Court should adjudge, and on payment of the costs of the application, though more than six months had elapsed since the decision of the Judge of Probates. *Ex parte Stockton, Hil. T.* 1872.

8—County Court—Interlocutory Order.
Quære, Whether there is any appeal to the Supreme Court under the Act 30 Vic. c. 10, from an interlocutory order of a Judge of a County Court: but an order absolutely to stay the proceedings in a suit, is a final decision, and may be appealed from. *Hannington* v. *Stewart, Hil. T.* 1873.

APPEARANCE.

Summons—Defect in, cured by appearance. See Justices of the Peace IV. 17.

Voluntary dispensing with time. See Pleading I. 37.

Filing Plea before appearance. See Summary Action 2.

Entering Special Bail.
Entering special bail and giving a notice thereof signed "Attorney for defendant" is a sufficient appearance, without adding express words of appearance. *Fleming* v. *Shaw, C. Ms.* 117.

APPOINTMENT OF OFFICER.

1—Harbour Master—Holding over—Recovery of Fees.
Where the Justices of the Peace at the General Sessions had always appointed the harbour master annually, including him in the annual list of the parish officers, and had from time to time made change in the list as regarded the office, there being no other minute or warrant of the appointment than the list entered on the Court minutes. Held, That the plaintiff, who was so appointed, could not hold over after the year against the defendant, appointed in his place, nor recover from him the fees of office received by the defendant while acting in the office under his appointment: the plaintiff's appointment was either not valid at all, or expired at the termination of his year and the appointment of his successor. *Stewart* v. *McDonald*, 1 *Kerr* 52.

2—Commissioners of Sewerage.
By the Act 18 Vic. c. 38, the Common Council of St. John is authorized and empowered to appoint, and also "to remove and re-appoint from time to time, as may be expedient," two Commissioners of Sewerage and Water Supply. Held, That the appointment was during the pleasure of the Common Council, and that they were the proper judges whether it was "expedient" to remove the Commissioners. *Ex parte Sears, Trin. T.* 1864.

Without limitation is an appointment for life. See Joplin v. Davidson, Ber. 308.

Under Medical Act. See Pleading I. 56. Peterson v. Harding, 4 All 583.

DIRECTORS OF BANK.

See Bank 3.

APPORTIONMENT OF DAMAGES.

Trespass on two lots—Claim—Verdict general. See Trespass IV. 6.

APPRAISERS.

Appointing of. See Landlord and Tenant 14.

APPRENTICE.

Infant—Conviction.
A conviction of an indented apprentice for making brooms contrary to an agreement contained in an indenture which he executed while an infant, is bad. *Regina* v. *Hawes*, 1 *All.* 100.

The provisions of the Rev. Stat. c. 134, s. 6, apply to all indentures, whether the apprentice is above or under fourteen years of age, and unless the requisites of that section are complied with, the apprentice is not liable to imprisonment by Justices under the 15th section of the Act. *Harris* v. *Roulston*, *Trin. T.* 1872.

APPROPRIATION OF PAYMENT.

Dealings with Old and New Firm—Remittances—Application of.
Defendant being indebted to a firm, of which one of the plaintiffs was a member, after the transfer of the debts and business of that firm to the plaintiffs, continued to deal with and make remittances to the new firm, with a knowledge of the transfer. Held, That the jury were warranted in finding that the remittances were intended to be, and were properly applied by the plaintiffs, to pay the debts due the old firm. *Esson* v. *Dunn*, *Mich. T.* 1862.

Want of Privity. See Bills and Notes V. 20.

Set Off. See Bills and Notes V. 17.

Application by law—Set off and payment—Right of defendant to show appropriation on cross examination of witnesses. See Evidence VIII. 7.

Work and Labour—Agreement to appropriate towards rent. See Assumpsit III. 20, 54.

Money Appropriated. See Assumpsit III. 35, and Bills and Notes V. 17.

APPURTENANCES.

See Crown Grant.

ARBITRATION AND AWARD.

I. Submission and Reference.
II. Revocation.
III. Matters Vitiating Award.
IV. Setting Aside Award.
V. Miscellaneous.

I.
Arbitration and Award.

1—Submission and Reference.
A submission to arbitration allowed to be made a rule of the Supreme Court under the Act of Parliament 9 and 10 Wm. 3. c. 15. *Doe d. Allen* v. *Murray*, 2 *Kerr* 359.

2—Must be made a rule of Court before moving to set aside award. *Nugent* v. *Barron*, 2 *All.* 621.

3—Enlarging Time.
When the time for making an award is enlarged by mutual deed of the parties, the effect will be the same as if the enlarged time had been that originally inserted in the submission. See *Ferguson* v. *Munro*, 2 *Kerr* 660.

II.
Revocation.

1—Joint Submission—Forfeiture of Bond—Damages.
One of two persons on the same side may revoke a joint submission to arbitration: and such revocation will be a forfeiture of a joint and several bond by both, conditioned to stand to, obey and perform the award. *Hatheway* v. *Cliff*, 2 *All.* 267.

When arbitrators, after a revocation, make an award which is unimpeached, the amount awarded is a proper measure of damages in an action on the arbitration bond. *Ibid.*

2—Notice to Arbitrators not to proceed—Party desirous to revoke—Practice.
On a reference under a rule of Court, notice given by one of the parties to the

arbitrators not to proceed, cannot, since the Act 7 Wm. 4, c. 14, s. 27, affect the validity of the award. If either party be desirous of revoking the submission, he should apply to a Judge. *Lloyd* v. *Hoskins*, 1 *Kerr* 132.

III.

MATTERS VITIATING AWARD.

1—Matters not included in Submission—Pleading in Bar.
To debt on a bond conditioned to perform an award, it is a good plea in bar, that part of one entire sum awarded by the arbitrators, arose out of a matter not included in the submission. *Hill* v. *Coy*, 1 *Kerr* 187.

2—Want of Notice.
Where a question upon a disputed boundary was left to reference, and the arbitrators informed the parties that they would employ a surveyor to make a survey of the land, which they were empowered to do under the terms of the submission, before they made their award; but they nevertheless proceeded to make their award without any such survey, and without any notice that they had changed their intention; the Court set aside their award. *Doe dem. Allen* v. *Murray*, 2 *Kerr* 439.

3—Award by two without notice to third.
Where a cause is referred to three arbitrators whose award, or that of any two of whom is to be final, two of these cannot proceed to make an award without giving notice to the third. *Raymond and another* v. *Luke*, *Ber.* 116.

4—Uncertainty.
An award directing "security to be given on a certain part of the property of A. B.," without stating what part, is void for uncertainty. *Burgoyne* v. *Burgoyne*, *U. Ms.* 120.

5—Interest—Partiality.
The Court will not disturb an award made under a rule of reference, on the grounds of interest and partiality in the arbitrators, unless the interest or partiality is very clearly shown; especially (*per Parker, J.*) where a party after discovering this had an opportunity of applying to a Judge to revoke the submission, of which he has not availed himself. *Lloyd* v. *Hoskins*, 1 *Kerr* 132.

Averment—Condition—Indenture. See Pleading I. 10.

6—Amount exceeding Penalty.
An award is not invalid because the amount awarded exceeds the penalty of the arbitration bond; neither will the recovery be limited to that penalty in an action on the award which proceeds on the mutual submission of the parties. See *Ferguson* v. *Munro*, 2 *Kerr* 660.

IV.

SETTING ASIDE AWARD.

1—Irregularity of Proceedings.
Where the proceedings of arbitrators had not been strictly regular, and the consequences of sustaining the award would be more serious than those of setting it aside, the Court set it aside, though the affidavits were contradictory,—it being doubtful whether the party had received notice of a meeting. *Brown* v. *Gurrier*, 2 *All.* 124.

It is necessary to give notice of an adjourned meeting, where the parties are not present at the adjournment. *Quære*, Whether notice of a meeting to the counsel in a cause which is referred, is notice to the party? *Ibid.*

2—Want of Notice—Mutuality.
The defendant having cut lumber on the plaintiff's land, agreed in writing to pay him such sum as two arbitrators should decide—it being understood at the time, that the plaintiff was to show the bounds of his land. The plaintiff afterwards, without notice to the defendant, pointed out his boundaries to the arbitrators, who awarded a certain sum to be due him. Held, That the award was bad for want of the notice. *Therriau* v. *Therriau*, 4 *All.* 48.

Quære, Whether the agreement to refer, being signed by the defendant only, was not bad for want of mutuality. *Ibid.*

3—Not signing within Time.
Under a submission at Nisi Prius to the award of A, B and C or any two of them, they agreed upon an award, and it was drawn up, signed by A and B and delivered to C to be signed by him and handed to the parties; C discovered a mistake, to which A and B consenting, the award was corrected and signed by all three, but not within the time limited. The Court refused to give effect to either. *Wilson* v. *Kerr and Campbell*, *Ber.* 280.

4—Arbitrators exceeding power.
An award made under a rule of reference,

set aside on account of arbitrators exceeding their power. See *Campbell* v. *Wilson*, *Ber.* 104.

5—Making award in favor of defendant under rule of reference to ascertain amount due plaintiff—Improper credits.

When a verdict was taken for the plaintiff for £1000 subject to the award of arbitrators to be agreed upon, and a rule of reference, subsequently drawn up, which, after reciting the agreement, directed that the award should be entered on the *postea* as a verdict of the jury—Held, That the award could not be made in favour of the defendant, and that the power of the arbitrators was confined to the *quantum* of damages only. Held also That as the submission was "all matters in the cause," they could not give the defendant credit for an item which could not come under the head of payment or set off in the cause. *Campbell* v. *Wilson*, *Ber.* 104.

6—Further information after close of evidence.

When after the evidence had closed, and the attorneys for the parties had left the room, the defendant's attorney made a communication to one of the arbitrators respecting a matter in controversy, in consequence of which the arbitrators obtained further information on the subject, and one of them swore that his decision was materially influenced thereby; an award in favor of the defendant was set aside, though the other arbitrators swore that they were not influenced by the subsequent information. *M'Causland* v. *Power*, *East T.* 1872.

7—Improper reception of evidence.

Where arbitrators improperly receive evidence *ex parte* the award will be set aside without reference to the probability of their having been influenced by the evidence. *Ibid.*

8—Swearing witnesses—Waiver.

An award will not be disturbed where the witnesses were examined without being sworn, although the rule of reference required them to be sworn if the party objecting to the award were present and consented to such examination. *Reilley* v. *Gillam*, *Ber.* 120.

a—An award made under a reference at *Nisi Prius* will not be set aside on the ground that witnesses were examined without being sworn if the objection was not taken before the arbitrators. *Serlyn* v. *Kelly*, *Hil. T.* 1827.

9—Objections—Merits.

An application to set aside an award will not be sustained on objections going only to the merits. *Forbes* v. *Lord*, *O. Ms* 60.

10—Discovery of new evidence.

An award made under a rule of reference at Nisi Prius, will not be set aside on the ground of the discovery of material evidence after the award, where the party who speaks as to the discovery of the paper, swears only in general terms, that he had made diligent search, etc., without stating the particular circumstances relating to the search and finding. *Woodward* v. *Merritt*, *O. Ms.* 86.

11—Awarding costs—Vitiating whole award.

A cause was referred—the costs to abide the event of the award. The defendant admitted that the sum claimed was due at the time of the arbitration, but objected to pay the costs because the action was commenced before the credit expired, and the arbitrators having found this to be the fact, awarded the amount admitted to the plaintiff, and directed that he should pay all the costs. Held, It appearing that the award had been made on condition that the defendant should not be subject to costs, and the whole award not being sustainable, that it was bad altogether. *Emms* v. *Neill*, 3 *All.* 438.

12—Laches.

The Court will not entertain an application to set aside an award made under rule of reference, when the award was to be entered on the postea as a verdict of a jury when the applicant has been guilty of laches. See *Foulis* v. *Kinnear*, *Ber.* 26.

Setting aside judgment on award for fraud. See Practice VI, 5.

13—Time of application to set aside award.

An application to set aside an award upon a submission made pursuant to the Statute 9 and 10 Wm. 3, c. 15, must be made before the last day of the term next after the publishing of the award. *Carter* v. *Adam*, 2 *All.* 211.

14—A motion to set aside an award under a submission with a clause of consent to make it a rule of Court, must be made before the last day of the term next after the award is published. *Nugent* v. *Barron*, 2 *All.* 621.

15—Where an award made under an order of Nisi Prius is entered on the *postea* as a verdict under the Act 12 Vic. c. 39, an application to set it aside may be made at any time before judgment is signed, if within twenty days after the award is filed with the Clerk of the Circuits. *Brown* v. *Harding*, 3 *All.* 351.

16—Subject to same rules as motion for new trials.

Motion to disturb award entered on postea as a verdict of jury, must be governed by same rules as motions for new trials. See *Foulis* v. *Kinnear*, *Ber.* 26..

17—Umpire—Joining with Arbitrators.

Where the submission to arbitration was by mutual bonds, conditioned to abide the award of two arbitrators if made by a certain day; but if they failed to make an award, then to abide by an umpirage to be made on the same day. Held, That an award made in due time would be valid as the award of the two arbitrators, although the umpire joined with them. *Ferguson* v. *Munro*, 2 *Kerr* 660.

The name of B. P. was inserted as umpire in the condition of the defendant's bond, but omitted in that of the plaintiff's, a blank left for his name not having been filled up. Held, That the award was not vitiated by B. P. joining with the two arbitrators in making it, although there was no mutual submission to him. *Ibid.*

Arbitrators competent to decide matters of Law. See Foulis *v.* Kinnear, *Ber.* 26.

18—Attachment.

Award must be before Court before an attachment will be granted for non-performance. See *Marks* v. *Marks*, 3 *Kerr* 486.

V.

MISCELLANEOUS.

1—Award good in part—Entry on postea.

An action of trover was referred by order of Nisi Prius; the arbitrators awarded that the defendant should restore the property to the plaintiff, or pay him £152. Held, That the award was good as to the latter alternative, and that the verdict should be entered on the postea for the amount. *Hughson* v. *White*, *East. T.* 1831.

2—Operation of award.

In trespass *quare Cl. fregit*, where the legal title to the land was in the defendant who, some time before the present action, had brought ejectment against the plaintiff to recover the land, which action was referred to arbitration, and the arbitrators awarded that the present plaintiff was entitled to retain the land as his own property, and that the present defendant should forthwith execute a deed of the land to the plaintiff or his heirs. Held, That the award did not operate as a conveyance of the land, and that the defendant was not estopped from setting up his legal title as a defence in this action. *Oliver* v *Elliott*, *Trin. T.* 1861.

3—Divisible—Affidavit of Arbitrator.

A cause was referred at Nisi Prius—the award to be entered on the postea, and costs to abide the event. The award ordered that defendant should pay plaintiff a certain sum, and that each party should pay his own costs. Held, That the award was divisible; that the part relating to the costs could be separated from the rest, and the award entered up as a verdict, with costs. Also, that an affidavit of the arbitrators was inadmissible to show that if they had known they had no power over the costs, they would have awarded a different amount to the plaintiff. *Hussey* v. *Ferguson*, *Hil. T.* 1864.

4—Married woman cannot bind herself by bond to refer.

A married woman cannot bind herself by bond to refer matters to arbitration, and her coverture is a good defence to an action for non-performance of an award made under such a reference,—there being no mutuality in the submission. *Harper* v. *Alexander*, *Mich. T.* 1866.

5—Reasonable certainty.

An agreement of reference recited that an action by defendant against plaintiff was pending; that the parties had agreed to refer the action and all claims, etc., between them relating thereto, or growing out of their dealings; that the action should be discontinued, and that the costs of the cause and of the reference should be in the discretion of the arbitrators. The arbitrators awarded that defendant should pay plaintiff £1000, in full payment and satisfaction of all accounts and transactions between them, and in full and final adjustment of all matters in difference; that defendant should pay plaintiff £12, the costs of the reference, and that on payment of these two sums, the parties should be *ipso facto* mutually discharged from all claims and demands which they had against each other. Held, That the award was reasonably certain, and in effect decided that each party should pay his own costs of the action. *Adam* v. *Carter*, *Hil. T.* 1864.

6—Amendment of Agreement of reference—Refusal to insert clause.

Where the plaintiff's attorney, in making a fair copy of an agreement of reference at Nisi Prius, by mistake omitted the clause that the award was to be entered on the postea as a verdict, the Court refused to allow that clause to be inserted in the agreement after the plaintiff had caused it to be made a rule of this Court. *Tobin* v. *Layton*, 2 *All.* 584.

7—Costs—Power to award—Postea—Separate actions.

An action of assumpsit and an action of debt pending between the parties, they agreed to refer them to arbitration—the award to be entered on the postea as a verdict, the costs of the causes to abide the event, and the costs of the reference to be in the discretion of the arbitrators. The arbitrators awarded that the action of debt should be discontinued, each party paying his own costs; that £40 were due the plaintiff in the action of assumpsit, and that each party should pay half the costs of the reference—the moiety payable by the defendant to be taxed as costs in the cause. The Court refused to make an order for entering the award for the plaintiff on the postea in the action of assumpsit, unless he consented that a verdict should be entered for the defendant in the action of debt. *Abbot* v. *Abbot*, 4 *All.* 87.

8—Power in Judge to order costs—Set off.

Where a case is referred at Nisi Prius, and judgment on the award is to be entered as a verdict, the Judge of the Court of Nisi Prius may make an order for full costs, where the plaintiff's demand is reduced by set-off; and such order may be made *ex parte*. *Scelye* v. *Styles*, 3 *All.* 246.

9—Referees—When considered as agents of parties in stating accounts.

Plaintiff being lessee of land, assigned one half of it to the defendant, who entered into a bond to pay the plaintiff for half the buildings, such sum as two arbitrators should determine before a certain day: the arbitrators not having been appointed under the bond, the parties afterwards agreed verbally to refer the valuation to arbitrators, who made an award of the value. Held, That the referees were the agents of the parties to settle the value, and that the plaintiff might recover the amount awarded by them, as an account stated. *Coram* v. *Wheten*, 4 *All.* 293.

10—Concurrent Acts—When not considered such.

An award directed that the defendant should pay the plaintiff [illegible] of money on a certain day, and th[illegible] such payment being made the defendant should be entitled to receive, and the plaintiff should deliver him two parcels of sleepers then lying at L. Held, That they were not concurrent acts, and in an action on the award for money, it was not necessary for the plaintiff to aver a readiness to deliver the sleepers. *Hassell* v. *Wilson*, 1 *All.* 618.

11—Breach of Bond for performance of award—particular breach must be stated in the declaration—general allegation is insufficient. See Burgoyne v. Burgoyne, C. Ms. 120.

12—Pleading in bar to action on bond or award.

Any facts which vitiate ar[illegible] ard (except misconduct of the arbi[illegible]) may be pleaded in bar to an act[illegible] the arbitration bond, or on the award, though such facts do not appear on the face of the award. *Rideout* v. *Stickney*, 1 *All.* 350.

13—Statute—Taking verdict—Time of signing Judgment.

The Statute 9 and 10 Wm. 3, c. 15, does not apply to references under the Act of Assembly.

It is not necessary that a verdict should be taken *pro forma* to authorize an award to be entered on the postea.

Quære—Whether judgment can be signed on the postea even in term, until the expiration of twenty days after filing the award. See *Brown* v. *Harding*, 3 *All.* 246.

14—Notice of adjourned meeting.

Necessary to give notice of an adjourned meeting when the parties are not present at the adjournment. *Quære*—Whether notice to the counsel in a cause which is referred is notice to the party. See *Brown* v. *Gurrier*, 2 *All.* 124.

15—Want of direction as to entering up award.
Reference to arbitration under Judges order. Costs to abide event; no direction as to how award to be entered; no judgment could be entered. See Costs 51.

ARBITRATORS.

See Arbitration.

ARREST.

1—Power to Arrest.
The House of Assembly in this Province has not the power to arrest and imprison the publisher of a libel on a Member of the House, touching his conduct and proceedings in the House. *Hill* v. *Weldon*, 3 *Kerr* 1.

The publishing of a newspaper containing libellous reflections on Members of the House of Assembly, is not such a breach of the privileges of the Assembly as will justify the arrest of the publisher, and subsequent commitment of him to prison, under the Speaker's warrant, made pursuant to the order of the House. *Ibid.*

No power of arresting, adjudicating, and punishing by imprisonment in such cases belonged to the House of Assembly in Nova Scotia, under the grant made of a General Assembly by King George the Second; nor appertained to the Assembly as a legal or necessary incident to a Colonial Legislature; nor has been obtained by usage and acquiescence; and consequently no such power is vested in the Assembly in New Brunswick from the circumstance of that Province having been formerly included within the bounds of Nova Scotia, neither was it obtained by the grant of a separate Legislature to New Brunswick in 1784. *Ibid.*

Colonial Assemblies are not vested with all the rights and powers of the Houses of Parliament, but such only as are essential to the discharge of their legislative functions. *Ibid.*

Quære, Whether the causing a newspaper, containing libellous publications on Members, to be sent into the House of Assembly, and distributed among the Members while engaged in their public duties, is such a contempt in the face of the House as would justify the arrest of the offender under the Speaker's warrant, and committing him to prison? An arrest and imprisonment cannot be justified on any

such ground, when it has not been charged as a distinct offence, and mentioned in the warrant of commitment. *Hill* v. *Weldon*, 3 *Kerr* 1.

Where an action of trespass has been brought against the Speaker of the House of Assembly for an arrest and imprisonment made under his warrant, if he claims exemption from personal liability in consequence of having acted under the order of the House, when the House had no authority to make the order, he should specially traverse with an *absque hoc*. If he justify generally, that question does not arise. *Ibid.*

Quære, Whether the order of the House of Assembly will excuse or justify the Speaker in issuing a warrant, which cannot be legally executed by the officer to whom it is directed. *Ibid.*

2—Privilege from.
A defendant is not exempt from arrest because he has been before arrested and discharged on ground of privilege. *Gilbert* v. *McLauchlan*, 2 *Kerr* 633.

3—The privilege of members of the House of Assembly from arrest during the session is for forty days, before and after the prorogation or dissolution. See *Rennie* v. *Rankin*, 1 *All.* 820.

A member of House of Assembly must be sued by bill and summons. *Ibid.*

4—Sheriff.
Sheriffs being required by rule of Court (East T. 2, Geo. 3,) to attend Court every term, are privileged from arrest when they come to Fredericton during term, and the particular cause of their so coming will not be enquired into. *Scott* v. *Clarke*, *Trin. T.* 1831.

5—Witness—Waiver.
Application to discharge defendant on the ground of being privileged as a witness, dismissed with costs, it appearing that he had waived his privilege at the time the arrest took place. *Gillespie* v. *Fogarty*, 1 *Kerr* 162.

6—Witness.
A witness attending *bona fide* before a sheriff's jury, in proceedings under a writ *de proprietate probanda*, is privileged from arrest; and if he be arrested *redeundo*, and give a bail bond, the Court will order the bail bond to be cancelled. *Burke* v. *Sutherland*, 1 *Kerr* 166.

7—Discharge of defendant by one of several plaintiffs.

If a defendant in custody on an execution, is discharged by one of several plaintiffs, he cannot be again arrested at the instance of a co-plaintiff. *Andrews* v. *Clarke*, *Ber.* 32.

8—Voluntarily allowing defendant to go at large.

If a judgment debtor arrested on a *ca. sa.* is voluntarily allowed by the creditor to go at large, he cannot be arrested again on a new *ca. sa.*, and if he should be so arrested, and give bail for the limits, these facts will be a good defence to an action on the limit bond for an escape. See *Andrews* v. *Dowdall*, (*Bond* 12.)

9—Arrest of judgment debtor—Use of criminal process.

Plaintiff recovered a verdict against defendant, but before judgment was signed, he left the Province and went to Nova Scotia. Plaintiff afterwards made complaint before a Justice of the Peace that the defendant had committed perjury in giving evidence on the action in which the verdict was obtained; upon which a warrant was issued against him, and delivered to a constable, who took it to Nova Scotia, and it having been indorsed there by a Justice of the Peace, the defendant was arrested on it, and brought into this Province, and taken before a Justice of the Peace who discharged him; he was then arrested on an execution issued on the plaintiff's judgment. Held, That unless the plaintiff had fraudulently made use of the criminal process for the purpose of bringing the defendant within the jurisdiction of this Court, the defendant was not privileged from arrest on the execution; and this being denied by the plaintiff, the Court refused to discharge the defendant from custody. *Oulton* v. *Hewson*, *Mich. T.* 1866.

10—Affidavit for order to hold to bail—Insufficiency of—Application to Court pending application to Judge.

An affidavit to hold to bail stated—that certain goods were shipped at Liverpool on board a certain vessel, of which the defendant was master, to be brought to St. John; that the defendant signed a bill of lading to deliver the said goods to the plaintiff at St. John; that the vessel arrived at St. John with only a part of the goods on board; that the defendant informed the plaintiff that he had sold certain goods (describing them) belonging to the plaintiff, of the value, etc. Held, That this affidavit disclosed no cause of action; that it was consistent with the statements in it, that the sale of the goods by the master of the vessel was justifiable; and therefore that an order for bail should not have been made. *Nevins* v. *Coll*, *Hil. T.* 1871.

Where a defendant has applied to a Judge at Chambers to set aside an arrest, on the ground that there is no *ac etiam* clause in the writ, he may afterwards, and while that application is pending, apply to the Court to rescind a Judge's order for bail in the case, on the ground that the affidavit to hold to bail is defective. (Fisher J., *dissentiente.*) *Ibid.*

11—Arrest without warrant.

To justify a private individual in arresting a person on a charge of felony, without a warrant, he must not only make out a reasonable ground of suspicion against such person, but must also prove that a felony has been committed. *Murphy* v. *Ellis*, *East T.* 1871.

12—Bankrupt.

A person resident in this Province who has been declared a bankrupt in England under the English Bankruptcy Act, and who has been afterwards arrested here for a debt incurred in this Province, is not entitled to have the bail bond which he has entered into upon such arrest given up and cancelled, upon affidavit that he was on his way to England to surrender himself to the Commissioners at a day appointed by them when the arrest took place. *The Mayor &c. of St. John* v. *Lockwood*, 2 *Kerr* 9.

13—A defendant who was in custody on execution at the suit of the plaintiff at the time of the Bankruptcy Act 5 Vic. c. 43, coming into operation, and who has since been declared a bankrupt under that Act and duly surrendered, is entitled to his discharge from custody under the twenty-fourth section. *Reynolds* v. *Hanford*, 2 *Kerr* 114.

14—A certificate under the present English Bankrupt Act is a discharge of debts incurred in this Province, and may be so pleaded in the Provincial Courts; but *Semble*, The certificate cannot be pleaded generally as in England, but the proceedings on which it is founded must be set out. *Jouett* v. *Lockwood*, 2 *Kerr* 674.

15—Where the defendant was arrested for a debt due on a bond, and it appeared that after the debt was contracted he had become a bankrupt, and received his discharge under the "Bankruptcy (Scotland) Act of 1856," the Court ordered his discharge on his entering a common appearance. *Gilbert* v. *McLean*, 2 *Han* 213.

Action for Misnomer—Defective execution —Issuing of second execution before return of first. See Trespass V. 8.

Justification — Process regular. See Trespass V. 7.

Arrest under execution from Justice's Court for excessive amount. See Execution IV. 10.

Refusing to discharge debtor after payment of debt — Legal determination of suit or discharge by law must be shewn. See Action at Law IX. 1, 2.

ARREST OF JUDGMENT.

See Practice VI.

ARTICLES.

See Shipping Law.

ASSAULT.

See Trespass V., and Criminal Law.

ASSESSMENT.

I. Parties Liable for. Land Damages.

II. Proceedings. School Assessments.

III. Miscellaneous.

I.

Parties Liable for.

1—Corporations are liable to be assessed under the Parish School Act 21 Vic. c. 9. *Ex parte The New Brunswick and Canada Railway and Land Co.*, 4 *All.* 376.

2—**Joint Stock Company — Saint John Suspension Bridge Co.**
The Saint John Suspension Bride Company is not rateable by the Rev. Stat. c. 53, s. 17, in the City of Saint John, because it has an office there and the annual meetings for the election of officers is held there. *Ex parte The Saint John Suspension Bridge Company*, 3 *All.* 190.

If a Joint Stock Company owns real estate in several Parishes, it is rateable under the Rev. Stat. as a resident of that Parish in which its principal business is carried on, and as a non-resident in the other Parishes. *Ex parte The Saint John Suspension Bridge Company*, 3 *All.* 190.

3—**Parish — No poor.**
By the Act 3 Geo. 4, c. 25, all the annual expenses of the York County almshouse are to be assessed on the several parishes mentioned in the Act, according to the number of poor each parish has in the house. Held, That a parish having no poor in the house could not be assessed at all. *Rex* v. *Justices of York*, *C. Ms.* 108.

4—**Upon whom—owner of Land.**
An assessment made by commissioners of sewers, under 22 Vic. c. 53, s. 10, must be upon the owner of the land by name, and not upon the land itself. *The Queen* v. *The Commissioners, &c., Germantown Lake*, 1 *Han.* 343.

5—**Railway Company.**
The E. & N. A. Railway Co. purchased land upon which there was a steam mill; part of the land only was used for the purposes of the Railway. Held, That the mill not being a part of the land so used, was not exempt from taxation by the Act 33 Vic. c. 46. *Ex parte The E. & N. American Railway Co.*, *Mich. T.* 1871.

The words "real and personal property" in the first section of the Act are limited and explained by sec. 2. *Ibid.*

6—**Lieutenant Governor — Salary of.**
The official salary of the Lieutenant Governor of the Province is not liable to be assessed under the City Charter of Fredericton, 22 Vic. c. 8, as an income "derived from any trade, profession or calling, within the Province." Wilmot and Ritchie J. J. *dissentiente*: per Barker J., that the Lieutenant Governor is not an "inhabitant" of the City within the meaning of the Act. *Ex parte the Hon. A. H. Gordon*, *Hil. T.* 1864.

7—**Inhabitant — Who not considered such.**
Plaintiff had a house and property in the parish of S. where he generally resided, and where he was assessed as an inhabitant. He held the Government appointment of Commissioner of Works, the office of which was kept in Fredericton, and was attended by him sometimes for a number

of days in succession without returning to his house in S. Held, That he was not an "inhabitant" of Fredericton, and that his being at the head of his department of Board of Works was not "carrying on business" in Fredericton, which subjected him to be assessed under the Act 26 Vic. c. 35. *Hatheway* v. *Cumming, Trin. T.* 1864.

8—Non-resident.
A non-resident carrying on business in a Parish, is liable to be assessed on his personal estate under 1 Rev. Stat. c. 53, s. 19. *Ex parte McLadd, Hil. T.* 1873.

9—Land Damages—Highways.
Assessment, when and how made—Warrant—Commissioners—New application. See Highways 20.

Damages—Highways. See Highways 23.

10—Railway—Damages—Assessment.
In assessing damages for land taken for railway purposes under the Act 28 Vic. c. 12, the jury, besides the value of the land taken for the track, may give damages for the inconvenience caused to the owner by the severance of one part of his farm from the other. *Glazier* v. *Fredericton Branch Railway Co.*, 2 *Han.* 3.

11—Subsequent damage.
The fact that the plaintiff has been paid damages for an alteration of a course of a stream flowing through his land done by Railway Commissioners under the authority of the Act 19 Vic. c. 17, will not prevent him from recovering damages caused by the subsequent overflowing of his land in consequence of the improper construction of the alteration. *McLeod* v. *Commissioners E. & N. A. Railway*, 1 *Han.* 574.

12—Private covenant as to compensation.
Where a company was authorised by Act to enter on private property, erect dams and reservoirs, and overflow land for the purpose of obtaining a supply of water on making compensation to the owners of the land, and in case they could not agree, the amount of compensation to be assessed by a jury in a manner directed by the Act, and the Company requiring to overflow land, entered into a covenant with the owner to build a bridge, over the overflowage, and keep it in repair while the overflowing continued. Held, That the parties having agreed upon the mode of compensation the statutory remedy by assessment did not apply. *Ryan* v. *Lockhart, East T.* 1872.

13—Entering on land—Provisions for compensation—Necessary evidence before right to issue writ—Agent—Owner—Notices.

See Joint Stock Company 15. Albert Mining Company.

II.

PROCEEDINGS.

On Default—Account—Affidavit. See Damages I ".

Writ of Inquiry. See Damages V.

Limit Bond—Damages—Assessment. See Bond 3, 10, 15.

Service of rule for assessing damages—Delay in service. See Practice VI. 14.

1—Notice—Parish School Act—Amount.
Where an assessment is made under the Parish School Act, the assessors must give notice thereof, in the same manner as in cases of assessment for County rates, under 1 Rev. Stat. cap. 53, sec. 12. *Ex parte Street*, 1 *Han.* 107.

2—Notice.
An assessment under the Act relating to sewers in the City of St. John, is not valid unless the notice required by the Rev. Stat. c. 53, s. 12, has been given by the assessors; and *Quære*, Whether such assessment can be made until the expiration of thirty days after such notice given. *Regina* v. *The Mayor of Saint John*, 3 *All.* 361.

An assessment which does not exceed the sum ordered to be levied by more than 10 per cent. is not illegal. *Ibid.*

3—Calling Meeting—Different objects.
An application to Trustees to divide a Parish into School districts, and to call a meeting of the inhabitants to determine upon an assessment under the Parish School Act, 21 Vic. c. 9, may be made at the same time; and if, on the division of the parish, three or more of the applicants are found to be resident freeholders in the district for which the assessment is required, the trustees may call the meeting without any new application. *Ex parte Yeats*, 4 *All.* 381.

A poll-tax may be levied under the Parish School Act. *Ibid.*

4—Separate statements—Mixed assessment.
A warrant directing an assessment for several purposes: as, for the poor; for County contingencies; and for schools, may be sufficient—provided the amounts required for each object are separately stated. But there must be separate assessments for each object, and if the whole are so blended together that this cannot be ascertained, the assessment is bad. *Ex parte McInerney, Hil. T.* 1873.

If an assessment is ordered by the Sessions the warrant may be issued by the Clerk of the Peace after the Sessions have adjourned. *Ibid.*

5—School assessment—Assessment list—Part defective—Certiorari.
Where the assessments for schools, and for the County purposes were stated in separate columns in the assessment list, and an objection was made to the legality of the school assessment, a certiorari was granted to bring up that part of the assessment only. *Ex parte Maher, Hil. T.* 1873.

6—Common School Act—Treasurer—Bond.
It will not invalidate an assessment made under "The Common Schools' Act 1871," s. 12, that the County Treasurer has not given a bond, as directed by the Act, to account for the money paid to him as the County School Fund—that part of the Act being directory only. *Ex parte Raymond, Mich T.* 1872.

7—General Assessment—Severance—Districts.
A County assessment in aid of Schools, under the 12th sec. of "The Common Schools' Act 1871," need not be separate from the general County assessment, provided the several amounts are distinguishable, nor is it necessary, in order to support such an assessment, to shew any division of School districts. *Ex parte Raymond, Hil. T.* 1873.

8—Common School Act—School purposes—Notifying Council of amount required.
By Act 22 Vic. c. 37, the Mayor, etc., of St. John, were authorized "on or before the 1st April in each year," to assess the City for certain purposes. By "The Common Schools' Act 1871," s. 58, the Board of Trustees was authorized to determine annually the amount required for the support and maintainance of Schools, etc., in the District, and "previous to the order for assessment for general City purposes," notify the Common Council of the amount required, and the Council was to cause the same to be levied and collected at the time of levying and collecting other City taxes. Held, That the Act was imperative as to the time of notifying the Common Council of the amount required for School purposes; and therefore, where the general City assessment was ordered on the 5th March, but the Board of Trustees did not notify the Council of the amount required for Schools till the 25th April, an assessment made for the latter purpose was bad. *Ex parte Carvill, Hil. T.* 1873.

9—School Assessment—Notice—Time—Amount.
A School assessment under the Act 21 Vic. c. 9, s. 15, is bad if thirty days have not elapsed between the publication of notice of the assessment, and the delivery of the warrant to the collector, according to 1 Rev. Stat. c. 53, s. 12. Also, if the amount ordered for assessing and collecting exceeds 15 per cent. on the assessment. *Regina* v. *Jardine, Mich. T.* 1863.

10—Corporation—Against whom—Stock—Actual value.
An assessment against a Joint Stock Corporation must be made against the President or Manager of the Company. *Ex parte The Bank of New Brunswick, Hil. T.* 1873.

Under the Act 22 Vic. c. 37, s. 12, the assessment should be made upon the actual value, and not upon the par value of the Stock of an incorporated Company. *Ibid*

III.

MISCELLANEOUS.

See Joint Stock Company.

1—Amount of assessment.
An assessment which does not exceed the sum ordered to be levied by 10 per cent. is not illegal. See *Regina* v. *Mayor of St. John,* 3 *All.* 361.

2—An assessment for poll tax, if not fixed by a particular statute, must be one-eighth of the amount ordered to be assessed according to 1 Rev. Stat. c. 53, s. 11. *Ex parte Sharkey, Mich. T.* 1872.

3—Certiorari to remove—Time of application.
An application for a *certiorari* to remove an assessment, should be made promptly. Where a party had notice of an assessment in December, and his property was

sold under execution for non-payment early in February, an application made in Easter term for a *certiorari* to remove the proceedings was refused, though the assessment appeared to have been improperly made. *Ex parte Gerow*, 4 *All.* 269.

4—General Sessions—Power to order.
The General Sessions has no power to order an assessment as for County contingencies, to meet the costs incurred by a party in making, and by the assessors in resisting an application to quash an assessment under the Parish School Act. *Regina* v. *Assessors of King's*, 1 *Han.* 520.

5—Summoning Freeholders—Private road—Justices issuing warrant—Presence of.
The two Justices who issue the warrant for summoning freeholders to determine on the necessity of a private road, under the Highway Act 50 Geo. 3, c. 6, must be present at the assessment of damages by such freeholders. *Pitt* v. *Lawson and others*, *C. Ms.* 57.

6—Commissioners acts not judicial—Interest.
The Acts of Commissioners of Sewers appointed under the Act 22 Vic. c. 53, are not judicial acts; therefore it is no objection to their proceedings to assess the proprietors of land for the purposes of the Act, that they are interested as owners of land in the district assessed. Ritchie J. *dissentiente*. *Ex parte Calhoun*, *Hil. T.* 1863.

7—Contractor voting—Interest.
K., a commissioner of sewers for the Germantown Lake District, became contractor for the execution of certain work executed under their direction, and afterwards sat and voted with the other commissioners, when they decided that the work had been satisfactorily performed, and ordered an assessment on the land owners to pay for it. Held, That the assessment was bad. *The Queen* v. *The Commissioners of Germantown Lake*, 1 *Han.* 343.

8—Assessment on person who had conveyed land assessed—Change by Commissioners of name—Certiorari refused.
An assessment was made upon A, as a proprietor of land in the district, it afterwards appearing that he had conveyed the land to B, the commissioners struck out A's name and inserted B's; the Court in the exercise of its discretion refused to grant a certiorari to buy up the assessment on B's application. *Ex parte Calhoun*, *Hil. T.* 1863.

As the insertion of B's name did not increase the assessment on any other proprietor of land in the district, it was held to be no ground for quashing the assessment on the application of such other proprietors. *Ibid.*

9—Refusal of warrant.
An application for a warrant to summon a jury to assess the damages to the owner of land through which the Saint John Water Company desired to lay pipes, etc., under the authority of the Act 2 Wm. 4, c. 26, was refused, where it was not shown that the Company deemed it absolutely necessary to lay down pipes through the land. *Ex parte The Saint John Water Company*, *Ber.* 128.

10—Commissioners—Liability—Neglecting to assess.
Quære, Whether Commissioners of Sewers would be liable to an action if they neglected to make assessment required by Act of Assembly. See *Peck* v. *Robinson*, 2 *Kerr* 687.

11—Power of Commissioners—Special Act.
Under the powers given to the Commissioners of Sewers by the Act 22 Vic. c. 53, and 1 Rev. Stat. c. 67, to assess for all expenses of draining, dykeing, etc., they may assess for the expense of purchasing a mill, erecting a dam across a river, making surveys and for interest on money borrowed—(these being necessary for carrying out the objects of the Act)—and for their own fees. *Ex parte Calhoun*, *Hil. T.* 1863.

12—Error—Intention to correct—Certiorari.
In showing cause against a rule for certiorari to remove an assessment, the assessors cannot shew that the matter objected to, is an error which they intended to correct, under the 31st sec. of 1 Rev. Stat. c. 53, unless the error has been corrected, the certiorari will issue. *Ex parte McGarr*, *Hil. T.* 1873.

13—Jury of Inquiry—No return of panel.
Sheriff not returning any panel on the writ; damages assessed by a jury summoned to try issues at the assizes no good ground for setting aside assessment. See *Wheeler* v. *Gove*, 1 *Kerr* 580.

14—Rector—Rents of Glebe—Liability to Assessment.
Under the Act 26 Vic. c. 35, which exempts from taxation the income of the inhabitants of Fredericton, derived from real or personal property, the Rector of the Parish is not liable to be assessed upon the income derived from the rents of his Glebe. *Lee* v. *Mayor of Fredericton, East. T.* 1873.

Promissory note given for amount of assessment. See Bills and Notes I. 9.

Interest — Instalment — Calls. Interest not allowed on assessment where Act silent as to. See Interest 2.

Assessment of Damages. See Bond.

Judgment by default—Damages—Inquiry — Venire — Setting aside Assessment. See Practice VI.

ASSETS.

See Executors and Administrators.

ASSIGNEE.

Of Judgment—Attorney claiming as such. See Attorney III. 7, 9.

Of Bankrupt. See Bankrupt.

Of Bail Bond—Executor of—Suing—Evidence. See Bond 15

Of Limit Bond. See Bond 2.

Of Covenant, binding Assignee. See Covenant 7.

Rights of—Breach of Warranty. See Covenant 4.

Of Policy of Insurance—Consideration. See Pleading I. 39.

Of Term—Deed—Project Evidence. See Landlord and Tenant VI. 2.

Of License. See License 2, 3.

Of Mortgage—Ejectment—Defence. See Mortgage 3.

Of Replevin Bond—Deputy—Delivery. See Bond 18.

Of Lease—Action by Assignee of a Lease against lessors on covenants to pay for improvements, plaintiff entitled to interest on amount appraised from time it became payable. See Landlord and Tenant VI. 2.

ASSIGNMENT.

Recognition of—Third party. See Chose in Action.

Acceptance of Rent—Recognition of Assignee. See Landlord and Tenant VI. 2.

By Partner — Assent of Co-partner. See Deed IV. 1.

Offer to assign—Bona fides—Notice. See Insolvent Debtor 5.

In Trust—Creditors. See Insolvent Debtor 5.

Of License to cut timber. See License.

By parol — To dig minerals. See License.

Of Land, without debt. See Mortgage 1, 2.

Of Premises—Mortgage debt. See Mortgage 1, 2.

Of Mortgage—Vesting of Power of Sale—Rights. See Mortgage 13.

Of Deed—Creditors not parties to—Bona fide. See Deed III. 1.

Trustee, also Creditor. See Deed III. 4.

1—Of Goods — Defeating Execution— Consideration—Delivery and Acceptance—Evidence.
An assignment of goods is not necessarily void, though the intent and effect of it may be to defeat an execution, if the assignment be made *bona fide* for the benefit of other particular creditors, and there be a delivery and acceptance of such goods under the assignment before the execution is delivered to the Sheriff. *Quære*, What acts will constitute a delivery and acceptance? *Kinnear* v. *White*, 2 *Kerr* 235.

It is a good consideration for such assignment, that the assignees were liable as security for certain existing debts of the assignors, and the goods were to be appropriated to the payment of those debts. Proof of the actual payment of the debts is not essential. *Ibid.*

Whether the consideration and transfer be real or fictitious, and whether there have been an actual delivery and acceptance of the goods, are questions for the jury, on the whole evidence. *Ibid.*

Where part of the alleged consideration was interest money due on a bond to a creditor in Nova Scotia, and a bill of exchange drawn by him on the plaintiff was given in evidence. Held, That a contemporaneous letter written by the creditor which specified that the bill was drawn for such interest was admissible in evidence. *Ibid.*

2—Previous Assignment—Execution—Bona fides.

In trespass against the defendant, Sheriff of Northumberland, for taking goods under an execution against P. as his property, which the plaintiff claimed under a previous assignment made by P. to him in payment of a debt; the question whether the transaction was *bona fide* or not being fairly left to the jury, who found for the plaintiff, the Court refused to disturb the verdict. *Doak* v. *Johnston*, 2 *Kerr* 310.

Declarations of the son of P., in whose possession the plaintiff had left the goods, as to the circumstances of the transfer, were held to have been properly rejected by the Judge at the trial; though the fact of such possession was proper for the consideration of the jury. *Ibid.*

The fact that the assignment was made to the plaintiff with intent to avoid an execution, does not in point of law make it void, if it be *bona fide*, and for a valid consideration. *Ibid.*

3—Of Lease—Privity of Estate—Covenant—Reversion—Action of Covenant.

Action of covenant by assignee of lessee against lessor on a lease made of land for eleven years, from 1st February 1830, on the usual Provincial building covenant, for not appointing an appraiser to value the buildings after the expiration of the term, and notice to the defendant on the 3rd May 1843, that the plaintiff had chosen an appraiser on his part, and request then made to the defendant to appoint an appraiser on his part. Plea, that the defendant at and from the end of the term, viz. 1st February 1841, was willing and ready to appoint an appraiser until the 1st May 1841, when the defendant granted, bargained and sold all his right, title and interest in the said land and the buildings and improvements thereon to B and C, after which the said B and C became and are the only persons capable in law to perform the covenants, whereof the plaintiff had notice; and that B and C had ever since been ready and willing to perform the covenant, but that the plaintiff had not applied to them to appoint an appraiser. Held, Bad on demurrer, there being nothing on the record to shew any privity of estate at the time of the assignment, or that the assignment was of a reversionary and not a possessory estate, or that the plaintiff remained in the possession of the demised premises, or that B and C were liable to the performance of the covenant. *Ansley* v. *Peters*, 2 *Kerr* 593.

Semble, The lessor would not be discharged from liability on his personal covenant by assignment of the reversion, although where he assigns during the term, and gives notice thereof to the lessee, application should be made to the assignee to appoint an appraiser. *Ansley* v. *Peters*, 2 *Kerr* 593.

The lessor by a bargain and sale of the land after the expiration of the term, does not incapacitate himself from the performance of the covenant, as he may still pay the appraised value; if he were incapacitated, the bargain and sale after the term and before appraisement would be a breach of the covenant. *Ibid.*

4—By Deed—Property passing by.

The defendant had in his possession as a pound keeper, timber belonging to H. who while it was in the defendant's possession, made a general assignment of his property by deed to the plaintiff. Held, That this was an assignment of the *property* in the timber, and not merely of a *chose in action*, and that the plaintiff, after tendering the amount of the defendant's lien on the timber, might maintain trover against him. *Jack* v. *Eagles*, 2 *All.* 95.

5—Policy of insurance—Invalid assignment.

Plaintiff, whose stock of goods in his store was insured by defendants by a policy under seal, sold them to A, taking notes in payment. Subsequently, at the office of defendants' agent, and by his consent, he indorsed on the policy that he thereby assigned it to A, having sold him the goods. This assignment was entered on defendants' books, but not made under seal, and A was not informed of it. The first note being unpaid, plaintiff by consent of A, took back the goods, and possession of the store. They were afterwards consumed by fire. Held, That the assignment on the policy was invalid, and that plaintiff could recover under the policy for the loss. Weldon, J., *dissentiente*; Fisher, J., *dubitante*. *Crozier* v. *The Phœnix Insurance Co.*, 2 *Han.* 200.

Of Lease—Exceptions—Obstructing Light, See Action on the Case IV. 4.

6—**Executor—Mortgage land of Testator.**
An executor cannot assign the legal estate in land mortgaged in fee to his testator, unless the land is devised to him. Without such devise, his assignment will only operate as a transfer of the mortgage debt. An assignment of a mortgage by an executor is not admissible in evidence without proof of the probate. See *Doe* v. *Hanson*, 3 *All.* 427.

7—**Of Administration Bond.**
In an application to put an administration bond in suit, the Court will not determine whether there has been a breach of the bond. If the applicant makes out a *prima facie* case of breach, and that he is a proper person to sue for it, he is entitled to an assignment. *In re Hunter*, 1 *Han.* 233.

8—An assignment will not be refused, though the bond varies from the form given by the Act,—the variance being slight. *Ibid.*

Of Replevin Bond. See Bond 21.

ASSUMPSIT.

I. Generally.
II. Parties.
III. Money Counts.
 a Account Stated.
 b Money Had and Received.
 c Money Lent.
 d Quantum Meruit.
 e Indebitatus Assumpsit.
 f Goods Bargained and Sold.
 g Money Paid.
IV. Miscellaneous.

I.

Generally.

Action—By and against whom Maintainable. See Action at Law IX.

Right to Action. See Action at Law IV.

For what Maintainable. See Action at Law X.

Rescinding Contract. See Action at Law V.

Remedy—Suspension of. See Action at Law VI.

Action before Expiration of Credit. See See Action at Law VII.

Foreign Judgment—Assumpsit maintainable upon. See Action at Law X.

Magistrate's Court—Judgment. See Action at Law X.

Former Recovery. See Action at Law VIII.

1—**Breach of Agreement.**
By agreement between the plaintiff and defendant, the latter undertook to manufacture and deliver to the plaintiff by a certain time 200,000 feet of deals, and the plaintiff agreed to advance to the defendant twenty shillings per thousand feet for all the deals delivered, but not to advance more than £50 over the quantity delivered; that the plaintiff should dispose of the deals and account to the defendant for the proceeds, the gain or loss to be divided equally, and the defendant's portion of the proceeds to be deducted from his private account with the plaintiff. The plaintiff advanced £200 to the defendant, who only delivered 74,000 feet of deals, which the defendant shipped to Scotland, where they remained unsold. Held, That the defendant was liable for breach of his agreement, and that the plaintiff's remedy was not suspended until the deals delivered were sold, but that he might recover the amount of the private account and the surplus advances as liquidated damages. *Lock* v. *Purdon*, 2 *All.* 33.

Held also, That any failure on the plaintiff's part in selling the deals did not affect the defendant's liability for breach of his agreement. *Ibid.*

2—**Mortgaged debt—Settlement of Accounts—Covenant existing.**
Defendant being indebted to plaintiff for supplies advanced to build a ship, and requiring further advances, mortgaged the ship to the plaintiff in September 1857, for £10,000, and covenanted to pay the amount due with interest in January 1858. In November 1857, the parties settled their accounts, when a balance of £9,749 was found to be due the plaintiff on the advances for which the mortgage was given. Held, That assumpsit could not be maintained for this balance. *Jardine* v. *McCauley*, *Trin. T.* 1862.

3—**Special averments—Failure in proof of—Recovery under Common Counts.**
The plaintiff and defendant entered into a contract, whereby the defendant agreed to supply the plaintiff with provisions, etc., at stated prices, for teams to be employed by the plaintiff in hauling logs during the winter; the logs to be driven

into the boom at B, as early the ensuing spring as the freshet would permit; defendant to make payment for the logs, after deducting his account for supplies, etc., in three and six months after the logs were driven to the boom. The action was brought before the expiration of six months from the delivery of the logs, and the plaintiff had a general verdict on both the special and common counts. Held, That having failed to prove the averments in the special counts, the plaintiff could not sustain the verdict on the common counts, not only because the credit had not expired, but because the whole estimate of damages had been based upon the contract. *Campbell* v. *Todd*, 3 *Kerr* 171.

Evidence under Common Counts. See Infra III.

II.

Parties. See Action at Law.

Corporation—Seal—Agents' Authority—Estoppel. See Corporation 4.

Tenants in Common. See Action at Law.

Parties—Rescission by. See Action at Law.

Parties not in *statu quo*. See Infra 29.

III.

MONEY COUNTS.

a—ACCOUNT STATED.

1—**Sufficiency of acknowledgment.** Upon an agreement made by B to purchase from C a quantity of saw logs, which C had previously bought of A, B agreed to pay A £75 from the proceeds of the lumber when it got to market; some time afterwards, upon an application for payment, B said "he had chartered a vessel, and that A would have his pay, one half in a fortnight, and the other half in two or th ee months." Held, That A could not recover the £75 on the count for an account stated, although more than three months had elapsed before bringing this action. *Lee* v. *Howe*, 1 *Kerr*. 569.

2—The defendant having purchased from P a mill, together with a quantity of logs, which had been sold by the plaintiff to P, accepted an order drawn by P on him in the plaintiff's favor for £75, the price of the logs, payable when the deals, into which the logs were to be sawed, were got to market and the proceeds realized; and some time after when the deals were at the market, the order being presented to him for payment, the defendant said he had chartered a vessel to take away the deals, and that he would pay the plaintiff one half the amount of the order in two or three days, and the remainder in two or three months. Held, That the plaintiff was entitled to recover the £75 under the account stated. *Lee* v. *Howe*, 2 *Kerr* 546.

3—An account containing items on both sides, and shewing a balance in favor of the plaintiff, was rendered by him to the defendant, who wrote upon the account a sum of money as a deduction from the balance claimed by the plaintiff. Held, That without the deduction there was no admission by the defendant, and that he had only admitted the balance of the account after the deduction. Held also, That the plaintiff could not increase this balance by reference to a previous account rendered to him by the defendant, in which a much larger balance was admitted to be due than the plaintiff claimed in this suit, without showing that one account referred to the other. *Spurr* v. *Allison*, 3 *All.* 454.

4—An account containing debits and credits was presented by the plaintiff to the defendant, who admitted it to be correct, but refused to sign it, alleging that there might be other credits to which he was entitled, and for which he required time to consider. Held, That this did not prove an account stated. *Harley* v. *Goodfellow*, 1 *Han.* 335.

5—When A delivered goods to B upon the understanding that B should deliver other goods in exchange, but subsequently A rendered an account to B of the same which B acknowledged to be correct and promised to pay, A may recover therefor under an account stated, notwithstanding his bill of particulars gives the items as the ground of his demand. *Grant* v. *Aiken & Shaw*, *Ber.* 259.

6—**Demand confined by particulars.** The plaintiff by his particulars confined his demand to damages for the breach of a special agreement which he failed to prove. Held, That he could not give evidence on the account stated of the acknowledgment of a sum due independent of the special agreement, but connected with the transaction to which it related. *Jackman* v. *Brown*, *Mich. T.* 1831.

7—Bill of Exchange admitted under account stated—Pleading.
If a Bill of Exchange is drawn for balance of account acknowledged to be due to the plaintiff from the drawer,—who has no funds in the drawers' hands,—the plaintiff may recover on the count upon the account stated, if in consequence of not alleging the excuse for non-presentment, he is unable to recover upon the special count. *Emerson* v. *Gardiner*, 1 *All.* 451.

8—The payee of a dishonored Bill of Exchange may recover the amount from the drawer in an action on the common counts, if no notice of dishonor has been given. *James* v. *McLean*, 3 *Allen* 164.

9—Payee against maker—Evidence.
In an action by the payee against the maker of a promissory note, although it is made payable at a particular place, yet it is admissible evidence under the common counts. *Merritt* v. *Woods*, *Ber.* 261.

A promissory note may be given in evidence under Account Stated. See Steadman v. Holstead, 3 Kerr 335.

Purchase money in Deed—Admission of. See Estoppel I. 17.

Stating Account by Referees—Agents of Parties—When? See Principal and Agent 16.

10—A writing addressed to defendant, requesting him to pay plaintiff £25, half cash and half goods, is not a Bill of Exchange. After payment of part, balance cannot be recovered as on an account stated. See Bills and Notes I. 14.

11—Acceptances—Evidence—Suspension of claim.
The defendant being indebted to the plaintiff, gave him three documents, intended to be acceptances of the defendant for $400 each, payable, with current rate of exchange on New York, in five, seven, and ten months from date respectively. Held, That they amounted to a special agreement, by which the plaintiff undertook to suspend his claim for payment till the intended acceptances were due; but that after that time, he could sue on the original consideration, or, on an account stated, of which the acceptances were evidence. *Stuart* v. *Kirk*, *Hil. T.* 1861.

b—Money Had and Received.

By and against whom action maintainable.

Stakehold—Horse race. See Action at Law.

Harbour Master—Holding over—Fees of Office. See Appointment of Officer 1.

12—Attorney—Money collected—Demand.
The defendant, an attorney, gave the plaintiffs a receipt acknowledging to have received from them several promissory notes for collection, one of the plaintiffs at the same time by letter requesting the defendant to collect the notes. Held, 1. That an action for money had and received was properly brought in the name of both plaintiffs, though the notes were in favor of one of them only. *Gilbert* v. *Palmer*, 1 *All.* 455.

13—A notice to an attorney demanding payment of money received by him in his professional capacity, signed by a person who was not shewn to have had any authority to make the demand, and served by one who had no authority to receive the money, is not a sufficient demand to support an action for money had and received, though the person who signed the notice was afterwards the attorney in the suit. *Robinson* v. *Palmer*, 2 *All.* 223.

14—Legacy—Payment to Executor by party holding.
H bequeathed to the plaintiff during her life, the profits of his stock and interest in the Saint Stephen's Bank, of which the bank had notice. After the death of H the bank declared a dividend on the stock, which was claimed by and paid to H's executor. Held, That in the absence of any agreement by the bank to hold the dividend for the plaintiff, an action for money had and received will not lie, and that payment to the executor discharged the bank. *Hill* v. *The Saint Stephen's Bank*, 3 *All.* 145.

15—Master and servant—Earnings for other services.
The plaintiff hired the defendant by the month to superintend certain work, and to devote the whole of his time to it: during this engagement, and without the plaintiff's knowledge, the defendant worked for another person and received wages; Held, [Ritchie, J. *dissentiente*] That the plaintiff could not maintain an action for

money had and received against the defendant for such wages, and that the only remedy against him was an action for damages for breach of his contract. Held, per Ritchie, J. 1. That by the agreement, the time and labour of the defendant became the property of the plaintiff, and that the subsequent hiring by the defendant was a wrong which plaintiff might waive, and recover the proceeds of the labour in an action for money had and received. 2. That the plaintiff might elect to consider the defendant as his agent in such hiring, adopt his contract, and recover the proceeds as money paid to the plaintiff's use. *Beardsly* v. *Copeland*, 3 *All.* 458.

16—Proceeds—Sale of Cargo.
The plaintiff and one F, shipped on board defendant's vessel at Saint Stephen, a cargo of lumber about half of which was the separate property of the plaintiff, kept apart from the rest in the vessel. The lumber was to be carried to the West Indies, and there sold by the defendant on the separate account of the plaintiff and F, and separate bills of lading were given. It was proved that the cargo had been sold by the defendant, and he admitted that he had received therefor $2,000. No account of sales or expenses was in evidence. The jury having found a verdict for the plaintiff for £200, on the count for money had and received, a rule *nisi* for a new trial was refused; the Court considering that there was sufficient evidence to support the verdict, although the exact amount due the plaintiff did not appear. *Benson* v. *Leeman*, 2 *Kerr* 118.

17—Voluntary Payment—Mistake.
The plaintiff being sued by the defendant, sent an agent with money to the plaintiff's attorney to pay a certain joint note and costs, supposing it to be the subject of the action; the agent, surprised by the attorney presenting him with a separate note for nearly a similar sum, of a previous date, on signifying there must be some mistake about it, the attorney told him that there would be no further costs of suit for thirty days; but the agent supposing the note shown him the result of a settlement of the first note, and that there had been a mistake in the dates, paid the separate note with costs, after which the plaintiff was sued on the joint note for the money contained in the first note, and paid it, and brought this action to recover back the money paid on the first note; and showed circumstances in evidence, upon which the jury found that the first note was paid without consideration, or had been fraudulently detained by the defendant, and was paid by the plaintiff's agent under a mistake of facts. Held, That the plaintiff could not recover back the money paid on the first note, as he should have defended the first action. *Johnson* v. *Brown*, 3 *Kerr* 264.

18—Public officer—Excessive demand.
If timber is seized for having been cut on Crown land without license, and the Government instead of proceeding to condemnation, authorize the seizing officer to release it upon payment of a certain sum per ton, which is paid by the claimant under protest; he cannot maintain an action for money had and received against the officer, because the amount demanded by him exceeds the rate allowed by law on granting licenses to cut timber. *Tibbits* v. *Allan*, 3 *Kerr* 280.

19—Purchaser—Deposit.
A purchaser of land has a right to a title free from incumbrances, and if the vendor is unable to give such a title the purchaser may recover back his deposit. *Scott* v. *Garnett*, 2 *All.* 624.

20—Appropriation of Money.
S. being indebted to the plaintiff, and having money in the defendant's hands, directed him to pay the plaintiff's debt, which the defendant agreed to do, the amount having been ascertained and known by the defendant. Held, That this was an appropriation of the money by S. and a receipt of it by the defendant to the plaintiff's use, for which he could maintain an action for money had and received. *Anderson* v. *Allison*, 3 *All.* 173.

21—A. having consigned goods to the defendants to sell, drew a bill for the amount in favour of B.; the defendants refused to accept the bill till the goods were sold, and it was protested for non-acceptance. Soon after drawing the bill, A. assigned his property to the plaintiff, who claimed the proceeds of the goods from the defendants, but afterwards wrote them that he found the amount had been appropriated by A. to pay a debt to B., and that he (plaintiff) had nothing to do with it. Held—1. That the plaintiff had renounced his claim, and could not recover the proceeds. 2. That his subsequently claiming the goods in consequence of the defendants' refusal to accept the draft, did not destroy the effect of his previous admission. *Cothren* v. *Kinnear*, 4 *All.* 251.

22—Contract rescinded.
The defendant agreed to deliver lumber to the plaintiff at a certain time, and the plaintiff agreed to make a payment in advance, and to pay the balance on delivery of the lumber; neither party was ready to perform the contract on the day specified for the delivery of the lumber. Held, That the contract was rescinded, and that the plaintiff could recover the advances under the count for money had and received. *McCann* v. *Kirlin*, 3 *All.* 345.

23—Contract—Failure in performance.
Where money has been received by a manufacturing corporation under a parol agreement to make payment for the same in articles of their manufacture, which they have failed to perform; an action of assumpsit lies to recover back the money. *Diamond* v. *The Saint George Lime Company*, 2 *Kerr* 537.

24—Purchase money—No fraud.
Where land has been sold and the deed executed, and there is no fraud, the purchaser cannot recover back the purchase money in an action for money had and received, although he may have been evicted by title paramount. The rule of *Caveat emptor* applies, and he should have protected himself by covenants. *Robinson* v. *James*, *Hil. T.* 1832.

25—Tenants in common—For share of Property sold with consent.
An action for money had and received will lie by one tenant in common against his co-tenant for a moiety of the price of the common property sold by the latter with the consent of the former. *Shaw* v. *Grant*, *Ber.* 110.

26—Waiver of Tort—Sale of whole Property without consent.
If one tenant in common of property, sells the whole, without authority from his co-tenant, the latter may waive the *tort* and recover his share of the price in an action for money had and received. *Doyle* v. *Taylor*, *Ber.* 201.

27—Rents and Profits.
One tenant in common cannot maintain an action for money had and received against his co-tenant for receiving more than his share of the rents and profits of the joint property, unless there is an account settled and balanced agreed upon, even though the defendant may have acted as bailiff of the other co-tenants in receiving the rents. *Frost et al* v. *Disbrow*, 1 *Han.* 73.

28—Infant tenant in common—Disputed account—Balance not agreed to.
Defendant being a tenant in common with the plaintiffs who were infants, rendered in an account in which he acknowledged a certain sum to be due from them to the plaintiffs, as their share of the rents of the joint property which he had received, the plaintiffs' guardian disputed the correctness of the account, and claimed a much larger sum from the defendant. Held, In an action for money had and received, that such balance not having been agreed to, the plaintiffs were not entitled to retain a verdict for that amount. *Ibid.*

29—Parties not in statu quo.
The defendant having sold certain real property to the plaintiffs, and received their acceptance for the payment of it, procured an assignment of a mortgage on the property to be made and delivered to the plaintiffs, and further agreed that if one L did not give a deed of the premises, the defendant would proceed against the property either by foreclosure or under the Absconding Debtors Act, so that one of the plaintiffs should receive a clear title to the property; which not being done, nor the assignment registered, the plaintiffs tendered back the assignment, demanded the purchase money, and brought an action for the recovery of it. Held, That there being no reassignment of the mortgage by the plaintiffs, nor an acceptance thereof, the parties were not in *statu quo*, and the action therefore was not sustainable. *Pingree* v. *Watson*, 3 *Kerr* 251.

30—Receipt—Promise to account.
A receipt given by the defendant to the plaintiff for certain orders, (stating the names of the persons and the amount due from each) "to be accounted in settlement," is not in itself sufficient to support an action for money had and received. *Lee* v. *Trefethen*, *Hil. T.* 1834.

31—Agreement to sell timber—Sale necessary.
Where timber was delivered to the defendant on an agreement that he should

sell it and pay a certain part of the proceeds to the plaintiffs, an action for money had and received will not lie unless the timber has been sold. *Scribner* v. *Betts, Hil. T.* 1833.

32—Amount paid on Execution—Land not liable to seizure.
Defendant recovered judgment against the executors of S. for a debt due from their testator, on which execution was issued to levy *de bonis testatoris*, and the real estate of S. sold by the Sheriff, and purchased by the plaintiff, who went into possession: the heirs of S. afterwards ejected the plaintiff—the real estate not being liable to seizure under the execution. Held, That the plaintiff could not recover from the defendant the amount paid to the Sheriff for the land, and which he had paid over to the defendant under the execution. *Robinson* v. *Jarvis, Hil. T.* 1832.

33—Displacement of Officer—Fees of office.
Where the General Sessions of a County appointed a Harbour Master under the authority of an Act of Assembly which did not limit the tenure of the office, and afterwards displaced him without reasonable cause, and appointed another, the former may bring an action for money had and received to recover the fees of office received by the latter since his appointment. *Joplin* v. *Davidson, Bert. R.* 308

34—Excessive demand by seizing officer.
Where timber was seized for having been cut on Crown land without license, and the Government, instead of proceeding to condemnation, authorized the seizing officer to release it on payment of a certain sum per ton, which was paid by the claimant under protest; he cannot maintain an action for money had and received against the officer, because the amount demanded by him exceeded the rate allowed by law on granting licenses to cut timber. *Tibbitts* v. *Allan*, 3 *Kerr* 280.

35—Money appropriated.
The master of a ship owned by the defendant having died, the defendant went on board, took charge of the captain's effects, and locked them up. Among them was a sum of money, which the mate claimed under an alleged agreement with the captain for £2 per month, extra wages; and he took the money as payment,—the defendant not trying to prevent him, but saying, he would let him have it if he could prove the bargain. Held, That *prima facie* the money was the private property of the captain, and that the defendant having taken possession of his effects, and afterwards allowed the mate to take the money, was liable to the representative of the captain for money had and received. *Dorman* v. *Anderson, Mich. T.* 1861.

36—No actual receipt of money.
Plaintiff employed defendant, an attorney, to collect a debt due to plaintiff from A: the defendant did not actually receive the money, but arranged the debt, by allowing the amount in the transfer of a mortgage from A to B, a creditor of the plaintiff. Held, That as the defendant had not received money or money's worth, an action for money had and received would not lie. *Neil* v. *Jack, Hil. T.* 1862.

37—Sale of Goods—Conversion—Waiver of tort.
Defendant agreed to deliver deals to H. on board a ship sent for the purpose—half the cargo to be paid for in cash: the deals were shipped, and H's agent paid the defendant £20 on account. H. became bankrupt in England on the 10th June, and on the 17th June, information of the bankruptcy was received in this country by H's. agent, who refused to make any further payment to the defendant, but gave him the bill of lading of the cargo, which he sold for his own benefit. Held, That the portion of the cargo shipped before the 10th June vested in the assignee of H, and that the sale thereof was a conversion for which the assignee might maintain trover, and that he might also waive the *tort* and bring an action for money had and received. *Carrick* v. *Atkinson, East. T.* 1863.

38—Fees of Witness—Criminal trial.
The fees of a witness attending a criminal trial, certified by the presiding Judge under 1 Rev. Stat. c. 160, s. 12, may be recovered in an action for mon[illegible] had and received, where it ap[illegible]ears that the County Treasure[illegible] [illegible]ucient funds in hand to pay the [illegible] *Mulligan* v *[illegible]ains-ford*, 2 *Ha*[illegible]

39—No receipt of money on check.
Defendant, at the requ[illegible]st of the cashier, and for the benefit of a Bank, bid in certain shares of the Bank-stock, which were advertised for sale. The defendant

had no funds in the Bank, but the cashier told him he could draw a check for the amount of the purchase money, which he did, and the amount was paid by the cashier to the seller of the shares, which were then transferred to the defendant. The purchase of its shares by the Bank was contrary to the charter. Defendant offered to transfer the shares to the Bank, but they refused to accept them, and repudiated the whole transaction—the cashier having in the meantime become a defaulter and absconded. Held, (Wetmore J. *dissentiente*) That no money having been received by the defendant on the check, and the money not having been paid for his use, but for the use and benefit of the plaintiffs, they could not recover the amount of the check. *Commercial Bank* v. *Stephenson, Hil. T.* 1872.

rporation—Money received by Mayor—Offset. See Corporation 16.

)—Work and labour—Agreement to credit on rent.

Plaintiff held land as tenant of defendant under a lease, and by an agreement outside of the lease, he was to do some ditching on the land, which was to be allowed him as a payment on account of the rent. The ditching was done during the summer, and the defendant afterwards issued a distress warrant for half a year's rent, due on the 1st of May previously, which rent the plaintiff paid. Held, That the amount of the ditching was a matter entirely in the knowledge of the plaintiff, and as he had not given the defendant any account of it before the distress issued, he had no means of crediting it on the rent; and that after submitting to the distress, the plaintiff could not maintain an action to recover back the value of the ditching. *Graham* v. *Gilbert, Hil. T.* 1873.

-Money Lent.

—Plaintiff having agreed to lend money to D, he drew a note for the amount in the plaintiff's favor and sent it to the defendant, who received the money from the plaintiff and gave her the note—indorsing his own name thereon. The plaintiff swore that she lent the money on the security of the defendant, believing at the time she got the note, that it was the joint note of the defendant and D. Held, That the defendant was liable in an action for money lent. *Douglas* v. *Disbrow*, 4 *All.* 197.

d—Quantum Meruit.

42—Contract—Deviations—Acquiescence.

The plaintiff contracted to build a bridge for the defendants according to a specification, for a certain price, but varied from the contract in many particulars, of which the defendants were aware, but made payments to the plaintiff while the work was going on and very shortly before its completion: the bridge was carried away by the ice, the spring after it was built. Held, That the defendants' conduct was evidence of acquiescence in the deviations, and that if the bridge was of any value, the plaintiff was entitled to recover on the common counts. *Foshay* v. *Baxter*, 1 *All.* 335.

43—Work and Labour.

In an action of *indebitatus assumpsit*, to recover payment for cutting wood and making fires for the House of Assembly, the plaintiff gave in evidence the contingent account of the Assembly, whereby it appeared that a sum of money had been allowed to the defendant for the plaintiff's services. Held, That the plaintiff was not bound by the amount allowed, but might recover more on the *quantum meruit*. *O'Brien* v. *Wetmore*, 1 *All.* 594.

44—Master and Servant—Stage Driver.

The plaintiff was employed as a driver by the proprietor of a stage coach. In an action against the master for wages, in which the plaintiff was proved to have received passage money from persons travelling by the stage, and which the defendant claimed to set-off against the demand for wages, the jury were directed that they might presume the plaintiff had paid over to his master the money so received, in the ordinary course of his employment. Held, That without some evidence that such was the course of dealing, the direction was wrong. *McRae* v. *McBeath*, 3 *Kerr* 446.

Held also, That money given to the servant by the owner of a horse, which was led behind the stage on one of its trips, was a mere gratuity to the servant for his trouble in looking after the horse, and that the master had no right to it. *Ibid.*

45—Repairs of Ship—Agent—Liability.
The defendant, having advanced money to D to build a ship, became the registered owner of three-fourths of the ship as a security for his advances, with an agreement that she should be sold in England and his debt paid out of the proceeds of the sale. The ship being at Saint John, and requiring repairs to enable her to go to England, D and the master of the ship employed the plaintiff to do the work, directing him to charge it to the owners. The ship was sent to England and sold, and the defendant got the proceeds. Held, That he was liable for the repairs. *Williams* v. *Wood*, 4 *All.* 362.

Extra Work. See Contract 14.

46—Hiring Horse.
A person hiring a horse to perform a journey is not liable for the value of the horse if he dies on the road, without the fault of the rider. *Quære*, Whether, in such a case, the owner of the horse is entitled to recover on the *quantum meruit* for the time the defendant had the horse? See *Dickie* v. *Campbell*, *U. Ms.* 44.

47—Ownership of Property—Liability.
The ownership of property alone will not render the owner liable to pay for work performed upon it without his request, though he receives it knowing that the work has been performed. *Hartley* v. *Fisher*, 1 *All.* 459.

e—INDEBITATUS ASSUMPSIT.

48—Special Contract—Recovery under common Counts.
Indebitatus assumpsit to recover the price of a quantity of spruce logs. Written agreement. No further acts remaining to be done by the plaintiff. Held, That he could recover on the common counts. See *Leslie* v. *Hanson*, 1 *Han.* 263.

49—Trees severed from freehold—Chattels—Recovery for, under common counts.
Plaintiff, by a written agreement, sold to defendant for £45, payable part that autumn and balance in one year, the logs on his and his son's land, with the right to cut, for five years. Defendant during the following winter cut and hauled off all the trees suitable for lumber. In the mean time, plaintiff conveyed to his brother, who brought an action of trespass against defendant, for cutting on the land, and recovered damages. Held, That the plaintiff was entitled to recover the amount, defendant having bound himself to pay on a certain day, and having got the logs: that the trees being severed, became chattels, and plaintiff's claim being merely a money demand, might be recovered on the common counts. *Murray* v. *Gilbert*, 1 *Han.* 545.

f—GOODS BARGAINED AND SOLD.

50—Merger—Set-Off.
Plaintiffs proved a demand of £41 against defendant for goods sold and delivered; defendant proved a large demand against the plaintiffs, which he promised to settle by his account for the goods, the amount of which was not ascertained at that time. Held, That the plaintiffs' demand was not merged in the defendant's, and might be recovered on the common count, there being no notice of set-off. *Cushing* v. *Goddard*, 3 *All.* 585.

51—Goods of Plaintiff—Execution against—Arrangement with Creditor.
Plaintiff sold defendant lumber, part of which was afterwards levied on under execution against the plaintiff, but was given up to the defendant by an arrangement with the judgment creditor, to which the plaintiff was no party. Held, That the plaintiff (having a right to sell the lumber) was entitled to recover the price notwithstanding the defendant's arrangement with the judgment creditor. *Johnson* v. *Crocker*, 4 *All.* 94.

52—Parties disabling themselves from performance of Contract—Rescission.
By agreement between the plaintiff and defendant, the plaintiff was to put up and enclose the frame of a house by a certain day, and the defendant was to make the doors and window sashes out of the plaintiff's lumber, finish the inside of the house, and be paid part in money and part in goods; the plaintiff furnished the lumber for the doors and sashes, which the defendant made and sold after the expiration of the time for completing the house. The plaintiff never put up the frame. Held, That as both parties had disabled themselves from performing it, the contract was rescinded, and the plaintiff could recover on the *quantum meruit* for goods delivered to the defendant under the contract. Held also, That as the facts were not disputed, the rescission of the contract was properly decided by the Judge. *McAuley* v. *Geddes*, 4 *All.* 526

g—Money Paid.

53—Contract—Transfer—Unfinished work.

D having a contract with the defendant to do work on a railway, transferred his contract to the plaintiff at the defendant's request, on receiving a *bonus* of one penny per yard on the work remaining to be done. Plaintiff gave D his note for the amount, on the undertaking of the defendant that if the plaintiff was prevented from completing the work, the defendant would pay the penny per yard for the amount unfinished. The plaintiff performed part of the work, and left the rest unfinished, at the defendant's request that he should work elsewhere. The plaintiff having paid the amount of the note to D—Held, That he could recover it from the defendant, as money paid to his use. *Hawkins* v. *McBean*, *East. T.* 1861.

54—Application of money.

The defendant being indebted to P in the sum of $1124, requested the plaintiff to pay the amount for him. The plaintiff did not pay the money to P, but, having had dealings with him, and having a demand against him for $624, placed the $1124 to his (P's) credit, intending thereby to pay his demand of $624. Part of the balance was paid to P and part was applied by the plaintiff in payment of some liabilities of P. The defendant had no knowledge of P's indebtedness to the plaintiff, or of the mode in which the $1124 was applied. Held, That there was not a novation of the original liability of the defendant, and no extinguishment of the debt due from the defendant to P; therefore the plaintiff could not recover against the defendant for money paid to his use. Per Ritchie, C. J.: That if P had agreed to extinguish his debt against the defendant, and the defendant had notice of the arrangement between the plaintiff and P, and had assented thereto, the action for money paid could have been maintained. Per Allen, J.: That if the plaintiff, with the assent of P, had retained the $624, and paid P the balance of the $1124, he could have maintained the action—such retainer being equivalent to a payment—and, in that case, no assent of the defendant was necessary. *Harris* v. *Robertson*, *Mich. T.* 1860.

IV.

Miscellaneous.

Partners—Liability. See Partnership 1.

See Commissioner of Sewers.

55—Collector of Taxes—Bond given.

Assumpsit on an account stated lies against a collector of taxes for a balance admitted by him to be due to his principal, though he has given a bond to the principal to account for monies collected. *The Mayor &c. of St. John* v. *Baldwin*, 3 *Kerr* 477.

56—Pleading—Sterling Currency—Damages—Particulars.

In an action brought in this Province for the value of goods sold and delivered in England, the plaintiff is entitled to recover such a sum, currency, as would be equivalent to the demand in sterling, according to the rate of exchange between this Province and England at the time of trial. Such an allowance may be recovered under the common counts, for goods sold and delivered without any specific averment that the debt was contracted in sterling money, or any allegation of the relative value of sterling and currency, this is matter of evidence. The particulars not covering such a specific charge were held sufficient, being dated at Liverpool and made up in sterling money. *Campbell* v. *Wilson*, *Ber.* 265.

57—Special Counts—Particulars—Recovery under Common Counts.

Where a Declaration contains Special Counts, with a count for money had and received, and the particulars also apply to the latter count, the plaintiff may give evidence under the count for money had and received though the Counsel did not claim to recover on that count in opening the case. *Currick* v. *Atkinson*, *East. T.* 1863.

Work and Labour.

Action for wages as Secretary of a Company—Recognition of Officer—Payment by Company of goods ordered by plaintiff. See Evidence I. 24.

Assumpsit maintainable for Top Wharfage under Act 5 Vic. c. 39, s. 6—Necessary Allegation and Proof. See Wharfage.

ASPORTAVIT.

Right to maintain trespass *de bonis asportatis*. See Trespass I. 11, 14, 15, 25, 27.

ATTACHMENT.

1—Against whom—
Corporations—Costs—not granted.
An attachment cannot be granted against a Corporation for non-payment of costs. *Doe* v. *Crawford*, 3 *All.* 266.

2—Sheriff—
Mode of former proceeding.
Until the general rule of the present term (Hilary, 4 Vic.) the mode of proceeding against a Sheriff when out of office, for not bringing in the body of a defendant, was by *distringas* and not by attachment, though the practice has been otherwise in England since the rule of King's Bench, Trinity term, 31 Geo. 3. *Henry* v. *Murphy*, 1 *Kerr* 207.

3—Sheriff—When not granted against —Deputation by Party.
An attachment will not be granted against a Sheriff for disobeying rule for returning a writ where special Deputy appointed by plaintiff. See *Sheriff Kingston* v. *O'Shea*, 1 *All.* 678.

4—Sheriff—Delay.
Delay, sufficiently accounted for, is not a cause for setting aside an attachment against a Sheriff where he has not been prejudiced by such delay. *Rex* v. *Sheriff of Glocester*, *Ber.* 187.

5—Witness.
An attachment will not be granted for not obeying a subpœna, when the witness is in custody at the time of service. *Regina* v. *Wetmore*, *Ber.* 244.

6—Witness—Wilful Absence—Calling on Subpœna.
An attachment will not be granted against a witness for not obeying a subpœna unless there is a clear case of contempt; but if his absence is wilful, the Court will not, in general, look to the materiality of his testimony. *Maloney* v. *Morrison*, 1 *All.* 240.

It is not necessary to shew that the witness was called on his subpœna, if it appears by other satisfactory evidence that he did not attend. *Ibid.*

7.—Witness.
A subpœna to attend on the 10th September, and so from day to day until the cause was tried, was served on the 11th September, and the witness attended for several days, and knew the cause was not tried. Held, That he was guilty of a contempt in subsequently absenting himself. *Johnson* v. *Williston*, 2 *All.* 171.

Where a witness accepted the conduct money, and went with the person who served him with the subpœna, and remained at the Court several days, an attachment was granted against him for subsequently absenting himself, though he and another person swore, in contradiction to the party who served the subpœna, that the original writ was not shewn to him, and he also swore that he attended the Court as a juror, and left in consequence of ill health, with the intention of returning; his absence appearing to be wilful. *Johnson* v. *Williams*, 2 *All.* 171.

8—Witness—Refusal to attend—Tender of Expenses.
Where a party is served with a subpœna to attend as a witness, and accepts a sum of money which is tendered to him for his expenses, without objecting to the amount, but refuses to attend on account of his own business, he is liable to an attachment for non-attendance, even though the sum tendered be less than he is entitled to receive under the ordinance of Fees. *Gilbert* v. *Campbell*, 1 *Han.* 258.

9—Time of application—Witness.
An attachment against a witness for contempt must be applied for at the next term after the contempt committed. *Doe dem Howe* v. *Mealley*, *Ber.* 121.

10—To enlarge Rule.
Motion to enlarge rule for an attachment against witness for not obeying subpœna on the ground that he could not be served with the rule, must be made at the term in which rule *nisi* is returnable. *Abbot* v. *Frink*, 3 *Kerr* 368.

11—Costs, refusal to pay—Agreement for Consent Rule.
A refusal to pay costs, taxed upon an *agreement* for a consent rule, will not entitle the opposite party to an attachment for non-payment. The rule should be first drawn up. *Doe* v. *King*, 3 *Kerr* 178.

12—Costs—Taxing under Consent rule.
In order to entitle a party to an attachment for non-payment of costs under the terms of the consent rule, it is necessary that the costs should be taxed *after* the consent rule is taken out. *Doe* v. *King*, 3 *Kerr* 206.

13—Costs—Improper taxation of.
Where the amount of a bill of costs, in which one item was improperly taxed, had been demanded, an attachment was granted for the balance. *Doe d. McCallum* v. *Roe*, 2 *All.* 143.

14—Costs—Subsequently incurred.
The defendant, after a demand of costs under a rule of Court by the plaintiff's attorney, paid the amount to the plaintiff; the attorney afterwards obtained a rule for an attachment for non-payment of the costs, but before the attachment issued, was informed of the payment to the plaintiff. Held, That he was not justified in afterwards issuing an attachment for the costs of an affidavit of the demand of payment, and the costs subsequently incurred. ... J. v. *Harper*, 2 *All.* 433.

15—Non-payment of Costs—Power of Attorney—Power of Attorney necessary to authorise demand of Costs.
The attorney in a suit referred by order of *nisi prius* has no authority to demand the amount awarded to his client, and an attachment will not issue. *Tobin* v. *Layton*, 2 *All.* 622.

16—Signature of Affidavit of due Execution of Power of Attorney—Verification.
Where the affidavit of the due execution of a power of attorney to demand costs under a rule of Court, was made in Nova Scotia before a Judge of the Supreme Court there—Held, That the signature of the Judge must be verified by an affidavit made here, in order to make the demand under such power sufficient to found an attachment. *Fraser* v. *Harding*, 2 *Kerr* 290.

17—Service of copy of Power of Attorney.
An attachment for non-payment of costs will not be granted, when the costs are demanded under a power of attorney, unless a copy thereof is served upon the party on whom the demand is made. *Gilbert* v. *Cyr*, *Mich. T.* 1870.

18—Power of Attorney—Must be executed by party—Attorney.
A power of attorney to demand costs must be executed by the party in the suit to whom they are payable. The attorney in the cause has no authority to give a power of attorney for that purpose. *Robicheau* v. *Turner*, *Trin. T.* 1871.

19—Demand of Costs out of Province—Place of demand.
A demand of costs in Nova Scotia is sufficient to support an application for attachment for non-payment. (Parker J., *dubitante.*) The place where the demand was made should be stated in the affidavit on which the motion is made, and a rule *nisi* only granted (per Parker J). *Regina* v. *Delaney*, *Mich. T.* 1864.

20—Time of Demand.
The affidavit of the demand of money in order to obtain an attachment must state the day on which the demand was made. *Campbell* v. *Todd*, 1 *All.* 199.

21—Costs—Demand—By whom made.
An attachment will not be granted for non-payment of costs, unless the demand is made by the party entitled to receive the costs, or his attorney in the cause, or a person authorized under a letter of attorney. *Marsh* v. *Rose*, *C. Ms.* 105.

22—Consent rule—Costs taxed under.
On motion for an attachment, for not paying costs taxed under a consent rule and a rule for judgment as in case of a nonsuit, it is unnecessary to show that a *ca. sa.* was taken out against the nominal plaintiff, and shewn to the lessor on the demanding of the costs; nor is it requisite that it should appear that final judgment had been entered up; but where the costs are demanded under a power of attorney, the practice requires that a copy of the power of attorney should be served on the party when the costs are demanded. *Doe* v. *King*, 3 *Kerr*, 492.

23—On Award—Award must be before Court.
A rule for an attachment against a party for not performing an award, will not be granted unless the award is brought before the Court. *Marks* v. *Marks*, 486.

24—Proceedings against Sheriff—Remedy on Judgment not Lost—When? See Discharge.

25—Judge's certificate that there was no reasonable cause to bring action in Supreme Court—Cannot be made a rule of Court to found an Attachment. See *Horner* v. *Crookshank*, 4 *All.* 375.

26—Exhibiting Interrogatories—Time.
If the prosecutor does not exhibit interrogatories against a defendant in custody on an attachment for contempt, a rule will be granted for his discharge unless the interrogatories are filed within four days. *Regina* v. *Salter*, 4 *All.* 51.

27—Married Woman—Marriage of female after verdict in Ejectment—Attachment against married female.
If the lessor of the plaintiff in ejectment (a female) marries after a verdict for the defendant, an attachment will be granted

against her for non-payment of the costs, after due demand. Doe dem. *Sargeant* v. *Sargeant, East. T.* 1864.

28—Attachment is in nature of a Mesne Process—Sheriff—Escape—Liability.
An attachment for non-payment of costs is in the nature of a mesne process, and a sheriff is not liable to an action for the escape of a person so imprisoned unless the plaintiff in the suit has sustained actual damage or delay in consequence of the escape. *Atkinson* v. *Mitchell, Trin. T.* 1865.

29—Election Law—Costs—Attachment.
Where the Judge who tries an election petition makes an order for costs under the 62nd sect. of the Act 32 Vic. c. 32, an attachment for non-payment of the costs should be granted by the Judge and not by the Court. *Kay* v. *Hannington, East. T.* 1873.

Cost of Appeal from decision of Judge in Equity, recoverable by attachment not by execution. See costs 79.

See General Rules 13.

ATTORNEY — BARRISTER — COUNSEL.

I. Admission.
II. Striking off Roll.
III. Privileges.
IV. Uncertificated.
V. Authority.
VI. Duties.
VII. Liability.
VIII. Bill of Costs.
IX. Taxation of Costs.
X. Miscellaneous.

I.

Admission.

1—See General Rules 15 to 25.

See Acts of Assembly 26 Vic. c. 23.
30 Vic. c. 7.
31 Vic. c. 3.

II.

Striking off Roll.

2—Some reason should be given for striking an Attorney off the Roll, even on his own application. *Ex parte McCully, Gent. one &c.*, 1 *Kerr* 521.

3—An application to strike an Attorney off the Roll for misconduct, must be founded on an affidavit adduced on the motion. *Ex parte Palmer*, 2 *All.* 533.

III.

Privileges.

1—A defendant, who is an Attorney of the Supreme Court, cannot be proceeded against summarily for a demand under £20. *Bennet* v. *Morse*, 2 *Kerr* 624.

2—Venue.
The plaintiff, an Attorney of the Supreme Court, by another attorney sued out a common *capias* against the defendant, and laid the venue in York county, describing himself in the commencement of the declaration as an attorney of the Supreme Court, and entitled to his privilege as attorney; on the defendant obtaining an order to change the venue to the county of Gloucester, on the usual affidavit that the cause of action arose there, the plaintiff by another order had the venue brought back, on the ground that as an attorney he is entitled to lay and retain his venue in York; and on motion to rescind the last order—Held, That the laying or retaining the venue in the county where the Court sits (viz. in the county of York), is a privilege inherent in the attornies of the Supreme Court of this Province. Held also, That this privilege was not waived by the plaintiff's not suing out an attachment of privilege, but as a common person by *capias*; the privileged character having been alleged on the record and allowed to remain there, without any prior objection to its regularity. *Desbrisay* v. *Baldwin*, 3 *Kerr* 379.

3—Lien.
An attorney has a lien on a judgment obtained by him for his costs, as between attorney and client. *Linton* v. *Wilson*, 1 *Kerr* 300.

4—Where the Court allowed a judgment to be set off against another, it must be subject to the attorney's lien generally, and not merely to the extent of the taxed costs in the particular suit. See *Rogers* v. *Ledden*, 2 *Kerr* 59.

5—An attorney, who also practises as a barrister, has no legal right to retain for counsel fees, money belonging to his client, without assent. *In re Bayard*, 1 *All.* 359.

6—Services—Fees.
A barrister cannot maintain an action against his client for professional services. *Kerr* v. *Burns*, 4 *All.* 604.

Quære, Whether such an action would lie on a special contract for a fixed sum, after the service was performed. *Ibid.*

A trial fee, under the Ordinance, is a fee to the counsel, and not to the attorney. *Ib.*

7—Judgment assigned.
Attorney has a right to receive the taxed costs of judgment assigned. See *Green* v. *Hendricks*, 1 *All.* 698.

8—Parties settling Suit.
The parties to a suit have a right to settle it without the consent of the attorney, and he is not justified after notice of the settlement in proceeding with the suit to recover his costs, unless the settlement was collusive for the purpose of defrauding him. *Ex parte Morse*, 3 *Kerr* 366.

9—Payment of Money—Assignee.
The Court will not compel an attorney, on a summary application, to pay over the proceeds of a judgment to a person claiming as assignee unless his right is clear. *Murray* v. *Johnston*, 1 *All.* 697.

10—Service of Bill upon Attorney
Should, in general, be personal service. See *Sayre* v. *Gilbert*, 2 *Kerr* 225.

11—Barrister.
A barrister has no legal remedy to recover remuneration for his services. *In re Bayard*, 1 *All.* 359.

12—A barrister against whom an action is brought has no right to conduct his defence both in person and by counsel. *Robinson* v. *Palmer*, 2 *All.* 223.

IV.

Uncertificated.

1—A writ issued by an uncertificated attorney, and all proceedings taken thereunder, will be set aside. *Desbrisay* v. *Mackay*, 1 *Han.* 138.

2—The proceedings in a suit by an attorney who has not taken out a certificate under the Act 22 Vic. c. 28, are a nullity; and the objection is not waived by the defendant's attorney attending the trial of the cause, after knowledge of the omission. *Ryan* v. *McIntyre*, *Hil. T.* 1870.

V.

Authority.

1—Written.
The Act 12 Vic. c. 40, s. 15, requiring attorneys to have written authority to sue is not limited to summary actions. If payment has been obtained in a suit with knowledge of the client, it will be presumed in absence of evidence to the contrary, that the attorney had written authority. Either party may apply to stay proceedings in an action brought without authority. *James* v. *McLean*, 3 *All.* 164.

2—Production of authority.
Counsel not required to produce his authority in making a motion before Court. See *In re Hunter*, 1 *Han.* 233.

3—Signing Cognovit.
An attorney has no authority to sign a cognovit in a suit without the authority of his client, but his client will be bound by a cognovit given without his consent, if he makes no objection when informed of it. *McNamee* v. *O'Brien*, 4 *All.* 548.

4—Presumption of authority to issue execution.
Where an attorney issued an execution in the name of the defendant, an attorney residing at a distance from him, and delivered it to the Sheriff, and afterwards attended before a Judge to oppose an application to set the execution aside. Held, in an action of trespass for taking property under the execution, that in the absence of evidence, to negative the authority and to show that the defendant did not receive the proceeds of the execution, it might be inferred that the attorney had authority to issue the execution. *Wilson* v. *Street*, 3 *All.* 251.

5—To give Power of Attorney to demand costs.
Attorney cannot give a power of attorney for his client to demand costs. See Attachment 18.

6—Counsel—Appearance in suit on trial without authority.
Where no notice of trial was given by plaintiff, and a counsel who had been retained in a former trial, in ignorance of this fact appeared without authority, defendant being absent, and defended, a verdict for the plaintiff was set aside. See *Doherty* v. *Desbrisay*, 1 *Han.* 404.

VI.

DUTIES.

1—Implied understanding to pay over money collected, on demand. See *Gilbert* v. *Palmer*, 1 *All.* 455.

2—What is a sufficient demand?
An intimation from a client to his attorney, who has collected money, that the client wishes it paid over, is a sufficient demand to support an action for money had and received. *Gilbert* v. *Palmer*, 1 *All.* 667.

It is not necessary that the demand should be made at the attorney's residence or place of business, unless he objects on that ground. *Ibid.*

Duty to communicate to client offer of compromise of suit. See Supersedeas, *Jones* v. *Steves*.

3—Counsel.
It is the duty of counsel to see that rules obtained by them are properly entered in the minutes of the Court. *Ex parte Glass*, 2 *All.* 88.

See Practice in Equity 21.

VII.

LIABILITY.

1—For Sheriff's Fees.
Attorney liable, as well as plaintiff, for Sheriff's fees on executing writ of *ca. sa.* See *Kavanagh* v. *McPhelim*, 1 *Kerr* 472.

2—Not liable for poundage on execution unless he receives the amount from the defendant, though the defendant has escaped from the limits and his bail has paid the debt and costs to attorney. *Caldwell* v. *Badger*, 2 *All.* 516.

Not Filing Papers—Forfeiture of Costs. See Practice VI. 48 *a*.

3—Improper Pleading.
If an attorney, without any assignable reason and without any precedent, adopts a new and unusual mode of pleading, in consequence of which his client suffers loss, the attorney is answerable in an action for negligence. *Carrigan* v. *Andrews*, 1 *All.* 485.

4—Issuing Void Writ.
An attorney is liable over to a sheriff who sustains damages by proceeding under what purports to be a writ of the Court but is not, when the same is put into the sheriff's hands by him. *Johnston* v *Winslow*, *Ber.* 53.

VIII.

BILL OF COSTS.

1—Delivery of before action.
It is not necessary for an attorney to deliver a taxed bill to his client before bringing an action. *Jack* v. *Clewes*, 3 *Kerr* 637.

2—The Act of Parliament 3 Jac. 1, c. 7, requiring the delivery of an attorney's bill of costs before action brought, extends to this Province, but the Act 2 Geo. 2 c. 23, requiring the delivery a month before action, is not in force here. *James* v. *McLean*, 3 *All.* 164.

3—Signing.
The Statute 3 Jac. 1, c. 7, requiring attorneys to deliver signed bills of costs to their clients, extends to this Province, and is not affected by its repeal in England by the 6 and 7 Vic. c. 73. *Kerr* v. *Burns*, 4 *All.* 604.

4—A general account, including the bill of costs delivered by an attorney to his client, though made out in the handwriting and headed in the name of the attorney, does not amount to a signing of the separate bills under the Statute. *Ibid.*

IX.

TAXATION OF COSTS.

1—Review of—Retaining of money by Attorney.
The defendant, after a verdict against him, placed in his attorney's hands £22, to be applied in part payment of the judgment; the attorney retained the money, and made an application to review the taxation of costs, which was refused with costs, because the defendant had in the mean time paid the amount of debt and costs to the sheriff. The Court ordered the attorney to repay the defendant the £22, but refused to compel him to pay the costs of dismissing the motion for review of taxation—not being satisfied that the defendant had instructed him not to take such proceedings. *Betts* v. *Chapman*, 2 *All.* 450.

2—Ordering Attorney to pay costs of dismissing motion for review.
Where on an application for a review of taxation of costs, it appeared that the bill was exorbitant, and the items disallowed

by the clerk, with trifling exceptions, illegally charged, the attorney applying for the review was ordered to pay the costs of dismissing the motion. *Doe* v. *Dobson*, 3 *All.* 531.

3—Allowance of Counsel Fees—Clerk's duty.
In taxing costs between attorney and client, counsel fees may be allowed without the Judge's fiat; but it is the duty of the Clerk to decide on the authority to make the payment, and the reasonableness of the charge. *Ex parte James*, 3 *All.* 286.

4—Outlays—Special Jury—Retaining Counsel.
An attorney is entitled to recover from his client a sum paid for a special jury, where the cause has been so tried with the client's knowledge, but the Judge has refused to certify. *Ex parte James*, 3 *All.* 286.

An attorney has no general authority to retain counsel in a cause at his client's expense, though such authority may be implied. If the attorney has an opportunity of conferring with his client, his consent should be obtained. *Ibid.*

5—Costs in Inferior Court—Clerk taxing.
In an action on an attorney's bill of costs incurred in the inferior Court, the reasonableness of the charges may be enquired into. The Clerk of the Supreme Court may tax a bill of costs in the inferior Court as between attorney and client. *James* v. *McLean*, 3 *All.* 164.

6—Taxable Charges—Services performed at request of client.
In taxing costs between attorney and client, the attorney is entitled to the taxable charges of drawing and copying a declaration in a suit brought by the client, though he is not the attorney in that suit; the service having been performed at the request of the client, and with the assent of the attorney in the suit. *In re Bayard*, 1 *All.* 571.

7—*Quære*, Whether an attorney can recover from his client money paid for counsel fees? See *Jack* v. *Clews*, 3 *Kerr* 637.

8—Recovery for services other than provided for in the ordinance.
In an action by an attorney to recover the amount of a bill of costs incurred in defending defendant against a criminal charge, the bill had been taxed by the clerk, who taxed only such items as the ordinance of fees provided for, and refused to recognize or touch the other items. Held, That the jury were bound by the clerk's taxation as to the taxable items, and as to the others they might find for the plaintiff for such services as were in the nature of attorney's work, but that plaintiff could not recover for counsel fees. *Quære*, Whether if the clerk had followed the English practice and taxed the whole bill it would have been sustained? *Peck* v. *Tingley*, 1 *Han.* 418.

X.

Miscellaneous.

1—Action for negligence—Preferring of judgment.
In an action against an attorney for negligence in conducting a suit for the plaintiff against M, it was proved that at the time the plaintiff employed the defendant, he was informed the defendant had a judgment against M, which would have priority over the plaintiff's claim. Held, 1. That it was no breach of duty on the part of the defendant to proceed on his own judgment against M, and exhaust his property before issuing execution on the plaintiff's judgment. 2. That evidence could not be given that the amount for which the defendant's judgment was signed against M, was not really due. *Alison* v. *Weldon*, 4 *All.* 631.

2—Record—Name of Attorney.
The Court consider it irregular for the name of more than one Attorney of firm to appear as Attorney on record. *Gilmour* v. *Bull*, 1 *Kerr* 94.

3—Partnership—Notice by one of firm.
Where two attorneys in partnership appear in a suit, a subsequent notice of a proceeding in the suit signed in the name of one of them is sufficient; the act of one partner in such a matter being the act of both. *Doe* v. *Taylor*, 3 *All.* 437.

4—Pleading—Action against.
Where Bill filed in vacation, Attorney must plead within twenty days from time of service of copy, and cannot wait till ensuing term. *Sayre* v. *Gilbert*, 2 *Kerr* 225.

5—Misconduct—Cognizance of, by Court.
Where a motion was made by the defendant against the plaintiff's attorney, requiring him to refund costs which had

been taxed for the plaintiff, on the ground that a payment had been made on the demand before action brought, reducing it within a Magistrate's jurisdiction, and that the attorney aware of it had incurred a large amount of costs, which the defendant had paid; and the application was accompanied by a draft of the bill of costs, which was said by the attorney to be lost or mislaid, in which draft there were apparent overcharges; the ground of application in regard to the payment was satisfactorily answered, but the Court considering that the attorney had not exercised sufficient forbearance towards the defendant, in going on with the suit when there was a very small sum due, ordered him to prepare a new bill to be taxed, to refund to the defendant the overplus, and pay the costs of the motion, although the attorney had offered before the application to refund a certain amount, or to abide the taxation of the opposite attorney. *Melanson* v. *White*, 3 *Kerr* 501.

6—Misconduct.

If an attorney of this Court is guilty of any misconduct in practising in an Inferior Court, this Court will take cognizance of it on a summary application. *Gilbert* v. *Soney*, 3 *Kerr* 679.

7—The Court will investigate a complaint made against an Attorney by his client, and make such order therein as justice requires. On such an investigation an attorney was ordered to refund money to his client and pay the costs of the application. *In re Lugrin*, *Trin. T.* 1831.

Proceeding in action after receipt given. See Receipt, *Moran* v. *Gallagher*.

Ordering Attorney to file writ. See Execution IV. 7.

8—Change of Attorneys—Attorney in contempt—Time of application.

Where a Judge's order had been made to change the attorney and file the papers in a cause, in ignorance of the original attorney being in contempt, a party wishing to take advantage thereof, should apply to rescind the Judge's order. *Kerlin* v. *Baillie*, 2 *All.* 115.

It is too late to apply after receiving a copy of declaration. *Ibid.*

9—Proper person to make application—Reasons.

An order for a change of attorney ought not to be made on the mere application of the attorney, on the ground that he is unable to proceed in the suit in consequence of non-payment of court fees. *Kelly* v. *Dow*, 4 *All.* 256.

Where such an order had been made and acted upon, and it did not appear that the client was aware of the disability of the attorney at the time he commenced the suit, the Court refused to set it aside. *Ibid.*

10—Taking Warrant of Attorney—Items improperly included—Ignorance of party.

It is improper for an attorney to include in an account against his client, claims for money lent, with professional charges, in order to take security for the whole; nor should he take a warrant of attorney from his client without affording him an opportunity of taking legal advice upon the nature of the demand and the security. *Smith* v. *Jones*, 2 *All.* 176.

Where an attorney, without any fraudulent intention, took from his client a warrant of attorney for costs of suits and money lent, etc., and for a settled account due from a former deceased client, whom the defendant represented, the Court refused to set aside the security and a judgment signed thereon, after two executions had been issued and money levied thereunder without objection by the defendant. But sums overcharged were deducted from the judgment, though it had been assigned to a third person. Such assignments should not be made by attornies, particularly when there is any question about the amount. *Ibid.*

Semble, That if the warrant of attorney had been taken for costs alone, the judgment would have been set aside. *Ibid.*

11—If an attorney, knowing that he is dealing with ignorant persons, takes from them on a settlement, a warrant of attorney for debt and costs, in which there are extravagant charges, such settlement may be opened up and examined within a reasonable time. *Gilbert* v. *Soney*, 3 *Kerr* 679.

12—Action on Attorney's Bill—Settlement of suit—Material question for jury—Defence.

Where the defence to an action on an attorney's bill is that the costs were incurred in a suit which the attorney had settled without the defendant's authority; it is a material question for the jury, in determining whether the defendant obtained any benefit from the plaintiff's services, to ascertain whether the previous suit was settled with his consent. *Dibblee* v. *Wood*, *East. T.* 1872.

13—Counsel—Witness.
Where a counsel in a cause is by consent allowed to go upon the stand to prove a particular fact, he becomes a witness in the cause generally, and may be cross-examined upon any fact in the cause. *Gilbert* v. *Campbell*, 2 *Han.* 55.

Examination as Witness—Objectionable. See New Trial.

14—Addressing Jury—Objectionable observations.
If a counsel in addressing the jury makes remarks which are considered objectionable by the opposing counsel, he should call the attention of the Judge to it at the time; if he does so, the Judge concurring will require the objectionable observations to be withdrawn. *Gilbert* v. *Campbell*, 2 *Han.* 55.

15—Admissions.
Where in an action of covenant brought by the assignee in fee on a warranty of title, the declaration alleged, as part of the damages, that by reason of the defect in the title, the plaintiff had not been enabled to obtain so large a price for the land as he otherwise might, and would have obtained; and the plaintiff's counsel stated, in his opening at the trial, that the plaintiff had before the commencement of the action sold and conveyed the land for an inadequate consideration, in consequence of such defect in the title; and afterwards put the deed in evidence. Held, That the defendant was entitled to the benefit of this admission and proof, as defeating the plaintiff's action, although he could not have been permitted to give evidence of such conveyance under any of the pleas upon the record. *Wallace* v. *Vernon*, 1 *Kerr* 5.

16—Where in an action for negligence as a surgeon, the defendant's counsel in addressing the jury relies on his client's skill as a surgeon, he cannot afterwards object on a motion for a new trial that there was no evidence that he was a surgeon. *Kelly* v. *Dow*, 4 *All.* 435.

Counsel not being able to attend trial—Excuse on motion for judgment. See Judgment, as in case of Non-suit II.

Actual signature of counsel not necessary to the copy of plea delivered. See *Oulton* v. *Palmer*, 2 *All.* 364.

Notice to Counsel of party.
Quære, Whether notice to counsel of a meeting of arbitrators in a cause which is referred, is notice to the party? See *Brown* v. *Currier*, 2 *All.* 124.

ATTORNEY GENERAL.

1—Privileges—Costs.
In suits where the Queen is a party and entitled to costs, a retaining fee of 25*s*. is allowed to the Attorney General; and for all papers properly termed "pleadings," a higher rate per folio is allowed for drafting and copying, than in suits between subjects. *Attorney General* v. *Twenty Casks of Spirits*, 3 *All.* 404.

2—Scire Facias—Fiat.
A *scire facias* at the instance of a private prosecutor, to repeal letters patent, can only issue on the fiat of the Attorney General, who may withhold his assent if no sufficient ground is shewn. A draft of the writ and a statement of the facts on which it is founded should be laid before the Attorney General, and if he is disqualified from acting, the Solicitor General or a Crown lawyer should decide on the application. *LeGall* v. *Duffy*, 3 *All.* 57.

3—Liability for Sheriff's Fees.
The Attorney General is liable in his personal capacity to a sheriff for such of the sheriff's fees of office on the execution of Crown processes, as are included in the Attorney General's taxed bill of costs, and received by him from defendants in the several Crown suits, after demand made, where no ground is shewn for retaining them. *White* v. *Peters*, 2 *Kerr* 329.

AUTHORITY.

Of Attorney. See Attorney.

Construction of Written Authority. See Contract 9.

AUTREFOIS ACQUIT.

See Bastardy.

AVERMENT.

See Pleading.

AWARD.

See Arbitration.

BAIL.

A DISCHARGE.

B RELIEF—APPLICATION FOR.

C LIMIT BOND (SURETIES)

D RENDER.

A

DISCHARGE OF.

1—Plaintiff procuring absence of Defendant.
Special bail discharged, although indemnified, when prevented from surrendering defendant by plaintiff's procuring his absence from the Province. *Pollock* v. *Short*, *Ber.* 279.

2—Surprise—Representation of Plaintiff's Attorney.
Where the plaintiff's attorney induced the bail to suppose that execution would be issued against the property of the principal, proceedings against the bail were set aside on the ground of surprise. *Hoynes* v. *Chalmers*, *C. Ms.* 1.

3—Delay.
Where special bail was entered in June 1826, and declaration delivered in March 1827, since which time no proceedings were taken by the plaintiff, the bail were discharged on account of the delay.—*Ganet* v. *McIntosh*, *C. Ms.* 140.

4—Omitting to enter cause in time.
When upon a summary writ returnable in Hilary term 1842, special bail was regularly put in and notice given, but the cause was not entered by the plaintiff in that or the next succeeding term; but an entry was irregularly made in Michaelmas 1842, and final judgment signed in the April following; the Court stayed proceedings subsequently taken on the recognizance of bail, and ordered an *exoneretur* to be entered on the bail piece, without costs. *Muldoon* v. *Beveridge*, 2 *Kerr* 532.

5—Proceedings stayed by Defendant.
Where the defendant obtained a stay of proceedings until security for costs was given, after sufficient time had elapsed, and no further proceedings in the cause taken by the plaintiff, the Court ordered an *exoneretur* to be entered on the bail piece. *Hill* v. *Rind*, *Ber.* 281.

6—Not giving security for costs after stay of proceedings.
Where the defendant in Hilary term 1854, had obtained an order to stay proceedings until security for costs was given, and the plaintiff had not given the security, the Court discharged the bail in Michaelmas term 1855. *Ratchford* v. *Morris*, 3 *All.* 245.

7—No ca. sa. against principal.
When no *ca. sa.* against the principal is found on file in the Clerk's office, proceedings against the bail will be set aside. *Merritt* v. *Lindsay*, *Hil. T.* 1828.

8—Affidavit not filed in time—Entry Docket.
It is no ground for setting aside proceedings against bail, that the writ and affidavit to hold to bail have not been filed within the time prescribed by rule of Court, provided the Entry Docket has been duly filed. *Gilmour* v. *Simpson*, *Mich. T.* 1861.

9—Variance—Affidavit—Declaration.
The cause of action stated in an affidavit to hold to bail, was the non-delivery of goods by the defendant as master of a vessel, according to a bill of lading. The contract set out in the declaration upon the bill of lading contained an exception of "the damages of the seas and breakage." Held, That there was a material variance between the declaration and affidavit, and that the bail were discharged. *Holderness* v. *McFarlane*, 3 *All.* 152.

Bankrupt—Right to have Bail Bond cancelled. See Bankrupt 5.

B

RELIEF—APPLICATION FOR.

10—Action on Recognizance—Render—Notice.
Where an action was brought on a recognizance of bail after render of the principal, but before notice thereof to the plaintiff, the Court refused to stay the proceedings except on payment of costs. *Duff* v. *Hunter*, 1 *Kerr* 499.

11—Reference—Pleading.
Bail cannot plead to an action on the recognizance, a reference of the original suit to arbitration. They should apply to the Court to have an *exoneretur* entered on the bail piece. *Sharp* v. *Connell*, 3 *Kerr* 125.

12—Special Contract—Common Affidavit—Verdict.
Where a party is held to bail on the

common affidavit for goods sold, and the declaration is framed with counts to recover a demand arising out of a special contract, together with a common count for goods sold; and on the trial a general verdict is given for the plaintiff on evidence however which only referred to the special contract. Held, That the bail were entitled to have an *exoneretur* entered on the bail piece, on motion, without first applying to have the verdict limited to the special counts, and that the affidavit did not include the demand arising out of the special contract and sounding in damages. *Ford* v. *Ladd*, 3 *Kerr* 287.

13—Cause not tried—Agreement to give confession.

Proceedings against bail were set aside on payment of costs, where notice of trial had been given for the Sittings after Trinity term 1858, but the cause was not tried in consequence of the defendants' agreement to give a confession, and the confession, though dated 1st June 1858, was not given till October 1859, when judgment was signed. *Raymond* v. *McMackin*, 4 *All.* 524.

14—Misnomer of Plaintiff—Delay in amending.

Where the defendant's attorney in entering special bail mistook the plaintiff's name, and was informed of the error by the plaintiff's attorney, but died soon after without having amended it, and the defendant employed another attorney, who made no application to amend the proceedings until it was too late to try the cause in the county where the venue was laid; the Court refused to set aside the proceedings on the bail bond and let the defendant in to defend, though the plaintiff's name was mis-stated in the entry docket; the defendant not having been misled thereby. *Riordan* v. *Dunn*, 3 *All.* 124.

15—Delay—Excuse.

Where an action was brought in August 1853, and notice of trial given for the January circuit following, which was countermanded, and no further step taken by the plaintiff; the Court refused in Trinity term 1855, to relieve the bail on the ground of delay; the plaintiff's attorney stating that the delay had been caused by the difficulty of obtaining evidence in a foreign country, and that he intended to proceed to trial at the next Circuit. *Jarvis* v. *Hardy*, 3 *All* 242.

16—Condition to pay costs not fulfilled.

In an action brought on a limit bond against the principal and sureties for an escape, it appeared that the plaintiff let the defendant go, upon the understanding that the defendant should pay all costs, the Court refused relief to the sureties under 6 Wm. 4, c. 41, s. 13, it not appearing that all costs had been paid. *Robertson, assignee of Sheriff* v. *Currie et al.*, *Ber.* 190

17—Attachment for costs in Equity Limit Bond given by prisoner —Application for relief.

When an action is brought in the Supreme Court on a limit bond given by a prisoner in custody on an attachment for costs in Equity, application for relief by the sureties must be made to the Supreme Court. *Bartlett* v. *Glasgow*, *Hil. T.* 1871.

18—Sureties on limit bond—Order for render Judge County Court.

Under the Act 12 Vic. c. 39, s. 14, the sureties in a limit bond may obtain an order for the render of the principal; and by 31 Vic. c. 13, s. 10, a Judge of the County Court may make the order. The term "bail" in those Acts, include the sureties in a limit bond. *Ibid.*

19—Pending pleading.

Bail cannot after pleading that no *ca. sa.* duly issued against the principal, and while that plea stands, apply to the Court to set aside the proceedings for irregularity, on the ground that the execution did not remain in the sheriff's office four days. *Fulton* v. *Andrews*, 2 *All.* 350.

After failure of such an application, a motion to withdraw the plea and set aside the execution for the same irregularity, was refused. *Ibid.*

20—Application on ground of delay in Plaintiff.

In an application to discharge the bail in a suit on the ground of delay in the plaintiff's proceedings, it must be sworn that the application is made on behalf of the bail. *Ritchie* v. *Porter*, 2 *All.* 360.

21—Objection to sufficiency of affidavit.

Quære, Whether it is too late for bail to object to the sufficiency of an affidavit, after the time for putting in bail has expired, if they did not see it before that time. *Simonds* v. *Simonds*, 2 *All.* 468.

22—Irregularity in affidavit to hold to bail—Waiver.

An irregularity in affidavit to hold to bail

is waived by pleading to the action. See *McPhelim* v. *Larson*, 4 *All.* 71.

Waiver.
Bailable Capias stating no cause of action. See Practice IV. 1.

23—Render to Gaol—Whence escape.
If a debtor escapes from the limits, and his bail apply to be relieved on rendering him to gaol under the Act 13 Vic. c. 31, such relief will only be granted on condition of his being rendered to the gaol whence he escaped. *Peters* v. *Perley*, 2 *All.* 585.

24—Bail Bond—Action—Insolvency of Principal—Affidavit.
An application by bail under the 1 Revised Stat. c. 124, to stay proceedings in an action on a limit bond, on account of the insolvency of the principal, was refused; it appearing that the principal had property sufficient to pay the debt. *Bradford* v. *Fenton*, 3 *All.* 407.

The affidavit to support such an application should state that it is made at the expense of the bail and without collusion with the principal. *Ibid.*

Quære, Whether, after application for relief, the bail can defend on the merit? See *Rippey* v. *Austin*, 4 *All.* 77.

25—Recognizance—Pleading to—Cause referred, should apply for an exoneretur. See Pleading V. 22.

26—Bail for principal debtor—Application by other bail for relief—Same subject matter of suit—Both bail fixed—Payment of debt by one.
A, the maker, and B the accommodation endorser of a note, were held to bail, and the bail in both cases fixed. B's bail settled the judgment on the understanding with the plaintiff's attorney that he should continue the proceedings against A's bail for their (B's bail) benefit. On application by A's bail for relief on the ground that the debt had been paid—Held, That they, being bail for the principal debtor, were not entitled to relief at the expense of B's bail, especially as it did not appear that they were not indemnified. *McFeason* v. *Callaghan*, *Trin. T.* 1863

27—Escape—No damages—No return of principal.
Matters which merely tend to shew that the plaintiff has sustained no damage by the escape of a debtor from the limits, do not afford a ground for summary relief to his sureties under the Act 10 and 11 Geo. 4, c. 30. The principal should have returned within the limits, or be prevented from doing so by inevitable accident before such an application will be granted. *Bonnell* v. *Ackerman*, *Mich. T.* 1834.

C

Limit Bond—Sureties.

28—Relief—Conditions.
Where an action had been commenced on a limit bond, the Court relieved the surety on his rendering the principal and paying the costs of the action on the limit bond, together with the costs of the application, within a period fixed by the Court. *McIntosh* v. *Allen*, 3 *Kerr* 362.

29—Insufficiency of affidavit on application—Answer.
In application for relief by the sureties in a limit bond, under the 1 Rev. Stat. c. 124, the affidavit neither stated when or at whose instance they became bail; what property the principal had at the time, whether the bond was given on arrest upon mesne or final process or render; or when the principal escaped. The affidavit in answer alleged that the principal had stated that he would have paid the debt if the defendants had not become his bail; that he had put property into the hands of L. to secure the person who might become bail; that the defendants became bail at the request of L without his knowledge, and that L. had become insolvent and transferred the property to one of the bail. Held, That the sureties were not entitled to relief. *Smith* v. *Leary*, 4 *All.* 162.

30—Defendant supersedable before escape.
The sureties on a limit bond entered into for a defendant in custody on *mesne* process, are entitled to be discharged, if the defendant before his escape had become supersedable. *Gordon* v. *French*, 2 *Kerr* 610.

31—Sureties not affected.
An agreement between the parties that no advantage should be taken of the omission to charge in execution, cannot affect the sureties, unless made with their privity. *Ibid.*

See Bond (Limit Bond.)

D

RENDER.

32—Fictitious name.
If two names appear on the bail piece as bail, it is sufficient for the purpose of render, though one of them is a fictitious person. *Wetmore* v. *Elliott*, 1 *All.* 720.

Quære, Whether, in such a case, the plaintiff might except to the bail? *Ibid.*

33—Bail may be entered by one person only for the purpose of rendering the principal. *Duncan* v *Barnes*, *Trin. T.* 1864.

34—Action on Limit Bond—Render after.
The render of the principal after an action brought for an escape on a limit bond, is not a ground for relieving the sureties. See Bond 8.

35—Notice of render—Omission—Waiver.
Quære, Whether a notice of render which omits to state the lodgment of the order for render with the gaoler, is sufficient? Such an objection to a notice is waived by the plaintiff opposing the defendant's discharge out of custody under the Insolvent Confined Debtors' Act, and by discontinuing and receiving the costs of an action brought against the bail before render. *Jackson* v. *Black*, 4 *All.* 79.

A notice of render signed by the defendant's attorney is sufficient even after judgment, if he continue to act as attorney. *Ibid.*

36—When may be made.
Bail to the Sheriff may render the defendant before the expiration of the time for putting in special bail. *James* v. *White*, *Trin. T.* 1866.

37—Exception—Entry.
Exception to bail not necessary to be entered in Judge's book. See *Porter* v. *Burns*, 1 *All.* 106.

38—Escape—Order for render after.
An order for render may be made after an escape from the limits, and proceedings on the bond against the sureties for the escape will be stayed on payment of costs. *McMillan* v. *Largen*, *Trin T.* 1865.

BAIL (COMMON.)

See Practice.

BAIL BOND.

See Bond 8.

BAILEE.

1—Pawnee may maintain replevin for pawned goods wrongfully taken.
A pawnee may maintain replevin against the pawnor for a wrongful taking of the goods pledged. Proof of such pawning is sufficient to enable the pawnee to recover in an issue joined upon the ordinary plea of property against the general owner. *Gibson* v. *Boyd*, 1 *Kerr* 150.

2—Conveyance to Trustees—Retaining part of goods.
Defendant conveyed all his property to trustees for the benefit of his creditors—certain goods of which the trustees had no knowledge, remained in his possession. Held, That the general property in the goods passed to the trustees, and that defendant could not be considered as holding the goods as their bailee. *McIntosh* v. *Hastings*, *Hil. T.* 1865.

BAILMENT.

1—Action by Bailor for negligence to horse.
The Court refused to set aside a verdict given for the plaintiff in an action by the bailor against the bailee of a horse for negligence, although the jury were not able to agree whether the bailment was a *commodatum* or *mutuum*, the injury being such as to make the defendant liable in either case. *Rainsbury* v. *Ross*, 2 *Kerr* 179.

2—Hiring horse—Death—Liability.
A person hiring a horse to perform a journey, is not liable for the value of the horse, if he dies on the road without the fault of the hirer. *Quære*, Whether, in such case, the owner of the horse is entitled to recover the hire on the *quantum meruit*, for the time the defendant used the horse? *Dickie* v. *Campbell*, *C. Ms.* 44.

3—Goods deposited in warehouse—Special instructions.
Plaintiff deposited goods in defendant's warehouse (which was also a bonding warehouse), with directions not to deliver them except to his order. F, for whom the goods were intended, but to whom the defendant was directed not to deliver them without payment, paid the duty at the custom house, and obtained a permit to release the goods from the public warehouse, and then got possession of them from the defendant's clerk. Held, That the defendant was liable to the plaintiff

for the goods. *Gunnison* v. *Thomas, East. T.* 1861.

BAILIFF.

Special—Appointment at Request—Liability of Sheriff. See Sheriff 21.

Special bailiff of plaintiff allowing defendant to go at large, cannot retake on a new *ca. sa.* See Execution II. 5.

BANK.

1—Authority to accept Bills of Exchange.

An incorporated banking company has authority to accept bills of exchange as a necessary incident to the transaction of its ordinary business; and such acceptance need not be under the corporate seal. *Berton* v. *The Central Bank, Hil. T.* 1863.

2—Provisions when directory only.

The provisions in the charter 4 Wm. 4, c. 44, that "every bond, bank bill, bank note, or other instrument, by the terms of which the Corporation may be charged or held liable for the payment of money, shall specially declare in such form as the Board of Directors shall prescribe, that payment shall be made out of the joint fund of the Corporation," is directory only. *Ibid.*

Liabilities of Stockholders. See Joint Stock Company 9.

3—Savings' Bank—Directors—Tenure of Office—Liability.

The Act 6 Geo. 4, c. 4, relating to Savings' Banks declared that all moneys, etc., belonging to the institution were vested in the trustees for the time being, for the use and benefit of the institution, and of the respective depositors therein. By regulations made under the authority of the Act, the management of the Savings' Bank was vested in a president and eight directors who were to be chosen annually. Held, That the president and directors so chosen were the trustees under the Act, and that they continued in office after the expiration of the year, none others having been chosen in their places,—and were liable to the plaintiff for money deposited in the Bank. *Gilchrist* v. *Wyer, Ber.* 219.

Banker Unlicensed—Unstamped Check. See Check 1.

BANK NOTE.

Bank Note payable to bearer.

Holder may maintain action on, though he has no beneficial interest in the note, and holds it merely as the agent of the owner for the purpose of demanding payment. See *Allison* v. *The Central Bank*, 4 *All.* 270.

Forgery of—What amounts to. See Criminal Law II. 20.

BANK STOCK.

Executors allowing Stock to remain undisposed of—Liability as contributories. See Winding Up Act 5.

BANKRUPT.

Privilege from Arrest. See Arrest.

Impeaching Certificate for fraud—Cannot be shewn on trial. See Evidence III. 18.

Judgment of Non-suit, although plaintiff a bankrupt. See Judgment as in case of Non-suit II. 22.

Plaintiff executing writ—No knowledge of bankruptcy—Trespass. See Sheriff 8.

Rent accruing due after issue of fiat. See Harding v. Baker, 1 All. 576.

Interest in case vesting in assignee. *Ibid.*

Provisional Assignee—Right to sue. See Beardsley v. Stephenson, 1 All. 631.

1—Claim provable under fiat—Liquidated damages.

The defendant conveyed land to A, with a covenant for title, which was broken by the existence of a prior mortgage, which A was obliged to pay. Held, That the amount so paid was liquidated damages, and was a claim provable under a fiat in bankruptcy afterwards granted against the defendant, and was discharged by his certificate under the Bankrupt Act, 5 Vic. c. 43 *Cunningham* v. *Scoullar*, 4 *All.* 385.

2—Fiat—Proof.

A fiat in bankruptcy under the Acts of Assembly 5 Vic. c. 43, and 6 Vic. c. 4, may be proved by a certified copy thereof without production of the Royal Gazette, except where title is to be shown in the assignee. *Ibid.*

3—Privilege from arrest—Pleading Certificate.

A certificate under the present English Bankrupt Acts, is a discharge of debts incurred in this Province, and may be pleaded in the Provincial Courts, but *Semble*, The certificate cannot be pleaded generally, as in England, but the proceedings on which it is founded must be set out. (See 6 C. p. 228, L. R. Ellis v. McHenry.) *Jouett* v. *Lockwood*, 2 *Kerr* 674.

4—Where defendant was arrested for a debt due on a bond, and it appeared that after the debt was contracted he had become a bankrupt, and received his discharge under the "Bankruptcy (Scotland) Act of 1856," the Court ordered his discharge on his entering a common appearance. *Gilbert* v. *McLean*, 2 *Han.* 213.

5—Bail bond given—Right to have cancelled.

A person, resident in this Province, who has been declared a bankrupt in England, under the English Bankruptcy Acts, and who has been afterwards arrested here for a debt incurred in this Province, is not entitled to have the bail bond which he has entered into upon such arrest, given up and cancelled upon affidavit that he was on his way to England to surrender himself to the commissioners at a day appointed by them when the arrest took place.

Quære, As to the liability of the defendant to arrest, and the mode of discharge? The Court is unwilling to decide questions of such importance upon a summary application, particularly where the defendant is not in confinement. *Mayor, &c., St. John* v. *Lockwood*, 2 *Kerr* 9.

6—Discharge from custody.

A defendant who was in custody on execution, at the suit of the plaintiff, at the time of the Bankruptcy Act, 5 Vic. c. 43, coming into operation, and who has since been declared a bankrupt under that Act, and duly surrendered, is entitled to his discharge from custody, under the 24th section. *Reynolds* v. *Hanford*, 2 *Kerr* 114.

Baron and Femme. See Husband and Wife.

BASTARDY.

1—Still-born child—Order.

An order of affiliation cannot be made under the Bastardy Acts where the child is still-born, although the parish has been put to expenses in the attendance on the mother. *Regina* v. *Murphy*, 1 *Kerr* 524.

2—Jurisdiction in Sessions.

A being charged as the reputed father of a bastard child of which B was then pregnant, appeared at the January Sessions and denied the charge; B was sworn as a witness, but it appearing to the Sessions that she did not understand the nature of an oath, the case was dismissed, and A's sureties discharged. After the birth of the child, A was again charged before a subsequent Sessions with being the father, and pleaded *autrefois acquit.* Held, (Parker J., *dubitante*, and Ritchie J., *dissentiente*,) that the January Sessions had power to try whether A was the father or not, though they could not make an order of filiation till the child was born, and that having acquitted him of the charge, he could not again be tried for the same offence. Held, per Ritchie J., That until the birth of the child, the Sessions had no power to hear evidence or make any adjudication; and that the order of the January Sessions discharging A was void, and could not be pleaded as an answer to the charge made against him after the birth of the child. *Ex parte Estabrooks*, 4 *All.* 273.

3—Proceedings not criminal—Witness.

A proceeding to obtain an order of affiliation under the 1 Rev. Stat. c. 57, is not a criminal proceeding on which the party charged is punishable on summary conviction, and therefore he is a competent witness by the Act 19 Vic. c. 41. *Ex parte Cook*, 4 *All.* 506.

Quære, Whether a Justice of the Peace who is a rate-payer in a parish on which a bastard child is chargeable, is disqualified from acting in proceedings to obtain an order of affiliation. *Ibid.*

4—Quashing order in part.

An order of affiliation may be quashed in part and confirmed as to the rest, if the defective part can be separated from the other. *The Queen* v. *Simpson*, 1 *Han.* 32.

5—Jurisdiction—Consent—Trial by single Justice.

Where in a bastardy case by consent of counsel a single Justice tried the matter alone and afterwards made an order of affiliation, the Court held that a court could not be constituted by consent, and ordered the proceedings to be quashed. *The Queen* v. *the Justices of Westmorland*, 1 *Han.* 468.

Held also, that the Court not being properly constituted there was no trial at all, and the party was required to enter into recognizances to answer the charge before the sessions. *Ibid.*

6—Order substantially good.
An order of affiliation, adjudging the father of the child to pay £10 12s. 9d. for the lying-in expenses of the mother, and for the support of the child up to the date of the order, is substantially good, though it does not follow the form given in 1 Rev. Stat. c. 57. *Ex parte Kennedy, Hil. T.* 1866.

7—Judgment on scire facias—Costs.
A judgment on *scire facias* on a recognizance in Bastardy proceedings, under 1 Rev. Stat. c. 57, is conclusive while it stands, and the defendant cannot object to the amount of costs taxed by the Sessions. If the costs are excessive, application should be made to the Sessions to reduce them. *Reg.* v. *Carson, Hil. T.* 1866.

8—Mayor of Fredericton—Right to sit in Sessions.
Under the Act 2nd Vic. c. 8, the Mayor of Fredericton has no right to sit in the Sessions on the trial of a Bastardy case arising outside of the city. *Ex parte Carson, Trin. T.* 1864.

See Acts of Assembly 33rd Vic. cap. 33.

Barrister. See Attorney, &c.

Bequest. See Will.

Bills of Exchange. See Bills and Notes.

BILLS AND PROMISSORY NOTES.

I. Requisites—Form—Operation.
II. Parties—Rights—Liability—Acceptance.
III. Presentment—Demand.
IV. Notice of Dishonour.
V. Defence.
VI. Miscellaneous.

I.

Requisites—Form—Operation.

1—Continuing Security—Time of payment not specified—Demand.
Where no time of payment is specified in a promissory note, it is payable on demand; and where such note is on interest, it does not become over due by mere lapse of time without demand of payment having been actually made. *Thorne* v. *Scovil*, 2 *Kerr* 557.

2—Blank Payee.
A promissory note payable to ——— or order, cannot be recovered by the person to whom it was given, either as payee or bearer, without inserting his name in the blank as payee. *Mutual Safety Insurance Company* v. *Porter*, 2 *All.* 230.

Any *bona fide* holder of such a note may insert his name in the blank as payee. *Ibid.*

3—Date contemporaneous with debt—Presumption.
There is no presumption that the date of a promissory note is contemporaneous with the debt which forms the consideration; therefore a note given for liquor after the passing of the Act 15 Vic c. 51, was held (R. Parker, J. *dissentiente*) not to be void without proof that the sale took place after the passing of the Act. *Mc Cann* v. *Reilly*, 3 *All.* 154.

4—Current Rate of Exchange.
A writing whereby the defendant promised to pay to his own order £42 3s. 9d., with current rate of exchange on Boston, is not a promissory note, either under the statute 3 and 4 Anne, c. 9, or the 1 Rev. Stat. c. 116. *Nash* v. *Gibbon*, 4 *All.* 479.

Semble, That even if a declaration on such a note could be sustained, it should have averred what the rate of exchange was, and what Boston was intended. *Ibid.*

5—Payable to maker's order.
A note payable to the maker's own order is not a promissory note within the statute of Anne, or the 1 Rev. Stat. c. 116; but when such a note is endorsed in blank by the maker, it becomes a note payable to bearer. *Ennis* v. *Hastings*, 4 *All.* 482.

It is no ground for motion in arrest of judgment that such an instrument has been declared on as a promissory note, and as having been indorsed to the plaintiff. *Ibid.*

6—Sum certain—Lex Mercatoria.
A bill of exchange must be drawn for payment of a sum certain; therefore an instrument drawn by A upon B, requesting him to pay to the order of A, five months after date, $400, with current rate of exchange on New York, is not a bill of exchange. *Cazet* v. *Kirk*, 4 *All.* 543.

A custom between merchants in this Province and the United States, to draw bills of exchange in this form, is not part of the *lex mercatoria*. *Cazet* v. *Kirk*, 4 *All.* 543.

7—Note payable to A or his heirs.
Right to recover vested in personal representatives.

Semble, Whether the instrument is a promissory note. See Doak Administrator, &c. *v.* Robinson, 1 Han. 279.

8—Principal and surety—Liability as makers—Property as security misapplied by surety.
One of the defendants in a joint and several note, signed it as surety for the other; the principal afterwards put property in the plaintiff's hands to sell and pay the note, but he applied the proceeds to the payment of another debt due to him from the principal. Held, That this was no defence at law, both the makers of the note being principals. *Morrison* v. *Kyle*, *East. T.* 1872.

9—No absolute transfer—Equities.
A note payable on demand was indorsed to the plaintiff as security for a liability he had incurred for the payee; the maker afterwards paid the amount of the note to the payee. Held, That the note not having been absolutely transferred to the plaintiff, he stood in the same position as the payee, and could not recover. *Estabrooks* v. *McKenzie*, *Hil. T.* 1827.

10—Note held by creditor taking proceedings under Insolvent Debtors Act—Right not divested.
The right to a promissory note held by a person who takes proceedings under the Insolvent Debtors Act, (21 Vic. c. 17) is not divested by the publication of the notice calling a meeting of creditors, and he may afterwards transfer the note,—neither is his right divested by a composition with his creditors under the Act. *Campbell* v. *Gilbert*, *Mich. T.* 1862.

11—Stamps.
Where no stamps are affixed to a promissory note at the time it is given, and no authority given to affix them, and only stamps of a single duty were upon it when produced at the trial, the note is void under the Statute of Canada, 31 Vic. c. 9. *Travis* v. *Glazier*, 2 *Han.* 215.

12—Cash or goods—Note Payable in.
A note payable in cash or goods comes within the meaning of the Act 4 Vic. c. 4. *Burnham* v. *Watts*, 2 *Kerr* 377.

13—Specific articles—Note for sum payable in.
A note for the payment of a certain sum in specific articles, becomes a money debt after the time for delivering the articles has elapsed; and a set off is admissible in an action upon it, under the Act 4 Vic. c. 4. *Steeves* v. *Hopper*, 1 *All.* 394.

Quære, Whether the plaintiff could declare for special damages for not delivering the articles? If he could, the consideration on which the contract was made should be stated. *Ibid.*

14—Half Cash—Half Goods.
A writing addressed to the defendant requesting him to pay the plaintiff £25, "half cash and half goods," is not a bill of exchange, nor can the plaintiff (after acceptance and payment of £12 10s. in cash) recover the balance as on an account stated. *Melville* v. *Bedell*, *Hil. T.* 1832.

15—Foreign Currency.
A note made in this Province for a certain number of dollars "payable in U. States currency" is a promissory note. (Fisher J. *dubitante.*) *Saint Stephen Branch Railway Co.* v. *Black*, 2 *Han.* 139.

16—Donatio—Mortis Causa.
A man in expectation of death indorsed a negotiable note specially to his wife and delivered it to her. Held, That the wife acquired no right by the indorsement and that it could not operate as a *donatio mortis causa*, the note not being transferable by delivery only. See *Weldon* v. *Weldon*, 2 *All.* 590.

17—Note on Demand.
Semble—A note payable on demand is, after demand of payment and refusal, to be treated as over due; and a note whereof payment has actually been made when demanded, cannot stand on a better footing. See *Dougan* v. *Small*, 2 *Kerr* 89.

18—Memorandum at foot of note.
A memorandum put by an indorser at the foot of a promissory note without the maker's authority, declaring it to be payable at a particular place, does not affect the maker's liability, it forming no part of his contract. *Cunard* v. *Toser*, 2 *Kerr* 305.

II.

Parties — Rights — Liability — Acceptance.

1.—Holder—No beneficial interest—Note payable to bearer.
Holder may maintain action although he

has no beneficial interest in note, and holds it merely as agent. See *Allison* v. *Central Bank*, 4 *All.* 270.

2—Holder.
Prima facie a person who has the possession of a note indorsed in blank is the legal holder. Per Ritchie J. See *Howard* v. *Godard*, 4 *All.* 452.

3—Indorsement contrary to agreement—Payment.
Defendant gave a negotiable note to G, who agreed to hold it as security for a liability he had incurred for the defendant; G, in violation of this agreement, indorsed and transferred the note to C, in order to raise money for G's benefit; C got the note discounted at a bank, and was obliged to take it up at maturity, and two years afterwards, he transferred it to the plaintiff. G never paid the money for the defendant, which formed the consideration for the note. Held, That unless C knew the circumstances under which G got the note, or was implicated in G's fraud, he would have had a right, on taking up the note from the bank, to recover the amount from the defendant; and that the plaintiff claiming under C, had the same rights. *Hastings* v. *O'Mahoney*, 4 *All.* 305.

Semble, That if C had taken up the note with G's money, it would have been extinguished, and he could not have recovered on it. *Ibid.*

4—Indorser—Original Liability—Participation in payments.
H gave the defendant a promissory note for the price of goods purchased from him, which note the plaintiff discounted for the defendant, who received the proceeds; when the note became due, it was renewed by H, and the new note indorsed by the defendant and held by the plaintiff. Held, That this was only an extension of the time for payment, and did not alter the original liability of the defendant as indorser. *The Commercial Bank* v. *Williston and another*, 1 *Han.* 283.

Before the renewal of the note, H, who was largely indebted to the plaintiff, as the drawer of a number of other notes, paid the plaintiff a sum of money without making any appropriation of it; he soon afterwards asked the plaintiff to give him credit for it, for the benefit of his indorsers; but the evidence left it uncertain whether it was for the benefit of his accommodation indorsers only, or for his indorsers generally, and a verdict having been given for the plaintiff for the amount of the note, without any deduction on account of the money paid by H, a new trial was granted, in order to ascertain whether the indorsers generally were entitled to participate in the payment by H. It being the defendant's duty to establish this fact, the new trial was granted on payment of costs. *Ibid.*

5—Infant.
A person after he comes of age is liable in assumpsit upon a note of hand made by him when an infant, if after coming of age he promise to pay it. *Fisher* v. *Jewett, et al. Ber.* 35.

6—Returning of original note—Fraudulent substitution—Rights of holder.
Plaintiff was managing agent of the Bank in which the defendant had discounted an indorsed note drawn by himself: When the note fell due, the plaintiff agreed to renew it on payment of a certain sum, and getting another indorsed note for the difference. Defendant brought a renewal note to the plaintiff—who (believing it to be duly indorsed) gave up the original note; but, soon afterwards discovering that the renewal note was not indorsed, he called on the defendant to rectify the error, which he refused to do. Held, That the original note having been obtained by the defendant fraudulently, it was still constructively in the plaintiff's possession, and he could sue thereon in his own name as holder. *Grover* v. *Watson*, *Hil. T.* 1866.

7—Bona fide holder—Failure of consideration between original parties.
The defendant made a note in favour of S for the amount of a bill of exchange. S failed and the bill was dishonoured. Before the note came due and before the failure of S, it was deposited by him with a number of other notes with the plaintiffs as collateral security for the payment of certain bills of exchange on which he was liable to the plaintiffs, the agreement being, that if the bills were not paid, the proceeds of the notes were to be applied in payment of the amount, but if the bills were paid, the plaintiffs were to collect the notes and place the amount to the credit of S. The amount of notes deposited by S with the Bank as collateral security never exceeded his indebtedness,

and at the time the note in question was indorsed to the plaintiffs and when S failed, there was a considerable deficiency. Held, That, the plaintiffs were *bona fide* holders for value and were not affected by the failure of consideration between the defendant and S. *Commercial Bank* v. *Page, East. T.* 1871.

8—**Executors of Drawer—Insufficiency of original consideration—Equities as against.**
A made a promissory note payable to his own order, which he indorsed, and gave to his son-in-law B as a gift by way of advancement to B's wife. After it was due, B transferred it to the plaintiff for valuable consideration. Held, That as the original consideration was not sufficient, it was subject to all the equities in the plaintiff's hands and he could not recover against the executors of A. *Thomas* v. *McLeod*, 1 *Han.* 588.

9—**Railway Company.**
The Saint Stephen Branch Railway Co. may take and recover on a promissory note given for amount of assessments on calls due by a stockholder on his shares. *St. Stephen Branch Railway Co.* v. *Black*, 2 *Han.* 139.

10—**Joint Liability—Separate interest.**
The jury having found defendants, joint promissors on a promissory note—Held, That they were liable although the interest of each in the purchase of vessel might be separate. See *Maynes* v. *Mahoney and McLean*, 2 *Han.* 23.

11—**Indorsement of name—No indorsement by payee—Liability.**
A party not appearing on the face of a promissory note as a maker, does not by indorsing his name thereon, render himself liable to the payee as a maker of the note. *Smith* v. *Bill*, 1 *All.* 213.

12—**Not producing or offering to deliver note.**
The maker of a negotiable note is not bound to pay it unless the party demanding payment produces and offers to deliver it up. *Jordan* v. *Coates*, 2 *All.* 107.

13—**Agent—Authority—Inference.**
The authority of an agent specially authorized to draw a bill of exchange for a a particular purpose, ceases on the acceptance, and if the drawer is discharged by want of notice of dishonour, the agent cannot, without further express authority, revive the liability by agreeing to waive the legal discharge. *McGhie* v. *Gilbert*. 1 *All.* 235.

14—The defendants gave a promissory note, which was endorsed in blank by the payee: after it was due it was in the hands of J, who demanded payment of the defendants, but refused to produce it, and a few days afterwards told the defendants' agent, who offered to pay the note, that they should not have it, and he would give them a hunt for it. The defendants afterwards tendered the amount of the note, when J said he had sold it, but refused to tell who the holder was, saying the defendants might seek it. On the following day the suit was commenced, and the defendants immediately afterwards paid into the Justice's hands the amount of the note and costs. The plaintiff was J's son, living in the house with him, and there was no proof of any actual transfer of the note by J. Held, That it might be inferred that the plaintiff was only the agent of J, and therefore that the jury were justified in finding a verdict for the defendants. *Jordan* v. *Coates*, 2 *All.* 107.

15—**Personal liability—Signing note as agent.**
Defendant as Commissioner of The New Brunswick and Canada Railway Company, drew a bill of exchange on the company, to pay for work done on the railway, and signed it "J. J. Robinson, Commissioner." The drawee knew for what purpose the bill was drawn, and that the defendant was the agent of the company. Held, In an action by an indorsee, that the defendant was personally liable. *Prele* v. *Robinson*, 4 *All.* 561.

16—**Recognition of authority—Evidence.**
In an action on a bill of exchange expressed to be accepted *"per procuration"* by the defendant's clerk, evidence was given of a conversation with the defendant in which he stated that A (the drawer) had drawn a bill on him which the plaintiff held, and that A ought to pay it, because it was drawn for his benefit. Held, Sufficient proof to leave to the jury of a recognition of the clerk's authority to accept. *Morrison* v. *Spurr*, 3 *All.* 288.

17—**Indorsement by request—Equities.**
Where a person indorsed his name upon a note at the request of the payee, at the same time informing the payee that it did not render him liable, he is not liable to

a party to whom the payee afterwards indorsed the note after it was due. *McQuinn* v. *Sorrell*, 2 *All.* 140.

18—Payee—Recovery on Common Counts.

The payee of a dishonoured bill of exchange may recover the amount from the drawer in an action on the common counts, if no notice of dishonour has been given. *James* v. *McLean*, 3 *All.* 164.

19—Wife—Donatio mortis causa—Assent of Executor—Evidence.

A man in expectation of death, indorsed a negotiable note specially to his wife and delivered it to her. Held, 1. That the wife acquired no right by the indorsement, and 2d, That it could not operate as a *donatio mortis causa*, the note not being transferable by delivery only. 3d. That the executor's allowing the widow to retain the note for two years and to receive legacies under her husband's will, without demanding the note, was no evidence of his assent to her retaining it, he having demanded payment from the maker. *Weldon v. Weldon*, 2 *All* 590.

Initialing of Inland Bill of Exchange, not an Acceptance. See Check 2.

III.

Presentment—Demand.

1—Excuse—Illness of maker.

In an action against the indorser of a promissory note. Held, That the circumstance of the maker lying dangerously ill will not excuse the want of presentment thereof at his residence or place of business; therefore a presentment to his brother in the street, near the residence, is insufficient. If such presentment could avail under the circumstances, it should be specially alleged. *Nowlin* v. *Roach*, 2 *Kerr* 337.

2—Settled account including note—Evidence.

In an action on a promissory note payable at a particular place, and a bill of exchange protested for non-acceptance, the only evidence to prove the presentment of the note and protest of the bill, was a settled account between the parties including the note and bill, and a charge for "protested exchange." Held, Sufficient to dispense with the preliminary proof of presentment and protest, and that it might be inferred that the protested exchange mentioned in the account referred to the bill in question, it being of the same amount, and no other bill being shewn between the parties. *Balloch* v. *Binney*, 1 *All.* 131.

3—Protest—Evidence of Presentment, &c.

In an action against the drawer of a foreign bill, the protest is evidence of an acceptance payable at a particular place, and of due presentment at that place. *Tarratt* v. *Wilmot*, 1 *All.* 353.

4—Sufficiency of Presentment—Indorser.

A letter written by the attorney of the indorsee to the maker, stating that the note in question, together with other notes, had been placed in his hands for collection, and requiring him to pay the interest, and give new security for the principal, is not such a presentment and demand of payment as would, upon notice thereof, make the endorser liable. This letter was sent on the 4th March, and not being attended to, the note was presented to the maker for payment on the 17th June following, and notice of dishonour given to the defendant as endorser on the 18th. Held, That the defendant was liable. *Thorne* v. *Scovil*, 2 *Kerr* 557.

5—Due diligence—Question of law and fact—Jury.

Whether due diligence has been used in the presentment of a bill of exchange to the drawee, is a mixed question of law and fact; and where the question has been properly left to the jury, the Court will not interfere with their verdict unless it clearly appears that they have come to a wrong conclusion. *Perley* v. *Howard*, 2 *Kerr* 518.

6—Waiver—Question left to Jury.

Where the defendant, who was the indorser of a promissory note which had not been duly presented to the makers, promised payment thereof, knowing that he had not received due notice of dishonour, and under circumstances from which it might be inferred that he was aware of the non-presentment, and the case had been left to the jury on the point of waiver of both these defects, who found for the plaintiff: the Court refused to disturb the verdict. *Watters* v. *Lordly*, 2 *Kerr* 15.

7—Waiver.

A subsequent promise by the indorser in ignorance of the defect in due presentment, though he was aware at the time that he was discharged for want of due notice, is a waiver only of the want of notice, not that of presentment. *Nowlin* v. *Roach*, 2 *Kerr* 337.

8—Presentment—Promise—Ignorance of non-presentment—Waiver.
A bill of exchange was drawn by defendant on T in Bangor, payable in Boston, and accepted generally by T who had no place of business in Boston. T died before the bill was due. There was no presentment in Boston, but presentment was made at T's place of business in Bangor, and answer given that there was no administration and no person authorized to pay acceptances. About six weeks after the bill was due, the defendant wrote to the plaintiff (indorsee) regretting the non-payment, requesting time for payment, and to be dealt leniently with, and offering notes at four and six months, which the plaintiff refused. Held, That as it did not appear that when defendant made the offer, he was aware the bill had not been presented in Boston, his promise was no waiver of the presentment. *Dana* v. *Bradley*, *East. T.* 1862.

9—Waiver.
In an action on a promissory note payable at a bank to order of maker, and indorsed by him, there was no proof of presentment. Held, That a subsequent promise to pay made by defendant admitted that all had been done by plaintiffs to entitle them to recover. *Saint Stephen Branch Railway Company* v. *Black*, 2 *Han.* 129.

10—Place—Dwelling house—Store closed.
The maker of a promissory note, who was a merchant residing and carrying on business in the city of St. John, having before the note became due closed his store and absconded. Held, That presentment at his late dwelling house was sufficient without proof of presentment at the store, or that the store remained closed on the day the note fell due. *Robinson* v. *Taylor*, 2 *Kerr* 198.

11—Admission.
The holder of a note swore that he went to the maker's store for the purpose of presenting it for payment, but finding the door locked made a formal presentment at the door. The maker of the note swore that he was at his store at the time stated, and that no presentment was made. The Judge left to the jury the question whether the holder had presented the note or not, and in answer to a question by the jury, told them that for the purposes of the suit such a presentment would be sufficient, no objection on that ground having been made by the defendant. Held, That there was no misdirection, and that the jury could not have been misled by the answer to their question. *Reed* v. *Kavanagh*, 4 *All.* 457.

An admission by a defendant that he had received notice of dishonour, in the absence of any proof that it was received too late, or any objection made to it, is evidence of its sufficiency. *Ibid.*

12—Necessity of presentment—Note drawn and payable in Boston.
Quære, Whether, in an action on a note drawn and payable in Boston, it is necessary to prove presentment there, there being no evidence that presentment is necessary by the law of that country. If necessary, it may be waived by a subsequent promise to pay the note. See *Allen* v. *McNaughton*, 4 *All.* 234.

13—Time and place of presentment.
In an action against the indorser of a note, the plaintiff must show that it was presented at a reasonable hour. *Patterson* v. *Tapley*, 4 *All.* 292.

Where a note was payable at a "store," and the only evidence was that when the holder went to present it, the store was closed; and the defendant objected that the presentment was not shown to have been made at a reasonable hour. Held, That in the absence of any evidence of the nature of the business carried on at the store, it might be inferred that it was closed in the due course of business, and therefore that the presentment was not made at a reasonable time. *Ibid.*

Semble, If no question is raised at the trial about the hour of presentment, and it is proved to have been made on the day the note falls due, it might be presumed to have been made at a proper hour. *Ibid.*

14—Presentment of a note at the maker's place of business is sufficient, although there is no person there at the time. *Kinnear* v. *Goddard*, 4 *All.* 559.

The maker of a note was proved to have occupied an office up to the 1st May, after which, there was no direct evidence of occupation, but his desk remained there as before. Held, In the absence of any proof of his having changed his office, that presentment of a note there after the 1st May, was sufficient. *Kinnear* v. *Goddard*, 4 *All.* 559.

15—Payable at particular place—Time of demand.

A demand of payment of a promissory note made payable at a particular place, need not be made on the very day it falls due to fix the maker, although there must be a demand at the place upon or after the day, before bringing the action.—*Ratchford* v. *Griffith*, 2 *Kerr* 112.

16—Payable "at any Bank"—Place of presentment.

A promissory note drawn on Boston, where both the maker and payee resided, was made payable "at any bank." Held, That this meant any bank in Boston.—*Baldwin* v. *Hitchcock*, 1 *Han.* 310.

17—Necessity of presentment.

In an action by the payee against the acceptor of a bill of exchange, payable at a particular place, which became due on the 3rd of November, the plaintiff averred presentment for payment on the 2nd. It appeared in evidence that the bill had been presented on the 2nd, and that on the 3rd, the day it became due, the defendant expressly refused to pay it to the plaintiff's agent, who called again, but it did not appear that the note was again produced. Held, That *proof* of presentment on the 3rd was admissible, and that the refusal to pay on the 3rd, rendered the actual presentment of the bill on that day unnecessary. *Chandler* v. *Beckwith*, *Ber.* 268.

Payable at particular place—Necessity of presentment—Suspension of remedy—Common Counts. See VI. 12 *a*.

18—Pleading.
See VI. 12.

IV.

NOTICE OF DISHONOUR.

See Bills and Notes III.

1—Evidence of.

Assumpsit by indorsee against drawers of a foreign bill of exchange, drawn by the defendants in this province on Duncan Brothers, London, payable sixty days after sight, and returned under protest for non-payment; the declaration averred in the usual form a presentment to, and acceptance by the drawees, presentment for payment, dishonour, protest and notice. There was no direct evidence of acceptance, but on the face of the bill appeared the following words: "Accepted 17th May, 1841, at Messrs. Jones, Loyd & Co.—Duncan Bro's.;" and the protest of the notary public stated that he went with the original afore copied bill of exchange to the house of Messrs. Jones, Loyd & Co., bankers, where the same drawn upon Messrs. Duncan Brothers is accepted payable, and demanded payment thereof, and was referred to the acceptors, whereupon he went with the bill to the counting house of the acceptors and demanded payment, whereunto a clerk answered that the said bill cannot be paid. Due notice of the dishonour was given to the defendants, and no objection made in regard to the acceptance. Held, That there was sufficient evidence of the dishonour to make the defendants liable. *Irvin* v. *Crookshank*, 2 *Kerr* 309.

2—Presumption of.

An action by the payee against the drawer of a dishonoured bill of exchange, was discontinued on terms of the acceptor paying the costs, and placing the amount of the bill to the payee's credit with a person to whom he was indebted; and on the representation of the acceptor that this had been done, the bill was given up to him. In trover against the acceptor for the bill (the amount not having been placed to the payee's credit), the jury were directed that under the circumstances they might presume that the payee had given notice of dishonour to the drawee, and that the plaintiff was entitled to damages to the amount of the value of the bill at the time of the conversion, which was the amount due on face of the bill. Held, That this direction was right. *McDonald* v. *Everitt*, 3 *Kerr* 569.

3—Sufficiency of.

A bill drawn in St. John was dishonoured in London on the 16th October, the plaintiff not then being the holder; a mail left Liverpool for St. John on the 19th October, by which the plaintiff could not have given notice of dishonour, but notice was given by the next mail on the 4th November which was as soon as the defendant was entitled to it. Held, That *prima facie* the notice was sufficient and that the plaintiff was not bound to show that he had received due notice from the holder of the bill at the time of the dishonour. *Tarrat* v. *Wilmot*, 1 *All.* 353.

4—By whom.
Notice of the dishonour by the cashier of a bank at which a note has been left by the holder for collection is sufficient. *Girvan* v. *Price*, 309 *All.* 4.

5—Where a note indorsed in blank, is left at a bank for collection, notice of dishonour may be given by the bank, though it has no interest in the note. *Howard* v. *Godard*, 4 *All.* 452.

6—Notice by letter—Posting.
Notice of dishonour to the defendant as indorser of a promissory note, put in the post office at Saint John, and directed as follows: "Mr. D. D. (the defendant) near Blake's mills, Nashwaak," is not sufficient without proof that a letter thus directed would probably reach the defendant in due course through the medium of the post office. *Robinson* v *Duff*, 2 *Kerr* 206.

7—In an action against the drawer of a bill of exchange, dated at Moncton—Held, That in the absence of any evidence of its locality, or the course of the post with regard to it, the mere putting the letter in the post office at Saint John, containing a notice of dishonour, directed to the defendant at Moncton, did not afford a reasonable presumption that the letter would reach its destination. *Bulloch* v. *Binney*, 3 *Kerr* 440.

Where by the copy of a notice of dishonor taken by a copying machine, it appeared to have been directed at the bottom to the defendant: *Semble*, That the letter put into the post office, containing the notice, will be presumed to be directed on the outside in the same way. *Ibid.*

8—Mistake in date of Note.
Notice of dishonour to the indorser of a promissory note is not voided by a mistake in the description of the note, E. G. stating it as a note dated 1st January 1841, whereas it was dated 1st January 1840, the note being otherwise correctly described, and there being no other note to which the notice could have applied. *Robinson* v. *Taylor*, 2 *Kerr* 198.

9—Admission.
An admission by the defendant that he had received notice of dishonour, in the absence of any proof that it was received too late, or any objection made to it, is evidence of its sufficiency. *Read* v. *Kavanagh*, 4 *All.* 457.

10—Place—Change of residence.
Defendant had resided and carried on business for several years at a place called Brandy Point, and was in the habit of receiving through the Post Office, letters addressed to him there. Held, That a notice of dishonour addressed to him at Brandy Point was sufficient, though he had changed his residence about that time—the plaintiff not being aware of such change, and having applied for information as to his residence, to the payee of the note, with whom the defendant was in the habit of transacting his business in St. John. *The Bank of New Brunswick* v. *Millican*, 4 *All.* 254.

11—Service of Notice—Entry in deceased Notary's book—Residence of party—Presumption.
Where the indorser of a note (the defendant) and several of his brothers lived with their mother, and the proof of service of notice of dishonour was an entry in a book by a deceased clerk of a notary, whose business it was to serve notices of dishonour and to make entries thereof in a book, and who had been directed to serve the notice at the residence of the defendant—"served on brother at residence." Held, In the absence of evidence that any brother of the defendant had any other residence than at their mother's house, that it was a fair presumption that the notice had been served there, and that the Judge was warranted in leaving it to the jury to find whether it had been duly served. *Canby* v. *Wright*, *Mich. T.* 1872.

12—Time—Waiver.
Where a bill drawn on persons residing in Dublin, Ireland, was protested for non-payment on the 3rd November, 1841, notice thereof to the indorsers, who resided at Saint John in this province (where the bill was drawn), on the 22d December following, was held not be in due time, it appearing the mails left Great Britain for this province on th 4th and on the 19th November, and that a notice sent by the mail of the 19th, would have reached Saint John about the 4th December. *Bank of New Brunswick* v. *Knowles*, 2 *Kerr* 219.

An offer to give promissory notes at three and six months for the amount due on the bill, which was not accepted. Held, To be no waiver of the laches *Ibid.*

13—Due diligence.
The defendant had a house in Mauger-

ville, where his family lived, and where he resided in the winter; but during the rest of the year—from May till about the end of December—he carried on business at Indiantown, and resided at the house of B, where his notes had several times been presented for payment, and notices of dishonour had been left for him, and which notes he had paid. In January 1857, a clerk in the bank, who had formerly delivered notices at the same place, left a notice of dishonour at B's house, addressed to the defendant, which notice he never received, having left Indiantown for Maugerville about three weeks before. The Judge left it to the jury whether the holder of the note had used due diligence to ascertain the defendant's residence and in giving the notice of dishonour. Held, per Carter C. J., Wilmot J., and Ritchie, J.—(N. Parker M. R., and R. Parker J., *dissentientibus*) that the direction was right; and that when reasonable diligence has been used to discover the place to which notice should be sent, and it has been sent accordingly, it proves the averment of due notice in the declaration; but that if, in consequence of the holder being unable to discover the indorser's residence, no notice of dishonour is given, the excuse should be averred. Per N. Parker M. R., —that the proper question for the jury was, whether B's house was the defendant's residence at the time the notice was left; and if it was not, that the verdict should have been for the defendant, though the plaintiff had used due diligence to ascertain his residence. Per Parker J., that as B's house was neither the defendant's residence or place of business at the time the notice was given, or the place designated by him on the note, the delivery of the notice there, did not prove the averment of notice in the declaration. *Patterson* v. *Tapley*, 4 *All.* 529.

14—Dispensation of presentment—Evidence of.

The payee of a note, indorsed it to the plaintiff as security for a debt: on the day the note came due (the maker having in the meantime left the country) the plaintiff went to the indorser and gave him the note, saying he supposed it was of no use to any one, the indorser handed it back to the plaintiff, and told him to keep it for the present. Held, That this was evidence of a dispensation of presentment by the indorser. *Masters* v. *Stubbs*, 4 *All.* 453.

15—Recovery under Common Counts, if no notice of dishonour given. See James v. McLean, 3 All. 164.

16—Mistake in name—Time of receiving notice—Admission—Inference for Jury.

A notice of dishonor sent through the post office, was addressed to "Edward T. Price." The defendant whose name was "Edward Price," admitted the receipt of the notice, but objected to pay because he was an accommodation indorser. Held, That the jury might infer that he had received the notice in due time, and therefore that he was liable notwithstanding the mistake in the name. *Girvan* v. *Price*, 3 *All.* 409.

V.

Defence.

1—Fraud.

Several of the creditors of the defendant entered into a composition agreement with him, whereby they engaged to accept payment of their debts at certain stated periods, and among the rest, the plaintiff agreed to grant three years for the payment of his debt. Held, That the plaintiff could not, before the expiration of that period maintain an action on a promissory note, which he had afterwards induced the defendant to give him for the amount of his debt, payable by annual instalments, but that such note was in fraud of the other creditors. *Willard* v. *Killman*, 1 *Kerr* 105.

2—Fraud—Question for Jury.

If in an action against the maker of a promissory note, the defence is, want of consideration, and that the note came into the plaintiff's possession by fraud, that question should be left to the jury. *Smith* v. *Fleming*, 2 *Han.* 147.

3—The indorsee of a bill of exchange, accepted by the defendant, for the accommodation of the payee, and of which there was some evidence of indorsement over due, having received property from the payee for the purpose of satisfying this bill and others, admitted that he had sufficient property in his hands for that purpose, and promised the defendant to destroy the bill. Held, That there was evidence of a good consideration for the promise, and that the Judge was right in leaving it to the jury to say whether the plaintiff had not, on such consideration, renounced his claim against the defendant on the bill. *Watson* v. *Porter*, 3 *Kerr* 137.

4—Consideration.
The plaintiff agreed to sell the defendant all his right and title to the timber growing on a track of land, which he had agreed to purchase from the Crown, and for which he had paid the principal part of the purchase money, but had not obtained a grant. The defendant cut a portion of the timber for which the plaintiff paid the duties, but the Crown prevented the defendant from cutting the remainder. Held, In an action on a promissory note given by the defendant to the plaintiff for the right to the timber, that there was not such an entire failure of consideration as to prevent the plaintiff from recovering. *Clark* v. *Ash*, 3 *Kerr* 211.

5—Defendant gave the plaintiff a promissory note for £150, because she thought a deceased brother (whose brother she inherited) would have left the plaintiff as much if he had made a will: a verdict for the plaintiff for £20 was set aside, though there was evidence that the deceased owed the plaintiff about that amount, this debt being no part of the consideration of the note. *McCarrol* v. *Reardon*, 4 *All.* 261.

6—Consideration—Assent of party.
Where the plaintiffs, who were an Insurance Company, refused payment of a partial loss to the assured in a marine policy, in consequence of the claims of W. P. & Co., to whom the amount of insurance was in case of loss made payable; but consented to advance the amount, upon the assured giving their promissory note indorsed by the defendant for the sum, which was to be paid at maturity unless they procured the assent of W. P. & Co. to their retaining the money; which assent was refused. Held, That the defendant was liable on the note, and could not defend himself on the ground of want of consideration or that the plaintiffs were not justified in requiring the assent of W. P. & Co. to the payment of the money for which the note was given. *New Brunswick Assurance Company* v. *Ansley*, 2 *Kerr* 106.

7—Defendant gave his note payable at a future day, to the plaintiff, for a debt due from A to the plaintiff, A agreeing, in consideration thereof, to convey land to the defendant. A afterwards refused to convey the land. Held, That the giving time for the payment of A's debt was a good consideration for the defendant's promise, and that the plaintiff's knowledge at the time the note was given, of the agreement between the defendant and A, respecting the land, did not affect the plaintiff's right to recover on the note, he not being a party to such agreement. *Moffat* v. *Duplissey*, 1 *Han.* 21.

8—Note for arrears of rent—No authority to lease—Note void.
The Justices of York were empowered by Act 10 Vic. c. 7, to lease certain lands at auction, but that no lease should be made unless the rent should have been fixed by the Justices, or till the land should have been sold, or offered for sale at auction. The right of the Justices was transferred to the Corporation of Fredericton, who agreed to lease the land to A, but no lease was executed, and A died, owing rent; the land was afterwards advertised at auction, but upon the sale, the defendant agreed to take a lease on the same terms that A held the land, and pay the arrears of rent, for which he gave his note to the plaintiff. Held, That they had no authority to lease the land except by auction, and that the defendant was not liable on the note. *City of Fredericton* v. *Lucas*, 3 *All.* 583.

9—Composition—Suspension of action—Fraud.
Several of the creditors of the defendant entered into a composition agreement with him whereby they engaged to accept payment of their debts in certain stated periods, and among the rest the plaintiff agreed to grant three years for the payment of his debt. Held, That the plaintiff could not before the expiration of that period, maintain an action on a promissory note which he had afterwards induced the defendant to give him for the amount of his debt, payable by *annual* instalments; but that such note was in fraud of the other creditors. *Willard* v. *Killman*, 1 *Kerr* 105.

9 a—Consideration—Composition—Release.
The defendant assigned to a trustee a portion of his annual income, for the purpose of paying his creditors a composition on the amount of their respective demands, and they covenanted that the payment of the composition should operate

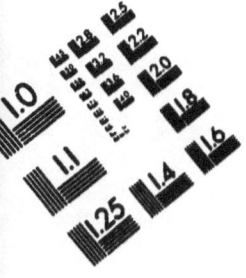

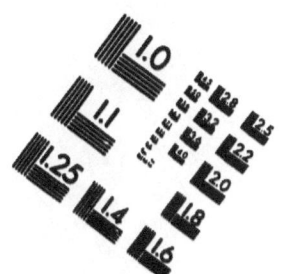

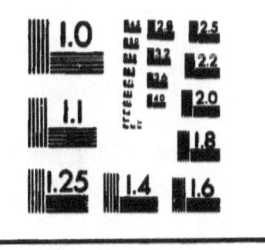

as a release of the original debts compounded for; C, one of the creditors, refused to execute the composition deed until the defendant gave him a note for £200, which he did without the knowledge of the other creditors, and after which C signed as a creditor for £723. Held, 1. That the sum stated in the deed must be taken to be the whole amount of C's debt, and therefore there was *prima facie* no consideration for the note, and it was a proper question for the jury whether the alleged consideration was real or not. 2. That the note was a fraud upon the other creditors, and that the plaintiff having become indorsee after it was due could not recover on it, though it would not affect that part of the defendant's income which was assigned for payment of his debts. *McCalmont* v. *Baillie*, 1 *All.* 572.

10—Objection—Lateness of to consideration.

The defendant having given a promissory note to the plaintiff, upon which the defendant's property was attached in the United States, gave a new note with security, in order to get the property released. Held, That it was too late to object that the consideration of this note was fraudulent. *Tuttle* v. *Smith*, 3 *Kerr* 643.

11—Note over due—Indorsement.

Where a promissory note made in 1836 at Bangor in the United States, where the maker and payee both resided, payable on demand (without specifying interest), was indorsed about two years afterwards by the payee to the plaintiff at Saint John in this Province, in payment of a debt, and it appeared that the amount of the note had been paid by the maker to the payee at Bangor a few days after the date, but the note had not been given up because the payee then stated it was lost or mislaid; an action having been brought by the indorsee against the maker, in which a verdict was found for the defendant; the Court refused a new trial. *Dougan* v. *Small*, 2 *Kerr* 89.

Semble, A note payable on demand is, after demand of payment and refusal, to be treated as over-due; and a note whereof payment has actually been made when demanded, cannot stand on a better footing. *Ibid.*

12—Note over-due—Evidence—Indorser's declarations.

In an action commenced in the autumn of 1840 by indorsee against C, the maker of a promissory note dated in March 1835, and payable in the November following, no evidence was given at the trial by the plaintiff of the time and circumstances of the transfer, but the defendant in order to shew that the note had been indorsed over-due, so as to let in evidence of the indorser's declarations, produced a witness who stated that the indorser had in August 1840, shewed him a note made by C in his (the indorser's) favour, which he proposed to assign to him in payment of a debt; which note witness believed to be the same as that now in suit, though he could not distinctly identify it; the Judge having refused to admit evidence of the indorser's declarations, and a verdict being found for the plaintiff, the Court granted a new trial on the payment of costs, on account of the staleness of the demand, and the strong presumption that the note had been indorsed over-due. *Hammond* v. *Clarke*, 2 *Kerr* 98.

13—Giving time to maker.

The plaintiff, who was indorsee of certain promissory notes made by J. & H. K., and indorsed by the defendants, which notes were given in payment of a bill of exchange drawn on persons in England, in the plaintiff's favour, and indorsed by him to J. & H. K., in anticipation of such bill coming back protested, entered into an agreement with J. & H. K. to hold over and return the promissory notes to them in case they took up the bill, with damages and costs, when it came back; the bill came back subsequent to the notes falling due, and the plaintiff was compelled to pay the amount to C the then holder, J. & H. K. failing to perform their agreement. Held, That the agreement amounted to a giving of time to the makers, and that the indorsers were discharged. *Bedell* v. *Eaton*, 2 *Kerr* 217.

14—Settlement of Note.

In an action on a promissory note for £30, made by J. B. to defendant, and by him indorsed to the plaintiff, the defence was that the note had been settled between the plaintiff and the maker, the plaintiff having received from him a new promissory note for £132, in which the £30 was included; but it appearing to have been agreed between the parties that the £30 was to stand—the amount when paid to be indorsed on the note: the Court set aside a verdict given for the defendant, and granted a new trial on payment of costs. *Thurgar* v. *Berry*, 2 *Kerr* 214.

15—Alteration—Negotiability.
Where, upon a purchase of goods by C from A, C agreed to give a promissory note for the amount, indorsed by B, and a note was accordingly drawn and taken to B, who indorsed it; but the words "or order" had been unintentionally omitted, which were afterwards inserted by A without B's privity. Held, That an action could not be maintained by A against B upon such note. *Lawton* v. *Millidge*, 2 *Kerr* 520.

16—Identity.
In an action by the indorsee of a promissory note against the maker, the handwriting of the attesting witness to the maker's signature, together with the handwriting of the indorser, were proved, but no evidence was given to identify the defendant with the person named in the note, and the Judge at the trial, for want of such evidence, non-suited the plaintiff; on motion for a new trial—Held, That the evidence given at the trial was sufficient, and accordingly a new trial was granted. *McCullough* v. *Shields*, 3 *Kerr* 391.

17—Set off—Appropriation.
Where the maker of a promissory note delivered the payee a quantity of hay, without making any specific appropriation of the amount towards the paying of the note, and on a subsequent demand of payment claimed no deduction on account of the hay. Held, In an action on the note, that the value of the hay could only be considered as a set-off, and that the plaintiff was entitled to costs, though the verdict was for less than £5. *Barlow* v. *Clark*, 3 *Kerr* 485.

18—Payment—Receipt of rent.
It is no defence to an action on a promissory note that the plaintiff had had possession of land belonging to the defendant, given as security for the note, and had an opportunity of receiving therefrom rent more than sufficient to pay the note; unless it is shewn that the plaintiff actually received such rent. *Simonds* v. *Travis*, 2 *Han.* 14.

19—Security for payment.
The defendant placed timber in the plaintiff's hands as security for the payment of a promissory note, under an agreement that the timber was not to be sold before 1st November without defendant's consent, but after that day, the plaintiff to be at liberty to sell, after giving the defendant fourteen days' notice: the plaintiff sold the timber after the 1st November, but without giving the notice. Held, (Ritchie, J., *dubitante*,) That though the defendant might be entitled to damages in an action of trover, or on the agreement for a wrongful sale of the timber, he was not entitled to credit as a payment, in an action on the note, for more than the proceeds of the sale, though that was less than the highest market value of the timber. *Kinnear* v. *Ferguson*, 4 *All.* 391.

20—Appropriation—Privity.
It is no defence to an action brought by the plaintiff, a merchant in Liverpool, as indorsee of a bill of exchange drawn by the defendant on one J. W., at Liverpool, and remitted to the plaintiff by his agent at Saint John in paying for moneys collected, that the bill was drawn against a ship and cargo, which the owners had consigned to the plaintiff instead of sending them to J. W., the defendant's agent, as had been originally intended; the plaintiff not having been privy to the arrangement, and having in fact applied the proceeds of the ship and cargo to the payment of other demands which he had against the owner. *Hatton* v. *Wilmot*, 2 *Kerr* 324.

21—Improper drawing—Forgery of signature—Estoppel.
It is not competent for the indorser of a note to set up as a defence to an action upon it, that the signature of the maker is forged. *McLeod* v. *Carman*, 1 *Han.* 592.

22—Indorsement by one of Firm—Authority—Fraudulent indorsement—Bona fide holder.
In an action by a *bona fide* holder against the indorsers of a note, it is no defence that the note was indorsed by one of the defendants (a firm) fraudulently, without the authority of the other defendants, and for matters not relating to the business of the partnership. *Ibid.*

Notice of such fraudulent indorsement given to the *bona fide* holder of a note will not affect his right to recover, nor will it affect the right of his indorsee though the last indorsement was made after the note was due. *Ibid.*

23—Release, before maturity of note.
The holder of a note may discharge the

indorser by a general release before the note is due, and such release will be a good defence to an action by a subsequent indorsee. *McLeod* v. *Carman*, 1 *Han.* 592.

24—Statute of Limitations.
To a plea of the statute of limitations in an action by the indorsee against the maker of a promissory note, the plaintiff replied that when the cause of action accrued to him he was beyond seas, and that he exhibited his bill within six years after his return. Rejoinder, that at the time the supposed cause of action accrued to the plaintiff, he was not beyond seas. Held, That the action accrued to the plaintiff when the note was transferred to him, and this being more than six years after it was due, his absence beyond seas was immaterial. *Bradbury* v. *Baillie*, 1 *All.* 690.

When the statute has begun to run, no subsequent indorsement to a person whether in or out of the Province, will stop it. *Ibid.*

25—To an action on a promissory note payable in four instalments, the defendant pleaded that he did not undertake or promise within six years. Replication—that the several causes of action, and each and every of them accrued to the plaintiff within six years, etc., on which issue was joined. Held, That though the plea might have been bad on demurrer, the proof of the issue was on the plaintiff, and the cause of action on the two first instalments having accrued more than six years before the action was brought, he could not recover them. *Montgomery* v. *McNair*, 2 *All.* 31.

26—The plaintiff sued on two promissory notes, made by the defendants while partners in trade more than six years before the commencement of the action; certain payments having been made within six years by one partner after the dissolution of the firm, as also an account in writing stated and signed by him, acknowledging a balance which included what was still due on the note. Held, Sufficient to entitle the plaintiff to a verdict against such defendant, and if the respective payments were actually made on the notes, they would be sufficient to take the case out of the Statute of Limitations against both defendants, the Act of Assembly 6 Wm. 4, c. 51, having expressly left the effect of payments on the same footing that they were before the passing of the Act. *Sands* v. *Keator*, 3 *Kerr* 329.

27—Statute of Limitations.
Assumpsit on three promissory notes; plea, Statute of Limitations. The notes, with several others, were given for land sold to the defendant by the plaintiff as executor of G, whose widow was entitled to the interest of the money for which the land was sold. The defendant within six years before action brought paid the widow £4 10*s.*, and directed her to tell the plaintiff to *indorse it on the notes*, without mentioning any particular notes, and no notes being produced; no indorsement was made on the notes, and there was no positive evidence that the other notes had been paid; but £4 10*s.* was the annual interest due on the three notes. The jury having found that the payment was made on the three notes—Held, That it was sufficient to take the case out of the Statute of Limitations. *Vanwart* v. *Roberts*, 3 *Kerr* 572.

28—Joint Payees—Indorsement by one.
A promissory note made to C and D jointly, was indorsed by C alone to B, and by B to A. Held, That B was liable as indorser, and could not set up as a defence to an action by A that D had not joined in the indorsement. *Thurgar* v. *Clarke*, 2 *Kerr* 370.

Semble, That A could not have maintained an action against the maker of the note without proving that C had authority to indorse. *Ibid.*

29—Extinguishment of original claim—Giving bill—Loss of.
Declaration in assumpsit on the common counts. Plea, admitting the sum of £526 12s. 4d. to have been due to the plaintiff, averred that for that sum the defendant at Saint Andrews, in this Province, drew his bill of exchange on one C. M., payable to the plaintiff, which was delivered to plaintiff, and by him received and accepted for and on account of the sum so due. Replication—that after the bill of exchange was so received, and before it became due and payable, the plaintiff sent the same by a vessel, of which the said C. M. was master, addressed to the plaintiff's agent in the West Indies, for the purpose of being presented on the said vessel's arrival, but that the vessel foundered at sea on the passage out, whereby the said C.

M., the drawee, perished, and the bill was destroyed and lost, and the plaintiff was unable to present the same, and the same remains wholly unpaid. Special demurrer, assigning for causes that the plaintiff's remedy for the original debt was lost by his taking the bill of exchange, and was not restored by the destruction and consequent non-payment of the bill, as set out in the replication; that the facts stated in the replication were immaterial; that after the receipt of the bill the liability for the original debt was only a secondary liability, and the plaintiff's primary remedy was against the personal representative of the drawee, and that the remedy, if any, was in equity only. Held, That the replication was not defective for any of the causes assigned, but afforded a sufficient answer to the plea. *Boyd* v. *McLauchlan*, 1 *Kerr* 210.

30—Plaintiff having an account against defendant and W. K., settled it by taking W. K.'s notes, payable at future days in favor of plaintiff and his partner, and gave a receipt at the foot of the account, stating that he had received payment by the notes (describing them). Held, That the original debt was extinguished by the notes. *Thompson* v. *Keith*, *East. T.* 1864.

31—Satisfaction of debt—Taking Bill.
Taking a bill of exchange is not, *per se*, a satisfaction of the debt, but operates only as a suspension of the plaintiff's right to recover on the consideration of the bill, until he has done all that is necessary to procure satisfaction by means of the bill. *Emerson* v. *Gardiner*, 1 *All.* 451.

32—Extinguishment of debt—Signing Composition deed.
The holder of a note, signing a composition deed by which he agreed to receive a certain dividend in full discharge of his claim against the maker, extinguishes his claim on the note, and he cannot maintain any action thereon against the indorser. *Thurgar* v. *Travis*, 2 *All.* 272.

33—No legal interest.
D agreed to purchase a vessel from the defendant, and to pay by relieving him of outstanding liabilities, or in approved payments on the transfer of the ship; in order to carry out this contract, D obtained outstanding notes of the defendant's by giving his own notes indorsed by W in the place of them, which notes he transferred to the plaintiff over due, telling the plaintiff at the time that he had no interest in them, and that they belonged to W. The defendant never transferred the vessel. Held, That the jury were properly directed that W never having had possession of the notes, had no legal interest in them, and that the defendant was legally liable on the notes, notwithstanding the agreement about the vessel might have been broken by D. *Raymond* v. *Wilmot*, 2 *All.* 80.

34—Usury.
A promissory note of £200 made by the defendant to one W. L., and indorsed to the plaintiff, which was affected by usury, was discounted at the Commercial Bank, and payment thereof when due demanded by the bank. The makers paid the bank £25, and the plaintiff the remaining £175; whereupon a new promissory note was given with the same parties as before for £175, on which the present action was brought. The £200 note was given up. Held, That it was open to the jury to consider the note for £175 as a new security not affected by the usury in the previous note; and they having found for the plaintiff, the Court refused to disturb the verdict. *Davis* v. *Chubb*, 2 *Kerr* 395.

35—In an action by the indorsee against the maker of a promissory note, there was positive and uncontradicted evidence of usury; but a verdict was nevertheless given for the plaintiff; the Court set aside the verdict, and granted a new trial on payment of costs. *Davis* v. *Leavitt*, 2 *Kerr* 397.

36—The defendant joined with one H. in a promissory note to the plaintiff for the price of goods sold to H. When the note became due, the defendant being called on for payment, gave a new note to the plaintiff, which was tainted with usury, and the old note was thereupon given up. Held, That the plaintiff failing on the second note on the ground of usury, could not recover on the first note which had been so given up to the defendant. The usury being clearly proved, the Court set aside a verdict given for the plaintiff on the second note, and granted a new trial on payment of costs. *Turner* v. *Gilbert*, 2 *Kerr* 404.

37—An agreement to discount a note on condition that the borrower would take part of the amount in bills of exchange, at a premium higher than the cash rate, is *prima facie* usurious; but that alone will not amount to usury if the excess of premium can be ascribed to any real contingency, or was taken as a fair equivalent for any risk incurred by the lender. *Bank of British North America* v. *Fisher*, 2 *All* 1.

38—Defendant indorsed a note for the accommodation of S, who gave it to B to raise money on it; B applied to the plaintiff who discounted the note, deducting more than the legal interest. Held, That it was a loan by the plaintiff, and not a purchase of the note, and therefore the transaction was usurious. *Peters* v. *Irish*, 4 *All.* 326.

39—In an action by the indorsee against the indorser of an accommodation note, to which the defence was, that the plaintiff in discounting the note had taken usurious interest, the maker of the note proved that he gave to B, a broker, to get it discounted. B could not identify the note as the one discounted for him by the plaintiff, but said if it was so, the transaction was usurious. A verdict having been found for the defendant, a new trial was refused—there being no evidence of any other note between the parties, and the plaintiff failing to show that he had not obtained it from B. *Hastings* v. *Henniger*, 4 *All.* 357.

40—The defendant made a note in favour of the plaintiff, which he indorsed in blank, and delivered to the defendant, who transferred it to N, to whom the plaintiff was obliged to pay the amount. Held, That the plaintiff could recover on the note as payee, though there was usury in the transaction between the defendant and N, the plaintiff being no party to that, and there being no usury in the inception of the note. *Lawrence* v. *Hammond*, 4 *All.* 612.

See Act of Assembly 22 Vic. c. 21, modifying laws relating to usury, limiting interest to 6 per cent., but contracts for more not void as to principal and legal interest.

VI.

Miscellaneous.

1—Damages.
Semble, That the acceptor of a protested bill of exchange, drawn in this country and accepted payable in England, is not liable to 10 per cent. damages under Rev. Stat. c. 116, in an action brought here. See *Morrison* v. *Spurr*, 3 *All.* 288.

2—Evidence—Declarations of principal.
In an action against one of the makers of a joint and several promissory note, signed by him as surety for the other maker, declarations of the latter made subsequent to giving the note are not evidence against the defendant. *Palmer* v. *Wilson*, 3 *All.* 443.

3—Note for Liquors.
In an action on a note for the price of liquors sold, the plaintiff need not prove that he had license to sell. *McAuley* v. *Lawlor*, 4 *All.* 600.

4—Equities—Holder—Payee.
If a promissory note is indorsed over as a security for advances only, the holder is subject to the same equities as the payee. *Estabrooks* v. *McKenzie*, *C. Ms.* 69.

5—Acceptance—Evidence of.
A bill of exchange was drawn payable in three equal instalments. When the first instalment became due, the holder presented it at the bank, where it was payable; the Cashier paid the first instalment and returned the bill to the holder with the following indorsement: "Paid on the within $741, August 12, '61." Held, An acceptance for the remaining instalments. *Berton* v. *The Central Bank*, *Hil. T.* 1863.

6—Check, if treated as an inland bill of exchange, the initialing by party's cashier does not amount to an acceptance. See Check 2.

7—Forgery relied on as defence—Consideration not required to be proved.
In an action on a promissory note for £700 the defence was that the defendant's signature was forged by the plaintiff, and in order to establish this, evidence was given (*inter alia*) of a legacy of £5000, payable by the defendant to the plaintiff's wife, which legacy had been paid independently of the note. The defendant's counsel relied upon the absence of evidence of any other transaction between the parties out of which the note could have arisen, and therefore the apparent want of consideration, as an ingredient to establish the forgery. The Judge left the question of forgery to the jury, who found a verdict for the plaintiff. Held, That as the de-

fendant had put his defence on the ground of forgery, the plaintiff was not called upon to prove the consideration, nor was the Judge to leave to the jury whether he had given any consideration for the note. (See Harvey v. Towers, 6 Exch. 656.) *Mathiavet* v. *Roach*, *Mich. T.* 1833.

8—Alteration of note—Evidence when made.
A joint note made by two persons appeared on its face to have been altered in the date. The note was delivered to the plaintiff by an agent of one of the makers (defendants) in its altered state; the other defendant was called as a witness, and stated that he could not write, or read writing beyond his own name, and could not say that the note had been altered since he signed it. Held, Sufficient for the jury to infer that the alteration was made before the note was signed. *Street* v. *Walsh*, *Trin. T.* 1862.

9—Interest recoverable from when.
A promissory note dated the 24th August 1857, payable with interest "from first August last," bears interest from the first August 1856. *Calhoun* v. *Colpitts*, *Mich. T.* 1862.

10—Partnership—Variance—Proof.
In an action against A and B carrying on business in partnership together with C, under the style of A. & Co., on a promissory note signed by A in the name of the firm, the declaration alleged that the note was made by A and B under the style and firm of A. & Co.; held no variance. The non-joinder of C could only be taken advantage of by plea in abatement. *Kelly* v. *Balloch*, 2 *Kerr* 699.

11—In an action by the payees against the maker of a promissory note payable to A B C and D, the declaration alleged that the defendant promised to pay the plaintiffs by the name, style and firm of A B C and D. Held, That it was not necessary to prove that the plaintiffs were partners, and that the words "name, style and firm" might have been struck out of the declaration. *Allen* v. *McNaughton*, 4 *All.* 234.

12—Averment—Proof—Special count—Recovery under common count.
If the holder of a bill of exchange relies upon there being no funds in the hands of the drawee, as an excuse for not presenting the bill and giving notice of dishonour, that fact should be stated in the declaration: and if presentment and notice are averred, they must be proved to enable the plaintiff to recover on the special count. If a bill of exchange is drawn for the balance of an account acknowledged to be due to the plaintiff from the drawer who has no funds in the drawee's hands, the plaintiff may recover the amount upon the count on account stated, if, in consequence of not alleging the excuse for presentment and notice, he is unable to recover upon the special count. *Emerson* v. *Gardner*, 1 *All.* 451.

12 a—Payable at particular place—Common Counts.
In an action by the payee against the maker, a promissory note is admissible in evidence under the common money counts, although it is in the body of it made payable at a particular place; the right of recovery, however, is suspended until presentment be made at the place, on or after the time of payment. *Merritt* v. *Woods*, *Ber.* 261.

13—Particulars referring to note—Evidence.
Where the declaration contained a count by the plaintiff, as indorsee of a note drawn by D. B. in favour of the defendant, and by him indorsed to the plaintiff; with the common money counts; and a bill of particulars had been delivered stating that the action was brought to recover the amount of the note. Held, That the plaintiff failing in proof on the count for the note, was not entitled to give evidence under the common counts of an admission by the defendant that he had received funds from D. B. for the purpose of paying the note, and had afterwards promised to pay it. *Topley* v. *McHenry*, 2 *Kerr* 57.

14—Defect supplied by Particulars.
The omission in a notice of set-off to state that a promissory note, which is otherwise sufficiently described, had been indorsed to the defendant, is not material, where the defect is supplied by the particulars, and the plaintiff has not been misled. *Bugbee* v. *McDonald*, 2 *Kerr* 61.

15—Evidence under Common Counts.
See Assumpsit. See also Supra 12.

16—Contribution—Liability for—Satisfaction.
See Consideration 8.

17—Variance.
Copy of Summons and Note—Summary process—Variance in—Cannot be taken

advantage of on trial if note corresponds with original which is the record. See *Steadman* v. *Holstead*, 3 *Kerr* 355.

BILL OF LADING.

Estoppel by—Evidence allowable to explain. See Carrier 1.

Refusal to deliver goods—No bill of lading produced. See Pleading II. 5.

Considered as an entire contract. See Contract 21.

BILL OF PARCELS.

Delivery of, after sale of goods—Parol Evidence as to quality. See Evidence V. 2.

BILL OF SALE.

Delivery up of unregistered vessel—Fraud. See Shipping Law 6.

BILL IN EQUITY.

See Equity. See Practice in Equity.

BILL OF EXCEPTIONS.

1—*Quære*, Whether the facts stated in a bill of exceptions can be contradicted? *Mills* v. *Vail*, 4 *All.* 239.

2—A bill of exceptions improperly obtained in the Court of Common Pleas, may be set aside by that Court before return made to a writ of error; and the order to set it aside may form part of the return. *Mills* v. *Vail*, 4 *All.* 629.

BOARD OF HEALTH.

Regulations—Not imposing penalty—Omission not invalidating. See Criminal Law 19.

BOARDING HOUSE KEEPER.

1—Lien.
A boarding house keeper has no lien on the goods of a person occupying rooms in his house under an agreement, for non-payment of his bill. *Light* v. *Abel*, *Trin. T.* 1865.

2—Character of keeping left to jury—Pleading.
In replevin the defendant pleaded that she kept a public boarding and lodging house, with rooms, etc. for the reception, public entertainment, boarding and lodging of all guests, boarders, etc., who might come to her house willing to pay an adequate price; that the plaintiff was accepted as a guest and boarder in the house for certain reasonable reward, and as such guest brought the goods and chattels to the defendant's house, and that she kept and detained them for a lien thereon, to insure payment of an account due to her for lodging and entertainment provided for the plaintiff. Replication—*de injuria*. Held, That the replication did not admit that defendant was an inn-keeper, that on the issue raised, it was properly left to the jury to find whether the defendant was an inn-keeper or a lodging house keeper, and whether the plaintiff was received at her house as a traveller, or transient boarder, or as a boarder under a special agreement. *Light* v. *Abel*, *Trin. T.* 1865.

BODILY HARM.

See Criminal Law.

BOOMAGE.

Liability to Payment of.
The Act 10, Vict. c. 72, authorized The South Bay Boom Company, to erect booms and piers between certain points on the River St. John, for securing timber, logs, etc., and the 15th sect. authorized them to receive certain boomage on all timber, logs, etc., which should be "carried or received, or which should enter into or within said piers or booms." Held, That the owner of a saw-mill at the mouth of a stream within the bounds of the boom, and whose free access to the River St. John was partially obstructed thereby, had no common law right as a reparian proprietor, to pass logs through the boom to his mill, without payment of boomage; and that as he came within the words of the Act, there was no implied exemption from the charge imposed by the 15th sec. of the Act. *South Bay Boom Co.* v. *Jewett*, *East. T.* 1862.

BOND.

I.

PARTICULAR BONDS.

A LIMIT BOND.
B BAIL BOND.
C REPLEVIN BOND.
D ADMINISTRATION BOND.
E ARBITRATION BOND.

II.

Miscellaneous.

Particular Bonds.

A Limit Bond.

1—Limit Bond—Defence—Action by Sheriff.
In an action of debt brought by a Sheriff upon a limit bond under 10 and 11 Geo. 4, c. 30, it is a good defence to shew that the Sheriff had received the defendant again into close custody either on being rendered by his bail or by such defendant rendering himself in discharge of his bail, but *non-damnifacatus* is not a good plea except only where the bond is merely to indemnify. *Campbell* v. *Henan et al*, *Ber.* 72.

2—Assignee of.
In an action by the assignee of a bond for the gaol limits, it is a fatal objection, even on motion for arrest of judgment after verdict, that it does not appear on the record that the assignee was the plaintiff in the suit on which the bond was taken, there being nothing to render proof of that fact necessary on the trial of the issue. *Semble*, The declaration should state the writ on which the defendant is in custody when the limit bond is taken. *Cameron* v. *Beardsley*, 2 *Kerr* 598.

3—Damages—Assessment.
In an action on a limit bond, the damages may be assessed by the jury; and the proper rule of damages when the bond has been taken from a person in custody under execution is the amount of such execution. *McKenzie* v. *Marsh*, 2 *Kerr* 629.

(See Nos. 10, 15.)

4—Limits of Gaol—Prisoner going beyond.
The Act 6 Wm. 4, c. 41, authorised the Justices of the Peace in the several counties to designate certain gaol limits, not to be less than 40 rods nor to exceed 160 rods from any gaol: the Justices of C. made an order that the gaol limits of that county should extend to 160 rods from the gaol, and that the sheriff should cause the same to be defined and designated by erecting posts at the extremities. In pursuance of this order the sheriff marked out limits in 1837, which had been since acted upon. Held, That a limit bond taken in reference thereto, was not forfeited, though the posts erected were afterwards found to be 174 rods distant from the gaol, and the prisoner had gone beyond the 160 rods, but not beyond the posts—it not appearing that he was aware of the excess. *Boyd* v. *Kennedy*, 1 *All.* 624.

Persons entering into a limit bond are not required to make a measurement to ascertain that the limits marked out by the Justices are in due conformity to the law. *Ibid.*

5—Payment of Sheriff's fee upon—Taking.
Payment of Sheriff's fee is necessary to the completion of limit bond, and the Sheriff is not bound to discharge defendant from gaol and give him the benefit of the limits without such fee being paid. See *Caldwell* v. *Winslow*, 2 *All.* 203.

6—Validity of—More than double amount—Non est factum.
A limit bond taken under the Act 6 Wm. 4, c. 41, for more than double the sum for which the execution issued, is valid; though if the penalty was unreasonable the obligor might be relieved by the Court. *Forster* v. *Pine*, 2 *All.* 215.

7—Defence—Non est factum—Different Court.
It is no defence under a plea of *non est factum* in an action on a limit bond, that it was brought in a different Court than that in which the original action was brought. *Ibid.*

8—Court—Suit.
An action on a limit bond need not be brought in the Court in which the suit in which the bond was given was brought. *James* v. *Roach*, *Hil. T.* 1864.

9—Taking assignment of first bond—Insufficient sureties—Taking second bond.
M. being a prisoner on the limits, escaped without the knowledge of the sheriff or the plaintiff, but returned again to the limits, and the sheriff being dissatisfied with the sureties, took a new limit bond: the plaintiff afterwards, (knowing that the second bond had been given,) took an assignment of the first bond, brought an action thereon, and recovered a verdict for the debt and costs in the original suit. Held, That he could not afterwards consider M. as remaining a prisoner on the execution, and take an assignment of the second bond and proceed thereon for the escape, even though the sureties in the first bond were insufficient. *Goodwin* v. *Murray*, 3 *All.* 595.

Taking a second limit bond is no defence to an action for a previous escape, unless the plaintiff consents to waive such escape. *Goodwin* v. *Murray*, 3 *All.* 595.

10—Action by assignee—Common Venire—Assessment of damages.

In an action by the assignee of a limit bond, to which *non est factum* is pleaded, the common *venire* to try the issue, is sufficient; and the plaintiff need not have damages assessed, but may take a verdict for nominal damages, and issue execution for the amount of his debt. *McElroy* v. *Getty and another, impleaded with Ellis*, 1 *Han.* 261.

11—Assignee—Action by—Proceedings to be set forth.

In an action by the assignee of a limit bond, it is necessary to set forth in the declaration the proceedings in the original action in which the defendant was in custody. *Baxter* v. *Sime*, *Hil. T.* 1833.

12—Defence—Action on a limit bond—Second arrest after voluntarily allowing to go at large.

If a judgment debtor arrested on a *ca. sa.* is voluntarily allowed by the creditor to go at large, he cannot be arrested again on a new *ca. sa.*; and if he should be so arrested, and give bail for the limits these facts will be a good answer to an action on the limit bond for an escape. *Andrews* v. *Dervdall*, *Trin. T.* 1832.

13—Order for discharge not served.

An order for the discharge of an insolvent debtor from the limits, not served upon the sheriff, nor acted upon by him, is no answer to an action on the bond for the escape of the debtor. (Wilmot and Ritchie J. J., *dissentiente.*) *James* v. *Roach*, *Hil. T.* 1864.

14—Escape—Different county—Judge's warrant—Limit bond—Sheriff no right to take.

A debtor in custody of the sheriff of Carleton on a *ca. sa.* escaped into the County of York, and was there arrested under a Judge's warrant for the escape and committed to the custody of the sheriff of York who gave him the limits. Held, That the sheriff had no right to take a limit bond; and the party being at large, the Court refused either to set aside the Judge's warrant, or to cancel the limit bond. *Ex parte Haines*, *Hil. T.* 1862.

See Bail. (Relief.)

B BAIL BOND.

15—Executor of assignee may maintain action—Evidence—Execution issuing—Amount.

The executor of the assignee of a bail-bond may bring an action upon it. *Scribner* v. *Gibbon*, 4 *All.* 182.

In an action by the assignee of a bail-bond where the only plea is *non est factum*, the plaintiff need not give any evidence of the original cause of action; but on proof of the execution of the bond, he is entitled to a verdict with nominal damages, and if execution issues for more than the debt due and costs, the defendant may be relieved by application to the Court. *Ibid.*

16—Erasure in—Avoidance.

Where in an action on a bail bond there was an erasure in the condition, and the name of the plaintiff in the suit appeared to have been altered, and there was no evidence when the alteration was made—Held, That this avoided the bond. *Weeks* v. *Hall*, *Hil. T.* 1834.

C REPLEVIN BOND.

17—Form of.

A replevin bond not in form given by the Rules of Court Mich. T. 4 Vic. is bad. *Pollock* v. *Gardner*, 2 *Kerr* 655.

18—Breach—Delay in Prosecuting—Assignment—Form.

A tenant replevied goods distrained for rent in November 1858; the landlord appeared, and the cause was entered for trial at the circuit in May 1859, but the plaintiff not appearing when it was called on, it was struck off the docket. Held, That this was a breach of the condition of the replevin bond, to prosecute without delay. The breach of the bond is necessarily a damage. *Steen* v. *Hanson*, 4 *All.* 459.

A replevin bond may be assigned on the request of the attorney of the defendant in the action of replevin, and may be given by the Sheriff to his deputy to be delivered to the assignee. *Ibid.*

It is no ground for arresting the judgment in an action on a replevin bond, that the bond as stated in the declaration, is not in the form prescribed by the Act, if the bond itself is correct. The variance might be amended even after notice of motion to arrest the judgment. *Ibid.*

19—Pleading—Excuse for breach.

In an action by the assignee against the

obligors of a replevin bond, the breach alleged was that the obligors did not appear at the day mentioned in the condition of the bond (Michaelmas term), and prosecute the suit with effect and without delay. Plea, that the defendant in replevin did not appear at the return of the writ (the second Tuesday in October), and in order that the plaintiffs might prosecute their suit according to the condition of the bond, they sued out a process against the defendant, returnable in Easter term, to which the defendant had appeared, and that the suit was at issue and being prosecuted with effect and without delay. Held, on demurrer, That the plea shewed a sufficient excuse for the plaintiff's breach; it not being specifically objected by the demurrer that they had not issued process against the defendant on the return of the writ of replevin, or within twenty days after. *Williams* v. *The St. Andrews Steam Mill Company*, 1 *All.* 580.

20—Claim of property—Inquisition—Breach—Immaterial mistake in name.

If a defendant in replevin claims property in part of the goods replevied, and the property is found in him on an inquisition under a writ *de proprietate probanda*, this constitutes a breach of the replevin bond, and entitles the defendant to an assignment of it, in order to recover the costs of the proceeding. *Berry* v. *Mitchell*, 2 *All.* 380.

Quære, As to the disposition by the Sheriff of the goods not claimed by the defendant. *Ibid.*

Property replevied was claimed by the defendant in the name of "Barry" instead of "Berry;" the property was found to be in the claimant, and the bond was assigned to him by his proper name. Held, That the mistake was immaterial. *Ibid.*

21—When bond cannot be assigned to defendant.

When on a writ *de proprietate probanda*, the finding is for the defendant, the replevin suit is terminated and the replevin bond cannot be assigned to the defendant. *Pollock* v. *Gardiner*, 2 *Kerr* 655.

22—One surety only—Objection cannot be taken by plaintiff.

A replevin bond with one surety is sufficient and may be assigned. Though the sheriff might object to take such a bond, or the defendant in the replevin suit to take an assignment of it, the plaintiff in the suit cannot take the objection. *Taylor* v. *Burpee*, *Trin. T.* 1861.

23—Handwriting—Proof—Assignment—Request—Defendant's Attorney.

In an action by the assignee proof of the obligor's handwriting is sufficient without calling the subscribing witness. The bond may be assigned at the request of the defendant's attorney. *Ibid.*

24—Action on bond—Prosecute without delay—Against whom.

Defendant M. issued a writ of replevin against B.;—the present plaintiff put in a claim of property but no writ *de prop. probanda* was issued. The plaintiff afterwards appeared in the replevin suit, but M. did not proceed therein, whereupon the plaintiff took an assignment of the replevin bond and brought an action thereon for not prosecuting the replevin. Held, Bad in arrest of judgment—the condition of the bond being that M. should prosecute the suit without delay, etc., against B., and not against the plaintiff. *Smith* v. *Millar*, *Hil. T.* 1866.

25—Staying proceedings—Power of Judge—Damages.

The provision in the Act 4 Wm. 4. c. 38, authorizing the Court to give relief in actions on replevin bonds, having been omitted from the Act 13 Vic. c. 53, which repealed the former Act, a Judge has no power, except under special circumstances, to stay the proceedings in such an action; where it is brought for the breach of the condition of the bond, to prosecute the replevin suit without delay, and the plaintiffs proceedings are regular. The Court will not enquire whether the defendant in the replevin suit has, or has not sustained damage by the breach of the bond. *Betts* v. *McGowan*, *East. T.* 1872.

D Administration Bond.

26—Application to put in suit.

In an application to put an administration bond in suit, the Court will not determine whether there has been a breach of the bond. If the applicant make out a *primâ facie* case of breach, and that he is a proper person to sue for it, he is entitled to an assignment. *In re Hunter*, 1 *Han.* 233.

An assignment will not be refused though there is a variance between the bond and the form given by the Act. *Ibid.*

The counsel moving for the assignment is not bound to shew that he is authorized to make the application. *In re Hunter*, 1 *Han.* 233.

It is sufficient to shew the substance of the proceedings against the administrator in the Probate Court without producing a copy of them. *Ibid.*

27—Breach—Non-payment of debt.
The non-payment of a debt does not, *per se*, constitute a breach of an administration bond, "well and truly to administer according to law" the goods and chattels of the intestate. *Sherlock* v. *McGee*, 1 *All.* 116.

28—Devastavit—Requisite statement.
In an action on an administration bond under the Act 3 Vic. c. 61, assigning as a breach a devastavit by the administrator, it must be stated that the estate of the intestate has sustained injury thereby to a certain amount. *Sherlock* v. *McGee*, 1 *All.* 346.

An allegation in the assignment of a breach that goods and chattels came to the hands of the defendant *as administrator*, necessarily shews that they were the goods of the intestate. *Ibid.*

E Arbitration Bond.

29—Revocation.
One of two persons on the same side may revoke a joint submission to arbitration, and such revocation will be a forfeiture of a joint and several bond by both, conditioned to stand to, obey and perform the award. *Hatheway* v. *Cliff*, 2 *All.* 267.

30—Breach—Pleading.
Particular breach in bond for performance of award, must be stated in declaration. See Pleading I. 43.

II. Miscellaneous.

31—Impeached for fraudulent representation—What defendant may prove.
Where a bond given for the purchase money of a lot of land, is impeached for fraud, on the ground that there was a fraudulent representation at the time of the bargain, and previous to the giving of the deed, as to a parcel of land included in the purchase, it must be affirmatively shewn as one of the requisites of such a defence, that the deed does not in fact contain the land bargained for. *Sisson* v. *Merithew*, 3 *Kerr* 284.

32—Escrow—Non-Execution by one of Obligors.
The condition of a bond recited that five persons named as obligors, had agreed to secure the payment of a sum of money to the plaintiff; one of the persons named did not execute the bond. Held, That in the absence of any circumstances attending the execution, beyond the mere fact of one of the parties named not having signed it, there was not sufficient evidence to be left to the jury that the bond was delivered as an escrow. Held also, That it was the joint bond of the obligors who executed it, and that the omission of one of the persons named in the bond to execute it, did not render it merely the several bond of each obligor who did. *Keator* v. *Scovil*, 3 *Kerr* 647.

33—Crown Bond—Neglect to enforce payment—Sureties—Application for relief.
One of the conditions of a bond given to the Crown by a deputy postmaster, required him to give three months notice to the postmaster general of his intention to resign his office, and to pay all sums of money chargeable against him as postmaster. At the time of his resignation, a postmaster was a defaulter, and died insolvent, about twenty-one months after. No proceedings were taken against him to enforce payment, though he was applied to several times, and promised payment, and no notice of his indebtedness was given to his sureties till after his death. Held, That his sureties were not entitled to be relieved from the bond under the 33 Hen. 8, c. 39, s. 79. *The Queen* v. *Hammond and another*, 1 *Han.* 33.

34—Corporation—Bond to—Condition—Notice—Seal of Company not necessary.
See Principal and Surety 1.

35—Obligees—Action by one.
A bond conditioned for the payment of money to A. or B., or either of them, cannot be sued on in the name of one of the obligees, unless the other is dead. See *Hazen* v. *Drummond*, 4 *All.* 267.

BOND & WARRANT OF ATTORNEY.

See Warrant of Attorney.

BOUNDARY,

See Crown Grant,

BOUNDARY LINES.

1—Agreement as to—Binding operation.

Where the respective owners of adjoining lots agree by parol to a division line, it is binding upon them, though it may differ from a line to which they had previously occupied. *Lawrence* v. *McDowell, Ber.* 283.

2—Where a boundary line has been run between adjoining proprietors of land by a surveyor mutually employed by them and acted upon for a number of years, and conveyances made according to it, it is binding upon them though it was incorrectly run and deviated from the description in the deeds under which they held, and gave one of the parties a much greater quantity of land than he was entitled unto. *Doe dem. Carr* v. *McCullough*, 1 *Kerr* 460.

3—Running and marking a line by one party, not in accordance with the true line between adjoining grants, having only been assented to on the condition that the true line should be ascertained and run, cannot establish it as a conventional boundary until it is acquiesced in and acted on by both parties. *Bevier* v. *Govane*, 4 *All.* 144.

4—Ascertained marks—Controlling courses.

Where the side line of a grant to H. was described as North 107 chains or to the Northwesterly angle of A's grant, such angle being capable of being ascertained, controls the course and distance of the side line of H's grant. *Hanson* v. *Mahoney*, 2 *Han.* 11.

Dispute as to boundary—Question for Jury. See Trespass II. 29.

BREACH.

Bond. See Bond.

Particular breach in bond for performance of an award must be stated in declaration. See Pleading I. 43.

Arbitration Bond. See Bond 27.

Covenant. See Pleading I.

Scire Facias on inquisition. See Practice IV. 3.

BREACH OF AGREEMENT.

See Agreement.

1—Unpaid instalment—Damages—Cross Action.

In an action for breach of an agreement to convey property to the plaintiff on payment to the defendant of a sum of money by instalments, and which agreement the defendant had disabled himself from performing, before the last instalment was due. Held, That the plaintiff not having paid the last instalment, could not recover it as part of the damages for breach of the agreement. Being part of the same transaction, the defendant is entitled to have the unpaid instalment deducted, and is not driven to bring a cross action for it. *Gilbert* v. *Campbell*, 2 *Han.* 55.

2—Partial Breach—Action.

Where goods are delivered under an agreement to be paid for by endorsed notes payable —— days after delivery, the vendor may, before the expiration of the term of credit, sustain an action against the vendee for a partial breach of his agreement, the vendee having in part paid for the goods according to agreement. *Brown* v. *Frink, Ber.* 363.

BREAKING OPEN DOORS.

Raising a window whereby a constable was enabled to reach and unbolt the door on the inside of a house, and thereby enter it, is a breaking. *Smith* v. *Burpee, Mich. T.* 1872.

See Distress—Notice of Action—Criminal Law—Constable.

Breaking into field under lawful fence—What does not constitute. See Trespass II. 2.

BRITISH NORTH AMERICA ACT 1867.

1—Provincial Legislatures—Powers of—Insolvency.

Insolvency being one of the subjects upon which the exclusive right to legislate is vested in the Parliament of Canada, the Legislature of New Brunswick has no right to pass an Act relating thereto, since the "British North America Act" came in force. *Reg.* v. *Chandler*, 1 *Han.* 548.

2—Imprisonment for debt.

The Act 33 Vic. c. 22 relating to imprisonment for debt, does not come within the prohibition of the 91st sec. of the British North America Act 1867, paragraph "Bakruptcy and Insolvency." *Valentine* v. *Hazleton.* Equity 1870.

(See Practice in Equity 22. Same case.)

3—Railways.
The Provincial Act 33 Vic. c. 47, authorizing the issue of Debentures to the Houlton Branch Railway Company, to aid in the construction of a railway from Houlton, in the State of Maine to the New Brunswick and Canada Railway in this Province. Held, To be beyond the powers of the local Legislature under the "British North America Act 1867." Sec 92. Sub sec. 10. *Ex parte Marks, Hil. T.* 1872.

4—Plaintiffs were incorporated in 1851 by an Act of the Legislature of New Brunswick for the purpose of constructing a railway from St. John to the boundary of the United States; the stock not having been subscribed, nor the assessments on the stockholders made according to the conditions of the Act, and it being doubtful whether subscribers for stock were liable to pay the calls, another Act (32 Vic c. 54) was passed to obviate the objections—declaring in what manner the subscribers for stock should be liable. Held, That this Act was not beyond the powers of the local Legislature under "The British North America Act." Sec. 92. Sub Sec. 10. *E. and N. American Railway Co.* v. *Thomas, Hil. T.* 1872.

5—Branch Pilots St. John—Regulations—Authority to make.
By Act 3 Vic. c. 70, the Corporation of Saint John was authorized to make laws and ordinances for the regulation of the Branch Pilots of St. John. Under this authority bye-laws were made before the passing of "The British North America Act 1867." Afterwards in 1869 the Corporation made another bye-law relating to pilots. Held, That the regulation of pilotage belonged to the Parliament of Canada under the 91st section of the British North America Act, and (per Ritchie C. J., Allen and Weldon, J. J.) that after that Act came in force, the powers of the Corporation to make bye-laws relating to pilotage ceased, and therefore the bye-law of 1869 was *ultra vires* (per Fisher and Wetmore, J. J.) that under the 129th Section of the British North America Act, the power of the Corporation to make bye-laws under the Act 3 Vic. c. 70 was continued until the Parliament of Canada legislate on the subject, and therefore the bye-law was valid. *Reg.* v. *Peters, Hil. T.* 1873.

The Act 33 Vic. c. 47 is *ultra vires* under the British North America Act 1867. Section 92. Sub sec. 10. *Reg.* v. *Dow, Hil. T.* 1867. (See Supra Ex parte Marks.)

Provisions for Non Sectarian Schools. See Common School Act.

Acts of local Legislature relating to attendance of Grand and Petit Jurors in criminal matters in County Courts are not *ultra vires*. See County Court 10.

BRITISH STATUTES.

1—Statutes not in force in New Brunswick.
The Act of Parliament 7 Geo. 2, c. 20, authorizing a stay of proceedings in ejectment on a mortgage, on payment of the debt and costs, does not extend to this Province. (But see 2 Wm. 4, c. 23, s. 3.) *Doe dem Owen* v. *Hatheway, Hil. T.* 1827.

2—The Acts of Parliament 5 Geo. 2, c. 19, and 13 Geo. 2, c. 18, relating to the proceedings for *certiorari*, do not extend to this Province. *Ex parte Ritchie*, 2 *Kerr* 75. *Ex parte Bustin*, 2 *All.* 211.

3—The Statute 1 Rich. 2, cap. 12, under which a Sheriff was held liable in an action of debt for an escape, is not applicable to this Province. *Wilson* v. *Jones*, 1 *All.* 658.

4—The Statute 29 Eliz. c. 4, relating to Sheriff's fees, is not in force in this Province. *Kavanagh* v. *Phelan*, 1 *Kerr* 472.

5—The Act 2 Geo. 2, c. 23, requiring the delivery of bill of costs a month before action, is not in force here. See No. 16.

6—The Statute 33 Hen. 8, c 39, s. 50, giving to bonds to the King the force and effect of a Statute Staple, extends to this Province. *Rex* v. *McLaughlin, Mich. T.* 1836.

7—The Statute of Uses 27 Hen. 8, c. 10, and the Statute of Enrolments 27 Hen. 8, c. 16, extend to and are in force in this Province. *Doe dem Hannington* v. *McFadden, Bert.* 153.

8—The Statute 33 Hen. 8, c. 39, s. 79, authorising the Court of Exchequer to give relief to Crown debtors, extends to this Province, and by virtue thereof the Supreme Court may relieve from an estreated recognizance (Parker, J., *dubitante*). *Rex* v. *Appleby, Ber.* 397.

9—The Act of Parliament 9 and 10 Wm. 3, c. 15, relating to submissions to arbitration, held to be in force. (See No. 13.) *Doe dem Allen* v. *Murray*, 2 *Kerr* 359.

10—The Statutes 43 Eliz. c. 6, and 13 Car. 2, c. 2, relating to costs, are in force in this Province. *Kelly* v. *Jones*, 2 *All.* 473; *Gilbert* v. *Sayre*, 2 *All.* 512.

11—The Statute 43 Eliz. c. 6, authorising a Judge to certify to deprive a plaintiff of costs, being part of the practice of the Court of King's Bench when the Supreme Court of this Province was established, is in force here, and is not affected by a subsequent repeal of it in England. *Kelly* v. *Jones*, 2 *All.* 473.

12—The Act of Parliament 3 Jac. 1, c. 7, requiring the delivery of an attorney's bill of costs before action brought, extends to this Province. See No. 16.

13—The Statute 9 and 10 Wm. 3, c. 15, does not apply to references under the Act of Assembly. See *Brown* v. *Harding*, 3 *All.* 351.

14—Certificate under English Bankrupt Act pleadable in this Province. See Bankrupt.

15—*Quære*, Whether the Statute 13 Eliz. c. 10, applies to Church Corporations in this Province? See *Bedell* v. *Rector &c. of Christ Church, Fredericton*, 3 *All.* 217.

16—**Bill of Costs—Delivery of.**
The Act of Parliament 3 Jac. 1, c. 7, requiring the delivery of an attorney's bill of costs before action brought, extends to this Province, but the Act 2 Geo. 2, c. 23, requiring the delivery a month before action, is not in force here. *James* v. *McLean*, 3 *All.* 164.

17—The construction given in England to the Statute 22 and 23 Chas. 2, c. 9, is part of the law of this Province, and is not affected by the Act of Assembly 13 Vic. c. 32. See Costs 24.

BYE-LAW.

Suing for calls—No bye-laws made. See Joint Stock Company. See Fredericton, (City of.)

1—**Proof—Necessity of.**
In a prosecution for a penalty under a bye-law of a Corporation, the bye-law must be proved. *Reg.* v. *Wortman*, 4 *All.* 73.

2—In a prosecution tried before the Mayor of Fredericton for violating a bye-law of the Corporation, the bye-law must be proved. *Ex parte Mulligan Mich. T.* 1862.

3—**Not fixing time for payment—Selling without License—Penalty—Right to recover.**
A Bye Law of Fredericton, to regulate the public market, required the stalls in the market to be leased annually, and declared that the lessee of a stall should receive from the Mayor a license to occupy, and that any person occupying without license should be liable to a penalty. Held, In a prosecution for the penalty, that the only question was whether the defendant had a license. *Ex parte Mulligan*, 2 *All.* 583.

Where the bye law fixes no time for payment of the purchase money of a stall, it may be done by conditions of sale. *Ibid.*

(See Justice of the Peace.)

4—**Power to make Bye-Laws—Authority to impose a toll.**
Power given to the Corporation of Fredericton by the Act. 22 Vic. c. 8, to make bye-laws "to regulate the anchorage, lading and unlading of vessels" does not authorise the imposition of a toll for anchorage. *Reg.* v. *Dowling*, *Mich. T.* 1862.

5—**Corporation limiting by Contract—Their power to make bye-laws.**
The Corporation of St. John being by Charter the conservators of the harbour, with power to regulate the navigation, anchoring and fastening of vessels, and to make bye-laws, etc., granted to the plaintiff the right to build a wharf extending into the harbour, and to receive the wharfage and emoluments to be derived from vessels lying at such wharf—the plaintiff built a wharf, and the Corporation afterwards passed a bye-law that no vessel should lie at that wharf with her bow to the south; in consequence of which the plaintiff lost the wharfage of a vessel. Held, In an action against the Corporation, that they had no right to limit by contract their power to make bye-laws relative to matters within their control under the charter, and that the plaintiff's grant must be taken subject to their right to make such bye-laws from time to time, as they should deem necessary for the anchorage of vessels. *Walker* v. *Mayor, &c. of St. John. Hil. T.* 1872.

Power in Corporation St. John to make bye-laws for pilotage since passing of "*The British North America Act* 1867." See *The British North America Act* 1867.

CALLS.

See Winding Up Act—Note may be given for assessment due on. See Bills and Notes I. 9.

CANADA.

Jurisdiction—Seizure of timber. See Timber.

CANADIAN COURT.

See Judgment III.

CAPIAS.

See Practice IV.

Misnomer. See Identity.

Wrong Name—Pleading. See Pleading II. 20.

It is not an irregularity in a capias *ad respondendum*, that it requires the defendant to answer the plaintiff in a plea of debt, instead of trespass, the usual form. *Campbell* v. *Mossop*, *C. Mo.* 154.

CARLETON WATER WORKS.

Issuing Notes. See Mandamus 9.

CARRIER.

1—Master of Ship—Loss by Jettison.
The master of a ship who has signed the usual bill of lading, is not liable for a loss by the jettison of goods, which have been laden on deck with the knowledge and consent of the shipper and consignee. Such master is not estopped by the bill of lading from shewing that the goods are to be laden on deck. *Johnston and another* v. *Crane*, 1 *Kerr* 356.

2—The master of a vessel is not liable for the loss occasioned by the jettison of goods, which have been laden on the deck with the privity and assent of the shipper. *Johnston* v. *Crane*, 2 *Kerr* 39.

Under the facts of this case as already reported, *ante*, vol. 1, p. 356, the Court did not think there was sufficient ground for reconsidering their former judgment, though they were not fully agreed upon the question, whether the shipper's assent to the goods being taken on deck would under all circumstances be a bar to his recovery for a loss by jettison. *Johnson* v. *Crane*, 2 *Kerr* 39.

3—Loss of Lumber—Jus tertii.
By agreement between the plaintiff and M., the latter was to furnish plaintiff with supplies to get lumber, which was to be the property of M., and was marked accordingly: a portion of the lumber was sold, and M. took part of the proceeds—allowing the plaintiff to receive the remainder—and afterwards sued him for the balance of his account for supplies. Held, That M. had thereby repudiated all claim to the rest of the lumber, and that in an action against the defendant as carrier for loss of part of it, he could not set up the right of property in M. under the agreement, as an answer to the action. *Forbes* v. *Holts*, 4 *All.* 611.

4—Railway Company—Liability.
The Commissioners of E. and N. American Railway in the absence of any regulations approved by the Governor in Council limiting their responsibility for the safe conveyance of goods and luggage, are subject to the same liabilities as common carriers. *Willis* v. *The Commissioners of the European and North American Railway*, 2 *Han.* 157.

5—Delivery to carrier—Acceptance for vender.
A delivery of goods by a vendor to a common carrier without any specific direction or authority from the vendee, will not amount to an acceptance by the latter within the Statute of Frauds. *Daley* v. *Marks*, *Ber.* 346.

6—Delivery not complete—Loss.
Plaintiff sent boards alongside of defendant's vessel to be shipped, but before being taken on board, they had to be surveyed and classified by the plaintiff, and before this was done, they were stolen. Held, That until the survey and classification, they were not in defendant's possession, and he was not liable for their loss. *Cushing* v. *Roberts*, *Hil. T.* 1861.

7—Negligence of servants.
A common carrier is liable for the negligence of his servants in taking goods on board his vessel in his absence, though he may have directed them not to receive goods—the plaintiff having no notice of such instructions. *Street* v. *Morrison*, *East. T.* 1862.

8—Negligence in using improper gear. In putting a large cask of brandy on board a vessel from a wharf, a carrier used can-hooks. In lowering the cask from the wharf one of the chains (by which the hooks held the cask) broke and the cask fell into the hold and was destroyed. Held, That it was negligence to use can-hooks instead of slings to lower the cask. *Street* v. *Morrison*, *East. T.* 1862.

CA. SA.

See Bail 7, 19. Practice IV.

CASUAL EJECTOR.

Judgment against. See Ejectment III.
" Practice VIII.

CAVEAT EMPTOR.

Sale and conveyance of land—No Fraud—Eviction of purchaser by title paramount—Action for money had and received for purchase money, not maintainable. See Assumpsit 24.

CERTAINTY.

See Justice of the Peace. (Conviction.)

CERTIFICATE OF JUDGE.

See Judge.

CERTIFIED COPIES OF DEEDS.

See Evidence VII.

Semble, Whether certified copies of deeds are properly receivable in evidence under Rev. Stat. c. 112, s. 12, without a new affidavit and notice since first trial of cause. See *Gilbert* v. *Campbell*, 2 *Han.* 55.

CERTIFIED FEES.

Constable—Right to Recover.

See Criminal Law IV.

CERTIORARI.

I. When it Lies. When Granted.
II. Time of Application. Delay.
III. Miscellaneous.

I.

When it Lies—When Granted.

1—Proceedings of Trustees of Schools. The Supreme Court has power to grant a *certiorari* to remove the proceedings of trustees of schools under the Parish School Act 15 Vic. c. 40, and to quash them if defective. *Ex parte Jocelyn*, 2 *All.* 637.

2—Judgment of City Court. A *certiorari* lies to remove a judgment from the City Court of Saint John; and the power will be exercised where the case involves questions as to the right of real property and the construction of Statutes, though the amount in dispute is trifling. *Ex parte McNichol*, 3 *All.* 493.

a—Important principle—City Court. Where an important principle was involved in a case tried before the City Court of St. John, the Court granted a *certiorari* to bring up the proceedings, though the case might have been reviewed before a Judge at Chambers. *Ex parte Foye*, *East. T.* 1873.

3—Proceedings of Justice of Peace. *Quære*, Whether a *certiorari* to remove proceedings before a Justice of the Peace in a civil suit, is not taken away by the Rev. Stat. c. 137. But if not, some reason must be shewn for not proceeding by review. *Ex parte Ellis*, 3 *All.* 601.

4—Insolvent Debtors Act. A *certiorari* lies to remove into Supreme Court the proceedings before Justices under the Insolvent Confined Debtors Act. *White* v. *Coleman*, 4 *All.* 630.

5—Insolvent Act of 1869. A demand was made upon a debtor under sect. 14 of the Insolvent Act 1869, requiring him to make an assignment of his estate and effects for the benefit of his creditors. The debtor presented a petition under section 15 to the County Court Judge, upon hearing which he decided that the demand was inoperative, and ordered that no further proceedings be taken. Held, That as there was an appeal from the Judge's decision, a *certiorari* would not lie to remove the proceedings. *Ex parte Thomas*, 2 *Han.* 163.

6—Summary convictions. The power given to a Judge by the Rev. Stat. c. 161, s. 32, to hear appeals from summary convictions before Justices of the Peace, does not take away the right of the Supreme Court to grant a *certiorari* to remove such convictions. *Ex parte Montgomery*, 3 *All.* 149.

Quære, Whether such mode of appeal is applicable to offences not created by the Rev. Stat. Also whether, in deciding a case on appeal, the Judge is to be governed by strict legal principles or by the equitable principles on which reviews of civil cases are determined? *Ex parte Montgomery*, 3 *All.* 149.

7—Commissioners altering road.
The granting a *certiorari* being discretionary it was refused to bring up the proceedings for the alteration of a public road, where the applicant had allowed one term to elapse, and the road had been opened in the mean time. *Rex* v. *Heaviside*, *Hil. T.* 1833.

8—Senate of University.
A *certiorari* is only granted to bring up the judicial acts of some inferior tribunal. The acts of the Senate of the University of New Brunswick in dismissing one of the professors are not judicial acts, and therefore not subjected to be reviewed by this Court. *Ex parte Jacob*, *Trin. T.* 1861.

9—Proceedings before Police Magistrate, St. John.
A conviction before the Police Magistrate of St. John for a breach of the bye-laws of the Corporation cannot be removed by *certiorari*, the provisions of the 36th and 37th sections of the Portand Police Act 11 Vic. c. 12, by which the *certiorari* is taken away, and an appeal given being incorporated in the St. John Police Act 12 Vic. c. 18. *Ex parte Harley*, *East. T.* 1862.

10—Assessment—Water Commissioners of St. John.
Certiorari refused to bring up an assessment of the Water Commissioners of St. John under the Act 18 Vic. c. 38, though the *certiorari* was not taken away by the Act. An appeal to the Common Council being given to persons aggrieved by the assessment. *Ex parte Nowlin*, *Trin. T.* 1864.

11—Question of Fact.
A *certiorari* will not in general be granted, when the case in the Court below depends on a mere question of fact. *Lord* v. *Turner* 2 *Han.* 13.

II.

Time of Application—Delay.

1—The time for granting a *certiorari* to remove proceedings of Trustees of Schools under Parish School Act 15 Vict. c. 40, is not limited by Act 13 Vic. c. 30, s. 2. *Ex parte Jocelyn*, 2 *All.* 637.

2—An application for a *certiorari* to remove proceedings under the Highway Act 13 Vic. c. 4, though no time is limited by law, should be made without unreasonable delay. A delay of one term held not unreasonable. *Ex parte Herbert*, 3 *All.* 108.

3—Where an appeal from a summary conviction is made to a Judge of the Court under the 1 Rev. Stat. c. 161, s. 32, and refused by him, a subsequent application to this Court for a *certiorari* should in general be made at the first term afterwards. *Ex parte O'Regan*, 3 *All.* 261.

The Court refused to interfere in such a case after the lapse of one term, where the conviction appeared to be sufficient on the merits. *Ibid.*

4—An application for a *certiorari* should be made at the first term after the conviction; but where the Justice had no jurisdiction in the matter, a *certiorari* was granted, though a term had elapsed. *Ex parte Mulhern*, 4 *All.* 259.

5—An application for a *certiorari* to remove an assessment, should be made promptly. Where a party had notice of an assessment in December, and his property was sold under execution for non-payment early in February, an application made in Easter term for a *certiorari* to remove the proceedings was refused, though the assessment appeared to have been improperly made. *Ex parte Gerow*, 4 *All.* 269.

6—When an order of affiliation was made in January 1865, but the defendant did not enter into recognizance to support the child, and in January 1866 the Sessions adjudged him to be imprisoned for not obeying the order. Held, Too late to apply for a *certiorari* to remove the proceedings for an alleged defect in the order of affiliation. *Ex parte Kennedy*, *Hil. T.* 1866.

7—Improper Entry—Delay.
Where a rule *nisi* for a *certiorari* was granted in Easter Term, and the rule improperly entered on the pleas side of the Court, in consequence of which it was discharged in Trinity Term; it is too late to renew the application in Michaelmas Term, and *Quære*, Whether it would have been granted in Trinity Term. *Robins* v. *Watts*, *Mich. T.* 1866.

8—When in time.
When an assessment was ordered on the

20th October and a rule *nisi* for a *certiorari* obtained at Chambers on 27th February returnable in Easter, the Court held the application to be in time. *Regina* v. *The Assessors of Rates, Kings*, 1 *Han.* 520.

9—Irregularity—Lateness in application.

Where the proceedings of Commissioners appointed to lay out a street under the authority of an Act of Assembly, had been filed in a public office, as directed by the Act, in November 1864, and the parties objecting to the laying out, and whose property had been taken by the Commissioners, applied to the Legislature for compensation in the following year. Held, That it was too late afterwards in 1865 to apply for a *certiorari* to bring up the proceedings of the Commissioners on the ground of irregularity. *Reg.* v. *Flewelling, East. T.* 1866.

10—Refusal to act—Payment of services.

It is no objection to the proceedings of the Commissioners that they refused to act until the Corporation of Saint John guaranteed the payment for their services, the street being in the city and the Act under which they proceeded having made no provision for paying them. *Ibid.*

III.

MISCELLANEOUS.

1—Bond before appeal—Certiorari not taken away by Act of Assembly.

The Act 18 Vic. c. 36, to prevent the traffic in intoxicating liquors, authorised a Justice of the Peace to impose fines and to order liquors to be destroyed in certain cases; and the 17th section declared that no order of the Supreme Court, or any other Court for review or removal, or other appeal from the judgment of the Justice, should be allowed, unless the appellant should give notice to the Justice of his intention to appeal, and within ten days after the conviction execute a bond with sureties to prosecute the appeal with effect, and to pay the fine and costs imposed upon him, in case the conviction was affirmed. Held, That the *certiorari* not being taken away by the Act, it was not necessary to give a bond to prosecute as a preliminary proceeding to applying for a *certiorari* to remove a conviction under the Act. *Ex parte Cliff, Mich. T.* 1856.

2—Allowing return to be amended—Ordering further Certiorari.

A *certiorari* having issued to bring up the proceedings and order made in the case of an insolvent confined debtor, the Justices stated in the return that the order was not in their possession, the return was allowed to be amended, by the Justices stating the substance of the order, if in their power to do so, or if not, by stating how the original order went out of their possession, or what has become of it, or otherwise, that a further *certiorari* might issue. *Reg.* v. *Vail, East. T.* 1861.

3—Costs—Conviction.

When a rule *nisi* for a *certiorari* to remove a conviction is discharged, the successful party is not entitled to the costs of opposing the rule. *Ex parte Daly*, 1 *All.* 435.

4—Judge in vacation.

A Judge of Supreme Court may grant a rule *nisi* for a *certiorari* returnable in Term. *Ex parte McNeill*, 3 *All.* 493.

5—Special provision in Act.

A Judge in vacation has no authority to make an order to shew cause in Term why a *certiorari* should not issue to remove proceedings under the Act 13 Vic. c. 53. *Ex parte Irvine*, 2 *All.* 516.

6—Short Service—Enlarging Rule.

Where an order *nisi* for a *certiorari* had been served only four days before the first day of the term at which it was returnable, the Court refused to make the rule absolute, and enlarged it till the next term. *Ex parte Lyons, Mich. T.* 1865.

7—Security for costs—School Act—Provisions of other Act—Application of.

The provisions in the School Act 21 Vic. c. 9, s. 16, that the proceedings for levying and collecting assessments shall be the same as provided for County and Parish rates, applies to the mode, machinery and forms by which these rates are levied and collected, and does not require security to be given for costs before a *certiorari* is granted to remove the assessment, nor give an appeal to the Sessions, as provided in the case of County rates by the Rev. Stat. c. 53, ss. 6, 22. *Reg.* v. *Jardine, Mich. T.* 1863.

8—The provisions of 1 Rev. Stat. c. 53, s. 6, requiring security for costs before granting a *certiorari* to remove a rate is not incorporated in the Parish School

Act. *Reg.* v. *Assessors of Rates, King's County*, 1 *Han.* 520.

9—Return not under seal—Objection.
A party appearing to support a conviction cannot object to the cause being proceeded with, because the Justice's return to the *certiorari* is not under seal. *Regina* v. *Oulton*, 1 *All.* 269.

10—Application to Judge at Chambers—Practice.
On an application to a Judge at Chambers for a *certiorari*, there should be a summons or rule *nisi* in the first instance. *Ex parte Howell*, 1 *All.* 584.

11—Contradictory Affidavits.
Where the affidavits in answer to an application for a *certiorari* to remove the proceedings in a prosecution under the Act 5 Wm. 4, c. 2, for non-performance of statute labour, stated that the party had been *duly notified*; the Court made the rule absolute in order to ascertain what the notice was—the applicant in his affidavit having denied notice. *Ex parte Ferguson*, 1 *All.* 663.

12—Return from Justice.
A return from Justice should be before the Court. See *Lord* v. *Turner*, 2 *Han.* 13.

13—Renewal of application.
When a rule for a *certiorari* is discharged because the affidavits are improperly entitled, the application may be renewed on amended affidavits. *Ex parte Bustin*, 2 *All.* 211.

14—Refusal.
An application for *certiorari* was refused where three former applications had failed, twice in consequence of a defect in the jurat of the affidavit, and once in consequence of the rule having been improperly granted by a Judge at Chambers. *Ex parte Irvine*, 2 *All.* 519.

15—Copies of proceedings—Return.
It is the duty of School Trustees to keep a minute of their proceedings, and if the original orders have been filed with the Clerk of the Peace or Assessors, copies may be returned with the *certiorari*. *Ex parte Jocelyn*, 2 *All.* 637.

16—Mistake in name of applicant—Quashing—Ordering new Certiorari.
Where the Christian name of the applicant for a *certiorari* was misstated in the writ, it was quashed, and a new *certiorari* ordered to issue. *Reg.* v. *Watters*, *Hil. T.* 1866.

17—Affidavits—When may be used.
After the return of a *certiorari*, affidavits may be used to shew want of jurisdiction in the Justice, when that fact does not appear on the return. *Reg.* v. *Simmons*, *Trin. T.* 1872.

18—Returnable when—Practice.
By the practice of the Court a *certiorari* is returnable (unless otherwise ordered) at the term next after that in which the rule for it is granted; and if not issued and served before such term, it is too late. *Reg.* v. *Harshman*, *Mich. T.* 1872.

19—Contradicting Return—Use of affidavits.
The affidavits on which a *certiorari* was obtained cannot be referred to, for the purpose of contradicting the return. *Ibid.*

(See Allen's Notes to The King *v.* Justices of York. C. Ms. 110.)

Statute 13, Geo. 2, c. 18 not in force. See British Statutes.

CESTUI QUE TRUST.

Relation of Trustee and Cestui que Trust created. See Equity 2 *a*.

CHALLENGE.

See Jury.

To fight a Duel.
Whether a letter be a challenge to fight a duel or not, left as question for the jury. It is no objection that the question has been left to them when their finding accords with the Judge's own opinion. *Dolby* v. *Kinnear*, 1 *Kerr* 480.

CHAMBER PRACTICE.

Attendance of competent agent—Taking out summons—One sufficient for attendance. See General Rules 9, 63.

CHATTEL.

Unregistered ship—Transfer—Revesting property—evidence. See Shipping Law 6.

Trees severed from land. See Assumpsit 49.

Manure, a chattel. See Trover 15, 16.

CHECK.

1—An unstamped check drawn upon a person, not being a chartered or licensed banker, or the manager of a savings' bank, is void under the Canadian Statute 31 Vic. c. 9, and cannot be received as evidence of payment. *Gandy* v. *Staples*, 1 *Han.* 615.

2—Initialing of by Cashier—Acceptance—Set-off.
In an action on a bill of exchange, the defendant claimed to set off the amount of a check payable to "bearer," drawn by one L. upon the plaintiffs, several years previously, upon which their cashier had written the initials of his name. In 1867 L. gave the check so initialed to G. who kept it till a few days before the trial of this cause (1871,) and then gave it to the defendant. Held, 1st, That if the check could be treated as an inland bill of exchange, the initialing of it did not operate as an acceptance within the statute. 2nd, That even if the initialing of the check could operate as an agreement by the plaintiffs to pay the amount to L., it was only a chose in action which the defendant could not avail himself of in this suit. *Commercial Bank* v. *Fleming*, *Hil. T.* 1872.

CHILD.

See Illegitimate Child.

CHOSE IN ACTION.

Recognition of assignment.
B. agreed, by a note in writing, to pay A. £20, in lumber, by a certain day, before which time A. assigned the contract to C. Held, That B. was not bound to recognize the assignment, but might deliver the timber to A. which would be a good discharge. See *Green* v. *Williston*, 3 *Kerr* 58.

Check operating as an agreement by plaintiff to pay amount. See Check 2.

CHURCH OF ENGLAND.

1—Land granted as a Glebe—Trespass—Right of Rector.
Where land is granted to the Rector, Church Wardens and Vestry of a Parish, incorporated under the Act 29 Geo. 3, c. 1, as a glebe for the use of the Rector, and he has been inducted and taken possession, an action of trespass for entering on the land and cutting down trees, must be brought in the name of the Rector. *Rector &c. of St. Stephens* v. *Tortelot*, 1 *Kerr* 537.

2—Style—No Rector appointed—Grant.
A Church Corporation may exist under the Act 29 Geo. 3, c. 1, by the style of "the Rector, Church Wardens and Vestry of &c.," though no Rector has at the time been appointed, and a grant to the Corporation by that name is good. *Doe dem. Rector &c. of Queensbury* v. *Guion*, 1 *All.* 6.

3—Powers of Church Wardens and Vestry.
The Church Wardens and Vestry may exercise the powers given to the Rector, Church Wardens and Vestry by the Act 29 Geo. 3, c. 1, as well where there never has been a Rector appointed, as where a vacancy is created by the death or absence of the Rector. *Ibid.*

4—Grant—Intention.
A grant of land to the Rector, Church Wardens and Vestry of a Parish "for a glebe," sufficiently indicates that it is intended to be for the use and benefit of the Rector under the Act 56 Geo. 3, c. 11. *Rector &c. of Hampton* v. *Titus*, 1 *All.* 278.

5—Rector—Incumbency—Legal Estate.
Under the provisions of the Act 56 Geo. 3, c. 11, the Rector of a Parish has, during his incumbency, a legal estate of freehold in glebe lands granted to the Church Corporation, and may make leases thereof, binding upon himself, without the assent of the Corporation. (Street J., *dissentiente.*) *Ibid.*

6—Lease by Rector.
Quære, Whether a lease of glebe lands by the Rector and Church Corporation for a term not exceeding 21 years would be binding on a succeeding Rector? Held, Per Street J., that it would. *Semble*, Per Carter J., that the lease should be confirmed by the Ordinary. *Ibid.*

7—Property in Trees—Trover.
The property in the trees growing on glebe lands is in the Church Corporation as the owners of the inheritance, and they may maintain trover for them, if wrongfully severed, against a tenant of the Rector, or any person acting under the tenant's authority. *Ibid.*

8—Statute.
Quære, Whether the statute 13 Eliz. c. 10, relating to leases by ecclesiastical persons, applies to Church Corporations in this Province. *Bedell* v. *The Rector &c. of Fredericton*, 3 *All.* 217.

9—No Rector—Action in name of Church Corporation.
An action of trespass for injury to a Parish Church may be brought in the name

of the Church Corporation in the absence of evidence of there being a legally inducted Rector. *Rector &c. of St. George's Church* v. *Cougle*, 1 *Han.* 609.

10—Closing Church—Unlawful act.
In an action of trespass for boarding up the doors and windows of a church, the defendants justified as Church Wardens, and that they had closed the church for repairs; but it was proved that they closed it to prevent a clergyman, who claimed to be Rector, from officiating there. Held, That even if the defendants were Church Wardens and there was no Rector, they had no right to close the church against other members of the corporation, or to prevent public worship being held there. *Ibid.*

11—Vacant Rectory—Right of presentation.
Prior to the Act 32 Vic. c. 6, the Lieut. Governor of the Province had by virtue of the Queen's prerogative, and the laws relating to the Church of England in this Province, the right to collate and to present to a vacant rectory. *Doe dem. Rector of St. George's Church* v. *Cougle*, 2 *Han.* 96.

12—Rector—Rents of Glebe—Liability to assessment.
Under the Act 26 Vic. c. 35, which exempts from taxation the income of the inhabitants of Fredericton derived from real or personal property, the Rector of the Parish is not liable to be assessed upon the income derived from the rents of his glebe. *Lee* v. *Mayor of Fredericton*, *East. T.* 1873.

CHURCH CORPORATION.

See Church of England.

CHURCH WARDENS.

See Church of England.

CITY COURT.

Practice in judgment by default.
A practice in the City Court of St. John of awarding to the plaintiff on judgment by default, the amount claimed in his particulars of demand filed at that time, without any proof of the amount, or any copy of the particulars served on the defendant, is bad, and cannot be rendered valid by the length of time the City Court has been in existence; neither is this practice confirmed by the Act 5 Wm. 4, c. 45, s. 7, never having been allowed by any superior legal tribunal before the passing of that Act. *Allen* v. *Mackay*, 1 *All.* 365.

CITY COUNCILLOR.

Election—Disqualification.
A contractor with the Commissioners of the Alms House for the County of York, is disqualified from being elected a City Councillor in Fredericton, under the Act 22 Vic. c. 8. *Ex parte Cameron*, 1 *Han.* 306.

CITY OF FREDERICTON.

See Fredericton (City of.)

COGNOVIT.

See Warrant of Attorney.

1—Costs—Estoppel.
Where a defendant has given a confession of judgment for £50, he is estopped from requiring that summary costs should be taxed, although the sum really due and for which execution is to issue, be under £20. *Foster* v. *Brown*, 1 *Kerr* 200.

2—Conditions—Liberty to enter up judgment.
By the terms of a cognovit it was agreed that in default of payment of a certain sum on a particular day, with costs to be taxed, the plaintiff should be at liberty to enter up judgment and sue out execution for such sum and costs. Held, That there was no forfeiture of the cognovit until the costs were taxed, and the amount made known to the defendant. *Snodgrass* v. *Wilson*, 1 *All.* 373.

3—Waiver.
A cognovit may be given before declaration filed, and is a waiver of any irregularity in the previous proceedings. *McNamee* v. *O'Brien*, 4 *All.* 548.

Motion to set aside—Dismissal—Costs. See Costs 85.

Costs. See Costs 19.

COLLECTOR OF CUSTOMS.

Liability for accidental fire destroying goods detained after request. See Action on the Case I. 1.

COMMISSIONER.

Of Highways.
See Justice of the Peace (Summary Conviction.)

See Action at Law (Notice) XI. 13, 14.
" Highways.
" Trespass V. 6.

Of Insolvency—Affinity—Disqualification.
A commissioner appointed to examine confined debtors, was held disqualified from holding an examination in a case in which the plaintiff was a first cousin to his wife. *Peck* v. *Barberie*, 1 *Han.* 115.

Commissioners of European and North American Railway—Duty of—Damage to land—Prevention of—Right of Action against. See Damages 30.

1—Of Sewers.
The acts of Commissioners of Sewers appointed under the Act 22 Vic. c. 53, are not judicial acts, therefore they are not disqualified from assessing the proprietors of land for the purposes of the Act, by reason of their being interested as owners of land in the district assessed. (Ritchie, J., *dissentiente.*) *Ex parte Calhoun*, *Hil. T.* 1863.

2—An owner of land in Germantown Lake District is disqualified from acting as a Commissioner of Sewers for that district, the duties of such Commissioners under the Act 22 Vic. c. 53, being of a judicial character—per Ritchie, C. J., and Weldon, J. Per Allen, J., That the Court was bound by the decision in *ex parte* Calhoun that the Commissioners were not disqualified by reason of their interest. (But see Act 32 Vic. c. 73.) *Reg.* v. *Commissioners of Germantown Lake*, 1 *Han.* 343.

3—A Commissioner of Sewers who is interested in a contract for the performance of work done under the Commissioners, is disqualified from acting with the other Commissioners in the approval of the work; and if he does so, an assessment on the proprietors of land, in which an amount for payment of such work is included, is bad. *Ibid.*

4—The intention of the Act 32 Vic. c. 73, being to remove the disqualification of Commissioners of Sewers, by reason of their being interested in the lands in the District to be assessed; it necessarily includes the interest of a Commissioner arising from relationship to a proprietor of such lands. *Ex parte Peck*, *Hil. T.* 1871.

5—**Swearing in of—Assessment without—Effect.**
By 1 Rev. Stat. c. 17, Commissioners of Sewers shall be sworn into office within one week after their election, or shall be deemed to have refused. Held, That the Act was imperative, and that a Commissioner elected on the 2nd August could not be legally sworn in on the 8th September—the office at that time being vacant; and that his joining with the other Commissioners in making an assessment, rendered it void. *Reg.* v. *Commissioners of Hopewell*, *Trin. T.* 1872.

6—*Semble*, That if an objection is made to a proposed assessment by the Commissioners of Sewers, and some of the proprietors of lands in the District give an undertaking to the Commissioners to indemnify them against all damages and costs in case they make the assessment, and they afterwards proceed with it, the assessment will be set aside. *Ibid.*

Commissioner to take affidavits in Supreme Court—Authority to administer Oaths. See Criminal Law II. 21.

Commissioners of Water Company—Owner of land—Compensation—Assessment of Damages—Proceedings—Construction of Act 2 Wm. 4, cap. 26—Application for Mandamus—Failure—Renewal of Motion. See Mandamus 11

COMMISSION MERCHANT.

See Warranty 5.

COMMON CARRIER.

See Carrier.

COMMON COUNTS.

See Assumpsit.

Recovery Under. See Assumpsit.

Counsel not claiming under common count in opening case. Right to recover under particulars. See Trial *Carrick* v. *Atkinson.*

COMMON SCHOOL ACT 1871.

Trustees—Duty—Inspectors authority.
If a requisition is made to the Trustees of Schools by a majority of the ratepayers of a district, to call a special meeting for a purpose authorized by "the Common School Act 1871," it is their duty to call the meeting under the 28th sec. of the Act; and if they refuse, the Inspec-

tor is authorised to appoint new Trustees, under the 37th sec. of the Act. *Ex parte Gilbert, Hil. T.* 1873.

Inspector—Appointing Trustees.
The Inspector of schools is authorized on a proper requisition made under the 37th sec. of "The Common School Act 1871," to appoint a new Trustee, either where a Trustee elected declines to accept the office; or, where after acceptance of it, he declines to do his duty. *Ex parte Kilby, Hil. T.* 1873.

Constitutionality—Non-sectarian.
The Parish School Act, (21 Vic. c. 9,) conferred no legal right upon any class of persons, with respect to Denominational Schools; therefore "The Common School Act 1871," which declares, that the schools conducted under its provisions shall be non-sectarian, is not *ultra vires*, as being contrary to "The British N. rth America Act 1867," s. 93. *Ex parte Renaud, Hil. T.* 1873.

Regulations—Effect of.
The constitutionality of "The Common School Act 1871," cannot be affected by any Regulations of the Board of Education, made under its authority; and, *Semble*, If the Board of Education have made regulations which they ought not to have made, or have not made regulations which they should have made—it is a case within sub-sec. 4 of "The British North America Act 1867," s. 93. *Ibid.*

ASSESSMENT FOR SCHOOL PURPOSES.

See Assessment II.

COMPARISON OF HANDWRITING.

See Evidence XI. 16. Practice in Equity 30.

COMPETENCY.

See Witness.

COMPOSITION—AGREEMENT.

See Bills and Notes V. 9.

COMPOSITION DEED.

See Deed. See Insolvent Debtor.

COMPULSORY LIQUIDATION.

Petition—Hearing of before Judge of County Court. See Insolvent Act of 1869.

CONDITION.

See Covenant 8. See Crown Grant II. 1.
" Deed I. 25. " Insurance.
" Pleading.

CONDITION PRECEDENT.

See Vendor and Purchaser.
" Landlord and Tenant.

1—Loss payable after proof.
The following clause in a marine policy of assurance, viz: "and in case of loss, such loss to be paid in sixty days after proof of loss and adjustment, and proof of interest in the said assured," has the operation of a condition precedent; and the judgment was arrested in an action by the assured against the insurer for the want of any averment in the declaration, that such preliminary proof had been furnished to or dispensed with by the defendant. *Watson* v. *Summers*, 2 *Kerr* 101.

Arbitration before Action. See Action at Law II.

2—Tender of Deed.
The defendant gave a bond to the plaintiff for the price of land, conditioned to pay £50 on the 1st June 1849, and the remainder in three annual instalments; and on making the first payment and receiving a deed from the plaintiff, to give a mortgage for the balance. Held, That a tender of a deed was not a condition precedent to the right to recover the first instalment. *Dykeman* v. *Craig*, 2 *All.* 265.

3—Where A. agreed to sell B. a piece of land, and B. agreed to pay £100 for the the same on or before 1st May, on payment whereof A. agreed to give B. a deed free from all incumbrances—Held, That A. was entitled to recover against B. for non-payment of the money, without proof of tender of the deed on or before the 1st May. *Hanford* v. *Gidney*, 1 *Kerr* 82.

4—Payment of costs—Insolvent debtor.
Payment of costs on failure of a previous application, not made a condition precedent to a second application. See *McFarlane* v. *Gordon*, 2 *All.* 201.

Contract—Driving logs—Performance. See Pleading I. 23.

Award—Concurrent Acts. See Arbitration V. 10.

Cognovit—Taxing Costs—Forfeiture. See Cognovit.

CONDITION IN RESTRAINT OF MARRIAGE.

See Will 8.

CONFESSION.

See Cognovit. See Criminal Law.

CONFUSION OF GOODS.

See Trover 26. Replevin 20.

CONSENT RULE.

See Ejectment VII.

CONSIDERATION.

See Assignment — Assumpsit — Bills and Notes—Contract—Declaration — Deed—Fraudulent Conveyance — Guarantee — Insurance—Pleading—Usury.

1—Executory promise—Compensation for injury.

An agreement, whereby B. who had permission to cut down a certain quantity of pine timber on public land belonging to the Crown, assigns his right and interest to A. by way of compensation for an injury he had done to A., being entered into without the privity or assent of the Crown is illegal and void, and no action can be maintained by A. against B. for continuing to cut timber on such land contrary to his promise contained in such agreement. The assignment being void, the promise was no more than an executory accord, for the breach of which no action lies. *Sharp* v. *McKeen*, 2 *Kerr* 524.

2—Forbearance.

On motion in arrest of judgment. Held, That the agreeing to forbear sending a substitute to exercise the plaintiff's rights in a schooner, of which he and defendant and others were possessed as part owners, is a good consideration to support a promise by the defendant to pay the plaintiff his proportion of the profits. *Murray* v. *Seelye*, 3 *Kerr* 212.

3—Value—Equality.

In order to constitute a valuable consideration to support a conveyance, it is not necessary that the money paid should be of equal value with the property conveyed; provided the transaction is *bona fide*. *Payson* v. *Good*, 3 *Kerr* 272.

4—Mutuality—Want of.

A. by deed poll agreed to make and haul all the timber he could find on B.'s permit, for which B. was to allow him whatever the timber sold for, after deducting B.'s supply bill and expenses, and that all the timber got should be the property of B. Held, That there was no mutuality, and that B. acquired no property in the timber without a delivery. *Coombes* v. *Hatheway*, 3 *Kerr* 592.

5—Illegal contract—Subsequent repeal of Statute.

A sale of liquor (not by a licensed manufacturer or agent) being illegal by the Act 15 Vic. c. 51, is not made good by a subsequent repeal of the Act. *Dever* v. *Corcoran*, 3 *All.* 338.

The original contract being illegal, a promise to pay, made after the repeal of the Act, is void for want of a consideration. *Ibid.*

Quære, If the liquor had been in the defendant's possession at the time of the subsequent promise, whether the plaintiff could have recovered? *Ibid.*

6—Valuable consideration—Deed.

To constitue a valuable consideration to support a deed, it is not necessary that it should be a money consideration: becoming bail for the grantor is sufficient. *Crockford* v. *Equitable Insurance Company*, *Mich. T.* 1863.

7—Lien—Parting with.

Parting with property on which the plaintiff has a lien, may be a good consideration to support an express promise, but not an implied one. See *Hartley* v. *Fisher*, 1 *All.* 439.

8—Evidence—Explanatory of consideration—Admission of—Contribution.

The plaintiff having purchased land from D. in May 1845, took a deed thereof to himself, and gave a mortgage thereon for the purchase money, as was stated by D. at the trial, and also the joint and several promissory notes of himself and the defendant, no stipulation having been made with D. for the security of the defendant. After the purchase, the defendant claimed and exercised a part ownership on the land. Afterwards, in March 1846, the plaintiff gave a conveyance of an undivided moiety of the land to the defendant, expressed to be "in consideration of £150 to the plaintiff in hand well and truly paid, the receipt whereof was thereby acknowledged." The subscribing witness was admitted to state that no money was paid at the time of the execution of the deed from the plaintiff to the defendant, but nothing whatever was then said about the purchase from DeVeber, or the defendant's joint liability on the notes. The plaintiff having afterwards paid the amount of one of the notes to D., brought an action for contribution on the ground that the purchase was made from D. for the joint interest of plaintiff and defendant, and the defendant was a principal and not a surety on the note. Held, (Parker J., *dissentiente*,) That he was entitled to recover, and that it might be inferred from the circumstances that the original purchase was on joint account; and that the plaintiff's acknowledgment of payment for the moiety in the deed might be explained by circumstances tending to shew that the condition was made up of the defendant's outstanding liability on the note, so as to leave it a question for the jury to say whether the consideration was so satisfied. *Reed* v *McClelan*, 1 *All.* 81.

9—Sheriff's sale of goods—Agreement as to bidding—Recovery of difference on re-sale.
Defendant being an execution creditor of the plaintiff, agreed with him that two persons named, were to bid in certain articles at the sheriff's sale, and if they were not bid up to near their value, that these persons and the plaintiff were to sell them within a certain time, and the plaintiff was to have the benefit of any advance in the price over the sheriff's sale. The goods were bid in, and sales of them afterwards made under the agreement at an advance. Held, That there was a sufficient consideration for the agreement and that the plaintiff could recover the difference on the re-sale. *Fraser* v. *Desbrisay Trin. T.* 1866.

CONSIGNEE.

Representations made by—Liability. See Warranty.

CONSTABLE.

See Action at Law (Notice of Action.)

1—Mileage.
Not entitled to, under Justice's Act, for each defendant, when more than one, unless he actually and necessarily travels twice to effect the service of summons. *Jordan* v. *Coates*, 2 *All.* 107.

Certified Fees—Right to recover.
See Criminal Law.

2—Refusing to Arrest—False Return—Liability.
A constable is liable in an Action on the Case at the suit of the bail in a cause in a Justice's Court for refusing to arrest the defendant on an execution issued by the Justice in that cause, and making a false return thereto, in consequence of which the bail were sued and compelled to pay the debt. *Power* v. *Stephenson*, *Hil. T.* 1861.

3—Breaking open doors—Warrant.
A constable has no right to break open the doors of a dwelling house to execute a warrant issued against the owner of the house, on a conviction for selling spirituous liquors without license. *Smith* v. *Burpee*, *Mich. T.* 1872.

4—Arresting Debtor—Duty as to levy on goods first.
A constable is liable in trespass, if he arrests a debtor under an execution issued out of a Justice's Court (1 Rev. Stat. c. 137) before he has used reasonable diligence to find goods to levy on. Where the debtor points out property to the constable, it is his duty to seize it, unless he has reasonable grounds for believing that it does not belong to the debtor, and this question should be left to the jury. *Hunter* v. *Maddox*, 1 *Han.* 162.

5—Notice of Action.
A constable appointed by the Sessions, under the Rev. Stat. c. 56, and acting under the Justice's Act 1 Rev. Stat. c. 137, is entitled to notice of action. *Robichcau* v. *Arsineau*, *East. T.* 1864. See further Action at Law (Notice of Action.)

When not entitled to Notice.
When executing process in which he is plaintiff. See Action at Law XI. 12.

CONTEMPT.

Commitment for—Justices Court.

See Nonsuit 11. See Attachment.

Power of Justices to commit for.
Justices of the Peace acting judicially are judges of record, and have power to commit to prison orally without warrant, for contempt committed in the face of the Court. *Armstrong* v. *McCaffrey*, 1 *Han.* 517.

They have no power to commit to lock-up house where that place is intended as a place merely of temporary security until prisoner can be taken to gaol. *Ibid.*

Witness in Contempt. See Attachment.

CONTINUING SECURITY.

See Warrant of Attorney.

CONTINUANCES.

Amending Roll by Entry of. See Amendment III.

After interlocutory judgment continuances may be entered at any time before final judgment. *McDonald* v. *Upton*, 3 *Kerr* 565.

CONTRACT.

See Agreement.

Parties disabling themselves from Performing—Recovery on Common Counts. See Assumpsit 52.

Immediate right of action attaching. See Action at Law IV.

Rescinding of—Can only be rescinded by the consent of all the parties contracting. See Action at Law 15.

Acquiescence — Deviation — Recovery on Common Counts. See Assumpsit 42.

Fixtures—Effect of Contract as to Gas Fittings. See Fixtures.

Contract under Seal—Partnership—Property—Liability of Firm. See Partnership 5.

Contract with Society supposed to be incorporated. See Equity 5.

Corporation—Entering into Contract under Seal—Estoppel. See Contract 12.

1—Sale—Vesting of Property—Sufficient delivery.
Defendant agreed to purchase from plaintiff for $800 the machinery of a mill, which was partly covered with sand, and paid him earnest money to bind the bargain. About ten days afterwards, the plaintiff signed a writing by which he guaranteed that certain of the machinery (specified) was under the surface of the ground where the mill had stood, and agreed to deliver all the machinery belonging to the mill for $800, and acknowledged the receipt of $2 on account of the sale. He afterwards made a formal delivery of part of the machinery in the name of the whole, but the defendant refused to take it unless it was put on the surface of the ground. Held, That the title to the machinery vested in the defendant by the verbal agreement when the earnest money was paid, no act remaining to be done by the plaintiff but that if by the writing any delivery was necessary, the plaintiff had made a sufficient delivery, and was not bound to put the machinery on the surface of the ground. *Allingham* v. *O'Mahoney*, *East. T.* 1873.

2—Construction of—Usage—Evidence.
Defendant having agreed to sell timber to the plaintiffs, made out and delivered to them an account charging them with the timber, "to be delivered by J. A.," and crediting them with a promissory note for the price. J. A. had no timber belonging to the defendant, but he accepted an order drawn by him for the delivery of the timber to the plaintiffs, on the defendant's promise that it should be in his (J. A.'s) hands at the time the plaintiffs required it. In an action against the defendant for not delivering the timber, (J. A. never having received it) the defendant gave evidence of a general usage in the timber trade by which the acceptors of such orders were alone responsible to the purchasers; and the plaintiffs gave evidence denying such usage. Held, 1st, That the defendant was liable to the plaintiffs on his contract for not delivering the timber, and that the jury were properly directed that there was no such proof of usage as would discharge him from his liability. 2nd, That the acceptance was only a prospective delivery order, designating the medium through which the timber was to be delivered, and that unless J. A. received it for delivery to the plaintiffs, they could not maintain any action against him on his acceptance. 3rd, That the contract was contained in the account signed by the defendant, and no time for the delivery being therein specified, it was properly declared on as a contract to deliver in a reasonable time. *Rankin* v. *Godard*, 4 *All.* 155.

Plaintiffs in their *prima facie* case having proved only the contract to sell and the breach. Held, That they could give evidence to rebut the usage set up by the defendant. *Ibid.*

3—Custom not affecting contract—Scowage—Loading ship.
Where a contract was made to load a ship for $1.60 per standard by the lump, and part of the load was brought alongside in wood-boats, the contract was held not affected by a custom of the port of Saint John, that in such case the amount of the

scowage went to the shipper. *McNichol* v. *Peck*, 1 *Han.* 428.

4—Property, in whom belonging—Debiting in Books.

S., who was building a ship for plaintiffs, being indebted to them, agreed to transfer the vessel to H., one of the plaintiffs, together with all materials for construction then procured, S. to finish the vessel at his own cost, and rig and equip her with rigging to be provided by plaintiff. The vessel, when finished, to be registered in the name of H. Canvas, cordage and wire were procured by L. at plaintiffs store; and while being prepared for the vessel were taken by the sheriff under an execution against S., when $150 worth of labor had been expended upon them. Held, That under the agreement the property in the sails and rigging remained in plaintiffs, and that the fact of the articles being charged to S. in plaintiffs' books was not conclusive to show a sale to S., but was a question for the jury. That the plaintiff was entitled to recover the value of the sails and rigging when taken. *Rankin et. al.* v. *Mitchell*, 1 *Han.* 495.

5—Guarantee—Considered as absolute contract.

The defendants entered into a written contract with T., by which he was to deliver them a quantity of lumber at a certain time. They afterwards agreed with the plaintiff to transfer to her the balance of lumber coming from T., for which they acknowledged to have received payment in full from the plaintiff, and guaranteed to see the lumber delivered at the time specified in the agreement with T. Held, That this was an absolute contract by the defendants to deliver the lumber; and not a guarantee that T. should deliver it, and that the plaintiff had nothing to do with T.'s contract except to ascertain the time of delivery. *Lindsay* v. *Rose*, 3 *Kerr* 576.

6—Partly written—Partly parol.

When a contract is to be made out partly by written documents, and partly by parol evidence, the whole becomes a question for the jury. *Macpherson* v. *Fredericton Boom Company*, 1 *Han.* 337.

7—Implied contract—Stevedore paying expenses.

There is no implied contract between the shipper of deals and the stevedore (who is employed by the owner of the vessel and undertakes to bring the deals from the wharf,) that the stevedore shall pay the expense of wood-boats employed by the shipper to bring part of the deals to the vessel. *Ward* v. *McNichol*, 3 *All.* 490.

8—Acceptance of offer of Logs—Extent of.

Plaintiffs on the 16th May 1854 made the following proposal to the defendant: "We hereby offer you our stock of spruce and pine logs, to be delivered to you at the usual place of delivery at Indiantown, with all possible despatch from Washademoak lake, at the rate of," etc., which the defendants accepted in the following terms: "We hereby accept your offer for all the logs that you will have during the season." The season for receiving logs from the Washedemoak lake was from about the 1st May to the 1st November. Held, That the agreement applied to all logs which the plaintiffs owned or had contracted for at the date of their offer. *Polley* v. *Waterhouse*, 3 *All.* 291.

Quære, Whether the defendant's acceptance would not extend the agreement to all the logs which the plaintiffs might have during the season in the ordinary course of their business. *Ibid.*

9—Construction—Authority—Question of law for Judge.

D. who resided at Fredericton, had dealings in lumber with F., who resided at Providence, R. I. D. wrote to F. asking him to join with him in the purchase at a price named, on joint account, of certain laths to be manufactured by M. F. telegraphed in reply, "Take the laths." M. was unable to manufacture without supplies; and I. at a meeting of E. M. and I., agreed to supply M., the laths cut by M. to belong to I. from the time they left the saw. I. being shewn the contents of the letter and telegram, agreed to furnish the laths to D. at the price named therein. The laths were delivered to D. and shipped by him to F., who sold them on joint account. Held, Fisher, J. *dissentiente*, In an action against D. and F. for the price of the laths, that D. had authority from F. to purchase from I. on joint account, the laths purchased being those cut by M. and referred to in the letter. That the authority being in writing, whether D. had authority to purchase or not was a question of law for the Judge to determine, and not for the jury. *Inches* v. *Fogg and Dowling*, 2 *Han.* 149.

10—Extra work—Special provisions.
Plaintiff agreed to build a house for defendant for £3,250, and that no allowance beyond that sum should be made for extra work or alterations, unless orders therefor in writing should be given by the architect in charge. During the progress of the work the plaintiff made alterations in the building by the verbal directions of the architect. After the building was finished, the architect made a valuation of the additional work and of certain omissions, deducting the latter from the former, and certified the balance to be due to the plaintiff. Held, That unless the defendant had dispensed with the proviso in the contract about the extra work, or had ordered the work to be done, or authorised the architect to do so, the plaintiff could not recover the amount. *Small* v. *McCullough*, 3 *All.* 484

Semble, That the defendant was not bound to pay the whole £3,250 unless the contract was fully performed, and that the value of any work left undone should have been deducted from the contract price, and the extra work stand on its own merits. *Ibid.*

11—Demand and refusal—Breach.
The defendant for value received promised to deliver the plaintiff 30 chaldrons of coal on demand. The only demand on the defendant and the only refusal by him to deliver the coal, was a refusal to allow the plaintiff to put the coal on board a certain vessel of which defendant claimed to be the owner, though he offered to deliver the coal to the plaintiff who refused to receive it, unless he was allowed to put it on board the vessel. Held, That as there was no contract about the vessel, the defendant's refusal was no breach of the agreement to deliver the coal. *Quære*, Whether such an agreement is within 1 Rev. Stat. c. 116. *Vanbuskirk* v. *Green*, 1 *Han.* 25.

12—Presumption—Re-survey of lumber.
Lumber sold and delivered subject to re-survey,—presumed to be according to provisions of Statute. See Rankin *v.* Emery, *Ber.* 330.

13—Fulfilment of—Accord and satisfaction—Settlement binding.
Defendant agreed to deliver plaintiff 100 tons of timber, of a specified size and quality, at a certain time. He delivered 101 tons, partly within the time, but not of the size and quality required. Disputes having arisen respecting it, and also as to the defendant's liability to pay the expense of putting the timber in shipping order, it was agreed between them that if the defendant would pay this expense, the plaintiff would allow the timber at 89 tons at the contract price. In an action for non-delivery of the timber, it was left to the jury, whether the plaintiff had agreed to receive the timber, and waive all claim for damages for breach of the contract; and the jury having found in the affirmative. Held, No misdirection—and that the performance of the contract being in controversy between the parties, such a settlement was binding—the defendant's agreement to pay for trimming the timber, being a sufficient consideration for the plaintiff's promise. *Semble*, That what took place between the parties, might be treated as an accord and satisfaction of the plaintiff's demand. *Turner* v. *Keiver*, 1 *Han.* 91.

14—When binding on parties—Enforceable in Equity—Statute of frauds—Substituted contract—Pleading—Infant—Party to suit.
C. (Plaintiff's mother) and M., daughters of S., were entitled to certain real estate in right of their mother, who died in 1826. S. married again, and subsequently in 1841, made a will whereby he provided that C. and M. should each receive £1000 on their marriage, and that when his youngest son became of age, an equal share with his other children, of his property should be invested for their benefit; after the death of either, her share to be divided amongst her children, the child to represent the parent in any division of property; no share to be deemed to have vested until paid, with the proviso that C. and M. should not be entitled to any benefit under his will unless they ratified his acts relative to their mother's real estate. In 1844, by deed in consideration of the legacies and provisions made for them by the last will and testament of S. they conveyed to him their real estate. C. married in 1847, and died in 1851. In 1852, S. revoked the provisions in his will in favour of C. bequeathing the plaintiff £1000 on his coming of age. In 1858 S. died. Held, 1st, That S. could not revoke the provisions in favour of his daughters in his first will, and that the transaction was a contract capable of be-

ing enforced in equity. 2nd, That there was a sufficiently signed contract to satisfy the Statute of Frauds. 3rd, That the fact of C. having received certain advances from S., after her marriage, was no proof to establish a substituted contract. 4th, That during coverture C. could not enter into a contract to abandon the rights she acquired under the will of S. 5th, That the provisions in the will for the benefit of C. inured for the benefit of the plaintiff her son. 6th, That the plaintiff's infancy was no bar to his enforcing the contract, as he was entitled during infancy to the interest of his mother's share. 7th, That in equity a party who intends to rely on the Statute of Frauds must specially plead it or raise the objection in his answer. 8th, That under 17 Vict. cap. 18, it was not necessary for M. to be a party to the suit. *Gilpin* v. *Scovil*, 1 *Han.* 379.

15—With Partnership or personally—Question for jury on whole evidence.

Where A. brings assumpsit for money had and received, against B., who defends on the ground that he is answerable to the representatives of A.'s deceased partner, and the testimony thereof is to be gathered from the entitling of accounts, the address of letters, as also from other circumstances. Held, That it was properly left to the jury on the whole evidence to determine whether B. had contracted with the firm, or personally with A. *Raymond* v. *Hay*, 1 *Kerr* 99.

16—Statute of Frauds—Operation of—Year.

A contract, not in writing, entered into on the 26th May, for the supply of a regiment with groceries for a year from the 1st June following, subject to be sooner determined in case the regiment should leave the Province, is void under Statute of Frauds. *Reed* v. *Harding*, 2 *Han.* 137.

17—Bill of Lading—Entire contract.

As a general rule the bill of lading, though containing different descriptions of goods belonging to the same person, is considered as an entire contract. *Neill* v. *Reid*, 4 *All.* 246.

18—Specific performance—Lapse of time.

Though in equity, time is not always the essence of a contract: *Semble*, That after a delay of four years, specific performance will not in general be decreed. *Purves* v. *Hume*, 3 *All.* 299. (See Equity 2.)

19—Want of acquiescence in terminating contract.

Where A. delivered timber to B., under an agreement that B. should ship as much as he could, and give A. credit for the amount, and B. having shipped what he thought fit, and given notice to A. to take away the remainder, and subsequent to such notice shipped a further quantity. Held, In the absence of any proof of acquiescence in such notice by A., that B. was not liable in an action of trover for the quantity shipped after the notice. *Hughes* v. *Sutherland*, 1 *Kerr* 574.

20—Rescission of contract—Evidence of—Substitution of new contract—Liability—Question for jury.

Defendant agreed with the plaintiff in March 1863, to carry deals from the plaintiff's mill at Fredericton to St. John during the whole of the coming season, at 2s. 6*d*. per thousand, and if plaintiff was obliged to give 2s. 9*d*. per thousand to others, he was to give that sum to the defendant. The plaintiff had made contracts for the delivery of deals in St. John, which he afterwards assigned to T. & P. (lumber merchants), together with the defendant's contract; and he also agreed to saw lumber by the thousand for T. & P.; and did saw for them under such contract from the beginning of the season till October. At the opening of the season the defendant went with his boats to the plaintiff's mill, but no deals were offered to him, and he heard that the plaintiff had sold his mill: in consequence of this, he agreed with T. & P. to carry their deals for 55 cents per thousand, and continued to carry them from the plaintiff's mill, where they were sawed, till the latter part of September, when the mill stopped. Held, per Fisher and Wetmore, J.J. (Weldon, J., *dissentiente*), That there was evidence of the rescission of the contract between the parties, and of the substitution of a new contract with T. & P., which ought to have been left to the jury; and that the defendant was not liable on the contract for not carrying deals which the plaintiff cut on his own account after the 1st October. *Morrison* v. *Gale*, *Mich. T.* 1872.

21—Liability to insure goods—Completion of contract.

Plaintiff applied to the agent of an Express Company in Fredericton, to forward a case of furs to Halifax, to be sent to London, stating that he wished to have them insured. The agent said that he could not get marine insurance in Fredericton, but that if the plaintiff would write to S., the agent of the Company at St. John, he had no doubt he would do it, as he had done so for others. On the following day, the agent of the Company at Fredericton received the furs from the plaintiff, and signed a receipt stating that they were to be forwarded and delivered to the nearest connecting Express,—nothing being stated in the receipt about insurance. The furs were sent to S. at St. John, and were by him forwarded to Nova Scotia, and there taken charge of by another Company, who shipped them to London, and they were lost. At the time the plaintiff delivered the invoice of the furs to the agent at Fredericton, he also delivered him a letter addressed to S., in which the plaintiff stated that he wished S. to insure $600 on the furs, and to forward them to Halifax immediately, as he wished to have them in London at a particular time. S. did not insure.—Held, In an action against the Company for neglecting to insure, that the contract was complete when the agent in Fredericton received the furs and gave the receipt, which contained the terms of the contract; and that the letter to S. was only a request to insure, and formed no part of the contract for the transmission of the furs. *McGoldrick* v. *Eastern Express Company*, *East. T.* 1872.

22—Quality of article—Description—Representation.

Defendants agreed to furnish the plaintiff with a quantity of coal from their mines. Coal from those mines, known as "Albert coal," was used almost exclusively for the manufacture of oil and gas, and the defendants knew that the plaintiff required the coal for the purpose of manufacturing it into oil, and they could have supplied an article fit for that purpose. Held, That the plaintiff was entitled to receive Albert coal of a fair merchantable quality, and fit for the purpose for which he required it; and that the contract was broken by the delivery of coal from the mines, so mixed with shale, as to be comparatively valueless for the purpose for which the plaintiff required it. *Spurr* v. *Albert Mining Co.*, *East. T.* 1871.

In contracts of this nature, it is not so much a question whether there has been a warranty, as, whether the article delivered by the defendant fairly answers the description of that which he agreed to sell. *Spurr* v. *Albert Mining Co.*, *East. T.* 1871.

Damages—Non-assignment of judgments, etc—Injury to business. See Damages I. 9.

CONTRIBUTION.

Loss of Goods by Jettison. See Shipping Law 10.

Action for, on note—Surety. See Consideration 8.

CONTRIBUTORIES.

Liability of Stockholder. See Winding Up Act.

Executors—Stock in name of, in bank—Liability. See Winding Up Act.

CONVERSION.

See Trover.

CONVEYANCE.

See Deed.

Wife should be party to—Seller of land should prepare Conveyance. See Vendor and Purchaser.

CONVICTION.

See Justice of the Peace.

CORONER.

See Venire.—Jury.

1—Authority to take limit bond where writ directed to, and arrest made by him.

The Coroner, though not specially named, has the same authority as the Sheriff to take a limit bond under the Act 6 Wm. 4, c. 41, where the writ has been directed to, and the arrest made by him. *Earle* v. *Deveber*, 1 *Kerr* 348.

2—Jury process—Sufficiency of.

Quære, Whether it is necessary to direct any other but jury process to a Coroner, where the only objection to the Sheriff is that he is related to the defendant. See *Stevenson* v. *Douglas*, *Ber.* 281.

3—Duty of—Judicial—Absence of any juror.

A Coroner's duty is judicial, and he can only take an inquest *super visum corporis*; and an inquest where the Coroner and jurors were not all present at the same time is void. *Ex parte Wilson, Trin. T.* 1871.

4—Inquest—Expenses.
Where an inquest has been duly taken—*Quære*, Whether the Sessions are justified in refusing to pay the expenses under 1 Rev. Stat. c. 132. *Ibid.*

CORPORATION.

1—Summary proceedings.
Since the Act 6 Wm. 4, c. 33, establishing the writ of summons, a Corporation may be proceeded against in a summary action; and, in cases where the proceedings ought to be summary, the plaintiff will only be entitled to summary costs. *O'Connor* v. *The N. B. and N. S. Land Company*, 1 *Kerr* 276.

2—Agent—Authority—Extent of.
The Tobique Mill Company (an incorporated company) authorized their agent, by power of attorney, "to manufacture logs into lumber at the mills, transport them to market, and dispose of them" for the company's benefit. Held, That this did not authorize the agent to deliver over lumber at the mills, in payment of securities given by him on behalf of the company for debts contracted in the course of his agency; and that such delivery vested no property in the creditor. *Lombard* v. *Winslow*, 1 *Kerr* 327.

3—Making promissory notes.
Quære, Whether the company could authorize their agent to make promissory notes; and if they could, whether he had a right to make notes in his own favour in payment of a debt due himself for his services? *Ibid.*

4—Contract not under seal—Agent—Authority—Estoppel by pleading.
A written contract made in the name and on behalf of a corporation, called "The Lancaster Mill Company," by their agent, with the plaintiffs, whereby the plaintiffs for certain stipulated payments, which would amount to over £600, to be made by the company, engaged to cut, raft, and drive to the company's mills a large quantity of logs in the course of the ensuing season, is of such nature and extent as could only be made under the common seal of the corporation. Held therefore, In assumpsit brought for the recovery of the stipulated payment after the delivery of the logs at the mills, that the corporation was not liable—per Chipman, C. J., Botsford, J., and Carter, J. The corporation was not liable on the contract, because there was no sufficient proof of the agent's authority, of a recognition of the contract by the corporation, of the mills being in the tenure of the corporation, or of the appointment of officers under the act of incorporation to manage the business of the company—per Parker, J. The defendant, being sued as a corporation, and appearing and pleading as such in bar to the action, is estopped at the trial from disputing its existence as a body corporate, and its ability to contract in that capacity. *Seelye* v. *Lancaster Mill Company*, 1 *Kerr* 377.

5—Assumpsit—When it lies against.
Where money has been received by a manufacturing corporation under a parol agreement to make payment for the same in articles of their manufacture, which they have failed to perform; an action of assumpsit lies to recover back the money. *Diamond* v. *The St. George Lime Company*, 2 *Kerr* 537.

6—Letters patent—Presumption of—Proper issue of.
Where a corporation is created by letters patent under the great seal of the Province, and under the signature of the Lieut. Governor, it will be presumed that such letters patent were properly issued. *Doe dem. Commercial Bank* v. *Williston*, 3 *Kerr* 101.

7—Admission of existence of corporation by what.
Giving a mortgage to a corporation, and entering into a consent rule in an action of ejectment brought by a corporation, are admissions of the existence of the corporation. *Ibid.*

8—Not liable to attachment for costs.
A corporation is not liable to an attachment for non-payment of costs; therefore where a peremptory undertaking was enlarged on the application of a corporation (plaintiffs), the defendants was allowed to sign judgment of non-suit if the costs were not paid in a limited time. *Trustees of Greenock Church* v. *Love*, 3 *Kerr* 179.

See also Doe *v.* Crawford, 3 *All.* 266.

9—Non-payment of money by collector—Action by.
Wh— an Act authorized the corporation of a city to raise money by assessment, and directed that the person appointed by them to collect the money, should pay it

over to the chamberlain of the city; the chamberlain, being only the servant of the corporation, cannot sue the collector for not paying over the money: the action must be brought by the corporation. *Mayor &c. of St. John* v. *Baldwin*, 3 *Kerr* 477.

10—Church Corporation—Existence of—Name.
A Church Corporation may exist under the Act 29 Geo. 3, c. 1, by the style of "The Rector, Church Wardens and Vestry" etc., though no rector has at the time been appointed; and a grant by that name is good. *Doe dem. Rector &c. of Queensbury* v. *Guiou*, 1 *All.* 6.

11—Powers—Exercise of by Church Wardens, etc.
The Church Wardens and Vestry may exercise the powers given to the Rector, Church Wardens and Vestry, by the Act 29 Geo. 3, c. 1, as well where there never has been a Rector appointed, as where a vacancy is caused by the death or absence of the Rector. *Ibid.*

12—Contract under Seal—Estoppel.
A Municipal Corporation with certain defined powers, is not, by entering into a contract under seal, estopped from showing its incapacity to make such a contract. *Jamieson* v. *The City of Fredericton*, 2 *All.* 128.

13—Authority by Statute to erect building—Implied power.
The Corporation of the city of Fredericton entered into a contract with the plaintiff for the erection of a building for a market house. Held, That sufficient authority was given them by the Act of Incorporation (11 Vic. c. 61), and therefore that the contract was valid. *Ibid.*

14—A power to establish Fairs, necessarily includes a power to establish Markets.—*Ibid.*

15—Crown right—Setting up same to invalidate Contract.
Quære, If the Corporation had no authority to establish a Market without license from the Crown, whether it could, after the performance of the contract, and in the absence of any interference by the Crown, set up the Crown right to invalidate the contract? and *Semble*, That after the performance of the contract, the corporation could not resist payment because of a defect in the title to the land on which the market-house was built—they retaining the possession of it. *Ibid.*

16—Seal—Resolution not under seal.
Defendant, a tenant of the Corporation of St. John, claimed compensation for some alleged damage to the land leased, caused by the corporation; and they passed a resolution, allowing him therefor, the amount of rent he would be liable to pay for the land for a certain time. Held, That not being under seal, the resolution was not binding on the corporation, and that the defendant could not set off the amount of rent so allowed, in an action by the corporation to recover money in his hands belonging to them. *Mayor &c. of St. John* v. *Wilmot*, 2 *All.* 565.

17—British Statute—Restraint of—Leases.
Quære, Whether the Stat. 13 Eliz. c. 10, restraining ecclesiastical persons from making leases for a longer term than 21 years, applies to Church Corporations in this Province. *Bedell* v. *The Rector &c. of Fredericton*, 3 *All.* 217.

18—Negligence—Liability for.
A Municipal Corporation is liable to an action for negligence in the discharge of any duty imposed on them by their charter. *Green* v. *The Mayor &c. of St. John*, 1 *Han.* 525.

19—Trespass—Action by Corporation—No Rector.
In the absence of proof of there being any Rector of a parish, an action of trespass for injury to the Parish Church may be brought in the name of the Church corporation. *Rector &c. of Saint George's Church* v. *Cougle*, 1 *Han.* 600.

20—Summons—Requisite statement of cause of action.
The summons issued against a corporation under the Act 12 Vic. c. 39, s. 16, should state the cause of action truly: where the summons was to answer in a plea of "debt," and the declaration was in *covenant*, an interlocutory judgment was set aside. *Gilmore* v. *The Liverpool &c. Assurance Co.*, *Hil. T.* 1871.

An affidavit of the service of a summons issued against a foreign Corporation, stated that the copy was served upon E. A., "the agent of the above named Company." Held, That as by the Act 12 Vic. c. 30, s. 16, service upon an agent was only good in a suit against a foreign Corporation, the affidavit was insufficient, as it did not state that the defendant was a foreign Corporation. *Ibid.*

21—Payment of money to a Society does not incorporate.

The mere grant by an Act of the Legislature of a sum of money to a Society for a particular purpose, does not constitute it a corporation. The Municipality of York was authorised by Act 23 Vic. c. 4 to issue debentures in a certain sum, to be appropriated in assisting The York County Agricultural Society to raise funds for the erection of permanent buildings for the purpose of holding annual shows and fairs. Held, That this did not create "The York County Agricultural Society" a Corporation. *Hodge* v. *Reid, Mich. T.* 1872.

22—Policies signed by president and countersigned by secretary as required by Act incorporating Insurance Company, valid without seal of company. See Evidence VI. 5.

Agent Accredited. See Principal and Agent 23.

23—Corporation of City of St. John.

Are not bound by their charter as grantees of Crown to build or keep in repair wharves or sea walls for the protection of the city lands from the sea. No such implied duty by charter. See *Coram* v. *Mayor &c. of St. John*, 1 *Han.* 441.

Water Company—Obligation to keep supply of water. See Water Company.

Corporation of Saint John have no right to limit by contract their power to make bye-laws within their control under the charter. See Bye-Laws 5.

See Joint Stock Company.

CORPORATE NAME.

See Church of England. See Corporation.

Misdescription.

Where the notices and orders upon which an action under the Winding Up Act was founded, were entitled "The President, Directors and Company of the Westmoreland Bank, in the County of Westmoreland,"—the corporate name being—"The President, Directors and Company of the Westmoreland Bank." Held, No misdescription, the words being merely an addition of the locality. *McKenzie* v. *Wiswell*, 1 *Han.* 503.

COSTS.

I. Record and Summary—(Allowance or Disallowance of Costs.)

II. Taxation of Costs—(What allowed.)

III. Notice of Taxation.

IV. Review of Taxation.

V. Particular Proceedings—Particular Persons.

VI. Several Defendants—Several Issues.

VII. Security for Costs.

VIII. Double Costs.

IX. Offer to Suffer Judgment by Default under Act 18 Vict. cap. 9.

X. Miscellaneous.

I.

Record and Summary—Allowance or Disallowance of full Costs.

1—Recovery under £5.

Where plaintiff recovered less than £5, in a case referred at *nisi prius*, the original demand being also less than that amount, a suggestion will be entered on the roll to deprive him of costs under the Act 50 Geo. 3, c. 17. *Ferguson* v. *Holmes*, *East. T.* 1831.

2—Verdict prima facie evidence of amount.

The amount of the verdict is *prima facie* the amount of the demand for which the action was brought; and where the amount recovered was under £5 the plaintiff was deprived of costs under the Act 50 Geo. 3, c. 17. *Dickenson* v. *Balloch*, *Ber.* 24.

3—Circumstances of case govern Court in depriving plaintiff of costs.

The Court will not deprive the plaintiff of costs in all cases *ex contractu*, where the verdict is under £5, but will look to all the circumstances of the case. *McIlhanny* v. *Wiswell*, *Ber.* 67.

4—Where the verdict in an action for use and occupation was for less than £5, but the plaintiff's right to the land and the construction of a deed under which he claimed were disputed, he will not be deprived of costs under 50 Geo. 3, c. 17. *Black* v. *Kirk*, *Ber.* 81.

5—Defendant disputing balance on account rendered.

Where the verdict was for £11, plaintiff was allowed full costs, though he had rendered an account to the defendant before action brought, showing credits and a balance due of less than £20—the defendant having disputed the balance and thereby rendered it necessary for plaintiff to sue for his whole demand. *Douglas* v. *Hanson*, *Ber.* 121.

6—Discretionary power.

Defendant gave plaintiff a note for £22, payable in timber; he afterwards delivered him some timber and an ox, which he claimed to have been received in satisfaction of the note: plaintiff recovered a verdict for £14. Held, That he was entitled to full costs under the discretionary power given to the Court by the Act 4 Wm. 4, c. 41. *Holland* v. *Close*, *Ber.* 344.

7—Important rights involved—Trover.

When important rights were involved in an action, the plaintiff was allowed full costs, though he recovered less than £20, and the action might have been brought under the Summary Act (4 Wm. 4, c. 41). *Coombes* v. *Caldwell*, 1 *Kerr* 127.

8—Reference to Arbitration—Award less than £5.

Where a cause was referred to arbitration, the award to be entered as a verdict, and an award was made in favour of the plaintiff for £3, he was allowed summary costs, it appearing by affidavit that his account, as allowed by the arbitrators, was about £20, and was reduced by the defendant's account,—notice of set-off having been given in the action, and it not being clearly shewn that the defendant's account was a payment. *Doyle* v. *Dougan*, 1 *Kerr* 161.

9—Assault and Battery—Verdict less than 40 shillings.

In an action for assault and battery where the verdict is for less than forty shillings, it is discretionary with the Judge whether he will certify or not, in order to entitle the plaintiff to costs under the Act 22 and 23 Car. 2, c. 9. *Ewing* v. *Scott*, *Trin. T.* 1834.

10—Title to Land.

The plaintiff is entitled to costs under the Act 30 Vic. c. 10 in an action for overflowing his land by means of a mill-dam; the defendant claiming his right to do so, by permission of a former owner of the land, and going into evidence of that right, though he afterwards abandoned it. *McLeod* v. *Murray*, 2 *Han.* 193.

11—Title to land—County Court.

Where the declaration contained counts for trespass *quare clausum fregit*, for assault, and for slander; but the plaintiff recovered for the assault only—there being no dispute about the plaintiff's title to the land—a certificate for costs was refused under the Act 30 Vict. c. 10, s. 21—the amount recovered, being within the jurisdiction of the County Court and the count for trespass to the land having been improperly included. *Bradley* v. *Ferguson*, *East. T.* 1871.

12—In trespass *quare clausum fregit*, and for an assault, the defendant gave notices of defence,—*liberum tenementum* as to the trespass, and a justification of the assault in defence of his possession. The question of title was principally in dispute, and the plaintiff recovered on both counts On motion for a new trial, the plaintiff abandoned the count for trespass, and the verdict, which was confined to the count for the assault, was excessive. Held, That as the defendant justified the assault as the owner of the land, the title to land came in question in connexion with the assault, and therefore the plaintiff was entitled to a certificate for costs under the Act 30 Vic. c. 10. *Burke* v. *Niles*, *East. T.* 1871.

12 a—Recovery for assault only.

Where in trespass *quare clausum fregit*, and for assault, the plaintiff recovers for the assault only; he is not entitled to the costs of the pleadings or evidence applicable exclusively to the issue, on which he was unsuccessful. *Burke* v. *Niles*, *Hil. T.* 1873.

13—Judge certifying under Act 30 Vic. c. 10.

Where a cause is referred to arbitration by an order of *nisi prius*, the presiding Judge has power to certify for costs under the Act 30 Vic. c. 10, s. 21. *Patton* v. *Harding*, *East. T.* 1871.

14—Assignee of Note for lumber—Delivery after action.

Where the assignor of a note payable in lumber obtained a verdict for nominal damages, in consequence of the debtor having delivered the lumber to the assignor after action brought, the Court granted the plaintiff a certificate for full costs. *Green* v. *Williston*, 3 *Kerr* 110.

15—Trespass—Claim of Title—Certificate.
Where the trespass is committed under a claim of title, or with the intent to oust the plaintiff from the possession of the land, the Judge may certify under the Statute 22 and 23 Car. 2, c. 9, to entitle the plaintiff to full costs. *Morrison* v. *McAlpin*, 2 *Kerr* 36.

16—Certificate—Time for granting.
Such certificate may be granted within a reasonable time after the trial, and an application therefor is not too late if made the day after the trial is over. *Ibid.*

17—Time of making application for Certificate.
An application to the Judge who tried the cause for a certificate to deprive an acquitted defendant of costs, under the Act of Assembly 7 Wm. 4, c. 14, s. 24, is not too late if made before the judgment is signed, though nearly two months after the verdict. *Crane* v. *Cunard*, 3 *Kerr* 407.

18—The Statute 43 Eliz. c. 6, authorising a Judge to certify to deprive a plaintiff of costs, is in force here. See British Statutes.

19—Cognovit—Damages laid at £50, conditioned for payment of £17.
Where A., an attorney, sued for a debt of £17 in an action not summary, and the defendant gave a cognovit in which he confessed the damages laid in the declaration (£50), but it was thereby stipulated that in case of default of payment of £17 with costs, to be taxed by a certain day, the plaintiff should be at liberty to enter up judgment for the £17.—Held, That he was entitled to summary costs only. *Harding* v. *Parker*, 2 *Kerr* 7.

20—Defendant suffering judgment over £5.
When the defendant suffers the damages to be assessed and final judgment signed for a debt over £5, the Court will not entertain a motion to deprive the plaintiff of costs on the ground that a payment had been made before action brought, whereby the debt was reduced below £5. *Bennett* v. *Morse*, 2 *Kerr* 624.

21—Set-Off—Appropriation.
Where the maker of a promissory note delivered the payee a quantity of hay without making any specific appropriation of the amount towards the paying of the note, and on a subsequent demand of payment claimed no deduction on account of the hay. Held, In action on the note, that the value of the hay could only be considered as a set-off, and that the plaintiff was entitled to costs, though the verdict was for less than £5. *Barlow* v. *Clark*, 3 *Kerr* 485.

22—Damages under £20—Assumpsit.
When the damages in assumpsit are under £20 the plaintiff is only entitled to summary costs though the defendant suffered judgment by default and took no steps to be present at the taxation and object to the costs. *Street* v. *The Saint Andrews Steam Mill Co.*, 1 *All.* 134.

23—Set-off—Goods furnished—Verdict below £5.
If a defendant gives a notice and particulars of set set-off which are principally made up of goods furnished the plaintiff, it shows *prima facie* that it was not intended as a payment, and the plaintiff is entitled to costs though the verdict is below £5. *White* v. *Dawson*, 2 *All.* 51.

24—Special notice of defence—Effect of.
The construction given in England to the the Statute 22 and 23 Car. 2, c. 9, is part of the law of this Province, and is not affected by the Act of Assembly 13 Vic. c. 32; therefore in trespass *quare clausum fregit*, the plaintiff is entitled to full costs though the verdict is under forty shillings, if the defendant gives notice under the Act, of leave and license, and relies solely on that defence. *Marks* v. *Gilmour*, 3 *All.* 170.

25—Cause referred at Nisi Prius—Order of Judge for full costs.
Where a cause is referred at *Nisi Prius*, and judgment on the award is to be entered as a verdict, the Judge of the Court of *Nisi Prius* may make an order for full costs, where the plaintiff's demand is reduced by set-off; and such order may be made *ex parte*. *Seelye* v. *Styles*, 3 *All.* 246.

26—Justices Court—No jurisdiction—Contract.
The Rev. Stat., c. 137, s. 43, depriving a plaintiff of costs where he does not recover more than £5, only applies to cases in which Justices of the Peace have jurisdiction; therefore in an action for nonperformance of a contract to deliver goods, the plaintiff is entitled to costs without a Judge's order, though he recovers less than that amount. *Rideout* v. *Stevens*, 1 *Han.* 28.

II.

Taxation of Costs.

27—What allowed—Commission to examine.
Cost of a Commission to examine witnesses are costs in the cause under Act Wm. 4, c. 34. *Fergus* v. *McIntosh*, *Ber.* 91.

28—Setting aside verdict—Offer to confess judgment — Costs of first trial—Commission.
A verdict for plaintiff in an action on a policy of insurance claiming for a total loss, was set aside for mis-direction: after notice given for a second trial, defendant offered to confess judgment for a sum amounting to a partial loss only, which the plaintiff accepted. Held, That he was not entitled to the costs of the first trial. *Wood* v. *Stymest*, *Hil. T.* 1863.

29—The expense of a Commission to examine witnesses taken before the first trial of a cause, but not used, will not be allowed to the plaintiff as a necessary preparation for the second trial. *Ibid.*

30—Attendance of Solicitor—Evidence not used.
The charges of a Solicitor attending the execution of a commission to examine witnesses in England, and the expense of taking evidence *de bene esse* in this Province, were not allowed on the taxation of costs, the evidence not having been used on the trial. *McGivern* v. *Stymest*, *Trin. T.* 1862.

31—A fee of one shilling only is taxable for an attorney attending a Judge on summons. *Ibid.*

32—Witnesses.
The expenses of a witness coming from England to this Province to give evidence will be allowed in the costs. *Light* v. *Abel*, *Hil. T.* 1866.

33—The mileage of a witness travelling from the State of Maine to the County of Northumberland in this Province, allowed in the taxation of costs. *Judkins* v. *Parker*, *C. Ms.* 151.

34—Materiality of witnesses.
Where issues are found for both parties, it must appear on taxing costs that the witnesses were material to prove the issue found for the party who charges for their attendance, and where the affidavits were not sufficient for that purpose, and copies had not been served on the opposite attorney, the Court set aside the judgment and ordered a new taxation. *Crookshank* v. *McFarlane*, 3 *All.* 18.

34 a—Election Law—Allegations—Materiality of witnesses to prove.
Where on the trial of an Election Petition, the Judge disallowed the costs of certain allegations in the petition, the affidavit of the attendance of witnesses used in taxing costs should shew that the witnesses were material to prove those allegations in the petition on which costs were allowed. *Herbert* v. *Hannington*, *East. T.* 1873.

34 b—Notices -Publication—Costs.
Publication of notices in a newspaper —"for three consecutive days"—under the 69th Sec. of the Act 32 Vic. c. 32, cannot be made in a weekly newspaper. The petitioner is not entitled to the costs of publishing notices in a newspaper, and of posting. *Ibid.*

35—Cause put off—Order to pay expenses—Prima facie taxable costs.
A trial being put off by a Judge's order upon the defendants paying to the plaintiff "all costs incurred in preparing for trial and the expenses of one D. M. from Canada who was sent for, should he attend as a witness." Held, That the *prima facie* construction of the order was the taxable expenses of the witness, and if any thing more was agreed to be paid, the *onus* was on the claimant to shew it. *Pollock* v. *Ritchie*, 3 *Kerr* 351.

36—Voluntary attendance.
If a witness attends voluntarily, it is not necessary to serve him with a subpœna in order to be entitled to charge for his attendance. *Flaglor* v. *Richards*, 1 *All.* 599.

37—Attendance as juror.
If a person subpœned as a witness attends the Court as a juror, or is too much intoxicated to be examined, he cannot recover his fees; but if they have have been paid, the party paying them is entitled to have them taxed, and the ordinary affidavit of the witness's attendance and materiality *prima facie* shows the payment. *Murray* v. *Williston*, 1 *All.* 492.

38—Sufficiency of affidavit—Payment by adverse party.
It is sufficient, in order to obtain the taxation of witnesses fees, to show by affidavit that they have attended during the period charged, and were material, with-

out shewing the payment of their fees; and it will be no answer that they were also subpœned and paid by the other party, unless he has given timely notice of such payment to the successful party. *Murray* v. *Williston*, 1 *All.* 492. (See General Rules 32.)

39—Affidavit should state belief that the witness attended the number of days charged. See *Taylor* v. *Travis*, 3 *All.* 505.

40—Evidence—Application to one count of declaration—Costs confined to same.

In an action for libel, consisting of five counts, and resulting in a verdict for defendant, a new trial was ordered; after which it was consented that the depositions of the witnesses, taken under a commission obtained by the plaintiffs, and made use of in evidence, might be used again on the next trial, whereat the witness himself appeared, and was examined for the plaintiff *viva voce;* after which his depositions under the commission was put in and read with the consent of all parties; and there was a verdict for the plaintiff on the first count of the declaration, and no finding on the other counts. Held, That the taxing officer was right in disallowing the expenses of the commission, and also the costs of the declaration, *nisi prius* record, and judgment roll, except so far as related to the first count of the declaration. *Andrews* v. *Wilson*, 3 *Kerr* 127.

41—Evidence generally—General issue.

In an action of trespass, in which the general issue only was pleaded, a verdict was given against the plaintiff on the ground of his not shewing sufficient possession. Held, That the defendant was entitled to the costs of all his evidence, though part of it was adduced to prove title in himself, in which he failed. *Gaudin* v. *McKilligan*, 2 *All.* 477.

Aliter, If the evidence had been offered under a plea of *liberum tenementum*, or a special notice of defence, not admissible under the general issue. *Ibid.*

If a clear case of over allowance for the attendance of witnesses is made out, the Court will review the taxation of costs. *Ibid.*

42—Allocatur.

A new trial having been granted on payment of costs, an *allocatur* allowed for shewing cause was taxed against the party who obtained the new trial. Held, That such taxation was wrong, and the costs accordingly deducted. *McEachern* v. *Ferguson*, 3 *Kerr* 355.

43—Bribery Act—Counsel Fee.

A Judge has no power to tax a higher counsel fee than five guineas on the trial of a cause under the Bribery and Corruption and Election Petition Act 1869. *Herbert* v. *Hannington*, *Trin. T.* 1872.

44—Copies of deeds.

Where copies of deeds are adduced under the Act of 7 Wm. 4, c. 15, the successful party is entitled to the costs of all copies actually read in evidence. *Doe d. Thomson* v. *Allanshaw*, 1 *Kerr* 93.

45—Change of Attorney—Subpœnas.

Costs of changing the attorney are not taxable against the adverse party. The number of subpœnas allowed must depend upon the particular circumstances of each case. *Roberts* v. *White*, *Trin. T.* 1831.

46—Replevin—Costs—Claim by third party.

Quære, Whether the plaintiff in replevin is entitled to recover against the defendant as part of the costs in the cause, the costs of the proceedings taken under a writ *de proprietate probanda* issued upon a claim of property put in by a third person under the 1 Rev. Stat. c. 126, s. 12? Held, per Ritchie, C. J., and Allen, J., That he is: N. Parker and Wilmot, J. J., *contra*. *Goddard* v. *Tuck*, *Hil. T.* 1866.

47—Different Issues.

In replevin, where some issues are found for the plaintiff and some for the defendant, each party is entitled to costs on the issues found in his favor. *Dickinson* v. *Ketchum*, *Ber.* 63.

48—Where a defendant pleads *non cepit*, and property on which issues are joined, and succeeds on the first issue only, he is entitled to the general costs of the cause and is liable to pay the costs of the other issue. *Stephenson* v. *Milliken*, 1 *Kerr* 56.

49—Inquisition.

When the verdict is for the defendant on an inquisition taken on a writ *de proprietate probanda*, under the Act 4 Wm. 4, c. 38, the defendant is not entitled to the costs of the inquisition. *Wilson* v. *Curry*, *Mich. T.* 1834.

a—Replevin bond—Counsel fees.

The plaintiff's attorney in an action on a replevin bond, cannot add to the taxed costs, a sum paid by the plaintiff for counsel fees. The costs mentioned in the condition of a replevin bond mean taxable costs. *Steen* v. *Hanson*, 4 *All.* 589.

50—Sheriff's Fees.
Sheriff's fees, on executing a writ of replevin, being part of the general costs of the cause, are not taxable in the costs of opposing a rule to set aside the writ, as having been improperly issued. *McGowan* v. *Betts*, *Mich. T.* 1871.

Replevin — Witnesses — Materiality. See No. 96 a.

51—Reference of cause to arbitration —No direction as to entering up judgment.
A cause was referred to arbitration, under a Judge's order, which directed that the costs should abide the event of the award, and that judgment should be entered up for the successful party, but without directing in what manner it was to be entered up—(the arbitrators made an award in favour of the plaintiff for £2 4s.) Held, That as no judgment could be entered up on the award, the plaintiff was not entitled to costs, either under the Act of Assembly 4 Wm. 4, c. 45, or the Statute of Gloucester. *Burns* v. *Chapman*, 3 *Kerr* 192.

52—Charge of Arbitrators—Taxed costs.
Where a cause was referred at *nisi prius* the award to be entered as a verdict—"with costs to be taxed"—the charge of the arbitrators for their services cannot be allowed in the costs. *McMahon* v. *Dibble*, *Trin. T.* 1831.

53—Motion for Judgment.
A counsel fee is taxable on a motion for judgment as in case of a non-suit, though the motion is not opposed. *York County Mutual Insurance Co.* v. *Hartley*, *East. T.* 1865.

54—Rule Nisi for new trial.
Where a rule *nisi* for a new trial is refused, a fee of 6s. 8*d.* is taxable to the opposite party for counsel attending to hear the motion. A charge for brief for argument is not taxable till until a rule *nisi* has been granted, even though notice of the motion has been given pursuant to the rule of Michaelmas Term 1st Vic. *Wright* v. *Merrithew*, 2 *All.* 520.

55—Judgment by default—Taxable items only allowed.
On a judgment by default on a summary action, no costs are taxable for items not specified in the table of fees in the Act 12 Vic. c. 40. *Snodgrass* v. *Johnston*, 2 *All.* 200.

56—Indorsement of Sheriff on writ, whether conclusive as to fees. See Sheriff 5.

57—Equity—Abbreviated Bill.
A copy of the abbreviated bill used on equity appeal not allowed in the costs, in addition to the copy used at the original hearing, where the same counsel argues both the original hearing and the appeal. *Gilbert* v. *Campbell*, *Hil. T.* 1863.

58—Costs of abbreviating pleadings and affidavits used in opposing an application for an injunction, not allowed in the costs of opposing a second application, the same counsel appearing on both motions, and it not being shewn that a second abbreviation had actually been made. *Hendricks* v. *Hallet*, 1 *Han.* 170.

59—Equity Appeal.
Where parties do not fairly state their cases, and their conduct does not appear to have been *bona fide*, neither of them will be entitled to costs on an equity appeal. *Hillock* v. *Frisle*, *Mich. T.* 1863.

60—No jurisdiction—Power to grant costs.
Where a Judge in Equity declines to hear an appeal because the Court has no jurisdiction, he has no power to give costs to the party opposing the appeal. *Ex parte Stockton*, *Mich. T.* 1871. (See also *Bustin* v. *Howell*, 1 *All.* 596.)

60 a—Appeal in Equity—Scale of Costs.
On an appeal from the decision of a Judge in Equity, the costs of appeal are to be taxed according to the Scale of Costs in Equity. *Hannington* v. *Harshman*, *East. T.* 1873

61—Foreclosure of mortgage—Mortgagor's equity of redemption transferred—Plaintiff's knowledge of.
A mortgagor was made defendant in a foreclosure suit, appeared thereto and answered, disclaiming any interest in the property. On motion to dismiss the bill as against the mortgagor—Held, That as the plaintiff either knew or had the means of knowing, before commencing the suit, that the mortgagor had conveyed away his equity of redemption in the property, the mortgagor was entitled to his costs. *Wilson* v. *Hornbrook and wife and McKenna*, 1 *Han.* 167.

62—Co-defendants—Practice.
In general, payment of costs between co-defendants is not directly ordered, but

the plaintiff is ordered to pay the costs to the defendants to whom they are decreed, and to add them to the general costs in the cause, and recover them from the other defendants. *Johnston* v. *McCartney*, 1 *Han.* 227.

III.

NOTICE OF TAXATION.

63—In all cases, between opposing parties, where the proceedings are not by default, there must be notice of taxation of costs, and a judgment signed without notice will be set aside, with costs. *Turner* v. *Crane*, *East. T.* 1833.

63 a—Taxing without notice.
Taxing costs and signing judgment without notice of taxation to the opposite party, is irregular; but where the attorney had offered to re-tax the costs and deduct any improper charges, an application to set aside the judgment was refused, and an item improperly charged in the costs was ordered to be deducted from the amount to be levied under the execution. *Thomson* v. *Green*, *Hil. T.* 1864.

64—An attorney having taxed costs and signed judgment without notice to the opposite attorney, contrary to an agreement made by his agent that notice should be given, and which was communicated to him—Held, That he was bound by the agreement of his agent, and that the judgment was irregular. *Cormick* v. *Wilson*, 3 *Kerr* 110.

65—Good Friday.
Taxation on that day not irregular. *Gilmore* v. *Gilbert*, 2 *All.* 50.

IV.

REVIEW OF TAXATION

66—Time.
Intended motion to review taxation must be given as soon after the taxation as circumstances will permit. See *Doe d. McCallum* v. *Roe*, 2 *All.* 143.

67—Where costs were taxed the 20th October and payment demanded 15th November, an application to review the taxation made without notice, on the first day of the following term was refused, the plaintiff being prepared to move for an attachment for non-payment of costs. *Ibid.*

68—Waiver.
The defendant's attorney was served with a copy of a bill of costs, in which neither the names of the witnesses, nor the sum charged for their attendance was stated, but reference was made for those particulars to an affidavit, no copy of which was served with the bill of costs; the defendant's attorney, by his agent, attended the taxation of costs without making any objection to the want of the affidavit. Held, That he had thereby waived his right to object, though the affidavit on which the witnesses' expenses were taxed, was afterwards contradicted in several particulars; and therefore the taxation could not be reviewed. *Chase* v. *Fawcett*, 1 *All.* 566.

The attendance of some of the witnesses having been denied, the amount charged and not paid by the plaintiff, was ordered to be deducted on a discharge being produced by the defendants, and the plaintiff before issuing execution was required to state on oath what witnesses he had paid. *Ibid.*

69—Where a party has attended taxation of costs, after due notice, without making any objection to the witnesses charged for in the bill, he cannot afterwards apply for a review of taxation, on the discovery of facts which he might have known at the time; unless a fraud has been practised upon him, or he has been greatly misled. *Flaglor* v. *Richards*, 1 *All.* 599.

70—New affidavits.
Quære, Whether, on an application for review of taxation, new affidavits are receivable by the Court, or by the clerk, in case a review is ordered. See *Murray* v. *Williston*, 1 *All.* 492.

71—Costs on review—Mistake of Clerk.
The costs of a review of taxation are not allowed where it was occasioned by the mistake of the clerk. *Snodgrass* v. *Johnston*, 2 *All.* 200.

72—Grounds for review—Mistake in entering Rule.
A mistake in entering a rule in the minutes is not a ground for reviewing taxation, it not appearing that the judgment was wrong, or the opposite party misled by it. Where there were mistakes on both sides, an application to set aside the judgment, and review taxation, was granted without costs. *Crookshank* v. *McFarlane*, 3 *All.* 18.

73—**Over-allowance—Witnesses.**
If a clear case of over-allowance for attendance of witnesses is made out, the Court will review taxation. See *Gaudin* v. *McKilligan*, 2 *All.* 477.

74—**Different Issues.**
If both parties are entitled to tax costs on different issues, an appointment for taxation should be obtained from the clerk. *Crookshank* v. *McFarlane*, 3 *All.* 18.

75—**Costs of Inferior Court.**
If an action is commenced in the Inferior Court, and afterwards removed into this Court, the clerk of Supreme Court may tax the costs incurred in the Court below, without referring them to the officer of that Court. *Milner* v. *Styles*, 3 *Kerr* 143.

76—**Making new motion—Withdrawing Affidavits.**
If, on an application for an order to review taxation of costs, the affidavits are insufficient, and the party intends making a new motion on additional affidavits, he ought to withdraw the first motion: if judgment is given upon it, he is precluded from making another application.

Semble, That notice should be given to the opposite party before applying for a review. *McLaughlan* v. *Wilson*, 3 *Kerr* 177.

77—**Equity—Taxation by Judge.**
The taxation of costs by the Clerk in Equity, under the Act 17 Vic. c. 18, may be reviewed by a Judge of the Court, and the application may be made by motion stating the objections to the taxation.

Time.
The application is not too late if made at the next sitting of the Court after the costs are taxed, though they were taxed during the sitting of the Court.

If the clerk in taxing costs, acts on a wrong principle, the Court will review the taxation. *Hendricks* v. *Hallet*, 1 *Han.* 170.

78—Where plaintiffs were dismissed in consequence of usury, the Court refused to interfere with discretion of Judge of Court in ordering that costs should follow the result of suit. *Jardine* v. *Mc Williams*, 1 *Han.* 579.

Appeals not generally entertained in questions of costs. See Supreme Court in Equity.

79—Where an appeal from the decision of a Judge in Equity is dismissed with costs, the costs of the appeal are recoverable by attachment and not by execution under the Act 17 Vic. c. 18. *Smith* v *Armstrong*, *Mich. T.* 1872.

V.

Particular Proceedings—Particular Persons.

80—**Persons—Executors.**
Executors are liable to costs on a non-suit in an action where *ne unques executor* is pleaded. *Mitchell* v. *Long*, *C. Ms.* 76.

81—Where an executor declared, upon promises to himself, and upon an account stated with him as executor, as well as upon promises to the testatrix, and was non-suited, the Court allowed the defendant her costs. *Executors of Grosvenor* v. *Agnew*, *Ber.* 29.

82—An administrator will not be relieved from his liability to the payment of costs under Act 7 Wm. 4, c. 14, s. 23, where he moves, not on matters appearing at the trial, but upon affidavits which are sufficiently answered by the defendant.

Semble, The Act extends only to cases in which executors or administrators were before that exempted from the payment of costs. *Thompson* v. *Allanshaw*, 1 *Kerr* 209.

83—**Insolvent Debtor—Application.**
Costs will not be given on refusing the first application of an insolvent debtor except in an extreme case: but the rule is otherwise on a second application, where the objections made to the former one are not fully answered. *McFarlane* v. *Gordon*, 2 *All.* 162.

84—**Payment of costs—Condition—Second application.**
Where an application to discharge an insolvent debtor was refused with costs, the Court refused to make the payment of the costs a condition precedent to another application. *McFarlane* v. *Gordon*, 2 *All.* 201.

85—**Motions—Cognovit.—Satisfactory answer.**
Where a motion was made to set aside a *cognovit* for fraud and collusion, and the charge was satisfactorily answered; the Court dismissed the charge with costs, to be paid by the applicant, though the matter had not been moved with costs. *Doe* v. *Crowley*, 3 *Kerr* 294.

86—**Quashing conviction.**
Court has no power to allow costs on

quashing convictions. *Regina* v. *Stevens*, 3 *Kerr* 356.

87—Mesne profits—Costs—Damages.
As a general rule the plaintiff after judgment against casual ejector is entitled to recover the costs thereof as part of the damages in an action for mesne profits. See *Doe* v. *Dobson*, 2 *All.* 446.

88—Discharging rule.—Mandamus.
No costs are allowed on discharging a rule *nisi* for a mandamus, on account of the affidavits being improperly entitled. *Regina* v. *Justices of York*, 1 *All.* 90.

89—A rule dischargeable without costs, if moved with costs will be discharged with costs. *Porter* v. *Burns*, 1 *All.* 106.

90—If a rule for setting aside proceedings with costs, is discharged on showing cause, the costs of opposing it do not follow as of course. *Kelly* v. *Wilson*, 1 *All.* 199.

91—The successful party should apply for costs at the time of discharging the rule. *Ibid.*

92—When a rule *nisi* for a *certiorari* to remove a conviction is discharged, the successful party is not entitled to the costs of opposing the rule. *Ex parte Daley*, 1 *All.* 135.

93—Where a rule was discharged on the authority of a modern English case altering the previous practice, the costs of opposing the rule were refused. *Simonds* v. *Simonds*, 2 *All.* 468.

94—Vexatious action—Staying proceedings until payment of costs.
Defendant obtained judgment as in case of a nonsuit because plaintiff did not try his cause pursuant to a peremptory undertaking; plaintiff having brought a second action for the same cause, the Court stayed the proceedings until the costs of the first suit were paid, the defendant's affidavit alleging his belief that the plaintiff was insolvent, and the second action vexatious—though the plaintiff stated that he was prevented from trying his first action by the absence of a material witness. (But See *Danvers* v. *Morgan*, 17 *C. B.* 530.) *Estabrooks* v. *McKenzie*, *C. Ms.* 41.

95—New trial.
Where a new trial is granted "the costs to abide the event of the suit" and the same party succeeds on the second trial, he is not entitled to the costs of showing cause against the rule for setting aside the first verdict. *Nice* v. *Coyle*, *Hil. T.* 1832.

96—If the rule for a new trial is silent as to costs, the successful party on the second trial is not entitled to the costs of setting aside the first verdict. *Weldon* v. *Weldon*, 3 *All.* 148.

96 a—Replevin—Plea—Witnesses—Materiality.
Where, in replevin, the substantial issue was the right to the property, which was found for the defendant, he is entitled to the costs of the witnesses called to support his plea, though their evidence may not have been exclusively applicable to that issue. *Fearon* v. *Murray*, *Trin. T.* 1861.

96 b—Mortgagee—Redemption of Mortgage.
As a general rule, a mortgagee is entitled to his costs in a suit for the redemption of his mortgage; but where he had been in possession of the property, and had not kept accurate accounts of the rents and profits, and claimed a considerably larger amount from the mortgagor than was ultimately found to be due, he was not allowed costs; and as the mortgagor had improperly disputed part of the amount claimed by the mortgagee, he was not allowed costs: each party being ordered to pay his own costs of the suit. *Livingston* v. *Bank of New Brunswick*, *Hil. T.* 1865.

VI.

Several Defendants—Several Issues.

97—Several Defendants—Acquittal.
Where four defendants, sued in trespass, entered a joint defence, in which issues were joined in fact and in law, the plaintiff obtained a verdict against one, but the other three were acquitted on the trial, and judgment was given for all the defendants on the issues in law, which did not go to the whole cause of action; after the lapse of more than one year from entering up the judgment, the defendant's agent having attended the taxation of the plaintiff's costs, and made objections without making any claim of costs, and soon afterward the defendant against whom the verdict was found voluntarily paid to the plaintiff the damages and costs; and it not appearing in

this application that the defendants who were acquitted incurred any costs, or that the other defendant had incurred any further costs in the joint defence than if he had been sole defendant: Held, That it would require a strong and clear case to authorize the Court to interfere at such a distance of time. Held also, That the issues in law not going to the whole cause of action, the defendants were not entitled to costs under the 7 Wm. 4, c. 14, s. 26. *McLauchlan* v. *Wilson*, 3 *Kerr* 105.

98—Allocatur.
By the Ordinance an allocatur is allowed to an acquitted defendant entitled to judgment for his costs under 7 Wm. 4, c. 14, s. 24. *Killeen* v. *Burke*, 3 *Kerr* 419.

99—Entry of Judgment.
Where, in an action of trespass against four defendants, the plaintiff obtains a verdict against one upon which judgment is entered, and the other three are acquitted, the acquitted defendants cannot enter up a separate judgment for their costs, but the award of costs should be entered on the plaintiff's judgment roll—same rule as to demurrer. *McLauchlan* v. *Wilson*, 2 *Kerr* 626.

100—Entry on Judgment Roll—Application—Lateness. See *Ibid*, 3 *Kerr* 105.

101—Several Issues—Different Findings.
In replevin, the defendant pleaded *non cepit*, and property in himself; a verdict was found for the defendant on the first issue, and for the plaintiff on the other. Held, 1st, That as the plea of *non cepit* went to the whole cause of action, the defendant was entitled to the general costs of the cause, but not to the costs of any evidence except such as was provided to support that issue. 2nd, That the plaintiff was entitled to the costs of the other issue, and to have them deducted from the defendant's costs. *Holderness* v. *McKendrick*, 2 *All.* 213.

It must clearly appear that witnesses whose expenses are claimed, were necessary to support the issues found for the party claiming. *Ibid.*

102—Where on an issue on a plea of property in replevin, the jury find the property in part of the goods to be in the plaintiff, and the remainder in the defendant, the plaintiff is entitled to the costs of all the pleadings; but each party is entitled to the costs of the evidence arising on that part of the plea which is found for him. *Read* v. *Botsford*, 4 *All.* 476.

Separate executions may be awarded; or the Court may order the costs of one party to be deducted from those of the other, and execution to issue for the balance. *Ibid.*

If, in such a case, the plaintiff neglects to enter up judgment within a certain time, the defendant will be entitled to the *postea*. *Ibid.*

103—Several Counts.
If the plaintiff obtains a verdict on one of several counts, and there is no finding on the other counts, he is only entitled to costs on that count on which he obtains judgment. *Walsh* v. *Fairweather*, 2 *All.* 423.

Taxation of costs on different issues. See Costs 74.

104—Nolle Prosequi.
Where plaintiff enters a *nolle prosequi* to one count of a declaration, the defendant cannot enter up judgment for his costs till the other counts are disposed of. *Allison* v. *Smith*, 4 *All.* 238.

VII.

Security for Costs.

1—A demand of particulars is not such a stop in the cause as to require the defendant to shew that at the time of making the demand, he did not know of the plaintiff's residence abroad. *Johnson* v. *Glasier*, *Hil. T.* 1828.

2—A company incorporated in Canada, and having no property in this Province, required to give security for costs. Where security was demanded before pleading, and refused, defendant was allowed to apply, and obtain security at the next term, though he had pleaded in the mean time. *Quebec and Halifax Steam Navigation Co.* v. *Williston*, *Mich. T.* 1834.

3—A demand for security of costs sent by post, held sufficient. *Abbot* v. *Ledden*, *Bert.* 33.

4—Defendant must apply promptly after knowledge of the plaintiff's absence; and if he allows a term to pass without applying, after he knows of the absence, security for costs will not be granted. *Gibbs* v. *De Veber*, *Ber.* 78.

5—Security for costs, without stay of proceedings, ordered by the Court after plea, and notice of trial, though the defendant might have applied sooner to a Judge at Chambers: the practice of making such applications at Chambers not being of long continuance in the Province. *Vance* v. *Campbell*, 1 *Kerr* 163.

6—Where an application to a Judge at Chambers for security of costs has failed on the merits, a new application may be made to the Court on amended affidavits. *Foster* v. *Amiraux*, 2 *All.* 541.

VIII.

Double Costs.

If judgment is affirmed after error assigned, the defendant in error is entitled to double costs under the Stat. 13 Car. 2, c. 2, s. 10. *Quære*, Whether the defendant is entitled to such costs where the writ of error is *non prossed*. *Gilbert* v. *Sayre*, 2 *All.* 512.

IX.

Offer filed under Act 18 Vic. c. 9, to suffer judgment by default.

Where the defendant, before pleading, filed an offer under the Act 18 Vic. c. 9, to suffer judgment by default for $250, which the plaintiff refused, and the defendant then pleaded and gave notice of set-off, and the plaintiff recovered a verdict for less than the sum offered, (defendant's set-off being allowed)—Held, That the offer must be taken with reference to the state of the pleadings at the time, and not having been renewed after the notice of set-off, that the plaintiff was entitled to full costs, and not merely to the costs up to the time of the offer. *Miller* v. *Lakeman*, *Mich. T.* 1866.

Defendant, in trover, about a month after the conversion, offered to confess a judgment under the Act 18 Vic c. 9, for $18, which the plaintiff refused. On the trial (upwards of two years afterwards), plaintiff recovered a verdict of $19,— a part, $15 30, being found by the jury as the value of the goods, and the balance as damages in the nature of interest since the conversion. Held, That as the amount tendered was more than the value of the goods and damages up to that time, the plaintiff was only entitled to costs up to the time of the offer, and that the defendant was entitled to the subsequent costs. *Belyea* v. *Stephenson*, *Mich. T.* 1866.

X.

Miscellaneous.

Bail—Staying Proceedings. See Bail 10.

Cognovit. See Cognovit.

Consent Rule. See Amendment III. 7.

Corporation—Summary Proceedings. See Corporation 1.

Corporation not liable to attachment for non-payment of Costs. See Attachment 1.

Certificate of Judge for full Costs. See Judge (Certificate of Judge).

Jury Challenge—Lateness of objection—Costs of day not allowed. See Oulton *v.* Morse, 2 Kerr 77.

Refusal to pay Costs. See Attachment 11.

New Trial. See Costs 42, 95, 96.
" Practice VIII. 9.

Award—Setting aside. See Arbitration.

Verdict—Setting aside—Costs to abide the event of suit where affidavits did not clearly state that defendant had no knowledge of suit pending. See Cameron *v.* Connell, 2 All. 398.

Conviction. See Justice of Peace VII.

Witnesses attendance—Affidavit of. See Affidavit IV.; General Rules 32.

Interlocutory Proceedings, Costs generally in discretion of Court. See Supreme Court in Equity 3.

Appeals not generally entertained in questions of costs. *Ibid.*

Ejectment—Improperly obtaining Rule to defend—Costs allowed Lessor. See Doe *v.* Fen, 1 All. 633.

Attorney—Right to receive Costs of judgment assigned. See Attorney III

Right to taxable charges between Attorney and Client. See Attorney III.

Counsel Fees. See Attorney III.

Inferior Court—Mandamus refused to compel Court to award costs. See Mandamus 8.

Judge's Certificate for costs cannot be made a Rule of Court. See Horner *v.* Crookshank, 4 All. 375.

Arbitrators power to award costs. See Arbitration.

Bill of Costs—Delivery of—Action on. See Attorney VIII.

Nolle Prosequi—Where plaintiff enters a *nolle prosequi* to one count of declaration defendant cannot enter judgment for costs until other counts are disposed of. See Allison *v.* Smith, 4 All. 238.

Motion for judgment, as in case of non-suit and for costs of day at same time for same default, latter motion discharged, with costs. See Stevens *v.* Hamilton, 1 Han. 335.

No jurisdiction.
If an order for review is made by a Judge in a case where he has no jurisdiction, the Court has no power to give costs to the party opposing the order, *Bustin* v. *Howell*, 1 *All.* 596. (See No. 60.)

Challenge to array.
Where defendant challenges the array on the ground of affinity between himself and the Sheriff, and the challenge is sustained, the defendant is entitled to the costs of the day as a general rule. See *Sirois* v. *Hammond*, 1 *Han.* 332.

Inquiry—Attendance—No sufficient notice of countermand—Costs allowed. See Practice IX. 10, 11.

New trial granted on payment of costs where the costs have been taxed and demanded of the attorney who obtained the rule, who was informed that unless the costs were paid an application would be made to discharge the rule; the Court granted a rule for that purpose absolute, unless the costs were paid in ten days after service. See *Scribner* v. *McLauchlin*, 1 *All.* 440.

Penalty—Bye-law—Fredericton.
Costs cannot be given for breach of bye-law: the word "costs" in 81st section means costs of distress and sale. See *Ex parte Mowry*, 3 *All.* 276.

Conviction sustained for penalty. *Ibid.*

Application discharged.
Reasonable grounds for making—Costs refused to plaintiff. See *Hardy* v. *Prince*, 3 *All.* 204.

Attorney General—Retaining Fee—Costs. See Attorney General.

COURTS.

See Admiralty—City Court.
" County Court—Exchequer.
" Portland (Town of).
" Inferior Courts—Justice of the Peace.
" Probate Court.
" Supreme Court of Judicature.
" Supreme Court in Equity.
" Surrogate.

COUNSEL.

Addressing Jury—Admissions by—Examination of—Fees. See Attorney X., Evidence I.

COUNTY COURT.

Judge making ex parte order for new trial.
In an action in the County Court, the jury having found a verdict for the defendant, contrary to the Judge's direction, he made an *ex parte* order for a new trial. On appeal, the order was reversed, and the case sent back to the County Court, with directions to issue an order calling on the defendant to show cause why a new trial should not be granted. *Commercial Bank* v. *Price*, *East. T.* 1872.

SUPREME COURT.

1—Jurisdiction—Necessary that proceedings should be first certified.
The Supreme Court has no jurisdiction over a cause in the County Court until the Judge has certified a copy of the proceedings, as directed by Acts 30 Vic. c. 10, s. 24, and 33 Vic. c. 20, s. 4; therefore, a party who has recovered a judgment in the County Court, against which proceedings for appeal had been taken, and notice of appeal given, but the proceedings had not been certified by the Judge, is not entitled to the costs of appearing to argue the appeal. *Ryan* v. *James*, *Mich. T.* 1870.

2—Illegible Certificate of Proceedings.
Where the proceedings, certified by the Judge of the County Court, on an appeal were generally illegible, the Court refused to hear the argument. *Dibblee* v. *Wood*, *Trin. T.* 1871.

3—Death of Judge after granting rule nisi—Proceedings.
Where the Judge of the County Court died after granting a rule *nisi* for a new trial on the ground of misdirection, but

no minute of his direction to the jury could be found. Held, That his successor might receive affidavits to shew what the direction was, in order to determine the application for a new trial. *Kinnear* v. *Calhoun*, *Mich. T.* 1871.

4—Jurisdiction—Offset—Recalling Evidence.
Where the plaintiff proved goods sold and delivered to the defendant, beyond the amount recoverable in the County Court, and also admitted the receipt of goods from and work done by the defendant, which, if deducted from the plaintiff's account, would have brought the amount within this jurisdiction; but omitted to prove any agreement that such goods and work were to be taken as payment, whereupon the defendant moved for a non-suit. Held, That it was discretionary with the Judge to allow the plaintiff to be recalled to prove that there was such an agreement. *Simpson* v. *Glass*, *Trin. T.* 1872.

5—Judge refusing to hear motion—Jurisdiction.
Where the Judge of the County Court refused a non-suit moved for on the ground that the case was beyond the jurisdiction of the Court, and the defendant afterwards moved for a new trial on the same ground before the successor of the Judge (who had died), and he, being of opinion that the Court had not jurisdiction, and that he had consequently no power to grant a new trial, declined to make any order. Held, That he should have ordered a non-suit to be entered; and the cause was remitted to the County Court for that purpose. *Boltenhouse* v. *Black*, *East. T.* 1872.

Action brought in Supreme Court—Title to land involved—Costs allowed. See Costs, 10, 11, 12.

6—Insolvent Act of 1869—Judge proper party to hear petition—Of what County.
The County Court Judge of the County in which the demand on the debtor to assign is made, is the proper party to hear the petition, although the debtor may reside and do business in another County. *Ex parte Thomas*, 2 *Han.* 163.

7—Taking examination of Debtor—County.
A Judge of the County Court may examine and make his order for the support or discharge of any debtor, in any County within his district, even if the debtor has been arrested and is in gaol, or on the limits in another County in his district. *Ex parte Jardine*, 1 *Han.* 572.

8—Sureties on Limit Bond—Render.
Judge may make order for render of principal; "*Bail*" in Act 12 Vic. c. 39, s. 14, includes sureties on limit bond. See *Bail* 18.

9—Right to stay proceedings—City Court—Interlocutory Order—Appeal.
The County Courts and the City Court of St. John, being both Courts of limited jurisdiction, and, in suits for the recovery of debts, of concurrent jurisdiction; a Judge of the County Court has no power to stay the proceedings in a suit brought to recover a debt in that Court, on payment of the debt without costs, on the ground that the suit might have been brought in the City Court, where the costs are less than in the County Court. *Hanington* v. *Stewart*, *Hil. T.* 1873.

Quære, Whether there is any appeal to the Supreme Court under the Act 30 Vic. c. 10, from an interlocutory order of a Judge of the County Court. But an order absolutely to stay the proceedings in a suit is a final decision, and may be appealed from. *Ibid.*

10—Acts relating to Grand and Petit Jurors in Criminal Matters.
The Acts relating to the attendance of Grand and Petit Jurors at the County Courts are within the powers of the Local Legislature, under "The British North America Act 1867," s. 92, as pertaining to the "Administration of Justice," and the "Constitution and organization of Provincial Courts," and do not belong to the Parliament of Canada under Sec. 91, as "Procedure in Criminal Matters." *Regina* v. *Foley*, *East. T.* 1873.

COUNTY COURT JUDGE.

See County Court.

COUNTERMAND.

Notice of—Time when given to save costs. See General Rules 77.

Notice of inquiry to save costs—Insufficiency of. See Practice IX. 10, 11.

COVENANT.

1—Construction—Mutual and Independent.

The defendant covenanted with the plaintiff to teach him the trade of a blacksmith, and the plaintiff covenanted to serve the defendant faithfully for five years, and not to absent himself from the defendant's service without leave. Held, That these covenants were mutual and independent, and that the non-performance by the plaintiff was no defence to an action against the defendant for breach of his covenant. *Hunter* v. *Gifford*, 1 *All.* 701.

2—Breach of.

A covenant "to keep up" a mill dam is broken by allowing it to remain out of repair after notice. *Leonard* v. *Young*, 4 *All.* 111.

3—To keep dam in repair, is a covenant running with the land. See Infra 10. Philps *v.* St. John Water Co.

4—Assignee of—Privity of estate—Conveyance.

Where the assignee of a covenant running with the land, had parted with his estate therein previous to bringing the action—Held, That he had parted with his action also. *Wallace* v. *Vernon*, 1 *Kerr* 5.

5—Action—Lessor against lessee—Reversion parted with—Rent.

An action of covenant for non-payment of rent does not lie by the lessor against the lessee, where the lessor has parted with his reversion in part of the property, since the lease; the rent being entire and not apportionable. *Rector &c. of Sackville* v. *Bacon*, *Trin. T.* 1864.

Particular Covenants—Assignee of Term—Improvements. See Landlord and Tenant VI. 2.

6—For quiet enjoyment—Dam overflowing.

The defendant by deed, containing the words "grant, bargain and sell," conveyed to the plaintiff a mill and mill privilege, and afterwards erected a dam on his own land further down the stream, by which the plaintiff's land was overflowed, and his mill prevented from working. Held, That this was a breach of the covenant for quiet enjoyment given by the Act 10 Vic. c. 42. *Wells* v. *Trenholm*, 2 *All.* 371.

7—Against Erections—Assignee—Estoppel.

Plaintiffs being owners of land below low-water mark in the harbour of St. John, granted to H., the owner of a lot fronting thereon, the right to extend below low-water mark, a wharf built upon his lot, and H. covenanted for himself, his heirs and assigns, that he would not erect any buildings on the wharf so to be built. H. afterwards extended his wharf beyond low-water mark and assigned to the defendant, who erected buildings on the wharf. Low-water mark had receded to the outer end of the wharf since the grant was made. Held, That the covenant bound the assignee, and that he was estopped from denying that the wharf was built and occupied subject to the conditions of the grant, and from claiming a right to build, as owner, of the land by accretion. *Mayor &c. of Saint John* v. *Smith*, 3 *All.* 103.

8—Lessee—Rights—Renewal of lease—Appraisement—Payment for improvements—Enforcing valid covenants.

A lease by a Church Corporation created by Act of Assembly 29 Geo. 3, c. 1, contained a covenant, that, if at the expiration of the term, the lessee should desire a new lease for twenty-one years he should be entitled to the preference; and in case he should refuse to take such new lease on the terms required by the lessor, that the buildings then on the demised premises, erected by the lessee, should be appraised, and that the lessor *first paying to the lessee the amount of such appraisement*, should be entitled to enter upon the premises and have the improvements: and in case the lessor should not consider it expedient to pay the amount of the appraisement, that then the lessee should be entitled to receive "a new lease of the premises for a further term of twenty-one years *upon the same terms and conditions of this present lease.*" Held, on renewal of the lease, that the lessee was entitled to the same covenants for payment for improvements and for delivering up possession on receiving such payment, as were contained in the former lease. *Bedell* v. *Rector &c. of Christ's Church, Fredericton*, 3 *All.* 217.

Quære, Whether by the words "first paying," etc. in the covenant, the lessor's right of re-entry at the end of the term, was suspended until the value of the buildings was paid to the lessee; or whether the lessor would only be liable on the covenant if he re-entered without payment. *Ibid.*

A covenant to do one of two things at the option of the covenantor, one of which is lawful and the other not, may be enforced as to that which is lawful. Thus a covenant in a lease by a Church corporation to pay the lessee for the buildings on the land at the end of the term, or grant him a new lease for a further term of twenty-one years on the same terms and conditions as the former lease, may be enforced so far as relates to the payment of the buildings, though that part which relates to the renewal may be void under the Statute 13 Eliz. c. 10. *Bedell* v. *Rector &c. of Christ's Church, Fredericton*, 3 *All.* 217.

Quære, Whether the Statute 13 Eliz. c. 10, applies to Church Corporations in this Province? *Ibid.*

9—Good Title—Existing Lease—Surrender.

The defendant demised land to M. for a term of years, by lease under seal, and afterwards, with the consent of M., conveyed the same land, with an adjoining piece, to the plaintiff in fee, and covenanted that it was free from incumbrances. M. remained in possession of the land after the conveyance, but paid no rent. Held, That this did not amount to a surrender of the lease by operation of the law, and therefore that there was a breach of the covenant. *Babbit* v. *Cowperthwaite*, 3 *All.* 254.

The mere consent of the lessee to a conveyance by the owner of the land, of his interest in the reversion, will not constitute a surrender of the lease by the operation of law. He must be a party to some act done, the validity of which he is estopped from disputing, and which would not be valid if the lease had continued to exist. *Ibid.*

10—To keep dam in repair—Construction.

Defendants being the owners of land through which a stream of water flowed, and across which they had built a dam connecting with a natural bank or point of land which formed part of the dam, leased the land adjoining below the dam to the plaintiffs and P. (who afterwards assigned to the plaintiffs) and their assigns, and covenanted to maintain and keep the dam in good repair at all times during the term: proviso, that if the supply of water should be cut off by the destruction or injury of the dam, the rent should be suspended. The bank was broken by an extraordinary flood, which overflowed and injured the plaintiffs' property. Held, 1st. That the covenant to repair only extended to the artificial dam built by the defendants, and not to the natural bank. 2nd. That even if it did extend to the natural bank, the accident was no breach of the covenant, if the defendants repaired the dam within a reasonable time. 3rd. That even if there was a breach of the covenant, the plaintiffs were not entitled to recover for the destruction of their property and suspension of their business, as damages resulting from such breach. *Philps* v. *The St. John Water Company*, 4 *All.* 24.

The covenant to keep the dam in repair is a covenant running with the land; and *semble* that the damages recoverable for breach of such a covenant, are confined to those sustained by the covenantee or his assigns, from the privation of the proper use of the demised premises by the default of the covenanter. *Ibid.*

Semble, That if the injury to the plaintiffs' property was caused by the negligence of the defendants in not keeping the dam in repair, the plaintiffs might recover the consequential damages in an action on the case. *Ibid.*

11—For title to land—Eviction.

The defendant conveyed land to A. in 1844, and covenanted that he had full power and authority to sell; A. put a tenant in possession who gave up the property to B., who claimed title to it as heir to his father. B.'s father took possession of the land in 1814, and died seized in 1824 leaving a widow, who a few years after conveyed her right and gave up possession to a person under whom the defendant claimed. Held, 1. That B. had a good title against every one but the original grantee, and therefore had a right to enter and evict A. 2. That B.'s entry having been made under his own title, and not under that of A.'s tenant, it amounted to an eviction, and that A. was not bound before bringing an action on the covenant, to resume possession of the land, or to give notice to the defendant of B.'s claim. *Beck* v. *Barlow*, 1 *All.* 465.

12—Breach—Pleading—Judgment non obstante veredicto—Right of immediate action.

To an action of covenant upon the words "grant, bargain and sell," in a conveyance of land, assigning as a breach the existence of a prior mortgage, the defendant pleaded that the mortgage was recorded in the public records, and that the plaintiff received the deed subject to such mortgage: an issue thereon having been found for the defendant, judgment was given for the plaintiff, *non obstante veredicto*, the plea being no answer to the action. The covenant is broken immediately, and the plaintiff need not wait until he is evicted before bringing his action. *Good* v. *End*, 1 *All.* 603.

13—Breach in Lifetime of Covenantee—Action—By whom—Heir—Executor.

If a covenant for title is broken in the lifetime of the covenantee, no estate descends to the heir, and an action for the breach is properly brought by the executor. *Beek* v. *Barlow*, 1 *All.* 465.

14—Where the breach of a covenant for title, and the damage arising therefrom, both occurred in the lifetime of the testator, the action for such breach should be brought by the executor. *Cunningham* v. *Scoullar*, 4 *All.* 385.

15—Policy of Insurance—Indorsement—Not under Seal—Covenant not maintainable.

A policy of insurance on goods against loss by fire was effected in the name of G. F. & Co.; the plaintiff H. F. having afterwards become the owner of the goods, the agent of the company made and signed the following indorsement on the policy: "This insurance is hereby continued in the name of H. F." Held (assuming that the agent had power so to continue the assurance for the benefit of the plaintiff), That the indorsement not being under the seal of the company, the plaintiff could not maintain covenant on the policy. *Frost* v. *Liverpool, London and Globe Insurance Co.*, *Hil. T.* 1871.

Assignee of Lease against Lessor—Privity of Estate—Possessory Estate.
See Assignment 3.

Property taken subject to Covenant.
See Equity 4.

CREDIBILITY.

See Witness.

CREDIT.

Repairs of Ship—Agent. See Assumpsit 45.

Unexpired Credit. See Action at Law VII. 2.

Privity—Personal Responsibility. See New Trial II. 22.

Salary of Preacher—Committee.

The plaintiff was engaged at a certain salary as a preacher at a meeting of the members of the church to which he belonged, and where a committee was appointed to collect subscriptions to pay his salary. The defendants were deacons of the church present at the meeting, and there was conflicting evidence whether they were the committee and whether they had made themselves liable to the plaintiff. Held, That it was properly left to the jury whether the plaintiff had engaged on the personal responsibility of the defendants, or whether he depended upon the voluntary subscriptions of the church.

Quære, Whether the mere nomination of a party on a committee renders him liable on contracts entered into by the other members, unless he has taken some part in the proceedings. *Lawton* v. *Wilder*, 2 *All.* 416.

Intoxicating Liquors.

The prohibition in the Act 17 Vic. c. 15, s. 13, against selling liquors on credit only applies to inn-keepers and tavern-keepers. See *McAuley* v. *Lawlor*, 4 *All.* 600.

Inquiry—Judgment by Default—Evidence.

After judgment by default on common counts, defendant, on execution of writ of inquiry, may shew that he contracted merely as agent of third person to whom credit was given. See *Fauls* v. *Sargent*, 3 *Kerr* 248.

Contract—Whether with Firm, or personal member of. See Contract 15.

Insurance Broker—Credit to—Agent. See Principal and Agent 1, 2.

Work and Labour—Agreement to Credit towards Rent. See Assumpsit III. 40.

CREDITOR.

See Insolvent Act of 1869.

Judgment Creditor—Remedy at Law before—Application in Equity. See Equity 6.

CRIMINAL LAW.

Summary Conviction. See Justice of the Peace IV.

I.

PROCEDURE AND PRACTICE.

1—Revenue Act—Operation.
The Revenue Act, 15 Vic. c. 28, s. 68, enacted that any penalty or forfeiture inflicted under that Act should be recovered by action of debt or information; section 72 enacted that if any person should assault any revenue officer in the exercise of his office, he should on conviction, pay a fine not exceeding £100, nor less than £50, which fine should be paid to the Provincial Treasurer; and in case of non-payment, the offender should be imprisoned for a term not exceeding twelve months, nor less than three months, at the discretion of the Court. Held, That the Act only limited the discretion of the Court as to the amount of fine and imprisonment on conviction for an assault under section 72, but did not alter the ordinary mode of proceeding by indictment. *Reg.* v. *Walsh*, 3 *All.* 54.

2—Alteration by Statute—Effect of.
An offence committed before, though tried after the Revised Statutes came in force, is not indictable under those Statutes, though the words creating the offence are not altered thereby. *Reg.* v *McLaughlan*, 3 *All.* 159.

The forms of indictment in the Schedule to Title XL. of the Revised Statutes are inapplicable to offences not referred to in that title. *Reg.* v. *McLauchlan*, 3 *All.* 159.

3—Necessary Allegation—Grievous Bodily Harm.
An indictment under the Act 12 Vic. c. 29, for causing grievous bodily harm, must allege the offence to have been committed "maliciously" in the words of the Act. It is not included in the word "feloniously." *Reg.* v. *Jope*, 3 *All.* 161.

4—Adjournment of Court.
Where a Circuit Court is adjourned to a future day, in consequence of unfinished civil business, the criminal jurisdiction of the adjourned Court is not confined to the trial of offences committed before the adjournment. *Reg.* v. *Dennis*, 3 *All.* 423.

5—Arrest of judgment—Objections.
Objections on motion to arrest judgment are confined to the questions in the case stated by the Judge under the Act. See *Reg.* v. *Fenety*, 3 *All.* 132.

6—Authority to find lesser offence—Mode of procedure established.
The Revised Statutes c. 159, s. 16, by which, on a trial for felony the jury is authorized to acquit of the felony and find a verdict of guilty of a misdemeanor, if the evidence warrants it, establishes a general mode of procedure in all criminal cases, and is not confined to felonies existing at the time of the passing of the Statute; therefore, on an indictment for a felonious assault under the Act 25 Vic. c. 10, the prisoner may be found guilty of an assault only. *Reg.* v. *Ryan*, 1 *Han.* 116.

7—Jury recommending no bill—Termination.
Where a bill of indictment laid before the Grand Jury was returned by them into Court with an indorsement "the Grand Jury recommend no bill," and no further proceedings are taken against the party, it is a termination of the prosecution. *Alward* v. *Sharp*, 1 *Han.* 286.

8—Assault—Revenue officer—Breaking open building—Justification.
By the Revenue Act 11 Vic. c. 2, a revenue officer is authorised to enter any building wherein he shall have cause to suspect smuggled goods to be concealed, provided that before entry, information on oath shall be given to a Justice of the Peace, that such officer has reasonable cause to suspect such goods are concealed therein, and that such Justice shall go

with the officer to such building, and authorise him to enter and search for goods, and if the doors be closed and admission denied, then after first demanding to be admitted and declaring the purpose of the entry, it shall be lawful for the Justice to direct the officer to enter the building and search for goods. Held, That to justify the breaking open a building, there should have been, 1st, a written information on oath; and 2nd, the actual presence of the Justice at the breaking; his being near to the place is not sufficient. *Reg.* v. *Walsh*, 2 *All.* 387.

Not opening a building after a proper demand, is a sufficient denial within the Act. *Ibid.*

If the breaking open is unlawful, the officer cannot justify the seizure of smuggled goods found within the building. *Ibid.*

Semble, That an order to enter, given to a police officer present with the revenue officer, would be sufficient, and that he would be presumed to be acting in aid. *Ibid.*

9—Information to recover penalties—Breach of Revenue Law—Dutiable articles.

By Act of Parliament 8 and 9 Vic. c. 93, gunpowder is prohibited from being imported into the British possessions in America, except from the United Kingdom or some British possession. Held, 1st. That gunpowder coming from a foreign country, could not be proceeded against as a non-enumerated dutiable article, under the Provincial Revenue Act 11 Vic. c. 1, for being imported into the Province at a place not a port of entry, contrary to the Act 11 Vic. c. 2, s. 21. But 2nd. That it was liable to seizure and forfeiture under the seventeenth section of that Act, for being landed without entry at the Treasury. *The Attorney General* v. *four hundred kegs of Gunpowder*, 2 *All.* 493.

The Provincial Legislature has power to impose additional grounds of forfeiture for breach of the revenue laws, on goods subject to forfeiture under an Act of Parliament. *Ibid.*

II.

Indictment.

1—Prosecutor—Grand Juror.

Where one of the Grand Jurors, by whom an indictment for forcible entry and detainer was found at the Sessions, was the prosecutor, the indictment having been removed into the Supreme Court, was quashed, though after plea. *Reg.* v. *Cunard et. al.*, *Ber.* 326.

Affidavits shewing that the prosecutor was not present when the bill was found by the Grand Jury, and took no part in the matter, were not received: his name appearing as one of the jurors in the caption of the indictment as returned on the *certiorari*. *Ibid.*

2—Allegation—Liability to Repair.

The Corporation of St. John being bound by public law to repair the highways in the city, it is sufficient in an indictment for not repairing, to allege that the defendants "ought of right" to repair, etc., without setting forth the particular ground of liability. *Rex.* v. *Mayor &c. of St. John*, *Hil. T.* 1828.

The Corporation is not bound to widen a bridge. *Ibid.*

3—In an indictment under 1 Rev. Stat. c. 147, for unlawfully and maliciously pulling down a building, it is not necessary to allege that it was done "riotously." *Reg.* v. *Elston*, *Hil. T.* 1861.

4—Malice.

If a building is pulled down unlawfully, and without any *bona fide* belief by the defendants that they had the right to do it, the jury may infer malice; malice may be inferred from the commission of a wrongful act, forbidden by law, without any personal malice against the owner of the property. *Ibid.*

5—For Stealing—Restoring Goods—Order by Judge.

On an indictment for stealing goods, the prisoner was acquitted, the defence being that the goods were his own. Held, That it was virtually a finding by the jury that the goods were not the property of the prosecutor, and therefore, that the Judge had no right to order them to be restored to him. *Reg.* v. *Eveleth*, *Trin. T.* 1861.

6—Stealing Goods in Foreign Country.

On an indictment for stealing, it appeared that the goods were taken in the State of Maine, and brought into this Province. Held, That in the absence of proof, that the taking was larceny according to the laws of Maine, the prisoner could not be convicted of larceny here. *Reg.* v. *Hill*, *Mich. T.* 1863.

7—Murder—Conviction for Assault.
On an indictment for murder, the jury found the prisoner guilty of an assault only, and that such assault did not conduce to the death of the deceased. Held, on this finding, That the prisoner could not be convicted of an assault under 1 Rev. Stat. c. 149, s. 20. *Reg.* v. *Cregan*, 1 *Han.* 36.

8—County—Vessel passing through.
By the Act 12 Vic. c. 30, s. 34, where any felony or misdemeanour is committed on any person on board any vessel employed on any voyage on any navigable river, etc., such offence may be dealt with, tried, determined, and punished in any county through any part of which such vessel shall have passed in the course of the passage in which the offence was committed, in the same manner as if it had actually been committed in such county. Held, In an indictment for an assault committed on board a steamboat, on its passage between A. and B., but before it came within the county of B., that it was sufficient to allege that the assault took place within the county of B. *Reg.* v. *Webster*, 1 *All.* 589.

9—Bodily Harm—Design—Setting out means used.
By the Act 12 Vic. c. 29, "whosoever shall maliciously by any means manifesting a design to cause grievous bodily harm, attempt to cause grievous bodily harm to any other person whether any bodily harm be caused to such person or not, shall be guilty of felony." Held, That an indictment charging the prisoner with having maliciously assaulted J. M. and cut him with a knife, with intent to do him grievous bodily harm, concluding *contra formam statuti*, was bad; the means used to manifest the design to commit a felony not being set out with sufficient particularity. *Reg.* v. *Magee*, 2 *All.* 14.

Held also, That the conviction could not stand for an assault, as the Act [Art. 17] did not apply where the indictment was defective, but where the evidence proved an assault under circumstances not amounting to a felony. *Ibid.*

If the indictment does not charge a felony including an assault, the prisoner cannot be convicted of an assault under Art. 17. *Ibid.*

10—Smuggling—Insufficient Allegation.
An indictment for smuggling, under the Revised Statutes, c. 29, charged in several counts: 1st. That the defendant unlawfully landed alcohol, subject to duty, and thereby smuggled the same. 2nd. That defendant unlawfully landed alcohol, subject to duty, without reporting to the Treasurer, and thereby smuggled, etc. 3rd. That the defendant landed the alcohol without a permit, and thereby smuggled, etc. 4th. That the defendant landed alcohol without paying the duties. Held, 1st. That the indictment was insufficient; as the mere unlawful landing of goods, without alleging any intent to defraud the revenue, did not constitute the offence of smuggling. 2nd. That the landing of goods without reporting them to the Treasurer, or without obtaining a permit, though it subjected the party to a penalty, did not amount to smuggling. 3rd. That the mere landing of goods without a previous payment of duties is not a breach of the revenue laws. *Reg.* v. *Cassidy*, 4 *All.* 623.

11—Furnishing copies of indictment after acquittal.
After an acquittal, no copy of an indictment should be furnished without the order of the Judge or the fiat of the Attorney General. *Heaney* v. *Lynn*, *Ber.* 27.

12—Embezzlement—Property not in prosecutor.
The prisoner was apprentice to a baker, and had authority from his master to deliver bills for bread to customers, and receive the amounts. In payment of one account he received a bank check payable to his master "or order," upon which he forged his master's name, and received the money from the bank. Held, on these facts, That he could not be convicted on an indictment charging that *he did, by virtue of his employment, as the servant of A. B., take into his possession a certain sum of money, for and on account of the said A. B., and did feloniously embezzle the said money, so being the property of the said A. B.*, the money received by the prisoner never having been the property of A. B. by reason of the forgery, but the property of the bank; and not having been received by virtue of the prisoner's employment as the servant of A. B. *Reg.* v. *Hatheway*, *Hil. T.* 1866.

13—Different Counts—Separate offence—Evidence.

Where a prisoner was convicted on an indictment containing two counts, charging separate offences and sentenced, and the evidence did not sustain the charge in one of the counts, but proved an offence of a different character, the judgment was arrested. *Reg.* v. *Hatheway*, *Hil. T.* 1866.

14—Larceny—Place of trial.

Larceny committed on the high sea on a voyage from Ireland to Saint John, does not come within the 1 Rev. Stat. c. 158, s. 10, relating to the place of trial of offences committed during a voyage, but may be tried under the Act of Parliament 18 and 19 Vic. c. 91. *Reg.* v. *Dillon*, *Hil. T.* 1864.

15—Fraudulent appropriation—Place.

The prisoner received from the prosecutor, in the County of Westmoreland, a quantity of boots and shoes to be sold on commission; he took them to the County of Kent, where he resided, and then to the County of Glocester, where he sold them, and fraudulently appropriated the money to his own use. On an indictment for larceny in the County of Kent, under the Act 27 Vic. c. 6, s. 1, which makes the bailee of a chattel, who fraudulently converts it, guilty of larceny,—the jury were unable to agree whether the prisoner fraudulently intended to appropriate the property in the County of Kent, or not until he had sold it in the County of Glocester. Held, That he could not be convicted on the indictment. *Reg.* v. *Cormier*, *Mich. T.* 1865.

16—Death caused by drowning.

An indictment charged the prisoner, being the mother of an infant of tender age, and unable to take care of itself, with feloniously placing it upon the shore of a river in an exposed situation, where it was liable to fall into the water, and abandoning it there with the intent that it should perish; by means of which exposure the child fell into the river and was suffocated and drowned, of which suffocation, etc. the child died. Held, That to support the indictment it was necessary to prove that the death was caused by drowning or suffocation. *Reg.* v. *Fenety*, 3 *All.* 132.

The objections on a motion to arrest judgment, are confined to the questions in the case stated by the Judge under the Act. *Ibid.*

17—Feloniously striking—Cause of death.

An indictment charged the prisoner with feloniously striking the deceased on the head with a handspike, giving him thereby a mortal wound and fracture, of which he died. It was proved that the death was caused by the blow on the head with the handspike, but that there was no external wound or fracture, the immediate cause of death being concussion of the brain, produced by the blow. Held, That the evidence supported the indictment. *Regina* v. *Shea*, 3 *All.* 129.

18—Resisting Constable—Form of execution.

An execution issued by a Justice of the Peace is sufficient, if it substantially follows the form K in the Schedule to the Rev. Stat. c. 137; and any person resisting a constable in executing it is liable to indictment. *Reg.* v. *McDonald*, 4 *All.* 440.

19—Regulations—Penalty—Misdemeanour.

By Act 3 Wm. 4, c. 28, s. 5, Boards of Health were authorized to make such rules and regulations for the preservation of the public health, and the prevention of infectious distempers, with such penalties and forfeitures for breach thereof, as they might deem necessary. By subsequent sections of the Act they were authorised to enter buildings and cause the removal of anything injurious to health; to close up streets, etc.; to prevent intercourse with vessels, and order them to quarantine; and by section 11 whoever should violate any of the orders of the Board, or wilfully neglect to act in obedience thereto, or should resist or obstruct the lawful execution of any such orders, should, for every offence "be deemed guilty of, and punishable as for a misdemeanor." The Board made a regulation against the use of slaughter houses within certain limits, but attached no penalty to the breach of it. Held, 1st. That the omission of a penalty did not render the regulation void; and that the defendant was liable to indictment for a breach of it either at common law or under the 11 section. 2nd. That the 11th section applied to the violation of any regulation or order the Board was authorized to make, and was not limited to the orders authorised by the sections of the Act, subsequent to the fifth section. *Regina* v. *Hartt*, *Trin. T.* 1833.

20—Forgery—Bank Note—What amounts to.

Forgery, or uttering in this Province a writing purporting to be a bank note issued by a Banking Company in the State of Maine, amounts to the crime of forgery, though it is not proved that the Company had power by its charter to issue notes of that description. *Reg.* v. *Brown*, 3 *All.* 13.

21—Perjury—Power to administer Oath.

A Commissioner authorised to take affidavits in the Supreme Court, has no power to take an affidavit of the service of an order in case of review of the judgment of a Justice of the Peace, and a party swearing falsely in such an affidavit cannot be indicted for perjury. *Reg.* v. *McIntosh*, 1 *Han.* 372.

22—*Semble*, Perjury may be assigned where the oath has been administered on the Common Prayer Book of the Church of England. See *McAdam* v. *Weaver*, 2 *Kerr*, 176.

See Perjury.

III.

EVIDENCE.

1—Evidence—Confession of Accomplice.

In an action of trespass for false imprisonment, the defendant pleaded that a felony had been committed, and he had reasonable grounds to suspect the plaintiff, and therefore arrested him and detained him until he was taken before a magistrate. Held, That the confession of a third person that he, together with the plaintiff, committed the felony, was not admissible in evidence as proof of the felony. *Blair* v. *Hopkins*, 1 *Kerr* 540.

2—Wife of one of two parties on trial not competent witness for either.

A. and B. were tried together on a joint indictment for an assault on a peace officer, and the wife of A. was offered as a witness to disprove the charge against B. Held, That her evidence was properly rejected, but had the husband not been on his trial she would have been a competent witness. *The Queen* v. *Thompson and Conroy*, 2 *Han.* 71.

Idem, (See *The Queen* v. *Thompson and others*, L. R. 1 Vol. Crown C. Reserved 377.)

3—Deceased Witness—Statement.

The statement of a deceased person, taken on oath by a magistrate, detailing the circumstances under which a felony was committed upon him, is admissible in evidence on the trial of the accused under 1 Rev. Stat. c. 156, s. 7, though it is headed, "The complaint," etc., instead of "The e[illegible]nation," etc., and does not appear c[illegible]ce to have been taken in the presence of the accused, it being proved that it was taken in his presence. *Reg.* v. *Millar*, *Hil. T.* 1861.

IV.

MISCELLANEOUS.

Constable—Fees—Judge certifying.

A Judge presiding at a Court of Oyer and Terminer has no power to make an order for the payment of constable for attending the Court, or swearing the attendance of witnesses in a criminal trial. (But see Acts of Assembly 35 Vic. c. 12.) *Mulligan* v. *Rainsford*, 2 *Han.* 1.

Certified fees of a constable may be recovered in an action before a Justice of the Peace, when suffic[illegible] funds in County Treasurer's hand[illegible]y them. *Ibid.*

Acts relating to att[illegible]ce of Grand and Petit Jurors in criminal matters at County Court are within powers of local Legislature. See County Courts 10.

CRIMINAL INFORMATION.

1—If the conduct of the prosecutor has been blameable, the Court will not grant a criminal information against a magistrate, at his instance; but if the conduct of the magistrate is not justifiable, the rule will be discharged without costs. *Rex* v. *Munro*, *East. T.* 1831.

2—A rule for a criminal information will be discharged with costs, where the facts upon which it was granted are disproved by the affidavit on shewing cause. *Rex* v. *Bates*, *Trin. T.* 1832.

CROSS ACTION.

See Damages 11.

CROSS EXAMINATION.

No right to prove justification upon, before defence opened.

Re-examination upon.

As to contents of written statement.

See Evidence VIII.

CROWN.

Right to enter on land used as a public road. See Highway 17.

CROWN BONDS.

The Statute 33 Hen. 8, c. 39, extends to this Province, and therefore the lands of a bond debtor to the King are bound from the date of the bond. *Rex.* v. *McLaughlan, Mich. T.* 1830.

1—Admission—No Estoppel.
In an action on a Crown Bond, in which the defendant pleaded *non est factum*, proof of an admission by him that it was his bond, is not an estoppel; and evidence having been given by the Crown of the handwriting of the subscribing witness, the defendant was allowed to give evidence that the signature of the witness was a forgery. *Reg.* v. *Robertson, Hil. T.* 1864.

2—Summary Application for Relief—Scire Facias.
Where the Attorney General had instituted a suit on behalf of the Crown by *scire facias* on a Treasury bond, conditioned for the payment of duties, the Court refused upon a summary application on affidavits for relief under the Statute 33 Hen. 8, c. 39, to determine the question as to the defendant's liability, the defendant not having pleaded to the *sci. fa.*, and the Attorney General not assenting to the application. *Regina* v. *Street*, 1 *Kerr* 373.

Sureties application for relief under 33 Hen. 8, c. 39, s. 79.

See Principal and Surety 7.

CROWN GRANT.

I. Construction. Boundaries.
Evidence.
Possession.
Meaning of Words.
Necessity of Inquest of Office.

II. Rights.
Mines and Minerals—Fishery—Glebe—Seizin—Ferry—Right to Soil.

III. Exceptions.
Mines—Minerals—Coals.

IV. Admission. Adverse Possession.
Against Crown.
Extention of boundaries by.
Subsequent Grant.

I.

Construction.

1—Controlling Line.
Letters patent granted land described as extending from a certain point thirty-two chains, or to a certain road, and thence to run a certain distance "on said road:" the road was sixty-nine chains distant from the starting point. Held, That the words of the grant necessarily imported that the second alternative in the description should be the controlling one, and that the land was bounded by the road. *Rex* v. *Wilson, Ber.* 1.

2—Bounded by lake—Margin.
A grant of land bounding on a lake, conveys the land to the margin only, and not to the centre of the lake. *Miles* v. *Burke, Hil. T.* 1873.

3—Dividing Lines—Boundaries—Several grants—Courses inconsistent.
The course laid down for the rear or dividing line between two several ranges of lots, granted by the Crown in two contemporaneous grants, founded upon one general survey of land lying between the Saint John and Kennebeccasis rivers, is not conclusive, where it is manifest that such course does not correspond with the delineation on the grant plan; is inconsistent with other parts of the description in both grants, and will not properly divide the land, or give the lots their several lengths and quantities. *Fowler* v. *Dowling*, 1 *Kerr* 581.

4—Boundaries—Protraction.
In construing the description of boundaries in a grant, ascertained lines, in the nature of fixed objects, will control courses and distances, when the course of a line is not expressed, protraction on the plan of the grant may be resorted to as an element for ascertaining the course. The marks of the original survey are to be sought for and adhered to in determining the boundaries of a grant. *Whelpley* v. *Lyons*, 2 *Kerr* 276.

5—Subsequent Grants—Reference to.
If the bounds of a lot of land are clearly ascertained by the grant, it cannot be extended by subsequent grants; but if there is any uncertainty as to the lines of a grant, subsequent grants of the Crown to other persons of adjoining lands on which the lines of the prior grant are described, may be referred to, in order

to shew where the Crown considered the lines of the prior grant to be. *Doe dem. Pensford* v. *Vernon*, 2 *Kerr* 351.

5 a—Adoption of Line by Crown—Description in Previous Grants.
Plaintiff claimed, under a grant issued in 1868, which described his land as running to the rear or last line of the Penobscott Association Grant, and referred to the plan annexed, which laid down that last line; but the plaintiff contended that the line so described on the plan was not the correct line of the old Penobscott grant, and that his land therefore would extend beyond that to where he contended the correct line was. The defendants shewed that by several other grants besides the one to the plaintiff, the same line as laid down on the plaintiff's plan had been described on the plans as the said last line, and the Court Held, That in that way the Crown had adopted that as the true line of the Penobscott grant, and that the plaintiff could only claim to it. *Arr..n* v. *McClure, East. T.* 1871.

6—Subsequent grant—Evidence of possession out of Crown.
Where land granted by the Crown in 1839 was described as being in rear of a certain lot No. 33, and *between that lot* and a lot No. 39, granted in 1784, subsequent grants from the Crown in 1786 and 1787 of adjoining lands to third persons, in which lot No. 33 is described as extending to and bounded on lot No. 39, an evidence to shew the Crown out of possession of the land described in the grant of 1839, so as to prevent that grant from operating without a previous inquest of office to re-vest the possession in the Crown. *Doe dem Pensford* v. *Vernon*, 2 *Kerr* 351.

7—Explanatory, but not to alter or vary.
If there is any uncertainty as to the lines of a tract of land granted by the Crown, subsequent grants from the Crown to other persons in which the prior grant is referred to, may be looked to for the purpose of considering where the Crown considered the lines of the prior grant to be; but not to vary its description, or alter its construction. *Doe d. Carpenter* v. *Jones*, 3 *Kerr* 155.

8—Evidence—Bounds.
A grant from the Crown is not conclusive evidence as to the bounds of any grant referred to therein, further than such bounds affect the premises of the grant itself. *Doe d. Carpenter* v. *Jones*, 3 *Kerr* 155.

9—Courses and lines by description in grant.
The true lines of a tract of land must be ascertained by the courses and distances specified in the grant, and particularly delineated on the plan of survey annexed. When there is no ambiguity in the description, and no proof of any actual survey contemporaneous with the grant, varying from the courses and distances therein specified. *Doe dem Morrison* v. *McAlpin*, 2 *Kerr* 467.

10—Prior and subsequent grants—Description.
A prior grant must have its effect, and the Crown cannot by a subsequent grant derogate from its own act, and limit the boundaries of the prior grant. Thus, where a grant to the plaintiff was described as commencing at a stake standing at the south east angle of lot No. 8, and by the plan annexed to the grant this stake was represented as distant 12 chains from the south east angle of lot No 7 (a fixed point), thereby showing lot No. 8 to be 12 chains wide, and by a subsequent grant of lot No. 8, also described as commencing at the south east angle of the same lot No. 7, it was represented as being 15 chains wide. Held, That this could not interfere with the prior grant to the plaintiff. *Robinson* v. *Wilson*, 3 *Kerr* 301.

11—Lines agreed and acted upon—Rectifying Error—Reasonable Time.
In ejectment, the lessor of the plaintiff for upwards of twenty years before the defendant's occupation, was in possession of the *locus in quo* as part of lot 43, granted in 1809, up to the rear of the boundary of that grant, ran by a Crown surveyor in 1828; and it appeared in defence that the line so run in 1828 was at the instance of the lessor, who took part in the survey and established the rear boundary, and this rear boundary was made the base line of a second tier of lots surveyed and returned to the land office, upon which a grant of such lots afterwards came out and was predicated, and the defendant became the purchaser of lot 43 at Sheriff's sale, and went into possession of the *locus in quo* as part of it about eighteen months before the trial;

the lessor in reply, showed that after such possession he, without the assent of the defendant, got another surveyor to run the rear line, who made it eight rods further in than the Crown surveyor had done, and endeavored to show by several witnesses a mistake in the first rear line, and that the lessor by reason of his long possession was entitled to the surplus as against the defendant's deed of lot 43. The learned Judge however ruled at the trial, that, whether a mistake or not, it could not be rectified after so long a period, but the first line having been agreed to at the time, and acted on by all parties interested, neither the Crown itself nor any person coming in under it, could then dispute such line. On motion for a new trial, on the ground of misdirection—Held, That such direction was right. *Semble*, That sixteen years is not a reasonable time within which to rectify such an error. *Doe dem. Belding* v. *Hallett*, 3 *Kerr* 359.

12—Lines ascertained by earlier grant—Exterior Boundaries and Interior Divisions inconsistent—Acquiescence.

The plaintiff and defendant being proprietors of adjoining tracts of land, the boundary between which tracts had not been ascertained by actual survey at the date of the grant and was in dispute—the tract belonging to the plaintiff being contained in a grant made by the Crown in 1809, and that of the defendant in a grant made in 1806. Held, That the true line must be ascertained by the terms of the earlier grant, regard being first had to the natural boundaries stated in the grant, and in subordination thereto, to the specified courses and distances—giving preference to the one or the other according to circumstances. *Brevier* v. *Govang*, 4 *All* 144.

The expression of quantity in a grant is descriptive, and is not to be disregarded where the boundaries are doubtful. *Ibid.*

The courses and distances of the exterior boundaries of a grant are rather adhered to, than those of the interior division of the tract into lots, where both cannot be reconciled, and the dispute relates to the exterior boundary. *Ibid.*

The running and marking of a line by one party, but not in accordance with the true line between adjoining grants, having only been assented to on the condition that the true line should be ascertained and run, cannot establish it as a conventional boundary until it is acquiesced in and acted upon by both parties. *Brevier* v. *Govany*, 4 *All.* 144.

13—Boundary by Shore of Tide River—Land below high water mark.

A grant bounded by the shore of a tide river does not convey any title to the land below high water mark, though it is described as one tract of land situated on both sides of the river. *Lock* v. *Cleveland*, 1 *All.* 390.

14—Controlling Distances—Ascertained Angle.

Where one of the lines of a grant was described as running a certain number of chains, or to the northwesterly angle of a grant to A., such angle being capable of ascertainment, controls the distances mentioned in the grant, whether it exceeds or falls short of the specified number of chains. *Hanson* v. *Mawheney*, 2 *Han.* 11.

15—Land Unimproved or Unoccupied within Twenty Years—No Adverse Possession.

The grantee of the Crown, according to the ordinary mode of granting wild land in this Province, being deemed *prima facie* in possession of the land granted when there is no adverse occupant, it is sufficient for a plaintiff in ejectment, who claims under such a grant more than twenty years old, to shew that the land within that period remained in its natural state and unenclosed. *Doe dem. Des Barres* v. *White*, 1 *Kerr* 595.

16—Recitals—Non-Registry—Inquest.

A grant of land from the Crown to A. in 1805 recited that a prior grant of the same land had been made to B. in 1765, under the great seal of Nova Scotia, and that such grant had not been registered in this Province, as required by the Act of Assembly 26 Geo. 3, c. 2, and also recited that it had been represented to the Government of this Province that the land had been sold and conveyed by B. to A. Held, 1st. That the recitals must be taken together, and that in the absence of any other evidence of the grant to B., and of the conveyance by him to A., the title of A., under the grant of 1805, was not disproved by the recital of the prior grant to B. 2nd. That the non-registry of the grant to B. under the Act 26 Geo. 3, c. 2, need not be found by inquest of office in order to enable the Crown to re-grant, at least, to the original grantee or his assigns. *Doe dem DesBarres* v. *White*, 1 *Kerr* 595.

17—Subsequent Grant—Recognition of Lines of Prior Grant—Presumption of Adoption by Crown.

A grant from the Crown to A. and others, was described as extending from the first bound 500 chains, or until it met the prolongation of the rear line of a prior grant. The line of A.'s grant was extended the 500 chains, and a rear line run at the end of that distance, upon which rear line the Crown afterwards bounded several grants of land by actual survey. Held, That as between the owners of lots in the grant to A., and the grantees in rear, that line must be considered as the boundary between the grants, though it appeared by a subsequent survey that it was twenty chains too far to the rear. Held also, That as the Crown, after discovering the error, took no steps to rectify it, it might be presumed to have adopted it as the rear line. *Gaudin* v. *McKilligan*, 2 *All.* 392.

18—Conditional Grant—Information for Intrusion—Inquest of Office—Authority to give Notice.

The Crown by letters patent under the great seal, granted to the defendant the right to occupy land for twenty-one years, unless the same should sooner be required by the Crown, on notice of which the grant was to cease and be void. Held, on an information for intrusion, after notice and refusal to give up possession, That as the removal of the defendant was not founded on any breach of condition, or forfeiture, no inquest of office was necessary to terminate his right. *The Queen* v. *Hebert*, 2 *All.* 427.

Semble, That a notice that the Government required the land, signed by the Surveyor General of Crown lands in his official character, was sufficient, without proof of any previous authority from the Crown to the give notice. *Ibid.*

The Crown, by subsequently laying out the land into lots and granting it, recognizes the authority of the Surveyor General to give the notice. *Ibid.*

19—Words "bank or edge," meaning of—Lake—Right to soil.

Where a grant from the Crown to B. was described as "beginning at a stake standing on the bank or edge of Round Lake, and (after describing other courses), thence south etc. to a stake standing on the westerly bank or edge of said lake, and thence following the several courses of the said bank or edge, to the place of beginning." Held, That the words "bank or edge," were intended to express the margin, and made the water's edge the boundary of A.'s grant.

N. received from the Crown a grant of Round Lake *eo nomine*, with all profits, hereditaments, etc., reserving to the Crown all mines and minerals. Held, That the grant conveyed the soil of the lake. *Burke* v. *Niles*, 2 *Han.* 166.

20—Contiguous Islands—Low Water—Meaning.

By a grant of an Island, "with all the contiguous small islands that are joined to, or connected with the said Island by a beach or shoal dry at low water," an Island that is connected with the principal one by a shoal which is only dry at extraordinary tides will not pass. *Doe* v. *Hill*, 2 *All.* 587.

"Low water" means low water at ordinary tides. *Ibid.*

II.

Rights.

1—Mines and Minerals—Condition—Construction—Necessity of Inquest of Office.

The Crown granted by letters patent to B., his executors, etc., the sole and exclusive right to make use of, work, occupy and enjoy for his benefit and advantage for the term of twenty-five years, all mines and minerals which might then have been discovered, or which might, during the continuance of the letters patent, be discovered within the bounds of certain described lands, paying therefor quarterly during the term to the use of the Queen, one shilling per chaldron for all coals which should be raised from the mines, and a duty of five per cent. on the value of all other minerals which should be raised during the term. Proviso, That if B., his executors, etc., should neglect to pay the rent or duty at the times specified, or should not commence to work the mines effectually within two years, the letters patent should cease and be void, and it should be lawful for the Crown to enter. Held, 1st. That until mines were discovered and entered upon, the instrument did not amount to a lease, but operated either as a license to dig for minerals or as a grant of an incorporeal right only; and therefore that no inquest of office was necessary to enable the Crown to take advantage of a breach of the condition. 2nd. That the patent was not absolutely void for breach of the condition, but voidable only at the election of the Crown, and that the intention of the Crown to take advantage of the breach was sufficiently manifested by the grant of a new patent to D. inconsistent with the previous patent to B., without any entry by the Crown. 3rd. That if the patent to B. had operated as a lease of the mines, or granted a corporeal hereditament, the Crown could not have taken advantage of a forfeiture, so as to re-grant the mines, without inquest of office or *scire facias*. *Le Gal* v. *Duffy*, 3 *All.* 57.

2—Fishery.
By the Act 14 Vic. c. 31, the Governor in Council was authorised to grant leases or licenses of occupation for Fishery Stations on the ungranted shores, beaches or islands of the Province. A grant was made to the plaintiff for the exclusive leave and license to occupy and enjoy as a fishing ground for the term of four years, a lot or beach abutted and described as follows, viz: "lot No. 4, on the outside of Portage Island; with the full and exclusive privilege of using the said lot or station as a fishing station." Held, That this grant did not convey any right of fishing, but merely a right to occupy a certain portion of the shore, and therefore that the defendant was not liable to an action for setting nets in front of the plaintiff's lot below low-water mark, and thereby preventing the fish from entering the plaintiff's nets. *Hierlihy* v. *Loggie*, 3 *All.* 204.

3—Glebe.
A grant of land to the Rector, Church Wardens and Vestry of a parish "for a glebe," sufficiently signifies it to be for the use and benefit of the Rector, under Act 56 Geo. c. 11. *Rector &c. of Hampton* v. *Titus*, 1 *All.* 278.

4—Seisin—Possession—Unoccupied Land.
A grant of land from the Crown under the great seal, conveys seisin to the grantee, and his possession will *prima facie* be deemed to continue, while the land remains unoccupied and unimproved. *Doe dem Kimpson* v. *Craft*, 1 *Kerr* 546.

5—A grantee of the Crown is deemed to be in possession while the land remains unoccupied and unimproved. *Doe* v. *Chace*, 3 *All.* 501.

6—Ferry—Infringement of right.
The Crown granted a ferry across the river Miramichi, between the parishes of C. and N., opposite the court house of the County, and communicating with the highway on each side of the river: the landing used on one side of the river was about two hundred yards above the court house. Held, That it was an infringement of the grantee's right to establish another ferry landing at the same place. *Fraser* v. *Drynan*, 4 *All.* 74.

7—Privilege—No right to Soil.
A grant from the Crown of a privilege to build mills in the bed of a river, does not convey any right to the soil, therefore the grantee cannot, before actual entry in the exercise of the privilege, maintain trespass against a person for building a mill upon the place where the privilege was granted. *Frink* v. *Hill*, *East. T.* 1831.

III.

Exceptions.

1—Mines and Minerals.
The Crown may grant land, and except the base mines and minerals therein.—*McMahon* v. *Berton*, 2 *All.* 321.

By a grant from the Crown of a tract of land "with the appurtenances and hereditaments thereto belonging, and mines and minerals; saving and reserving all mines of gold, silver, copper, lead, and coals;" coal mines are excepted, though no other minerals have been discovered in the land. Such an exception, without reserving a right to enter and dig, will not, as a legal incident thereto, give a right to do any act on the land which will injure the surface; and *Quære*, Whether a bare right of entry would be given as incident to such exception. *Ibid.*

Semble, That if the mine had been opened and worked by the Crown before the grant of the land, the rights incident to the exception would have been more extensive. *Ibid.*

2—All Coals—Construction—Injury to surface—License.
An exception in a Crown grant of "all coals, and all gold and silver and other mines and minerals" extends to all carbonaceous minerals; and therefore a

mineral, though not strictly coal, is excepted. *Gemer* v. *Cairns*, 2 *All.* 595.

The construction of a Crown grant cannot be limited by the Royal instructions, directing the Governor of the Province to reserve to the Crown certain minerals. *Ibid.*

A license from the Crown to dig minerals in granted land where the mines are excepted out of the grant, will not justify an injury to the surface soil. *Ibid.*

IV.

ADMISSION—ADVERSE POSSESSION AGAINST CROWN.

1—An admission in a grant from the Crown under the great seal of the Province, is evidence against the Crown. *Rex* v. *Wilson*, *Ber.* 1.

2—Adverse possession against Crown—Sufficiency.
To prevent a Crown grant from taking effect on the ground that the Crown had been out of possession for twenty years before that grant issued, the adverse possession should be defined, continuous and unequivocal. Mere isolated acts of trespass, without visible limit, and merely lumbering on the wilderness land of the Crown, without clearly defined bounds, are not sufficient. *Smith* v. *Morrow*, *Mich. T.* 1872.

3—Extending boundaries by Crown after grant.
The Crown may by a subsequent grant extend the boundaries of former grant beyond the distance mentioned therein, so far as relates to the rights of the parties claiming under the respective grants, *inter se*, though the Crown may not be estopped thereby as against the grantee in the first grant. *Aiton* v. *Demill*, *Trin. T.* 1872.

CROWN TIMBER.

1—Seizure of Timber—Place—Onus probandi.
Certain sticks of white pine timber having been seized by the proper officers of the Crown, as forfeited under the Acts of Parliament 8 Geo. 1, c. 12, and 2 Geo. 2, c. 35—Held, That upon the prosecution of such seizure, the *onus probandi* as to the place where the sticks were cut being private, and not Crown property, lies upon the claimant. *Regina* v. *Beveridge*, 1 *Kerr* 58.

2—Liability to seizure—Disputed Territory.
If timber has been cut upon Crown lands over which this Province has exercised and continues to exercise jurisdiction, it is liable to seizure here, though the territory where it is cut is claimed by the Government of Canada as being part of that Province, and license to cut timber has been granted by that Government. *Tibbits* v. *Allan*, 3 *Kerr* 280.

CROWN OFFICE.

See General Rules 98.

CURRENCY AND STERLING.

Bills of Exchange—Premium—Standard.
Where accounts are kept in Sterling money, the premium on bills of exchange drawn on England is not to be taken as the standard to ascertain the difference between currency and sterling, unless the money is payable in England. *Quære*, Whether in such a case the value of sterling money, fixed by the Act 15 Vic. c. 85, should not be taken as the standard. *Spurr* v. *Allison*, 3 *All.* 454.

CUSTOM AND USAGE OF TRADE.

As to Bills of Exchange—Drawing—*Lex Mercatoria*. See Bills and Notes I. 6.

Signing Judgment by default. See City Court.

Practice contrary to regulations of Government—License cutting Timber—Whether evidence of practice allowable. See Evidence III. 13.

Issue on Invalid Custom. See New Trial III. 33.

As to Payment of Rent. See Landlord and Tenant III. 13.

Timber Trade—Acceptors of Timber Orders. See Contract 2.

Port of Call and Discharge and Loading—Construing Policy of Insurance in reference to. See Insurance 21.

Scowage—Loading Ship. See Contract 3.

Goods laden on board Ship deck according to custom of particular trade—Owner is entitled to contribution in general average for a loss by jettison. See Shipping Law 10.

Pond Keeper—Lien on Timber. See Lien 7.

Loss of Logs by Storm—Liability. See Pond Keeper.

CUSTOM DUTIES.

1—British North America Act—Foreign Goods—Onus probandi.
Certain liquors manufactured in Ontario, prior to July 1867, warehoused for exportation and having paid no excise duty, were exported to Portland, U. S., where they were landed and immediately exported to St. John, N. B., where they arrived after the British North America Act came in force, being under the control of the Customs authorities during the whole period of transit until they left Portland. Held, That by passing through the United States they did not become foreign goods, and were entitled to be admitted free of duty under the 121st section of the British North America Act. That coming from a foreign country they were *prima facie* foreign goods, and the burden of proving that they were not so, to the reasonable satisfaction of the Custom House authorities, was on the importer. *Kinnear and another* v. *Robinson*, 1 *Han.* 559.

2—Lumber—Defence in action for penalty.
Where the proper steps have not been taken to obtain exemption of the duty imposed by the Act of Assembly 7 Vic. c. 18, on lumber shipped for exportation after the 1st May 1844, it cannot be set up as a defence to an action for the penalty imposed on shippers who omit to give the requisite bond for such duty, that the lumber would have been free from duty had the proper steps been taken to obtain exemption. *Watson* v. *Marks*, 2 *Kerr* 604.

3—Forfeiture of Goods.
An entry at the Custom House declared that the packages contained articles not subject to duty; but some of them contained contraband goods. Held, That it was but one entry, and that being false as to some of the packages, the goods were not duly entered, and the whole were forfeited under 1 Rev. Stat. c. 27, s. 10.—*Regina* v. *Six barrels of Hams*, 3 *All.* 387.

COURTESY.

See Tenant by Courtesy.

DAM.

See Mill Dam. See Assumpsit—Covenant—Negligence—Damages—Waste—Action on the Case.

Erection of Dam in stream capable of being used as a highway—Persons not injured have no right to destroy Dam—Injunction to restrain. See Water Course.

DAMAGES.

I. Principles. Recovery.
II. Evidence.
III. Pleading.
IV. Default.
V. Setting aside Assessment.
VI. Excessive.
VII. Miscellaneous.

I.

Principles—Recovery.

1—Action on the Case—Waste—Damages confined to actual injury—Tenant in Common—Proportion.
In an action on the case for waste by one tenant in common against his co-tenant, the damage must be confined to the actual injury done to the premises, and to such portion thereof as the plaintiff's undivided share bears to the whole estate. *Linton* v. *Wilson*, 1 *Kerr* 223.

2—Erection of Dam--Overflowing Land.
A., the owner of land through which a river flows, is entitled to recover damages in an action on the case from B., the owner of the land adjoining, situate lower down the stream, for erecting a mill-dam upon his own land, which caused the water to flow back upon A.'s land. *Smith* v. *Scott*, 1 *Kerr* 1.

3—Obstructing River—Corresponding Advantages.
In an action for obstructing a river by erecting a mill-dam, it is not a proper question for the jury, whether the benefit derived by the public from the mill is sufficient to outweigh the inconveniences occasioned by the dam. *Rowe* v. *Titus*, 1 *All.* 326.

4—Sterling and Currency.
In an action brought in this Province for the value of goods sold and delivered in England, the plaintiff is entitled to recover such a sum in currency as will be equivalent to the demand in sterling money, according to the rate of exchange at the time of trial. (See Currency and Sterling.) *Campbell* v. *Wilson*, *Ber.* 265.

5—Such allowance recoverable under Common Counts, without specific averment of contract in sterling money, or statement of relative value of money, this, matter of evidence. *Campbell* v *Wilton*, *Ber.* 265.

6—Trespass—Several Defendants.
In trespass against several defendants, two of them left when forbidden by the plaintiff, and took no part in subsequent acts of trespass; the plaintiff's counsel elected to go against all the defendants for the trespass. Held, That the damages were properly confined to such trespasses as were committed when all the defendants were upon the land. *McMillan* v. *Fairley*, 1 *Han.* 325.

7—Failure on delivery—Fall in Market Price.
In an action for the wrongful detention of timber, the plaintiff is entitled to damages for a loss sustained by reason of a fall in the market, between time when the timber should have been delivered to him, and the time he received it. *Goddard* v. *Fredericton Boom Co.*, 1 *Han.* 536.

8—Detention of Alcohol—Measure of Damages.
In an action for wrongfully detaining a quantity of alcohol belonging to plaintiff from September 1867 till May following, when it was delivered to plaintiff, short 408 gallons; the proper measure of damages is—interest on the value of the alcohol during its detention, the value of the 408 gallons short, with interest from September 1867, and any depreciation in the value of the alcohol during its detention. *Kinnear* v. *Robinson*, 2 *Han.* 73.

9—Injury to Business—Agreement to assign Judgments, etc.
In an action for a breach of a contract to assign to the plaintiff certain judgments and mortgages upon his property, he cannot recover damages for injury done to his business and credit in consequence of the sale of his property under a decree in a suit for the foreclosure of the mortgage. *Gilbert* v. *Campbell*, 1 *Han.* 471.

10—Wrongful Taking of Goods—Measure of Damages.
Where the plaintiff has the immediate right to the possession of goods, the proper measure of damages in an action against the sheriff for wrongfully taking them is, the value of the goods at the time of the conversion, though they were taken under an execution against a person who had performed labor upon them, and for which the plaintiff would be bound to account to such person. *Rankin* v. *Mitchell*, 1 *Han.* 495.

11—Disabling from Performance—Deduction of Money—Breach of Agreement to convey—Cross Action.
In an action for breach of an agreement to convey property to the plaintiff on payment of a sum of money by instalments, and which agreement the defendant had disabled himself from performing before the last instalment was due; the plaintiff not having paid the last instalment, cannot recover it as damages for breach of the agreement; being part of the same contract, the defendant is entitled to have the unpaid instalment deducted from the damages, and is not driven to bring a cross action for it. *Gilbert* v. *Campbell*, 2 *Han.* 55.

12—Escape—Final Process—Debtor returning to custody.
If a prisoner in execution on final process escapes, and afterwards returns into custody, the proper measure of damages is not necessarily the whole debt, but such sum as the jury think the detention of the debtor's body would have been worth during his absence. If there is no actual loss proved, the plaintiff is entitled to nominal damages. *Kelly* v. *Jones*, 2 *All.* 465.

13—Mesne Process—Sheriff not arresting.
Sheriff not liable for neglecting to arrest on *mesne* process, unless some damage sustained by his neglect. See *Curran* v. *Beckwith*, 3 *All.* 365.

14—Limit Bond—Rule of Damages—Execution.
Damages may be assessed by a jury, and the proper rule of damages where the bond has been taken from a person in custody under execution, is the amount of such execution. (See Limit Bond.) *McKenzie* v. *Marsh*, 2 *Kerr* 629.

15—Master and Servant—Entire Contract.
The defendant agreed to employ the plaintiff for three years at an annual salary, commencing on the 1st April 1848, but dismissed him without sufficient cause before the end of the second year. Held, That the plaintiff had an immediate right of action for breach of the agreement, in which he was entitled to recover damages for the loss sustained by the breach of

the entire contract, and was not limited to the sum due at the time of his dismissal. *Meade* v. *Doherty*, 2 *All.* 195.

16—**Tenant in Common—Sale of Goods.**
In case of sale of goods by one tenant, his co-tenant may affirm the contract and sue the former in assumpsit for his share; in such case the produce of sale would be the measure of damages. See *Doyle* v. *Taylor*, *Ber.* 201.

17—**Replevin—Plea Non Cepit.**
The defendant in replevin is entitled to damages on a verdict in his favor on the plea of *non cepit* if he gives such evidence as would have supported an avowry under the former law. See Pleading II. 28.

18—**Interest—Instalment—Act silent as to.**
Interest not allowed on the instalment in assessment of damages. See Interest 2.

19—Illegal exaction of Duty—Interest not recoverable on money paid, as damages. See Interest 1.

20—**Covenant to pay for Improvements—Appraised Amount—Interest recoverable on.**
See Landlord and Tenant VI. 2.

21—**Nuisance—Owner of House not in actual occupation.**
The owner of a house of which he is not in the actual occupation, may recover from a person who has placed an offensive nuisance on adjoining premises, damages for the injury sustained in not being able to let the house advantageously in consequence of the nuisance. An owner is liable if he let a building which required particular care to prevent the occupation from being a nuisance, and the nuisance occurs for want of such care on the part of the tenant. *Smith* v. *Humbert*, 2 *Kerr* 602.

22—**Trover for Bill of Exchange—Non-fulfilment of Agreement.**
An action by the payee against the drawer of a bill of exchange was discontinued on the terms of the acceptor placing the amount of the bill to the payee's credit with a third person; and on the acceptor's representation that this had been done, the bill was given up to him. Held, in an action of trover for the bill against the acceptor—(the amount not having been placed to the payee's credit)—That it might be presumed, under the circumstances, that the payee had given notice of dishonour to the drawer, and that the plaintiff was entitled as damages to the value of the bill at the time of the conversion, which, *prima facie*, was the amount of the bill. *McDonald* v. *Everitt*, 3 *Kerr* 569.

23—**Revocation of Arbitration Bond—Award.**
Where arbitrators, after a revocation, make an award which is otherwise unimpeached, the amount awarded is a proper measure of damages in an action on the arbitration bond. *Hatheway* v. *Cliff*, 2 *All.* 267.

24—**Mesne Profits—Costs.**
As a general rule, the plaintiff, after judgment against casual ejector, is entitled to recover the costs thereof as part of the damages in an action for *mesne* profits. (See II. 7.) *Doe* v. *Dobson*, 2 *All.* 446.

25—**Counsel Fees.**
The plaintiff in replevin cannot recover as part of his damages, an amount paid to counsel on the execution of a writ *de proprietate probanda* issued on a claim to the property put in by the defendant. *Davis* v. *Cushing*, *Mich. T.* 1863.

26—Substantial damages may be recovered in replevin, though no special damage is alleged in the declaration. (Per N. Parker, J., special damage should be alleged. *Firth* v. *Fitzgerald*, *Hil. T.* 1866.

27—**Tort—Actual Damage—Jury not limited to.**
In actions of tort, the jury are not limited to the actual damage sustained by the plaintiff; therefore, where the actual damage was only $2, and the jury gave a verdict for $40, it was held not excessive. *Rose* v. *Belyea*, 1 *Han.* 109.

28—**Bill of Exchange—Damages.**
Semble, That the acceptor of a protested bill of exchange drawn in this Province, and accepted payable in England, is not liable to 10 per cent. damages under 1 Rev. Stat. c. 116, in an action brought here. *Morrison* v. *Spurr*, 3 *All.* 288.

29—**Vendor—Sum agreed to be paid for Land by Vendee.**
In an action by a vendor, for breach of an agreement to purchase land, the plaintiff cannot recover as part of his damages the sum which the defendant had agreed to pay for the land. *Pugsley* v. *Gillespie*, *Mich. T.* 1872.

30—**Subsequent neglect—Damage to Land.**
A stream diverted into a new channel by

the Commissioners of the European and North American Railway under 19 Vic. c. 17, became obstructed in consequence of the new channel filling up and overflowing plaintiff's land. Held, 1st. That the Commissioners were bound to keep the channel open, and were liable to an action for the damage to the plaintiff's land. 2nd. That the fact of the plaintiff having been paid by the Commissioners, land damages for the diversion of the stream, was no bar to his recovering damages for their subsequent neglect to keep the channel open. *McLeod* v. *Commissioners of E. and N. A. Railway*, 1 *Han.* 574.

31—Exemplary Damages—Wilful act—Wrongful intent.
In an action on the case for pulling down a house, and thereby preventing a Sheriff from executing a writ of restitution awarded under 1 Rev. Stat. c. 126, the jury may give exemplary damages if the defendant has acted wilfully, and with a determination to prevent the process of the law from being executed. (See Emblen *v.* Myers, 6 H. & N. 54.) *Allenach* v. *Desbrisay*, *East. T.* 1865.

32—Special Damage—Necessity of statement in declaration.
In replevin for iron, the plaintiff cannot recover for loss sustained by not being able to get the iron at a certain time, for the purpose of manufacturing it, unless such special damage is alleged in the declaration. *Domville* v. *Kevan*, *East. T.* 1871.

Land Damages—Subsequent damage. See Assessment I. 10, 11.

Splitting up claim for.
A party cannot split up his claim for damages and proceed for a part of the trespass at one time, and part at another. See Trespass III. 5.

II.

EVIDENCE.

1—In Reduction—Mitigation.
In an action for breach of a written contract, whereby defendant in consideration of £500 paid to him by the plaintiffs, agreed to convey to plaintiff a mill at P. as soon as he obtained a grant thereof. Held (Chipman, C. J. *dissentiente*), That the defendant could not show in reduction of damages that at the time the agreement was entered into, he had delivered a quantity of logs to the plaintiffs as a part of the consideration for the bargain. *Smith* v. *Millidge*, 2 *Kerr* 408.

2—Warranty—Price—Unsoundness.
In an action for the price of fish, warranted sound, the defendant may give the unsoundness of the fish in evidence in mitigation of damages, and is not obliged to resort to an action on the warranty. *Smith* v. *Dunham*, 2 *Kerr* 630.

3—Slander—Character of Plaintiff.
In an action of slander for charging the plaintiff with stealing, evidence of the general bad character of the plaintiff is not admissible in mitigation of damages. *Williston* v. *Smith*, 3 *Kerr* 443.

4—Plaintiff's Negligence—Destruction of third person's property by—For which Defendant liable.
In an action for work and labour in unloading a ship, the defendant cannot give evidence in reduction of the contract price, of the value of property in the ship belonging to a third person, which was destroyed by the plaintiff's negligence in discharging the cargo, and for which the defendant would be liable to the owner of the property. *Wilson* v. *Jarvis*, 3 *Kerr* 671.

5—Special Damage—Allegation—Admissibility.
Evidence of special damage in not being able to fulfil a contract for the delivery of logs, is not admissible under an allegation in the declaration that the plaintiff was prevented by the act of the defendant from getting the logs to market, and thereby lost the freight and sale thereof. *Rowe* v. *Titus*, 1 *All.* 326.

6—Expense of attending before Sheriff's Jury.
In trespass for taking goods, the expense of attending before a jury called by the sheriff to inquire into the right of property, is not evidence under an allegation of special damage by reason of loss of time, etc., in regaining the possession; and *Quære*, Whether it would be evidence in any case. (See 2 *Han. Mercer* v. *Cosman.*) *Wilson* v. *Ellis*, *Ber.* 324.

7—Mesne profits—Taxed Costs—Payment must be shewn.
Where the declaration, in an action for *mesne* profits alleged that the plaintiff was obliged to, and did necessarily lay out and expend a large sum of money in recovering the possession of the land, he cannot recover, as part of the damages, the costs

of the judgment by default in the ejectment, on the mere production of the taxed bill of costs, without proof of payment. *Doe* v. *Cahill*, 2 *All.* 650.

8—Bail Bond—Assignee of—Evidence.
In an action by the assignee of a bail bond, when the only plea is *non est factum*, the plaintiff need not give any evidence of the original cause of action; but on proof of the execution of the bond, he is entitled to a verdict with nominal damages, and if execution issues for more than the debt due and costs, the defendant may be relieved by application to the Court. See I. 14. (See Bond—Limit Bond.) *Scribner* v. *Gibbon*, 4 *All.* 182.

9—Admission—Action against Sheriff.
Quære, Whether in an action against the sheriff for an escape, evidence of the admission of the judgment debtor of his ability to pay the debt was properly rejected. See *Kelly* v. *Jones*, 2 *All.* 465.

10—Nuisance—Erection of Steam Mill.
The evidence of persons living in other adjoining premises as to the injurious effect of the steam mill upon them is admissible in order to shew by necessary inference the damage done to the plaintiff by the erection. No other damage need be shewn than the abridgement of the plaintiff's enjoyment in the occupation of his premises. *Barlow* v. *Kinnear*, 2 *Kerr* 94.

11—Notice of action—Statement.
Where special damage is claimed in consequence of an unlawful imprisonment by a Justice of the Peace, *e. g.*, the cost of obtaining the plaintiff's discharge from prison, it should be stated in the notice of action, otherwise evidence cannot be given of it. *Sewall* v. *Olive*, 4 *All.* 394.

III.

Pleading.

1—Statute of Limitations—Limiting recovery.
In an action on the case for overflowing plaintiff's land by a dam, erected more than six years before bringing the action—Held, That the effect of the plea of the Statute of Limitations was not to bar the action, but to limit the recovery of damages to six years. *Conners* v. *McLaggan*, 2 *Kerr* 446.

2—Detention of Lumber—Subsequent replevy by plaintiff—Damages too remote.
In an action for wrongfully detaining the plaintiff's timber, in which the declaration stated that, by reason of the detention, the plaintiff was prevented from manufacturing the lumber, and lost the sale of it, and his saw-mill was kept idle; it is no answer to the plaintiff's claim for damages that after the alleged detention the defendants had placed the lumber in the hands of T. from whom the plaintiff replevied it; the damages claimed in this action being anterior to the time when the lumber was placed in T.'s hands. But the plaintiff is not entitled to damages for any depreciation in the value of the lumber subsequent to the delivery to T., as such damages might have been recovered in the action against him; nor to damages for the loss of the use of the mill, they being too remote and not a necessary consequence of the detention of the lumber. *Godard* v. *Fredericton Boom Co.*, *Trin. T.* 1866.

IV.

Default.

See Practice V. VI.

Where damages had been assessed on an account by a Judge at Chambers, but the affidavit on which it was made did not support all the items of the account, the Court reduced the damages to the amount warranted by the affidavit. *Scoullar* v. *Webb*, 1 *Kerr* 520.

See Judgment by Default.

V.

Setting aside Assessment of Damages.

1—It is no ground for setting aside the assessment on a writ of inquiry executed at the Assizes, that the Sheriff has not returned any panel on the writ, and the damages have been assessed by the jury summoned to try the issues at the Assizes. *Wheeler* v. *Goss*, 1 *Kerr* 580.

2—Where, on a writ of inquiry before a Sheriff's jury to assess damages for the wrongful detention of liquor from September 1867 till May following, the plaintiff gave evidence of transactions respecting the liquor prior to September, and also the expense of warehousing, insurance, and legal expenses, and no rule was laid down by the Sheriff for the guidance of the jury as to the measure of damages, the Court set aside the assessment, being unable to ascertain by the evidence how the jury arrived at the amount. *Kinnear* v. *Robinson*, 2 *Han.* 73.

VI.

EXCESSIVE.

See Supra I. 27.
" New Trial II. 34, III. 13, 14, 16, 17, 18.
" Malicious Arrest, etc. 7.

VII.

MISCELLANEOUS.

Good and bad Counts.
Evidence on trial applicable to good Counts, no inference that damages were given on bad Counts. See Amendment III. 5.

Assumpsit—Breach of Agreement—Non-suspension of Action—Liquidated Damages. See Assumpsit I. 1.

Damages too remote. See Covenant 10.

Breach of Covenant, and damage arising in lifetime of testator, action should be brought in name of executor. See *Cunningham* v. *Scoullar*, 4 *All.* 395.

Conflicting Evidence — Damages large — Verdict not disturbed. See New Trial III. 17.

Highway—Jury assessing, on view of land where no witnesses produced. See *Ex parte Hebert*, 3 *All.* 108. See Highways 20.

Jury not confined to value of land merely. See Highways 26.

Mandamus, requiring appraisers to assess damages. See Mandamus 6.

Private Road—Presence of Justices. See Assessment III. 5.

Apportionment of Damages—Trespass on two distinct lots of land. See Trespass IV. 6.

Nominal Damages—Question fairly left to jury. See New Trial III. 18 a.

Note payable in specific articles.
Quære, Whether plaintiff can declare for special damage for not delivering articles. See Bills and Notes I. 13.

Liquidated Damages—Claim for, provable under Bankruptcy. See Bankruptcy.

Writ of Inquiry.
Assessing damages on second writ held regular where jury gave no verdict, and were dismissed. See *Ward* v. *Dow*, *Ber.* 21.

Assessment by Jury—Limit Bond. See Venire.

See Assessment, Practice, Judgment by Default.

DAMAGE FEASANT.

When Cattle may be taken—Place.
A field driver appointed under the Act to impound cattle going at large contrary to the Sessions regulations can only take them while at large in the parish for which he is appointed. The place of taking is a question for the Justices' decision, and unless it is clearly against evidence the Superior Court will not interfere. *Sterling* v. *Jones*, 2 *All.* 522.

Replevin for—Justice of the Peace—Jurisdiction. See Justice of the Peace II. 11, 12.

DEATH.

1—Of Husband—Abatement of Action.
Action brought by husband and wife to recover money had and received to the use of the wife, does not abate by the death of the husband. *Hannington* v. *McMananin*, 4 *All.* 509.

2—Summary Action.
On death of one of several defendants, before interlocutory judgment, suggestion should be made on memorandum of judgment. See *Crane* v. *Goodine*, 4 *All.* 371.

Absconding Debtor. See Absconding Debtor 12.

3—Of Defendant pending motion for new trial.
Where defendant died after verdict, and pending the determination of a motion for a new trial, the Court refrained from granting a new trial until the plaintiff had an opportunity of applying to have terms imposed. *Key* v. *Thomson*, 2 *Han.* 224.

Death of Intestate—Letters of Administration—Evidence of. See Evidence IV. 1.

Affidavit endorsed on Deed of Administrator, not evidence of death of intestate. See Deed I. 24.

4—Equity—Re-swearing—Answer—Death of one of several defendants.
Where one of the persons named as defendant in a suit had died before the summons issued, the pleadings were amended by striking out his name, and the answer was re-sworn. *Byers* v. *Harrigan*, 1 *Han.* 231.

DEBT.

1—Action—Sheriff.
Action of debt will not lie by a sheriff on a limit bond, when he had received the prisoner into close custody after taking the bond. See *Campbell* v. *Henan*, *Ber.* 73.

Action of debt against a sheriff for an escape cannot be maintained in this Province under the Statute 1 Rich. 2, c. 12, which is not applicable to this Province. *Wilson* v. *Jones*, 1 *All.* 658.

2—Legacy—Termination of trust—Action by Legatee.
See Action at Law IX. 16.

3—Legatee.
A legatee may maintain an action of debt against an executor for a certain legacy given by his testator. *Ibid.*

4—Bequest—Defence—Property unsold.
A bequest by a debtor to his creditor of a legacy to the amount of the debt, payable out of the proceeds of certain property which remains unsold, is no defence to an action by the creditor for his debt. See *Bishop* v. *Robinson*, 1 *Han.* 68.

DEBTOR.

See Insolvent Debtor.

Discharge of—At Suit of Executor—Persons beneficially interested agreeing to release. See Discharge.

Discharge of defendant by one of several plaintiffs. See Discharge.

By consent of plaintiff—Remedy on judgment. See Discharge.

Refusal to discharge—Equitable satisfaction. See Action at Law IX. 1.

DECK LOAD.

Loss by Jettison—Contribution—Liability of master of ship for loss. See Shipping Law.

DECEIT.

See Warranty.

DECLARATION.

See Pleading—Practice.

DECREE.

See Supreme Court in Equity.

DEDICATION.

1—Of Highway—Presumption.
Dedication of a road to the public may be presumed from long user and the expenditure of Statute labor on the road, and a party may be convicted under the Act 5 Wm. 4, c. 2, s. 16, for encroaching upon such a road as well as upon highways duly laid out under the Act. *Reg.* v. *Buchanan*, 3 *Kerr* 674.

2—A public highway may be established in this country by dedication and user. See Highways 16.

By Crown—Presumptive Evidence. See Highways 30.

DEED.

I. Deed.
II. Voluntary Conveyance.
III. Trust Deed.
IV. Composition Deed.
V. Miscellaneous.

I.
Deed.

1—Registry—Relation.
A deed, when registered under the Act of Assembly 26 Geo. 3, c. 3, conveys the estate by relation from the time of the delivery of the deed, when there is no *meme* incumbrance which has obtained a priority. *Doe dem. Bridges* v. *Quint*, *East. T.* 1828.

2—Adverse Possession—Registry not giving Possession.
A deed registered under the Act 26 Geo. 3, c. 3, will not enure to give possession to the grantee, so as to enable him to maintain trespass against a person in the actual adverse possession of the land, and who took possession subsequent to the registry of the deed and the entry of the plaintiff under it, and continued such possession for several years before the alleged trespass. *Dunham* v. *King*, *Trin. T.* 1831.

3—Words "remise, release and quit claim"—Execution, acknowledgment and registry—Good deed.
A deed, whereby the grantor, for valuable consideration, did "remise, release and quit claim" to the grantee, his heirs and assigns, all his right, title and interest in certain described lands, having been duly executed, acknowledged and registered, pursuant to the Act 26 Geo. 3, c. 3, is a good conveyance of land, within the meaning of the 10th section of the Act. *Doe dem. Wilt* v. *Jardine*, *Bert.* 142.

4—Statute of Uses and Enrolments in force.
The Statute of Uses 27 Hen. 8, c. 10, and the Statute of Enrolments 27 Hen. 8, c. 16, extend to, and are in force in this Province; therefore, a deed of bargain and sale, not enrolled according to the provisions of the latter Statute, nor registered according to the Provincial Act 26 Geo. 3, c. 3, does not pass any estate to the bargainee. *Doe dem. Hanington* v. *McFadden*, *Bert.* 153.

5—Words, privileges and appurtenances, etc.—Right to use stream.
A deed by which the grantor conveys a certain piece of land, "together with the "saw-mill thereon, with all and singular "the privileges and appurtenances belonging thereto; together with the "mill-pond, mill-dam, and any other "privilege connected with, or belonging "to the said premises," does not convey a right to use a stream flowing through the grantor's land, for the purpose of taking logs to and from the mill, though the grantor had used the stream for that purpose previous to the deed. *Rogers* v. *Peck*, *Bert.* 318.

6—Grantor disseised—No estate passing.
If, at the time of the execution of a conveyance of land, the grantor is actually disseised, no estate passes to the grantee. *Doe dem. Thomson* v. *Barnes*, *Bert.* 426.

7—Deed destroyed—Evidence—Feoffment.
Where the only evidence of the contents of a deed destroyed many years ago, and under which the plaintiff claimed title, was that of witnesses who had read it, and heard it read; and who stated that it was a deed of the land in dispute, from A. P., the grantee, to his daughter R. E. (one of the lessors of the plaintiff), of the land where she lived, either sixty or eighty rods; that the names of A. P. and his wife were signed to it; that it bore date some time in the last century, and was to R. E., her heirs and assigns, for ever. Held, That sufficient did not appear to enable the Judge to direct the jury that it was a deed of feoffment, or to determine its legal operation. *Doe dem. Edgett* v. *Stiles*, 1 *Kerr* 338.

8—Execution—Proof of.
The execution of a deed of conveyance is not proved by the magistrate's certificate of acknowledgment indorsed, without the certificate of registry. *Joplin* v. *Johnson*, 2 *Kerr* 541.

9—Identity of Lot.
Where the description in a deed designated the lot by number, and referred to an inventory, which was not produced—Held, That there being sufficient evidence from the other part of the description of the identity of the lot to go to the jury, the deed was sufficient. *McEachern* v. *Ferguson*, 3 *Kerr* 242.

10—No memorandum of acknowledgment.
Where a certified copy of a deed tendered in evidence under the Act 7 Wm. 4, c. 15, contained no memorandum by the Justice of the acknowledgment of the due execution of the deed, according to the Act 26 Geo. 3, c. 3. Held, That the deed was not duly registered. *Doe dem Lyons* v. *Slavin*, 3 *Kerr* 258.

11—Valuable consideration—Inequality of value.
In order to constitute a valuable consideration to support a conveyance, it is not necessary that the money paid should be of equal value with the property conveyed, provided the transaction is *bona fide*. *Payson* v. *Good*, 3 *Kerr* 272.

12—Acknowledgment—Proof of person taking, being a Justice of the Peace.
Where the memorandum of acknowledgm[illegible]sed on a registered deed, was su[illegible]d, "Josophus M[illegible]re, J. Peace," bu[illegible]d not state in the body of it, that he was a Justice of the Peace for the County; he was allowed to be called as a witness to prove that he was so. *Robinson* v. *Wilson*, 3 *Kerr* 301.

13—Acknowledgment before Deputy Mayor.
A deed acknowledged before a Deputy Mayor of a borough in Great Britain, with the common seal of the borough affixed, is a sufficient acknowledgment

under the Act 52 Geo. 3, c. 20. *Blair* v. *Armour*, 3 *Kerr* 341.

14—Subscribing Witness—Proof by.
A power of attorney, proved by the oath of a subscribing witness before a competent authority in Ireland, is sufficient under the Act 52 Geo. 3, c. 20: it need not be acknowledged by the person executing it. *Maloney* v. *Purdon*, 3 *Kerr* 515.

15—Certificate of Proof—Signature—Judicial Notice.
Where the certificate of proof of the execution of a deed was subscribed "Geo. D. Ludlow," without any description of his official character, either in the certificate or annexed to his signature. Held (Carter, J. *dissentiente*), That the Court would take judicial notice that a person named George D. Ludlow was Chief Justice of the Province at the time the deed appeared to have been executed; and that it was competent for the Registrar of Deeds to recognise the certificate as an authentic act of the Chief Justice. *Watson* v. *Hay*, 3 *Kerr* 559.

16—Escrow—Need not be by express words.
It is not necessary that the delivery of a deed as an escrow should be by express words, though it is in form an absolute delivery; yet, if from the circumstances attending the execution, it can reasonably be inferred that the delivery was only conditional, it will operate as an escrow. *Keator* v. *Scovil*, 3 *Kerr* 647.

17—Foreclosure—Master in Chancery—Evidence of Proceedings.
The deed of a Master in Chancery, purporting to be made in pursuance of a decree of foreclosure, duly registered, is evidence that all the proceedings on which it is founded were rightly done, without producing the decree. *Jarvis* v. *Edgett*, 1 *Allen* 66.

18—Words "adjacent and adjoining."
Semble, That there is no distinction between the words "adjacent" and "adjoining," used in the description of the property in a deed. *Doe dem Dunn* v. *Pitt*, 1 *Allen* 385.

19—Witness deceased—Absence of other—Proof of Deed.
A deed appeared to have been executed in the presence of two witnesses, one of whom, a Justice of the Peace, authorised to take acknowledgment of deeds, was dead; no account could be given of the other by persons who had the best means of obtaining knowledge of the inhabitants of the place where the deed was executed. Held, That it was properly received in evidence on proof of the handwriting of the deceased witness. *Doe dem Chubb* v. *Hatheway*, 2 *All.* 69.

20—Unregistered conveyance—Vendee in possession.
An unregistered conveyance of land operates as a release, if the vendee is in possession at the time; if he takes possession immediately after, it may operate as a feoffment, as livery of seisin may be presumed after a long possession. *Doe dem McKay* v. *Allen*, 2 *All.* 191.

21—Easement—Soil not passing.
A, the owner of a saw-mill to which a piling place was attached, conveyed the mill with "the privileges and appurtenances" thereto belonging: the purchaser ceased to use the piling place, as such, and built upon it. Held, That no title to the soil of the piling place passed by the deed; but only an easement as appurtenant to the mill, which ceased when the purchaser built upon the land. *Doe dem Hill* v. *Todd*, 2 *All.* 261.

21 a—Soil of Mill-pond—Easement.
A deed of a piece of land "together with the mill privilege, saw-mill and erections belonging to the same; and also "all the pond or flowage above the said mill," conveys no right to the soil of the mill-pond, but only an easement to dam the water and overflow the land for the purpose of the mill below. *Herbeson* v. *Cunningham*, *Hil. T.* 1873.

22—Registry before proof—Inadmissibility in evidence.
Where, by the certificate endorsed on a deed, it appeared to have been registered before it was proved, it is not admissible in evidence as a registered deed by relation from the time of proof. *Doe dem Blair* v. *Rideout*, 3 *All.* 502.

23—Two deeds on one sheet—One Certificate of Registry—Registry Book evidence.
Where two deeds were written on the same sheet of paper, and registered at the same time, but only one certificate of registry and one number were indorsed, it may be proved by the Registry Book that both deeds were registered. *Doe dem Kerr* v. *McCulley*, 3 *All.* 194.

Quære, Whether a proper certificate of registry could not be indorsed at the trial. *Ibid.*

24—Affidavit endorsed on deed—Not evidence of death of Intestate—Evidence of due sale, etc.

The affidavit indorsed on a deed purporting to be made by an administrator under license from the Probate Court, is not evidence of the death, or of the granting of administration; but only that the land has been duly advertised and sold. *Doe dem Simpson* v. *Donovan*, 4 *All.* 116.

25—Condition—Estate in possession—Immediate right of entry.

A deed of land, subject to a condition that the grantor should receive and enjoy all the profits and emoluments accruing therefrom during his life, *habendum*, to to the grantee, his heirs and assigns, with a general covenant of warranty, conveys an immediate estate in possession, and not an estate in remainder after the death of the grantor; and the grantee's right of entry accrues on the execution of the deed. *Doe d. Baxter* v. *Baxter*, 4 *All.* 131.

26—Conveyance from grantor to himself and others.

A man cannot convey land to himself; therefore a deed of bargain and sale from B. to C., M. and himself, and their heirs being inoperative as to B., vests the whole estate in C. and M. as joint tenants, and an action of trespass cannot be maintained by the three on such title. *Cameron* v. *Steves*, 4 *All.* 141.

27—Preparation of conveyance—Vendor.

It is the duty of the seller of land to prepare the conveyance; and if he has a wife who would have a right of dower in the land in case she survived him, she should be a party to the conveyance. *Sweeney* v. *Godard*, 4 *All.* 300.

28—Acknowledgment in Great Britain—Seal of Corporation.

The acknowledgment of a deed in Great Britain was in the following form: "Be it remembered that on, etc., before me, T. G., Mayor of the town of Southampton, in England, personally appeared, etc. Given under my hand and seal the day and year first above written," and signed by the Mayor, with a seal affixed having the words "Southampton Villa" inscribed around what appeared to be the City arms. Held, That it imported to be the corporate seal of Southampton, and not the private seal of the Mayor, and therefore the acknowledgment was sufficient under the 1 Rev. Stat. c. 112. *De Veber* v. *Britain*, 4 *All.* 330.

29—Description—Whole lot passing.

A deed of conveyance described the land, as a piece of land, "*being lot number seven*" in the division of a certain property, and running from Crooked Creek etc. Held, That the whole of lot No. 7 passed by the deed, though the line of that lot did not run from Crooked Creek. *Stiles* v. *Kiever*, *East. T.* 1862.

30—Description in part inaccurate—Effect.

Where part of the description is inaccurate, effect is to be given to the description first in order, and to the name; and a cumulative description, if it fails in point of accuracy, will be rejected. *Ibid.*

31—Barrister's Deed—Sale—Immediate execution.

The Equity Act (17 Vic. c. 18), directs that on sales by a Barrister, he shall execute a conveyance of the land "*immediately* upon such sale." Held, That this meant without any improper delay; and that three weeks after the sale was not an unreasonable time. *Doe dem Jardine* v. *Coigley*, *Trin. T.* 1863.

32—Consideration—Becoming bail.

Becoming bail for the grantor, is a sufficiently valuable consideration to support a deed against a prior unregistered conveyance. *Crockford* v. *Equitable Insurance Co.*, *Mich. T.* 1863.

33—Escrow—Delivery of deed.

To make the delivery of a deed operate as an escrow, it must be delivered to a stranger,—not to the grantee. *Haggarty* v. *O'Leary*, *Hil. T.* 1866.

34—No declaration of use—Consideration—Money blank.

Under the Registry Act (1 Rev. Stat. c. 112) a deed from A. to B., expressed to be "for and in consideration of the "sum of —— lawful money of the Province," *habendum* to B., his heirs and assigns, but without any declaration of the use, is a sufficient conveyance of the land to B.

Semble, That it sufficiently appeared that the consideration of the deed was money, and the amount of consideration being unimportant, that the deed might operate either as a deed of bargain and sale or as a feoffment. *Wortman* v. *Ayles*, 1 *Han.* 63.

35—Lunatic.

The deed of a lunatic is not absolutely void, but voidable, and can only be avoided by the grantor or his representatives. *Doe dem. Hickman v. King*, 1 *Han.* 330.

36—Date—Sheriff's deed—Affidavit differing.

The date mentioned in a deed is not conclusive, and the actual date of the execution may be shewn. Where a sheriff's bore date in 1841, and the affidavit of the due advertising and sale was made in 1843—Held, That evidence was admissible to prove that the deed was executed at the time the affidavit was sworn. *Doe dem Connell v. Dickerson*, 1 *Han.* 456.

37—Sheriff's deed—Date of deed and affidavit—Executing at same time.

The affidavit of the sheriff under the Act 4 Wm. 4, c. 22, of the duly signing and selling land taken in execution, must be made at the same time that the sheriff's deed is executed, and in the absence of evidence to the contrary, the deed must be presumed to have been executed on the day it bears date. Such an affidavit, purporting to have been sworn on the 2nd February, when the deed bore date on the 2nd January previous, is insufficient, there being no other proof of the time of the execution of the deed. *Doe dem Bustin v. Donelly*, 3 *Kerr* 66.

38—Fraud—Want of consideration—By whom may be set up.

Fraud or want of consideration for a deed, can only be set up by the grantor or those claiming under him. *Hickman v. North British Ins. Co.*, 2 *Han.* 235.

39—Description—Rejection of part—Construction.

D. conveyed to his daughter a piece of land in Saint John, described as "a lot on the corner of St. James and Sidney streets, now in the occupation of P. M. and wife (the defendants), subject to any charge or mortgage now against the same." At the time of making this conveyance, D. the grantor, owned parts of two lots, Nos. 1085 and 1086, adjoining each other, and purchased at different times. No. 1086 was situated on the corner of St. James and Sydney streets, and was occupied by the grantor's daughter and her husband, P. M.; and was also subject to a mortgage given by the grantor. No. 1085 was situated altogether on St. James street, and was occupied by tenants of D., who received the rents—his daughter having only the use of a wood-shed and outhouse thereon, in common with the other tenants. Held, per Ritchie, C. J., Allen and Wetmore, J. J., That no part of the description in the deed could be rejected; that the lot No. 1086 exactly fitted and corresponded with the description in the deed, and therefore that lot only passed by the deed. Per Weldon and Fisher, J. J., That the words of the deed, coupled with the surrounding circumstances, shewed an intention to convey both lots to the defendant. *Doe dem Donaghue v. McGarrigle, Hil. T.* 1873.

40—Defendant's deed under sale by license of Probate Court—Objection to proceedings in Probate Court—Remedy by Appeal—Irregularity of proceedings cannot be objected to on trial—Deed cannot be avoided on trial.

The lessors of the plaintiff claimed as devisees under the will of H. P.; the defendant claimed under a deed from H. P.'s executor, under a license from the Probate Court. The plaintiff contended that the license was void, because H. P. had left sufficient personal property to pay his debts, and that the executor had improperly expended large sums in costs in the Probate Court, in proceedings which he had no right to take; that he had acted fraudulently towards the estate; and that the defendant, who had been his attorney in the proceedings in the Probate Court, was cognizant of the fraud of the executor, and had no right to purchase from him. A verdict having been found for the defendant—Held, on motion for a new trial, That though a large amount of costs appeared to have been unnecessarily incurred in the Probate Court, and the proceedings there were irregular, it did not avoid the defendant's deed; that the parties interested under the will should have appealed from the decree of the Probate Court, granting license to sell the real estate, and could not object to the regularity of the proceedings in this action. *Doe dem Sullivan v. Currey, Trin. T.* 1872.

Fraudulent Conveyance—Resulting Trust—Equitable Estate. See Ejectment II. 10.

II.

Voluntary Conveyance.

1—Father to son—Creditors—Taking upon execution.

A voluntary conveyance of land made by a father to his son, is void as against creditors, and the land may be taken and sold by the Sheriff under an execution against the father, founded upon a judgment obtained since the conveyance. *Doe dem Barlow v. Hatfield*, 2 *Kerr* 122.

Although a valuable consideration be specified in the deed, it is a question for the jury whether the same is real or fictitious; and where the consideration is set up as arising out of services performed by the son as clerk to his father, evidence of the mode of living and extravagant habits of the son, and the father's complaints of the son's extravagance, and of payment of moneys for him from time to time, is admissible to disprove the validity of the consideration. *Ibid.*

Where the conveyance to the son was attacked as well on the ground of fraud as want of consideration, and evidence has been given of other conveyances made by the father at the same time to this and other of his children, the effect of which would be to defeat creditors: *Semble*, Evidence of the circumstances under which these other deeds were given, in order to rebut the inference of fraud is relevant, but the Court refused to grant a new trial on account of the rejection of such evidence; the verdict of the jury having proceeded upon the single ground of the want of consideration for the conveyance, upon which the present defence rested, the evidence as to the other conveyance became immaterial. *Ibid.*

2—A. made a voluntary conveyance of land to the plaintiff, his infant son, but without any fraudulent intent; fourteen years afterwards, the defendant obtained a judgment against A., under which the land previously conveyed to the son was sold by the sheriff, and purchased by the defendant with notice of the prior conveyance. Held, per R. Parker, J. and Wilmot, J. (N. Parker, M. R. *dissentiente*), That under the Act of Assembly 26 Geo. 3, c. 12, s. 5, the defendant was a purchaser for valuable consideration, in the same situation as if he had purchased from A., and therefore that the deed from A. to his son was fraudulent and void under the Statute 27 Eliz. c. 4. Held, per N. Parker, M. R., 1st. That at the time of the judgment against A. he had no interest in the land which could be sold under the Act 26 Geo. 3, c. 12, and therefore the sheriff's deed to the defendant was a nullity. 2nd. That a purchaser at sheriff's sale was not such a purchaser as was contemplated by the Statute 27 Eliz. c. 4. *Doe v. McCulley*, 3 *All.* 194.

3—A., without any fraudulent intent, made a voluntary conveyance of land to the plaintiff, his infant son; fourteen years afterwards the defendant obtained judgment against A. in an action of *tort*, under which the land previously conveyed to the plaintiff was sold by the Sheriff, and purchased by the defendant with notice of the prior conveyance. Held, per Carter, C. J., Parker, J. and Wilmot, J., (N. Parker, M. R. and Ritchie, J., *dissentiente*), That under the Act of Assembly 26 Geo. 3, c. 12, s. 5, the defendant was a purchaser for a valuable consideration, in the same situation as if he had purchased from A., and therefore the deed from A. to the plaintiff was fraudulent and void under the Statute 27 Eliz. c. 4. Held, per N. Parker, M. R. and Ritchie, J., 1st. That at the time of the judgment against A. he had a bare power of sale, and no estate in the land which could be seized under execution; and therefore that no interest passed to the defendant by the Sheriff's deed. 2nd. That to invalidate the plaintiff's deed, a second conveyance by A. for valuable consideration was necessary. And per N. Parker, M. R., that the defendant was to be considered as a subsequent creditor of, and not as a purchaser from A., and therefore that the plaintiff's deed was good against him. *Doe v. McCulley*, 3 *All.* 508.

4—Subsequent Creditor—Sheriff's deed.

A voluntary conveyance of land (without fraud) is good against a subsequent creditor claiming under a Sheriff's deed, since the 1 Rev. Stat. c. 113. *Doe dem Roup v. Trentowsky*, *Mich. T.* 1863.

In 1852, A. without valuable consideration conveyed land to B. in trust to hold for the benefit of A.'s wife for life, and after her death to be divided among his children. In 1855, the lessor of the plaintiff obtained judgment against A. under which the land conveyed to B. was levied on by the Sheriff, and purchased by the lessor of the plaintiff in 1859. The defendant claimed under a lease from B. in 1857. Held, That the conveyance to B.

was good, and that nothing passed by the Sheriff's deed. *Doe dem Roup* v. *Trentowsky*, *Mich. T.* 1863.

III.

Trust Deed.

1—Fraud—Execution of Deed—Intention.

In trover for timber seized by the defendant, as sheriff of Saint John, under a *fi. fa.*, issued against P. at the suit of S. & B., which timber was claimed by the plaintiffs, as trustees under a deed of assignment made by P. to them, expressed to be for the general benefit of the creditors, and executed just before the signing of a judgment in S. & B.'s suit, and the intent of which was to prevent his property being taken under the execution upon such judgment, the case went to the jury upon the question of fraud in the assignment, who found for the defendant. A new trial was granted on payment of costs, it appearing that P. was insolvent at the time of the assignment, that an actual delivery of the timber had been made to the plaintiffs before the issuing the *fi. fa.*, and the evidence being insufficient in the opinion of the Court to shew that the deed was not intended to be for the benefit of the creditors as expressed on the face of it. *Hayward* v. *White*, 2 *Kerr* 304.

The question in cases of this sort is whether the transaction is *bona fide*, and really what it purports to be—for the benefit of creditors—or a mere pretext or cover in order to protect the property for the benefit of the debtor. *Ibid.*

A condition in the trust deed that each trustee shall only be answerable for his own neglect or default, is not unusual or improper. *Ibid.*

It is not essential to the validity of a trust assignment for the benefit of creditors, that the creditors should be parties to the deed. *Ibid.*

2—Bona Fides—Question for jury—Interference of Court—Insufficient evidence—Fraudulent clause.

Although the *bona fides* of a trust deed, whereby the debtor's property is all assigned to trustees for the benefit, in the first instance, of certain preferred creditors, and afterwards for the benefit of all the creditors generally, is a question for the jury, and has been so left to them by

the Judge, yet the Court will set aside the verdict, and grant a new trial, where the evidence does not appear sufficient to warrant the inference of fraud which the jury have drawn. *Burnham* v. *White*, 2 *Kerr* 571.

The question upon which the validity of the deed depends is whether the assignment was really intended to operate, as it purports to operate, for the benefit of creditors, or was merely colorable, and made to protect the property for the use of the debtor. *Ibid.*

A clause in the deed of assignment, whereby the trustees agree to become bail for the assignors in case they are arrested, or their security for the gaol limits, and are to be indemnified out of the trust property, is not fraudulent; such clause, though the terms are general, will be necessarily confined to arrests for debts existing at the time of the assignment. Neither is a clause, whereby the responsibility of each trustee is confined to his own acts or defaults, unusual or improper. *Ibid.*

3—Appointment of Trustees in case of death or discharge—Vesting of Estate.

The Mayor etc. of Saint John conveyed real estate to five persons, their heirs and assigns, upon certain trusts; and the deed declared that in case either of the trustees should die or be desirous of being discharged from, or become incapable to act in the trusts, it should be the duty of the other trustees for the time being, to call a general meeting of the creditors of the said mayor, etc., and that it should be lawful for a majority of the creditors present to nominate, substitute, and appoint any other person to be a trustee in the place or in addition to the trustees thereby appointed, with the like powers to such new trustee to act and perform the trusts as fully as if he had been originally a trustee. Held, That the nomination of S. by the creditors as a trustee in the place of M., one of the five trustees named in the deed, vested no estate in the land in S., but that the legal estate vested in M. by the deed remained in him until he parted with it by a legal conveyance. *Wright* v. *Robertson*, 3 *Kerr* 78.

4—Trustee and Creditor also—Execution by—Impeachment for fraud.

Where parties to a deed of assignment,

in trust for the payment of creditors generally, were described as trustees of the second and creditors of the third part, and it appeared in evidence that when the deed was executed one of the trustees was also a creditor of the assignor. Held, That such trustee, in the absence of evidence to the contrary, must be considered to have executed the deed both as creditor and trustee. Held also, That such trust deed could not be impeached for fraud and misrepresentation by the plaintiff, who claimed through a party whose demand was released by the deed—the same not having been repudiated by the parties to it. *Hammond* v. *Barker*, 3 *Kerr* 634.

IV.

COMPOSITION DEED.

1—Partners—Assent of—Proof of execution by trustees.
One of three partners assigned to trustees for payment of the partnership debts, property which had originally belonged to the firm, the deed reciting that the other partners had conveyed to him. Held, 1st. That such assignment would be valid if assented to by the other partners. 2nd. That such assent appearing, the recital of the conveyance from them did not make its production necessary for the construction of the subsequent assignment. And 3rd. That proof of the execution of the deed by the trustees was not necessary to enable them to recover the property assigned. *McMillan* v. *Ritchie*, 2 *All.* 242.

2—Schedule—Omission of.
A composition deed recited that the grantor was indebted to certain persons in the sums set opposite their names in a schedule annexed. Held, That the omission of a schedule did not vitiate the deed. *Tharper* v. *Travis*, 2 *All.* 272.

V.

MISCELLANEOUS.

1—Exchange of lands—Agreement in writing—Possession—Operation—Feoffment—Tenancy at will.
An agreement in writing between A. and B. for the exchange of lands, although accompanied by possession, will not operate as a conveyance by way of feoffment to pass the life estate to A., where the terms used do not clearly denote that it was to operate as a conveyance, and a deed of bargain and sale has been since given from A. to B. of the same land in which the agreement is recited as a contract for the conveyance of the fee. *Sutherland* v. *Walter*, 1 *Kerr* 141.

2—A writing under seal, accompanied by livery of seisin, may operate as a feoffment where such intent of the parties is clearly expressed. Where such an agreement will not operate as a conveyance, possession under it is only a tenancy at will. *Ibid.*

3—Parol license to enter.
A parol license from the owner of land in which mines are excepted, to the grantee of the mines to enter and dig them, vests no estate in the licensee, and is no breach of the implied warranty in a deed of bargain and sale. *Gesner* v. *Cairns*, 2 *All.* 595.

4—Right of way—Rights of public.
The owner of land laid out and opened an alley-way leading from a street through his land, and leased the lots on each side of the alley. After the alley had been used by the public and the tenants occupying the lots for more than twenty years, G., the administrator of one of the tenants, assigned to the defendant, and by the description of the land in the deed, conveyed to him the alley as a part of the property leased. Held, That this conveyance could not affect the right of the public to use the alley, and that the defendant was liable for obstructing it, though the plaintiff was the tenant of a house fronting on the alley, and also claimed under G. as representing another lessee of the property. *Leary* v. *Armstrong*, 1 *Han.* 22.

5—Acquiescence—Estoppel.
The acquiescence of the judgment debtor in a Sheriff's sale, and subsequent possession of the land by the purchaser short of twenty years, though presumptive evidence that all the necessary proceedings have been taken, will not give a title to the purchaser by estoppel. *Doe* v. *Hazen*, 3 *All.* 87.

6—Estate in remainder, or in presenti—Acquiescence in sale.
The plaintiff claimed fifty acres of land under a deed in fee from his father J. B. in 1822, of a tract of 400 acres, of which the fifty acres were part, which deed was subject to a condition that J. B. should receive and enjoy all the profits and emoluments accruing from the land during

his life. J. B., in order to pay a debt, about two years after the conveyance to the plaintiff, and with his consent, caused the fifty acres to be sold by the Sheriff; the plaintiff bid at the sale, and afterwards agreed with the purchaser upon a division line between that and the remainder of the land. There was no proof of any judgment or execution against J. B., or of any advertisement by the Sheriff under which the land was sold. Held, That if the plaintiff had a present estate in the land at the time of the Sheriff's sale, his acquiescence in such sale would not divest him of his estate. *Doe* v. *Baxter*, 3 *All.* 232.

Quære, Whether the plaintiff took an estate *in presenti* under the deed, or an estate in remainder after the death of his father? If the latter, *Semble*, That his acquiescence in the sale and division of the land during his father's life would not operate as an estoppel *in pais*. *Ibid.*

7—Executor's Deed—Affidavit—Evidence.

Quære, Whether the affidavit required by the Rev. Stat. c. 136, s. 42, to be indorsed on an executor's deed, is evidence of any of the proceedings except the advertising and sale of the land. *Doe* v. *Thompson*, 4 *All.* 483.

8—Water-course—Right to make.

A. being the owner of lot No. 13, through which a stream ran, granted to B., his heirs and assigns, the right to the waters of the stream and the privilege of making a dam or dams, and cutting a trench therefrom across lot 13 and lot O, into lot P, on which B. had a mill. B. made a dam and trench, which did not cross lot 13, and which not answering the purpose, he made a parol agreement with C., who had become the owner of lot 13, under which he made a second dam and trench. Held, That he had a right to do this under the deed, and that his parol agreement with C. did not affect that right, particularly as regarded the defendant, who shewed no title to lot 13. *McKendrick* v. *Purdan*, 2 *All.* 28.

9—Water Privilege—Easement.

A deed granting all the right, title, interest, etc. of A. in and to the water privilege of a piece of land described, conveys only an easement, and no interest in the land itself, therefore the grantee cannot by virtue of the deed, maintain trespass for an entry on the land. *Watson* v. *Sinclair*, 3 *All.* 343.

10—Mortgagee in Fee—Estate passing—Requisites.

The estate of a mortgagee in fee of land cannot pass by deed of bargain and sale, without enrolment or registry, nor by feoffment without livery of seisin. *Doe dem Burkham* v. *Watts*, 2 *Kerr* 441.

11—Valuable Consideration.

To constitute a valuable consideration to support a deed, it is not necessary that it should be a money consideration; becoming bail for the grantor is sufficient. *Crockford* v. *Equitable Insurance Company*, *Mich. T.* 1863.

12—Registry of Deed before Lease—Operation.

A. leased land to the plaintiff for twenty-one years, and afterwards conveyed to B. in fee, by metes and bounds, a piece of land, including that leased to the plaintiff,—the deed containing the following words: "a portion of which, on the west side of the brook, is under lease to D. (the plaintiff), which lease is not yet expired." B. conveyed the whole of the land to the defendant, and both the defendant's deed, and the deed from A. to B., were registered before the plaintiff's lease. Held, 1st. That B. was only a purchaser of the reversionary interest in the land leased, and the lease was not therefore void as against him under the Registry Act. 2nd. That as B. was not a subsequent purchaser of the land leased, he could not, by conveying to the defendant, give him a better title than B. himself had. 3rd. That though the lease would have been void as against a subsequent purchaser from A. for valuable consideration, under a registered deed, A. could not by conveying to a third person, expressly subject to the lease, place such person in the same position as the law had placed A. as the general owner. *Downes* v. *Gordon*, *Trin. T.* 1861.

13—Registry Book—Best evidence of registry.

The best evidence of the registry of a deed is the Registry Book. Where a deed, by the memorandum indorsed, appeared to have been acknowledged on the 6th June, but the certificate of registry was dated the 5th, the Registry Book was admitted in evidence to show that the deed was registered on the 5th June, and that the memorandum of acknowledgment was then upon it. *Doe dem Simpson* v. *Falls, Trin. T.* 1863.

14—Proof of deed—Foreign Country.
A deed executed in a foreign country, may be proved in this Province by the subscribing witness. The provision of the Registry Act as to the proof of deeds executed in a foreign country is permissive. *Crockford* v. *Equitable Ins. Co., Mich. T.* 1863.

15—Deed Poll—Want of mutuality.
A. by deed poll agreed to make and haul all the timber he could find on B.'s permit, for which B. was to allow him whatever the timber sold for, after deducting B.'s supply bill and expenses, and that all the timber got should be the property of B. Held, That there was no mutuality, and that B. acquired no property in the timber without a delivery. *Coombes* v. *Hatheway*, 3 *Kerr* 592.

Livery of Seisin—Sufficiency of. See Livery of Seisin. *McLardy* v. *Flaherty*, 3 *Kerr* 655.

Evidence of—Allowed on Trial—Deed not acknowledged. See Evidence VIII. 12 a.

Breach—Covenant for Quiet Enjoyment. See Covenant 6.

Warranty, breach of. See Supra 3, Gesner v. Cairns.

Trustee—Right to pass Estate.
A person having the legal estate in land may by conveyance at law pass such estate, though it was given him in trust. See *Doe* v. *Gilbert*, 1 *All.* 520.

Delivery to, or assent of Grantee necessary. See Evidence XI. 34 a.

Estoppel—Mortgagor—Setting up Title of Mortgagee. See Estoppel I. 12, 13.

Title after acquired by Deed. See Estoppel I. 18.

Admission of Receipt of Purchase Money. See Estoppel I. 17, III. 2.

Exception in Lease—Construction—Obstruction of Lights. See Action on the Case IV. 4.

Sheriff's Deed—Recitals of Judgments—Proof of not necessary. See Sheriff's Sale 1.

Miscalling Writ in Sheriff's Deed. See Sheriff's Deed 1.

Defective Deed—Use of to show extent of—Claim of Possession. See Trespass II. 28.

Presumption of Regularity of Proceedings in Sheriff's Sale. See Sheriff's Deed 2.

DEFAMATION.

Actionable Words.
Privileged Communication.
Actionable Writing.
Averments.
Pleadings—Proof.
Mitigation of Damages.

1—Actionable words—Rebel.
The term Rebel is not actionable unless it is used in a treasonable sense, which must appear on the record, otherwise jugdment will be arrested. See *Beardsley* v. *Dibble*, 1 *Kerr* 246.

2—Slander.
In an action of slander the declaration alleged that the plaintiff was a clerk or servant at the store of J. Cunard & Co., at R., and that the defendant intending to injure the plaintiff, etc., and to cause him to be reputed a dishonest person and unfit to be employed as a clerk or servant, spoke the following words to the plaintiff, "you was turned out of Cunard's store at R. for robbery—you are a d—d parcel of robbers." Held, That the words being actionable in themselves, proof of the particular employment of the plaintiff as alleged, was not necessary. *Hea* v. *McBeath*, 2 *Kerr* 301.

3—Not libellous to write of a man that his outward appearance is more like an assassin than an honest man. See *Lang* v. *Gilbert*, 4 *All.* 445.

4—Privileged Communication.
The declaration in an action of slander stated that the defendant spoke of the plaintiff as a clerk of H. the following words: "That miserable fellow C. (the plaintiff) has just robbed H., he has taken money from him, and put his hand in the chest. I could see it all along. C. is a robber. You don't know him,—he deceived my poor boy, and has robbed H. of seventy pounds, and I can prove it;" meaning that the defendant intended to charge the plaintiff with theft. The defendant was H.'s father-in-law, and used the words to H.'s attorney. Held, 1st. That as the defendant had no interest in H.'s business, the communication was not privileged, though it was made confidentially to the attorney alone. 2nd. That

though the words might amount to a charge of embezzlement, they were not intended to impute larceny. *Carvil* v. *McLeod*, 4 *All.* 332.

5—A written paper charging the plaintiff with having wrongfully taken the defendant's logs, sawing them up and selling the lumber, is libellous, without any averment or proof that larceny was thereby imputed. *Connick* v. *Wilson*, 2 *Kerr* 496.

The charge in question was contained in a letter written by the defendant to McK., an intimate friend of his, who was a near relative to the plaintiff, but in no way interested or concerned in business with either party, with the avowed object of the defendant's availing himself of McK's influence and good offices in his controversies with the plaintiff, and to warn the plaintiff and his mother against the consequences of law suits, and the alleged interested motives of his attorney. McK. being absent from the country, the letter was opened by his agents and relatives, and became public. Held, That this was not a privileged communication. *Ibid.*

6—Actionable Writing.
A writing which tends to vilify and degrade a person, is actionable, although no crime be imputed. *Connick* v. *Wilson*, 2 *Kerr* 617.

7—Prefatory Averments.
In a declaration for a libel prefatory averments are not necessary, where the charge is apparent on the face of the paper, without reference to extrinsic facts. The question after verdict is, whether enough appears on the record to sustain the action. *Ibid.*

8—Professional misconduct—Charge.
A written paper charging the plaintiff (an attorney) with being governed entirely by a craving after his own gains, without regard to the interest of his clients, and reckless of bringing them to ruin, is libellous; and if the jury find a verdict for the defendant, the Court will grant a new trial if they think the verdict is wrong, though the Judge left the question of libel to the jury, without expressing any opinion upon the writing. The charge in question was contained in a letter written by the defendant to McK., a friend of his, but who had no interest in the business, with the object of obtaining McK.'s influence in settling certain law suits in which the defendant was engaged. Held, That this was not a privileged communication. Held also, That the defendant, intending the letter to be confidential, would not justify him in casting injurious imputations on the plaintiff's character. *Andrews* v. *Wilson*, 3 *Kerr* 86.

9—Forswearing Allegiance—Charge—Proof of Slanderous Matter.
Libel, charging the plaintiff, an Englishman, with having forsworn his allegiance to his country by enlisting in the American army, and afterwards deserting therefrom. Plea of justification. Held, That an Englishman who enlists in the army of a foreign country, and takes an oath of allegiance thereto, forswears his allegiance to his native country; and that the plaintiff's admission that he had enlisted in the American army and deserted, might as against him be taken to be true, and therefore was evidence to prove the justification. *Hill* v. *Hogg*, 4 *All.* 108.

10—Perjury—Imputation of.
The defendant wrote a letter to A. relative to an affidavit made by the plaintiff about the service of a writ on him as A.'s agent, containing among others, the following statements: "If L. (the plaintiff) swears that I did not serve him with a copy of that writ on the 31st October last he swears to a lie. * * * I think from the experience you have of mankind, you will admit that the outward appearance of L. is more like an assassin than an honest man; you must admit that he is exceedingly low bred and ungentlemanly, and consequently cannot appreciate the feelings, conduct or character of a gentleman." In an action for a libel contained in this letter, the declaration charged the defendant with imputing perjury to the plaintiff. The defendant justified the truth of the charge, and the jury found—contrary to the evidence of the plaintiff—that the defendant had served him with the writ on the 31st October. Held, 1st. That if the plaintiff had made an affidavit respecting the service of the writ, the jury having found it to be untrue, the justification was proved, and the plaintiff could not recover. 2nd. If the plaintiff did not make the affidavit, the letter was not libellous, because it only stated the matter hypothetically. *Lang* v. *Gilbert*, 4 *All.* 445.

11—Action for defamation—Allegation of perjury—No jurisdiction to administer oath—Plaintiff cannot recover. See McAdam v. Weaver, 2 Kerr 176.

Averment of perjury—Facts necessary. See Perjury.

12—Pleadings—Notice of defence.
A notice of defence, in an action for a libel, stating that the allegations contained in the writing are true, is sufficient under the Act 13 Vic. c. 32, there being no affidavit of the plaintiff that he was misled by the generality of the notice. *Lang* v. *Gilbert*, 4 *All.* 359.

13—Averment.
In calling a woman a whore, it is sufficient to aver in declaration that the defendant intended to impute unchastity. *Martindale and wife* v. *Murphy and wife*, *Ber.* 85.

14—Proof of innuendoes.
In an action of slander for charging the plaintiff with perjury, some of the counts stated in the inducement that the words were spoken of and concerning the plaintiff, and of and concerning a certain affidavit, etc., the defendant justified, setting out the affidavit, and alleging certain statements therein contained to be wilfully false. The affidavit referred to two papers which were annexed, but there was no positive proof that they were annexed when the affidavit was sworn to by the plaintiff. Held, That there was sufficient *prima facie* evidence to let in the whole of the affidavit, and that the admission of part to be read without the papers annexed was not correct, and the innuendoes not sufficiently proved. *Milner* v. *Gilbert*, 3 *Kerr* 617.

The verdict being for plaintiff—*Quere*, Whether this was a sufficient ground for a new trial; the statement alleged by the defendant to be false, and on which he founded his charge of perjury, being contained in that part of the affidavit which was read, and the defendant being obliged to make use of it to support his plea. *Ibid.*

In other counts the words were, "He perjured himself in an affidavit in C.'s suit." without any inducement stating the words to have been spoken of and concerning the affidavit. Held, That it was not necessary for the plaintiff to prove any affidavit, but that the *onus* was on the defendant in support of his pleas of justification to prove that the plaintiff had sworn wilfully false in an affidavit in C.'s suit. *Ibid.*

15—Proof of words.
It is not necessary in slander to prove all the words as laid in the declaration, if the words proved do not qualify those alleged. The words alleged were, "you perjured yourself in the suit between Thomas and me before Lawlor." The words proved were, "you perjured yourself in the suit between *your brother* Thomas and me, etc. Held, No variance. *Vye* v. *Newman*, *Hil. T.* 1866.

16—Mitigation of damage—Evidence.
In an action of slander for charging the plaintiff with stealing, evidence of the general bad character of the plaintiff is not admissible in evidence in mitigation of damages. *Williston* v. *Smith*, 3 *Kerr* 443.

17—Limitations—Other action for same offence—Evidence.
To a plea of the statute of limitations in an action on the case for slander, the plaintiff replied, under one of the exceptions in the Statute, that another action was brought in this Court within due time for the said identical grievances, in which a verdict was given for the plaintiff, but the judgment afterwards arrested *prout patet per recordum*, and that the present action was commenced within one year; the defendant rejoined *nul tiel record*. Held, That the replication was sufficiently proved by the production of a record in which the declaration contained substantially the same actionable words, although the venue was different, and material omissions in the innuendoes were supplied in the new action. *Beardsley* v. *Dibblee*, 2 *Kerr* 254.

Where the same evidence would be applicable to both actions, the identity of the grievances is a question of fact for the jury, although the additional allegations may make further proof necessary in the new action. *Ibid.*

DEFEASANCE.

See Warrant of Attorney. General Rules 27.

DEFENCE.

See Evidence VIII.

Notice of. See Pleading III.

DEFENDING WARRANTED TITLE.

Recovery of Costs. See Warranty.

DE INJURIA.

De injuria may be a good replication in an action of assumpsit, and is not confined to actions of tort.

In an action by the indorsee against the maker of a promissory note, the defendant pleaded that the note was discounted by the plaintiff on a usurious contract. Replication—*de injuria*, held good. *Bank of British North America* v. *Fisher*, 1 *All.* 606.

DELAY.

See Bail 14, 15.
" Certiorari II.
" Specific Performance.

Objecting to Partition. See Partition.

Enlarging rule *nisi*, not allowed unless delay satisfactorily accounted for. *Ex parte Glass*, 2 *All.* 88.

DELIVERY.

1—Sufficiency of—Direction to Jury.
Where A., the owner of a quantity of timber, being largely indebted to the plaintiffs, who were to be paid by means of such timber, directed his agent B. to take possession of and hold it for the plaintiffs, and B. accordingly took such possession, and put his mark upon the timber, and communicated this direction of A. to the plaintiffs, who assented thereto, although it did not appear that any absolute delivery of the timber, or the survey bills thereof, had been taken by the plaintiffs, nor any credit therefor given in the plaintiffs' books. Held, That the Judge was right in directing the jury that such acts and directions amounted to a delivery, and that such timber could not be afterwards taken in execution by the defendant against A., the original owner. *Crookshank* v. *White*, 1 *Kerr* 367.

2—Construction of Contract—Necessity of delivery.
A. agreed in writing to cut 100 M. feet of logs on land of which he had the permit, and deliver them to the plaintiff in the following spring, the logs to be the property of the plaintiff; and that plaintiff might at any time take possession of the logs and sell them, and after deducting from the price the amount of his supplies, and all expenses he might be put to with them, to pay the balance, if any, to A. Held, That without a delivery, or some act done by the plaintiff under the agreement, he had no property in the logs cut thereunder by A. *Tompkins* v. *Tibbits*, 1 *Han.* 317.

3—Necessary acts—Actual or constructive.
A., the owner of timber in possession of the Fredericton Boom Company, for the purpose of being rafted, agreed verbally to transfer it to the plaintiff, to be sold to pay certain creditors of A., and gave the plaintiff a written order upon the agent of the Boom Company, to deliver to the plaintiff all the lumber in the boom belonging to A. of certain marks. When the order was presented, the Secretary of the Company said it would be all right; but no transfer was made in the books of the Company, nor any delivery of the timber to the plaintiff, nor any dealing with it by him. Held, That no property passed to the plaintiff, and that the timber was liable to an execution subsequently issued against A. *Allen* v. *Ferguson and White*, 1 *Han.* 149.

4—Bulky article.
A symbolical delivery of a bulky article, such as timber, is sufficient to pass the property to the purchaser. Therefore, where A., the manufacturer of timber, which was hauled by B. on the shares, agreed to sell the plaintiff 500 tons out of a larger quantity lying on the bank of the river, and sent his agent, with the plaintiff, to deliver this quantity to him, which the agent did by putting his hand on one stick in the name of the whole, B. being present and agreeing that his men should assist the plaintiff's men in rafting the timber, which they did, and the plaintiff and B., each had separate rafts. Held, That there was a sufficient delivery to the plaintiff, as against a person claiming under an execution against B.; and that if B. had a lien on the timber for the hauling, he had lost it by parting with the possession. *Fiddes* v. *Henderson*, *C. Ms.* 47.

Assignment—Bona fides—Execution—What constitutes delivery.
See Assignment 1.

Delivery when not necessary. See Trover 5.

Re-delivery of ship. See Shipping Law 6.

Sufficiency of delivery. See Contract 1.

DELIVERY ORDER.

Usage—Acceptance. See Contract 2.

DEMAND OF PARTICULARS.

Not a step in cause. See Affidavit III. 6.

Not a waiver of necessity of filing plea before appearance in summary action, nor a step in cause. See Andrews v. Hanson, 1 All. 509.

DEMAND OF PAYMENT.

See Bills and Notes I. 1, 17. III. 15.

DEMAND OF PLEA.

See Practice VII. 15.

DEMAND OF POSSESSION.

Effect of. See Partition.

Termination of Tenancy. See Tenant at Will 3.

DEMAND AND REFUSAL.

See Trover. Contract 11.

DEMURRER.

See Pleading—Practice—Amendment.

DEPARTURE IN PLEADING.

See Pleading.

DEPOSITIONS.

See Evidence IX.

DEPUTY.

See Sheriff.

A sheriff may appoint a special deputy to execute a writ without requiring security from him. The 1 Rev. Stat. c. 131, only applies to the general deputies of the sheriff appointed under the Act. *Patterson* v. *Tingley*, *Trin. T.* 1863.

DEPUTY TREASURER.

Appointment—Are revenue officers—Bond—Continuance in Office—Liability.

Deputy Treasurers, appointed under the revenue laws in this Province are substantive revenue officers of the Crown, although appointed by the Province Treasurer, and the appointment does not terminate with the life of the Province Treasurer from whom it has proceeded, and consequently the surety bond given to the Crown by a deputy Treasurer on this appointment continues in force, and the sureties are liable for misconduct or defalcation committed by the deputy during the time of a subsequent Province Treasurer, such deputy continuing to act without any new appointment. *The Queen* v. *Kerr*, 2 *Kerr* 137.

The surety bond extends to moneys received by the deputy under ordinary revenue acts passed subsequently thereto, and also to moneys collected for special purposes by the deputy under acts in force at the time of the appointment, such as the sick and disabled seamen's fund, the emigrant fund, beacon and buoy money; and also to the Governor's share of seizures made by such deputy, but not to the surplus revenue received at the Customs under acts of the Imperial Parliament, which is only properly payable to the Province Treasurer. *Ibid.*

The deputy who may have received such surplus revenue in his official capacity from the collector of the Customs is liable therefor to the Crown, although his sureties may be exempt; and the Crown may apply the moneys levied under extent against the deputy, to any part of the demand for which the extent has issued, to which he is liable. *Ibid.*

DERELICT LAND.

Where a navigable river recedes gradually and imperceptibly, the derelict land belongs to the riparian proprietors. See *Burke* v. *Niles*, 2 *Han.* 166.

DESCRIPTION.

See Abuttal. Crown Grant.

Of parties as Executors. See Executors and Administrators V. 6.

DESCENT CAST.

The doctrine of descent cast enures to the benefit of the heirs only, and not to strangers. *Doe dem Thompson and wife* v. *Purvis*, *Ber.* 426.

DEVASTAVIT.

Allegation of devastavit without specific averment of value of goods wasted, is bad. See *Therlock* v. *McGee*, 1 *All.* 110.

Averment of injury to estate. See Bond (Administration Bond.)

DEVIATION.

Voyage. See Insurance 29, 34, 35.

Contract. See Assumpsit 42.

DEVISE—DEVISEE.

See Will.

DIES NON.

Good Friday, though a public holiday, is not a *dies non*, and a taxation of costs on that day is not irregular. *Gilmore* v. *Gilbert*, 2 *All.* 50.

DIRECTOR.

See Corporation—Bank.

DISABILITY.

See Limitation of Actions.

DISCLAIMER.

Tenancy under wife—Refusal to pay rent to husband.

Defendant held as tenant from year to year under an agreement with plaintiff's wife, and with his consent, the rent to be paid to the wife. Held, That refusal to pay rent to the plaintiff, and a denial of *his* right to the property, but at the same time, claiming to hold it under the lease from the wife, did not amount to a disclaimer. *Doe dem Andrews* v. *Taylor*, *East. T.* 1861.

Claim of right to property.

B. let land to the defendant as tenant from year to year, and died leaving an infant heir. The guardian of the child demanded the rent and gave notice to quit. The defendant refused to pay, saying she would have kept the land and taken care of the child, if she had been allowed, and that she had as good a right to the property as any body else. After the time mentioned in the notice for giving up possession, the guardian again demanded it. The defendant refused to give up the property, and said she had a better right to it than any one else.—Held, That although it might be doubtful whether the defendant's first refusal amounted to a disclaimer of the right of the heir; the second refusal, being unequivocal, was a disclaimer, and entitled the heir to recover in ejectment. *Reed* v. *Brown*, 2 *All.* 366.

DISCHARGE.

See Arrest. Bankrupt. Insolvent Debtor. Bail.

1—Action by Executor—Release by Devisee.

The Court will not order the discharge of a debtor in custody at the suit of an executor, on the ground that the persons beneficially interested under the will have agreed to release the debt, and have directed the executor to grant a discharge. *Percival* v. *McKenzie*, 1 *Kerr* 498.

2—Plaintiff discharging Debtor—Remedy on judgment.

The plaintiff by proceeding against the Sheriff by attachment for not returning the execution, and afterwards consenting to discharge him on making the return and paying costs, does not lose his remedy against the defendant on the judgment, unless from the circumstances attending the proceedings against the Sheriff, his consent to discharge the defendant can be implied. *Carman* v. *Mott*, 3 *Kerr* 131.

Refusing to discharge an Equitable Satisfaction. See Action at Law IX. 1.

3—By one of several Plaintiffs—Second Arrest.

Where a defendant was discharged by one of several plaintiffs, he cannot be arrested a second time at the instance of a co-plaintiff, and a rule *nisi* obtained by consent of defendant's counsel in order to file affidavit to get license of the Court to issue a second *ca. sa.* was discharged with costs. *Executors of Andrews* v. *Clarke*, *Ber.* 32.

Improper discharge of Debtor by Judge's order—Issuing *fi. fa.* before order rescinded. See Execution IV. 19.

Insufficient Affidavit for order to hold to Bail—Application to rescind order. See Arrest 10.

DISCONTINUANCE.

Plaintiff has power to discontinue his suit before decree. See *Gilbert* v. *Campbell*, 1 *Han.* 471.

Service of rule to discontinue without payment of the costs. Party entitled to move for judgment as in case of nonsuit. See *White* v. *Barton*, 1 *Han.* 1.

DISCOVERY OF NEW EVIDENCE.

See New Trial I. 8, II. 13, III. 9.

DISHONOUR (NOTICE OF).

See Bills and Notes IV.

DISMISSAL OF CAUSE.

Non-entry of Cause. See Practice V. 3.

DISSEISIN.

See Limitation of Actions 22. Deed.

Question of disseisin left to jury—Verdict for plaintiff undisturbed. See Possession 1.

1—Grantor conveying whilst disseised—No Estate passes.
If, at the time of the execution of a deed of conveyance of land, the grantor is disseised, no estate passes to the grantee. *Doe dem Thompson* v. *Barnes*, *Ber.* 426.

2—Facts constituting disseisin must be clearly apparent.
All the facts which constitute a disseisin should be clearly made out, and no presumptions allowed in favour of disseisin. Where it is doubtful whether certain acts amount to a disseisin, or are mere acts of trespass; or, whether the occupation was adverse or permissive, the question should be left to the jury. *Ibid.*

3—Original entry not wrongful—Wrongful continuance.
Where the original entry of a person upon land is not wrongful, there can be no disseisin except at the election of the owner: a wrongful continuance in possession will not work a disseisin. Where A. went into possession of land with the consent of the grantee, and held for a number of years, paying rent, and acknowledging the title of the grantee, and died in possession; after which, his widow let the defendant in possession, who refused to give up the land. Held, That the defendant's wrongful continuance in possession was not a disseisin, and did not prevent the operation of a deed from the heirs of the grantee. *Doe dem Strange* v. *Thompson*, 1 *Kerr* 564.

4—Disseisin—Question for Jury.
Disseisin is a question of fact for the jury to decide; and if on a trial in ejectment a verdict is taken for the plaintiff by consent, subject to a motion for a nonsuit, on the ground that the party through whom the plaintiff derives title was disseised at the time he conveyed to the plaintiff; the Court will not decide the question, but send the case down to a jury. *Doe d. Dowling* v. *Pearson*, 3 *Kerr* 135.

5—Possession—Conveying Land—Subsequent conveyance, and prior registry.
A. conveyed land to the plaintiff, who entered into possession. A. afterwards conveyed the same land to B., who registered his deed before the plaintiff's deed, and subsequently conveyed to C., who conveyed to the defendant. Held, That the possession of the land by the plaintiff, not being wrongful, would not prevent the operation of any of the deeds under which the defendant claimed title. *Payson* v. *Good*, 3 *Kerr* 272.

6—Continuance in possession as against registered Deed.
Where a party enters under an unregistered deed his continuance in possession, though wrongful as against a subsequent purchaser claiming under a registered deed, does not amount to disseisin. *Ibid.*

DISTRESS.

1—Replevin—Distress for rent—Averments—Surrender by operation of law—Questions left to jury.
In replevin for scows, the defendants averred the taking as a distress for rent of a slip, due them from W. The plaintiff pleaded—1st. That the slip was a place over which the tide ebbed and flowed, and was with the knowledge and consent of the defendants used by all persons as a public slip or landing place, in which their ships, etc., were accustomed to lie in the ordinary course of loading and unloading their cargoes, and other purposes connected with shipping and trade, paying to the occupier certain wharfage; and that the scows at the time of the distress were lying in the slip for the purposes aforesaid in the course of trade, with the consent of the defendants. 2nd. That before the rent became due, all the estate and interest of W. in this slip were duly surrendered to the defendants by operation of law. Replication—1st. That the scows were not lying in the slip in the course of trade, with the knowledge, etc. 2nd. That the estate of W. in the premises was not surrendered to the defendants by operation of law before the rent became due. Held, That these were proper questions for the consideration of the jury, and they having found for the plaintiff on both issues, the Court refused to disturb the verdict, though they might not have come to the same conclusion as the jury on the first issue. *Hammond* v. *Johnston*, 3 *Kerr* 161.

2—Avowry—Agreement as to suspension of remedy—Question for jury.
To an avowry for rent due on the 1st

February, the plaintiff pleaded that before the distress, on the 29th February, it was agreed between him and defendant, that the plaintiff should deliver to H. certain goods to be sold on account of the plaintiff, and should sign an order on H. to pay the proceeds as far as the amount of the rent to defendant, and if the goods were not sold before the 1st May then next, that H. should be under the direction of the defendant in the sale; in consideration of which the defendant agreed that he would not distrain for the rent in arrear before the 1st May. Averment of the delivery of the goods to, and the acceptance of the order by H., who held the proceeds of the sale to the amount of the rent for the use of the defendant. Replication, taking issue on the agreement not to distrain before the 1st May. Held, That it was a question for the jury whether the agreement of the parties was, that the right of distraining should be suspended. *Green* v. *Kehoe*, 3 *Kerr* 494.

3—Trover—Distrainable goods—Bailiff—Question of felony.

In trover against a landlord for goods alleged to have been taken by his bailiff under a distress for rent, some of which were not distrainable and were not included in the inventory, a verdict was found for the plaintiff, though the bailiff swore that the goods claimed were not taken. Held, That as the only question at the trial was whether such goods were taken, the landlord was liable for the act of his bailiff; and that it was not the duty of the Judge to raise the question whether the goods were feloniously taken by the bailiff. *Myers* v. *Smith*, 4 *All.* 203.

Quære, Whether if the taking had been felonious, it would have been a defence to the action. *Ibid.*

If a locked trunk is distrained, the landlord is responsible for the value of its contents; and per Ritchie, J., the bailiff should open the trunk and take an inventory of the contents. *Ibid.*

4—Breaking outer doors—Effect on legality of proceedings.

Breaking open the outer door of a dwelling house to distrain for rent, does not render the distress void, and is no answer to an avowry for rent in arrear, in an action of replevin for the goods. (Carter, C. J., *hesitante*, and Ritchie, J., *dissentiente.*) *Myers* v. *Smith*, 4 *All.* 207.

Held, per Parker, J., That the unlawful act of breaking the door, came within the term "irregularity" in cap. 126, s. 7 of the Rev. Stat., for which an action on the case would be the remedy. *Ibid.*

Per Ritchie, J., 1st. That the distress was illegal, and that replevin was the peculiar remedy therefor. 2nd. That section 7 of the Statute applied only to cases where the distress was legally made, but the subsequent conduct of the distrainer was irregular. *Ibid.*

5—Fraudulent or Clandestine removal of goods.

Where goods are fraudulently or clandestinely removed without a distress, the landlord may follow them and distrain within thirty days thereafter, under 1 Rev. Stat. c. 126, s. 4, although the rent may not have been due, or in arrear at the time of removal. *Hoyt* v. *Stockton*, 2 *Han.* 60.

6—The mere removal of goods by the tenant from the demised premises, when rent is in arrear, is not conclusive evidence of a fraudulent intent to prevent the landlord from distraining, although the effect of such removal may be to prevent the landlord from thus recovering the rent. In order to justify the landlord in pursuing them, it must appear that they were removed with a view to elude the distress; and it is a question for the jury whether the removal is fraudulent within the Act of Assembly 50 Geo. 3, c. 21. *Martin* v. *Gilbert*, 1 *Kerr* 202.

7—Distrainable interest in goods—Disputed right to goods—Wrongdoer.

Defendant leased a house to P., who shortly afterwards gave a bill of sale of goods to plaintiff, and received from him a lease of the goods for two years. A few days before a quarter's rent came due, P. moved the goods off the premises: the defendant followed them and distrained for the rent: plaintiff gave notice that he was the owner of the goods, and forbade the sale; but the defendant, believing the bill of sale to be fraudulent, sold the goods under the distress. In trespass for taking the goods, the principal question was, whether the bill of sale was *bona fide*, but the Judge directed the jury that the tenant had no distrainable interest in the goods, and if the bill of sale was *bona fide*, the plaintiff must recover. A verdict having been found for the plaintiff—Held, per Weldon, Fisher and Wetmore, J. J. (Ritchie, C. J., *dubitante*), That the tenant had no distrainable interest in the goods. Per Ritchie, C. J., That even if he had a distrainable interest, the defendant was liable for having sold the goods as the absolute property of the tenant. Per Allen, J., That the tenant had a distrainable interest in the goods, and that as there was misdirection on this point, there ought to be a new trial, as it would materially affect the damages, whether the defendant was altogether a wrongdoer or not. *Pidgeon* v. *Milligan*, *Trin. T.* 1871.

8—Trespass—Pleading distress for rent —Subsequent irregularity after distraint.

It is a good plea to a declaration in trespass for taking goods, that the goods were distrained for rent and not being replevied within five days were appraised, and after such appraisement kept and detained in satisfaction of the rent; although the defendant should have proceeded to sell the goods, yet the omission to do so will not enable the owner to maintain trespass, the original taking being lawful. The option granted by the Act 50 Geo. 3, c. 21, s. 7, to bring trespass or case, is to be understood according to the subject matter of the grievance, and not the mere election of the party. *Rogers* v. *Buntin*, 2 *Kerr* 230.

Execution—Claim for rent—Reasonable time for Sheriff to make enquiries. See Landlord and Tenant II. 15.

Damage Feasant—Replevin—Justice of Peace may grant. See Justice of the Peace II. 11.

Non-payment of rent—Power of re-entry sufficient distress—Affidavit. See Ejectment IV 2, 3.

Impounding Cattle. See Damage Feasant.

Work and Labour—Agreement to credit on rent—Distress—Payment—Action for money had and received. See Assumpsit III. 40.

Excessive distress. Necessary allegation. See Pleading I. 53.

DISTRESS WARRANT.

Distress Warrant—Irregular proceedings.

The Act 18 Vic. c. 38, relating to Sewerage and Water Supply in St. John, authorised two of the Commissioners to issue a distress warrant for a rate, but no warrant was to issue till thirty days after a demand in writing under the hands of the Commissioners or any two of them of the amount due: one of the Commissioners signed a warrant in blank without any proof of a demand made for the rate, and the other Commissioner afterwards filled it up and issued it. Held, That it was illegal. *Nowlin* v. *Sears*, *Mich. T.* 1864.

The 25th section of the Act declared that no proceedings should be taken for the recovery of any rate after the expiration of one year from the time of the assessment. Held, That a distress levied on the 17th July 1862, based on an assessment made on the 11th July 1861, was bad, though the warrant was issued within the year—the distress being a "proceeding." *Ibid.*

DISTRIBUTION.

See Heir at Law.

DISTRINGAS.

A distringas is not the proper remedy against a Sheriff in office, to compel him to sell goods levied on. *Phillips* v. *Dickenson*, *Trin. T.* 1831.

Prior to Rule of Court of Hil. T. 4th Vic., the mode of proceeding against a Sheriff when out of office, for not bringing in the body of a defendant, was by distringas, and not by attachment. *Henry* v. *Murphy*, 1 *Kerr* 207.

DIVERSION OF STREAM.

See Damages I. 30.

DIVORCE.

1—On ground of Cruelty—Necessary acts of violence.

To entitle a wife to a divorce *a mensa et thoro* on the ground of cruelty, there must be acts of violence or ill treatment by the husband, by which her life or health is endangered; or, there must be evidence of threats of such violence or ill treatment, under circumstances which lead to a conclusion that there was an intention on his part of carrying the threats into execution. A slight blow, given without premeditation, and in consequence of very insulting remarks made to him by his wife, does not amount to cruelty. *Hunter* v. *Hunter, Trin. T.* 1863.

2—Dower barred by Adultery—Alteration of decree so as to bar Dower —No notice—Wife not having appeared in suit.

In a decree of divorce *a vinculo matrimonii*, on the ground of the wife's adultery, where the conduct of the husband has been free from blame, the wife should be barred of her dower. *Leeman* v. *Leeman, East. T.* 1872.

Where, in such a case, the decree of the Court of Divorce did not bar the dower, the Supreme Court, on appeal by the husband, under the Act 23 Vic. c. 37, ordered the decree to be altered in that respect, though no notice of the appeal had been given to the wife—she not having appeared to the suit. *Ibid.*

DOCKETING OF JUDGMENT.

It is not necessary for a person claiming property by virtue of a Sheriff's sale under execution, to prove the docketing of the judgment by the Clerk under 8 Geo. 4, c. 7. *Doe dem Barlow* v. *Hatfield*, 1 *Kerr* 417.

DONATIO MORTIS CAUSA.

A man in expectation of death, indorsed a negotiable note specially to his wife, and delivered it to her. Held, That this did not operate as a *donatio mortis causa*, the note not being transferable by delivery only. *Weldon* v. *Weldon*, 2 *All.* 598.

A., shortly before his death, gave his wife a box containing certain things under circumstances which would amount to a *donatio mortis causa* of the box and contents. In the box was a deposit receipt for £300, which A. had in the bank. Held, That this record being only evidence of a debt, and not a document that could have been transferred so as to make the bank liable to a third party, this money did not pass to the wife as a *donatio mortis causa*. (See Aniss *v.* Witt, 33 Beav. 619, that money due on a banker's deposit note passes as a *donatio mortis causa* by the delivery of the note.) *Ex parte Gerow, East. T.* 1863.

DOWER.

1—View—Assignment—Particulars.

In an action of ejectment for dower, under the Act 21 Vic. c. 35, there must be a view of the premises, and if the plaintiff recovers, the dower must be assigned by the jury in giving their verdict. The declaration may be substantially the same in form as in an ordinary action of ejectment, and the defendant if necessary may obtain particulars of the plaintiff's claim. *Doe dem Johnston* v. *Jardine, Trin. T.* 1872.

2—Equity of redemption in Land.

A widow cannot maintain an action at law for dower in land in which her husband had only an equity of redemption during the coverture; even though the husband's right has been sold since his death, and purchased by the defendant expressly subject to the right of dower, or though the mortgage may have been paid, if it is not discharged on the records. *Doe dem McDonald* v. *Estabrooks*, 4 *All.* 455.

3—Husband tenant in common.

If the husband was seised as tenant in common, the widow can only be endowed in common under the Act 21 Vic. c. 25, and not by metes and bounds. *Doe dem Johnston* v. *Jardine, East. T.* 1873.

4—View—Proceedings.

Where an order for view is made in an action for dower under the Act 21 Vic. cap. 25, the proceedings should be the same substantially as under the writ of view under the Act 4 Ann c. 16. *Ibid.*

5—Arrears of Dower.

Semble, That arrears of dower cannot be recovered unless the husband died seised of the land. *Ibid.*

Objection to trial of Action for Dower by common jury. See Judgment as in case of Nonsuit III. 13.

EASEMENT.

See Deed. Crown Grant III. 1.

1—Privileges and Appurtenances—Words in a Deed not creating a right of way. See *Rogers* v. *Peck, Ber.* 318.

2—Words in Deed—Water privilege—Interest.

A deed granting all the right, title, interest, etc., of A., in and to "the water privilege of a piece of land described," conveys only an easement, and no interest in the land itself; therefore, the grantee cannot, by virtue of the deed, maintain trespass for an entry on the land. *Wilson* v. *Sinclair*, 3 *All.* 343.

3—Exclusive enjoyment—Acquisition of right—Cessation of use—Effect—Question for Jury.

An easement to appropriate the water of a stream in a particular way (as by a dam to turn the water in a particular direction), may be acquired by an exclusive enjoyment for twenty years; and where such a right is once created, it is perpetual, and passes with the inheritance. *McLean* v. *Davis*, *Hil. T.* 1865.

4—A short cessation of the use of the easement, occasioned by the burning of a mill with which it was connected, will not affect the right, if there was an intention to rebuild the mill carried into effect within a reasonable time. *Ibid.*

5—The removal, by a tenant, of a mill-dam by which an easement has been acquired, without the assent of the owner of the inheritance, will not destroy the right; and after the expiration of the tenancy, the owner of the freehold may restore the dam. *Ibid.*

6—In a case relating to the right to an easement of this description, it is a question for the jury to determine—1st. Whether a right has been acquired by a diversion of the water for twenty years; and 2nd. If so acquired, whether it has been relinquished or abandoned. *Ibid.*

7—Mill-pond—Soil.

A deed of a piece of land, "together with the mill privilege, saw-mill, and erections belonging to the same; and also the pond or flowage above the said mill," conveys no right to the soil of the mill-pond, but only an easement to dam the water and overflow the land for the purposes of the mill below. *Herbeson* v. *Cunningham*, *Hil. T.* 1873.

8—Demise—Construction of—Wharf.

Plaintiff leased to defendant part of a wharf forty feet wide by one hundred feet in length, "together with a right of way or passage for foot passengers, horses, carts, etc., in, through, over, and upon the wharf to the southward, westward and northward" of the part leased (the eastern part fronting on a highway). *Habendum*, the demised premises, "together with the privilege and enjoyment of the said wharf and the said right of way or passage hereby demised," etc. The plaintiff covenanted to keep the wharf in good repair and fit for the transportation of goods and merchandise, and for the passage of horses, etc., so that it may be used by the lessee, his executors, etc., "for all purposes of ingress, egress, etc., and as a highway," etc. Held, That the demise only extended to the portion of the wharf forty feet by one hundred feet, and that the lessee had only a right of way over the remainder of the wharf, and was liable to pay wharfage for landing goods upon it. *Lawton* v. *Reed*, *East. T.* 1373.

Conveyance of Mill with privileges and appurtenances—Soil of piling place not passing. See Deed I. 21.

ECCLESIASTICAL CORPORATION.

See Church of England.

EJECTMENT.

I.

Lessor's Title.

1—Bargain and Sale—Judgment Lien—Relation of execution to prior judgment.

Ejectment was sustained by a lessor of the plaintiff under a deed of bargain and sale from A. against the defendant, who claimed under a purchase from the Sheriff by virtue of an execution issued upon a judgment which had been obtained upon a former judgment of the Court against A., which latter judgment was prior to the deed of bargain and sale to the lessor of the plaintiff, the Court holding that the execution could not have relation back to the first judgment. *Doe dem. Peabody* v. *M. Knight*, *Ber.* 370.

2—Lessee, Estate for years—Necessity of actual entry.

The estate of a lessee for years is not complete without actual entry; therefore, where a lessor in ejectment made title under a lease from D., without shewing any entry under the lease, and it appeared also that the defendant had been several years in possession. Held, That the lessor's title was incomplete. *Doe* v. *Munro*, 1 *All.* 92.

3—Remainderman.
The tenant of a devisee for life may, after the death of such devisee be ousted by the remainderman without any notice to quit. *Doe dem Fields* v. *McKay*, 2 *Kerr* 435.

Lot No. 8, containing two hundred acres, was granted by the Crown to one W. in 1787, but it did not appear that he ever used or improved it. The lot remained in a wilderness state until 1811, when E. H. entered upon it, cleared and cultivated seven or eight acres, and resided there until her death in 1813. By her will in August 1813, she devised fifty acres of the lot to one S. for her life, with the remainder to G. F. and the heirs of his body. At the death of S. in 1842, the defendants were found in possession of the fifty acres; and it appeared that they came on th lot under S., and paid rent to her, though the particulars of the demise did not appear. They now set up an adverse possession against G. F.—Held, That they, occupying as tenants of S., could not set up title by adverse possession against G. F., the remainderman. *Ibid.*

Held also, That under the circumstances, it was fairly to be presumed they held the whole fifty acres under S., and not merely the part actually improved by E. H., and that at the death of S., the devisee for life, G. F. or his assignees were entitled to recover possession of the fifty acres. *Ibid.*

Maintaining Ejectment without demand of possession. See Will 8.

Heir—Disclaimer. See Disclaimer.

4—Lessor's Title—Rebuttal by adverse possession proved and uncontradicted.
Where the evidence of the plaintiff's right to recover in ejectment, arising from documentary title, and constructive possession in the person who conveyed to the lessor of plaintiff, was rebutted by actual adverse occupation for twenty years past in the defendant, and those from whom he claimed, which was uncontradicted, the Court set aside the verdict given for the plaintiff, and ordered a new trial. *Doe d. McMackin* v. *Devine*, 1 *Kerr* 411.

Title by Estoppel. See Acquiescence.

5—Grantee of Crown—Unoccupied land—Possession.
The grantee of the Crown, according to the ordinary mode of granting the wild lands in this Province, being deemed *prima facie* in possession of the land granted where there is no adverse occupant, it is sufficient for a plaintiff in ejectment, who claims under a grant to his lessor more than twenty years old, to shew that the land within that period remained in its natural state and unenclosed. See *Doe dem Des Barres* v. *White*, 1 *Kerr* 595.

6—Grantee—Adverse possession—Disseisin—Descent cast—Demise of wife's property before marriage.
When, at the time of the execution of a deed of conveyance from A. to B. of certain lands, the grantor is disseised thereof, no estate passes to B. All the facts which constitute a disseisin must be clearly made out, and no presumptions should be allowed in favor of a disseisin. The doctrine of descent cast enures only to the benefit of the heirs, and not to strangers. A demise in name of husband and wife of the wife's property, laid previous to the marriage, is not good. *Doe dem Thomson and wife* v. *Barnes*, *Ber.* 426.

7—Prior possession.
Prior possession is a sufficient title in ejectment against a mere wrong-doer. *Doe dem Dowling* v. *Pearson*, 3 *Kerr* 135.

8—The plaintiff in ejectment claimed under a conveyance from A. in 1847 A. had then been in possession of the land about six years, and continued to occupy till 1850, when he left the country and the defendant took possession. Held, Ritchie, J., *dissentiente*, That in the absence of any title in either party, the prior possession of the plaintiff (claiming through A.) was sufficient to enable him to recover against the defendant. *Doe* v. *Thomson*, 4 *All* 461.

Per Ritchie, J., That less than twenty years' possession in the plaintiff, was not evidence of title in ejectment, unless the defendant entered under the plaintiff, or the plaintiff was wrongfully deprived of possession by actual ouster, or by force or fraud. *Ibid.*

9—Vacant Crown Land.

Quære, Whether a mere priority of possession of vacant Crown Land is sufficient title in ejectment against a wrong-doer in any case? It is not certainly against a person who has applied to the Crown for a grant of the land, and obtained an order for survey thereof. *Doe dem Morrison* v. *McAlpin*, 2 *Kerr* 467.

10—Title out of Lessor—Limitations—Payment of rent.

It is a sufficient defence in an action of ejectment, to prove title out of the lessor of the plaintiff. *Doe ex dem McGowan* v. *McColgan*, 1 *Han.* 533.

Where the lessor of the plaintiff derives his title from his ancestor, acquired by the Statute of Limitations, it is sufficient to prove, for the defence, that such ancestor paid rent for the *locus in quo*, while the Statute was running. *Ibid.*

Re-entry—Lease—Forfeiture. See Infra IV. 3.

11—Title in third person—Mortgage.

Defendant in ejectment may show that at the time of the demise laid, the legal title was vested in a third person, to whom the lessor of the plaintiff had mortgaged the property, though the defendant does not claim under the mortgagee. (But see 2 Wm. 4, c. 23, s. 4.) *Doe dem Munro* v. *Hanson*, *Mich. T.* 1831.

Possession of widow—Continuance after death of husband—Holding for whom considered—Making out title by adding possession. See Possession 4.

II.

BETWEEN PARTICULAR PERSONS.

1—Tenant at will—Adverse possession—Statute of Limitations.

Where B. being put into possession of premises by A. under an agreement for purchase, continued to hold such possession for upwards of twenty-one years, and receive the rents, profits, etc., the Court considering B. strictly a *tenant at will*, held in an action of ejectment brought by the heirs of A. against B.'s grantee, that the plaintiff's right of action was barred by the 7th section of the Act of Assembly of 6 Wm. 4, c. 43. *Doe d. Purdy, et al* v. *Peters*, *Ber.* 350.

2—Merger of tenancy at will—Possession under agreement for sale.

An agreement was made by A. and B. by mutual bonds, for the sale and conveyance of lands by A. to B. on payment of a certain sum on or before the 1st of May 1829, *together with lawful interest for the first three years, and eight per cent. for the last two years, as a consideration for the use of the land.* Held, That B., who was let into possession under this agreement, was not tenant at will to A., but tenant for years until the 1st May 1829. Before that day A. died, and by his will devised the land to his widow for her life, and after her death to his children (the lessors of the plaintiff.) He appointed his widow his executrix, and the defendant, who was B.'s assignee, paid the purchase money of the land to the widow, and received from her the deed of bargain and sale. Held, That the defendant could not, after this, set up a *tenancy at will* under the agreement, such tenancy if any having merged in *the life estate* conveyed by the widow's deed; and that after the death of the widow an ejectment might be maintained by the children without any notice to quit, or demand of possession. *Doe dem Cliff et al* v. *Connaway*, *Ber.* 382.

3—A person taking possession of land under an agreement to purchase, which specified no time for the continuance of the possession in the event of the purchase not being completed, becomes a tenant at will; and such tenancy must be terminated by some act of the parties, before he can be ejected on non-completion of the purchase. *Doe* v. *Denny*, 3 *All.* 50.

The Act 6 Wm. 4, c. 43, s. 7, does not apply to such a case; but only to questions arising under the Statute of Limitations. *Ibid.*

4—Landlord and Tenant—Expiration of lease—Notice to quit—Holding over.

Where a tenant, under a parol lease for seven years, holds over the term (no rent having been paid), no notice to quit is necessary before ejectment brought by the landlord. *Doe* v. *Parkinson* v. *Hawkman*, *Ber.* 434.

5—Landlord—Defence by—Necessity of shewing title against.

In ejectment, where the landlord defends the action, the plaintiff must show a title against him, otherwise he cannot recover. As where A. defended as landlord of B., who he admitted by the consent rule to be in possession, and the plaintiff only proved conveyances from C. to B., and from the Sheriff to the lessor of the plaintiff under an execution, of B.'s right and title to the property, without showing any actual possession in B. or C. Held insufficient. *Doe dem Hatheway* v. *Hatch*, 3 *Kerr* 687.

6—Mortgagors — Defence by Tenant under title of Mortgagee.

In ejectment by mortgagors against a tenant, who had received the possession from them, under a lease made after the giving of the mortgage, but while the mortgagors were in possession; the tenant may defend under the mortgagee's title by showing that he subsequently became tenant of the premises to the mortgagees, and had paid rent to them. *Doe dem Diffin* v. *Simpson*, 3 *Kerr* 194.

7—Heir and Tenant by courtesy.

A married woman, whose husband had left the country, let the defendant into possession of her land, and died; her daughter, claiming as heir, brought ejectment, and there was conflicting evidence of the death of the husband, upon which the jury found in favor of the life. Held, That as the husband had the possessory right as tenant by the courtesy, the verdict was properly given for the defendant. Held also, That though the defendant having received possession from the mother, might be estopped from disputing the right of the lessor of the plaintiff to inherit the land, he was not estopped from showing that she had not the right to the immediate possession. *Reed d. Burchell* v. *Brown*, 2 *All.* 168.

The heir's right of entry is suspended until the death of the tenant by the courtesy. *Ibid.*

Lessee and Lessor—Defence by Lessor—Surrender of lease—Facts for jury. See Surrender.

8—Persons beyond seas—Right of action.

The right given by 1 Rev. Stat. c. 139, s. 16, to persons beyond seas, to bring an action for the recovery of land within ten years after the disability ceases, does not suspend the right of action during the person's absence. *Doe dem Fitzgerald* v. *Maxwell*, *Hil. T.* 1865.

9—No documentary or possessory title.

Defendant let into possession under written agreement, necessary to produce it, or give secondary evidence after notice to produce. See Evidence VII. 23.

10—Fraudulent conveyance — Resulting trust—Equitable estate.

R. N., the plaintiff's father, agreed to purchase land from F., and paid for it; but being somewhat in debt, he requested F. to make the conveyance to the plaintiff—then about two years old—which was accordingly done, and R. N. took possession of the land. Upwards of a year after this, a judgment was obtained against R. N. and execution issued, under which the land was seized by the Sheriff and sold to the defendant. In ejectment by the son—Held (Fisher, J., dissenting), That though the purchase by R. N., in the name of his son, might create a resulting trust in favor of the former, he would only have an equitable estate, and the defendant, claiming his right under the Sheriff's deed, had no defence against the legal title of the plaintiff under the deed from F. *Nixon* v. *Romerille*, *Mich. T.* 1871.

III.

Practical Procedure.

1—Service of Declaration.

A service of declaration in ejectment on the tenant's son on the premises, is not sufficient without proof that it came to the tenant's knowledge. *Doe dem True* v. *Fen*, 1 *Kerr* 458.

2—Service of a declaration by reading it in a loud voice, and passing the copy and notice under the door of the dwelling-house, the tenant being in the house at the time and refusing to open the door, or listen to the explanation of the service. Held sufficient. *Doe dem Beatty* v. *Roe*, 2 *Kerr* 169.

3—Landlord — Affidavit — Name of Tenant.

In ejectment brought by the landlord for non-payment of rent under Act 50 Geo. 3, c. 21, where half a year's rent is in arrear, and no sufficient distress found on the premises, the affidavit of service of declaration by affixing a copy to the door of the house, the possession being vacant, should state the name of the tenant from whom the rent is due. *Doe dem White* v. *Roe*, 2 *Kerr* 360.

4—Service of a declaration in ejectment on a daughter of the tenant, on the premises, is not sufficient to obtain a rule for judgment against the casual ejector. *Doe d. Disbrow* v. *Fen*, *Ber.* 234.

5—Service of a declaration in ejectment on the wife of the tenant, at his dwelling-house, is sufficient. *Doe dem Peabody* v. *Roe, Ber.* 347.

6—Where the tenant could not be found, and no person was in actual possession, and a copy of the declaration had been affixed on the most conspicuous part of the premises, a rule *nisi* for judgment was granted, to be served in the same manner as the declaration. *Doe dem Tredwell* v. *Roe*, 1 *All.* 585.

7—Rule Nisi—Statement—Name of tenant—Number of days for appearance.

The rule *nisi* for judgment against the casual ejector, need not state the name of the tenant, nor the number of days allowed him to appear. *Doe dem Taylor* v. *Roe*, 1 *All.* 1.

Service of—Where tenant could not be found. See Supra 1.

8—Non-entry of rule—Excuse.

Where the rule for judgment against the casual ejector was not entered at the term in which the notice directed the tenant to appear, in consequence of a proposition made by him to settle the claim, and which he afterwards refused to carry out, a rule for judgment was allowed to be entered at the next term. *Doe dem N. B. and N. Scotia Land Co.* v. *Roe, East. T.* 1865.

9—Claim as landlord—Allowing to defend as such.

If the relation of landlord and tenant does not clearly exist, there should be a summons or rule *nisi* before a person claiming as landlord can be allowed to defend an action of ejectment in that character. *Den d. Fauls* v. *Fen*, 1 *All.* 585 *and* 633.

10—Judgment against casual ejector—Acknowledgment of service of declaration.

An acknowledgment by the tenant before the day of appearance, that he had received the copy of a declaration in ejectment, is sufficient to entitle the plaintiff to judgment against the casual ejector. *Doe dem Kirk* v. *Roe*, 2 *All.* 453.

11—Objections as to proof of possession—Must be taken at trial.

If the defendant in ejectment wishes to limit the plaintiff's right to recover, to part of the land, in consequence of its being chiefly wilderness, and no actual possession proved, the objection must be taken at the trial. *Doe* v. *McGloyn*, 4 *All.* 189.

IV.

Setting aside or staying Proceedings.

1—Judgment against casual ejector—Non-Fulfilment of agreement—Right to enter judgment.

Where by the terms of an agreement entered into by the parties pending an action of ejectment, that the tenant should give up possession of ten acres of the land in question, situate along a certain shore, wherever the same might be selected, but that if the selection included the house where the tenant lived, he was to be allowed to hold it until the 1st May ensuing; and on failure to perform the stipulations of the agreement on the part of the tenant, the lessor was at liberty after the 1st May to sign judgment, etc.; and it appearing that the selection along shore was to be such as to suit one W. C., and that he, with the lessor and a surveyor, went about 1st April following and made the selection of the ten acres, which included the house where the tenant resided, and afterwards the tenant in possession being dissatisfied with the selection, without the assent of the lessor got another surveyor, who made a selection of the ten acres, which excluded the house; and upon the lessor and others on his behalf coming on the premises to ascertain whether there were any mistake in the first survey, the tenant refused to let them proceed, threatened to shoot them, and refused to give up the house on the 1st May; whereupon the lessor of the plaintiff entered up judgment against the casual ejector, and sued out execution. Held, That the lessor was right in so doing. *Doe dem Scovil* v. *Roe*, 3 *Kerr* 511.

2—Vacant premises—Re-entry—Distress.

Affidavit should state that the party had searched for property on the demised premises on a particular day, and that none could be found—the bald statement that no sufficient distress was to be found, not sufficient. *Doe dem Gilbert* v. *Roe*, 2 *Han.* 5.

3—Re-entry for non-payment of rent—Insufficiency of distress to satisfy rent not shewn—Lease—Renewal—Necessity of realising portion of distress if any found, before bringing ejectment on clause of forfeiture.

A lease was made by A. to B., for fourteen years from 1st May 1849, with a covenant by A. to pay for improvements, or renew the lease at the end of the term. A. conveyed the reversion to the plaintiff in October 1869, at which time it was alleged that $1,200 arrears of rent were due from B., who had left the country. In ejectment, for a forfeiture for non-payment of the rent, the plaintiff claimed the arrears, and also $72 for a half year's rent, due since he became the owner of the reversion. The affidavit of the bailiff stated that when he served the declaration there was not sufficient distress on the premises to satisfy the arrears of rent stated to be due, and that the value of the goods on the premises at that time did not exceed $50 in his estimation. Held, 1st. That as this affidavit referred to the whole arrears of rent claimed by the plaintiff, it did not clearly shew that there was not sufficient distress on the premises to satisfy the half year's rent accruing due since the plaintiff became the owner. 2nd. That as it did not appear that the lease had been renewed, or that B. held over after the expiration of the lease, or that the tenant in possession held under B., there was nothing to shew that a new tenancy was created, to which the proviso for re-entry in the lease would attach. If the goods on the demised premises are not sufficient to satisfy half a year's rent, the landlord may bring ejectment on the clause of forfeiture, without realising a part by distress. *Doe d. Boyd* v. *Roe*, 2 *Han.* 49.

4—Judgment by default—Merits.

When a judgment by default in ejectment had been signed, in consequence of the neglect of the attorney instructed by the tenant to enter an appearance, the Court set it aside on an affidavit of merits, the writ of possession not having been executed. *Doe dem Thomson* v. *Roe*, 2 *All.* 259.

5—Staying proceedings until payment of costs of previous action.

The lessor of the plaintiff claimed under a deed from A. in 1847, and the defendant under a subsequent deed from the assignee of A., who had become bankrupt, under which deed the defendant brought ejectment against A. and obtained possession. The Court refused to stay proceedings in ejectment brought by the lessor of the plaintiff till the defendant's costs in his suit against A. were paid, though the lessor of the plaintiff had employed the attorney to defend that action. *Doe* v. *Thomson*, 4 *All.* 596.

6—Second Trial—Refusal to enter into consent rule—Costs.

Where a second ejectment was brought in consequence of the tenant's refusal to enter into a consent rule containing a proper description of the premises, the Court refused to stay the proceedings until the costs of the first suit were paid. *Doe dem Morrice* v. *Roe*, 3 *All.* 84.

V.

Miscellaneous.

1—Demise expired—Amendment.

Where demise stated in a declaration had expired, the Court refused, after a delay of three years, to allow the plaintiff to amend by extending the demise, though it was suggested the defendant would set up the Statute of Limitations as a defence to a new action. *Doe* v. *Todd*, 1 *All.* 601.

2—Consent Rule—Lands included by mistake.

The defendant in ejectment entered into a general consent rule; at the trial the Judge directed a verdict for the defendant for all but a small part of the land described, but the jury did not agree, and after the trial the defendant obtained an order to amend the consent rule by striking out that portion of the land, on the ground that it was included by mistake. Held, That as the plaintiff was entitled to a verdict for that part of the land, and consequently to the general costs of the cause, the amendment could only be made on payment of such costs by the defendant. *Doe* v. *Day*, 3 *All.* 440.

3—Special Consent Rule.

The lessor of the plaintiff is not bound to enter into a special consent rule without the order of the Court or a Judge. A consent rule for part of the land is special. *Ibid.*

Verdict against Evidence—Statute of Limitations operating against second trial. See New Trial II. 16.

See General Rules 47, 48, 102, 103.

Landlord and Tenant—Writ of Restitution—Title—Right to bring Ejectment. See Landlord and Tenant VII. 5.

Ejectment for Dower. See Dower.

VI.

MESNE PROFITS.

1—Evidence to sustain action.
Where a declaration in ejectment had been served on A. and B. as tenants in joint possession, and upon A. appearing to defend, the common consent rule was entered into with him alone, whereby he was declared to be in possession of the whole premises in question, and the plaintiff nevertheless in default of B.'s appearance proceeded to enter up judgment against the casual ejector, and issue a writ of possession for the whole premises, under which a *pro forma* possession was delivered by the Sheriff to the lessor of the plaintiff. Held, That such judgment and possession were not sufficient to enable the casual ejector to maintain an action for mesne profits against B., the suit being still pending with A.; and *Semble*, The lessor of the plaintiff ought not to have executed an *habere* under judgment against the casual ejector, while the issue joined with A., involving the title to the whole premises, remained undetermined. *Doe* v. *Esterbrooks*, 1 *Kerr* 119.

2—An action for mesne profits against husband and wife alleging a joint trespass, is not supported by proof of a judgment in ejectment against the wife before marriage, the marriage not being averred. *Burnham* v. *Watts*, 1 *All.* 89.

3—*Quære*, Whether an action for mesne profits can be maintained without a judgment in ejectment. See *Doe* v. *Dobson*, 2 *All.* 446.

Judgment receivable in evidence. See Evidence III. 5.

4—Costs—Damages.
Plaintiff entitled to recover cost of judgment against casual ejector. See Damages I. 24.

Actual payment of costs necessary before recovery as damages. See Damages II. 7.

VII.

CONSENT RULE.

Special—Plaintiff not bound to enter into without order. See Supra V. 3.

Amendment of. See Amendment III. 7.

Lateness in application for extension of demise. See Supra V. 1.

Lateness of amendment. See New Trial III. 54.

Lands included by mistake. See Supra V. 2.

1—Evidence.
Rules from the office of the Clerk of the Office of the Pleas, should be signed by the officer himself, and not by his clerk; though a consent rule in the handwriting of such clerk is admissible in evidence before a Sheriff's jury on a writ of inquiry. *Jarvis* v. *Edgett*, 1 *All.* 264.

2—Effect of Consent Rule.
The lessor of the plaintiff and another person, each named J. M., applied for different lots of land; by mistake, the grant intended for the lessor of the plaintiff, got into the possession of the other J. M., who conveyed to the defendant. In ejectment, the consent rule described the land as "granted to J. M. and by him conveyed to the defendant." Held, That the object of the consent rule was only to settle the local situation of the premises, and that the plaintiff was not estopped by the admission from giving proof of his title. *Doe dem Mallet* v. *Robicheau*, 1 *All.* 419.

3—Estoppel.
Quære, Whether an estoppel which binds one defendant will bind another because he has joined in the consent rule. *Doe* v. *McDonald*, 1 *All.* 673.

4—Corporation.
Quære, As to the effect of a consent rule in an action brought by a Corporation. See *Doe* v. *Guion*, 1 *All.* 6.

ELECTION.

Of Directors. See Joint Stock Company 4.

Tenure of Office—Liability. See Bank 3.

Members of Assembly. See Election Law.

1—Polling—Completion—Equal number of votes—Double Return.
"Polling," under the Act 11 Vic. c. 65, s. 21, is complete when the elector declares the name of the candidate for whom he votes, and the officer enters such vote in the poll-book; after which it is too late to require the elector to take the oath of qualification. *Stiles* v. *Gilbert*, 4 *All.* 421.

Per Parker, J., That where two candidates have an equal number of votes, the Sheriff should make a double return. *Stiles* v. *Gilbert*, 4 *All.* 421.

2—Presiding Officers—Right to vote.
The presiding officer at an election under the Act to incorporate the Town of Moncton, 18 Vic. c. 66, has no right to vote, except to give the casting vote where the numbers are equal. By acting as returning officer a person abandons his right to vote as a rate-payer. *Ex parte Tuttle*, 4 *All.* 615.

Disqualification. See City Councillors. See Fredericton (City of.)

Of Counts in Declaration. See Trespass II. 8, 12, 13, 25.

Of Credit. See Principal and Agent 1, 2.

Of Commissioner—Taking necessary oath of office. See Commissioner 5.

ELECTION LAW.

1—Petitioner—Qualification.
A person who has been nominated as a candidate at an election for representatives for the Local Legislature, and has made the declaration of qualification required by the Act of Assembly 18 Vic. c. 37, and whose name has been entered by the Sheriff as a candidate in the poll book, and has contested the election and received votes as a candidate, is entitled to present a petition complaining of the due election and return of a member, under "The Bribery and Corruption and Election-Petition Act 1869;" and it is not competent for the respondent, on the trial of such a petition, to shew that the petitioner was not qualified as required by the Act. 18 Vic. c. 37. *Hebert* v. *Hanington*, *Trin. T.* 1872.

2—Bribery—Knowledge of Candidate—Re-election.
The election of the defendant as a member of the Local Legislature was set aside under "The Bribery and Corruption and Election-Petition Act 1869," for bribery and treating by his agents—the Judge certifying that the bribery was not committed by or with the knowledge or consent of the defendant. At an election held to fill the vacancy, the defendant was again elected. Held, That he was not disqualified for re-election, the Act not having declared any such disqualification except where personal bribery had been committed; and that the practice of the Imperial Parliament in such cases did not apply. *Kay* v. *Hanington*, *Hil. T.* 1872.

3—Costs—Taxation—Scale.
The costs on the trial of an election petition are to be taxed, as near as may be, according to the scale of costs in actions at law, and no greater sum can be taxed for counsel fees than is allowed by the Ordinance of Fees. *Hebert* v. *Hanington*, *Trin. T.* 1872.

4—False Return.
By the Act 11 Vic. c. 65, s. 30, all false returns which shall be wilfully made of any member to serve in the Assembly of this Province, are prohibited and declared to be illegal; and in case any person shall return any member to serve in the Assembly contrary to the right of election established by the Act, such return shall be adjudged to be false, and the party aggrieved, to wit, every person that shall be elected to serve in such Assembly, by such false return may sue the Sheriff or Returning Officer, and persons wilfully making and procuring such false return, and recover the damages he shall sustain by reason thereof. Held, That an action would not lie against a Sheriff under this Act, for a false return to a writ of election, without proof of actual malice. *Stiles* v. *Gilbert*, 4 *All.* 421.

Per N. Parker, M. R. *Quære*, Whether a person returned by the Sheriff as a member, but who, upon a scrutiny before the House of Assembly, fails to maintain his right to the seat, is a person "elected," and therefore entitled to maintain an action under the Act as "the party aggrieved?" *Ibid.*

Per Parker, J. That a person having the majority of votes, and who ought to have been returned by the Sheriff, did not lose his right of action for the false return by a decision of the House of Assembly against his petition; though the *quantum* of damages might be doubtful. *Ibid.*

5—Costs—Attachment.
Where the Judge who tries an election petition, makes an order for costs, under the 62nd section of the Act 32 Vic. c. 32, an attachment for non-payment of the costs should be granted by the Judge and not by the Court. *Kay* v. *Hanington*, *East. T.* 1873.

6—Notice—Publication.
Publication of notice in a newspaper "for three consecutive days," under the 69th section of the Act 32 Vic. c. 32, cannot be made in a weekly newspaper. *Hebert v. Hanington, East. T.* 1873.

Costs of publishing and posting. See Costs 34 a.

Allegations in petition—Materiality of witnesses to prove. See Costs 34 a.

ENTRY OF CAUSE.

See Practice III. (Entry Docket.)

Insufficient excuse for non-entry.
The Court refused, after trial and verdict for the plaintiffs, to allow a cause to be entered, though the defendant's attorney consented; the only excuse alleged for not entering it at the return of the writ being that the plaintiff's attorney expected it would have been settled. *Doherty v. McGrath, Hil. T.* 1866.

ENTRY BY A CLERK IN COURSE OF DUTY.

See Evidence III. 16.

ENGLISH STATUTES.

See British Statutes.

ENLARGING RULE.

1—Delay in Service.
Where a rule to shew cause has not been served in time, it will not be enlarged, unless the delay is satisfactorily accounted for. *Ex parte Glass*, 2 *All.* 88.

2—A rule *nisi* for quashing a conviction was granted in Easter Term, returnable at the next term, the rule was not served upon the Prosecutor of Justice until the day preceding Trinity Term, the Court refused to enlarge the rule, no satisfactory reason being shewn for the delay. *Regina v. Harshman, Trin. T.* 1868.

3—Ignorance of Practice.
Where a rule for *certiorari* was made in Trinity Term, but the writ was not taken out, the Court refused in Michaelmas Term to enlarge the rule on an affidavit of the attorney that he was not aware that by the practice he ought to have taken out the writ before Michaelmas Term. *Regina v. Harshman, Mich. T.* 1872.

EQUITABLE MORTGAGE.

Debenture Bond—Railway Company—Undertaking—Seizure of Land under fi. fa.
The defendants, being indebted to the plaintiff in the sum of £1000, executed a bond to him, declaring that for the purpose of securing the debt and interest they granted to him (*inter alia*) the undertaking of the Company, and all moneys to arise from the sale of their lands, with a condition that on failure of payment on a certain day, the plaintiff might, upon giving three months notice, enter upon the receipt of the proceeds of the sales, tolls, etc., and upon the absolute possession of the railway, etc., and reimburse himself the amount due, provided that "nothing therein should be held to limit the powers of sale or appropriation by the Company, of any of their lands, nor constitute a charge upon the same." Held, That this did not constitute an equitable mortgage on the lands of the Company, and that judgment creditors of the Company, without notice of the bond, could not be restrained by injunction from selling the lands under execution. *Wickham v. The N. Br.'h and Canada Railway & Land Company.* [S. C. Law R. 1 P. C. 64.] *Mich. T.* 1864.

Quære, If an equitable mortgage was complete, how it would be affected by a subsequent judgment and execution. *Ibid.*

EQUITY.

See Practice on Equity.

1—Bill filed by Administrator against Executor for an account of Estate—No complaint in lifetime of Administrator of Estate—Not keeping separate accounts—Exceptional circumstances—Right to call for an account.
W. C. was the administrator of the estate of W. H., and previous to the year 1824 sold considerable portion of the estate for payment of debts: in that year partition was made among the heirs of W. H. (the mother of W. C. being one) of the remainder of the estate. At that time W. C.'s mother was a widow, residing with her son, and having a considerable property, both in her own right as one of the heirs of her father, and also under the will of her husband. W. C. also had an equal share with his mother under his father's will, of which he was sole execu-

tor, and he had the entire management and control of his mother's property, and was her confidential adviser in all matters of business. For several years, regular and full accounts were made up annually of the receipts and expenditure by W. C. on account of his mother, though it did not appear that those accounts had been rendered to her; but about the year 1836 he ceased to keep any separate accounts of her estate. At this time W. C. was in the receipt of a large official income, and kept up a well-appointed household, of all the comforts of which his mother partook equally with him. In 1848 she made a will, bequeathing all her personal estate to W. C., and devising her real estate to another relative. W. C. died without issue in 1851, before his mother, and consequently the bequest to him by her will lapsed. A bill was filed by her administrator against his executors for an account of the estate of W. H., which had come to the hands of W. C. as administrator; and also for an account of all moneys received by him as agent of his mother up to the time of his death. Held, 1st. That as no complaint had ever been made during the lifetime of W. C., it might be presumed that the heirs of W. H. were satisfied with his administration of the estate, before they executed the deed of partition in 1824, and therefore his estate was not liable to account. 2nd. That though under ordinary circumstances the fact of a fiduciary agent or trustee not keeping separate accounts of the trust-moneys would be regarded with suspicion in a Court of Equity; this, from the peculiar relation of W. C. and his mother, and the terms of affection and confidence in which they had lived together, was an exceptional case; and that, in the absence of any evidence that advantage had been taken by him of his position, and of the confidence reposed in him, or that he had kept his mother in ignorance of what was necessary to be known for her protection, or of any information which would be likely to induce her to abstain from merging her income in his, the abandonment of the separate accounts in 1836, acted on up to the death of W. C., put an end to all right on the part of his mother or her representative to call for an account of her estate. *Botsford* v. *Hazen*, *Hil. T.* 1861.

1 a—**Executor's accounts—Impeaching agreement—Liability as Stockholder—Knowledge of Agent—Trustee holder of Stock, entitled to indemnity.**

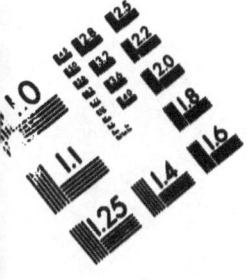

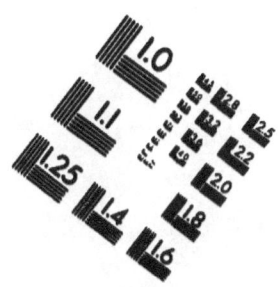

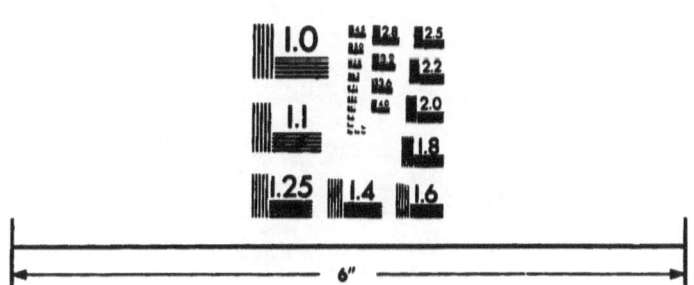

A. died in 1853, having appointed B. his executor. B. proceeded to collect the assets of the estate, and invested part of them in bank stock in his own name, as executor, the dividends of which were credited to the estate from time to time; but before the estate was fully settled, and before he had rendered any account of his administration, he died, leaving C. his executor. After this, in 1863, the widow of A. obtained administration *de bonis non* on his estate, and left the Province, appointing C. her agent; who managed the estate of A., collected the remaining assets, and received the dividends from the bank stock, and paid or credited the amounts to the widow. A full inventory of the estate of A., shewing the bank stock and other investments, was made under the direction of C. and filed in the Probate Court, and a copy sent to the widow, to which she made no objection. In 1866, the widow and residuary legatees of A. returned to the Province for the purpose of having the estate settled: they claimed to be entitled to an account of B.'s administration, which C. said he could not furnish, but offered to produce B.'s books for their examination. C. claimed a considerable sum from the estate for B.'s services as executor of A., which the widow and legatees refused to allow. After a good deal of negotiation, an agreement was entered into between the widow and legatees of A. of the one part, and C. as executor of B. on the other part, reciting all the facts and the claims on both sides; that no accounts had been rendered by B., or by C. as his executor, since his death; that legal questions might hereafter arise as to the liability of B. as executor, which all parties were desirous of avoiding; and in order to arrive at an immediate settlement of all questions arising out of the administration of the estate it was agreed (*inter alia*) that all money, deeds, notes, bank stock, securities, books, etc., belonging to the estate of A. [illegible] should be delivered up by C. to the widow of A. at a certain time; and that the estate of B. and his heirs, etc., should be released and discharged from all liability in connection with the administration of A.'s estate. In pursuance of this agreement, C. delivered to the widow all the securi-

ties, certificates of bank stock, books, etc. belonging to A.'s estate, and she afterwards received the dividends of the bank stock, though the stock was not transferred to her in the books of the bank. In 1867 the bank suspended, and proceedings having been taken to wind up its affairs, under the Act 27 Vic. c. 44, C. (as the holder of the shares) was placed on the list of contributories and compelled to pay $7000 as an assessment on the shares. The widow and legatees having refused to pay this sum to C. and to indemnify him against any future calls on the shares, a bill was filed to compel them to do so, and to obtain a decree that the agreement was valid and binding. On the hearing, the defendants claimed to show that the agreement was fraudulent; that they were compelled to enter into it in order to get possession of the assets of the estate, and because they could not get any accounts of the administration. Held, 1st. That B.'s accounts as executor were not in issue, and that if the defendants wished to impeach the agreement, they should have filed a cross bill. 2nd. That the widow of A. had the means of knowing her liability as a stockholder in the Bank, and was bound by the knowledge of her agent. 3rd. That C. only held the Bank stock as a trustee for the widow, and was entitled to be indemnified for any calls made upon him as the holder of the stock, under the Act 27 Vic. c. 44. Decree made against the defendants according to the prayer of the bill. *Botsford* v. *Crane*, *East. T.* 1873.

2—Remedy at Law—Suit for specific performance not maintainable.

The defendants, D. F. & S., entered into partnership in 1866 for purchasing and selling shingles and clapboards. D. resided in Fredericton, and the other defendants in Boston. D. was to purchase the shingles, etc., and ship them to F. and S., who were to control the sales, and the proceeds were to come to them: the capital to be furnished equally by the parties, and the profit and loss to be equally divided. D. being unable to furnish his share of the capital, applied to the plaintiff in February 1866, who agreed to make advances to him on condition that he should ship shingles, etc., to the plaintiff to secure him, D. agreeing (with the assent of F. and S.) to ship every alternate cargo to him for that purpose. The plaintiff claimed that the money was advanced to all the defendants; but F. and S. denied this, alleging that it was made to D. alone, and that they did not require it, having sufficient means to furnish their share of the capital; they also claimed that the amount to be advanced by the plaintiff was limited to $20,000, and that the shipments to him by D. were sufficient to cover that sum. Held, That even if the amount was not limited, the agreement gave the plaintiff no lien on the partnership lumber; that if there was a breach of the agreement, the plaintiff had a remedy therefor at law, and therefore he could not maintain a suit for the specific performance of it. *Fogg* v. *Dowling*, *Trin. T.* 1870.

3 a—Remedy in Equity for specific performance—Adoption of agreement—Relation of trustee and cestui que trust created.

M. being indebted to the plaintiff for logs and lumber, and to others in various amounts, and being also largely indebted to the defendants, gave them a warrant of attorney to confess judgment, subject to a defeasance, stating that it was given to secure the defendants in the amount due them from M., and in all sums which they might pay under a certain agreement then made between them. By this agreement the defendants undertook and agreed to pay (*inter alia*), by three instalments, all balances due by M. on logs and timber delivered to him since a certain day, the amounts to be fixed by orders drawn by him on the defendants: the defendants to have power to issue execution on the judgment forthwith, and sell all the real and personal estate of M., and after paying all expenses, to retain the proceeds till the purposes of the agreement were satisfied, and if any surplus remained, to pay the same to M. The plaintiff and M. having settled the amount due plaintiff for lumber, M. drew an order on the defendants for the amount, which order was presented to the defendants, and the first instalment paid to the plaintiff, and indorsed on the order. When the second instalment came due, the defendants refused to pay, because M.'s property, sold under the judgment, fell short of what he had represented, and was insufficient to pay the several amounts mentioned in the agreement. Held, 1st. That the plaintiff having assented to, and acted upon the agreement between the defendants and M., the relation of trustee and *cestui que trust* was thereby created. 2nd. That the defendants were absolutely bound by the agreement to pay the plaintiff the amount stated in the order; and 3rd. That the plaintiffs had a remedy in equity for a specific performance of the agreement. *Pickard* v. *The Central Bank*, *Hil. T.* 1868.

3—Deposit of Policy of Insurance—Mortgage right—Equitable claim perfected.

Defendant mortgaged a house to A. to secure a debt, and covenanted to insure a certain sum on the house, and, if required, to assign the policy to A. Defendant insured the house, but afterwards becoming indebted to B., and being pressed for payment, deposited the policy of insurance with B. as collateral security. B. had no notice of A.'s mortgage. On the 5th March, a few days after the deposit of the policy with B., the house was burnt. On the following day A. gave notice to the Insurance Company of his mortgage, and claimed the amount of the insurance: he also applied to the defendant for an order to the Insurance Company to pay the amount, but the defendant declined to give it, stating that he had already appropriated the money to the payment of his debt to B. On the 21st March, B. presented the defendant's order on the Insurance Company for the amount of the insurance, and claimed payment. Held, That A., by giving notice to the Company of his equitable claim under the mortgage, had perfected his right to the insurance money, and had priority over B., notwithstanding the deposit of the policy with him. *The Queen Insurance Co.* v. *Macpherson*, *East. T.* 1868.

4—Property taken subject to covenant—Knowledge of party—Equitable rights—Specific performance—Restraining by injunction until fulfilment of covenants—Remedy at law not ousting jurisdiction of equity—Agreement for compensation—Statutory remedy for assessment not applicable.

If a party takes property, with knowledge that the person through whom he claims has covenanted to use it in a particular way, he takes it subject to the equity created by that party; and a specific performance of the agreement will be enforced against him. *Ryan* v. *Lockhart*, *East. T.* 1872.

The St. John Water Company, under the authority of their Act of Incorporation, 2 Wm. 4, c. 26, covenanted with the owner of land, which they required to overflow, that they would build a bridge over the overflowage to enable him and his assigns, etc., to pass from one part of his farm to the other, and would keep the bridge in repair so long as the overflowage continued. The bridge was built and kept in repair until all the rights and property of the Company, subject to the outstanding liabilities, were vested in Commissioners (the defendants) by Act 18 Vic. c. 38; saving to every person all rights and remedies in law or equity, and all actions or suits pending, or thereafter to be brought against the Company for or by reason of any malfeasance or misfeasance, or any act done or committed, or by reason of any contract or agreement theretofore made, which rights and remedies should continue as if the Act had not been passed. The defendants continued the overflowage, but refused to keep the bridge in repair. The plaintiff having become the owner of the land, filed a bill for specific performance of the covenant, and to restrain the defendants from overflowing his land. Held, 1st. That the defendants, having taken the property of the Water Company subject to the outstanding liabilities, were bound by the covenant to keep the bridge in repair. 2nd. That the reservation in the Act of rights and remedies against the Company, only applied to actions pending, and rights of action accrued before the passing of the Act; and not to a breach of contract, or wrong done, by the Commissioners, though such contract had been entered into by the Company. 3rd. That the plaintiff had a remedy in equity against the Commissioners for a specific performance of the covenant, and that they should be restrained by injunction from overflowing his land until the bridge was put in a proper state of repair. 4th. That though the plaintiff might have a remedy at law on the covenant, that did not oust the jurisdiction of equity. 5th. That the mode of compensation for the overflowage having been agreed upon between the Company and the owner of the land, the statutory remedy of assessment by a jury did not apply. *Ryan v. Lockhart, East. T.* 1872.

5—Contract with Society supposed to be incorporated—Personal liability—Estimate of work not an award—Not affected by consideration of matters not referred—Concurrent Remedies—Objection to jurisdiction—Time of taking.

Plaintiff entered into a contract with the York County Agricultural Society to erect a building within a specified time, for a certain sum, and by the terms of the contract, the Society, if dissatisfied with the progress of the work, was authorised to take possession of and complete the building, and charge the expense to the plaintiff. The contract was under a seal represented to be the corporate seal of the Society, and it was declared that the members of the committee of the Society (who managed the business) should not be personally or individually liable to the plaintiff. The building was not completed within the time agreed, and the Society took possession, and proceeded with the work. It was afterwards agreed that the unfinished work, to complete the building according to contract, should be estimated by two mechanics, one chosen by each party, and that from the sum determined by them as necessary for that purpose, the Society should deduct a certain sum, and charge the balance to the plaintiff. This was done, and after making all deductions, a balance was due plaintiff on the contract. The Society never was in fact incorporated, and the plaintiff failed to recover the balance in an action at law against the Society. Held, 1st. That there being no Company liable on the contract, the members of the Committee of the Society, who had taken the benefit of the plaintiff's work, were personally liable. 2nd. That the clause in the contract against their personal liability was only intended to apply in case there was a Corporation liable on the contract, and there not being any such liability, it was repugnant and void. 3rd. That the estimate of the unfinished work was not an award in the legal sense of the word, but a mere valuation or appraisement, and therefore was not invalid in consequence of the arbitrators having taken into consideration matters not referred to them—it being substantially a decision of what was referred. 4th. That though the plaintiff might have had a remedy at law against the defendants, it did not follow that there was not a concurrent remedy in equity; but at all events, the objection was too late at the hearing, and should have been taken by plea on demurrer. *Hodge v. Reid, Mich. T.* 1872.

6—Judgment Creditor—Remedy at law before application in equity.

A judgment creditor cannot file a bill in equity to enforce his judgment against the land of his debtor until he has taken all necessary proceedings to enforce his judgment at law, and is unable there to obtain the relief to which he is entitled. *Black v. Hasen, Hil. T.* 1871.

7—Bill in Equity—Allegation—Interest in subject of suit.

An allegation in the bill, that the plaintiff had purchased the rights of two of the heirs, and obtained conveyance thereof, shows a sufficient interest in the subject matter of the suit. *Coy v. Coy*, 1 *Han.* 177.

8—Foreclosure of mortgage after death of mortgagee.

In a suit for foreclosure of a mortgage in fee, after the death of the mortgagee, the bill must show in whom the legal estate is vested. Alleging that the plaintiff is executor and trustee of the mortgagee is not sufficient. *Wiggins and others v. Floyd*, 1 *Han.* 229.

9—Bill for payment of Legacy.

In a suit to obtain payment of a legacy; *Quære*, Whether, if the bill shows the personal estate insufficient for payment of the debts, it must not also show that the legacy was charged on the land, if the plaintiff seeks payment therefrom. *Wallace and Wife v. Woods*, 1 *Han.* 230.

10—Plaintiff purchasing property without leave to bid at sale.

The plaintiff in a foreclosure suit may purchase the property at a sale under the decree, without having obtained leave to bid at the sale. The want of such leave is only an irregularity. *Gaskin v. Phœnix Insurance Company, Trin. T.* 1866.

11—Foreclosure—Mortgagor having no interest—Plaintiff's neglect of knowledge—Costs.

A mortgagor was made defendant in a foreclosure suit, appeared thereto and answered, disclaiming any interest in the property. On motion to dismiss the bill as against the mortgagor—Held, That as the plaintiff either knew or had the means of knowing before commencing the suit, that the mortgagor had conveyed away his equity of redemption in the property, the mortgagor was entitled to his costs. *Wilson* v. *Hornbrook et al*, 1 *Han.* 157.

12—Mortgage—Payments—Liability of land mortgaged.

A. the father, and B. and C. his sons, being joint owners of two lots of land, mortgaged them to the plaintiff. A. afterwards conveyed to the plaintiff land of which he was sole owner, in payment of half the mortgage debt, and then released all his interest in the mortgaged lands to B. and C., who occupied the land in common for several years, and made several joint payments to the mortgagee on account of the mortgage debt. B. and C. afterwards divided the land equally between them by deed of partition. In a suit for foreclosure of the mortgage, B. claimed that as between himself and C., his portion of the land had been released by the mortgagee at the time A. conveyed the land to him, and that C.'s lot should be first sold to satisfy the mortgage.—Held, 1st. That in the absence of any written agreement by the mortgagee, the whole of the land remained equally liable to the mortgage, and should be sold in one lot. 2nd. That if a verbal agreement, and the appropriation of the payment by A., would be sufficient to release a particular part of the mortgaged lands, it would not bind C. who was no party to it. 3rd. That the subsequent partition of the land between B. and C., in ignorance by the latter of the agreement by which the portion of the land allotted to B. was to be released from the mortgage, was a fraud upon C., and that such agreement would not be carried out for B.'s benefit. *Johnston* v. *McCartney and others*, 1 *Han.* 220.

ANSWER IN EQUITY.

13—Answer in Equity—Practice.

An objection that a suit is defective for want of parties, cannot be taken on the argument of exceptions to the defendant's answer. *Hendricks* v. *Hallet*, 1 *Han.* 185.

In answering interrogatories, the defendant must confess, or traverse the substance of each charge in the bill. Particular charges must be answered particularly and precisely, and not in a general manner. *Ibid.*

Where defendant is interrogated as to the receipt of particular sums of money, it is not sufficient to refer to an account annexed to his answer, as shewing what he had received, unless he states that it is the best account he can give. *Hendricks* v. *Hallet*, 1 *Han.* 185.

If he states that an account annexed to his answer, contains all the information he is able to give on a particular question, it is sufficient; though it was his duty to have kept a more particular account. *Ibid.*

Defendant is bound to answer an interrogatory if it is pertinent to the case made by the bill, though it is not founded on any specific charge in the bill: and *Semble*, That he should answer an interrogatory whether it is material or not. *Ibid.*

Defendant, filling the offices of trustee and executor, is bound to answer an interrogatory, whether his accounts distinguish the receipts and charges as trustee, from those as executor. It is not sufficient to refer the plaintiff to the accounts. *Ibid.*

Defendant is bound to answer as to his own transactions; and, if necessary to obtain information to enable him to do so; but he is not bound to seek information as to transactions not his own, and of matters equally accessible to the plaintiff. *Ibid.*

As a general rule, if defendant professes to answer, he must do so fully; and he cannot protect himself from the consequences of an insufficient answer, by objecting that the interrogatory is not warranted by the bill, or that the plaintiff has no equity. *Ibid.*

An answer which states a conclusion of law, is insufficient. *Ibid.*

When an answer denies or ignores a matter inquired after, it must be as to the defendant's knowledge, information, or belief. *Ibid.*

Defendant may be interrogated as to the contents of writings, decrees, etc. *Ibid.*

Where the discovery would be material to the case made and the relief prayed by the bill, a defendant may be interrogated as to the amount of his property, and his ability to pay; but he is not bound to answer a mere hypothetical interrogatory. *Ibid.*

14—Time allowed to answer.

A defendant is entitled to a month to answer after filing of the bill; and notice of motion to take the bill *pro confesso* cannot be given till the expiration of that time, though a copy of the bill and interrogatories may have been served on the defendant more than a month before the notice. *Godfrey* v. *Oglesby*, 1 *Han.* 233.

15—Amendment—Death of defendant.
Where one of the persons named as defendants in a suit had died before the summons issued, the pleadings were amended by striking out his name, and the answer was re-sworn. *Byers* v. *Harrigan*, 1 *Han.* 231.

16—Adding plaintiffs—Further allowance of time to answer.
Where an amendment was made in a foreclosure suit, by adding plaintiffs after the filing of the bill, the defendant was allowed a month to answer after service of the order to amend, and of a copy of the amended bill. *Wright* v. *Evanson*, 1 *Han.* 232.

See Supreme Court in Equity.

EQUITY APPEAL.

See Supreme Court in Equity.
" Practice in Equity.

EQUITY OF REDEMPTION.

See Equity.

Purchase of, by Mortgagee—Effect. See Mortgage 17.

ERROR (WRIT OF).

1—If it lies for not awarding judgment Non obstante veredicto.
Quære, Whether a writ of error lies for not awarding judgment *non obstante veredicto*, particularly where the Court below might have awarded a repleader; or whether the Court of Error may award such judgment *non obs. veredicto*? *Kinnear* v. *Gallagher*, 1 *Kerr* 424.

2—Mistake in entry of warrant of Attorney on roll—Taking advantage of.
A mistake in the entry of the warrant of attorney on the roll, and in the *incipitur* of the judgment in stating the action to be "trespass on the case," instead of "debt," cannot be taken advantage of on the general assignment of errors. *Ibid.*

3—Application to amend, pending writ of error.
Pending a writ of error, the Supreme Court may allow application to be made to the Court below to amend formal errors on the record, and may suspend judgment in the meantime. This was allowed where the award of the *venire* and the day of trial were left blank in the record below. *Kinnear* v. *Gallagher*, 1 *Kerr* 424.

4—Objection must be taken in Court out of which writ issued.
No objection can be taken to a writ of error in the Court below: it must be made in the Court out of which the writ issued. *Coffin* v. *Marsh*, 3 *Kerr* 427.

5—Rule to assign errors is a four day rule—Double costs—Delay in assigning error.
The rule to the plaintiff in error to assign errors, is a four day rule—the English practice not having been altered by rule of this Court. *Gilbert* v. *Sayre*, 2 *All.* 512.

If judgment is affirmed after error assigned, the defendant in error is entitled to double costs, under the Statute 13 Car. 2, c , s. 10. *Ibid.*

Quære, Whether the defendant is entitled to such costs where the writ of error is *non prossed.* *Ibid.*

A plaintiff in error not having assigned errors, the defendant, after the lapse of nearly nine years, issued and served on the plaintiff in error a *scire facias qu. executionem non*, and a rule to assign errors. The plaintiff not having assigned errors, the defendant signed judgment on the *scire facias*. The Court refused to set aside this judgment after the expiration of a term, but granted a rule to shew cause why the plaintiff in error should not be allowed to assign errors in bar of judgment of *non pros.* *Ibid.*

6—From what Court should issue.
A writ of error to remove a cause from the Court of Common Pleas into this Court should issue out of the Court of Chancery; and if issued out of this Court it is a nullity. *Mills* v. *Vail*, 4 *All.* 239.

7—Filing of—Time.
An assignment of errors cannot be filed till after the return of the writ of error; and a *scire facias ad audiendum errores* issued before the return of the writ of error will be set aside for irregularity. *Wetmore* v. *Levy*, 4 *All.* 502.

8—On judgment of Inferior Court—Matter ex debito justitiæ.
A writ of error on the judgment of an Inferior Court, being grantable *ex debito*

justitiæ can only be taken away by the express words of an Act of Assembly; and therefore it lies on summary judgments in the Court of Common Pleas. *Wetmore* v. *Levy*, 4 *All.* 510.

A writ of error to remove a cause from the Common Pleas, should issue out of the Court of Chancery, be tested in the name of the Lieutenant Governor, and be returnable at Fredericton. *Ibid.*

9—Affirmance of judgment—Interest—Notice necessary.
Notice should be given of an application to be allowed interest on the affirmance of a judgment in error. *Mills* v. *Vail*, 4 *All.* 629.

10—Issuing of writ sci. fa. ad. aud. errores.
It is not necessary that a *scire facias ad audiendum errores* should issue of the same term in which the writ is returnable. *Wetmore* v. *Levy*, *Hil. T.* 1861.

ESCAPE.

On Final Process—Measure of Damages. See Damages I. 12.

1—Right to issue fi. fa. after escape.
The recovery of judgment in an action against the Sheriff for an escape, unless it produces satisfaction, does not destroy the plaintiff's remedy against the debtor. After an escape from execution, the judgment creditor may issue a *fi. fa.* against the debtor's property. *Kelly* v. *Wilson*, 2 *All.* 4.

2—Application by Bail to render after escape.
If a debtor escapes from the limits, and his bail apply to be relieved on rendering him to jail, under the Act 13 Vic. c. 30, such relief will only be granted on condition of his being rendered to the jail whence he escaped. *Peters* v. *Perley*, 2 *All.* 585.

3—Damage—Attachment for non-payment of costs is in the nature of mesne process.
An attachment for non-payment of costs is in the nature of mesne process, and a Sheriff is not liable for the escape of a person in custody on such process, unless the plaintiff has sustained actual damage or delay in consequence of the escape. *Atkinson* v. *Mitchell*, *Trin. T.* 1865.

4—Sheriff—Justification—Order for discharge.
The production of an order of a Judge of a County Court, valid on its face for the discharge of a debtor, under the 1 Rev. Stat. c. 124, is a justification to the Sheriff in an action for the escape of the debtor; and he is not bound to prove the regularity of the previous proceedings. *Clementson* v. *Coombes*, *East. T.* 1871.

Prisoners delivered over by old Sheriff to new—Chargeable for escape. See Sheriff 13.

Debt—Action of, against Sheriff for escape, not maintainable. See British Statutes 3.

Action on limit bond for escape—Assignment of first bond—Taking second bond. See Bond II. 9.

ESTATE.

See Deed—Mortgage—Will—Landlord and Tenant—Tenant at Will.

ESTOPPEL.

I. By Acts—Conduct—Admissions.
II. Acquiescence.
III. Opening up of Estoppel.
IV. Miscellaneous.

I.

By Acts—Conduct—Admissions.

1—Leasing premises—Setting up title in a third person afterwards.
Ejectment. By indenture bearing date 1st May 1829, the land in question was leased by the lessor of the plaintiff to the defendant for two years, at the rent of £6; the defendant remained in possession several years after the expiration of the lease, but there was no proof of payment of rent. Held, That notwithstanding this, and that the defendant had not been actually let into possession by the lessor of the plaintiff, yet he was estopped from denying his right to lease, and from setting up a title in a third person at the time of making the lease, under whom the defendant was entitled to claim, there being no proof of fraudulent misrepresentation or concealment to mislead the defendant when he accepted the lease. *Doe dem Sands* v. *Phillips*, 1 *Kerr* 86.

2—Running boundary lines by Surveyor mutually chosen—Acquiescence.
Where a boundary line has been run between adjoining proprietors of land by a surveyor, mutually employed by them, and acted upon for a number of years, and improvements and subsequent con-

veyances made according thereto. Held, That the parties were bound by it, although it proved to have been run very incorrectly, and to deviate materially from the description of the boundaries in the title deeds under which the parties were holding, and to give the defendant 150 instead of 100 acres of land. *Doe dem Carr* v. *McCulloch*, 1 *Kerr* 460.

3—Accepting lease.
Where B., being in possession of land, accepted a lease of the same from A., who claimed title thereto. Held, That B. was thereby estopped from denying A.'s right to the possession at the termination of the lease, no other person having interfered with B.'s holding under the lease, and no fraud or deception having been practised by A. in order to induce B. to accept the same. *Doe dem Sands* v. *Phillips*, 1 *Kerr* 533.

4—Appearance and pleading—Corporation.
The defendant being sued as a Corporation, and appearing and pleading and as such in bar to the action, is estopped at the trial from disputing its existence as a body corporate, and its ability to contract in that capacity. *Seelye* v. *Lancaster Mill Company*, 1 *Kerr* 377.

5—Payment of rent—Outstanding title.
The plaintiff being in possession of land, a grant of it was made by the Crown to the Rector, Churchwardens and Vestry of W., of which the Rector informed the plaintiff, who agreed to hold the land from the Rector at an annual rent, and paid the rent two or three years. Held, That the plaintiff could not dispute the Rector's title by shewing a previous grant of the same land to B., through whom he did not profess to claim. *Hughes* v. *Holmes*, 1 *All.* 12.

6—After a conveyance of land made by a person of unsound mind, a tenant for years, of the land paid rent to the grantee. Held, After the death of the tenant that his widow was estopped by the payment of rent, from denying the title of the grantee. *Doe dem Hickman* v. *King*, 1 *Han.* 330.

7—Agreement under Seal—Payment—Explanation of delivery of goods.
By agreement, under seal, between the plaintiff and B., the latter agreed to purchase a vessel, then building by the plaintiff, and to pay him a certain sum per ton when the vessel was launched, $1,400 which had been advanced to the plaintiff, to be deducted from the purchase money. In an action on the agreement for the price of the vessel, the defendant under notice of set-off, claimed payment for goods delivered to the plaintiff, subsequent to the agreement. Held, That the plaintiff was not estopped by the agreement from showing, in answer to the set-off, that the goods were not delivered as an additional payment on account of the vessel, or as a sale, but on account of the $1,400, which sum was not paid at the date of the agreement. *Bishop* v. *Robinson and others, Executors of C. E. Bishop*, 1 *Han.* 68.

8—Entering into recognizance—Cannot plead fraudulent representation as to.
The sureties in a recognizance entered into under the Rev. Stat. c. 98, "Of Controverted Elections," cannot plead that they entered into it by a fraudulent representation of the nature of it, believing it to be the obligation of the principal only. *The Queen* v. *Sparrow and others*, 1 *Han.* 113.

If the recognizance was obtained by fraud, the sureties should apply to the Court to vacate it; but while it stands as a record, they are estopped from denying the truth of it. *Ibid.*

9—Purchasing at Sheriff's sale.
Where property claimed by the plaintiff is seized by an execution against A., and the plaintiff forbids the sale, he is not, by purchasing at the Sheriff's sale, estopped from denying that it was A.'s property. *Pelton* v. *Temple*, 1 *Han.* 275.

10—Representations—Party acting upon.
Where a party makes a representation to another, with reference to the title to lands, which induces him to alter his previous position and advance money upon them, he is estopped from denying the truth of such representation. See No. 27.

11—Adoption of Devise.
Assenting to a devise and going into possession of land under the will, estops parties from setting up a new title in other party. *Ibid.*

12—Giving Deed—Title at time.
In ejectment against a mortgagor by a purchaser of the equity of redemption under a warranty deed, the defendant is estopped from showing that he had no title when he gave the deed; nor can he

set up the title of the mortgagee in bar of the action. *Doe* v. *Power*, 1 *All.* 271.

13—In ejectment by mortgagee against mortgagor to whom the land had been granted by the Crown, the defendant proposed to show that the land was paid for by his son, who occupied it as owner till his death. Held, 1st. That the mortgagor was estopped by his deed from saying that he had no title. 2nd. That such evidence was also inadmissible on behalf of the son's widow, who defended the action jointly with the mortgagor. *Doe* v. *McDonald*, 1 *All.* 673.

Quære, Whether an estoppel which binds one defendant, will bind another, because he has joined in the consent rule. *Ibid.*

14—Admissions not made in connexion with matter of action.
The admissions of a party made to a stranger to the suit, are not conclusive upon him as an estoppel. Thus where the plaintiff stated to R. that property in his possession belonged to his brother, and R. communicated this to the defendant, who had a judgment against the plaintiff's brother, and thereupon issued an execution and seized the property, for which the plaintiff brought trespass. Held, That as the statements to R. were not made in connexion with the subject of the action, they were not conclusive on the plaintiff. *Murray* v. *Johnston*, 1 *All.* 409.

15—Corporation entering into contract.
A Municipal Corporation with certain defined powers, is not by entering into a contract under seal, estopped from shewing its incapacity to make such a contract. *Jameison* v. *The City of Fredericton*, 2 *All.* 128.

16—Assent to mortgage of cattle.
The plaintiffs, living with their father, assented to his mortgaging and delivering cattle to the defendant, as security for a debt due from him. Held, in trover against the defendant, That the plaintiffs were estopped from setting up title in the cattle. *Lyon* v. *Perkins*, 2 *All.* 375.

17—Purchase money in deed—Receipt of.
Quære, Whether one who has conveyed land and acknowledged in the deed the receipt of the purchase money, can recover a balance unpaid, on an admission by the purchaser that he owes it. *McAllister* v. *Day*, 4 *All.* 37.

18—Conveyance—Title after acquired.
S. conveyed to the defendant by deed poll of bargain and sale, land of which he had neither title nor possession, but he afterwards acquired a title, which was purchased by the plaintiff at Sheriff's sale, without notice of the prior conveyance. Held, 1st. That the defendant had no estate by estoppel. 2nd. That the plaintiff, not claiming under, or recognising the deed to the defendant, was not estopped as a privy in estate with S. from setting up the legal title which S. had acquired since the conveyance to the defendant.

Quære, Whether a deed poll will create an estate by estoppel. *Doe* v. *Wetmore*, 3 *All.* 140.

19—License—Disputing title—Disproving license.
In trespass, the plaintiff proved that the defendant had gone on the land by his permission, and afterwards disputed his title. Held, That the defendant was not estopped from giving evidence to disprove the license, and to shew that he entered under a claim of right. *Hazen* v. *Bryson*, 3 *All.* 101.

20—Lease—Estoppel by—Third party.
In ejectment against A. and B. the plaintiff proved possession of the land in 1827; that in 1835 he had ejected A.; that in 1848 B. had leased the land from him for a year and paid rent, and that A. retook possession immediately after being ejected. Held, That B. was estopped by the lease from disputing the plaintiff's title, but that A. was not estopped, and might shew title in a third person. *Doe* v. *Brown*, 3 *All.* 433.

After foreclosure, a stranger to the mortgage may dispute the title of the mortgagor. *Ibid.*

21—Landlord and Tenant—Representation of title.
The defendant obtained possession of land from the plaintiff's tenant, by representing that he had the title to it, and threatening to eject the tenant. Held, in an action of ejectment by the landlord, That the defendant was estopped from disputing his title, and setting up an adverse title in himself. *Doe* v. *Estey*, 3 *All.* 489.

22—Mortgage title of Lessor—Ignorance of prior mortgage.
One D. P. having mortgaged the premises in question to the lessor of the plaintiff,

after which the Church corporation, claiming the premises by a Crown grant, brought ejectment against B. R., who about being evicted compromised, and took a lease from the corporation, and then mortgaged such leasehold premises to one J. B., and J. B. mortgaged the same to the defendant, who entered; and while so in possession of part of the premises admitted that he had gone in under D. P., but referred to his mortgage from J. B., without any apparent knowledge of the mortgage from D. P. to the lessor. Held, That he was not estopped from contesting the mortgage title of the lessor. *Doe dem Eels* v. *Garnett*, 3 *Kerr* 535.

23—Counsel addressing Jury.
When in an action for negligence as a surgeon, the defendant's counsel, in addressing the jury, relies on his client's skill as a surgeon, he cannot afterwards object on a motion for a new trial, that there was no evidence that he was a surgeon. *Kelly* v. *Dow*, 4 *All.* 435.

See Evidence I. (Admissions.)

24—Agreement to indemnify against loss—Acquiescence of plaintiff with defendant.
Plaintiff purchased timber from J., which was seized under an execution issued by the defendant against J. An action having been brought by J. against the plaintiff, for the price of the timber, it was agreed between the plaintiff and defendant that the latter should indemnify the former against all loss, in case J. recovered in the action against him, which was defended on the ground that the timber was rightfully seized under the execution. J. recovered in the action, and the defendant paid the amount of the judgment. Held, That the plaintiff was estopped from afterwards setting up a right to the timber against the defendant. *Crocker* v. *Hutchison*, *Hil. T.* 1861.

25—Admission of execution of bond.
To a *scire facias* on a Crown bond, the defendant pleaded *non est factum*. Held, That evidence of an admission by him that it was his bond was not an estoppel; that he might give evidence to prove that the supposed signature of one of the subscribing witnesses was a forgery; and that it was a question for the jury upon the issue raised, whether the defendants had executed the bond or not. *Reg.* v. *Robertson*, *Hil. T.* 1864.

26—Sheriff's return—Particular action.
A Sheriff's return to an execution is only an estoppel in the particular action in which the execution issued. *Miller* v. *Weldon*, 2 *Han.* 188.

27—Representation—Title—Party lending money on faith of representation.
S. B. being in possession of a tract of 300 acres of land, made a will devising 150 acres thereof to his son Robert, and 75 acres to his sons William and Thomas respectively: the will was proved, Robert being one of the executors, and the three sons divided the land according to the will. Thomas afterwards applied to one M. to borrow money on the security of his portion of the land, and the three brothers then pointed out to M. their respective portions of the land, telling him that they held it under their father's will, and referring him to the County Records in order to see the will, and satisfy himself as to the title. In consequence of this, M. examined the will, and finding the property devised as they had represented to him, lent money to Thomas on a mortgage of his 75 acres. Held, That Robert and William having acted under the will, and having by their representations induced M. to lend money to Thomas, were estopped from denying their father's title to the land, or that Thomas had a title under the will to the 75 acres; and that they could not, in an action of ejectment by the assignee of M.'s mortgage, set up title in themselves under a deed from the heirs of a third person to whom the land had been granted. *Doe dem Armstrong* v. *Bridges*, *Mich. T.* 1869. (See 1 Han. 490.)

Giving Confession—Costs. See Cognovit 1.

II.

Acquiescence.

1—Of Judgment Debtor in Sheriff's sale—Title by estoppel not given.
The acquiescence of the judgment debtor in a Sheriff's sale, and subsequent possession of the land by the purchaser short of twenty years, though presumptive evidence that all the necessary proceedings have been taken, will not give a title to the purchaser by estoppel. *Doe* v. *Hazen*, 3 *All.* 87.

2—In sale of land—Agreement as to division line.
The plaintiff claimed fifty acres of land

under a deed in fee from his father J. B. in 1822, of a tract of 400 acres, of which the fifty acres were part, which deed was subject to a condition that J. B. should receive and enjoy all the profits and emoluments accruing from the land during his life. J. B. in order to pay a debt, about two years after the conveyance to the plaintiff, and with his consent, caused the fifty acres to be sold by the Sheriff; the plaintiff bid at the sale, and afterwards agreed with the purchaser upon a division line between that and the remainder of the land. There was no proof of any judgment or execution against J. B., or of any advertisement by the Sheriff under which the land was sold. Held, That if the plaintiff had a present estate in the land at the time of the Sheriff's sale, his acquiescence in such sale would not divest him of his estate. *Doe* v. *Baxter*, 3 *All.* 232.

Quære, Whether the plaintiff took an estate *in presenti* under the deed, or an estate in remainder after the death of his father? If the latter, *semble*, that his acquiescence in the sale and division of the land during his father's life would not operate as an estoppel *in pais*. *Ibid.*

Nuisance—Plaintiff's presence while work proceeding. See Action on the Case III. 1.

III.

Opening up of Estoppel.

1—An estoppel by record must be pleaded if there is an opportunity of doing so, otherwise the truth may be shewn. *Weldon* v. *Weldon*, 2 *Han.* 188.

2—An estoppel arising from an admission in a conveyance of land, of the receipt of the purchase money, is opened by a bond from the purchaser to the vendor conditioned to pay such sum for the property as arbitrators should determine. *Coram* v. *Whelen*, 4 *All.* 293.

IV.

Miscellaneous.

1—**Judgment against several—Non-service of process upon one—No knowledge of suit—Judge's order setting aside arrest in reply to judgment recovered.**

A judgment was obtained against A. and two others, without service of process on A., or his having any knowledge of the suit. (An attorney retained by the other defendants having appeared for A. also.) He was afterwards arrested on a *ca. sa.* issued on the judgment, and was discharged by a Judge's order on an affidavit denying knowledge of the suit and of any authority to the attorney to appear for him. Held, in an action for false imprisonment against the plaintiff in that suit, That A. was not estopped by the judgment from denying his liability; but that in reply to the plea of judgment recovered, he might shew the Judge's order setting aside the arrest. *Sulis* v. *Ferguson*, *Hil. T.* 1861.

2—**Judgment on scire facias.**

A judgment on *scire facias* in proceedings in bastardy, under 1 Rev. Stat. c. 57, is conclusive while it stands, and the defendant cannot object that the amount of costs is excessive. *Reg.* v. *Carson*, *Hil. T.* 1866.

3—Judgment in defended cause—Filing papers—Motion to set aside—Defendant estopped from taking advantage of papers not being filed. *Lynot* v. *Seelye*, 1 *All.* 35.

4—**Bail.**

Quære, Whether an application by bail for relief, under 1 Rev. Stat. c. 124, estops them from afterwards applying to defend on the merits. See *Rippey* v. *Austin*, 4 *All.* 77.

5—**Bills and Notes.**

Indorser, non-joinder in indorsement of joint payee, cannot be set up by payee who indorsed. See Bills and Notes V. 28.

Indorser delivering Note to Bank, cannot set up forgery of signature of maker. See Bills and Notes V. 21.

Carrier—Master of Ship—Not estopped by bill of lading. See Carrier 1.

Consent Rule—Plaintiff not estopped by. See Ejectment VII.

6—**Corporation.**

Presumption of Letters patent being properly issued, title of Corporate body being recited in instrument, and consent rule by party making objection. See Corporation 7. See Supra I. 4.

Crown Grant—Bounds—Reference to other grants. See Crown Grant 8.

7—**Evidence.**

Plaintiff relying on estoppel, defendant taking possession under a written agreement, it must be produced. See Evidence VII. 3.

Tenant by Courtesy — Disputing title of Lessor. See Ejectment II. 7.

Covenant binding Assignee. See Covenant 7.

EVIDENCE.

I.

Admissions—Declarations—Acts.

See Acknowledgment.

1—Admissions under Great Seal of the Province—Evidence against the Crown. *Rex* v. *Wilson*, *Ber.* 1.

2—By professed owner of land—Payments.
Where the defendant deduced his title by several *mesne* conveyances from W. K., the declaration of W. K. while the professed owner of the estate, that he never paid any thing for it, are properly admissible in evidence to shew that the recorded deed to W. K. was not made, as it purports to be, for a valuable consideration. *Payson* v. *Good*, 3 *Kerr* 272.

3—Res Gestæ—Counter Evidence.
The declaration of a party accompanying the act of shewing the point of beginning on the boundary of a grant, are admissible in evidence as part of the *res gestæ*, but the truth and correctness of such declarations are open to be controverted by other evidence. *Doe dem Lonchester* v. *Murray*, 3 *Kerr* 335.

4—Contradicting Deed.
The declaration and admissions of a party filling the character of surviving partner and administrator, and also of another party as heir of a person through whom the defendants claim title, were offered by the plaintiff in evidence, but rejected by the Judge on the ground that such admissions went to contradict the terms of a deed between the parties who made the admissions. Held, That the learned Judge was right in rejecting such evidence. *Maloney* v. *Purden*, 3 *Kerr* 515.

5—At time of making bargain.
Evidence of what the parties said at the time of making a bargain for the purchase of land, is admissible to shew what they meant by certain expressions used in the conveyance. *Doe* v. *Pitt*, 1 *All.* 385.

6—By grantee—Effect of.
The verbal declaration of the grantee of land, that he had sold it to a person under whom the defendant claims, is not sufficient to shew title out of the grantee. *Doe* v. *Todd*, 2 *All.* 261.

7—Commissioner of Highway—Intention.
The declaration of a commissioner of highways, at the time of laying out a road, that he intended to lay it out four rods wide, is not admissible. *Basterach* v. *Atkinson*, 2 *All.* 439.

8—Judgment Debtor—Ability to pay.
Quære, Whether in an action for an escape, evidence of the admission of the judgment debtor of his ability to pay the debt, was properly rejected. *Kelly* v. *Jones*, 2 *All.* 465.

9—Trover—Statement at time of demand.
A. executed a bill of sale to the plaintiff and delivered it to the defendant, who agreed to hold it as the agent of both parties. Held, in trover for the bill of sale, That the defendant's declarations made at the time of a demand, stating his reasons for refusing to give up the bill of sale, were admissible in evidence. *Dever* v. *Myshrall*, 3 *All.* 354.

10—Fraudulent conveyance—Declaration as to state of affairs.
Where the issue was whether a conveyance from A. to the defendant was fraudulent, a declaration made by A. as to the state of his affairs, is not admis-

sible in evidence, unless made at, or about the time when the deed was given. *Doe* v. *Fraser*, 3 *All.* 417.

A letter written by the plaintiff to A. several years after the conveyance and not referring to it any way, is not evidence for the defendant in such a case; nor is a subsequent conveyance of land from the defendant to A. admissible evidence to rebut the charge of fraud in the conveyance from A. to the defendant. *Ibid.*

Where the declaration of a third party is offered in evidence, the circumstances relied on to make it admissible should be stated to the Judge. *Ibid.*

11—Maker of note—Declarations.

In an action against one of a joint and several promissory note signed by him as a surety for the other maker, declarations of the latter made subsequent to giving the note are not evidence against the defendant. *Palmer* v. *Wilbur*, 3 *All.* 443.

12—Statement of affairs—Exhibit—Schedule.

A debtor, for the purpose of making a settlement with one of his creditors, exhibited to him a statement of his affairs, which the creditor copied in his presence. *Quære*, Whether such copy was admissible in evidence as a duplicate original or as a statement made by the debtor without notice to produce the original. A schedule referred to on a mortgage, but not annexed to it, is not admissible in evidence without proof that it was signed at the same time as the mortgage. *Lawton* v. *Tarrat*, 4 *All.* 1.

13—Entry in books—To whom credit given.

In an action for money lent, where the question in dispute was whether the loan had been made on the credit of the defendants, who were Aldermen of the city of St. John, and borrowed the money for the use of the city—of which the plaintiff was aware at the time; an entry made in the plaintiff's books debiting the Corporation with the money, is not conclusive; it not having been communicated to the defendants, and no authority from the Corporation to contract the loan, having been proved. *Gilbert* v. *Porter*, 1 *Kerr* 390.

14—Fraudulent transfer—Entries in books—Admissions as to state of business.

B., who was largely indebted, and several suits pending against him, transferred all his property to the plaintiff for £7,000, and took as payment the plaintiff's promissory notes payable in five years, without security. Held, in an action brought by the plaintiff against a creditor of B., who had seized the property under an execution, That the value of the plaintiff's notes in the market, and his probable means of paying them, was relevant testimony to shew that the transfer was fraudulent and made to defraud B.'s creditors. Held also, That entries in B.'s books relative to the property, though made by his clerks, might be referred to by him on cross-examination, and by his clerks on examination in chief by the defendant, in order to shew the value of his property and the state of his business at the time of the transfer. *Lawton* v. *Tarrat*, 4 *All.* 1.

In order to establish fraud in the transfer, declarations and admissions by B., both before and after the transfer, as to the general state of his business and the value of the property transferred, are admissible in evidence on the part of the defendant. *Ibid.*

The reasons for objecting to such evidence where its admissibility is doubtful, are much diminished by the Act 19 Vic. c. 41, allowing the parties to testify. *Ibid.*

15—Insurance—Verbal declarations of owner of vessel as to part ownership.

In an action upon a policy of insurance for the loss of a vessel, the verbal declarations of the plaintiff, the sole registered owner, that another person a foreigner was part owner, are not sufficient to disprove the allegation of interest in the plaintiff, who had obtained the register upon his own declaration, and acted as owner in procuring the insurance, and in the other affairs of the vessel. *Watson* v. *Summers*, 2 *Kerr* 62.

16—Ejectment—Examination in Bankrupt Court—Acknowledgment of title.

Plaintiff in ejectment relied upon a declaration made by the defendant in his examination in the Bankrupt Court, that the land in dispute had belonged to O., who conveyed it to the plaintiff, with his (defendant's) consent. Held, Not to be such an acknowledgment of title in the plaintiff as to prevent the operation of the Statute of Limitations. *Doe* v. *Taylor*, 4 *All.* 165.

17—Statements in bill in Equity.
The statements in a bill in Equity, under oath, are evidence against the party filing it, in an action at law. *Doe dem Palmer* v. *Ross, Trin. T.* 1862.

18—Consideration—Satisfaction—Admissions explainable by circumstances. See Consideration 8.

19—Trespass—Possession—Conversation.
The defendant in an action of trespass justified under A., and in order to show title in him, offered evidence of a conversation between A. and B.—not made upon the land, but several miles distant from it—in which A. gave B. permission to build a mill on the land in dispute. B. built the mill more than twenty years before the action, but did not further recognise A.'s right to the land. Held, That this was not sufficient evidence of A.'s possession, and that the justification was not proved. *White* v. *Smith*, 4 *All.* 335.

20—Declarations of members of Committee—Agents.
In an action against the Corporation of St. John for negligence in constructing a sewer, whereby plaintiff's land was overflowed, declarations of Aldermen, members of the Corporation, relative to the sewer are not evidence against the defendants; but declarations of members of a committee appointed by the Corporation to superintend the construction of the sewer, made while the work was in progress, and relative thereto, are evidence—being the declarations of an agent relative to a matter within his authority. *Riley* v. *The Mayor etc. of St. John, Hil. T.* 1865.

21—Boundaries of land—Declaration must be made while party in possession—Or against interest—Or privity shewn.
The declaration of a person as to the boundary of land is not evidence, unless it is made while he is in possession of the land, and is against his interest, or, unless there is privity between him and the person against whom his declaration is offered. *Sartall* v. *Scott, Trin. T.* 1864.

21 a Boundaries—Declarations by person in possession.
Declarations respecting the boundaries of land by a person in possession, and under whom the defendant claims, are evidence against him in an action in which the boundaries of the same land are in dispute. *Niles* v. *Burke, Hil. T.* 1873.

22—While the Crown is the owner of land it may, by its declarations, explain or control a previous grant, and a party claiming under a grant, subsequent to such declarations may be bound thereby. *Carter* v. *Saunders, Trin. T.* 1864. (See Crown Grant.)

23—Action against Sheriff—Taking goods on execution—Declarations of third person as to transfer.
In an action against a Sheriff for taking goods under an execution against P., which the plaintiff claimed under a previous assignment made to him by P. in payment of a debt, declarations of P.'s son, in whose possession the plaintiff had left the goods, as to the circumstances of the transfer, are not evidence against the plaintiff; though the fact of such possession is proper for the consideration of the jury in determining the *bona fides* of the transfer. *Doak* v. *Johnson*, 1 *Kerr* 219.

24—Action for Wages—Evidence—Recognition of plaintiff's right to give orders—Official character—Company.
In an action for wages as Secretary of an incorporated Company, the plaintiff relied on the defendant's having used and paid for goods ordered by him, and having paid for work done for their benefit also by his direction. Before the goods were ordered, the defendants had notified the plaintiff that he was not the Secretary of the Company. Held, That the payment by the Company for the work and goods was not a recognition of the plaintiff's right to give the orders, or an acknowledgment that he was the Secretary of the Company. *Ansley* v. *Albert Mining Company, Mich. T.* 1862.

Fieri Facias—Delivery—Intention to have executed—Letter to debtor. See Execution I. 5.

Account rendered. See Assumpsit III. 3.

Bills and Notes—Admissions. See Bills and Notes IV. 9.

To party stranger to suit—Matter not affecting suit. See Estoppel I. 14.

Receipt of purchase money in Deed. See Estoppel I. 17.

Counsel addressing Jury. See Attorney X. 15. Estoppel I. 23.

Estoppel opened by Bond. See Estoppel III.

Admission of party that Bond was his—Not conclusive. See Estoppel I. 25.

Libel—Justification from Admission. See Defamation 9.

Subsequent act not affecting previous admission. See Assumpsit III. 21.

Offer to confess Judgment. See Judgment II. 4.

Payment of money into Court. See Infra X. 9, 10, 11.

II.

JUDICIAL, OFFICIAL, AND OTHER DOCUMENTS.

1—**Plan—Grant.**
A plan produced by the heir of one of the grantees of the Crown, which had been in his possession for twenty-five years, and which had been seen in his father's possession for fifteen years before that, and which was kept with the grant, was held to be sufficiently authenticated as the plan referred to in the grant as "annexed," though the witness had never seen it annexed to the grant. *Rex* v. *Wilson, Ber.* 1.

2—**Subsequent grants—Reference—Effect.**
Where land in dispute was contained in a grant from the Crown to the defendant in 1827, but was claimed by the plaintiff as part of a grant made in 1784, to one D., under whom he made title, if there is any uncertainty as to the rear line of the grant to D., subsequent grants from the Crown to other persons, prior to the defendant's grant, in which the D. grant is referred to, are evidence for the purpose of ascertaining where the Crown considered the rear line of the D. grant to be; but not to vary its description, nor alter its construction. *Doe dem Carpenter* v. *Jones*, 3 *Kerr* 155.

3—Where the lessor of the plaintiff claimed the land in question as being part of lot No. 33, granted by the Crown in 1784, and the defendant claimed it as a lot in rear of No. 33, granted in 1830; other grants of the Crown of adjoining lands, made in 1786, and between that date and 1830, may be referred to for the purpose of showing what the Crown considered to be the true rear line of lot No. 33; provided there is any uncertainty as to the line. *Doe dem Ponsford* v. *Vernon*, 2 *Kerr* 551.

4—Where land granted to the defendant in 1839, was described as being in rear of lot No. 33 (granted in 1784,) and lying between that lot and lot No. 39; subsequent grants of adjoining lands in 1786 and 1787, in which lot No. 33 was described as extending to, and bounded on lot No. 39, are evidence to shew the Crown out of possession, for more than 20 years, of the land described in the defendant's grant, so as to prevent that grant from operating without a previous inquest of office. *Ibid.*

5—Where the question in dispute is the dividing line between two tracts of land granted by the Crown, a grant issued subsequent to both these grants is not evidence for the purpose of explaining any ambiguity in either of them, and ascertaining where the Crown intended the line to be: while the Crown is the owner of the land, it may by its declarations explain or control a previous grant, and a party claiming under a grant, subsequent to such declarations, may be bound thereby. *Carter* v. *Saunders, Trin. T.* 1864.

6—**Surveyor's return—Ambiguity in grant.**
A return of a survey of land filed in the Surveyor General's office, upon which a grant issues, is admissible in evidence to explain an ambiguity in the grant, though the handwriting of the Surveyor who made the return is not proved—it being an official document coming from the proper custody, and the Surveyor being dead. *Wiggins* v. *McLean*, 1 *All.* 671.

7—A return of a survey of Crown Land filed in the Surveyor General's office, is not evidence to prove that the Surveyor has run the lines stated in the return, although it is an ancient document, and the Surveyor is dead. *Maynes* v. *Dolan*, 3 *All.* 573.

8—**Decree of partition.**
A decree of partition is evidence in an action of ejectment, to show that the land in dispute, formerly part of an undivided estate, had been assigned as the separate property of the plaintiff. *Doe* v. *Estey*, 3 *All.* 480.

9—**Deed—Pleading—Assent of grantee.**
To an action for the breach of a written contract whereby B., in consideration of £500 paid to him by A., agreed to convey to A. a mill and mill privilege at P., as soon as he obtained a grant thereof.

B. pleaded 1st. *non assumpsit;* 2ndly. That he executed and delivered a conveyance to A.; and 3rdly. That a conveyance was tendered and refused. At the trial a registered deed was offered in evidence under the pleas, but without proof by the subscribing witness of the execution in the ordinary way. Held, That such evidence was properly rejected, it not being competent for the grantor to make a deed evidence by mere force of the registry and acknowledgment, without delivery to or the assent of the grantee. *Smith* v. *Millidge*, 2 *Kerr* 408.

10—Proof of Deed, before received in evidence.
A deed appeared to have been executed in the presence of two witnesses, one of whom, a Justice of the Peace authorized to take acknowledgment of deeds, was dead: no account could be given of the other by persons who had the best means of obtaining a knowledge of the inhabitants of the place where the deed was executed. Held, That it was properly received in evidence on proof of the handwriting of the deceased witness. *Doe* v. *Hatheway*, 2 *All.* 69.

11—The execution of a deed of conveyance is not proved by the Magistrate's certificate of acknowledgment endorsed thereon, without registry. *Joplin* v. *Johnston*, 2 *Kerr* 541.

12—Registry of Deed before proof.
A deed offered as a registered conveyance, appeared by the certificate endorsed, to have been registered before it was proved. Held, That it could not operate as a sufficient registry by relation, and that the deed was improperly admitted in evidence. *Doe* v. *Rideout*, 3 *All.* 502.

13—Registry Book—Two deeds written on one sheet—One Certificate.
Where two deeds were written on the same sheet of paper and registered at the same time, but only one certificate of registry and one number were endorsed—Held, That the Registry Book was properly admitted in evidence to show that both deeds were registered. *Doe* v. *McCulley*, 3 *All.* 104.

Quære, Whether a proper certificate of registry could not have been indorsed at the trial. *Ibid.*

14—Probate of Will.
The probate of a will, though registered, is not evidence of a due execution to pass real estate. *Hamilton* v. *Love*, 2 *Kerr* 243.

15—Judgment of Foreign Court
Is evidence only of debt. See *Fergus* v. *Wardlaw*, 3 *Kerr* 665.

16—Seal of Foreign Judgment.
It is sufficient that the seal affixed to a foreign judgment is the seal used by the foreign Court, though it purports on its face to be the seal of a different Court from that in which the judgment was obtained. See *Cyr* v. *Sanfacon*, 2 *All.* 641.

17—Foreign Judgment—Proof of.
A judgment of the Court of King's Bench in England may be proved in this Province by an examined copy verified by an affidavit sworn before the Lord Mayor of London, under the Act of Parliament 5 Geo. 2, c. 7; such affidavit by the Act being tantamount to the *viva voce* testimony of the witness. *Champion* v. *Long*, *Hil. T.* 1834.

18—Record of Judgment—Debt on Bond—Date.
Semble, That the record of a judgment in an action on a bond, is evidence of the date of the bond, in an action of ejectment by a person claiming title under the obligor, to shew that he was indebted at the time of the conveyance, and that it is therefore fraudulent. *Doe* v. *Gilbert*, 1 *All.* 520.

19—Writ—Execution.
An altered *fi. fa.* is not receivable in evidence. See *Johnston* v. *Winslow*, *Ber.* 53.

20—Original fi. fa. not returned.
In making title to land under a Sheriff's deed, the original execution under which the land was sold when not returned and filed in Court, is admissible in evidence. *Linton* v. *Wilson*, 1 *Kerr* 223.

21—In an action against a Sheriff to recover money levied by him under an execution, the original execution with the Sheriff's return thereon in the hands of the attorney is not evidence; after being returned the execution is a record, and the evidence should come from the proper custody. See Supra 20. *Stuart* v. *Andrews*, *Hil. T.* 1827.

22—Contemporaneous Letter.
Where part of the alleged consideration for an assignment of goods was interest money due on a bond to a creditor in Nova Scotia, and a bill of exchange drawn by him on the plaintiffs was given

in evidence. Held, That a contemporaneous letter written by the creditor, which specified that the bill was drawn for such interest, was admissible in evidence. *Kinnear* v. *White*, 2 *Kerr* 235.

23—Agreement for consent rule—Judgment in ejectment.

In trespass for *mesne* profits against one who came into possession under the tenant in the action of ejectment, the agreement for the consent rule, signed by the Attorney of the tenant in possession, and the judgment in ejectment against the casual ejector are evidence for the plaintiff—the first as a proceeding to connect the tenant, under whom the defendant in this action claimed, with the action of ejectment, and the latter, to shew the plaintiff's right to the possession of the property. *Fraser* v. *Harding*, 3 *Kerr* 94.

24—Agreement.

In an action for obstructing a water course an agreement between the plaintiff and defendant, whereby the latter agreed to enlarge the water course and did so, and was paid by the plaintiff for it, is evidence for the plaintiff, and relevant to the matter in dispute. *Palmer* v. *Turner*, *East. T.* 1862.

25—Newspaper—Report not authorised.

In an action against the Corporation of St. John for negligence in the construction of a sewer, whereby the plaintiff's land was overflowed, a newspaper, purporting to contain a report of the proceedings of a meeting of the Corporation at which the question of the sewer, and its effect on the plaintiff's property were discussed, was put in evidence by the plaintiff. Held, That in the absence of evidence that the report was authorized by the defendant to be published, it was not evidence; and that as the statements in it had a material bearing on the plaintiff's case, and did probably influence the jury, a verdict for the plaintiff was set aside. *Riley* v. *The Mayor etc. of St. John*, *East. T.* 1864.

Newspaper—Notice—Authority. See Joint Stock Company 3.

26—Nisi Prius Record—Merger of Defendant's claim.

A judgment recovered by the defendant against the plaintiff after the commencement of the plaintiff's suit, cannot be pleaded as a set-off, even though the verdict on which the judgment is founded was given before the commencement of such suit. The defendant's original cause of action being merged in the judgment, the *nisi prius* record in the defendant's suit is not evidence of the plaintiff's indebtedness before the commencement of his suit. *Hammond* v. *Mott*, 3 *All.* 426.

27—Assignment of mortgage by executor.

An assignment of a mortgage by an executor is not admissible in evidence without proof of the Probate. *Doe* v. *Hanson*, 3 *All.* 428.

28—Receipt.

A written receipt, signed by the mortgagee, is not admissible in evidence to prove payment of rent to him. *Joplin* v. *Johnston*, 2 *Kerr* 541.

29—Judgment of Non Pros.—Nova Scotia.

In an action on a Nova Scotia judgment signed 7th March, 1855, in pursuance of a Judge's order setting aside the defendant's plea as frivolous, the defendant produced a certificate from the Prothonotary of the Court, entitled in the same cause, stating that judgment of *non pros.* for want of a replication was marked on the 11th December, 1854. Held, That in the absence of any record of such judgment, or of any evidence to shew that "marking" was equivalent to "signing," there was not sufficient evidence of a judgment of *non pros.* to affect the validity of the plaintiff's judgment. *Dennison* v. *Taylor*, 3 *All.* 313.

Quære, Whether, in such case, further evidence than the mere identity of name was not necessary, to identify the defendant with the defendant in the judgment sued on. *Ibid.*

30—Minutes of Court of Session.

The minutes of the Court of General Sessions are evidence in the same Court of the facts therein stated, without any other proof that the matter therein recorded took place; therefore a recognizance in a case of bastardy taken under the Act 2 Vic. c. 42, is proved by the production of the minutes of the Sessions containing the entry. *Ex parte Daley*, 1 *All.* 424.

31—Proceedings before Justice of Peace returned to Supreme Court.

An information and other proceedings before a Justice of the Peace, returned to the Supreme Court with a *certiorari* and filed with the Clerk of the Crown, becomes a record, and may be proved by an examined copy, taken before the original was filed. *Sewell* v. *Olive*, 4 *All.* 394.

32—A copy of the Minutes of the Supreme Court, stating the reversal of the judgment of a Justice of the Peace on *certiorari*, is not evidence of such reversal, it being of itself a judgment which should be made up of record and proved accordingly. *Douglas* v. *Hinkley*, *Hil. T.* 1828. (See Sewell *v.* Olive, Supra 31.)

33—Memorial—Incumbrance.
A registered memorial of a judgment against the vendor is evidence of an incumbrance on his land. *Scott* v. *Garnett*, 2 *All.* 624.

III.

PARTICULAR ACTIONS AND SUITS.

1—Promissory Note—Evidence under Common Counts. See Bills and Notes VI. 12. See Assumpsit III. a.

2—Defamation—Affidavit of defendant before magistrate—Malice.
In an action for oral slander an affidavit made by the defendant before a magistrate as the foundation of a criminal proceeding against the plaintiff, which is still pending, is not admissible evidence to show malice in the defendant. *Rankine* v. *Clarke*, *Ber.* 303.

3—Charge of Stealing—Evidence of general bad character of plaintiff not admissible in mitigation of damages. *Williston* v. *Smith*, 3 *Kerr* 443.

4—Allegations—Affidavits—Innuendoes.
In an action of slander for charging the plaintiff with perjury, some of the counts stated in the inducement that the words were spoken of and concerning the plaintiff and of and concerning a certain affidavit, etc., the defendant justified, setting out the affidavit, and alleging certain statements therein contained to be wilfully false. The affidavit referred to two papers which were annexed, but there was no positive proof that they were annexed when the affidavit was sworn to by the plaintiff. Held, That there was sufficient *prima facie* evidence to let in the whole of the affidavit, and that the admission of part to be read without the papers annexed was not correct, and the innuendoes not sufficiently proved. *Milner* v. *Gilbert*, 3 *Kerr* 617.

5—Mesne profits—Judgment—Agreement for consent rule.
In trespass for *mesne* profits by A. against C., who claimed under B. for an alleged wrong by C. between the time of the demise to A. and his recovery against B., a judgment in ejectment by A. against the casual ejector (B. being the real defendant, and by C. his attorney, having entered into the usual agreement for a consent rule) was offered, together with the agreement for a consent rule, and admitted in evidence; and it appeared that after such judgment obtained, the plaintiff's agent had taken possession of the premises, though no *habere facias* had been executed. Held, That such judgment was rightfully received in evidence against C., he having come in under B. Held also, That the agreement for the consent rule was admissible as a proceeding in the action of ejectment, which served to connect B. with the ejectment suit, as tenant in possession. *Fraser* v. *Harding*, 3 *Kerr* 94.

6—Inspection of Pickled Fish.
Quære, Whether any evidence is admissible of the bad quality of pickled fish inspected and marked under the Act of Assembly 5 Wm. 4, c. 43, other than the re-inspection provided for in the thirteenth section of that Act; or without such re-inspection having been made? *Smith* v. *Dunham*, 2 *Kerr* 630.

7—Sheriff—Action against for false return—Malice—Past practice.
In an action against the Sheriff of A. for a false return to a writ of election, where the charge was, the unlawfully striking out the names of voters who had refused to take the oath of qualification after having polled, evidence of such a practice at elections in the county of W., of which A. was formerly a part, is admissible on the question of malice. (Per Ritchie, J., Parker, J., *dubitant.*) *Stiles* v. *Gilbert*, 4 *All.* 421.

8—Limit bond—Defence—Discharge of Debtor—Fraud.
Where the defence to an action against the sureties on a limit bond is, that the debtor was discharged by the Justices for non-payment of the weekly allowance, evidence is not admissible to show that the discharge was fraudulently obtained, by the debtor concealing himself to avoid the payment, unless the sureties are implicated in the fraud. *Jones* v. *Fletcher*, 4 *All.* 550.

9—Partners—Proof.
In an action by partners, brought after the Act allowing parties in a cause to be witnesses, it is not necessary to call the plaintiffs to prove the partnership—it may be proved by other evidence—in the usual way by parties having dealings with them as such, or by persons having means of knowing who composed the firm. *Rankin* v. *Harley*, 1 *Han.* 271.

10—Negligence as Surgeon — Differing statements made to different persons.
In an action against the defendant for negligence as a surgeon, in his treatment of the plaintiff, whose hands and feet had been amputated in consequence of his having been frozen, it was proved by the plaintiff that when the defendant first visited him, he said that the plaintiff would not lose any of his limbs. Held, That a statement made by the defendant on the same occasion, to another person in the house where the plaintiff was, that he would lose his hands and feet, was evidence for the defendant as part of the *res gestæ*, it appearing that his practice was always to encourage his patients, and prevent a depression of their spirits. *Key* v. *Thomson*, 1 *Han.* 297.

When the plaintiff gives the evidence of medical men as to the proper treatment of cases of frozen limbs, the necessity of frequent visits, and their practice in particular cases; the defendant may give evidence of the treatment of other cases of a similar character, and of the results, in order to rebut the inference of negligence arising from the evidence on the part of the plaintiff. *Ibid.*

11—Disproof of wrongful intent in action for negligence against a surgeon not admissible. See *Kelly* v. *Dow*, 4 *All.* 435.

12—Assumpsit not accepting timber—Contract with other parties—Irrelevant testimony made relevant.
In an action for not accepting timber according to agreement, the plaintiff gave evidence of the purchase of timber by the defendant from C. and W. about the same time. Held, That although the defendant's contract with C. and W. would otherwise have been irrelevant testimony, the plaintiff had thereby made it material, and that it was open to the defendant to go into evidence to explain the whole of the transaction with C. and W., without calling them as witnesses. *Connell* v. *Smith*, 3 *Kerr* 483.

13—Trover—Custom.
By regulations of Government, no timber was to be cut on ground applied for until the license had issued. *Quære*, Evidence of a practice to the contrary is admissible. *Coombes* v. *Hatheway*, 3 *Kerr* 592.

14—Negligence of Plaintiff—Reduction of Contract Price.
In an action for work and labour in unloading a ship, the defendant cannot give evidence in reduction of the contract price, of the value of certain property in the ship belonging to a third party, which was destroyed by the plaintiff's negligence in discharging the cargo, in consequence of which the defendant would be liable in damages to the owner of such property. *Wilson* v. *Jarvis*, 3 *Kerr* 671.

15—Special Contract—Relation to part only of work.
In *indebitatus assumpsit* for building a house, the plaintiff proved the value of the work to be £140, in answer to which it was shewn that the principal part of the work was done under a special contract for £55. Held, That evidence of a special contract which related to part of the work only, was inadmissible in reply. *Robertson* v. *Miles*, 1 *All.* 27.

16—Entry in books—Bond—Principal and Surety.
In a joint action against a principal and surety on a bond conditioned for the fidelity of the principal as a clerk, entries of the receipt of sums of money made by the clerk in books kept by him in the course of his duty, are evidence against the surety of the receipt of the money; but *Semble*, That an entry by the clerk in the margin of the check book of the drawing of a check, without showing that it has been paid, is not evidence against the surety. *Mechanics' Whale Fishing Company* v. *Kirby*, 1 *All.* 223.

By the condition of the bond the obligors agreed to make good to the plaintiffs, a Corporation, any loss sustained by the misconduct of K. as a clerk, within three months after due proof thereof either by confession of K. or otherwise, and notice or warning thereof in writing given to the obligors. Held, That a notice from the Solicitor of the Company to the obligors of the general nature of K.'s default, accompanied by an account of entries made by him in the Company's books, shewing the moneys received and paid, and a notification that the books were open for the inspection of the obligors, was sufficient proof, and that an affidavit verifying the accounts was unnecessary. Held also, That neither the notice nor the Solicitor's appointment need be under the seal of the Company. *Mechanics' Whale Fishing Company* v. *Kirby*, 1 *All.* 223.

17—Former Recovery—Admissible in Replevin.
A former recovery in replevin is admissible in evidence in a subsequent action between the same parties without being pleaded, where the matter in dispute is in substance the same, and relates to the title of the land from which the trees were cut and carried away. *Stewart* v. *McFarlane*, 1 *All.* 233

18—Bankruptcy—Certificate—Fraud.
Evidence that the bankruptcy was fraudulent and collusive, is inadmissible on a trial at *Nisi Prius* to impeach a bankrupt's certificate duly obtained from the Commissioner, and certified by the Court of Chancery under the Acts 5 Vic. c. 43 and 6 Vic. c. 4. *Morrison* v. *Albee*, 2 *All.* 145.

19—Trespass—Laying out road Justification—Plaintiff's original case—Rebutting evidence.
The defendants in trespass justified entering, under the Act 13 Vic. c. 4, as Commissioners of highways to lay out a road through the land, and proved a return of the road sufficient upon its face. Held, That evidence of excess in laying out the road wider than the law allowed, must be given as part of the plaintiff's original case, and was not admissible as rebutting evidence. *Downing* v. *Gault*, 2 *All.* 569.

Quære, Whether evidence of a person not present at the laying out, but who afterwards examined marks on the trees where the road was laid out, is admissible to prove excess? *Ibid.*

20—Special damage—Contract.
Evidence of special damage in not being able to fulfil a contract for the delivery of logs, is not admissible where the damage alleged in the declaration is that the plaintiff was prevented from getting the logs to market, and thereby lost the freight and sale thereof. *Rowe* v. *Titus*, 1 *All.* 326.

21—Record of judgment—Date of bond.
Semble, That the record of a judgment in an action on a bond, is evidence of the date of the bond in an action of ejectment by a person claiming title under the obligor, to shew that he was indebted at the time of the conveyance, and that it is therefore fraudulent. *Doe* v. *Gilbert*, 1 *All.* 520.

22—Entry on books—Delivery of timber.
Where both the plaintiff and defendant claimed to have had a delivery of timber from M., the original owner, an entry by the plaintiff in his books, of a credit to M. of the amount of the timber, dated at the time of the alleged delivery, but not actually made till a year after, and without the knowledge of M. is not evidence for the plaintiff. *McMillan* v. *Fraser*, 2 *All.* 615.

23—Penalty—Prosecution for—Selling liquor without license.
In a prosecution for a penalty for selling liquor without license, proof that the sale was made by a person in the defendant's shop in his absence, and without shewing any general or special employment of such person by the defendant in the sale of liquors, is sufficient *prima facie* evidence against him. *Ex parte Parks*, 3 *All.* 237.

The prosecutor need not prove that the defendant had no license. *Ibid.*

24—Action against administrator.
In an action against an administrator to which he pleads an outstanding judgment, and *plene administravit præter*, and the plaintiff proves assets in the defendant's hands, more than sufficient to satisfy the judgment, the defendant will not be allowed to give evidence of the payment of debts before the recovery of the judgment and before the receipt of the assets. *Backhouse* v. *Palmer*, *Hil. T.* 1828.

25—Action against Sh[illegible]—[illegible]oof of judgment to w[illegible]ution.
In an action against [illegible], where he justifies under an exec[illegible] against a third person, he must [illegible] in evidence the judgment on which the execution was founded. *Crane* v. *Clarke*, *Hil. T.* 1828.

26—Trespass—Title in foreign country.
In an action of trespass *de bonis asportatis*, evidence of title to land in a foreign country is admissible to prove the plaintiff's right to the property taken. *Mann* v. *Chamberlain*, *Hil. T.* 1828.

27—Action on Guarantee—Joint or several interests.
Defendants gave a guarantee that the wages due W. K. and G N. from J. H. for making timber, should be paid when they brought the timber up. Held, in an action on the guarantee by G. N., That evidence was admissible to shew that he and W. K. were separately employed by J. K., and had separate wages, in order to shew that their interests under the guarantee were several. *Neville* v. *Joseph*, *Hil. T.* 1832.

Ejectment—Sheriff's Deed—Sale under an *alias*, the original execution need not be proved. See Sheriff's Deed 6.

Replevin. See Pleading II. 27–30.

IV.

Particular Facts.

1—Administration—Letters of are evidence of the intestate's death. See *Scribner* v. *Gibbon*, 4 *All.* 182.

2—Administrator's deed—Affidavit—Evidence of what.
The affidavit indorsed on a deed purporting to be made by an administrator under a license from the Probate Court, is not evidence of the death or granting of administration; but only that the land has been duly advertised and sold. *Doe* v. *Donovan*, 4 *All.* 116.

3—*Quære*, Whether the affidavit required to be indorsed by the Rev. Stat. c. 136, s. 42, on an executor's deed, is evidence of any of the proceedings except the advertising and sale of the land. *Doe* v. *Thompson*, 4 *All.* 483.

4—Agency.
Semble, That the fact of agency may be proved by parol, though the appointment was in writing. See *Welsh* v. *Street*, 3 *All.* 251.

Agent Accredited. See Corporation 4.

5—Lease—Duplicate originals—Primary evidence.
The defendant let land to the plaintiff, and a lease having been written, A. by their direction, and in their presence, affixed seals and signed their names to it; it was then agreed that A. should make a copy of the lease, and execute it for them in the same manner; he did so, and a few days afterwards, in the presence of both parties, delivered one copy to the plaintiff and the other to the defendant Held, That they were duplicate originals, and that either of them was primary evidence. *Leonard* v. *Young*, 4 *All.* 111.

6—Proceedings against Administrator.
It is sufficient to shew the substance of the proceedings against an administrator in the Probate Court, without setting out the proceedings themselves. *In re Hunter*, 1 *Han.* 233.

7—Coal—Merchantable quality—Evidence.
In an action on a contract to deliver "Albert Coal," an article known to be used in the manufacture of oil, the breach being that the defendants had delivered coal of an inferior quality, yielding less oil per ton than coal of a good merchantable quality, evidence is not admissible on the part of the defendant to shew how much oil per ton was obtained by another manufacturer from Albert Coal, without also shewing that it was the same quality of coal as that delivered by the plaintiff. *Spurr* v. *Albert Mining Co.*, *East. T.* 1871.

Alien—Evidence of being one. See Alien.

Appeal—Evidence produced—Examination before Master—Court not bound to use it—When? See Supreme Court in Equity 4.

Unstamped Check—Void—Not receivable in evidence. See Check 1.

Bankrupt—Fiat proveable by certified copy. See Bankrupt 2.

Bills of Exchange. See Bills and Notes.

Bye Law—Must be proved. See Bye Laws.

Chattel—Unregistered Ship—Revesting of possession. See Shipping Law 6.

City Court—Judgment by default—Proof of particulars—Custom. See City Court.

Composition Deed — Execution of. See Deed IV.

Crown Grant — Boundaries — Lines. See Crown Grant.

Custom Duties — Goods liable for. See Custom Duties.

Deed—Acknowledgment—Execution. See Deed I.

Deed of Master in Chancery—Prima facie evidence of proceedings. See Deed I. 17.

Deed Registry Book—One registry of two deeds on same paper. See Deed I. 23.

Deed Registry Book best evidence of registry of deed. See Deed V. 13.

Deed of Sheriff—Recital of other judgments—Proof not necessary. See Sheriff's Sale 1.

Deed receivable in evidence as part of *res gestæ* without proof of judgment or execution. See Doe v. Baxter, 4 All. 131.

Docket of Judgment—Not necessary to prove docketing of judgment, under claim by virtue of Sheriff's sale under execution. See *Doe dem Barlow* v. *Hatfield*, 1 *Kerr* 417.

Foreign Law—Written law how proved. See Foreign Law.

Insurance—Preliminary proof. See Insurance 38.

Insurance—Waiver of proof of loss. See Insurance 33 a.

Identity. See Identity (Name).

Limitation—Payment relied on to take case out of operation of Statute—Necessity of affirmative evidence. See Limitation of Actions II. 2.

Marriage. See Infra VI. 3.

Memorial of Judgment registered against the Vendor is evidence of an incumbrance on the land. See *Scott* v. *Garnet*, 2 *All.* 624.

Mesne Profits—Evidence in action for.—See Ejectment (Mesne Profits).

Negligence. See Action on the Case II.

Contributory Negligence. See Negligence.

Usage—Evidence admissible to prove doubtful contract, but not to contradict one that is plain. See *McGivern* v. *Provincial Insurance Co.*, 4 *All.* 64.

Voluntary Conveyance. See Deed II.

V.

Parol Explanations.

1—Contents of Deed destroyed—Sufficiency of proof—Lost Deed—Ancient Deed.

Where the only evidence of the contents of a deed that was destroyed many years ago, was that of witnesses who had read it and heard it read, who stated that it was *a deed from A. P. and his wife to their daughter R. E. of the land where she lived, either sixty or eighty rods; that it had the name of A. P. and his wife to it, and was to R. E. her heirs and assigns for ever, and the date was some time in the last century.* Held, That sufficient did not appear to enable the Judge to direct the jury that such was a deed of feoffment, or to determine its legal operation and effect.

Quære, Whether the contents of an "ancient deed" can be proved by parol evidence, or whether the deed itself must not be produced? *Doe dem Edgett* v. *Stiles*, 1 *Kerr* 338.

2—Bill of parcels—Representation as to quality.

The delivery of a bill of parcels after the sale of goods, on which a receipt was given for the price, does not exclude parol evidence of the representation as to quality. *Magee* v. *Street*, 1 *All.* 242.

3—Term "grandson."

The term "grandson" in its primary sense means a legitimate grandson; and where there is a legitimate grandson to take by this description, and nothing on the face of the will to the contrary, parol evidence is not admissible to shew that an illegitimate grandson was intended. *Doe* v. *Taylor*, 1 *All.* 525.

4—Agreement—Reference to account.

Defendant agreed, in writing, to deliver plaintiff a quantity of logs, for which the plaintiff agreed to pay him, after paying the amount of the defendant's account due the plaintiff, at the rate of sixteen shillings per thousand feet. Held, in an action on this agreement, That parol evidence was admissible on the part of the defendant, to show what the account referred to in the agreement was, and to identify an account rendered to him by the plaintiff, as the account so referred to. *DesBrisay* v. *Glencross*, 1 *Han.* 106.

5—Written Lease—Lot to be occupied.

Where a written lease of a farm excepted a part of it, described as Lot No. 2, parol evidence is inadmissible to show that it was agreed between the parties at the time of the bargain that the tenant should also occupy Lot No. 2. *McElveney* v. *McKilligan*, 1 *Han.* 322.

6—Sheriff's Deed—Affidavit—Different dates.

Where a Sheriff's deed and his affidavit of due execution and sale, bear different dates, parol evidence is admissible to prove that they were executed on the same day. *Doe d. Connell* v. *Dickinson*, 1 *Han.* 456.

7—Explanations—Agreement in writing.
Plaintiff and M. built a vessel, of which defendant became master, purchasing a sixteenth from M. and a sixteenth from plaintiff, which he did not pay for. The vessel being in difficulties at Boston, U.S., and $1,240 due defendant for wages, he, in consideration of $1,000, by deed of sale transferred to plaintiff all his right in the vessel, and released all claim on account of wages. Held, in an action to recover the price of the sixteenth, That parol evidence was admissible to prove that plaintiff, at the time of the deed being executed by defendant, verbally agreed to renounce all claim to the purchase money. *Lingley* v. *Smith*, 1 *Han.* 589.

Parol Evidence not allowed to amend Sheriff's endorsement of return on writ. See Johnston *v.* Winslow, Ber. 53.

Sale of Land—Property referred to—Parol explanation. See Sale.

VI.

PRESUMPTIVE EVIDENCE.

See Presumptions.

1—Surrogate—Person acting as such.
It will be presumed that a person acting as Surrogate has taken the oath of office; but if he has not, his acts will not be invalid if he has been appointed to the office. *Crookshank* v. *McFarlane*, 2 *All.* 544.

2—Necessary affidavit—Court confirming Certificate.
It will be presumed that the Court of Chancery in confirming a certificate, acted on a sufficient affidavit of the bankrupt, as required by the Act 6 Vic. c. 4, s. 25. *Morrison* v. *Albee*, 2 *All.* 145.

3—Marriage—Commissioner's Acts.
In an action for *crim. con.* the fact of the plaintiff's marriage may be proved by any person present at the ceremony, and if performed by the Commissioner under the Act of Assembly 8 Geo. 4, c. 9, it will be presumed (at least in the absence of proof to the contrary) that he was acting within his authority, and followed the requisition of the Acts as to the notification and form of the solemnization. *Montgomery* v. *McLeod*, *Ber.* 375.

The original certificate of marriage filed with the Clerk of the Peace, as directed by the Act 52 Geo. 2, c. 21, may be given in evidence, without calling the subscribing witness. *Montgomery* v. *McLeod*, *Ber.* 375.

4—Prima facie proof of Marriage.
The land in dispute in an action of trespass, was granted to A. The defendant claimed under a deed from B., and in order to prove that B. was a daughter of A. called a witness, who stated that he knew A and his family—enumerating them—and including B. as one of the daughters: the witness was not cross-examined. Held, Sufficient *prima facie* evidence of the marriage of A., and that B. was one of his daughters. *Power* v. *Howie*, *Mich. T.* 1864.

5—Corporation—Persons acting as president and secretary.
The Act 7 Wm. 4, c. 54, incorporating the New Brunswick and Marine Assurance Company, required that policies should be subscribed by the president and countersigned by the secretary. Held, That a policy so signed was valid without the seal of the Company, and that evidence of these persons having acted as president and secretary was *prima facie* evidence of their appointment. *Dimock* v. *New Brunswick and Marine Assurance Company*, 1 *All.* 398.

6—Person practising as Surgeon.
Evidence that the defendant practised as a surgeon is sufficient proof that he was such. See *Kelly* v. *Dow*, 4 *All.* 435.

7—Rebuttal of presumption—Payment of debt—Omission in schedule of debtor—Evidence to shew mistake.
As a defence to an account stated, the defendant shewed several payments since the settlement, and also that the plaintiff had applied for relief under the Insolvent Act 7 Vic. c. 32, and in his schedule of debts sworn to and exhibited before the Master of the Rolls, the demand in question was not included, but the plaintiff's clerk stated that the list of debts was made out by him, and that the demand was omitted by mistake. Held, Sufficient to rebut the presumption that would otherwise have arisen that the debt was paid. *McDonald* v. *Cother*, 3 *Kerr* 394.

Sheriff's Deed—Regularity of Proceedings. See Sheriff's Deed 2.

8—Sheriff's Deed more than twenty years old.
In making title under a Sheriff's deed

more than twenty years old, where the sale was under a *venditioni exponas*, and the land had been advertised in the Gazette—Held, in the absence of evidence to the contrary, 1st. That a legal levy had been made under a *fi. fa.* 2nd. That no newspaper was published in the county. 3rd. That the other notices required by the Act had been given; and 4th. That the sale took place during the hours prescribed by law. *Doe* v. *Hazen*, 3 *All.* 87.

9—Presumption against defendant, not being called as a witness.
Where the defendant knew all the circumstances, and might have been called as a witness to shew the exact quantity of the property in dispute which came to his possession—Held, That it was not a mis-direction to tell the jury they might infer that if the defendant had been called, his evidence would not have benefitted his case,—an inference, though slight, that the whole of the property in dispute came into the defendant's possession is much strengthened by the fact that it was in his power to show the exact amount, and that he has not done so, and the jury are thereby warranted in adopting such inference. *Tufts* v. *Hatheway*, 4 *All.* 62.

10—Absence of evidence by defendant.
In an action to recover the price of logs, the plaintiff, in order to prove the quantity received by the defendant, shewed the average size and number of logs put in and driven down a stream, at the mouth of which defendant had a saw-mill, and that the defendant had sawn a portion of them. Held, in the absence of any evidence by the defendant of the quantity he had sawn, That the jury were justified in presuming he had received the whole quantity driven down the stream by the plaintiff. *Leslie* v. *Hanson*, 1 *Han.* 263.

11—Conduct of party—Implied recognition.
A recognition may be implied from the conduct of a party, as where knowing of a warrant of attorney and judgment against him, he allows them to stand for three years without objection, and continues to deal with the plaintiff on the security of them. *Hutchinson* v. *Johnston*, 4 *All.* 40.

12—Right of way—Presumption of deed.
To sustain a plea of right of way by lost deed, no proof is requisite of such deed having actually existed, but the jury have a right to presume such deed from long and uninterrupted usage of a way exercised as a matter of right, and necessary to the convenient enjoyment of the land to and from which the road leads. *Jones* v. *Jones*, 2 *Kerr* 265.

13—Master and servant—Payment of passage money from travellers.
No presumption that same was paid over in ordinary course of employment without proof that such was course of dealing. See *Rae* v. *McBeath*, 3 *Kerr* 446.

14—Issue of Writ.
In the absence of evidence of the actual time of issuing a writ of *mesne* process, it will be presumed to have issued on the day it bears date. *Pomeres* v. *Provincial Ins. Co.*, *Hil. T.* 1873.

Doubt raised by Evidence—Presumption that note was given in accordance with agreement set out in declaration. See Pleading I. 26.

No Administration Bond — Presumption that no administration granted. See Executors and Administrators IV. 1.

Attorney—Authority to issue Execution. See Attorney V. 4.

Re-survey of Lumber, presumed to be made according to Act. See Rankin v. Emery, Ber. 330.

Unlawful Act — Knowledge — Master and Owner of Ship. See Principal and Agent. 22.

Letters Patent—Proper issue of. See Corporation 6.

Publications in newspaper—Authority. See Joint Stock Company 3.

Commission to examine witnesses — Presumption as to. See Infra IX. 2.

Presumption that Payee had given notice of dishonour of bill. See Bills and Notes IV. 2.

VII.

Secondary Evidence—Notice to Produce.

1—Certified copy of Will.
Semble, That a certified copy of a will cannot be given in evidence under the 1 Rev. Stat. c. 112. *Connell* v. *Haley*, 4 *All.* 636.

2—Will.
Secondary evidence of a will devising real

estate in this Province, the original will being filed in the office of the Surrogate General of Nova Scotia, is not admissible, there being no evidence of any law of Nova Scotia prohibiting the removal of the will. *Doe d. Gilmour* v. *Whitney, Ber.* 339.

3—License to sell Land—Copy.
A license by the Governor in Council to an administrator to sell land, granted under the Act 26 Geo. 3, c. 11, need not be under seal; and it may be proved by a copy from the records of the Council, certified by the Clerk of the Executive Council, under the Act 21 Vic. c. 3, s. 7. *Caughey* v. *Inman, Mich. T.* 1862.

4—Inventory—Examined copy.
An examined copy of an inventory, filed by the administrator in the Registry of the Court of Probates, pursuant to the Act of Assembly 3 Vic. c. 61, is admissible in evidence, and the original need not be produced. *Cunliffe* v. *Morehouse*, 2 *Kerr* 311.

5—Affidavit—Exemplification.
In an action for a malicious arrest upon a bailable capais issued out of this Court, the affidavit upon which the writ issued having been filed, may be proved by an exemplification under the seal of the Court; and proof of the defendant's signature to the original affidavit is not necessary, if it appears that the arrest was made by his procurement. *Wentworth* v. *Hallett*, 2 *Kerr* 560.

6—Surrogate's book—Private entry.
An entry of the grant of administration in a book kept by a Surrogate, which is stated to be a private book, is only secondary evidence, and therefore not admissible without proof of search for the letters of administration. *Doe* v. *Read*, 1 *All.* 31.

7—Judge's notes.
The Judge's notes of the testimony of a witness since deceased, are evidence in a subsequent trial of the same cause to prove that witness's testimony, though the second trial is before a different Judge. *Doe* v. *Murray*, 1 *All.* 216.

8—The evidence of a witness who has left the Province since a former trial between the parties, may be read from the Judge's notes. *Abel* v. *Light, Trin. T.* 1866.

9—Notice to produce—Time—Record improperly held.
In an action of replevin, both parties filed *Nisi Prius* records. The cause was tried on the defendant's record, and the plaintiff obtained a verdict. The Clerk of the Circuits, by mistake, indorsed the *postea* on the record filed by the plaintiff, and gave it to his attorney: the defendant's attorney afterwards got the other *Nisi Prius* record. In an action of assumpsit afterwards brought by the defendant in the replevin suit against the plaintiff, it became necessary, in order to admit from the Judge's notes, the testimony of a witness examined in the replevin suit, to prove that trial: notice to produce the *Nisi Prius* record which had been given by the Clerk to the defendant's attorney (the plaintiff's attorney in the present action) was served on him about seven o'clock in the evening previous to the trial, but he, objecting that the notice was too short, refused to produce it. Held, in the absence of any affidavit from the attorney explaining why he took the record, or why he could not produce it, That the notice was sufficient—the record being improperly in his possession; and that, under the circumstances, it was his duty to use more than ordinary exertions to return it to the Clerk. *Abel* v. *Light, Trin. T.* 1866.

10—*Quære*, Whether a copy of a notice from the plaintiff to defendant, complaining of delay in furnishing certain materials for a building, was admissible in evidence without a notice to produce. *Small* v. *McCullough*, 3 *All.* 484.

11—*Semble*, That a notice to produce "all papers, memoranda, receipts and accounts *settled* relating to this suit," is not sufficient to let in secondary evidence of an unsettled account. See *Ross* v. *Lindsay*, 3 *Kerr* 645.

12—Entries transcribed—Contents of Logs.
Logs were measured as they were sawed in a mill, and their contents marked on a board by the persons who sawed them. At the end of each week, the figures on the board were transcribed into a book by a person who had made a part of the measurements, but who could not tell, from the character of the figures on the board, what portion of them was made by either of the other parties. Held, That the book was not evidence to prove the the quantity of logs sawn, without calling all the persons who had measured the logs. *Leslie* v. *Hanson*, 1 *Han.* 263.

13—Payment under written agreement—Production of agreement necessary.

One item in an account of money paid by the plaintiff for the defendant, appeared on cross-examination to have been paid under a written agreement by the defendant to deliver goods to the plaintiff. Held, That without production of the agreement the plaintiff could not recover on this item. *Harley* v. *Goodfellow*, 1 *Han.* 335.

14—Loss of document—Proof of—Sufficiency—Question for Judge.

The sufficiency of preliminary proof of the loss of a document to entitle secondary evidence to be received, is a question for the Judge at the trial to determine. *Gilbert* v. *Campbell*, 1 *Han.* 471.

15—Necessary search.

Where a person is in the habit of preserving and filing away letters of importance, secondary evidence of the contents of a letter of that description is not admissible without search among his letters, there being no proof of its loss. *Little* v. *Johnston*, 1 *Kerr* 496.

16—Lost paper.

Where an agreement for a right of way had been made ten or twelve years before the trial, and the road laid out and used in pursuance of it, secondary evidence of the contents of the agreement was received, it appearing by the testimony of the person in whose possession it was left, that he had searched thoroughly for it, and was sure it was not in his possession, that he might have burnt it as a useless paper, or given it to one of the parties, but had no distinct recollection of what he had done with it, and it was just as probable he had burnt it, as that he had given it to one of the parties. *Basterach* v. *Atkinson*, 2 *All.* 439.

17—Search for note.

Slight evidence of search for a note which has been paid and taken up by the maker, is sufficient to account for its non-production, and to admit secondary evidence of it. *Lyman* v. *Cain*, 3 *All.* 259.

18—Certified copy of deed—Affidavit.

An affidavit made by an attorney, that the lessor of the plaintiff resides in Halifax, N. S., had never been in this Province, had not the deed in his possession, and did not know where it was to be found, is not sufficient to entitle a certified copy of the deed to be given in evidence under 1 Rev. Stat. c. 112, s 12. Fisher, J., *dissentiente*. *Doe ex dem Trider* v. *McIntosh*, 1 *Han.* 502.

19—Document partly destroyed—Contents.

If part of an original document be lost or accidentally destroyed, the part which is preserved may be admitted in evidence and secondary evidence given of the remainder. *Doe* v *Jack*, 1 *All.* 476.

When a person has made extracts from a paper, he may, after the loss of the original, refresh his memory by reference to such extracts; and where other secondary evidence is produced of the whole instrument, a witness may speak to the contents of a part which he has abstracted, although he has not seen or does not recollect the remainder. *Ibid.*

20—Certified copy of grant.

A certified copy of a grant under the Act 3 Vic. c. 65, is admissible in evidence without accounting for the non-production of the original. *Doe* v. *McDonald*, 1 *All.* 673.

21—Former testimony of witness—Proof of.

Where the plaintiff has been examined as a witness on a former trial respecting the same subject, it is necessary, in order to prove his testimony, that the witnesses should swear to the words used by him, and not merely to the effect of them. *Fraser* v. *Black*, 2 *All.* 312. (See Infra. VIII. 17.)

22—Absence of attesting witness—Handwriting.

Whether due diligence has been used to discover an attesting witness must depend upon the circumstances of each case. *Crane* v. *Ayre*, 2 *All.* 577.

Where the attesting witness to a bond left the plaintiff's employment in the country fifteen years before the trial and went to Saint John, and about two years afterwards told two persons of his acquaintance in the country that he was going to Australia, after which neither of them had ever seen him, though one of them had resided in Saint John for three years afterwards, and the other was there frequently, and there was no proof that the witness had been in the Province for thirteen years. Held, Sufficient presumptive proof of his absence to admit secondary evidence of his handwriting. *Ibid.*

23—Ejectment—Title under agreement—Production necessary.
Where a plaintiff in ejectment proves no documentary or possessory title, but relies upon the estoppel arising from his having let the defendant into possession of the land, and it appears in the plaintiff's case that the defendant took possession under a written agreement; the plaintiff cannot recover without producing the agreement, or giving secondary evidence of it after notice to produce. *Doe* v. *Blanche*, 3 *All.* 180.

Statement of affairs by debtor to creditor—Copy made in presence of debtor. See Supra I. 12.

Lease—Duplicate originals—Primary evidence. See Evidence III. 5.

VIII.

EXAMINATION OF WITNESSES ON TRIAL.

1—Rebuttal of testimony.
A witness for the plaintiff denied on cross examination having made a statement in presence of L., who was afterwards called, by the defendant, and contradicted him. Held, That the plaintiff might call evidence in reply to rebut L.'s testimony and confirm that of his own witness; such evidence not being properly part of the plaintiff's case in the first instance. *Whelpley* v. *Riley*, 2 *All.* 275.

2—The defendants in trespass justified entering, under the Act 13 Vic. c. 4, as Commissioners of Highways to lay out a road through the land, and proved a return of the road sufficient upon its face. Held, That evidence of excess in laying out the road wider than the law allowed, must be given as part of the plaintiff's original case, and was not admissible as rebutting evidence. *Downing* v. *Gault*, 2 *All.* 569.

Quære, Whether evidence of a person not present at the laying out, but who afterwards examined marks on the trees where the road was laid out, is admissible to prove excess? *Ibid.*

3—Calling Witnesses in reply—Surprise.
Plaintiff and defendant owned adjoining lots in the city of St. John, and the question was, whether a cellar wall running at right angles with the street on which the lots fronted, was wholly within the bounds of the plaintiff's or the defendant's lot,—the breadth of the wall being the land in dispute. The defendant's witness was asked on cross examination, whether after a fire which burnt the houses on both lots, B., under whom the defendant claimed, had not employed F. to remove a stone wall adjoining that in dispute. Held, That the Judge was right in allowing the plaintiff to call F. in reply to the defendant's case, and that the admission of his evidence was not such a surprise on the defendant as to entitle him to a new trial. *Adams* v. *Ferguson*, 4 *All.* 102.

4—Where a witness on cross examination, denied having signed a paper, but which was not then shown to him, and the opposite party afterwards produced the paper, and gave evidence to prove the witness's signature to it, the witness may be re-called to disprove the signature.—*Tompkins* v. *Tibbits*, 1 *Han.* 317.

5—Re-examination of witness as to statements concerning matter involving penalty.
Where a witness called to prove that the consideration of a note was usurious, declined to state what amount he gave on discounting the note, because his answer might render him liable to a penalty, but on cross examination said that he gave what he thought it was worth. Held, That he was bound on re-examination to state what he gave. *Peters* v. *Irish*, 4 *All.* 326.

6—Proving justification on cross examination of plaintiff's witnesses.
The defendant has not a right on the cross examination of the plaintiff's witness, and before the defence is open, to prove a justification of which he has given notice, and the affirmative of which lies on him; no question leading to it having been asked on the examination in chief. *Atkinson* v. *Smith*, 4 *All.* 309.

7—Payment—Set-off.
A defendant cannot prove his set-off in plaintiff's case, but a payment rests on a different footing, and in the absence of any evidence of appropriation, the law will *prima facie* apply it to the payment of outstanding indebtedness; and a defendant has a right to shew payment on cross examination of plaintiff's witnesses.—*Fredericton Boom Co.* v. *McPherson*, 2 *Han.* 9.

8—Paper not in evidence.
Though as a general rule (except by legislative enactment) a witness cannot

be examined as to the contents of a paper not in evidence, it does not necessarily follow that this is a sufficient ground for setting aside a verdict, where the paper is afterwards put in evidence and the opposite party has an opportunity of examining upon it, and it has been allowed to go before the jury—no injustice appearing to have resulted from the evidence. *Lawton* v. *Tarratt*, 4 *All*. 1.

9—False imprisonment—Policeman making arrest—Asking question as to whose direction arrest made.

Defendant lost a cow, which he suspected to have been stolen by the plaintiff; he reported the facts to the Chief of the Police, who told him, in the presence of a policeman, that he had better arrest the plaintiff. He then went to the plaintiff's shop with the policeman, and directed him to take the plaintiff in charge, and the policeman arrested the plaintiff and detained him several hours, when the cow was found, having strayed from the defendant's field. In an action for false imprisonment, the policeman stated, in answer to a question from the plaintiff's counsel, that he would not have arrested the plaintiff without the direction from the defendant. Held, That the question was proper. *Quære*, Whether the defendant's counsel had a right to ask the policeman on cross-examination, whether he did not make the arrest, in consequence of the direction from the Chief of the Police. Though the evidence was improperly rejected, it is no ground for a new trial, as the defendant, being a trespasser, by directing the arrest, the verdict must have been in favor of the plaintiff. *Foley* v. *Tucker*, 1 *Han*. 52.

10—Discretion of Judge—Contents of written statement.

It is discretionary with the Judge at *Nisi Prius*, under the power given by the Act 19 Vic. c. 41, s. 10, whether he will allow a witness to be cross-examined as to the contents of written statements made by him, without the writing being produced. *Lawton* v. *Chance*, 4 *All*. 411.

11—It is discretionary with a Judge at *Nisi Prius* to receive evidence at any time during the trial. *Stiles* v. *Brewster*, 4 *All*. 414. (See New Trial III. 35.)

12—May admit evidence even after the counsel has addressed the jury, and the Court will not interfere if the evidence is not in itself inadmissible, or no injustice has been done. *Doe* v. *Connelly*, 3 *All*. 337.

Recalling Witness — Discretionary with Judge. See County Court 4.

12 a—Livery of seisin—Evidence after close of Case.

A deed was put in evidence without objection as a registered deed, but was afterwards discovered not to have been duly acknowledged, whereupon the defendant's counsel objected, in his address to the jury, that it did not give livery of seisin. *Semble*, That the objection was not too late; but that in such a case the Judge might allow the opposite party to give evidence of livery of seisin. *Scribner* v. *McLauchlan*, 1 *All*. 379.

13—Withdrawing Evidence.

It is discretionary with the Judge at the trial to allow the counsel to withdraw evidence. (Per Ritchie, C. J., where evidence is pressed in against the opinion of the Judge, the counsel must stand by it.) *Pelton* v. *Temple*, 1 *Han*. 275.

14—Scientific Witness.

A scientific witness cannot be asked questions, the answers to which are based upon previous evidence given by other witnesses, and upon which conclusions are drawn which are for the jury to determine. See *Key* v. *Thomson*, 2 *Han*. 224.

15—Party to suit—Hostile witness.

Where one of the parties to a suit is called as a witness by the other, it is discretionary with the Judge to allow him to be examined as a hostile witness, and to restrict his own counsel to the style of an examination in chief. The opposite party on the record is not necessarily a hostile witness, his conduct on the stand is the proper test. *Atkinson* v. *Atkinson*, *East. T.* 1862.

16—Different statement—Proof of—Tender of evidence—Time.

It is not competent to prove on the cross-examination of a witness, that he has made a different statement relative to the subject matter of the suit in his examination in bankruptcy in England, without producing the original proceedings in bankruptcy. *Campbell* v. *Gilbert*, *Mich. T.* 1862.

If, for the purpose of affecting the credibility of a witness (a proper foundation having been laid) and showing that he had made a different statement on a former occasion. *Quære*, Whether a duly certified copy of his examination in bankruptcy would not be evidence? If so, the evidence should have been distinctly tendered after the close of the case in which the evidence sought to be contradicted was given. *Campbell* v. *Gilbert, Mich. T.* 1862.

17—Discrediting Witness—Statements on former trial—Proof of.

A plaintiff examined as a witness in his own cause may be asked on cross examination for the purpose of discrediting him, whether, in giving his evidence on a former trial relating to the same matter, he had not made certain statements respecting it without proving by the record that a former trial took place. And where he denied making the statements, a person who heard his evidence on the former trial, and took it down in writing, so far as he was able, may be called to contradict him, if he can speak positively as to the statements denied by the plaintiff, though he did not take down the whole of his evidence. (See No. 21.) *Bryson* v. *Hamilton, East. T.* 1873.

18—Party producing Papers on cross-examination.

Papers proved on cross-examination are to be treated as the evidence of the party producing them. *Crane* v. *Clarke, Hil. T.* 1828.

19—Recalling Witness.

Where on the trial of an action against one of the sureties in a bond given by a Deputy Treasurer, the Treasurer was examined as a witness on the part of the Crown, and on cross-examination, proved a number of letters written by him to the Deputy,—partly relating to official business, and partly to private transactions and land speculations in which they had been engaged, and had suffered losses,—from which it was intended to be argued by the defendant that moneys received by the Treasurer from the Deputy and carried to his private account, were in fact Crown moneys, and should have been so credited; and these letters were afterwards put in evidence by the defendant. Held, That the Treasurer might be recalled by the Crown, after the close of the defendant's case, to explain the transaction, and to prove that all moneys remitted by the Deputy on account of the revenue, were duly credited. *Regina* v. *Kerr*, 2 *Kerr* 137.

20—Where a witness on cross-examination proves documents for the defendant, it must in general be subject to the implied condition that the witness may be recalled by the opposite party after the documents are in evidence. *Ibid.*

21—Second trial—Testimony—Particularity.

Where the plaintiff has been examined as a witness on a former trial respecting the same subject, it is necessary, in order to prove his testimony, that the witness should swear to the words used by him, and not merely to the effect of them. *Fraser* v. *Black*, 2 *All.* 312. (See No. 17.)

22—Examination as to matters in writing—Partnership.

Where, on the cross-examination of plaintiff, the defendant's counsel examined him as to the time he entered into a partnership, and his interest in it, the plaintiff was held to be entitled to go into the contents of the whole agreement, although it appeared there were written articles. *Tozer* v. *Hutchinson*, 1 *Han.* 540.

23—Privileged communication.

The rule of evidence that a communication respecting a suit between the agent of the client and his attorney is privileged, is not altered by the Act 19 Vic. c. 41, s. 1, allowing the parties to be examined as witnesses. *Lawton* v. *Chance*, 4 *All.* 411.

24—Defendant's witness—Contradicting by plaintiff—Confirming plaintiff's case.

Evidence is admissible to contradict a statement of a fact made by a witness for the defendant, though the effect of such evidence may be to confirm the plaintiff's original case. The time at which evidence is admissible is in the discretion of the Judge. *Heavy* v. *Odell, East. T.* 1863.

25—Counsel.

Where a counsel in a cause is by consent allowed to go upon the stand to prove a particular fact, he becomes a witness in the cause generally, and may be cross-examined upon any fact in the cause. *Gilbert* v. *Campbell*, 2 *Han.* 55.

26—Lease—Production necessary.

In an action of trespass for cutting down a mill-dam, the plaintiff relied on, and gave evidence of possession only. On cross-examination, he admitted that he held the property under a written lease from G., and stated that he was bound by the lease to keep the premises in repair. Held, That the plaintiff was bound to produce the lease, to enable the Judge properly to direct the jury as to the effect of it, and as to the amount of damages which the plaintiff, as tenant, would be entitled to recover. *Betts* v. *Venning*, *Hil. T.* 1873.

27—**Examination of defendant—Recalling.**
If the plaintiff calls and examines the defendant as a witness, he is not, when afterwards examined as a witness in his own case, to be treated as a recalled witness; but his counsel has a right to examine him, and to prove his defence as fully as if the defendant had not been previously called as a witness by the plaintiff. *Ibid.* (See New Trial IV. 11.)

Defendant's Counsel cross-examining on matter—Objection made at opening of case. See New Trial II. 15.

IX.

COMMISSION—INTERROGATORIES—DEPOSITION.

1—**Deposition taken abroad—Presumption that oath rightly taken.**
Depositions taken abroad under a Commission issued pursuant to the Act Wm. 4, c. 34, and returned with the commission, are admissible in evidence without proof that the commissioners had taken the oath prescribed by the commission, or return by them to that effect. Such oath is required to be taken, but the Court will presume that this has been done, nothing appearing to the contrary. *Wilmot* v. *Haws*, 1 *Kerr* 351.

2—**Papers, annexing of—Commission.**
Papers enclosed and returned with a commission to examine witnesses, and referred to by the witnesses, need not be annexed to the depositions, if sufficiently identified. It will be presumed that a commission produced in Court is in the same state as it came from the Commissioners, and that the exhibits enclosed are those referred to in the depositions. *Lawton* v. *Tarratt*, 4 *All.* 1.

3—As a general rule, where evidence is taken under a commission, and documents are proved, such documents should be returned enclosed with the commission. There may be exceptions where the document cannot by law be removed from its place of custody; in such case, an office copy, or an examined copy, should be returned with the commission. *Thompson* v. *Reed*, *Hil. T.* 1861.

4—If there is clear evidence to identify papers as those referred to in the depositions taken by the Commissioners, they may be received in evidence, though not returned with the depositions. *Ibid.*

5—The mere proof of the handwriting of one of the Commissioners upon a paper purporting to have been referred to in the depositions, is not sufficient evidence of identity. *Ibid.*

6—**Second commission to examine same witness.**
Where a commission to examine a witness abroad has been executed and returned, another commission to examine the same witness on matters not gone into on the first commission, can only be granted under very peculiar circumstances, and the necessity of it must be clearly shewn by affidavit. The second commission should be limited in its terms. *Light* v. *Abel*, *East. T.* 1865.

7—**Addressing to Court—Sufficiency.**
The depositions of a witness taken *de bene esse* under the Act 5 Wm. 4, c. 34, sealed up and indorsed "in the Supreme Court," with the title of the cause, the date and the Commissioner's name are sufficiently addressed to the Court within the meaning of the Act, to be receivable in evidence. *Waterhouse* v. *Marine Assurance Company*, 3 *Kerr* 639.

8—**Commission addressed to several—Execution by part—Waiver.**
Where a commission for the examination of witnesses abroad was issued directing the depositions to be taken before four Commissioners, one of whom, though notified, did not attend, and the commission was executed by the other three, in the absence of any protest at the time, or suggestion that defendant had been injured by its execution by three only, and where he had an opportunity of applying at term to suppress the depositions, the Court held that the objection was waived, and it was too late to object to their reception in evidence at the trial. *Gilbert* v. *Campbell*, 1 *Han.* 471.

9—Wrong entitling—Misnomer.
A commission issued out of the Supreme Court of this Province for the examination of a witness in Ireland, in which the plaintiffs were named "Hugh James and Heatley W. his wife," the depositions returned with the commission were entitled "In the Supreme Court, Nova Scotia," and the plaintiff's wife was called "Heatley Ann" in the title of the cause.—Held, That the depositions could not be received in evidence. *Doe dem James* v. *McLauchlin*, *Mich. T.* 1861.

X.

Admission from Pleading.

1—Admission by Plaintiff's Counsel.
Plaintiff may avail himself of a fact which is admitted by the plaintiff in his opening, and made part of the plaintiff's case, although as the pleadings stood the defendant could not have given evidence of such fact. *Wallace* v. *Vernon*, 1 *Kerr* 5.

2—Different Pleas.
Semble, An admission on one plea does not qualify the issue joined on another distinct plea, nor affect the recovery on the latter issue. *Kinnear* v. *Gallagher*, 1 *Kerr* 424.

3—Reference to description of lot in declaration—Plea—Plan.
Description of lots in plan of city of St. John, plea not guilty in so far as relates to the said close described by number, and as mentioned in declaration in specific count. Held, That the reference in plea to the said close being specific and plain, the plea incorporated the description as far as it related to the lot in question, and was an admission of the identity of the lot on the face of the plea; that further proof was unnecessary, and that reference to plan was surplusage. *Merritt* v. *Cuxater*, 2 *Kerr* 385. See Trespass II. 19, same case.

4—Intestate's goods—Allegation.
An allegation in the assignment of a breach, that goods and chattels came to the hands of the defendant as administrator, necessarily shows that they were the goods of the intestate. *Sherlock* v. *McGee*, 1 *All.* 346.

5—Execution of Lease.
In an action against the assignee of a lease made by the plaintiff to A., the defendant pleaded that it was not the deed of A. Held, That the execution of the lease by the plaintiff was admitted by the pleadings. *New Brunswick and Nova Scotia Land Co.* v. *Kirk*, 1 *All.* 443.

6—Replevin — Replication, property in plaintiff—Plea admitting property in custody of law. See Pleading II. 30.

7—Corporation sued as such—Appearing and pleading—Estopped from disputing existence as body corporate. See Estoppel I. 4.

8—Demurrer—Plea—Leave to amend.
Where a cause has been set down for argument on demurrer to a plea, and the defendant obtains leave to amend on payment of costs, he thereby admits the plea is bad. See *Howe* v. *Carson*, 3 *Kerr* 111.

9—Payment of money into Court.
Payment of money into Court generally, in a declaration containing a count on a promissory note, and the common counts does not prevent the defendant from disputing the consideration of the note. *McCann* v. *Riley*, 3 *All.* 154.

10—Payment of money into Court in an action of *indebitatus assumpsit*, only admits a cause of action to the amount paid, but has no other effect. *Anderson* v. *Allison*, 3 *All.* 173.

11—In *indebitatus assumpsit* on the summary side of the Court, for goods sold and delivered, and for the hire of a warp and buoy rope, the particulars to the writ were £10 for a warp sold, and £2 for the hire of an anchor and rope; the defendant paid £3 into Court generally, and the only contract proved on the trial was one for the hire of a warp. On verdict for the plaintiff for £7, and rule *nisi* to set it aside—Held, That the payment of money into Court only amounted to an admission that the defendant was liable in respect to some contract to the amount of the money so paid in; and that it was incumbent on the plaintiff to show not only that a larger sum was due, but that a contract existed in respect of which the defendant was liable beyond the amount so paid into Court, and that the case was not altered by the Act of Assembly 4 Wm. 4, c. 41, s. 2, relating to particulars in summary actions, and a new trial was accordingly granted. *Taylor* v. *Barker*, 3 *Kerr* 614.

12—The declaration stated that the defendant was indebted to the plaintiff in £1000 for salvage of "a certain ship," by the plaintiff's vessel before then saved, and delivered to the defendant; and in the further sum of £1000, for work and labor of the plaintiff, done and performed with his steamer in and about the defendant's business, and at his request; there was also a common count for work and labor. The defendant paid £15 into Court on the declaration generally. Held, That this did not admit any contract for salvage beyond the amount paid, as the contract set out in the declaration was not specifically for salvage of any particular ship, but applied to more than one transaction. Where a specific contract is declared on, payment of money into Court admits that contract; but where a contract is set out which may apply to more than one transaction, payment only admits a contract to the extent of the amount paid. *Walker* v. *Pendleton*, *Mich. T.* 1862.

Offer to confess judgment. See Judgment II. 4.

XI.

MISCELLANEOUS.

1—Authority of Officer—Proof—Affidavit on Sheriff's Deed by Deputy.
Where the affidavit indorsed on a Sheriff's deed of land sold under execution, as to the regularity of the proceedings, pursuant to the Act 4 Wm. 4, c. 22, appears to have been made by the Deputy Sheriff—Held, That the authority of such Deputy may be proved by evidence of his acting in that capacity, although his appointment was under a written deputation, which is not produced. *Doe d. Barlow* v. *Hatfield*, 1 *Kerr* 417.

2—Surveyor General—Notice signed in official character—Authority. See Crown Grant I. 18.

3—Assignment of Mortgage by an Executor is not admissible in evidence without proof of Probate. See *Doe* v. *Hanson*, 3 *All.* 427.

4—Consideration — Evidence to explain. See Consideration 8.

5—Objection after admission of evidence.
A deed was put in evidence without objection as a registered deed, but was afterwards discovered not to have been duly acknowledged, whereupon the defendant's counsel objected in his address to the jury, that it did not give livery of seisin. *Semble*, That the objection was not too late; but that in such case the Judge might allow the opposite party to give evidence of livery of seisin. *Scribner* v. *McLaughlin*, 1 *All.* 379.

6—Tender of Evidence.
The expression of wrong opinion of Judge on effect of evidence offered, upon which counsel withdraws it, is not a ground for new trial, the evidence should be distinctly tendered. *Ruel* v. *McElroy*, 3 *All.* 212.

7—Evidence offered to show a statement made by a deceased witness in giving evidence on a former trial in the hearing of plaintiff in the present suit, rejected.

Quære, Whether other evidence than appears on Judge's notes could be given; if it could, it should be distinctly tendered on that ground. *Prescott* v. *Walton*, 2 *Han.* 230.

8—Evidence rejected at a certain stage of cause, but not absolutely, and not again tendered, is no ground for new trial. *Tufts* v. *Hatheway*, 4 *All.* 62.

9—When evidence is tendered, the Judge has a right to ask the particular purpose for which it is offered, and if the counsel refuses to state it, he may reject it. *Key* v. *Thomson*, 1 *Han.* 297.

10—Judge admitting evidence at any time during trial. See Supra VIII. 11.

11—Improper admission of evidence—Withdrawal.
Though improper evidence of damage has been given, if it has been expressly withdrawn by the Judge from the consideration of the jury, and by subsequent evidence in the cause, it becomes immaterial; the Court will not disturb the verdict on the ground of its improper admission. *Spurr* v. *Albert Mining Co.*, *East. T.* 1871.

12—Surveyor—Reference to plan—Loss of field notes.
A surveyor who had made a survey of land by direction of the Government, may refer to a plan of it made by himself shortly after the survey filed in the Crown Land office, and upon which survey a grant of the land issued, for the purpose of enabling him to state the courses and distances which ran, his field notes of the survey having been lost. *Niles* v. *Burke*, *Hil. T.* 1873.

13—Debits and credits—Account containing.
One side only of an account containing debits and credits cannot be given in evidence; but it is competent for the party to whom the account has been rendered, to put it in evidence and disprove the debits. *Palmer* v. *Gilbert*, 1 *All.* 505.

14—Promissory Note—Evidence under Common Counts. See Bills and Notes VI. 12. See Assumpsit III. a.

15—Feigned Issue—Evidence under. See Practice XII.

16—Handwriting—Proof of—Comparison.
The defendant's signature to a disputed note was proved on a former trial by comparing it with the signature to a bond which he had signed. The witness who proved this, had since died, and on the second trial his testimony was read from the Judge's notes, and evidence given of the defendant's signature to the note in dispute, by comparing it with the signature to a bond shewn to the witness. Held, That without proof to identify this as the bond proved at the first trial, or that the defendant's signature was genuine, the evidence was improperly admitted. *Palmer* v. *Wilbur*, 3 *All.* 443.

17—A witness who once had in his possession, a promissory note acknowledged by the defendant to have been signed by him, is competent to prove the defendant's handwriting, though his only means of the knowledge of it is the signature to the note formerly in his possession. *Patterson* v. *Gillis*, *East. T.* 1831.

18—Onus probandi—Timber cut without license—Crown land.
Where timber is seized by the Crown as being liable to forfeiture under the Acts of Parliament 8 Geo. 1, c. 12, and 2 Geo. 2, c. 35, for being cut without license, and is claimed on the ground that it was not cut on the property of the Crown; the *onus* of proving that it was cut on private property, is on the claimant. *Regina* v. *Beveridge*, 1 *Kerr* 58.

19—Selling Liquor.
In a prosecution for a penalty for selling liquor without license, proof that the sale was made by a person in the defendant's shop in his absence and without shewing any general or special employment of such person by the defendant in the sale of liquors, is sufficient *prima facie* evidence against him. The prosecutor need not prove that the defendant had no license. *Ex parte Parks*, 3 *All.* 237.

20—Onus Probandi.
The *onus* of proving that liquor was not intended for sale, in order to save it from forfeiture under section 15 of 18 Vic. c. 36, is thrown on the owner. *Reg* v. *Salter*, 3 *All.* 321.

In action of replevin. See Replevin. See Pleading II. 27, 30.

21—Attesting witness—Diligence in discovering.
Whether due diligence has been used in discovering attesting witness must depend on the circumstances of each case. See *Crane* v. *Ayre*, 2 *All.* 577.

22—Relevancy—Bill of Sale—Subsequent burning of house.
Where the question in issue was whether the plaintiff had fraudulently set fire to a house in which he lived, evidence that he had given a bill of sale of his furniture, and subsequently insured it and claimed the insurance after the fire, is relevant, being an act of the plaintiff tending to shew a motive for the destruction of the house. *Whelan* v. *Wetmore*, 3 *All.* 482.

The bill of sale was altered in a material part after execution. Held, That it was not thereby void from the beginning, but was admissible to prove that the plaintiff had sold the furniture. *Ibid.*

22 a—Damage to land—Irrelevant questions.
In an action for overflowing plaintiff's land by means of a mill-dam, and thereby destroying his growing trees, the plaintiff cannot be asked for what purpose he purchased the land, or how much he paid for it, such evidence being irrelevant to the question of damages. *Lowell* v. *McAdam*, *East. T.* 1873.

23—Admissibility of evidence under plea—Lateness of objection—Waiver.
In trespass for impounding cattle, the defendant pleaded "not guilty," and at the trial his counsel opened a defence, justifying impounding the cattle *damage feasant* and examined several witnesses to prove it, and the plaintiff's counsel then objected that the evidence was not admissible under the plea; but further evidence was received, and the defendant obtained a verdict. The Court refused a new trial

on the ground of the improper admission of the evidence, the damage, if any, being very small.

Quære, Whether the plaintiff had not waived the objection, by not taking it before the defendant gave any evidence of justification. *Campbell* v. *Wheeler*, 1 *Han*. 269.

24—Defective Title Deeds

May be used to shew extent of claim of possession. See Trespass II. 28.

25—Usage—Rebutting proof of.

See Contract 2.

26—Nuisance—Erection of steam mill.

Evidence of adjoining residents as to the injurious effects of steam mill upon them, admissible. See *Barlow* v. *Kinnear*, 2 *Kerr* 94.

27—Mining—Injurious effects on adjoining soil.

Evidence of the injurious effects of mining coal on other lands in the neighbourhood of the plaintiff's, is properly received. See *McMahon* v. *Berton*, 2 *All*. 321.

28—Witness not remembering statements.

When a witness called by the plaintiff to prove a payment, says that he does not remember any statement made by the defendant at the time, explaining the payment, it is competent for the defendant to call evidence for that purpose. *Flaglor* v *Richards*, 1 *All*. 514.

29—Agreement not affecting prima facie case—Non-production—Contract partly written, partly oral.

Contract partly written and partly parol, the plaintiff making out a *prima facie* case of possession of lumber, it is unnecessary to produce an agreement in writing relating to matter of suit, but not affecting the *prima facie* case. When a contract is to be made out partly by written documents and partly by parol evidence, the whole becomes a question for the jury. *Macpherson* v. *Fredericton Boom Company*, 1 *Han*. 337.

30—Conflicting statements—Application to compel Sheriff to pay over money—Non-production of receipt.

An application was made on behalf of B. to compel the Sheriff to pay over a sum of money deposited by him in lieu of bail in certain suits in which S. was arrested, but in which he had since been rendered. B.'s affidavit set forth that the Sheriff agreed, when the money was deposited, to return it if S.'s was rendered. This statement Sheriff denied, alleging that he gave a receipt to B., and that the creditors of S., who were proceeding against him, under Absconding Debtors' Act, claimed the money as the property of S. Held, That the receipt not being produced, and the evidence being conflicting, the Court would not grant the application. *Oulton* v. *Scovil*, 1 *Han*. 498.

31—Winding up act—Judge's order.

A Judge's order settling list of contributories, only *prima facie* evidence of liability. See *McKenzie, Curator, etc.* v. *Seaman*, 1 *Han*. 621.

32—Debit on Books. See Credit.

33—Credit—Contracting as Agent—Judgment by default—Inquiry.

After judgment by default in an action on the common counts for work and labor, etc., the defendant, on the execution of a writ of inquiry, may shew that he contracted merely as the agent of a third person to whom the credit was given. See *Falls* v. *Sargent*, 3 *Kerr* 248.

34—Serving paper—Making evidence.

A party cannot make evidence for himself by serving an account on the opposite party. See *Gilbert* v. *Palmer*, 1 *Han*. 667.

Nor by writing letters. See *do*., 1 *Han*. 471.

34 a—Registered deed—Delivery to, or assent of grantee must be shewn.

To an action for the breach of a written contract, whereby B., in consideration of £500 paid by him to A., agreed to convey to A. a mill and mill privilege at P. as soon as he obtained a grant thereof. B. pleaded—1st. *Non assumpsit*; 2ndly. That he executed and delivered a conveyance to A.; and 3rdly. That a conveyance was tendered and refused. At the trial a registered deed was offered in evidence under the pleas without proof by the subscribing witness of the execution in the ordinary way. Held, That such evidence was properly rejected, it not being competent for the grantor to make a deed evidence by mere force of the registry and acknowledgment, without delivery to, or assent of the grantee. *Smith* v. *Millidge*, 2 *Kerr* 408.

35—Shewing fraud in obtaining judgment.

Evidence of fraud in obtaining a judgment by the plaintiff against A. is admissible at *Nisi Prius*, where the plaintiff claimed title under a sale on execution issued on such judgment, and was party to the fraud; the defendant being also a judgment creditor of A., and having purchased under an execution issued after the plaintiff's execution. *McKay* v. *Crocker*, *Hil. T.* 1861.

36—Plaintiff and defendant had both obtained judgments against A., and issued executions thereon, but the plaintiff's execution was first in the Sheriff's hands; the Sheriff sold under both, and the plaintiff purchased under defendant's protest, at the sale on his execution, and the defendant purchased the same property under the sale on his execution. Held, That the defendant had a right in an action of trover brought against him by the plaintiff (the property being in the defendant's possession) to shew fraud in the plaintiff in obtaining his judgment against A. *Ibid.*

37—Disclosure of Writing—Formation of Association.

Defendants were the committee of an Association who employed M. to publish a newspaper under a written agreement which prohibited him from pledging the credit, or creating any liability against them. Plaintiff acted as Reporter for the paper, but proved an agreement with the members of the Association, having been referred by them to M. for the financial arrangements. In an action against the committee for work as Reporter, one of the defendants on cross-examination stated, that there was a writing under which the Association was formed previous to the agreement with M. Held, That the writing was properly admitted in evidence on the part of the defendants, 1st. Because the plaintiff had shewn by the agreement he put in, that the defendants represented an Association; and 2nd. Because he had shewn by the cross-examination that there was a writing previous to the agreement out of which it grew, and it was therefore competent for the defendants to shew the origin of the Association. *Beardsley* v. *Scovil*, *East. T.* 1864.

38—Statement of belief—Previous statements—Effect.

On the trial of an indictment for burning a barn, a witness for the prosecution stated that he had examined foot tracks in the snow leading from the barn to the prisoner's house, that they were double tracks, and appeared as if the person had gone and returned on the same track. On cross-examination, he stated that it appeared to be a double track going and coming, but he could not state positively as the snow was mealy in the bottom, and he could not see distinctly; and on re-examination he said he believed the tracks each way were the same tracks. Held, That the statement of the witness' belief did not make his evidence on this point inadmissible, but that the effect of it was properly left to the jury. *Regina* v. *Foley*, *East. T.* 1873.

39—Damage—General assertion insufficient.

A plaintiff giving evidence on his own behalf cannot be allowed to state that he has sustained a certain amount of damage by the act of the defendant: he should state the facts on which he relies to prove his damages, from which the jury are to determine the amount. *Domville* v. *Keevan*, *East. T.* 1871, and *Ryan* v. *James*, *East. T.* 1872.

Replevin—Plea *non cepit*—Evidence under. See Pleading II. 28.

Proving property. See Pleading II. 29.

Trespass—Place not proved—Sufficiency of evidence to entitle plaintiff to recover on *asportavit* count. See Trespass I. 25.

Place properly described—Reference to original grant—Correspondence in proof—Evidence of plan in Clerk's office not essential. See *Merrit* v. *Coxeter*, 2 *Kerr* 385. (See same case, Supra X. 3.)

Mesne profits—Action for—Husband and wife—Judgment against wife—Action against husband and wife for joint trespass, not supported by proof of judgment against wife before marriage—Marriage not being averred. See Ejectment VI.

Confessions of third persons—Proof of felony. See Criminal Law.

Res Gestæ—Sheriff's deed received in evidence as forming part of *res gestæ* in action of ejectment, without proof of judgment or execution to warrant it. See *Doe* v. *Baxter*, 4 *All.* 131.

Latent ambiguity—Intention. See Release.

Evidence in particular actions and suits.

See further under the following heads:

Account stated. See Assumpsit.

Administrators. See Executors and Administrators.

XII.

Questions of Fact proper for Decision of Jury.

Disseisin.
Disseisin is a question of fact for the jury to decide; and if on a trial in ejectment a verdict is taken for the plaintiff by consent, subject to a motion for nonsuit, on the ground that the party through whom the plaintiff derives title was disseised at the time he conveyed to the plaintiff; the Court will not decide the question, but send the case down to a jury. *Doe dem Dowling* v. *Pearson*, 135.

Easement—Acquisition—Relinquishment, or Abandonment. See Easement 6.

Fraud. See New Trial III. 29.
" Fraud.

Fraudulent Removal. See Distress.

Foreign Law. See

Inferences from Facts. See Malicious Prosecution.

Nuisance—Effect of erection of Dam. See Action on the case III. 1.

Partnership. See Contract 15.

Possession (Adverse). See Limitation of Actions.

Trust Deed. See Deed.

Insurance. See

Parties—Same Name—Intention. See Identity.

Surrender. See

XIII.

General Issue—Evidence under.

1—Sheriff.
Neglecting to execute process may shew under general issue that debt was barred by Statute of Limitations. See *Curran* v. *Beckwith*, 3 *All.* 365.

2—Acceptance; payable half cash, half goods—Tender of goods.
In an action on an acceptance, payable half in cash and half in goods, a tender of the goods cannot be given in evidence under the general issue. *Turner* v. *Crane*, *Hil. T.* 1832.

3—Trespass—Easement.
An easement or privilege granted by deed to turn the water of a river for the use of mills, and to build mill dams, does not convey the right of soil, and cannot be

given in evidence under the general issue in trespass. *Wallace* v. *Milliken*, *East. T.* 1831.

4—License—Digging land.
In trespass for digging up the plaintiff's land, the defendant justified his entry under a license from a former owner of the land to work the mines therein. Held, That evidence of such license was not admissible under the general issue, either to justify the defendant's entry or to shew a previous possession in him. *Gesner* v. *Cairns*, 2 *All.* 595.

Pew—Joint occupation of. See Use and Occupation.

Information for Intrusion. See Intrusion 1.

Admissibility of evidence under—Objection not made in time. See Supra XI. 23.

Plea when considered as traversing whole declaration. See Pleading II. 40. Atkinson *v.* Desmond.

EXCEPTION.

See Bail, Practice, Error, Crown Grant.

EXCESSIVE DAMAGE.

See Damages.

EXCESSIVE DISTRESS.

See Distress—Necessary allegation in declaration. See Pleading I. 53.

EXCHANGE.

Agreement for Exchange of Lands. See Deed V. 1.

Agreement for Exchange of Wagons—Warranty of ownership. See Warranty 4.

EXCHEQUER.

See Supreme Court.

1—Where logs were seized as having been cut on Crown land without license, an order for their sale as "perishable articles" was refused; the only ground alleged being the expense of their custody pending the proceedings for condemnation. *Rex* v. 726 *Saw Logs*, *Trin. T.* 1833.

2—A summary action, in which the rights of the Crown are involved, may be removed into the Court of Exchequer by an order. *Wilson* v. *Brisson*, 2 *All.* 535.

EXECUTION.

I. Fieri Facias—Levy.
II. Capias ad Satisfaciendum.
III. Setting Aside and Staying.
IV. Miscellaneous.

I.

Fieri Facias.

Receivable in Evidence though not returned. See Evidence II. 20.

1—Right to seize goods—Different County.
Goods of a judgment debtor were sold and delivered to the plaintiff in the County of Carleton, and were afterwards brought into the County of York. Held, That the Sheriff of the County of York could not seize them under an execution subsequently issued against the debtor, though at the time of the delivery to the plaintiff there was an execution against the debtor in the same suit in the hands of the Sheriff of Carleton. *Connell* v. *Millar*, 1 *Kerr* 302.

2—Binding Lands.
A writ of *fieri facias de bonis et terris*, issued upon a judgment in a summary action binds the lands from the time of the delivery thereof to the Sheriff to be executed, and it is not necessary that any prior memorial of the judgment should be registered in the county records to prevent a conveyance, made by the judgment debtor of the land after the delivery of the *fi. fa.* to the Sheriff, taking precedence of the Sheriff's sale and conveyance. *Doe dem Nesmith* v. *Williston*, 2 *Kerr* 459.

3—Against estate of mortgagee in fee.
The estate of a mortgagee in fee who has not taken possession of the land, is not seizable in execution on a judgment against him. The fact of there being no bond or covenant to pay the money does not affect the question. *Doe* v. *White*, 4 *All.* 314.

4—Delivery—Operation—Intention to levy.
An execution put in the Sheriff's hands, with instructions not to levy on it unless it should become necessary to prevent another execution from taking precedence will not bind the goods of the defendant, nor defeat a purchase of them before a seizure actually made under the execution. *Crane* v. *Clark*, *Hil. T.* 1828.

5—Where a *fieri facias* issues, and there is no evidence of intention beyond the mere delivery of the writ to the Sheriff, it may be inferred that it was intended for immediate execution; but circumstances may be shewn which will negative this presumption, and tend to the inference that at the time the writ was delivered, it was not the intention of the judgment creditor that it should be executed without further instructions. A letter from the judgment creditor while an execution is in the Sheriff's hands, advising the debtor about the management of his business and the disposition of his property to raise money to pay his debts, is evidence of the intention of the creditor that the execution should not be put into immediate force. *Johnson* v. *Crocker*, 4 *All.* 94.

6—Where a *fieri facias* was delivered to the Sheriff for the purpose of binding the debtor's lands, and not for the purpose of a sale, and the Sheriff informed the debtor that he had the execution and indorsed upon it that he had levied on the lands, but did no other act for more than five years, when he advertised the land for sale. The Court, doubting whether this amounted to a levy on the land, set it aside on the application of the debtor and a mortgagee of his land. *Hamilton* v. *Bryson*, 1 *Han.* 618.

7—Before judgment obtained.
An execution placed in the Sheriff's hands before judgment, will be treated as fraudulent, and will be set aside at the instance of a judgment creditor of the defendant. For the purposes of justice, the Court will take notice of the particular time of a day when certain proceedings took place. *De Veber* v. *Colling*, *Hil. T.* 1834.

Miscalling Writ in Sheriff's Deed.
See Sheriff's Deed 1.

8—Levy under.
Where an execution is correct in itself, though indorsed to levy more than the amount due, the Court will allow the levy to stand for the sum really due, if there is no fraud in the transaction. See *Lunt* v. *Estabrooks*, 3 *Kerr* 144.

9—The Sheriff need not make an actual entry on the land to levy: the advertisement is proof of the levy. See *Doe* v. *Hazen*, 3 *All.* 87.

10—An actual levy is not necessary. Where, after an execution had been delivered to the Sheriff, the defendant gave a written acknowledgment that a levy had been made on his property under the execution, and afterwards paid the amount to the Sheriff—Held, That the Sheriff was entitled to poundage on the amount paid, under 1 Rev. Stat. c. 163. *Central Bank* v. *McKeen*, *East. T.* 1863.

11—Sale—No actual seizure or overt act by Sheriff.
The property of a judgment debtor in goods is not divested by a sale by the Sheriff, unless there has been some overt act of seizure by him, such as marking or taking possession of them or separating them from others. The Sheriff must have done some act to enable him to deliver possession of the property to the purchaser, and he cannot by a general sale of all a debtor's goods, pass the title to property not in his view, and on which he has made no actual levy. *Reynolds* v. *Ayre*, *Trin. T.* 1862.

12—Retaining money—Other execution.
The Court will not order the Sheriff to retain in his hands money which he has levied on an execution at the suit of the plaintiff, in order to satisfy an execution against the plaintiff at the suit of one of the defendants in the Sheriff's hands at the same time. *Bradley* v. *Hopley*, *Hil. T.* 1828.

13—Second execution—Satisfaction out of proceeds of first—Sheriff's right.
If a second execution comes into the Sheriff's hands after he has sold under a former one, he has no right to apply any money remaining in his hands after satisfying the first execution, towards the second one. *Stevenson* v. *Douglas*, *Ber.* 281.

14—Teste—Issue.
An execution tested on the day it is issued in vacation upon a judgment entered up as of the preceding term, although irregular, is not a nullity since the Act 5 Wm. 4, c. 37. (Chipman, C. J., *dubitante.*) *Power* v. *Johnston*, 2 *Kerr* 43.

See Acts of Assembly 21 Vic. c. 20.

15—Sheriff's Return—Uncertainty.
A return of a Sheriff to a writ of *fi. fa.* that he had "taken from the defendant a horse claimed by the defendant's son, and placed it in charge of H., from whose

custody he said it was stolen; and that nothing else was found with the defendant," is bad for uncertainty. *Ketchum* v. *Muscroll*, 3 *All.* 347.

Amending Return—Wrong Levy. See Amendment II.

16—Variance between *fi. fa.* and the judgment amount—Sale not affected thereby. See Variance, *Linton* v. *Wilson*.

17—Irregularity—Purchaser.
Any irregularity in issuing the *venditione exponas* will not affect a purchaser under the Sheriff's deed. See *Doe dem Hazen* v. *Hazen*, 3 *All.* 87.

18—*Fieri Facias* may issue after escape of debtor. See *Kelly* v. *Wilson*, 2 *All.* 475.

19—Alteration.
An execution which has been in the hands of the Sheriff, and was by him returned to the plaintiff's attorney, who altered it to an *alias*, and re-issued it, is void. *Johnston* v. *Winslow*, *Ber.* 53.

II.

Capias ad Satisfaciendum.

1—Issuing second ca. sa.
If no original execution issued within a year and day after judgment is found on file, a second *ca. sa.* is not warranted, without a *scire facias* to revive the judgment. *Brown* v. *Partelow*, 3 *Kerr* 324. (See 2 Rev. Stat., extending time, 12 Vic. c. 39, s. 35.)

2—Amendment of.
An application to amend a *ca. sa.* issued sixteen years ago will not be granted unless the writ is found on file, or some record of it is produced. *Quære*, Whether such an amendment would be made after such a lapse of time, and after the defendant had been arrested on a second execution, which was also irregular. *Brown* v. *Partelow*, 3 *Kerr* 324.

3—Testatum.
The want of an original *ca. sa.* in the County where the venue is laid, if not amended, is a valid objection to arrest under a *testatum ca. sa.* *Sewell* v. *Burpee*, 3 *Kerr* 363.

4—Irregularity—Difference between judgment.
Ca. Sa. differing in amount only from the judgment upon which it is issued, is not void, but only irregular. *Spence* v. *Stuart*, *Ber.* 219.

Bail, pleading that no *ca. sa.* issued against principal—Application to Court to set aside proceedings for irregularity. See Bail 19.

5—Defendant permitted to go at large by special bailiff of plaintiff.
If a defendant in custody upon a *ca. sa.* is permitted to go at large by a special bailiff named by the plaintiff to execute the writ, and his servant and agent, for that purpose, he cannot afterwards be retaken on a new *ca. sa.* These facts will be a good defence to an action on the limit bond given on the second arrest. *Andrews* v. *Dowdall*, *Trin. T.* 1832.

III.

Setting aside Execution.

1—Suspending—Staying.
If not warranted by the judgment will be set aside—Debt—Execution in assumpsit. See Practice VI. 3.

2—Second execution for balance—Recital.
If a part of a debt has been levied the execution should be returned and filed before a second execution issues for the balance, and the latter execution should recite the former levy, or it will be set aside for irregularity. *Smith* v. *Jones*, 2 *All.* 176.

3—A Judge of Common Pleas has power to set aside an execution irregularly issued, upon a judgment in that Court. *Wilson* v. *Street*, 3 *All.* 80.

Suspending Remedy. See Judgment.

4—Staying Execution—Administrator—Estate insolvent.
The Court will stay an execution on a judgment duly obtained against an administrator for the full amount of a debt due by his intestate, upon affidavits shewing the estate to be insolvent, and that the plaintiff will, if such execution issues, obtain an undue share of the assets of the estate. *Cunliffe* v. *Morehouse*, 2 *Kerr* 347.

IV.

Miscellaneous.

Excessive Amount. See Supra I. 8.

Injunction to restrain selling under execution—Contesting Sale at Law. See Practice in Equity II. 4.

Replevin—Separate Execution. See Costs 102.

Insolvent Debtor discharged — Refusal to allow second execution against. See Insolvent Debtor 17.

Memorial—Priority over subsequent judgment and execution. See Memorial.

Poundage. See Sheriff.

Costs of Appeal from decision of Judge in Equity recoverable by attachment, not by execution. See Costs 79.

1—Unsatisfied Execution—Right to issue for balance.

Where a Sheriff, having a *ca. sa.* against a defendant, received from him a horse in full satisfaction of the execution, without any authority from the plaintiff; and several months afterwards sent the horse to the plaintiff, who sold it to the best advantage, though for much less than the value agreed upon between the Sheriff and defendant—Held, That the Sheriff had no authority by law to receive the horse, and that it was no satisfaction of the judgment, although the horse might have produced enough to pay the amount due if the Sheriff had sold it at that time; but that after crediting the amount produced by the sale, the plaintiff could issue an execution for the balance. *Carman* v. *Mott*, 3 *Kerr* 131.

2—Issue of—When considered.

An execution issued in the week which includes the third return day of the term, is deemed to be issued in term, and may be tested on the first day of term though the judgment on which it is founded is not signed until after the first day. *Coffin* v. *Marsh*, 3 *Kerr* 427.

3—A writ of execution is considered duly issued within the meaning of the Act 7 Vic. c. 32, s. 7, when it is sent by the attorney for the *bona fide* purpose of its reaching the hands of the Sheriff in the usual course for the transmission of such documents. *Lunt* v. *Estabrooks*, 3 *Kerr* 291.

4—Justification under execution.

A process, regular on its face, is a justification to the officer. See *Carter* v. *Purington*, 2 *All.* 226.

5—An execution issued on a summary judgment is a justification to the Sheriff, or a person clothed with his authority, for any act done under it, without proof of the filing of the bill of costs. *Patterson* v. *Tingley*, *Trin. T.* 1863.

Quære, Whether such proof would be necessary to render the execution a justification to third parties? *Semble*, That the execution is only voidable for the omission to file the bill of costs. *Ibid.*

6—Sale of personal property after levy on land.

Where logs were cut by the plaintiff, and carried away from the land of a judgment debtor, after the defendant, as Sheriff, had received an execution, under which he had advertised the land for sale, and the defendant under the same execution seized the logs and sold them before the time for selling the real property arrived. Held, That he was justified in so doing, and might avail himself of such a defence under the general issue. *Fitzsimmons* v. *J*‸*nes*, 3 *Kerr* 596.

7—Ordering Writ to be filed.

Where an action was pending against an attorney for imprisoning the plaintiff on an irregular execution, which was wanted as evidence on the trial, the Court ordered the attorney to file the writ in the Clerk's office. *Roberts* v. *Watson*, 1 *All.* 94.

8—Impeaching sale at trial for irregularity of execution.

The validity of a sale under an execution cannot be impeached on a trial at *Nisi Prius*, on the ground that the execution is irregular for having issued on a judgment more than a year old without a *scire facias*. *Doe* v. *Watson*, 1 *All.* 675.

Variance in recital of Judgment. See Variance.

Sale by Sheriff under an *alias* the original execution need not be proved. See Sheriff's Deed 6.

9—Justice of the Peace—Sufficiency of execution issued by.

An execution issued by a Justice of the Peace is sufficient, if it substantially follows the form K in the Schedule to the Rev. Stat. c. 137; and any person resisting a constable executing it, is liable to an indictment. It is sufficient if the execution is made returnable in a certain number of days from the date, so that it may be ascertained by calculation. *Reg.* v. *McDonald*, 4 *All.* 440.

10—Alias Writ—Excessive amount—Arrest.

If an execution issues upon a judgment in a Justice's Court within the time limited by the 1 Rev. Stat. c. 137, s. 38, an *alias* or pluries may afterwards issue, though more than three years have elapsed since the judgment. *Semble*, That an execution issued by a Justice of the Peace for more than the amount of the judgment, is irregular only, and the mere arrest of the defendant under it, is not necessarily a wrong; but otherwise, if he is imprisoned under it for a greater number of days than is allowed by law according to the sum actually due. *Ryan* v. *James*, *East. T.* 1872.

11—Execution for lesser amount than judgment—Tender—Refusal—Imprisonment.

Defendant recovered judgment against the plaintiff in a Justice's Court for £3 7s.; the execution issued stated the amount to be *thirty-seven shillings*, which sum the plaintiff tendered to the defendant, who refused to receive it. Held, That the execution was not a nullity, and that trespass would not lie against the defendant and the constable for imprisoning the plaintiff on the execution after the tender of the thirty-seven shillings. *Carman* v. *Wilson*, *Trin. T.* 1864.

12—Debtor pointing out property to Constable—Duty to seize it.

Where the debtor points out property to the constable to levy on it, it his duty to seize it, unless he has reasonable grounds for believing that it does not belong to the debtor. *Hunter* v. *Maddox*, 1 *Han.* 162.

13—Direction of execution to any Constable.

The Act 22 Vic. c. 27, authorising Constables to serve processes in any part of the County in which they are appointed, an execution issued out of a Justice's Court, under 1 Rev. Stat. c. 137, may be directed to any Constable *of the County*. The deviation from the form prescribed by cap. 137, does not affect the substance of the execution. *Atkinson* v. *Desmond*, *Trin. T.* 1863.

14—Property liable to seizure—Interest in Logs.

Plaintiff obtained a license to cut logs, and agreed with A. to cut and haul the logs, put the plaintiff's mark on them and take them to the mouth of the Oromocto for him; plaintiff to furnish the supplies, pay the wages, and sell the logs at Saint John; and after deducting stumpage, freight, supplies, etc., pay A. any balance that might remain. Held, That A. had no interest in the logs that could be seized under execution. *Pelton* v. *Temple*, 1 *Han.* 275.

15—Husband and Wife—Separate property.

Land was conveyed to a married woman, for life, for her separate use; it was managed under her directions, and the labor paid for by the produce of the land, the husband not interfering except as her agent. Held, 1st. That under the Rev. Stat. c. 114, the crop, when severed, did not become the property of the husband, and was not liable to seizure under an execution against him. 2nd. That an action for seizing the crop, under execution against the husband, was rightly brought in the name of the husband and wife. *Dow and wife* v. *Dibblee*, 1 *Han.* 55.

16—When a husband and wife reside on land of which the wife has the fee, the husband is tenant by the courtesy, and the crops raised by his labor and the labor of his servants and children, are his and liable to seizure for his debts, and the Sheriff may enter to make a levy. In the absence of title, the possession is the possession of the husband. *Pourrier and Wife* v. *Raymond*, 1 *Han.* 512.

17—Real estate, in *remainder* or *reversion*, may be taken in execution, and sold at Sheriff's sale, under the Act 26 Geo. 3, c. 12. See *Doe* v. *Hazen*, 3 *All.* 87.

Estate of Mortgagee in fee, not liable. See Supra I. 3.

18—Real estate of testator.

Land which belonged to a testator cannot be taken in execution on a judgment recovered against his executor for a debt due by the testator, either under the Act of Parliament 5 Geo. 2, c. 7, or the Act of Assembly 26 Geo. 3, c. 12. Real estate descends to the heir. License to sell requisite before divested. *Doe dem Hare* v. *McCall*, *C. Ms.* 90.

19—Improper discharge of debtor by Judge's order—Issuing fi. fa.

One of two joint debtors in custody on execution, was improperly discharged by a Judge's order; the plaintiff's attorney, without applying to rescind the order, issued a *fi. fa.* Held, That it was not absolutely necessary to rescind the Judge's order before issuing the *fi. fa.*, and it was allowed to stand—the plaintiff undertaking not to issue another *ca. sa.* or take any proceedings against the defendant's sureties in consequence of his discharge. *Hogan* v. *Whitehead*, *Hil. T.* 1871.

EXECUTORS AND ADMINISTRATORS.

I. Actions by and against.
II. Rights and Liabilities.
III. Executor De Son Tort.
IV. Administration — Grant of — Proof — Probate.
V. Miscellaneous.

I.

Actions by and against.

1—Debt for specific legacy.
A legatee may maintain an action of debt against an executor for a certain legacy given by his testator. *Livingstone* v. *Powell et. al., Executors of Powell, Ber.* 225. (See Action at Law IX. 16.)

2—Suspension of action.
Actions against executors or administrators for the recovery of debts due from the testator or intestate, are not suspended for eighteen months under the Act 3 Vic. c. 61; the thirty-fifth section has no such operation. *Cunliffe* v. *Morehouse*, 2 *Kerr* 311.

3—Set-off—Bond—Penalty.
In an action against an administrator on a promissory note given by the intestate, he pleaded *plene administravit*, and gave notice under the Statute of a bond debt due and outstanding, and no assets *ultra*. Held, That the sum actually due on the bond, and not the penalty, was the amount which the defendant was entitled to set off against the assets in hand. *Sherlock* v. *McGee*, 2 *Kerr* 508.

4—Assets not accounted for—Insufficiency to pay—Limitation of recovery.
It is competent for a creditor in an action at law against the executor, where the amount of assets is in question, to shew that assets came to his possession for which he has not accounted in the Surrogate Court; but where it appears that the executor has assets sufficient to pay a larger dividend than that alleged in his plea or notice under the Act, but not enough to pay the whole debts, the recovery will be limited to the rateable proportion which the creditor is entitled to receive from the assets. *Harrison* v. *Morehouse*, 2 *Kerr* 584.

Representative character—Liability for money bequeathed—No averment of receipt of money. See Pleading I. 25.

5—Administration by two out of three defendants—Small assets in hands of third—Verdict for defendants.
In an action against three defendants, as executors, two of whom had fully administered, and the amount in the hands of the other defendant was very small, the Court refused to set aside the verdict in favor of all the defendants. The plaintiff might have had a verdict against the defendant shewn to have assets in his hands. *Crookshank* v. *McFarlane*, 2 *All.* 544.

6—Executor of the assignee of a bail bond may bring an action upon it. *Scribner* v. *Gibbon*, 4 *All.* 182.

7—Executors appointed by power in will—Right to sue.
A testator named seven executors in his will, and directed that if any of them should die or renounce, the remaining executors should by writing appoint others in their place, so that the same number should always exist. Two of the executors named in the will died, and the survivors appointed two others, who were sworn as executors, and probate granted to them by the Judge of Probates, after the original probate granted. Held, That these seven persons could sue as executors. *Wright* v. *Stackhouse, Hil. T.* 1863.

8—Covenant—Breach in life time of testator.
Where breach of a covenant for title and the damage resulting therefrom, both occurred in the life time of the testator, the action for such breach should be brought by the executor. See Covenant 13.

9—If covenant for title is broken in the life time of the covenantee, no estate descends to his heir, and an action for the breach is properly brought by his executor. See Covenant 14.

10—Proving promise.
In an action by an administrator for work and labor of the intestate, and alleging only a promise to the administrator, the plaintiff must prove the promise as laid. *Stevenson* v. *Perley*, 3 *Kerr* 398.

II.

Rights and Liabilities.

1—Executors of deceased administrator.
The executors of a deceased administrator have no right to file an account of his administration in the Probate Court; nor

has the Judge of Probates any authority to pass such an account if filed. *In re Frost*, 1 *Han.* 127.

2—An administrator *cum testamento annexo* died without having filed any accounts of his administration. Held, That the Probate Court, on the application of the residuary legatees under the will, had no jurisdiction to pass accounts filed by the executors of the deceased administrator; that the proper course would be to appoint an administrator *de bonis non, cum testamento annexo*, who would be bound to account, and to whom the executor of the deceased administrator would be liable in the first instance. *In re Frost's estate, Mich. T.* 1866.

3—License to sell—No waiver of right to sell by will.

Executors obtaining license to sell from the Governor and Council, do not waive any right they have to sell under the will. *Doe dem Pike* v. *Tierney, Hil. T.* 1831.

4—Claim by administrator—Allowance.

A claim of an administrator against the estate for maintenance of the intestate may be included in, and allowed in his account passed by the Probate Court; but the claim must be limited to six years. *Ex parte Holly, Trin. T.* 1863.

5—Where the Probate Court allowed the administrator's claim for maintenance for ten years, but during the first four years of that period he had received the proceeds of the intestate's farm, the amount of which he had a right to appropriate towards the payment of his charge for maintenance, the Supreme Court, on appeal, ordered the difference between the two sums to be deducted from the administrator's account. *Ibid.*

6—Application of assets to payment of Executor's claim.

Where there is no fraud or collusion, an executor may apply the assets of the testator in payment of his own debt; though in case of a deficiency of assets to pay debts or legacies, the alienee of the property (knowing that it belonged to the estate) may be liable in equity to creditors or legatees, or the next of kin. *Allingham* v. *Daniel, Trin. T.* 1871.

7—No right to pay debts in preference, nor retain.

Where the Act 26 Geo. 3, c. 11, s. 18, directing executors, where an estate is insolvent, "to divide it in due proportion to and among the creditors,"—it is their duty to pay debts according to the common law priority of classes, and *pari passu* in each class, and they have no right to pay any one creditor in preference, nor to retain for the whole of their own debts of the same class. *Joseph* v. *McLeod, Trin. T.* 1833.

8—Costs—Liability to.

If an executor declares on promises to himself, he is liable for costs. *Executors of Grosvenor* v. *Agnew, Ber.* 29.

9—An administrator will not be relieved from his liability to the payment of costs, under Act 7 Wm. 4, c. 14, s. 23, where he moves, not on matters appearing at the trial, but upon affidavits which are sufficiently answered by the defendant. *Semble*, The Act extends only to cases in which executors or administrators were before that Act exempted from the payment of costs. *Thompson* v. *Allanshaw*, 1 *Kerr* 209.

10—Absconding debtor holding property as administrator—Trustees not entitled to. See Absconding Debtor 4.

11—Assignment of mortgaged land.

An executor cannot assign the legal estate in land mortgaged in fee to his testator, unless the land is devised to him: without such devise, his assignment will operate only as a transfer of the mortgage debt. See *Doe* v. *Hanson*, 3 *All.* 427.

12—Deposit of money by two persons—Death of one—Right of administrator.

A sum of money was deposited in a bank, for which a receipt was given in the following words: "Received from P. C. and H. C., to be drawn by either of them, or the survivor, $1400, for which we are accountable with interest, on receiving fifteen days notice." P. C. sent the receipt to the bank, and applied for the money, but the Manager not being satisfied that the person who brought the receipt had authority to receive the money, declined to pay it. P. C. died three days after this. Held, That on his death, the right to receive the money vested in H. C., and that P. C.'s administrators could not recover it from the bank. *Condon* v. *Bank of B. N. America, Trin. T.* 1870.

13—Bank Stock undisposed of—Suspension of payment by bank—Liability of Executors.

A testator died possessed of bank stock, which his executors allowed to remain undisposed of, and received the dividends. By the the terms of the bank charter the Stockholders were individually liable for the payment of the debts of the bank, in proportion to the stock they held. About two years after the death of the testator, the bank suspended payment, and was wound up under the Act 27 Vic. c. 44, and a call made on the executors as contributories. Held, That they were liable therefor in their representative capacity, and that the payment of legacies under the will could not be allowed against their contingent liability to calls under the charter. *McKenzie, Curator, &c.*, v. *King*, *Mich. T.* 1871.

III.

EXECUTOR DE SON TORT.

1—Wife continuing business after the death of husband.

The wife of a grocer and liquor seller, who continues after his death to keep the house open and sell liquors left therein at his decease, is made thereby an executrix *de son tort;* and cannot protect herself under the plea of *ne unques executrix* against a demand by a simple contract creditor of her husband, by showing that there was an outstanding judgment against her husband for an amount exceeding all the assets of the estate. *Keith* v. *Perks*, 2 *Kerr* 552.

2—Brother of deceased—Agreement to take property and pay debts—Parties to agreement—Subsequent discharge.

The brother of a deceased person, at the request of several of his creditors, made an agreement with them to take the property of the deceased and pay them a proportion of their respective claims on getting a discharge. The property was placed in the hands of a third person by the creditors till the agreement could be performed, but it was soon afterwards abandoned. Held, That all the parties to the agreement were liable as executors *de son tort*, but that they discharged themselves from liability by afterwards delivering the property to the administrator before action brought. *Crookshank* v. *McFarlane et. al.*, 2 *All.* 544.

IV.

ADMINISTRATION—GRANT OF—PROOF—PROBATE.

1—Acting as Administrators—Entry in book.

The plaintiff claimed under a deed from two persons as administrators, but there was no positive proof that letters of administration had been granted, and no administration bond could be found or was known to have existed; the Court refused to disturb a verdict for the defendant, finding that no letters of administration were granted, though the vendors had acted as administrators for several years, and though it appeared by an entry made at the time in a book kept by the Judge of Probates that administration was so granted: it being uncertain whether this entry was an official act—the case having been tried before—and the plaintiff's right to recover being doubtful on other points. *Doe* v. *Read*, 1 *All.* 68.

Semble, Administration, if granted, is not void for want of an administration bond; but the absence of one is a strong fact to rebut a presumption that administration was granted. *Ibid.*

2—Remaining good until revoked—Seal—Surrogate's Acts.

Administration irregularly granted (as to a creditor without citing the next of kin,) remains good till revoked by the proper Court. Letters of Administration must be under seal, but no particular impression is necessary. Any seal used by the Surrogate for the purpose is sufficient, till a particular seal is provided. It will be presumed that a person acting as Surrogate has taken the oath of office; but if he has not, his acts will not be invalid if he has been appointed to the office. *Crookshank* v. *Giberson*, 2 *All.* 544.

3—Affidavit endorsed on deed, not evidence of grant of administration. See Evidence IV. 2.

What it is evidence of. See Evidence IV. 3.

4—Letters of Administration—Evidence of intestate's death. See Scribner v. Gibbon, 4 All. 182.

5—Probate of Will, though registered, is not evidence of a due execution to pass real estate. See Hamilton v. Love, 2 Kerr 243.

6—Foreign, Probate—Pleading.

Probate of a Will in Nova Scotia gives no title in this Province; nor will probate granted in this Province, after declaration and issue joined, support an action by the executor. *Mitchell* v. *Long*, *C. Ms.* 76.

V.

MISCELLANEOUS.

Assumpsit on Promises and Foreign Judgment. See Pleading I. 19.

Promises laid to Plaintiff as Administrator. See Pleading I. 18.

Estate insolvent—No ascertaining of insolvency — Distribution of Assets. See Pleading II. 36.

1—Execution — Real Estate.
Lands of a Testator cannot be taken in execution under the Act 26 Geo. 3, c. 12, on a judgment against the executor for a debt of the testator. *Doe dem Hare* v. *McCall, C. Ms.* 90.

2—Notice to sell Land—Extent of time —Posting up—Publication.
A Notice to sell Land by Executors, by virtue of a license from the Governor and Council, under the Act 26 Geo. 3, c. 11, s. 18, must be given thirty days, exclusive of the day of sale, both by posting up notices and by publication in the newspaper; but it is not necessary to prove that the notices posted up continued up till the day of sale. *Doe d. Pike* v. *Tierney, Hil. T.* 1831.

3—Acknowledgment of Debt—Statute of Limitations.
The mere acknowledgment of a debt by an administrator is not sufficient to take the case out of the Statute of Limitations: there must be an express promise to pay. *Gibbs* v. *Sewall, Trin. T.* 1833.

4—Property bequeathed to Executor —Rent—Charge against same.
A testator bequeathed property to his executor, out of which he directed him to pay all his just debts. Held, That rent arising upon a lease executed by the testator, which accrued due after his death, was a charge upon the property bequeathed to the executor. *Wetmore* v. *Ketchum, Mich. T.* 1862.

5—Legacy—Bill filed for payment of—Distribution of Assets—Reference to take account.
The plaintiff and defendant were executors of A. who bequeathed a legacy of £50 to the plaintiff's wife, charged upon land devised by the will to the defendant. On a bill filed for the payment of this legacy, it appeared that the plaintiff, as executor, had received assets belonging to A's estate, which he had not accounted for, and that the defendant had in consequence been obliged to charge the real estate devised to him, to raise money to pay the testator's debt. At the hearing, a reference was directed to inquire what moneys belonging to the estate had been received by the plaintiff, and how he had applied them. On appeal by the plaintiff from this order: Held, The inquiry was proper; and that if the plaintiff had caused the fund from which the legacy was to be paid, to be used for the payment of the testator's debts, the defendant should hold that fund discharged from the legacy, or so much thereof as the plaintiff had virtually received from the assets in his hands. *De Veber* v *Andrews*, 3 *All.* 383.

6.—Description—Character—Proof.
The plaintiff in ejectment claimed under a lease from the corporation of Saint John to J. H. and C. H., describing them as executors of J. G. H. deceased; and an assignment of that lease to the plaintiff from the said J. H. and C. H., also describing themselves as executors of J. G. H. Held, That by the lease from the corporation the title vested in J. H. and C. H., and that it was not necessary to prove that they were executors as described. *Doe d. Hatheway* v *Rogers, Mich T.* 1866.

Judgment against executor—Staying execution—Estate insolvent. See Execution III. 4.

Plaintiff's remedy against executor in equity —Money received by executor. See Assumpsit III. 14.

Death of husband—Separate earnings of of wife. See Husband and Wife.

Promissory note to A. or heirs—Right to. See Bills and Notes I. 7.

Surrogate Court—Decision—Finality. See Surrogate Court.

Discharge of Debtor by persons beneficially interested under will. See Discharge.

Acts of personal representative enuring to benefit of heirs and minor children of deceased to shew possession. See Trespass II. 28.

Application to put bond in suit. See Bond D.

Injunction to restrain Administrator from selling land—Sufficiency of assets—Application to dissolve, refused until defendant showed deficiency of assets. See *Coy* v. *Coy*, 1 *Han.* 177.

FILING PAPERS.

See Practice—General Rules 94.

FINES.

See Justice of the Peace (Conviction.)

FIRES.

An action of debt will not lie to recover damages sustained in consequence of a fire kindled by the Defendant, the remedy by action of debt, given by the Act 26 Geo. 3, c. 30, relating only to the recovery of the penalty thereby imposed, and not interfering with the common law remedy. (See Wiley v. Crawford, 1 B. & S. 253.) *Russel* v. *Sutherland, C. Ms.* 80.

Water Company—Duty of keeping water to prevent fire. See Water Company.

Action by Landlord—Premises burnt by fire by alleged negligence of tenant. See Action on the Case I. 2.

Accidental Fire—Liability for. See Action on the Case I. 1

FISHERY.

1—Right of.
By the Act 14 Vic. c. 31, the Governor in Council was authorised to grant leases or licenses of occupation for Fishery Stations on the ungranted shores, beaches or Islands of the Province. A grant was made to the plaintiff for the exclusive leave and license to occupy and enjoy as a Fishing ground for the term of four years, a lot or beach abutted and described as follows, viz: lot No. 4, on the outside of Portage Island; with the full and exclusive privilege of using the said lot or station as a Fishing station. Held, That this grant did not convey any right of fishing, but merely a right to occupy a certain portion of the shore, and therefore that the defendant was not liable to an action for setting nets in front of the plaintiff's lot below low water mark, and thereby preventing the fish from entering the plaintiff's nets. *Hierlihy* v. *Loggie*, 3 *All.* 204.

2—The right of fishing in a public navigable river belongs to the public, and not to the owners of the lands bounded on the river. *Rose* v. *Belyea*, 1 *Han.* 100.

3—Weir—Erection of.
No action can be maintained for erecting a fish weir between high and low water mark in an arm of the sea, whereby fish, which otherwise would have been caught in the plaintiff's weir, were caught by the defendant. *Cheney* v. *Guptail, East. T.* 1871.

FISHING VESSEL.

See Foreign Fishing Vessel.

FIXTURES.

Landlord and Tenant—Agreement.
An agreement by a tenant of a shop, that if the landlord would make certain improvements, the tenant would put in gas fittings and leave them there when the lease expired, is executory only, and vests no property in the gas fittings in the landlord unless they are left by the tenant in the shop. If they are removed by the tenant before he leaves, the landlord cannot maintain trover for them. *Dunn* v. *Garrett*, 2 *All.* 218.

FORECLOSURE.

See Equity.
" Practice in Equity.
" Mortgage.

FOREIGN CORPORATION.

See Corporation.

FOREIGN FISHING VESSEL.

Defendant, an officer appointed by the Canadian Government for the protection of the Fisheries, seized a vessel belonging to the plaintiff in the harbour of Gaspe, in the Province of Quebec, on the 18th August, for an alleged breach of the Act relating to fishing by Foreign Vessels, (31 Vict. c. 61,) and on the 22nd August brought the vessel to the Port of Shediac, in the Province of New Brunswick, but did not deliver her to the Collector of Customs there. The Act directed that vessels seized should be "*forthwith* delivered to the Collector or other principal officer of Customs at the port *nearest* to the place where seized." There was a Collector of Customs at Gaspe, and at several other ports nearer than Shediac. No proceedings having been taken towards the condemnation of the vessel, the plaintiff replevied her on the 5th Sept. Held, per Ritchie, C. J., Allen and Weldon, J. J., That by taking the vessel to Shediac and retaining her there in his own possession the defendant became a trespasser *ab initio*, and that replevin would lie. Per Fisher and Wetmore, J. J., That by the seizure the vessel was in custody of the law, and therefore replevin would not lie. *McGowan* v. *Betts*, *East. T.* 1871.

FOREIGN GOODS.

See Custom Duties.

FOREIGN JUDGMENT.

See Judgment.

FOREIGN LAW.

1—Plaintiff became surety for the defendant in an administration bond in Massachusetts. On passing the defendant's accounts in the Probate Court there, a balance belonging to the estate was found to be in h[illegible], which he neglected to pay, w[illegible] ond became forfeited: the def[illegible] resigned the office of administrator, and the plaintiff was appointed administrator *de bonis non*. In an action in th[illegible] Province, for money paid by the plaintiff to the defendant's use, it was proved that by the law of Massachusetts the amount for which the plaintiff was liable as surety in the administration bond was considered as paid by him by operation of law on his appointment as administrator—he being thereby made liable for the amount—and that he could therefore maintain an action against his principal for money paid. Held, That such being the foreign law, the action was maintainable here. *Valentine* v. *Hazelton*, 1 *Han.* 110.

2—Foreign law is a question of fact, to be found by the jury, and not to be determined by the Judge; therefore, when the plaintiffs, in order to prove their right to sue, as Receivers of a Foreign Corporation, put in evidence the Statutes of New York, providing for the winding up of Insolvent Corporations and the appointment of Receivers by the Court of Chancery; and also proved by the evidence of a witness, that Insolvent Corporations were wound up, and Receivers appointed by the Supreme Court of the State, without any explanation to show that the Statute had been altered, and the jurisdiction taken away from the Court of Chancery; and no question was left to the jury as to what the foreign law was; a verdict for the plaintiff was set aside. *Osgood* v. *Hatch*, *Mich. T.* 1872.

The written law of a foreign country may be proved by a skilled witness, without the produc.ion of the law itself; but where it can be produced, it is more satisfactory than verbal testimony. *Osgood* v. *Hatch*, *Mich. T.* 1872.

FOREIGN PROBATE.

See Executors and Administrators.

FORFEITURE.

See Crown Grant.
" Custom House Entry.
" Justice of Peace (Conviction.)

FORGERY.

See Criminal Law.

FORMER RECOVERY.

See Action at Law VIII.
" Justice of the Peace V. 5.
" Landlord and Tenant VII. 5.

A verdict recovered without judgment signed cannot be pleaded in bar to an action between the same parties. *Gilbert* v. *Graham*, *East. T.* 1873.

When admissible in evidence in Replevin without being pleaded. See Evidence III. 17.

FORMER DECISION.

Reversal.

Where it appeared to the Court that a former decision was inconsistent with the right application of a clear and well established principle of law, it reversed the former decision without the intervention of a Court of Appeal. Allen, J., without differing from the rest of the Court as to the principle of law, thought that the Court having, in Calhoun's case, decided that persons were not disqualified from acting as commissioners by reason of being land owners, the Court was bound by that decision until reversed by a Court of Appeal.—*Regina* v. *Commissioners of Sewers, Germantown Lake*, 1 *Han.* 343.

FARMS.

See Justice of the Peace IV. V.
" Bond C.

FOUR DAY RULE.

See Error 5.

FRAUD.

Assignment of goods—Defeating execution—Bona Fides. See Assignment 1.

Goods claimed under previous assignment—Taking on execution bona fides. See Assignment 2.

Estate conveyed for fraudulent purpose—Trustee bound to convey—Avoidance by infant *cestui que* trust—Fraud a question for jury. See Infant 5.

Judgment on award — Setting aside for fraud. See Practice VI. 5.

Lease—Contravention of agreement—Cognisance. See Landlord and Tenant VI. 1.

Release—Surviving plaintiff setting aside for fraud. See Practice VI. 1.

False Declaration—Ownership of ship. See Shipping Law 6.

Trust deed—Creditors—Fraud. See Deed III.

Warrant of Attorney — Setting aside for fraud. See Warrant of Attorney.

Contesting receipt on ground of fraud—Attorney proceeding to trial after receipt given. See Receipt.

FRAUDS (STATUTE OF).

See Contract—Agreement—Guarantee.

1—Interest in land — License to cut timber.
A license to cut a quantity of timber within certain prescribed limits, *and to remove the same*, does not convey any interest in lands under the Statute of Frauds, or give any property in the standing trees. *Kerr* v. *Connell*, *Ber.* 133.

2—Delivery of goods—Acceptance.
A mere delivery of goods by the vendor without an actual acceptance by the vendee of some part thereof, is not sufficient within the Statute of Frauds. *Doley* v. *Marks*, *Ber.* 346.

The receipt of goods by a common carrier from the vendor, without any specific direction or authority from the vendee, will not amount to an acceptance by the vendee within the Statute. *Ibid.*

3—Justice's Court.
The Statute of Frauds is equally applicable to cases brought in the Justice's Courts, as to actions brought in other Courts. *McKeen* v. *Brown*, *East. T.* 1831.

4—Debt of third party.
B. applied to plaintiff to hire a horse and was refused, defendant then said to plaintiff "Let him have the horse and I'll be responsible if anything goes wrong." Plaintiff thereupon let B. have the horse and he injured him. Held, That such promise was within the Statute of Frauds, and not being in writing, defendant was not liable. *Hamm* v. *McAfee*, *Mich. T.* 1862.

FRAUDULENT CONVEYANCE.

See Deed.
" Ejectment II. 10.

FRAUDULENT REMOVAL.

See Distress.

FRAUDULENT REPRESENTATION.

See Warranty.

L., residing in St. John, drew bills of exchange on plaintiff at Liverpool, which he accepted for the accommodation of the defendants, who agreed to guarantee the payment of them at maturity: these bills would fall due on the 2nd Sept. 1868, on the 11th August L. drew other bills on the plaintiff, also for the defendants' accommodation. The plaintiff received L.'s letter advising the drawing of these bills, on the 24th August, and not having at that time received funds from the defendants to take up the bills falling due on the 2nd Sept., telegraphed to L. that unless those funds were sent he would not accept the bills drawn on the 11th August. At this time L. had become insolvent and left the Province, having assigned his property to trustees for the benefit of his creditors. The trustees received the plaintiff's telegram, and took it to the cashier of the Bank who knew that L. had absconded, and an answer was sent to the plaintiff by cable, in the name of L., stating that funds had been sent by the last mail, which was the fact. In consequence of this answer the plaintiff accepted the bills drawn on the 11th August, and was obliged to pay them, L. not having shipped cargoes of lumber as he had agreed. The telegram sent to the plaintiff was in the handwriting of one of L.'s trustees, but was sent to the telegraph office by the cashier of the Bank, and the cost of transmitting it charged to L. in the Bank books. The cashier swore that it was sent by direction of the President of the Bank, but he, and also the Directors, denied all knowledge of it till several months afterwards, and after the cashier had become a defaulter and absconded. Held, in an action against the Bank for falsely representing by the telegram that L. was in St. John, whereby plaintiff was induced to accept the bills, (per Allen and Fisher, J. J., Weldon, J. *dissentiente*,) That answering the telegram addressed to L. was not within the scope of the cashier's duties, and therefore that it should have been left to the jury to find whether the answer was sent by the authority of the Directors: and *quære*, whether the Stockholders would be liable even if the Directors had authorised it.

Per Weldon, J., That as the telegram to L. related to the payment of the bills of exchange in which the Bank was interested, the cashier had authority to answer it, and the defendants were liable for his false representation. *McKay* v. *The Commercial Bank*, *Hil. T.* 1872.

FRAUDULENT TRANSFER.

See Evidence I. 14.

FREDERICTON (CITY OF).

See Bye-Laws—Corporation—Costs—Justice of the Peace.

1—Offences—Trial—Justice of Peace of County not an Alderman—No right to sit with Mayor.

Under the Act 26 Vic. c 33, which requires all offences committed in Fredericton, and punishable by summary conviction, to be tried before the Mayor and an Alderman; a Justice of the Peace for the County, who is not an Alderman, has no jurisdiction to sit with the Mayor and try an assault. *Ex parte Hughey*, *Hil. T.* 1864.

2—Mayor—Jurisdiction.

The jurisdiction of the Mayor of Fredericton as a Justice of the Peace, under the Act 22 Vic. c. 8, s. 82, is limited to matters arising within the limits of the City; therefore, he has no right to sit in the Sessions of the County of York on the trial of a bastardy case arising outside of the city. *Reg.* v. *Carson*, *Trin. T.* 1864.

3—Right to vote—Assessment in each Ward.

A person assessed on property in several Wards of the City of Fredericton, has a right to vote in each Ward in which he is assessed, under the Act 22 Vic. c. 8, s. 17. The election for each Ward is a different election. *Ex parte Grieves*, *Hil. T.* 1864.

4—Contractor—Interest—Disqualification—Quo Warranto.

A contractor with the Commissioners of the Alms House for the County of York is disqualified from being elected a City Councillor in Fredericton, under the Act 22 Vic. c. 8; and a decision of the City Council in favour of the election, on complaint of an elector, under the 24th section of the Act, does not preclude the elector from applying for a *quo warranto* to try the right. *Ex parte Cameron*, 1 *Han.* 306.

When a person elected a City Councillor has entered upon, and is exercising the office, a *quo warranto* is the proper mode of trying his right to it. *Ibid.*

5—Complaint—Prosecution for engaging in occupation without license—Information.

A complaint against a party, under 26 Vic. c. 33, s. 2, for engaging in an occupation in the City of Fredericton, not being a rate-payer of the City or County, or licensed, should be prosecuted in the name of the City Treasurer. For the recovery of all fines and penalties under any Act relating to the municipal affairs of the City of Fredericton, the information should be laid by the City Treasurer, or by his authority; and a conviction therefor, founded on the information of a common informer, cannot be sustained. *Ex parte Eagles*, 2 *Han.* 51.

6—Mayor a ministerial officer—Refusal to swear in person properly returned.

The Mayor of Fredericton, in swearing in an Alderman elect, under the Act 22 Vic. c. 8, is merely a ministerial officer, and has no power to refuse to swear in a person properly returned by the presiding officer as duly elected; on the ground that he was (in the opinion of the Mayor) disqualified by law from being elected. *Ex parte Richards*, 2 *Han.* 131.

7—Quo Warranto—Discretion of Court in granting—Mayor—Collection of moneys by.

The granting a *quo warranto* being discretionary, it was refused, without costs, on an application against the Mayor of Fredericton, on the ground that he was disqualified from holding the office, by reason of his having improperly held money in his hands belonging to the City; no corrupt motive being charged against him, the amount being small, and the object of the relator in making the application, not free from suspicion. *Ex parte Torrens*, 2 *Han.* 196.

Semble, That the 8th section of the 22 Vic. c. 8, and the 2nd section of 32 Vic. c. 87, do not apply to moneys collected by the Mayor as fines imposed for violation of the City bye-laws. *Ibid.*

8—Sale of right to collect market tolls.

A sale by the Corporation of Fredericton of the right to collect market tolls for a year, is not illegal under the City Charter, 22 Vic. c. 8; and a bond given to the City by the purchaser for the amount of the purchase money may be enforced. Such sale, being a demise of the tolls, may be by parol, though tolls are incorporeal hereditaments. (Ritchie, J., *dissentiente.*) *City of Fredericton* v. *Mulligan*, *Trin. T.* 1863.

9—Bye-Laws—Authority—Public Landings—Wharfinger—Bond.

The charter of Fredericton authorizes the Corporation to make bye-laws to regulate the public landings in the City, though the title to the land is held by the Justices of the County. *Ex parte Mowry*, 3 *All.* 276.

A vessel lying at a private wharf in Fredericton, but extending beyond it, and partly across a public landing, is subject to the orders of the wharfinger of the City, and the master of the vessel is liable under the City bye-laws for disobeying such orders. *Ibid.*

By the 48th section of the Charter of Fredericton, "No person shall be capable of acting as wharfinger until he shall have entered into a bond to the City, with two sufficient sureties to be approved of by the City Council, in such form as the Mayor shall approve," &c. A Wharfinger was appointed in April, and gave a bond which was approved by the Mayor: Held, in a prosecution for disobeying the orders of the Wharfinger, That having performed the duties of the office for two months without objection, the approval of the bond by the City Council might be implied. *Ibid.*

Quære, Whether the giving or approval of a bond were necessary preliminaries to any legal act by the Wharfinger. *Ibid.*

The office of Wharfinger being annual, the liability of his sureties ceases at the end of the year for which he was appointed, and is not revived by his re-appointment. *Ex parte Mowry*, 3 *All.* 276.

10—Leasing land—Giving New Lease—Auction.

The Act 10 Vict. c. 7, empowering the Justices of York to lease certain lands at auction, provided that no lease should be made unless the upset price or rent should have been previously fixed by the Justices, and after such land should have been sold, or once offered for sale at public auction, after ten days notice. The right of the Justices having been transferred to the Corporation of Fredericton, they agreed to lease to A. who died before executing the lease, owing rent: the land was afterwards advertised to lease by auction, but before the sale the defendant agreed to take a lease on the same terms that A. held it, and pay the arrears of rent, for which he gave his promissory note. Held, That the Corporation had no authority to lease the land except by auction, and that the defendant was not liable on the note. *City of Fredericton* v. *Lucas*. 3 *All.* 583.

Semble, [per Parker, J.] That though the land had been *once* leased by auction, on the expiration of that lease the Corporation was bound to offer it again at public auction before giving a new lease. *Ibid.*

Power to Contract for building Market House. See Corporation 13.

FREIGHT.

Shipowners. See Lien.

FRIVOLOUS DEMURRER.

Power in Court to set aside. See *Petty* v. *Hammond*, 3 *Kerr* 684.

GENERAL ASSEMBLY.

Election of Members—Return of. See Election Law.

Powers—Privileges. See Arrest.

GENERAL ISSUE.

See Pleading II. 24, Evidence XIII.

GENERAL RULES.

See Appendix.

GERMANTOWN LAKE.

See Commissioners.

GIVING TIME.

See Bond II. 33.

GLEBE.

See Church of England.
" Corporation. Trespass I. 8.

GOOD FRIDAY.

See *Dies Non*.

GOODS SOLD.

See Assumpsit (c.)

GRAND JURY.

See Criminal Law.

GRANT.

See Crown Grant.

GRIEVOUS BODILY HARM.

See Criminal Law.

GUARANTEE.

I. CONSIDERATION.
II. OPERATION OF STATUTE OF FRAUDS.
III. CONSTRUCTION MUST BE STRICTLY PURSUED.
IV. PARTIE'S INTEREST—RIGHT TO SUE.

I.

CONSIDERATION.

Consideration not appearing by the agreement. See Pleading I. 6.

1—**Consideration not inferred from terms of guarantee.**
The plaintiff agreed to advance money to D. T., to enable him to get logs, on receiving security for the delivery of the logs: the defendant having agreed to become security, an agreement for the delivery of the logs by D. T., and payment thereof by the plaintiff was signed by them, and the defendant then wrote upon the agreement and signed the following memorandum: "I guarantee the performance of this contract on the part of D. T.;" and the agreement was then delivered to the plaintiff. Held, That no consideration for the defendant's promise could be inferred from the terms of the guarantee; and that the same rule would apply, whether the guarantee was written on the same paper with the agreement, or on a separate paper referring to it. *Aiton* v. *Bulloch*, 4 *All.* 321.

2—An agreement in writing was made between the plaintiff and one D., whereby the plaintiff was to deliver 600,000 feet merchantable spruce logs, at certain times and places, for a certain specified price per thousand; the logs to be surveyed by one W. A., by Emery's table; and at the foot of the agreement was the following memorandum, signed by the defendant at the same time that D. signed it: "I guarantee the above payments to John S. Taylor" (the plaintiff.) Held, That there was a sufficient consideration expressed by reference to the agreement. *Taylor* v. *Harris*, 2 *Kerr* 343.

Held also, That the whole of the 600,000 feet not having been delivered, and the survey of part of the logs which were delivered not having been made by W. A., the defendant was not liable on his guarantee. A surety is entitled to a strict performance of the contract which he guarantees, and any deviation made without his assent discharges him. *Ibid.*

3—A writing by defendant in the following words: "We guarantee that the wages due W. K. and G. N., from J. H., for making timber shall be satisfied when they bring the timber up, according to their own arrangements," shews a sufficient consideration of forbearance by W. K. and G. N. to sue for their wages till the timber was brought up. (See Act 23 Vic. c. 31.) *Neville* v. *Joseph*, *Hil. T.* 1832.

4—The rights of W. K. and G. N. for wages, being separate and distinct—Held, That each might sue separately on the guarantee. *Ibid.*

5—A guarantee in the following words:—"We hereby guarantee to you the payment of £50, by J. G., in three years from this date," shews a sufficient consideration on the face of it. *Johnston* v. *Fraser*, *Mich. T.* 1832.

II.

OPERATION OF STATUTE OF FRAUDS.

1—Where a bill of sale, by way of mortgage of certain cattle, was given by B. to A., which were to be delivered on a future day in case B. failed in payment of a promissory note, and a written collateral guarantee given by the defendant to A to secure such delivery: Held, That such guarantee not stating the consideration on which the same was made, is invalid under the statute of frauds. *Marks* v. *Scott*, 2 *Kerr* 638.

(See Act 23 Vict. c. 31.)

2—C. was getting timber for defendant under a contract, and being in want of hay, sent a message to him to that effect. Defendant said to the messenger "You can tell C., or any one that will supply him with hay, that I will accept C.'s order payable in the spring." This message was communicated to the plain tiff, who afterwards supplied C. with hay. Held, in an action for goods sold and delivered, That the defendant's undertaking was either collateral, to answer for C.'s debt, or an agreement to accept an order from C. for the value of the hay; and in either case the plaintiff could not recover. *Semble*, That it was a guarantee. *Cohrell* v. *Hatfield*, *Trin. T.* 1831.

III.

Construction must be strictly pursued.

1—Where the defendant undertook, in writing, that if the plaintiff would advance to one T. H. C. to the amount of £1000, he would guarantee that T. H. C. paid the plaintiff £500 in the month of July next; and the plaintiff advanced £281, and was ready to advance the remainder if T. H. C. would have received it. Held, That the defendant was not liable to any extent on his guarantee, as he only agreed to be responsible if the advances amounted to £1000. The contract of guarantee must be strictly construed. *Thorne* v. *Carman*, 2 *Kerr* 381.

2—**When an Absolute Contract.** The defendants entered into a written contract with T., by which he was to deliver them a quantity of lumber at a certain time. They afterwards agreed with the plaintiff to transfer to her the balance of lumber coming from T., for which they acknowledged to have received payment in full from the plaintiff, and guaranteed to see the lumber delivered at the time specified in the agreement with T. Held, That this was an absolute contract by the defendants to deliver the lumber, and not a guarantee that T. should deliver it, and that the plaintiff had nothing to do with T.'s contract except to ascertain the time of delivery. *Lindsay* v. *Rose*, 3 *Kerr* 576

3—**Contract—Delivery of Shingles—Quality—Liability.** In March 1871, P. agreed to sell and deliver to plaintiff all the sawed cedar shingles his mill manufactured during that season, to be paid for on delivery, at certain rates, according to quality. The plaintiff at the same time made an advance of $500 to P. on the contract, and the defendant agreed as follows: (all being written on the same paper,) "I guarantee to D. G. (plaintiff,) that on or before the 10th May next, P. will deliver to him sufficient sawed cedar shingles at the rate specified in the within contract, to make good to him the above advance of $500; he failing to do so, I hereby hold myself liable to said D. G. for the sum of $500, or such portion of said advance as may be due, it being understood that I am to get credit for whatever portion of shingles may be delivered by said P., supposing the amount does not come to $500." P. delivered a quantity of shingles, some under the contract, (but not to the amount of $500) and some of a different description and under a separate contract of which the defendant had no knowledge. Held, in an action on the guarantee, That the defendant was only entitled to credit for such shingles as P. had delivered of the description and quality described in his contract with the plaintiff, and not for *all* the shingles delivered; and that the plaintiff was not bound to give notice to the defendant that P. was not fulfilling his contract. *George* v. *Brayley*, *Hil. T.* 1873.

IV.

Partie's Interest in Guarantee—Right to Sue.

See Agreement 8.

A guarantee by one partner in the name of the firm for a matter not relating to the partnership business, will not bind the firm. *Marks* v. *Wright*, *Hil. T.* 1828.

See Supra. Neville *v.* Joseph I. 4.

GUARDIAN IN SOCAGE.

Widow holding possession for heir. See Possession 4.

GUNPOWDER.

See Revenue Act.

HABEAS CORPUS.

Proceedings issuing after *habeas corpus* to remove cause—Irregularity in writ of—Setting aside proceedings. See Practice VI. 46.

HALF BLOOD.

The half brothers and sisters of a person who dies intestate and without children, are not entitled to the whole real estate, under the Act of Assembly 26 Geo. 3, c. 11; but as "the next of kin" they are entitled to the remainder of the estate after the portion of the heir at law is deducted. *Doe* v. *Troughton*, 3 *All.* 414.

If no heir at law can be found, *quære*, in whom will this portion of the estate vest? *Ibid.*

The person entitled as heir by the common law, is not excluded under the Act, though he is not one of the next of kin to the intestate; neither are the next of kin prevented from taking the *remainder* because they are not in equal degree with the heir, but nearer in degree. *Ibid.*

HARBOUR MASTER.

Appointment of. See Appointment of Officer 1.

Recovery of Fees. See Assumpsit III. 33.

HEIR.

See Half Blood.

Widow holding for heir. See Possession 4.

Right of entry suspended until death of tenant by the Courtesy. See *Reed* v. *Burchill*, 2 *All.* 168.

HEIR AT LAW.

1—Intestate without children.
If A. die intestate and without children, leaving a brother and two sisters, the brother as heir at law will be entitled to a double portion or two-fourths of the real estate of A. in this Province, under the Act of Assembly 26 Geo. 3, c. 11, s. 12, and the sisters to one-fourth each. The words in the Act do not confine the double portion to the eldest son or lineal heir, but extend to collaterals. *Doe dem. Thompson* v. *Allanshaw*, 1 *Kerr* 84.

2—Advancement.
Under the Act of Assembly 26 Geo. 3, c. 11, the eldest son and heir at law of an intestate must bring into hotchpot his advancement of the realty, as well as the younger children, if he seek a portion of the real estate left by the father. He will be entitled to two shares or a double portion of the aggregate of what has been advanced and left—per Botsford [illegible] and Parker, Justices; Chipman [illegible] *dissentiente*. *Doe dem. Shore* v. *Saunders*, 2 *Kerr* 18.

3—Next of Kindred.
If a person dies intestate and without children, leaving a mother and brother and sisters, the brother and sisters are entitled to his real estate under the Act of Assembly 26 Geo. 3, c. 11, s. 12, as "the next of kindred in equal degree," to the exclusion of the mother. *Doe d. Mahoney* v. *Crane*, 3 *Kerr* 228.

The eldest brother is entitled to a double share, as heir at law. *Ibid.*

(See Half Blood.)

HIGHWAYS.

(See Justice of the Peace.)

1—Saint John Highway Act—Confirming roads—Obstructions—Non-user.
The Saint John Highway Act 50 Geo. 3, c. 16, s. 3, confirms all highways used as such, to the extent and width to which they were originally laid out; and a party is liable for placing an obstruction within the limits of the road as laid out, though that part of it has never been used as a road by the public. *Rex* v. *Bennett*, *Mich. T.* 1825.

2—Road through private property—User.
A road through private property (parallel to a public road, as laid out and recorded but opened through the whole distance), is not deemed a highway, nor dedicated to the public, though it had been used for twelve years by persons having occasion to travel in the direction to which the public road extended. *Rex* v. *Vail*, *Mich. T.* 1826.

3—Presence of Justices at assessment.
The Justices who issue the warrant to summon a jury to lay out a private road, under the Act 50 Geo. 3, c. 6, s. 12, must be present at the assessment of the damages. *Pitt* v. *Lawson*, *Hil. T.* 1827.

4—Corporation of St. John—Obligation—Indictment.
The Corporation of St. John being bound by public law to repair the highways in the City, it is not necessary, in an indictment for not repairing, to set forth the particular ground of the obligation. *Rex v. the Mayor &c. of St. John, Hil. T.* 1828.

5—Proceeding for alteration of road.
A proceeding under the Act 50 Geo. 3, c. 6, to obtain an alteration of a road, must be a continuous proceeding; therefore, if a proceeding on one application fails, there must be a new application of freeholders for a warrant to summon another jury. *Rex v. White, Commissioner of Waterborough, East. T.* 1831.

6—Laying out—Return of Commissioners not evidence of.
A road must be laid out before it is recorded: the return of the Commissioners of Highways is not evidence of the laying out of a road under the Act 50 Geo. 3, c. 6. *Rex v. Sterling, Ber.* 22.

7—Neglect of Commissioners to file return—Laying out not invalid thereby.
The laying out of a public highway by Commissioners, under the Act 5 Wm. 4, c. 2, does not become invalid by the neglect of the Commissioners to file a return of the laying out with the Clerk of the Peace, as directed by the Act. *Brown v. McKeel,* 1 *Kerr* 311.

8—Trespass—Justification—Width of Road.
The defendant in trespass pleaded that the *locus in quo* had been laid out and recorded as a public road, three rods wide. Held, No justification; the Act requiring that no public highway should be laid out of less width than four rods. *Perlee v. Dibblee,* 1 *Kerr* 514.

9—Conviction—Obstruction—Place.
A conviction for obstructing a highway, is bad, unless it appears on the face of it that the place where the alleged obstruction took place was a public highway. *Reg. v. Brittain,* 2 *Kerr* 614.

10—Certainty of description—Laying out.
The record of a road laid out by Commissioners under the Act 5 Wm. 4, cap. 2, should so describe the road that a person going on the land with the return, may be able to ascertain and trace the road; and if the return does not point out the width of the road, or if it does not appear whether the line described is to be the centre, or the side of the road, it is defective. *Boyaington v. Holmes,* 3 *Kerr* 74.

Semble, That making one line on the ground may be a sufficient laying out, if it appears how the width of the road is to be formed in reference to such line. *Ibid.*

11 — Intended alteration — Objecting Parties—Notice.
Where the proceedings of Commissioners in altering a road under the Act 5 Wm. 4, c. 2 were objected to, whereupon the inhabitants applied to two Justices to obtain a warrant for a jury. Held, That no notice was necessary to be given to the objecting parties of the time and place of the jury's meeting to inquire into the intended alterations. *Reg v. Commissioners of Highways for Johnston,* 3 *Kerr* 583.

12—Justice Presiding—Relationship—Summoning Jury—Parish.
It does not render a Justice incompetent to preside at an inquest of a jury summoned under the Highway Act, that he is married to a sister of the party applying for an alteration of the road: nor is it necessary that the jury should be summoned from a different Parish from that in which the alteration is to be made. *Ibid.*

13—Dedication—User.
Dedication of a road to the public may be presumed from long uses and the expenditure of statute labor on the road; and a party may be convicted under the Act 5 Wm. 4, c. 2. for encroaching on such a road, as upon a highway duly laid out under the Act. *Reg. v. Buchanan,* 3 *Kerr* 674.

14—Title to Land—Justice of Peace—Trial.
If in a prosecution before a Justice of the Peace, under the Act 5 Wm. 4, c. 2, for obstructing a highway, the title of land comes in question, it must be gone into by the Justice if he entertains the suit. *Ibid.*

15 — Removal of Fence — Commissioner's Duty.
If a road is laid out over land on which a fence is standing it is the duty of the Commissioner of Highways to move the fence, and the owner of the land, omitting to do so, is not punishable under the Act

5 Wm. 4, c. 2, for obstructing the highway. *Ex parte Morrison*, 1 *All.* 203.

16—Dedication—Evidence.
A public highway may be established in this country by dedication and user; but if the question arises between the public and the owner of the land in a newly settled part of the country, stronger evidence may be required than in a more populous neighborhood. *Reg.* v. *Deane*, 2 *All.* 233.

17 — Crown Reservation — Right—Evidence.
Land was granted to the Corporation of St. John in 1785, reserving a right to the Crown to enter at any time and erect barracks, batteries, &c. Held, 1st. That this did not prevent the Corporation from dedicating a part of the land to the public for a highway; 2nd. That neither the running of lines across the land by officers of the Royal Engineers in 1816 and 1818, without proof of their instructions, nor the subsequent erection of a gate across the road by the military authorities, and occasionally closing the same, was sufficient evidence of the exercise of the reservation to vest the exclusive right to the land in the Crown, the road having from that period been constantly used by the public, and by the Military only as a road. *Ibid.*

18—Record—Certainty—Entry of Commissioner or Surveyor.
The record of the laying out of a road under the Highway Act 12 Vict. c. 4, should state the width and courses of the road; and if defective in these particulars, it will not justify the Commissioner and Surveyor of roads in entering on land to open a road. *Basterache* v. *Atkinson*, 2 *All.* 439.

19—Expenditure of Public Money—Extent.
The expenditure of public money on a road laid out thirty feet wide, can only make it a public highway to that extent, and will not have the effect of making it a highway four rods wide. *Ibid.*

20—Assessment of damages—When made—Instance of owner.
The assessment of damages to a person through whose improved land a public road is laid out under the Act 13 Vic. c. 4, need not be made concurrently with the laying out, but may be subsequent to it. If made before the road is laid out, it is a nullity. It should be made at the instance of the owner of the land, and not of a person applying for the road. *Ex parte Hebert*, 3 *All.* 108.

21—Warrant to summon Jury—Direction—Delivery.
The warrant to summon a jury should either be directed to a particular constable, or, if generally, "to any constable," should be delivered by the Justice who issues it to some particular constable to execute, and not left with the party applying for the jury to select a constable. *Ibid.*

22—Assessment on view.
The jury may assess the damages on view of the land, without examining witnesses, if none are produced. *Ibid.*

23—Levy of Damages.
The Sessions cannot order the damages assessed by the jury to be levied upon the inhabitants of part of a Parish unless the Commissioners recommend it. If the Commissioners recommend the assessment to be levied on a certain district, under sec. 9 of the Act, they must name the persons to be assessed, and must include all the resident rateable inhabitants within the district. *Ibid.*

24—Return to Sessions.
Semble, That the Commissioners may amend their return to the Sessions before an order made to levy the assessment. *Ibid.*

25—Assessment set aside—Application de novo.
If an assessment is set aside for irregularity in the proceedings, the owner of the land may apply for a warrant and assessment *de novo*. *Ibid.*

26—Damages—Value of Land—Keeping up fences.
In assessing damages under the Highway Act, to the owner of improved land in consequence of a public road being laid out through it, the jury are not confined to the value of the land, but may take into consideration the expense of keeping up fences. *Reg.* v. *Justices of Kent*, 3 *All.* 118.

27—Excessive Damages—Refusal to set aside.
Where the quantity of land taken was two acres, and the jury awarded the owners £75 damages, the Court refused to set aside the award, though it was sworn the land was not worth more than £5 per acre, and that some of the jurors had stated they gave the high damages to prevent the road being opened. *Ibid.*

28—Order of Sessions—Levy—Damages.

Where the jury recommended that the damages should be levied upon a certain part of the Parish in which the road was, and the Commissioners sent the assessment to the Sessions, requesting that it might be "dealt with according to law," but not stating their opinion that the road was only for the convenience of a portion of the Parish: Held, That the Sessions were warranted in ordering the amount to be levied on the whole Parish. *Ibid.*

29—Recommendation of Commissioners not binding on Justices.

The Justices are not bound by a recommendation of the Commissioners that the damages should be assessed upon a certain district. If they disagree with the Commissioners, *quære*, whether they have power to assess the whole Parish. An order of the Justices to assess the amount of damages awarded by a jury, is a sufficient order for the payment. *Ibid.*

30—Dedication of Crown.

To establish a highway by dedication of the Crown, the particular land must be expressly reserved in a grant from the Crown, or be defined in the plan of a grant containing a reservation of roads. *Cole* v. *Maxwell*, 3 *All.* 183.

In the absence of any evidence of a plan attached to an ancient grant of land "*with allowance for roads*" by which a particular part of the land is dedicated as a highway, and without any use of such road by the public, a dedication by the Crown will not be presumed, though several of the old proprietors of lots in the grant spoke of a *planned road* over the land, and one of them caused the lines of the supposed road to be marked on his land about 40 years before the trial. *Ibid.*

The declaration of the owner of the land that there was a road through it, without any proof of use or of the locality of the road, does not amount to a dedication of it to the public. *Ibid.*

In trespass to land and ploughing up the soil, defendant pleaded that there was a public highway over the land, by reason whereof he entered. Held, That if it was a highway, ploughing up the soil was not justified. *Ibid.*

31—Recording as laid out—Commissioner's duty.

When Commissioners of Highways have laid out a road, it is their duty to record it as laid out. They have no right to abandon a part of it, and make a return of the other part. *Ex parte Weade*, 3 *All.* 307.

32—Shutting up road—Necessary return before.

To justify the shutting up a highway under the 1 Rev. Stat. c. 66, the return of the Commissioners must show, either expressly or by necessary implication, that the road is not required for the convenience of the inhabitants of the parish. The words "not required for the inhabitants," and "not required for the convenience of the inhabitants" are not identical in meaning. *Oulton* v *Carter*, 4 *All.* 169.

River—Obstructing use of as highway. See Action on the Case IV. 1.

Erection of dam in public stream—Destruction of same by persons not injured—Injunction to restrain. See Water Course.

HIRING.

A person who hires a horse to perform a journey, is not liable for the value of the horse if he dies on the road, without the fault of the hirer; and *quære*, whether in such case, where the hiring was not by the day, the owner of the horse could recover on the *quantum meruit* for the time the defendant used the horse. *Dickie* v. *Campbell*, *Hil. T.* 1827.

HOMICIDE.

See Criminal Law.

HORSE.

See Hiring—Warranty.

HORSE RACE.

Money deposited upon — Stakeholder — Right to recovery back of deposit. See Action at Law I. 3.

A deposit of money with a stakeholder in this Province to abide the result of a horse race in Nova Scotia, is not an illegal transaction under the Revised Statutes, and may be recovered back, if the race is not run. See *Kenney* v. *Stubbs*, 4 *All.* 126.

HOUSE OF ASSEMBLY.

See General Assembly.
" Arrest (Privilege from.)

HUSBAND AND WIFE.

I. Actions by and against.
II. Necessaries.
III. Separate Property of Wife. (Liability of, to Execution.)
IV. Miscellaneous.

I.

Actions by and against.

1—**Release of action by husband.**
The husband may release an action brought in the name of himself and his wife, to recover a debt due to the wife before marriage, though she is living separate from him, and the action is brought for her benefit, and no consideration was paid for the release. *McLellan* v. *Cougle*, 4 *All.* 237.

2 — **Abatement of Action — Death of Husband.**
An action brought by husband and wife to recover money had and received to the use of the wife, does not abate by the death of the husband. *Harrington* v. *McMonamin*, 4 *All.* 599.

3 — **Action by wife alone — Husband insane.**
A married woman, whose husband is insane and confined in a Lunatic Asylum, and who is compelled to support herself by keeping a boarding house, may sue and recover in her own name, the amount due from a boarder lodging in the house after her husband's insanity, under the Rev. Stat. c. 114, s. 3.

The amount due from a boarder under such circumstances, vests in the wife as her separate property, and will not pass to the husband's representatives on his death. *Abell* v. *Light*, 1 *Han.* 97.

4 — **Legacy — Husband maintaining action as representative of wife.**
If a legacy is bequeathed to a married woman, who dies before any act done by her husband to reduce it into possession, he can only maintain an action for it as the representative of his wife, though he may be beneficially entitled to it. *Collins* v. *Cahir*, 2 *All.* 103.

5 — **Rent — Tenant dying, leaving a widow—Continuance of possession by second husband — Non-joinder of wife.**
A tenant died in possession of premises, leaving a widow. Held, That the defendant, who had married the widow and continued in the occupation of the premises, was liable for rent during his occupancy, and that the wife need not be joined in the action as a co-defendant. *Matthew* v. *Chittick*, 2 *Kerr* 696.

6—**Action for Dower.**
A widow cannot maintain an action at law for dower in land, in which her husband had only an equity of redemption during the coverture, even though the husband's right has been sold since his death, and purchased by the defendant, expressly subject to the right of dower; or, though the mortgage may have been paid, if it is not discharged on the records. *Doe* v. *Estabrooks*, 4 *All.* 455.

II.

Necessaries.

7—**Liability of husband for.**
The defendant turned away his wife without cause, and afterwards offered to take her back and provide for her, but she refused to return. The jury were directed that this offer did not relieve the defendant from liability to a third person, who had afterwards supplied the wife with necessaries. Held, per Wilmot, J., and Ritchie, J., (Parker, J., *hesitante*, and N. Parker, M. R., *dissentiente*), A misdirection; and that the question for the jury should have been, whether the defendant made a *bona fide* request to his wife to return, and if so, whether she had refused on a well-founded belief that his ill-treatment to her would be renewed. Held also, That the liability of the husband depended upon the implied authority of the wife, as his agent, to bind him; and that when the necessity for the authority ceased, her right to bind him ceased also. Held, per N. Parker, M. R., That a husband who wrongfully turns away his wife, continues liable at law for her support, except in case of her misconduct; and that the question whether she was bound to return to his home on his offer to take her back, could only be determined in the Spiritual Court, in a suit for the restitution of conjugal rights. *Bennett* v. *Jones*, 4 *All.* 307.

III.

Separate Property of Wife.

8—Land was conveyed to a married woman,

for life, for her separate use; it was managed under her directions, and the labor paid for by the produce of the land, the husband not interfering except as her agent. Held, 1st. That under the Rev. Stat. c. 114, the crop, when severed, did not become the property of the husband, and was not liable to seizure under an execution against him. 2nd. That an action for seizing the crop, under execution against the husband, was rightly brought in the name of husband and wife. *Dow and Wife* v. *Dibblee*, 1 *Han.* 55.

9—When a husband and wife reside on land of which the wife has the fee, the husband is tenant by the courtesy, and the crops raised by his labour and the labour of his servants and children, are his and liable to seizure for his debts, and the Sheriff may enter to make a levy. In the absence of title, the possession is the possession of the husband. *Pourrier and wife* v. *Raymond*, 1 *Han.* 512.

IV.

MISCELLANEOUS.

Infant subsequently married — Right of entry of husband. See Limitation of Actions IV. 16.

Mesne profits—Judgment against wife before marriage—No averment of marriage.

An action for *mesne* profits against husband and wife alleging a joint trespass, is not supported by proof of a judgment in ejectment against the wife before marriage—the marriage not being averred. *Burnham* v. *Watts*, 1 *All.* 89.

Costs—Attachment against married woman. See Attachment 27.

Deed—Joinder by wife. See Deed I. 27.

Partition — Infancy — Long acquiescence. See Partition.

Decree barring right of dower of wife. See Divorce.

Tenant by Courtesy. See

Property passing to husband's representatives. See Supra, *Abell* v. *Light*.

Wife not competent to submit by bond to arbitration. See Arbitration, &c., V. 4.

Delivery of note to wife by husband—Delivery of box. See *Donatio Mortis Causa*.

IDENTITY.

See Name.

Identity of person—Two surveyors of lumber same name—Left to jury to decide upon the evidence which of the two was intended. Rankin *v.* Emery, Ber. 330.

Identity of defendant with person named in note—Sufficiency of evidence. See Bills and Notes V. 16.

Trespass—False imprisonment—Not shewn that party was commonly known by name by which he was arrested. See Pleading II. 20.

Judgment — Action on — Averment that the defendant and person named are the same, sufficient. See Pleading I. 28.

Alias description — Sufficiency of proof. See Pleading I. 57.

Judgment—Action on—*Quære*, As to sufficiency of name of defendant, with person named in judgment. See Evidence II. 29.

Arrest — Insufficiency of affidavit to discharge defendant for arrest under mistaken name. See Affidavit III. 5.

Replevin—Mistake in name of party claiming property. See Replevin 21.

Identity of Commissioner taking deposition. See Evidence IX.

ILLEGITIMATE CHILD.

Liability of father for support of.

The father of an illegitimate child is not liable to a third person for the expense of supporting such child, unless it has been incurred upon his authority; or he has contracted to pay for it. *Forrest* v. *McRea*, 2 *Kerr* 174.

Grandson — Legitimate and Illegitimate Child—Same name—Devise—Operation. See Will 2.

IMPERIAL STATUTES.

See British Statutes.

IMPLIED CONTRACT.

See Contract.

INCUMBRANCE.

Registered Memorial of judgment against vendor is evidence of incumbrance on his land. See Lien.

Purchaser of land entitled to land free from incumbrance. See Vendor and Purchaser.

Registry of Mortgage not a notice of an incumbrance to a subsequent purchaser. See Doe v. Power, 1 All. 271.

INDEMNITY.

Master and owner of ship—Risks—Implied contract to indemnify—Negligence. See Principal and Agent 22.

INDICTMENT.

See Criminal Law.

INDORSEMENT.

See Bills and Notes.

INDUCTION.

See Trespass I. 8.

INFANT.

1—Promissory Note.
The promissory note of an infant is voidable only, and he may confirm it after he comes of age. *Fisher* v. *Jewett*, *Ber.* 35.

2—Deed—Voidable.
The deed of an infant is voidable only; and the infancy cannot be given in evidence to invalidate the deed, in a suit between third parties. *Donohoe* v. *Hallett*, *Trin. T.* 1828.

3—Avoidance by heirs.
The conveyance of an infant is voidable only, and may be confirmed after he comes of age; but if he dies soon after coming of age, having done no act to confirm the deed, his heirs may avoid it. *Doe d. Foster* v. *Lee*, *Mich. T.* 1871.

4—Covenant not to trade.
A covenant by an infant in an indenture of apprenticeship, that he will not carry on a trade within certain limits, is not binding on him. *Reg.* v. *Harris*, 1 *All.* 100.

5—Conveyance to infant—Fraudulent intent—Subsequent conveyance by grantor and infant.
Land was conveyed to an infant by direction of his father for the purpose of defrauding the father's creditors, the father having afterwards been arrested by the creditors, he and his son joined in a mortgage of the land to secure the debt. Held, That the mortgage was good; that the infant being only a trustee for his father was bound to convey the land as he directed; and that neither of them could set up the infancy to defeat the mortgage. *Doe dem Diffin* v. *Simpson*, 3 *Kerr* 194.

6—Scire Facias on judgment—Infant not served.
Judgment by default was signed against A. and B. on a joint and several promissory note. B. was not served with process, and on a *scire facias* against him, under the Act 26 Geo. 3, c. 24, to obtain execution on judgment, proceedings were stayed—it appearing that at the date of the note he was an infant, and had not authorised A. to sign the note for him, and had no knowledge before the judgment of its having been done. Neither the fact of the note having been given for a balance due the plaintiff on a lumber transaction, in which A. and B. were jointly concerned; nor of B.'s having offered after coming of age to compromise and pay a portion of the debt, will deprive him of his right to relief. *Mitchell* v. *Astle*, 2 *Kerr* 86.

Right of entry accruing to female infant—Marriage—Action not brought within time. See Limitation of Actions IV. 16.

Infancy no bar to enforcing contract. See Contract 14.

Infant apprentice—Conviction. See Apprentice.

INFERIOR COURTS.

Taxing Costs by Clerk of Supreme Court. See Costs 75.

Mandamus to try Cause. See Mandamus 2.

Mandamus refused to compel Court of Common Pleas to award costs. See Mandamus 7.

Mandamus refused to compel Magistrate to proceed in a criminal cause at suit of private prosecutor. See Mandamus.

Prohibition to restrain action brought against Clerk of the Circuits for recovery of fine imposed. See Prohibition.

Removal of Cause—Issue of Writ of Error. See Error (Writ of.)

The Inferior Courts of Common Pleas have no power to grant new trials, and a mandamus will issue to compel them to enter judgment for a party in whose favor a verdict has been given in that Court. *Rex* v. *Justices of Northumberland*, *Hil. T.* 1826.

The Inferior Courts of Common Pleas are

Courts of Record in regard to summary actions, as well as other actions. *Wheeler* v. *Grant*, *Mich. T.* 1832.

INFORMATION.

See Justice of the Peace.
" Criminal Law.
" Crown Grant I. 18.

1—An information of debt, filed by the Attorney General, is sufficient, though it is stated to be on the relation of the Deputy Treasurer: if such allegation is unnecessary, it might be rejected as surplusage. *Attorney General* v. *Patterson*, *East. T.* 1826.

2—An information, alleging the offence to be the importing goods into the Province from the United States, contrary to the Acts of Assembly, does not state any offence against the Act 6 Wm. 4, c. 4, which declares a forfeiture of all goods *landed* before they are reported at the Treasurer's office, and a permit obtained. The "*importing*" goods, and "*landing*" them, are distinct acts. *Attorney General* v. 250 *Barrels of Fish*, *Ber.* 419.

INJUNCTION.

See Practice in Equity—Equity.

INNKEEPER.

Prohibition as to selling liquor on credit.

The prohibition in the Act 17 Vic. c. 15, s. 13, against selling liquor on credit, only applies to innkeepers and tavern keepers. *McAuley* v. *Lawlor*, 4 *All.* 600.

See Boarding House Keeper.

INNUENDO.

See Defamation—Pleading.

INQUEST OF OFFICE.

See Crown Grant I. 18.
" Licence.
" Intrusion.

INQUIRY (WRIT OF.)

See Practice X.

INROLLMENT.

Statute of Inrollments is in force in this Province. See British Statutes.

INSOLVENT ACT OF 1869.

1—County Court Judge—Hearing petition.

The County Court Judge of the County in which the demand on the debtor to assign is made, is the proper party to hear the petition, although the debtor may reside and do business in another County. See *Ex parte Thomas*, 2 *Han.* 163.

Removal of proceedings had before Judge of County Court not allowed. See *Certiorari* I. 5.

2—Creditor—Debt not matured.

A creditor whose debt has not matured may take proceedings to subject the estate of his debtor to compulsory liquidation under the Act, section 20. *In re Perks*, 2 *Han.* 121.

3—Property—Third party—Claim—Attachment.

If property claimed by a third person has been attached as the property of an insolvent, under a warrant issued under the 20th section of "The Insolvent Act of 1869," such person has no right to apply, under section 50, to set aside the attachment, or to have the property restored to him by the assignee: he must resort to his common law remedy. *Clementson* v. *Hammond*, *East. T.* 1871.

A third party cannot object to the regularity of the proceedings taken against a debtor under the Insolvent Act of 1869. *Ibid.*

4—Execution—Setting aside—Right of Insolvent.

Plaintiff, a judgment creditor of defendant, proved his claim before the assignee under the Insolvent Act; afterwards, and before defendant obtained his discharge, the plaintiff issued execution on his judgment, and levied upon property which the insolvent had not included in his schedule of assets. Held, That whether the property belonged to the defendant at the time of his insolvency, or was the property of a third person, he had no right to apply to set aside the execution, as in either case, he could have no right to it. *Jones* v. *DesBrisay*, *Trin. T.* 1871.

5—Where proceedings for compulsory liquidation are taken under "The Insolvent Act of 1869," and an attachment is issued, money which has been levied by the Sheriff under an execution against the debtor, but which has not been paid over to the

Judgment creditor, passes to the assignee, under the 59th section of the Act. *Bullen* v. *Harding*, *Mich. T.* 1871.

6—Compulsory liquidation—No petition presented—Proceedings.
M., a creditor of defendant, made a demand upon him to assign his estate, for the benefit of his creditors, under the 14th section of "The Insolvent Act of 1869." No petition against this demand was presented within five days, as required by the Act, but after that time the defendant settled his debt with M., who took no further proceedings. Held, That the estate of the defendant was nevertheless subject to compulsory liquidation, and that the demand of M. enured to the benefit of the other creditors of the defendant. *Dever* v. *Morris*, *Hil. T.* 1872.

7—Sections 92 and 93—Quasi penal.
The 92nd and 93rd Sections of "The Insolvent act of 1869" being *quasi* penal, are to be strictly construed, and to warrant imprisonment under their provisions the case must be brought within the express words of the Act. *Jones* v. *Bigeau*, *East. T.* 1873.

8—Offer to suffer judgment—Effect.
In an action on a promissory note made by the defendant in favor of the plaintiff, the declaration alleged fraud and false pretences in obtaining credit according to the 92nd section of the Act, the defendant pleaded the general issue and gave a notice of defence denying the alleged fraud; he also filed an offer under the Act 18 Vict. c. 9, to suffer judgment by default for the amount of the note, which offer the plaintiff accepted. Held, That this was not such a judgment by default as was contemplated by the 93rd section of the Act; the acceptance of the defendant's offer having settled all the issues in the suit, and therefore no order for imprisonment could be made. *Ibid.*

INSOLVENT CONFINED DEBTOR.

Application for Relief — Discharge — Refusal.

Discretionary power in Court — County Court Judge.

Order — Non-compliance with — Notice— Execution after discharge — Legal payment—Certiorari.

Costs—Miscellaneous.

See Insolvent Act of 1869.

1—Application for relief—Accounting for property.
An affidavit for relief under 1 Wm. 4, c. 43, must account for all the property the defendant may appear to have possessed. Applications for relief may be made in the suit, or may be considered as distinct judicial proceedings. *Wilmot* v. *Cornwell and Babine*, *Ber.* 31.

2—Confinement—Time.
To entitle a debtor to a discharge on the ground of having been confined for a year, it must explicitly appear that he has been in confinement for the whole time in the suit to which the application refers. *Ex parte Hennigar*, *Ber.* 209.

3—Accounting for property—Voluntary disposition.
A confined debtor, applying to be discharged under the Act 6 Wm. 4, c. 41, s. 4, must account fairly and fully for any property of which he may have been in possession at the time of commencing the action, and relief will not be granted if his inability to discharge the debt arises from a voluntary disposition of his property made pending the action, the value of which is not properly accounted for. *Wyer* v. *Goss*, 1 *Kerr* 193.

4—Assignment of property—Deed—Production.
Where a person who has assigned his property to trustees for the benefit of his creditors, applies for discharge under the Insolvent Debtors' Act, a copy of the trust deed must be brought before the Court. *McFarlane* v. *Gordon*, 2 *All.* 162.

5—Assignment—Offer—Notice.
Where a confined debtor, possessed of property, has not offered to assign it to the plaintiffs, at whose suit he is in custody, in the manner directed by the Act 13 Vic. c. 31, he must clearly shew that such deviation has not been made with any unfair object, before he can claim the assistance of the Court. An assignment of property by a confined debtor to a third party, without notice to the execution creditor, in trust for the benefit of such of his creditors as shall execute the trust deed, within two months from its date and release him, is an undue preference within the meaning of the Act. *Charlotte County Bank* v. *Williams*, 2 *All.* 183.

5 *a*—An assignment by an insolvent confined debtor in trust for the benefit of

such of his creditors as should execute the deed within a limited time, and release him from his debts, is *prima facie* an objection to his being discharged from confinement under the tenth section of the Act 13 Vic. c. 31; but where a debtor had no means of paying his debts, nor any interest in the property assigned, and had been a prisoner twenty months, the Court discharged him. *Charlotte County Bank* v. *Williams*, 2 *All.* 258.

6—**Variance—Deed—Consideration.**
Where an insolvent debtor having been confined more than a year, applied to the Court for relief, and in setting forth the sum he had received for a lot of land, there appeared a variance of £50 between the price alleged by him and the consideration expressed in the deed of conveyance. Held, That this circumstance, unexplained, was a sufficient ground for refusing the application. *Ex parte Goss*, 1 *Kerr* 164.

7—**Conveyance to Son.**
Between the signing of the judgment and issuing the execution, the defendant conveyed his land to his son, who gave a bond to support the defendant for life; the Court refused to discharge him under the Insolvent Debtors' Act, though he had been in custody over twelve months, and though the land had since been sold by the Sheriff under an execution against the defendant; it not appearing that the son had lost the possession of the land, or that the bond was not still in force. *Kelly* v. *Wilson*, 1 *All.* 375.

8—Where an insolvent debtor had conveyed his property to trustees for the benefit of such of his creditors as should execute the deed within two months and release him, the Court refused to discharge him out of custody—no satisfactory account being given of the amount of property received by the trustees. *McFarlane* v. *Gordon*, 2 *All.* 201.

9—It is no answer to an application for discharge by a debtor who has received the weekly allowance for six months under the Insolvent Confined Debtors' Act (1 Rev. Stat. c. 124), that he has the means of supporting himself; that is a ground for suspending the order for support, under the 8th section of the Act. *DesBrisay* v. *Mooney*, *Hil. T.* 1861.

10—Defendant having been arrested on *mesne* process, applied for support under the Insolvent Confined Debtors' Act (1 Rev. Stat. c. 124), and was refused: he afterwards entered special bail, and judgment having been signed in the suit, and a *ca. sa.* issued, he was again arrested, and remained on the limits for upwards of six months. Held, That an application to two Justices for support was necessary after the second arrest, before the Court could relieve him under the 9th section of the Act. [By Act 26 Vic. c. 10, application is to be made to a Judge of the Supreme Court.] *Small* v. *Coleman*, *Hil. T.* 1861.

11—**Power in Court to discharge—Confinement for year.**
The Court is empowered to discharge an insolvent confined debtor after he has been a year in prison, although he may not have applied for weekly support. An objection to the discharge, on the ground that such an application has not been made, must come from the creditor; otherwise the Court will not notice it. *Fairbanks* v. *Dolby*, 2 *Kerr* 80.

12—**Discretionary power—Preference without fraud.**
The Supreme Court has a discretionary power to discharge an insolvent debtor under the Act 6 Wm. 4, c. 41, and will exercise such discretion where the debtor has not acted fraudulently, though he has given a preference to creditors which would prevent his discharge by two Justices under the second section of the Act. *Barker* v. *Bois*, 1 *All.* 722.

13—**Quashing order of Justices.**
Where Justices make an order for support under the Insolvent Debtors' Act—(1 Rev. Stat. c. 124,)—and it appears by the examination of the debtor that he has given an undue preference to one of his creditors—this Court has power to quash the order. *McDonald* v. *Watt*, 1 *Han.* 24.

14—County Court Judge has power to discharge debtor in any county within his district, or to bring debtor from any county within his district, and possesses same power as Supreme Court Judge to discharge. *Ex parte Jardine*, 1 *Han.* 572.

15—**Order—Justices—Discharge for non-payment.**
An order for discharge for non-payment of weekly allowance, under the Insolvent Debtors' Act, 1 Rev. Stat. c. 124, need not be made by the same Justices that made the order for support. Parker, J.

and Ritchie, J., *dissentientibus*. *Jones* v. *Fletcher*, 4 *All.* 550.

16—Notice of order.
Where the creditor's attorney was in Court, and heard the order for support made, notice of it is not required. *Ex parte Jardine*, 1 *Han.* 572.

17—Execution after discharge.
Where an Insolvent Debtor had been discharged under the 1 Rev. Stat. c. 124, the Court refused to allow a new execution to issue against him, though the weekly allowance had been tendered to the gaoler of the county upon the limits of which he was confined, and at the house where he lodged. *Doe* v. *Holmes*, 4 *Kerr* 557.

Semble, That if the order for discharge had been irregularly obtained, it should be set aside before any proceedings are taken against the Debtor. *Ibid.*

See Act of Assembly 23 Vic. c. 28, authorizing payment to gaoler at gaol.

18—Legal payment.
Payment of the weekly allowance to a confined debtor may be made in coins which are not a legal tender, if not objected to. *Hatheway* v. *Day*, 4 *All.* 595.

19—Certiorari.
A certiorari lies to remove into Supreme Court the proceedings before Justices under Insolvent Confined Debtors' Act. *White* v. *Coleman*, 4 *All.* 630.

20—Costs.
Costs will not be given on refusing the first application of an insolvent debtor, except in an extreme case, but the rule is otherwise on a second application where the objections made at the former, are not fully answered. See *McFarlane* v. *Gordon*, 2 *All.* 162.

21—Where an application to discharge an insolvent debtor was refused with costs, the Court refused to make the payment of the costs a condition precedent to another application. See *McFarlane* v. *Gordon*, 2 *All.* 201.

Non-suit—Defendant becoming insolvent. See Judgment, as in case of Non-suit II. 6, 11.

Partner—Power to compound debt. See Partnership 8.

Ascertaining Insolvency. See Pleading II. 36.

Pleading Discharge — Replication Fraud. See Pleading II. 3.

Sheriff's Poundage on *Ca. Sa*—Debtor obtaining discharge. See Sheriff 16.

Application for *Certiorari* to bring up proceedings before Justices. See *Certiorari* I. 4.

INSPECTOR.

See Common School Act 1871.

INSTALMENT.

See Joint Stock Company.

INSURANCE.

1 — Insurance on house — Title — Interest.
Plaintiff being in possession of a house effected insurance upon it as owner. The property on which the house stood was leasehold, and the legal title prior to the insurance was in W., under whom plaintiff claimed by a writing (said to have been burnt,) not under seal, and stating no consideration. It appeared that W. had, before the insurance, assigned the lease to B. by deed duly registered. Held, That the title was in B. by the registry of the assignment, without any entry, and that plaintiff had no insurable interest. *Crockford* v. *London and Liverpool Insurance Co.*, *East. T.* 1861. S. P.—*Crockford* v. *Equitable Insurance Co.*, *Mich. T.* 1863.

2—Declarations—Evidence.
In an action against the Secretary of the Society of Underwriters, under the Act 21 Vic. c. 61, the declarations of an underwriter on the policy, relative to the subject matter, are evidence against defendant. *Duffy* v. *Stymest*, *Trin. T.* 1861.

3—Fraud—Entire Contract.
Plaintiff insured two buildings, and the merchandise in one of them, against loss by fire. One of the conditions of the policy declared that if there should be any fraud, overcharge or false swearing, the claimant should forfeit all claim under the policy. One ground of defence to an action brought on the policy was, that the plaintiff made a false declaration as to the value of the goods lost by the fire. Held, That the contract was entire; and if the plaintiff was guilty of fraud or false statement in reference to the goods, he could not recover any part of the insurance. *Cushman* v. *London and Liverpool Ins. Co.*, *Hil. T.* 1862.

4—General Average—Rule.

A vessel sailed from Shields, G. B., bound for Providence, Rhode Island, and was obliged to put into Cowes and Cork to refit. A jettison occurred during the voyage, and on her arrival at Providence, a general average was made up, according to the rule of that port, which included an allowance for seamen's wages and maintenance. Held, That the rule prevailing at the port of destination was to be adopted in making up the adjustment of general average charges; and not the rule in England, where such charges would be excluded. *McGivern* v. *Stymest*, *East. T.* 1862.

5—Repairs—Not seeking instructions—Sale of vessel—Liability for total loss—Damages.

A vessel sailed from Havana for New York, and the next day struck on a rock: she continued on her voyage for ten days, and then put back to Havana, which she reached in five days. A survey was held, and it was found that she could not safely proceed to New York without repairs, which the captain said would cost there more than the vessel was worth, though they could have been made in this Province for about £75. The vessel was safe in the harbour of Havana without repairs; and instructions respecting her, might have been received from the owners within a month. Held, That the captain was not justified in selling the vessel, and that the underwriters were not liable for a total loss, without notice of abandonment. *Semble*, That even if the plaintiff could have recovered for a partial loss, it could only be for nominal damages, as there was no evidence by which the amount of loss could be estimated. *Wood* v. *Stymest*, *East. T.* 1862.

6—Certificate of nearest Magistrate—Interest—Disqualification.

One of the conditions of a policy required, that persons sustaining loss should procure a certificate of a magistrate or notary "*most contiguous* to the place of the fire, and not concerned in the loss, as a creditor or otherwise, or related to the insured or sufferers," that he was acquainted with the insured, and verily believed that he had sustained the loss without fraud, etc. Held, That where the nearest magistrate was also a sufferer by the same fire which destroyed the plaintiff's property, he was disqualified from certifying under the words of the condition, "concerned in the loss as a creditor, *or otherwise*."

Quære, Whether the fact of the nearest magistrate being a creditor of the insured disqualified him from certifying. *Semble*, No. *Ganong* v *The Etna Ins. Co.*, *East. T.* 1864.

7—Transfer of Ship—Security—Intention.

Where a bill of sale of a ship has been executed, it may be shown that the transfer, though absolute in its terms, was intended only as a security, and that the transferror has an equity of redemption. *Millidge* v. *Stymest*, *Trin. T.* 1864.

8—Notice of abandonment must be given by legal owner—Notice by equitable owner—Recovery.

Notice of abandonment must be given by the legal owner of a vessel. Where such notice was given by an equitable owner, and a verdict recovered against the underwriters as for a constructive total loss, the verdict was set aside: the plaintiff only being entitled, as equitable owner, to recover for partial loss. *Ibid.*

9—Preliminary proof—Waiver.

The mere fact that an Insurance Company states no objection to the preliminary proof given of a loss, at or after the time of its being received, is no evidence of a waiver by them of objections to it; but where objections are made on other grounds, and no objection taken to the sufficiency of the preliminary proof, it may be evidence of a waiver. *McManus* v. *The Etna Ins. Co.*, *Trin. T.* 1865.

10—Constructive total loss.

An insurance on fish was declared in the policy to be "against total loss." Held, That a constructive total loss came within the words of the policy. *O'Leary* v. *Stymest*, *East. T.* 1865.

11—Claim for constructive total loss—Evidence of partial loss—No evidence of amount of repairs—Damages.

Plaintiff claimed for a constructive total loss, but the evidence showed a partial loss only—the vessel having been repaired and sailed again. No evidence was given as to the amount of the repairs, and the plaintiff was non-suited. Held, That the non-suit was wrong; and that plaintiff was entitled to a verdict for nominal damages at all events. *Millidge* v. *Stymest*, *East. T.* 1866.

12—Mortgagee—Foreclosure—Sale—Extinguishment of interest.

Plaintiff insured his interest in a house as mortgagee: the mortgage was afterwards foreclosed, and the property sold under the decree, and purchased by the plaintiff. Held, That his mortgage interest was extinguished by the foreclosure and sale, and that he could not recover for a loss happening afterwards. *Gaskin* v. *The Phœnix Ins. Co., Trin. T.* 1866.

13—Mortgagee—Insurance by—Debt paid.

Where a mortgagee insures, solely on his own account, it is only an insurance of his debt; and if the debt is afterwards paid, or the mortgage discharged, the policy ceases to have any operation. *Ibid.*

14—Continuance of Policy on Goods—Change of Ownership—Agent—Want of Seal—Covenant not maintainable.

A policy of insurance on goods, against loss by fire, was effected in the name of G. F. & Co., H. F., the plaintiff, having afterwards become the owner of the goods, the agent of the Company made and signed the following indorsement on the policy: "This insurance is hereby continued in the name of H. F." Held, (assuming that the agent had power so to continue the assurance for the benefit of the plaintiff,) That the indorsement not being under the seal of the Company, the plaintiff could not maintain covenant on the policy. *Frost* v. *The Liverpool, London & Globe Insurance Co., Hil. T.* 1871.

15—Insurance—Value—Recovery.

Plaintiff insured $5,000 on his interest as mortgagee, in the undivided half of a mill and machinery. The mill was burnt, and the plaintiff furnished the agent of the Company with the preliminary proof required by the policy, which he considered sufficient, and agreed to pay the loss, but requested the plaintiff to allow the Company sixty days to pay it, to which he assented; and the agent then gave the plaintiff a letter, stating that he had examined plaintiff's claim; that the loss appeared satisfactory, and that he agreed to pay it within sixty days from that date. Soon after this, one G. wrote to the agent, stating that he owned half the mill property, and claimed half the amount insured, as the mill was insured to its full value. The agent thereupon wrote again to the plaintiff, and after referring to a proposal by G that the Company should re-build the mill, stated that under any circumstances the Company were bound to protect him from loss, and that they held themselves liable to indemnify him fully. There was evidence that the mill was not worth more than half the amount insured upon it. In an action on the policy, the defendant paid $2,500 into court, and pleaded that the plaintiff's interest did not exceed that sum. The jury were directed that the plaintiff could only recover the actual value of his interest in the mill; that if the defendants' agent, with knowledge of the facts, had adjusted the loss with the plaintiff, and there was no fraud, it would be evidence of the amount of the loss, though not conclusive on the defendants. The jury found that the adjustment was made by the agent with a full knowledge of all the facts, or with the means of knowledge; and that he affirmed the adjustment after he had the knowledge. They gave no answer to questions as to the value of the mill at the time of the fire, and the amount of loss sustained by the plaintiff by the fire, but found a verdict for the plaintiff for the amount claimed. Held, That there was no misdirection, and that the verdict was warranted by the evidence. Held also, That the fact that other property besides the mill, was conveyed to the plaintiff by his mortgage, as security, did not affect his right to recover on the policy. *Thomson* v. *The Liverpool, London & Globe Ins. Co., Hil. T.* 1871.

16—Insurable interest—Agreement for re-conveyance.

Plaintiff being a mortgagor in possession of a mill, conveyed it away by a deed, absolute on its face, taking an agreement for a re-conveyance on payment of a certain sum which he owed the grantee. Held, That this was in effect a mortgage, and that the plaintiff had an insurable interest. *Kelly* v. *The Liverpool, London and Globe Ins. Co., Hil. T.* 1871.

17—Other insurances avoiding policy—Meaning of condition.

One of the conditions of a policy declared that it should be void in case any other insurance was made on the property, unless notice thereof was given to the Company. Held, That this only referred to other insurances made by the assured, or with his knowledge or consent; and not to an insurance made by his mortgagee, without his knowledge. *Ibid.*

18—Policy—Construction—Time risk.
A policy of insurance on a vessel "for four calendar months on a fishing voyage, beginning the adventure from the 11th June instant, and to continue until the said expiration of four months," without stating where the vessel was to sail from, or whither she was to return, is a time risk, and is not terminated by the vessel returning from a fishing voyage within that period. *Dimock* v. *New Brunswick Marine Assurance Company*, 3 *Kerr* 654.

19—Fire policy—Increase of risk.
A policy of insurance against fire upon a dwelling house, contained a condition that if, after the insurance was effected, the risk was increased by any means within the control of the assured, or if the building should, without the assent of the assured, be occupied in any way so as to render the risk more hazardous than at the time of insuring, the insurance should be void. Held, That the assured afterwards ceasing to occupy the house without any fraudulent intent, was not an increase of the risk within the meaning of the condition, unless it was proved that under the circumstances and situation of the building insured, its destruction by fire was more probable when unoccupied, than if the assured had continued to reside in it. *Foy* v. *The Ætna Ins. Co.*, 3 *All.* 29.

20—Signing by accredited Agent—Validity—Prima facie proof—Corporate seal.
A policy of insurance of a Foreign Company declared that it should not be valid until countersigned by W. the agent at Saint John. In an action on the policy, proof that it was signed by W. and that he acted as the agent of the Company at Saint John, and had paid a loss on a similar policy, is sufficient under the Act 13 Vic. c. 37, if uncontradicted, to shew that he was the accredited agent of the Company, and to dispense with proof of their corporate seal. *Robertson* v. *The Provincial Mutual and General Insurance Co.*, 3 *All.* 379.

21—No Patent Ambiguity—Usage of Trade.
A policy of insurance on a vessel, described the voyage to be "from St. John to a port of call and discharge and loading in the West Indies." Held, That there was no patent ambiguity, and that the words of the policy meant one port both for discharge and loading: and not two ports—one for discharge, and another for loading. *McGivern* v. *The Provincial Insurance Company*, 4 *All.* 64.

Quære, Whether, if it had appeared by the usage of trade, that a peculiar meaning was attached to the words "a port of call and discharge and loading," the policy might not have been construed according to such usage. But also, *Semble*, That such usage and construction should be averred in the declaration. *Ibid.*

22—Issue of Policy—Time—Notice to broker.
The business of an insurance company was managed by an agent residing in St. John, to whom application for insurance in other parts of the province were made through brokers. Held, (per Ritchie, J.) That a policy was issued when the agent forwarded it to the broker for delivery. Notice of a prior insurance to an insurance broker, is not notice to the company. *McLachlan* v. *Ætna Insurance Co.*, 4 *All.* 173.

23—Interest of assured—Declarations.
In an action upon a policy of insurance for the loss of a vessel, the verbal declarations of the plaintiff, the sole registered owner, that another person, a foreigner, was part owner, are not sufficient to disprove the allegation of interest in the plaintiff, who had obtained the register upon his own declaration, and acted as owner in procuring the insurance, and in the other affairs of the vessel. *Watson* v. *Summers*, 2 *Kerr* 62.

24—Preliminary proof—Conditions precedent.
In an action on a policy of insurance containing a proviso that the loss was to be paid within sixty days after proof of loss and adjustment, and proof of interest in the property, such preliminary proof is a condition precedent to the plaintiff's right to recover, unless there is an averment that it has been waived. *Robertson* v. *The New Brunswick Marine Insurance Company*, 3 *All.* 333.

25—Mortgagor—Incumbrance—Disclosure.
A mortgagor may insure to the value of his property without disclosing the incumbrance, unless there is a stipulation in the policy requiring it. *Parker* v. *Equitable Ins. Co.*, 4 *All.* 562.

26—Abandonment—Refusal to accept—State of facts governing recovery.

A vessel was driven on shore, and being supposed to be a total loss, notice of abandonment was given to the underwriters. They refused to accept the abandonment, got the vessel off, brought her to St. John, her port of destination, in a place of safety, before action brought, and required the owner to take charge of her. The cost of repairing her after she was brought to St. John by the underwriters, would be less than her value when repaired. Held, That the right of the assured to recover depended upon the state of facts existing at the time the action was brought, and that he could only recover for a partial loss. *Taylor* v. *Smith*, 1 *Han.* 120.

27—Over-Valuation.

A house was insured by plaintiff for £250, and proved to have been worth at least £400. Held, That if the plaintiff was only entitled, as widow, to half the estate, there was not an over-valuation. *Lingley* v. *Queen Ins. Co.*, 1 *Han.* 280.

28—False statements—Statements in affidavit—Account of loss—Delivery of.

A condition of a policy of insurance on clothing, provisions, etc., in St. John, required that persons sustaining loss should forthwith give notice thereof to the Company, and within fourteen days thereafter deliver in as particular an account of the loss as the nature and circumstances of the case would admit of, and make proof of the same, etc., and if there appeared any fraud or false statement, or that the fire happened by the wilful means, or connivance of the insured, he should be excluded from all benefit under the policy. The plaintiff's affidavit furnished to the Company under this condition, claiming a loss of furs, clothing and bedding by fire, stated that he was in the County of Sunbury at the time of the fire, and was unable to ascertain in what manner it originated. In his evidence on the trial, the plaintiff swore that he left St. John about 7 o'clock p. m., on his way to the County of Sunbury, where he arrived the following morning; the fire broke out at 9 o'clock, at which time the plaintiff would have been in the County of Kings, on his way to Sunbury, and only a few miles from St. John. The house was locked when the fire was discovered, and on being broken open it was found to be in a room in which there was neither fire-place nor stove, and no appearance of any clothing or bedding; a candlestick was found in a barrel in this room, containing straw partly consumed. Held, That it was the duty of the plaintiff to state in his affidavit that the house was locked at the time of the fire, the circumstances connected with his leaving, and where he was at the time, and that his statement that he was in the County of Sunbury, was a false statement and avoided the policy. Held also, That an account of the loss delivered within fourteen days after knowledge thereof by the assured was in time, though more than fourteen days had elapsed since the fire. *Smith* v. *The Queen Ins. Co.*, 1 *Han.* 311.

29—Deviation—Intention—Change of risk—Detention—Justifiable delay a question of law—Reasonable delay a question for jury.

A ship was insured for a voyage from Liverpool to Cardiff, thence to Aden, and from thence to India or Burmah. She was chartered for and set sail from Cardiff to Aden, with the intention of proceeding from Aden to Chincha, instead of India or Burmah, and was lost before reaching Aden. Held, No deviation, and that the underwriter was liable. *Reed and another* v. *Weldon*, 1 *Han.* 458.

A ship was insured for a voyage from Dundee to St. John, N. B., thence to a port of discharge in the United Kingdom. She started on her voyage and arrived at St. John, where she was put on the blocks, detained 17 days, repaired and re-classed. Held, That this changed the risk, was equivalent to a deviation, and avoided the policy. *Ibid.*

Whether delay in a voyage is unjustifiable or not, is a question of law for the Judge; but whether unreasonable or not, is a question for the jury. *Ibid.*

30—Not communica[illegible] [illegible]mportant facts.

Plaintiffs applic[illegible] [illegible]efendants on N[illegible] 12th to insure [illegible]eir vessel on a time policy for six months, beginning on the 9th Sept. previous, the da[illegible] on which she left Swansea for St. Thomas, where she was then over-due. In the written application in reply to the question "where bound," the plaintiff's reply was "a port in the West Indies." The news of a hurricane having occurred at St. Thomas had been published in the newspapers that morning, and was known to plaintiffs but not to defendants. Held, in an action to recover for a total loss, That the destination of the vessel and the fact of there being a hurricane at her port of destination, should have been communicated to defendants, and this not having been done, the plaintiffs were non-suited. *Mahoney* v. *The Provincial Ins. Co.*, 1 *Han.* 622.

31—Re-Insurance—Relation of policy. Plaintiff's premises were insured in The London and Liverpool Company, from 2nd October 1865, to 2nd October 1866. Before the term expired he received notice from W., the agent at Newcastle, that the London and Liverpool Company would renew the policy on the same terms, and accordingly he paid W. the premium money and got his receipt. A., the general agent at St. John, declined to renew the policy, and paid the premium to defendants, who issued a policy (taking the description of the premises from the London and Liverpool's books) dated the 16th October 1866, but insuring from the 2nd October 1866 to 2nd October 1867. The premises were destroyed by fire on the 13th October, before the policy issued; but the plaintiff did not know that he was insured by defendants until he received the policy from W., who also acted for them. Held, That this amounted to a re-insurance, and there being no fraud, plaintiff was entitled to recover; that the policy related back to the 2nd October, and that the condition in the policy, that all facts relating to the state of the premises must be disclosed, must be taken to relate to the time from which the policy took effect. *Giffard* v. *The Queen Ins. Co.*, 1 *Han.* 432.

32—Insurable interest—Widow. A widow having continued, for four years after her husband's death, in possession of a house built on land of which he was the lessee for years, and paid the ground rent, insured the house in her own name. No administration was taken out on the husband's estate. Held, That she had an insurable interest—1st, as the presumptive owner of the house; 2nd, as ex-cutrix *de son tort*; 3rd, as the widow under the Statute of Distribution. *Lingley* v. *The Queen Ins. Co.*, 1 *Han.* 280.

33—Promise by Underwriter to pay—Knowledge of facts. Where it was proved on the trial of a case against an underwriter on a policy of insurance for a loss, that the defendant had promised to enquire as to the particulars of the loss, and if correct, pay it; and that after several days he did promise to pay, the Court refused to disturb a verdict for the plaintiff, although there was evidence of a deviation, which otherwise would have avoided the policy. *Reed* v. *McLaughlin*, 2 *Han.* 128.

33 a—Waiver of proof of loss. Plaintiff, whose stock of goods in his store was insured by defendants by a policy under seal, sold them to A., taking notes in payment. Subsequently, at the office of defendants' agent, and by his consent, he indorsed on the policy that he thereby assigned it to A., having sold him the goods. This assignment was entered on defendants' books, but not made under seal, and A. was not informed of it. The first note being unpaid, plaintiff, by consent of A., took back the goods, and possession of the store. They were afterwards consumed by fire. Held, That the assignment on the policy was invalid, and that plaintiff could recover under the policy for the loss. Weldon, J., *dissentiente;* Fisher, J., *dubitante*. Where, in an action to recover insurance, the defendants' witness contradicted the plaintiff as to the value of the goods lost by fire, but the jury were properly directed as to the measure of damages, the Court refused to disturb their verdict, even though they might have given less had they been on the jury. The plaintiff's attorney testified that he met defendants' agent in the street, and said he had the proofs ready except a certificate, which he feared he could not get in the time required by the policy; that defendants' agent said it made no difference, but to get the proofs as soon as he could. Defendants' agent denied this conversation. Held, This was evidence of waiver to go to the jury. *Crozier* v. *The Phœnix Ins. Co.*, 2 *Han.* 200.

34—Detention—Re-classing—Deviation—Seaworthiness at inception of voyage. A vessel was insured for a voyage from Dundee, Scotland, to St. John, thence to a Port in the United Kingdom. On her arrival at St. John she was placed on the blocks, repaired and re-classed, being detained 17 days. Held, In an action to recover the amount of the insurance, that in the absence of any evidence of the vessel having sustained damage on the voyage from Dundee to St. John, such detention for re-classing was a deviation, and avoided the policy. A vessel insured for a round voyage is bound to be sufficiently seaworthy at its inception to make it without repairs, in the absence of any damage from extraordinary perils of the sea. *Reed* v. *Philps*, 2 *Han.* 172.

35—Deviation.
Insurance on a ship "at and from Saint John to a port of call and discharge and loading in the West Indies, and from thence to a port of call and discharge in the United Kingdom." The ship sailed from Saint John to Havana, discharged her cargo, and then sailed to Matanzas, another port in the West Indies, where she took in a cargo and sailed for Cork, and was lost on the voyage. Held, That going to Matanzas was a deviation. *McGivern* v. *Provincial Insurance Co.*, 3 *All.* 311.

Quære, Whether calling at a port for orders, before going to a port of discharge, would have been a deviation. *Ibid.*

36—Losses—Jettison—Recovery—Contribution.
Where the owner of a ship is also the owner of part of the cargo, which was thrown overboard for the preservation of the ship in the course of the voyage, on which insurance was effected. Held, That such owner might recover from the insurer on the ship the average proportion which the ship would be liable to contribute to the loss sustained by such jettison of the cargo. *Marks* v. *Watson*, 2 *Kerr* 211.

Where the goods are laden on deck according to the custom of a particular trade, the owner thereof is entitled to contribution in general average for a loss by jettison. *Ibid.*

37—Defence—Previous insurance—Foreign law.
One of the conditions of a policy of insurance was, that if the assured should have any other insurance on the property, not notified to the insurers and indorsed on the policy, the insurance should be void. At the time of insuring his house with the defendants, the plaintiff had an insurance thereon in the name of M., in an office in the State of Maine. Held, That as by the law of this country, neither the plaintiff nor M. could recover on that policy, the defendants, in order to avoid their policy for want of notice of the previous insurance, should have shown that by the law of Maine the plaintiff could recover on the policy effected by M. *McLachlan* v. *The Ætna Insurance Company*, 4 *All.* 173.

38—Requisite proof—Preliminary proof—Affidavit—Materiality of description.
One of the conditions of a policy of insurance required, that all persons sustaining loss should give notice to the agent through whom insured, and within one month after the loss, deliver in as particular an account thereof as the nature of the case would admit, and, if required, make proof of the same by their oath or affirmation, and by the production of their books of account, etc., and should, if required, procure a certificate under the hands of three of the nearest householders, etc. The plaintiff having sustained a loss, furnished an affidavit and certificate in the terms of the condition, without being required to do so. In an action on the policy, one of the notices of defence was that the proof and certificate required by the condition were not given by the plaintiff after the alleged loss; but the defence on the trial was, concealment at the time of effecting the policy. Held, 1. That the affidavit and certificate were admissible as part of the preliminary proof. 2. But if not strictly admissible, it was immaterial evidence, and therefore no ground for a new trial. *Perkins* v. *The Equitable Insurance Co.*, 4 *All.* 562.

The plaintiff in his application to insure a building, stated that it was owned by himself and P., and worked by them as a mill. At that time the mill was in the possession of a tenant under a lease for five years, was mortgaged to its full value, and a line of railway had been laid out through the land, for which the plaintiff claimed damages, alleging that it destroyed the mill. There being nothing in the policy requiring such matters to be described, it was left to the jury, and they found, that the non-disclosure was not material. Held, That these questions were properly left. *Ibid.*

39—Answers to questions—Warranty.
An Insurance Company required applications for insurance to be made on printed forms containing certain questions which were to be minutely answered, and were

declared to form the basis of the insurance. One of the questions was: "Is the property involved in law, or mortgaged; if the latter, to whom, and for what amount?" The answer was: "There is a mortgage on the house for £300"—which was untrue. This application was referred to in the policy, one of the conditions of which was, that if the buildings were described otherwise than they really were, the insured should not be entitled to any benefit under the policy. Held, 1. That the answer to this question amounted to a warranty, and being untrue, rendered the policy void. 2. That being an essential part of the contract, its materiality was not a question for the jury. *Marshall* v. *The Times Fire Ins. Co.*, 4 *All.* 618.

40—Months—Commencement of action—Issue of writ.

A policy of insurance is a mercantile instrument; therefore the term "Months" used therein, limiting the time for bringing an action for a loss, means calendar months. *Pomares* v. *Provincial Insurance Co.*, *Hil. T.* 1873.

Where one of the conditions of a policy declared that no action should be brought thereon, unless within 12 months after the loss; it will be presumed, in the absence of evidence of the time the writ actually issued, that it issued on the day it bears date. *Ibid.*

41—Loss payable to plaintiff—Action—Conditions—Partial loss—Preliminary proof—Deviation—Suspicious circumstances—Fraud left to Jury.

Where the plaintiff procures an insurance on a vessel belonging to M., and by the terms of the policy the loss is to be paid to the plaintiff, he may maintain an action thereon in his own name. *Dimock* v. *The New Brunswick Marine Assurance Company*, 1 *All.* 398.

By the conditions of a policy the insurers agreed to pay within sixty days after proof of loss, etc., but that no partial loss should be paid for unless it exceeded five per cent. The plaintiff delivered the master's protest describing the loss, and the certificate of a ship carpenter that the vessel was not worth repairing. Held, 1. That there was sufficient preliminary proof to enable the plaintiff to recover for a partial loss, and that a certificate from the custom house that the register of the vessel had been deposited there as a condemned vessel, was not necessary. 2. That the plaintiff might recover for a partial loss, though he claimed a total loss; and that in the absence of any evidence by the defendant of the extent of the injury, there was sufficient evidence to sustain a verdict for a partial loss, though the vessel was afterwards partially repaired, and the value of the repairs was not shewn. *Dimock* v. *The New Brunswick Marine Assurance Company*, 1 *All.* 398.

Whether going to Saint Stephen on the river Saint Croix was a deviation, or in prosecution of the necessary purposes of a fishing voyage, upon a time policy, was considered a question proper for the jury upon the evidence. *Ibid.*

Though the circumstances of a loss are suspicious, if there is some evidence of its being accidental, which is uncontradicted, and the question of fraud has been fully left to the jury, who find for the plaintiff, the verdict will not be disturbed. *Ibid.*

Deposit of Policy of Insurance—Mortgage right—Equitable claim. See Equity 3.

Action on Policy—Fire Insurance—Interest—Conditions—Preliminary Proof—Pleadings—Averments—Waiver. See Pleading I. 37.

Assignment of Policy—Consideration to support promise by Insurer to Assignee. See Pleading I. 39.

Defence—Deposit of Gunpowder contrary to Provisos—Plea—Replication. See Pleading II. 9.

Objecting to pay loss on different ground than want of preliminary proof—Waiver. See Waiver.

Seal of Company when not necessary—President and Secretary—Prima Facie evidence of appointment. See Evidence VI. 5.

INSURANCE BROKER.

Action by—Re-insurance—Money paid—Evidence.

Policies of insurance effected by a broker, declared that preliminary proof and evidence of the loss were to be given to the broker, and payment of losses to be made within sixty days thereafter. The practice of the broker was to receive the premiums in money or notes, crediting the underwriters with the amount, whether actually paid or not, the assured being liable to him alone for the premium Proofs of losses were furnished to the broker from time to time, and on being satisfied of their correctness, he paid the amounts, and the policies were cancelled. Half yearly accounts were furnished by the broker to the underwriter, containing full particulars of all the risks, premiums, losses and charges, to which he made no objection until the account was rendered shewing the balance claimed in this action. Held, in an action against the underwriter to recover the amount paid by the broker for losses, That the jury were warranted in inferring that the defendant had authorized the broker to decide upon the proof of loss in each case, and had assented to his decision. Held also, That the plaintiff could recover from the defendant the amount of premium of a re-insurance effected for him without proof of actual payment to the underwriter. *Ranney* v. *Gregory*, 1 *Han.* 152.

INTEREST.

Covenant to pay for improvements—Plaintiff entitled to interest on amount appraised. See Landlord and Tenant VI. 2.

1—Interest is not recoverable in the nature of damages in an action for money had and received, brought to recover an amount of duty illegally exacted at the Treasury. *Hammond* v. *Robinson*, 1 *Kerr* 295.

2—Interest cannot be recovered on a bond given to secure the payment of instalments of stock in a Joint Stock Company, under the Act 5 Wm. 4, c. 48, though the bond is in a penal sum conditioned to secure the payment of a lesser sum at a certain day. *St. John Bridge Company* v. *Woodward*, 1 *Kerr* 29.

3—Where a verdict was obtained on a policy of guarantee, including interest up to that time, and a rule *nisi* for a new trial was granted, and afterwards discharged; interest was allowed on the amount of the policy, (but not on the amount of the verdict,) from the date of the verdict till the rule was discharged, under the Act 12 Vic. c. 30, s. 20. *Commercial Bank* v. *The European Assurance Society*, *Hil. T.* 1871.

4—Notice should be given of an application to be allowed interest on the affirmance of a judgment in error. See Mills v. Vail, 4 All. 620.

Excessive Claim—Mortgage—Payment—Mortgagor allowed interest. See Mortgage 14.

INTERLOCUTORY JUDGMENT.

See Judgment by default.
" Practice V. 30, 31, 32.
" " VI. 15, 16, 17, 18.
" " VII. 10, 11, 12

INTERROGATORIES.

See Evidence.

INTESTATE.

See Heir at Law.

INTOXICATING LIQUORS.

See Justice of the Peace. (Summary Conviction.)

INTRUSION.

1—If on the trial of an information for intrusion on Crown land, it appears that the Crown has been out of possession for twenty years, the defendant is entitled to a verdict on the general issue, under the Stat. 21, Jac. 1, c. 14. *Rex* v. *Watson*, *Hil. T.* 1828.

2—The Crown granted to the defendant the right to occupy land for twenty one years, unless the same should be sooner required by the Crown, on notice of which the grant was to cease and be void. Held, in an information for intrusion, after notice to the defendant, and refusal to give up possession, that no inquest of office was necessary to terminate his right, his removal not being founded on any breach of condition or forfeiture. *Reg.* v. *Hebert*, 2 *All.* 427.

3—*Semble*, That a notice to the defendant that the Government required the land, signed by the Surveyor General of Crown Land in his official character was sufficient, without proof of any previous authority from the Government to give the notice. By subsequently laying out the land into lots and granting it, the Government recognized the authority of the Surveyor General to give the notice. *Ibid.*

4—The right to the soil between high and low water mark in a navigable river being in the Crown, it has also the constructive possession, and may maintain trespass and intrusion against a person for erecting a building thereon; and the defendant cannot set up as a defence the public right of navigation over the place, his building not having been placed there in the exercise of any such right. *Reg.* v. *Taylor, Hil T.* 1862.

5—*Quære*, Whether damages can be recovered, unless they are alleged in the information. *Ibid.*

IRREGULARITY.

See Practice VII.

ISSUE (NO PLEA).

See Practice VII.

Of Writ. See Writ.

INVENTORY.

See Evidence VII. 4.

JEOFAILS.

See Error (Writ of).

JETTISON.

See Insurance 36. See Shipping Law.

JOINT DEBTORS.

See *Scire Facias.*

JOINT LIABILITY.

See Contract 9.

All not served with Process. See Practice VII. 8.

See Practice IV. 5, 6.

Infant not served—Judgment *Scire Facias.* See Infant 6.

JOINT INDICTMENT.

See Criminal Law.

JOINT TENANCY.

Conveyance of Land by grantor to himself and others. See Deed I. 26.

JOINT TRESPASS.

See Trespass II. 9, 10.

Separate Acts—Abandonment.

See do. II. 8, 12, 13, 25.

Joint Conversion. See Trover 24.

JOINT STOCK COMPANY.

See Assessment.

1—Calls—Lapse of time—Instalments. The Act 5 Wm. 4, c. 48, incorporating the St. John Bridge Company, required thirty days' notice to be given of the calls for the payment of each instalment of the capital stock, and that no greater amount than ten per cent. should be called in at any one time Held (Chipman, C. J., *dissentiente*), That the full time of thirty days must elapse between the time appointed for the payment of each instalment, and that it was not sufficient, in one notice, to call for payment of several instalments at intervals of less than thirty days. Held also (*per totam curiam*), That though one call could not be enforced for want of sufficient notice, it did not vitiate other calls in the same notice, where the full time was given. *St. John Bridge Co.* v. *Woodward*, 1 *Kerr* 29.

2—Right to sue for calls—Bye-Laws. An Act incorporating a Joint Stock Company, directed that the stock should be divided into two hundred shares, to be secured in such manner as the bye-laws of the Company should direct, and should be paid in such sums, and at such times as the Directors should appoint. Held, That it was not essential to the right of the Company to sue for calls of stock, that bye-laws for securing the same should be made, provided the Directors who made the calls were duly appointed. *Portland and Lancaster Steam Ferry Co.* v. *Pratt*, 2 *All.* 17.

3—Notice—Newspaper—Time. The Act of Incorporation required the first meeting of the Company to be called by A., by giving notice in one or more of the newspapers published in St. John, "for not less than three consecutive weeks immediately before the day appointed." Held—1st. That a newspaper containing such a notice, and having the name of A. thereto, was evidence of the notice, and that A. having attended the meeting, it would be presumed that the notice was published by his authority; 2nd. That it was not necessary that three weeks should elapse between the publication of the first notice and the day of meeting; but that a publication in the newspaper for three consecutive weeks was sufficient; 3rd. That it would not be presumed that the newspaper was published more than once a week—that fact (if material) should have been shewn affirmatively. *Portland and Lancaster Steam Ferry Co.* v. *Pratt*, 2 *All.* 17.

4—Annual Meeting—Election—Presence of Stockholders.

Where an Act of Incorporation required that an annual meeting for the choice of Directors should be held at such time "as by the laws and regulations of the corporation should be appointed," an election made at a meeting held under an order of the Directors, at which meeting all the stockholders were not present, is invalid. The law regulating the annual meeting should be made by the stockholders, and not by the Directors merely. *Semble*, That in the absence of any bye-law on the subject, an election at a meeting so called, at which all the stockholders were present, and voted, would not be void *Ibid.*

5—Membership.

A person named in the act of incorporation and in the list of subscribers, who never authorized his name to be used, or hold any shares in the Company, ceases to be a member thereof after the first meeting to organize the Company, and is therefore not disqualified as a juror in an action brought by them. *Portland and Lancaster Steam Ferry Co.* v. *Pratt*, 2 *All.* 17.

6—Liability to rates.

If a Joint Stock Company owns real estate in several Parishes, it is rateable under 1 Rev. Stat c. 53, as a resident of that Parish in which its principal business is carried on, and as a non-resident in the other Parishes. *Ex parte St. John Suspension Bridge Co.*, 3 *All.* 190.

7—Officer summoning Jury—Disqualification as Stockholder.

In an action for calls on stock in a Company, the officer who summoned the jury was a stockholder, (the whole amount not being paid up,) but before receiving the *venire*, transferred his stock to the President of the Company. The act of incorporation declared that no shareholder should be entitled to transfer his stock unless all calls were paid. Held, That he had not divested himself of his interest as a stockholder. *Woodstock Railway Co.* v. *Tupper*, 1 *Han* 454.

8—Right to sue for Assessments—Remedial Act.

The plaintiffs were incorporated by Provincial Act, 27 Vic. c. 43, for the purpose of constructing a railway from St. John to the boundary of the United States—the capital stock to be two millions of dollars, and the Company to proceed to locate and complete the road as soon as $50,000 of the stock were paid in. The Directors were authorized to make equal assessments on the shares from time to time, as they might deem necessary, to be paid to the Treasurer, and in case any subscriber for stock neglected to pay the assessment on his shares for thirty days after notice, the Directors might order his shares to be sold at auction, and in case of any deficiency, he should be accountable to the Company for the balance. By Act 32 Vic. c. 54, to amend the act of incorporation, after reciting that it was doubtful whether the subscribers for shares were legally liable to pay assessments unless the whole amount of the capital stock had been subscribed for, and the $50,000 paid in, and also, whether the notices of assessments had been given in accordance with the act of incorporation,—it was enacted, 1. That the subscribers for stock should be liable in the same manner and to the same extent as if the whole capital stock had been fully subscribed, and as if the $50,000 had been paid in, in the manner directed by the act of incorporation, and as if all assessments on the shares and the notices given thereof, had been made and given according to the said act. 2. That to entitle the Company to recover against any stockholder, two months notice of the assessment should be published in a newspaper, and after the expiration of that time, the Company should be entitled "to "sue for, recover, and receive from any stockholder the amount due for unpaid subscribed stock *in the same manner* as if the calls for assessment had been regularly made" in accordance with the requirements of the act of incorporation. Held, 1. That the Act 32 Vic. c. 54, was not *ultra vires*, under the "British North America Act, 1867," s. 92, subsection 10; 2nd. (Per Ritchie, C. J., Allen and Weldon, J. J., Fisher, J., *dubitante*) That an action of debt could not be maintained under the Act of Incorporation, for the assessments on stock; but that the proceeding by sale of the shares must be adopted; 3rd. (Fisher, J., *dissentiente*) That the preamble of the Act 32 Vic. c. 54, showed that the object of the Legislature was, not to alter the remedy given by the Act of Incorporation for the recovery of assessments, but to remove other difficulties; and that the words of section 2 did not give the Company a right to sue for assessments. *European and North American Railway Co. v. Thomas, Hil. T.* 1872.

9—Stockholders of Bank—Liability.

The stockholders of the Westmorland Bank, by their charter, in addition to the liability of the stock held by them for payment of the debts of the bank, are liable in their private and individual capacity for an amount equal to the sum of their stock. *McKenzie, Curator of Westmorland Bank v. Wiswell,* 1 *Han.* 503.

10—Executors investing in Bank Stock in their own names—Liability—Register.

The executors of the estate of C. invested a portion of its funds in bank stock in their own names, but for the benefit of the estate, by which the dividends were received. After their death their representative, by writing, agreed to transfer the stock to the widow of C., who had taken out letters of administration *cum testamento annexo de bonis non.* The stock certificates were handed over to her and she afterwards received the dividends, but no transfer was made on the books of the bank as required by its charter and bye-laws. The bank suspended, and the estates of the executors were placed by the Judge on the list of contributories for the stock standing in their names on the register. Held, That they being *prima facie* legally liable, the Judge was right in not altering the register by substituting the party equitably entitled to the stock. *In re President, &c., Westmorland Bank;—Ex parte Allison,* 1 *Han.* 506.

11—Judge's order—Winding-up Act—Evidence.

A Judge's order settling the list of contributories under the Winding-up Act (27 Vic. c. 44) is only *prima facie* evidence of liability, and the defendant, in an action brought against him to recover a call on the stock, may give evidence to shew that he is not a stockholder. *McKenzie v. Seaman,* 1 *Han.* 621.

12—Action for calls—Judge's order prima facie evidence of liability.

In an action against a Stockholder for calls under the Winding-up Act, the order of a Judge of the Supreme Court authorizing such calls, is *prima facie* evidence of the defendant's liability. *McKenzie v. Scovil,* 2 *Han.* 6.

13—Judicial Notice—Signature of Judge.

A Judge at *Nisi Prius* is bound to take judicial notice of the signature of another Judge of the Court, to an order made under the Winding-up Act. *Ibid.*

14—Taking Promissory Note from Stockholder for assessment.

A Joint Stock Company may take a promissory note from a stockholder for an amount due by him on an assessment on his stock,—there being nothing in the act of incorporation to prohibit it. *St. Stephen's Branch Railway Co. v. Black,* 2 *Han.* 137.

15—Provisions for assessment of damages—Appointment of arbitrators—Procedure towards assessment—Agent—Seal—Rights of parties—Lessee for years—Owners.

The Albert Mining Company Act, (15 Vic. c. 87, s. 8,) declared that if the Company deemed it necessary to enter on the private property of any person for the purpose of carrying on their mining operations, they should allow the owners of such land such compensation by way of rent or otherwise, as might be agreed on, for the damages such owner might sustain by reason thereof, and if they should not be able to agree with the owner of the soil as to the amount of compensation, then the amount should be determined by three arbitrators, one to be chosen by the Company and one by the owner of the land, which arbitrators should choose a third; and if the owner of the land should decline making such agreement, or appointing an arbitrator, then the Company should make application to the Supreme Court or a Judge, stating the grounds of such application, and such Court or Judge was thereby required from time to time on such application to issue a writ to the Sheriff of the County, commanding him to summon a jury to assess the sum of money or annual rent to be paid as compensation to the owner of the land. Held, 1. That in order to justify the issuing of a writ, it must be shewn to the Judge by legal evidence, that an application for an agreement and arbitration had been made by the Company to the owner of the land and declined; and that an affidavit of such an application sworn before a British Consul in a foreign country, was not legal evidence. 2. That the authority of an agent of the Company to make the agreement with the owner of the land and appoint an arbitrator, need not be under the Company's seal. 3. That the word "owner" applied to a lessee for years of the land. 4. That the jury in assessing the damage, might either award a sum in gross or an annual rent. 5. That if the preliminary notices to the owner of the land were proved, the writ might issue without a summons to the owner to shew cause. *Ex parte The Albert Mining Company*, 3 *All.* 39.

The 10th section of the act declared that nothing in the act contained should interfere with the rights of the respective parties between whom suits were pending for anything which had happened or been committed before the passing of the act. Held, That an owner of land who had a suit pending for trespass by mining operations on his land at the passing of the act, was not thereby excluded from the operation of the 8th section. *Ibid.*

Authority to cut down street. See Railway Company.

South Bay Boom Company—Right to receive boomage. See Boomage.

JUDGE.

I. Reviewing Decision of.
II. Power at Chambers.
III. Discretionary Power at Trial.
IV. Certificate of Judge.

I.

Reviewing Decision of. (See Trial.)

1—The Court will not review the decision of a Judge refusing an amendment at *nisi prius*, unless satisfied that injustice has been done by his refusal. See *McAllister* v. *Day*, 4 *All.* 37.

II.

Power at Chambers.

2—A Judge at Chambers has power to grant further time to plead in abatement. See *Ross* v. *Hammond*, 3 *Kerr* 631.

3—Where damages were assessed by Judge at Chambers in a default cause on an insufficient affidavit as to some items, the Court reduced the assessment to amount warranted by affidavit. *Scoullar* v. *Webb*, 1 *Kerr* 520.

III.

Discretionary Power at Trial.

Discretionary power as to reception of evidence at trial. See Evidence VIII.

IV.

Certificate of Judge.

4—Finality of Decision.
When a Judge having a discretionary power, grants an order to the plaintiff on the trial of a cause for full costs, his decision is final. *Sturks* v. *Malcolm*, 3 *Kerr* 581.

5—Time—Application.
An application to the Judge who tried the cause for a certificate to deprive an acquitted defendant of costs under Act of Assembly 7 Wm. 4, c. 14, s. 24, is not too late if made before the judgment is signed, though nearly two months after the verdict. *Crane* v. *Cunard*, 3 *Kerr* 417.

6—When a trespass is committed under a claim of title, or with the intent to oust the plaintiff from the possession of the land, the Judge may certify under the Statute 22 and 23 Chas. 2., c. 9, to entitle the plaintiff to full costs. *Morrison* v. *McAlpin*, 2 *Kerr* 36.

Statute 43 Eliz. c. 6, in force in this Province. See British Statutes.

Fees on Entry of Cause. See Doe v. Christopher, 2 All. 420.

7—Cannot be made a rule of Court.
A Judge's certificate that there was no reasonable cause for bringing action in Supreme Court, cannot be made a rule of Court. *Horner* v. *Crookshank*, 4 *All.* 375.

JUDGE (COUNTY COURT.)

See County Court Judge.

JUDGE'S NOTES.

See Evidence VII. 7.

JUDGE'S ORDER.

Application to rescind. See Practice V. 5.

Prima facie evidence of defendant's liability as stockholder. See Joint Stock Company 11 and 12.

Finality of order granting leave to appeal. See Practice V. 5 *a*.

Necessity of rescinding Judge's order for discharge of joint debtor before issuing execution. See Execution IV. 19.

Order for discharge of debtor.
Production of an order of Judge of County Court, valid on its face, a sufficient justification to Sheriff. See Escape 4.

Insufficient affidavit for order to hold to bail — Application to rescind Judge's order—Previous application pending on other matter. See Arrest 10.

JUDICIAL NOTICE.

1—Place.
The Court cannot take judicial notice that a vessel lying "near the mouth of Richibucto Harbor" is in the County of Kent. *DesBrisay* v. *The Commissioners of the E. & N. A. Railway*, 1 *Han.* 48.

2—It will not be judicially intended that a deed purporting to have been made at Birmingham, was made at Birmingham, England. *Hasluck* v. *McMaster*, *C. Ms.* 4.

3—It cannot be judicially noticed that an Hotel is a place for selling liquors. See Justice of the Peace IV. 15.

4—Person.
The Court cannot take judicial notice that the person who signs a certificate of registry, endorsed upon a deed, was not the Registrar at the time the deed was recorded: and in the absence of any such proof, it must be presumed that the Registrar rightly certified. A certificate dated in 1806, stated that the deed had been registered the 29th April, 1836. *Quære*, Whether the certificate should not have been made at the time the deed was registered. *Doe on the demise of Robinson* v. *Chassey*, 1 *Han.* 50.

5—Where the certificate of proof of the execution of a deed was subscribed "Geo. D. Ludlow," without any description of his official character, either contained in the certificate, or annexed to the signature. Held, (per Chipman, C. J. and Parker, J., Carter, J., *dissentiente*,) That the Court should take judicial notice that a person named Geo. D. Ludlow was Chief Justice of the Province at the time the deed appeared to have been executed. *Watson* v. *Hay*, 3 *Kerr* 559.

6—Order of Judge under Winding-up Act.
A Judge at nisi prius is bound to take judicial notice of the signature of another Judge of the Court. *McKenzie*, *Curator*, *&c.*, v. *Scovil*, 2 *Han.* 6.

7—Judgment Roll.
Quære, Whether the Court could judicially notice an indorsement on a judgment roll of a rule setting aside the judgment. See *Wilson* v. *Andrews*, 1 *All.* 715.

Public Law—Authority to repair Streets. See Pleading I. 62.

JUDGMENT.

I. GENERALLY.
II. OFFER TO SUFFER JUDGMENT BY DEFAULT.
III. JUDGMENT (FOREIGN).

I.

GENERALLY.

Plaintiff's remedy on, not lost by proceeding against Sheriff. See Discharge 2.

1—Satisfaction of—What amounts to.
Where the defendant, after judgment, indorsed a note of a third party to the plaintiff, to be collected by him, and the proceeds applied in payment of the judgment, accompanied also by a request that the plaintiff would carry on the suit against such third party in his own name; and on the plaintiff's suing such third party, the suit was settled between them by the plaintiff receiving a sum of money on account and taking a new note in his own name for the balance, of which he informed the defendant. Held, That this was a satisfaction of the original judgment. *Sewell* v. *Burpee*, 3 *Kerr* 363.

2—Suspension of remedy on — Taking negotiable note.
Where a negotiable note is given as collateral security for a debt secured by a judgment on a warrant of attorney, the remedy on the judgment is suspended until the maturity of the note; and where the creditor had transferred the note, and it had been mislaid, the execution on the judgment was suspended until the defendant was indemnified against his liability on the note. *Hardy* v. *Price*, 3 *All.* 264.

3—Lien.
A judgment is not such a lien on land as to prevent the judgment debtor from conveying the legal estate and seisin to a third person. (See Act 8 Geo. 4, c. 87.) *Doe d. Peabody* v. *McKnight*, *Ber.* 376.

4—Enforcing judgment—Resort to equity.
A judgment creditor cannot file a bill in equity to enforce his judgment against the lands of his debtor, until he has taken all necessary proceedings to enforce his judgment at law, and is unable there to obtain the relief to which he is entitled. *Black* v. *Hazen*, *Hil. T.* 1871.

5—Subsequent creditor—Rights—No Fraud.
A subsequent judgment creditor of the defendant has no right to complain of an irregularity in the plaintiff's judgment, as that it was signed too soon. It is only in case of fraud that a subsequent creditor can apply to set aside a judgment. *Robinson* v. *N. B. and Canada Railway and Land Co.*, *Mich. T.* 1863.

6—Judgment nunc pro tunc—Lost roll.
The Court refused to allow a judgment roll to be filed *nunc pro tunc* on the ground that a former judgment roll had been lost or mislaid, without satisfactory proof that such roll was once actually in existence. *Shedden* v. *Smith*, *C. Ms.* 136.

7—Setting aside—Conditions imposed.
On setting aside an irregular judgment and execution, it was made a condition that defendant should not bring an action of trespass for the levy, the plaintiff's attorney having proceeded under a mistake of the practice. *Fleming* v. *Shaw*, *C. Ms.* 117.

Setting Aside. See Practice VI.

Set-off. See Set-off.

Amendment. See Amendment III.

Arrest of Judgment. See Practice XIII.

Judgment on Bond and Warrant of Attorney. See Warrant of Attorney.

Record of Judgment—Evidence as to date of Bond. See Evidence II. 18.

Judgment—Action on Evidence—Identity. See Evidence II. 29.

A Judgment changes the nature of a debt. See Set-off 9.

II.

Offer to suffer Judgment by Default.

1—An offer, under the Act 18 Vic. c. 9, to suffer judgment by default, must be signed by the defendant in the cause, and not by his attorney. *Wetmore* v. *DesBrisay*, 4 *All.* 356.

2—An offer to suffer judgment by default, under the Act 18 Vic. c. 9, may be made before declaration filed. *Gibson* v. *Bateman*, 4 *All.* 598.

3—Where the plaintiff's attorney was unable, in consequence of the non-payment of Court fees, to file an acceptance of an offer to confess judgment within the time allowed by the Act 18 Vic. c. 9, and a Judge's order was made granting him further time, the Court refused to set it aside. *Carrick* v. *McLeod*, *Trin. T.* 1864.

4—Where a defendant, after giving notice and particulars of set-off, files an offer to confess judgment under the Act 18 Vic. c. 9, without withdrawing the set-off, or giving notice that the offer was made without reference to it, it is *prima facie*, an admission that the sum stated in the offer, is the balance due the plaintiff after giving the defendant credit for the amount of the set-off. *Turner* v. *Hamilton*, *Trin. T.* 1864.

5—The plaintiff, by filing an acceptance of an offer to confess judgment, signed by the defendant's attorney, and taxing the costs, up to that time, does not waive the objection to the want of defendant's signature to the offer; but may afterwards treat the offer as a nullity and proceed to trial. *Wilson* v. *Maxwell*, *Mich. T.* 1864.

6—Where the defendant, before pleading, filed an offer, under the Act 18 Vic. c. 9, to suffer judgment by default for $250, which the plaintiff did not accept, and the defendant then pleaded to the action and gave notice of set-off, and the plaintiff recovered a verdict, (after allowing an amount for the defendant's set-off,) for less than the sum tendered. Held, That the tender must be taken with reference to the state of the pleadings at the time, and, not having been renewed after the notice of set-off, that the plaintiff was entitled to full costs. *Miller* v. *Lakeman*, *Mich. T.* 1866.

7—Defendant in trover, about a month after the conversion, offered to confess a judgment under the Act 18 Vic. c. 9, for $18, which the plaintiff did not accept. On the trial, (upwards of two years' afterwards,) plaintiff recovered a verdict for $19, a part—$15.30 being found by the jury as the value of the goods, and the balance for damages, in the nature of interest. Held, That as the amount tendered was more than the value of the goods and interest up to that time, the plaintiff was only entitled to costs up to the time of the offer, and that the defendant was entitled to the subsequent costs. *Belyea* v. *Stephenson*, *Mich. T.* 1866.

Offer to suffer judgment in suit brought under 92nd and 93rd sections of Insolvent Act of 1869. See Insolvent Act of 1869. 8.

III.

JUDGMENT (FOREIGN).

1—Not debt of record.
A foreign judgment is not a debt of record, but only evidence of a debt; and the simple contract on which it is founded, is not merged in it. *Fergus* v. *Wardlaw*, 3 *Kerr* 665.

2—Pleading in Bar.
The judgment of the Canadian Court in a suit between the hired men and the plaintiff relative to timber, is no bar to an action against the defendant for a tort committed by him before the timber came within the jurisdiction of Canada. *McMillan* v. *Ritchie*, 2 *All.* 242.

If the proceedings in a foreign Court do not operate as an estoppel, this Court may inquire into the grounds of the judgment. *Ibid.*

The whole of the proceedings in a suit in a foreign Court should be produced to prove the judgment. *Ibid.*

3—Action on—Seal—Proof—Jurisdiction.
No action will lie in this country on a foreign judgment, if the defendants were not resident within the jurisdiction of the foreign Court, and had no property or agent there, and were neither served with process in the foreign country, nor defended the suit; though they were served in this country with notice of the pendency of the suit, and the judgment may have been obtained according to the practice of the foreign Court in similar cases. *Cyr* v. *Sanfacon*, 2 *All.* 641.

It is sufficient that the seal affixed to a foreign judgment is the seal used by the foreign Court, though it purports on its face to be the seal of a different Court from that in which the judgment was obtained. *Ibid.*

(See Schibsby v. Westenholz, *et. al.*, 6 Q. B. 155, L. R.)

4—Authentication of.
The judgment of a foreign Court is not sufficiently authenticated by a copy certified to be correct by the clerk, although the clerk's signature and authority are verified by a certificate annexed thereto under the hand of the Judge and the seal of the Court; the copy of the judgment itself should be authenticated under the seal of the Court. *Pool* v. *Hill*, 2 *Kerr* 184.

Judgment of Court of King's Bench in England—Proof of. See Evidence II. 17.

JUDGMENT AS IN CASE OF NON-SUIT.

I. MATTERS RELATING TO PRACTICE.
II. ANSWERS—EXCUSE—SUFFICIENCY—INSUFFICIENCY.
III. DISCHARGING RULE ON PEREMPTORY UNDERTAKING — ANSWERS —ENLARGING RULE.

I.

MATTERS RELATING TO PRACTICE.

1—Entertaining Motion—Compliance with Rule of Court.
The Court will not entertain motions for judgment as in case of non-suit unless the requisites of the rule of Hilary Term 6 Wm. 4, have been complied with. *Harris* v. *Beamont*, 2 *Kerr* 172.

2—Remanet.
Where a cause has been entered for trial, and made a remanet, the defendant cannot move for judgment as in case of a nonsuit for a subsequent default. *Embree* v. *Hatheway*, *Trin. T.* 1827.

3—Not proceeding to Second Trial.
Where a cause has been tried and the verdict set aside, judgment as in a case of a nonsuit cannot be granted for not proceeding to a second trial. *Turner* v. *Crane*, *Trin. T.* 1831.

4—Subsequent notice after Remanet.
Where a plaintiff has once taken down his cause to the assizes, and it has been made a remanet, the defendant cannot obtain judgment as in case of a nonsuit, though the plaintiff may have given a subsequent notice of trial, on which he has made default. *Bennett* v. *Stockford*, 1 *Kerr* 300.

5—Fresh Default.
A cause was entered for trial at the Circuit in 1865, and struck off, and the

plaintiff paid the costs of the day. No notice of trial was given for the next circuit. Held, That this was a fresh default, and that the defendant was entitled to judgment as in case of a non-suit. *Thomson* v. *Keith, Mich. T.* 1866.

6—Time.

There is no limit of time for a defendant to move for judgment as in case of a non-suit, nor is a term's notice necessary where four terms have elapsed without any proceedings. *Scoullar* v. *Payson, Trin. T.* 1833.

7—Cause postponed with assent of defendant.

If a plaintiff has once taken his cause down to trial, and the trial be postponed to the next Circuit with the assent of the defendant, the defendant is not entitled to judgment as in case of a non-suit for not then proceeding to trial. *Gilbert* v. *Dunham*, 2 *Kerr* 361.

8—Two defendants—Settlement with one.

Where two defendants appeared by the same attorney and pleaded jointly, and afterwards one of them settled with and paid the plaintiff, the other defendant cannot move for judgment as in case of a non-suit. *McGlynn* v. *Falconer, Hil. T.* 1861.

9—Trial by record—Notice—Statute not applicable.

Where the plaintiff has given notice of trial by the record, but failed to bring the cause on for trial, the defendant cannot obtain judgment as in case of a non-suit. The Statute only applies where the plaintiff could be non-suited on the trial. *Kelly* v. *Coughlan*, 3 *Kerr* 104.

10—Summoning Jury—Number.

A *venire* to summon 12 jurors to try a cause is correct, but as the number stated is not for the officer's guide in summoning, he should summon 24. If he only summons 12, and for that reason the cause is not tried, the plaintiff is not liable for costs of the day or to judgment as in case of a non-suit. *Hazen* v. *Bryson*, 2 *All.* 580.

11—Service of notice.

A notice of motion for judgment, as in case of non-suit, must be served on the plaintiff's attorney. Service on the plaintiff is insufficient. *Murphy* v. *Close*, 3 *All.* 83.

11 *a*—What will be deemed a sufficient service of notice of motion, for judgment as in case of non-suit, on the plaintiff's attorney who has left the Province. See *Wheelock* v. *Alden*, 2 *Kerr* 172.

12—Offer to suffer judgment.

A rejected offer to suffer judgment by default, under the Act 18 Vic. c. 9, does not prevent the defendant from obtaining judgment as in case of a nonsuit. *Thomas* v. *Demill*, 3 *All.* 407.

13—Replevin—Not grantable in.

Judgment as in case of a non-suit cannot be granted in replevin. *McGeehan* v. *Hale*, 3 *All.* 507.

Where such a judgment was inadvertently granted, the nature of the action not having been stated, the Court set it aside, notwithstanding the omission of the plaintiff's counsel to take the objection on the motion for the judgment. *Ibid.*

14—Demurrer pending.

A party is not in a condition to move for judgment as in case of a non-suit for not proceeding to trial pursuant to notice, where a demurrer is pending to one part of the cause of action. In such cases the motion may be for costs occasioned by not proceeding to trial pursuant to notice; but this cannot be done in a proceeding of which fourteen days notice has been given to move for judgment as in case of a nonsuit. *Kinnear* v. *Watts*, 3 *Kerr* 300.

15—Venue—Affidavit.

The affidavit to found a motion for judgment as in case of a nonsuit for not proceeding to trial according to the practice of the Court must state where the *venue* is laid. *Doe* v. *Wry*, 2 *All.* 311.

16—Double motion—Costs of day.

Where a motion for judgment, as in case of a nonsuit, was pending, the Court discharged with costs, a motion for costs of the day for the same default. *Stevens* v. *Hamilton*, 1 *Han.* 335.

17—Defect in affidavit.

The Court refused without costs, a rule for judgment *quasi* non-suit, for not proceeding to trial pursuant to notice, where the name of the Commissioner was omitted from the *jurat* in the copy of the affidavit stating the plaintiff's default, served on plaintiff's attorney. *Belyea* v. *Hamm*, 2 *Han.* 26.

18—Joinder of Issue—Affidavit.

An affidavit stating that issue was joined as of Michaelmas term last past is *prima facie* sufficient to support a motion for judgment as in case of a nonsuit.

19—Terms elapsing.
There is no arbitrary rule that two terms or two assizes should pass after issue joined in order to sustain a motion for judgment as in case of a non-suit for not proceeding to trial, according to the practice of the Court, but the plaintiff is bound to proceed to trial at the first *nisi prius* held next after the term immediately succeeding that in which issue is joined, provided there is sufficient time to give notice of trial. (See next cases.) *Sprague* v *Matthews, Ber.* 433.

20—A plaintiff is bound to try his cause at the first Circuit after issue joined, unless issue be joined of the term immediately preceding. *Samuel* v. *McAndrews, Ber.* 278.

21—Where issue is joined in vacation, it refers to the next subsequent and not the preceding term, although joined as of the preceding term; in such case therefore judgment as in case of a non-suit cannot be moved for until two terms have elapsed after issue joined. *McDonald* v. *Ryder,* 2 *Kerr* 645.

22—Where issue is joined in vacation, two subsequent terms must elapse before judgment, as in case of a non-suit for not proceeding to trial pursuant to the practice of the Court, can be obtained. *McClelan* v. *McClelan,* 3 *Kerr* 223.

23—After a review of all the cases—Held, That where two circuits or sittings have passed after issue joined, at either of which the plaintiff might have tried the cause, the defendant may move for judgment as in case of a non-suit for not proceeding to trial according to the practice of the Court. *Oliver* v. *Campbell, Hil. T.* 1871.

24—Limit of time for motion—Term's notice.
There is no limit of time for a defendant to move for judgment as in case of a non-suit; nor is a term's notice necessary where four terms have elapsed without any proceedings. *Scoullar* v. *Payson, Trin. T.* 1833.

25—Entry of cause.
Judgment as in case of a non-suit cannot be signed unless the cause has been duly entered by the plaintiff in the Clerk's office. *Miller* v. *Weldon,* 1 *Han.* 376.

II.

Answers—Excuse.

1—Sufficiency.
An affidavit of the plaintiff, stating that the record was withdrawn at the trial "because he was advised by counsel that the testimony of one W. B. was material and necessary, and that the said W. B. now resides at Boston in the United States, and the plaintiff hopes to be able to procure his testimony at the next circuit." Held, A sufficient excuse on the first default. *Desmond* v. *Yeomans,* 3 *Kerr* 71.

2—The absence of material documentary evidence, which belonged to a person who was willing to produce it, but could not then procure it in time for trial, is a sufficient excuse in opposing a rule for judgment as in case of a non-suit. *Doe d. Scott* v. *King,* 3 *Kerr* 72.

3—The evidence of a material witness in a distant part of the Province, who was unable to attend without serious loss and inconvenience, greatly disproportioned to the amount in controversy, is a sufficient excuse for the plaintiff not taking his cause to trial at the first assizes. *Scovil* v. *Eaton,* 3 *Kerr* 73.

4—The affidavit, in answer to a motion for judgment as in case of a non-suit, stated that the case arose out of circumstances similar to those existing in a case of W. against the defendant in this suit, tried at the same assizes, and the plaintiff withdrew the record in consequence of the Judge who tried the cause having decided the question of law against W. A motion for a new trial in that case having been refused, and the facts shewing that the plaintiff in this case could not recover, the rule for judgment as in case of a non-suit was granted. *White* v. *McDonald,* 3 *Kerr* 220.

5—In answer to a motion for judgment as in case of a non-suit, the affidavit of the plaintiff's attorney stated that a commission had been issued to examine witnesses on the part of the plaintiff, at W. in the United States; that one of the plaintiffs residing at W. had written to the other plaintiff residing in this Province, that the commission had been received, and would be executed; in consequence of which he gave notice of trial, but was obliged to countermand the same, the commission not having been returned; that the plaintiff residing at W. had since written to the other plaintiff, assigning as a reason for not executing the commission, his necessary absence on pressing business, and the residence of one of the required witnesses at a distance from the place where the commissioners resided; and stating that the commission should be executed and returned. Held, A sufficient excuse. *Doe dem McTavish* v. *Roulstin*, 3 *Kerr* 221.

6—It is a sufficient excuse for not proceeding to trial, that the defendant has since the commencement of the action taken the benefit of the Insolvent Debtors' Act; and in such case, a motion for judgment as in case of a non-suit will be dismissed with costs, unless the defendant consents to a *stet processus*. *Ketchum* v. *Murray*, 2 *All.* 94.

7—The absence of a material witness from the Province during the sitting of the Court, is a sufficient answer to a motion for judgment as in case of non-suit upon the first default. *Kirk* v. *Payne*, 1 *Kerr* 525.

8—It is a sufficient answer to an application for judgment as in case of a non-suit in an action of trespass *qu. cl. fregit*, that the plaintiff's attorney had by mistake laid the venue in the wrong county—the plaintiff offering a peremptory undertaking and paying costs. *Peters* v. *Drawyer*, 3 *All.* 432.

9—Where plaintiff, after notice of trial, was induced by the defendant to agree to refer the cause to arbitration, a motion for judgment, as in case of a non-suit, was refused with costs. *McDonald* v. *McIntyre*, *Ber.* 280.

10—Where a cause was entered for trial, and withdrawn on an agreement to refer, which the defendant afterwards refused to carry out, an application for judgment as in case of a non-suit was refused with costs. *Hanson* v. *Gove*, *Hil. T.* 1863.

11—**Insufficiency.**
Judgment as in case of a nonsuit, for not proceeding to trial pursuant to notice, will be granted, although the plaintiff became bankrupt, and an assignee appointed. *Hammond* v. *Wheeler*, 2 *Kerr* 560.

12—Where the cause had been at issue, and noticed for trial more than three years, and the only excuses offered for the delay were a hope that had been entertained of avoiding the expense of a commission by getting the cause referred to arbitration, but which was finally refused—an intention to apply for a commission, and a belief that the cause would be ready for trial at the next circuit. Held, Insufficient to discharge a rule for judgment as in case of non-suit on a peremptory undertaking. *Fletcher* v. *Hippesley*, 3 *Kerr* 299.

13—An affidavit of the plaintiff's attorney, stating that he sent the *nisi prius* record to the circuit for entry, but when he arrived there discovered it had not been received, without stating when or how it was sent, is not sufficient to discharge, on a peremptory undertaking, a rule for judgment as in case of a non-suit, for not proceeding to trial at such circuit pursuant to notice. *Kinnear* v. *Watts*, 3 *Kerr* 440.

14—An affidavit stating that the deponent was informed and believed that the defendant had run off to the United States without leaving any property in this country, is no answer to a motion for judgment as in case of a non-suit. *McGarrigle* v. *Smith*, 1 *All.* 509.

15—Where the plaintiff did not try his cause in 1849, in consequence of the absence of a witness, it is no excuse for not going to trial at the circuit in the following year; that during the summer of 1849 the defendant expressed a wish to the plaintiff's attorney to settle the suit amicably—the plaintiff not appearing to have assented thereto, and not stating any intention to go to trial. *Wetmore* v. *Wood*, 1 *All.* 703.

16—It is no answer to a motion for judgment as in case of a non-suit, that the plaintiff instructed his attorney to send him subpœnas for his witnesses, after the opening of the Court at which the cause was entered for trial, and that in consequence of not receiving the subpœnas, he was unable to get the necessary witnesses. *Curran* v. *Gilmour*, 2 *All.* 87.

If a sufficient excuse is offered, it is admissible in a *qui tam* action as well as in any other; but in judging of the excuse, the Court will not altogether lose sight of the nature of the action. *Ibid.*

17—Notice of trial was given for the circuit in 1850, and countermanded in consequence of discovering that a material witness was in England; notice of trial was again given for the circuit in 1851, but the cause was not tried, a commission which had issued to examine the witness in England not having been returned. It was not stated that the commission had issued in time to be returned before the circuit. Held, That the defendant was entitled to judgment as in case of a non-suit. *Ritchie* v. *Porter*, 2 *All.* 360.

18—It is no excuse for not proceeding to trial according to notice, that the plaintiff's attorney was so much engaged in the House of Assembly as to be unable to attend the trial, and that the counsel spoken to on the previous day to try the cause, was occupied in another Court—it not appearing that the counsel was prevented attending by any unforeseen cause, or that no other sufficient counsel could be procured. *Estabrooks* v. *Tapley*, 2 *All.* 454.

19—An affidavit stating that the reason for not going to trial was the absence of a witness who resided in Calais; without alleging that he was a material witness, or that any effort had been made to procure his attendance or his evidence, is not a sufficient answer to a motion for judgment as in case of a non-suit. *Nicholson* v. *Marks*, 3 *All.* 21.

20—Service of a rule to discontinue, without payment of the costs, will not prevent the defendant from obtaining judgment as in case of a non-suit. *White* v. *Barton*, 1 *Han.* 1.

21—An affidavit of the plaintiff's attorney, stating the absence of a material witness, and his belief that the testimony of the witness could be procured at the next circuit, is not sufficient to oppose a rule for judgment as in case of a non-suit for not going to trial pursuant to notice, without stating the grounds of his belief, or shewing that anything had been done to procure the attendance of the witness; but time was allowed to obtain further affidavits. *Mitchell* v. *Cuppage*, *Ber.* 277.

III.

Discharging Rule on Peremptory Undertaking—Answers Enlarging Rule.

1—An application for judgment as in case of a non-suit for not proceeding to trial pursuant to notice, is sufficiently answered by showing that the plaintiff was ready and desirous to proceed to trial, but was prevented from doing so by the defendant's attorney objecting to the insufficiency of the notice of trial. And in making such application, if it appear that the default really was for not proceeding to trial according to the practice of the Court, the motion will not succeed. *McDonald* v. *Ryder*, 3 *Kerr* 218.

A mistake in reference to an almanac in giving the notice of trial, which was defective, the plaintiff being ready at the Court with counsel and witnesses to try the cause, and the refusal of the defendant's attorney to waive the objection to the notice, is a sufficient excuse on a first default for enlarging a rule, on a peremptory undertaking. *Ibid.*

2—Where in an action against the Sheriff, the plaintiff's attorney issued the *venire* to a Coroner who was connected with the plaintiff (but of which the attorney was ignorant) in consequence of which the defendant challenged the array and the cause was not tried; the Court discharged a rule for judgment as in case of a non-suit, on the plaintiff's giving a peremptory undertaking and paying costs. *Stiles* v. *Gilbert*, 3 *All.* 262.

3—It is a sufficient answer to an application for judgment as in case of a non-suit in an action of trespass *qu. cl. fregit*, that the plaintiff's attorney had by mistake laid the venue in the wrong county—the plaintiff offering a peremptory undertaking and paying costs. *Peters* v. *Drawyer*, 3 *All.* 432.

4—Issue was joined in 1854, and by the consent of the defendant's attorney the cause was not tried during the following year: no further proceedings having been taken, the Court, in Hilary term 1858, dismissed a motion for judgment as in case of a non-suit, on the plaintiff's giving a peremptory undertaking to try the cause—it appearing that he had a good cause of action, and the defendant not stating any defence. *Doe* v. *Sentill*, 4 *All.* 58.

5—Where two defendants had appeared and pleaded by separate attorneys in two suits brought by the same plaintiff, and notice of trial had been given in one suit for the Sittings after Hilary term 1859, but it was not tried, in consequence of one of the defendants having compromised the suits, the Court refused a rule for judgment as in case of a non-suit on application of the other defendant, on the plaintiff entering a *stet processus* and defraying the costs of the application in both cases, and the costs of the day in the suit in which notice of trial had been given. *Rankin* v. *Anderson*, 4 *All.* 635.

6—It is sufficient ground for enlarging a peremptory undertaking, that the plaintiff, who claimed under a will, was unable to discover the residence of the subscribing witness. *Connell* v. *Haley*, 4 *All.* 636.

7—Where the plaintiff countermanded notice of trial twice, first, because the presiding Judge at the Court was incapable from interest from trying the cause, and secondly, in consequence of the absence of the plaintiff's counsel from the country, a rule for judgment as in case of a non-suit was discharged on a peremptory undertaking. *Shepherd* v. *Hallett*, 1 *Han.* 43.

8—In answer to an application for judgment as in case of a non-suit, where the cause had not been tried in consequence of a challenge to the array, the plaintiff's attorney stated, that he did not issue a *venire* to the Coroner, in consequence of a statement of the defendant's attorney leading him to believe that there was no relationship between the Sheriff and the defendant, the Court ordered the application to stand over, in order that the defendant's attorney might answer the affidavit. *Hoyt* v. *Stockton*, 1 *Han.* 327.

9—An affidavit stating the temporary mental derangement of a witness, and his subsequent recovery, is sufficient to discharge a rule for judgment as in case of a non-suit, upon giving a peremptory undertaking and paying costs. *Samuel* v. *Saunders*, *Ber.* 278.

10—An affidavit of the plaintiff stating that he left the country on important business expecting to return in time for the trial, but was unable to do so, is not a sufficient answer to a motion for judgment, as in case of a non-suit. The affidavit should state all the circumstances which prevented the plaintiff's return, in order that the Court might judge whether his conclusion of inability to return was justified. *Desbrisay* v. *Livingston*, *Hil. T.* 1862.

11—There is a distinction between cases where the record is withdrawn in consequence of the absence of the plaintiff, and where it is caused by the absence of a third party. *Ibid.*

12—An action of Dower, under the Act 21 Vic. c. 25, was not tried, because the defendant's counsel objected, and the Judge thought it could not be tried by the common jury, nor until an order for a view had been made, as directed by the Act: a motion for judgment, as in case of a non-suit, was refused, without costs. *Doe d. McCullough* v. *Dowd*, *Mich. T.* 1862.

13—**Peremptory undertaking.**

A peremptory undertaking will not be discharged on an affidavit stating that the defendant had left the Province, and had stated that he did not intend to return. *Leslie* v. *Rae*, *Ber.* 32.

14—A peremptory undertaking will not be enlarged merely on the ground that when the cause was called on for trial, a witness who resided in town, was not in Court, and therefore the record was withdrawn. *Doe dem Kinnear* v. *Wiswell*, *Bert.* 127.

15—The Court will enlarge a peremptory undertaking to go to trial where suspicion attaches on the defendant that he has been instrumental in keeping material witnesses out of the way of being served with subpœna. *Robertson* v. *Crandall*, 1 *Kerr* 56.

16—Where the defendant had given notice of trial by proviso, and had afterwards countermanded it when it was too late for the plaintiff to give notice; the Court enlarged a peremptory undertaking, the plaintiff appearing to have been misled by the defendant's notice. *Gilbert* v. *Gooden*, 2 *Kerr* 374.

17—A peremptory undertaking will not be enlarged unless the plaintiff show that he has used all reasonable and ordinary means to fulfil it. *McDonald* v. *Thompson*, 2 *Kerr* 700.

18—Affidavit of the plaintiff's attorney stated that he did not go to trial at the Court at W. because he understood that an objection had been sustained to the legality of the jury by the Court at Saint John, in consequence of the Sheriff not having filed a list of persons qualified to serve as jurors; and knowing that the Sheriff of W. had not filed any list, he expected a similar objection would be taken by the defendant. Held, A sufficient ground for enlarging a peremptory undertaking. *Sidell* v. *Best*, 3 *Kerr* 640.

The plaintiff being in contempt for non-payment of the costs incurred by his first default, it was made a condition of enlarging the rule that those costs, the costs of the day on the second default, and the costs of the motion, should be paid within a month. *Sidell* v. *Best*, 3 *Kerr* 640.

19—A rule absolute for not proceeding to trial according to peremptory undertaking, cannot be moved for until the term succeeding the sittings in which plaintiff undertook to bring on the cause, notwithstanding time has gone by for giving notice of trial. The plaintiff may move for enlarging the undertaking during the term. The condition is not broken until time for trial is past. *Groves* v. *Sisson*, 1 *Kerr* 102.

20—A peremptory undertaking will not be enlarged on the ground that the plaintiff's counsel advised on the first day of the Circuit, that the declaration must be amended—in consequence of which, the cause was not tried. *Marshall* v. *Winslow*, *Mich. T.* 1833.

JUDGMENT BY DEFAULT.

See Interlocutory Judgment.
" Practice X.

1—Signing of—Plea treated as a nullity.

In a summary action on a promissory note, the defendant pleaded as to part, that the plaintiff had sustained damage by the non-performance of the promises to the amount of £7. 9s. which he confessed and was ready to pay; and as to the residue non-assumpsit. The plaintiff treated the plea as a nullity, and signed judgment. Held, That the judgment was regular, it not being shewn that the plea was filed in time. *Sayre* v. *Smith*, 2 *All.* 164.

Quære, Whether such a plea was good in a summary action? But if pleaded in time, it should not have been treated as a nullity. *Ibid.*

Semble, That being accompanied by a notice of set-off, the plaintiff could not have signed judgment for the sum confessed. *Ibid.*

2—Setting aside—Costs.

In Hilary term an interlocutory judgment was set aside on payment of costs, and on terms of the defendant paying £7. 9s. into Court within ten days after taxing costs, and if defendant would not accede to these terms, the motion to be dismissed without costs. The rule entered by the clerk of the Court and served on the defendant was unconditional, "that the motion be dismissed without costs." The defendant afterwards paid part of the amount, and agreed to pay the plaintiff the balance in two months. The defendant afterwards discovered that the rule had been improperly entered, and in Trinity term applied to set aside the judgment. The Court considering that the defendant's attorney might have ascertained the decision of the Court, refused the application. *Sayre* v. *Smith*, 2 *All.* 363.

3—For want of plea—Pleas and notice of defence.

Judgment by default for want of a plea cannot be signed after the plea is filed and a copy delivered to the plaintiff's attorney, though the filing and delivery were after the time for pleading had expired. *Oulton* v. *Palmer*, 2 *All.* 364.

If two pleas are pleaded, and a notice of other matters of defence given under the Act 13 Vic. c. 32, the plaintiff is not justified in treating them as a nullity; but should apply to a Judge to set them aside. *Ibid.*

The actual signature of counsel is not necessary to the copy of plea delivered. *Ibid.*

4—Signing too Soon.

By the Act 12 Vic. c. 40, a defendant in a summary action has thirty days to plead from the last day of the term exclusively, though the writ may have been returnable on the first day of the term; therefore where the term ended on the 20th October, judgment by default signed on the 19th November, was too soon. *Glass* v. *Corrigan*, 3 *All.* 295.

5—Summary Costs.

The defendant allowed judgment by default to be signed against him for a sum above £20, though the amount due the plaintiff was under that sum; the Court refused, after final judgment signed, to stay the proceedings on payment of the sum due, and summary costs. *Collins* v. *McArthy*, 3 *All.* 504.

6—Setting aside after execution of writ of inquiry.

A judgment by default in an action of *tort*, set aside on payment of costs after the execution of a writ of inquiry, on an affidavit of merits, and that the omission to appear was through ignorance and mistake—no trial having been lost. *Burrell* v. *James*, 3 *All.* 599.

7—Effect as evidence.
In an action of covenant on a deed purporting to have been executed at Birmingham, judgment by default admits the deed as declared on, and no proof of it is necessary on an inquiry of damages. *Hasluck* v. *McMaster*, *Mich. T.* 1825.

8—Judgment by default—Assessment—Affidavit.
In assessing damages under the act after judgment by default, the plaintiff must establish the amount of his debt or damages by legal proof. Where the only evidence of the debt was an account shewing several sums of money due from the defendant to the plaintiff on various transactions, with an affidavit of the plaintiff, that "the account was just and true;" it was held insufficient, and the judgment was set aside. See Practice VI. 50.

Judgment by default in Ejectment—Setting aside—Merits. See Ejectment IV. 4.

Summary action—Filing plea before appearance—Letting defendant in to defend. See Andrews v. Hanson, 1 All. 509.

What not a waiver of irregularity in signing. See Practice VII. 11, 12.

JUDGMENT (INTERLOCUTORY).

See Judgment by Default.
" Practice V. 30, 31, 32.
" do. VI. 15, 16, 17, 18.
" do. VII. 10, 11, 12.
" do. X.

JUDGMENT NUNC PRO TUNC.

Making up new record. See Judgment.

JUDGMENT NON OBSTANTE VEREDICTO.

Covenant—Immaterial Plea. See Covenant 12.

Replevin—Pleading. See Pleading II. 29.

JUDGMENT OF NON PROS.

See Practice VI. 8–12.

JUDGMENT ROLL.

See Amendment III. See Judgment.

JUDGMENT (RULE FOR).

See Practice VIII.

JURAT.

See Affidavit V.

JURISDICTION.

See Bastardy—Justice of the Peace—Courts—Criminal Law—Writ of Error—Foreign Judgment—Fredericton (City of)—Replevin.

JURORS.

Affidavits of. See Affidavit IV. See New Trial II. 41.

Conduct of. See New Trial II. III.

Fees as witness—Right to recover See Costs II. 37.

JURY.

See Evidence XII.

1—Summoning of—Highway.
Where the proceedings of Commissioners in altering a road under the Act 5 Wm. 4, c. 2, were objected to, whereupon the inhabitants applied to two Justices to obtain a warrant for a jury. Held, That it was not necessary that the jury should be summoned from another parish. *Reg.* v. *Commissioners of Highways for Parish of Johnston*, 3 *Kerr* 593.

2—Venire.
A *venire* to summon twelve jurors to try a cause is correct, but as the number stated is not for the officer's guide in summoning, he should summon twenty-four. *Hazen* v. *Bryson*, 2 *All.* 580.

Quære, Whether thirty jurors ought not to be summoned under the Act 13 Vic, c. 43. *Ibid.*

(See Venire.)

3—Qualification of.
A person named in the Act of Incorporation and in the list of subscribers, who never authorised his name to be used or hold any shares in the Company, ceases to be a member thereof after the first meeting to organize the Company, and is therefore not disqualified as a juror, in an action brought by them. *Portland Ferry Company* v. *Pratt*, 2 *All.* 17.

4—Challenge of.
It is not a ground of challenge to the array, that some of the jurors named in the Sheriff's panel are not on the list of persons qualified to serve as jurors, filed under the Act 18 Vic. c. 24. *Dow and Wife* v. *Dibblee*, 1 *Han.* 55.

5—It is no ground of challenge to the array, that the action is based upon a lease made by the Mayor, etc., of St. John to the lessor of the plaintiff; that the Mayor, etc., had, or claimed to have, a reversionary interest in the land in dispute; and that the Sheriff who summoned the jury, and the jurors, were Corporators of St. John—it not being alleged that the Corporation of St. John had any interest in the suit. *Doe dem. Grant* v. *Boyne*, 1 *Han.* 431.

It is no ground of challenge to a juror in an action brought by a Corporation, that he is in the employ of one of the stockholders in the Company. *Fredericton Boom Co.* v. *Murpherson*, 2 *Han.* 8.

6—Where the Sheriff and Coroner had married sisters, it is a good ground of challenge to the array, that the jury have been returned by the Coroner in a cause where the Sheriff is defendant; and the death of the wife of the latter without issue does not destroy the affinity. *Oulton* v. *Morse*, 2 *Kerr* 77.

The objection, however, not having been taken by the defendant until the cause was called on for trial, at a late day of the Court, the costs of the day for not proceeding to trial pursuant to notice were refused. *Ibid.*

7—It is no principal cause of challenge to the array, that the Sheriff by whom the jury were returned was married to a sister of the person who was security for the costs, and who had aided the plaintiff with money to carry on the suit; but the Court would in such case, on application by the defendant, award the *venire* to the Coroner. *Murchison* v. *Marsh*, 2 *Kerr* 608.

8—The defendant may challenge the array if affinity exists between the Sheriff who summoned the jury and himself. *Wetmore* v. *Levi*, *Trin. T.* 1861.

9—**Illness of—Trial—Waiver.**
If one of the jury is taken ill during a trial, the Judge cannot, without consent of the parties, swear another juror in his place, and continue the trial. The objection is not waived by the defendant's counsel afterwards addressing the jury. *Noble* v. *Billings*, 3 *All.* 85.

10—**Disqualification.**
The fact of a man being in the employment of a stockholder of an Incorporated Company, does not disqualify him from serving as a special juryman in the trial of a case to which the Company is a party. *Fredericton Boom Co.* v. *McPherson*, 2 *Han.* 8.

A challenge for cause to a special juryman must be supported by affidavits. (Per Weldon, J. at *Nisi Prius.*)

Jury of View—Lodging and boarding with plaintiff. See New Trial III. 46.

Special Jury—Talesmen.
Talesmen may be sworn on special jury. See *Rankin* v. *Godard*, 4 *All.* 155.

Striking Panel — Abandonment of Rule. See Practice VII. 1.

JUSTICE OF THE PEACE.

I. Courts.
II. Jurisdiction in Civil Cases.
III. Duties—Liability.
IV. Summary Convictions.
  A. Jurisdiction.
  B. Information.
  C. Proceedings for Penalties.
V. Convictions.
VI. Generally.
VII. Costs.
VIII. Notice of Action.

See Criminal Law—Bastardy.

I.
Courts.

1—Courts of Justices of the Peace established by the Act 4 Wm. 4, c. 45, are not Courts of Record. *Young* v. *Woodcock*, 3 *Kerr* 554.

2—A limited power given to a Court to fine and imprison does not constitute it a Court of Record. *Ibid.*

Power of Justices to commit for contempt —Acting judicially are Courts of Record. See Contempt.

II.
Jurisdiction in Civil Causes.

1—**Civil Cause—Trespass to land—Title in question.**
A Justice of the Peace has no jurisdiction to try an action of trespass to land under the Act 4 Wm. 4, c. 45, where the defendant claims an interest in, or a right to the use of the land; as where the question was whether there was a public highway over the land. *Sloan* v. *Davis*, 2 *All.* 593.

2—A Justice of the Peace has not jurisdiction under the Act 56 Geo. 3, c. 17, to try an action where the title to land comes in question, and if the defendant in an action trespass justifies entering on the land, as being a highway, the jurisdiction of the Justice is ousted. *Colwell* v. *Purdy*, *Trin. T.* 1831.

2 *a*—If in an action of trespass to land, tried before a Justice of the Peace, the defendant sets up title and offers a deed in evidence, and the plaintiff also gives evidence of deeds and of a title arising by estoppel, on which the Justice undertakes to decide; the title is *bona fide* in question, and the Justice has no jurisdiction. *Regina* v. *Harshman, East. T.* 1873.

3—**Seamen's Wages.**
By the Act of Parliament 7 & 8 Vic. c. 112, s. 15, in all cases of wages not exceeding £20 which shall be due and payable to any seamen, it shall be lawful for any Justice of the Peace in and for any part of her Majesty's Dominions where, or near to the place where the ship shall have ended her voyage, &c., to make an order for payment of the wages. Held, 1. That any Justice in the county where the voyage ended, had jurisdiction 2. That if there had been a deviation from the voyage agreed upon, or the ship was unseaworthy, the seamen had a right to determine the contract, and to recover wages to the time of leaving the ship. 3. That the jurisdiction of Justices under s. 15 extended to all cases where wages were due and payable, and not merely to the cases specified in s. 11. 4. That the order of the Justice need not fix any time for the payment of the wages. *Regina* v. *Wheaten*, 3 *All.* 269.

4—**Money demand—Review from Justice's Court.**
Where the particulars of the plaintiff's demand in a Magistrate's Court, were 3d. over £5, though the amount stated in the summons was for £5, and the demand proved, which had not been reduced by actual payment, was less than £5, and the verdict for 2s. 9d. Held, That the Magistrate had no jurisdiction. *Draper* v. *Monroe*, 3 *Kerr* 438.

5—**Waiving Balance.**
A Justice of the Peace has no jurisdiction under the Act 4 Wm. 4, c. 45, in cases of debt where the amount exceeds £5, unless reduced to that sum by actual payments. A creditor has not the power of bringing such a debt within the jurisdiction of a Justice, by waiving the balance of his claim so as to bring the demand within the sum to which the Justices' Courts are limited. *White* v. *Macklin*, 1 *Kerr* 94.

See Revised Statutes (Justice's Act) allowing abandonment.

6—An objection, that a defendant was a commissioner for laying out public money, and as such contracted with the plaintiff, and is not therefore personally liable, cannot be set up upon review of the Justices' judgment, where it was not made at the trial before the Justices. The proceedings in Magistrates' Courts are regulated by the same general rules as in other Courts. *Cormier* v. *Tibideau*, 1 *Kerr* 297.

7—In the case of a review from a Justice's Court, it is not a sufficient ground for reversing the judgment that the evidence to support the verdict is slight and contradicted by that on the other side, if the whole case be such as the Justice was warranted in submitting to the jury for their decision. *Lee* v. *Breen*, 2 *Kerr* 323.

8—On review from a Justice's Court, the defendant against whom judgment had been rendered did not deny his liability, but contended that he was jointly liable with another person, and that although the action had been commenced against both, judgment had been rendered against him alone. It appearing on the Justice's return that he was the only defendant who had been served with summons and appeared, and that the judgment had been so entered at his request; the Court affirmed the judgment. The Court refused to receive affidavits to falsify the return. *Buckstaff* v. *Doten*, 2 *Kerr* 366.

9—On review of the judgment illegally rendered for a defendant in a Justice's Court, the same may not only be reversed, but judgment will be awarded for the plaintiff for the amount sought to be recovered, where the right is clear and the facts undisputed. *Watson* v. *Marks*, 2 *Kerr* 694.

10—The Court is very reluctant to disturb a Justice's judgment on a strict rule of law, where the substantial justice of the case is in favor of the verdict. *Jordan* v. *Coates*, 2 *All.* 107.

11—**Replevin.**
A Justice of the Peace may grant reple-

vin for cattle impounded, for breach of regulations of Justices in Sessions made under the Act 13 Vic. c. 30, it being in the nature of a distress damage feasant. See *Sterling* v. *Jones*, 2 *All.* 522.

12—A Justice has jurisdiction, though the value of the cattle impounded exceeds £5, if the amount required to obtain their release does not exceed that sum. *Ibid.*

13—Granting new trial.
A Justice of the Peace has no power to grant a new trial in an action tried before him under the Act 50 Geo. 3, c. 17. *Rose* v. *Marsh*, *Trin. T.* 1827.

14—Proceeding with trial—Different Justice.
Where a Justice of the Peace commences the trial of a civil suit, but is unable to proceed because he is required as a witness, and another Justice is called upon to try the cause under 1 Rev. Stat. c. 137, s. 28, he must continue the proceedings to the end of the suit, the first Justice has no further jurisdiction. *Sumner* v. *McMonagle*, *Mich. T.* 1864.

15—Commission.
A new Commission of the Peace, in which the name of one of the former Justices is omitted, does not determine his authority until he has express or implied notice of the new Commission. *Turner* v. *Doyle*, *Trin. T.* 1833.

16—Nearest Justice—Meaning.
An Act directed that the damages caused by an alteration of a road, should be assessed by five freeholders, to be appointed by "the nearest Justice of the Peace." Held, That this necessarily meant the nearest disinterested Justice. *Rex* v. *Heaviside*, *Hil. T.* 1833.

17—No jurisdiction—Issuing execution—Liability.
The judgment of an Inferior Court, involving a question of jurisdiction, is not conclusive; therefore, a Justice of the Peace is liable in an action of trespass for issuing an execution on a judgment recovered before him, in a case in which he had no jurisdiction because the title to land came in question, though the judgment remains unreversed. See *Pickett* v. *Perkins*, 1 *Han.* 131.

Issuing execution—Regular if in Statutory form. See Execution IV. 9.

Proceedings for breaking into field under lawful fence. See Trespass II. 2.

III.

Duties—Liability.

1—Paying over money.
A Justice of the Peace to whom money is paid on a judgment recovered before him, is bound to pay it over to the plaintiff in the suit, and if he does so and the judgment is afterwards reversed on appeal, he is not liable to repay the defendant, though he promised to retain the money till the appeal was decided. *Wilson* v. *Boyd*, 2 *All.* 537.

Quære, Whether a Justice is entitled to a notice of action for money had and received in such a case. *Ibid.*

2—Refusing to proceed in cause.
Where a Magistrate commenced the examination of a party on a criminal charge, and after hearing a portion of the evidence refused to proceed with it further, the Court refused to grant a mandamus at the instance of a private prosecutor to compel him to do so. *The Queen* v. *Duvaney*, 1 *Han.* 511.

3—Liability of—Trespass—Issuing execution.
A Justice of the Peace is not liable to an action of trespass for issuing a second execution for a balance due upon a judgment recovered under the Act 4 Wm. 4, c. 45, before the first execution is returned—the matter being within the Justice's jurisdiction. *Stewart* v. *Hazen*, 2 *All.* 254.

Such an execution may be irregular, but is not void. *Ibid.*

4—Defective conviction—Prior acts.
Where a Justice of the Peace has jurisdiction to try a complaint, and there has been a regular information, but the conviction and warrant of commitment are defective, he is not liable in trespass for any thing done prior to the conviction. See *Sewall* v. *Olive*, 4 *All.* 394.

See Trespass V. 2. 10.

Criminal Information against. See Criminal Information.

IV.

Summary Convictions.

A. Jurisdiction.

1—If, in a prosecution before a Justice of the Peace, under the Highway Act 5 Wm. 4, c. 2, the title to land comes in question, it must be gone into by the Justice if he entertain the suit. *Regina v. Buchanan*, 3 *Kerr* 674.

2—Proceedings taken in Foreign country.
A Magistrate has no jurisdiction to administer an oath and take examination within the limits of a Foreign country, and a commitment founded on such proceedings is void, and affords no justification in an action of trespass against the Magistrate. *Nary v. Owen, Ber.* 377.

3—Adjourning proceedings—Power.
One Justice of the Peace has power at the return day of the summons, to adjourn the proceedings till a future day, under the Summary Conviction Act, (1 Rev. Stat. c. 138, s. 21) though jurisdiction to hear the case is given to two Justices. *Ex parte Holder, Hil. T.* 1866.

4—Same Justices—Trial.
Quære, Whether a complaint, under the Act 15 Vic. c. 51, should be tried by the same Justices who issued the summons. To be available, this objection should be taken at the trial. See *Ex parte Cole*, 3 *All.* 48.

5—One Justice issuing summons—Penalty before two.
One Justice may issue the summons on a complaint under the Act 33 Vic. c. 23, though the penalty is recoverable before two Justices. *Reg. v. Simmons, Trin. T.* 1872.

6—Interest—Disqualification.
If the Justice is interested in the prosecution, as where he was a member of a Division of the Sons of Temperance, by which a prosecution for selling liquor was carried on, he is incompetent to try the cause, and a conviction before him is bad. *Ibid.*

7—Two parties acting—Authority to one.
An authority given to one Justice to recover penalties may be exercised by two. *Ex parte Dunlop*, 3 *All.* 281.

8—Summons—Warrant—Authority.
Complaint under oath of an assault was made before a Justice, on which he issued a summons: the defendant not appearing, the Justice, on proof of service of the summons, issued the warrant (B) under the Summary Convictions Act of Canada, 32 and 33 Vic. c. 31, upon which the defendant was arrested, brought before the Justice and convicted,—protesting against the proceedings. Held, That as there was a complaint under oath, the Justice had authority to issue a warrant in the first instance, and that his having used the form (B) instead of (C) did not make the arrest illegal, and that he had power to convict, though the summons served was defective in not stating the day the defendant was to appear. *Reg. v. Perkins, Trin. T.* 1872.

9—Omission of words.
Where the law directs the application of a penalty, it is no objection to a conviction for such penalty, that it omits the words, "to be paid and applied according to law," given in the forms of conviction under the Summary Conviction Act. *Ibid.*

10—Place—No objection—Conviction.
Where the jurisdiction of the Justices appeared upon the conviction, which was in form prescribed by 1 Rev. Stat. c. 138, and the place of sale spoken of at the trial appeared to be known by all parties, and no objection was then made that it was not within the jurisdiction of the Justices. Held, That the jurisdiction sufficiently appeared. *Ex parte Dunlop*, 3 *All.* 281.

11—Injuring fence.
The offence of wilfully injuring a fence under cap. 153 1 Rev. Stat. is not punishable by summary conviction. *Ex parte Mulheron*, 4 *All.* 259.

B. Information—Conviction—Proof.

12—Variance.
A variance between the information and the evidence in summary proceedings before Justices of the Peace is not fatal, since the Summary Conviction Act, 1 Rev. Stat. c. 138; therefore, on an information for selling various kinds of spirituous liquors, a conviction for selling brandy only is sufficient. *Ex parte Parks*, 3 *All.* 237.

13—It is no ground for quashing a conviction for selling spirituous liquor without license, that the information on which it is founded, and the warrant issued thereon, state the offence to be, selling "liquor" without license; or, selling contrary to the Acts of Assembly, when there is but one Act to regulate the sale; or, selling to divers persons unknown to the informant—provided the evidence proves a sale to a particular individual, and no objection was taken by the defendant at the trial to the variance between the information and proof, and it does not appear that he was in any way misled by it. *Reg.* v. *Harshman*, *Mich. T.* 1872.

14—On an information for selling spirituous liquors without license contrary to the bye-laws of the Town of Moncton, the illegal sale was proved, but there was no evidence of the bye-laws, and the Justices convicted the defendant of selling contrary to the Statute to regulate the sale of spirituous liquors (17 Vic. c. 15). Held, That as it did not appear that the defendant was misled, or had any defence on the merits, the variance between the information and the conviction was not fatal since the Rev. Stat. c. 138, s. 1. *Ex parte Dunlap*, 3 *All.* 281.

15—A warrant to search for liquors in a dwelling house in which a family resides, and no part of which is used as a shop or place for the sale of liquors, cannot issue under the Act 18 Vict. c. 36, without the oath of three persons stating their reasons for believing that liquors have been sold, or are kept in such dwelling house for illegal sale. *Reg.* v. *Salter*, 3 *All.* 321.

Proof that the house in which the liquor was seized was kept as an hotel, will not justify a search-warrant on the information of one person, as it cannot be judicially noticed that an hotel is a place for the sale of liquor. *Ibid.*

Where liquor legally imported is condemned under section 15, as being kept for illegal sale, the Justice has no power to order the casks containing the liquor to be destroyed. *Ibid.*

The *onus* of proving that the liquor was not intended for sale in order to save it from forfeiture under section 15, is thrown on the owner; but to subject him to the penalty under section 16, it must be proved that he intended the liquor for illegal sale. *Ibid.*

An information under the Act need not state that the informer is a reputable person. *Ibid.*

16—Right of party to know informer.
In a proceeding under Act 18 Vic. c. 36, s. 15, the person summoned to shew why the liquors seized should not be forfeited has a right before going into his proof to be informed who the complainant is, and what he has sworn to in the information. *Ex parte Stevenson*, 3 *All.* 391.

16 a—No complaint on oath—Party appearing.
Where power is given by an Act to a Justice of the Peace to issue a summons upon complaint made on oath, and the party to be summoned appears and defends the suit without any summons being issued, he cannot afterwards object that there was no complaint on oath—this being only a preliminary step to authorize the summons to issue. *Ex parte Wood*, 1 *All.* 422.

C. PROCEEDINGS FOR PENALTIES.

17—Summons—Service—Selling liquor.
A proceeding for a penalty under the Act 15 Vic. c. 51 for selling intoxicating liquors is not a civil suit within the Justice's Act 4 Wm. 4 requiring six days service of summons. *Semble*, Such an objection to the summons would be cured by the appearance of the defendant. *Ex parte Coll*, 3 *All.* 48.

18—Action of debt—Cumulative remedy.
The action of debt given by Act 15 Vic. c. 51, is a cumulative remedy, and does not take away the mode of proceeding prescribed by the Summary Convictions Act 12 Vic. c. 31. *Ex parte Hartt*, 3 *All.* 122.

19—Recovery before Mayor.
The penalties imposed by the Act 3 Vic. c. 47, for selling liquor without license, are recoverable before the Mayor of Fredericton, under the Act of Incorporation 14 Vic. c. 15, s. 67. *Reg.* v. *Allen*, 2 *All.* 435.

The Mayor being *ex officio* a Justice of the Peace, may in that character proceed for penalties which by the city charter are made recoverable before the Mayor. *Ibid.*

20—Under charter of the city of St. John, the fine imposed upon persons carrying on trade within the city, without having been admitted as freemen, is properly recoverable before the Mayor, although the warrant must be under the seal of the city. *Reg.* v. *Small*, 2 *Kerr* 48.

21—In whose name—No provision in Act.
A prosecution to recover a fine or penalty where no other mode is provided, must be in the name of the Queen. The common law mode of proceeding is not taken

away by 1 Rev. Stat. c. 161, s. 32. *Reg.* v. *Armstrong, East. T.* 1864.

See Fredericton (City of.)

V.

CONVICTIONS.

1—Selling liquor—No day specified.
A conviction for selling spirituous liquor without license is bad, if it does not specify the day on which the offence was committed. (But see 23 Vic. c. 33.) *The Queen* v. *French*, 2 *Kerr* 121.

2—Exceptions.
In a conviction under the Act 15 Vic. c. 51, which prohibits the sale of intoxicating liquors, except beer, ale, porter and cider, it is insufficient to allege that the sale was "contrary to the Act of Assembly." The conviction should negative the exceptions in the Act. *Ex parte Clifford*, 3 *All.* 16.

3—Persons selling—License—Onus probandi.
In a prosecution for a penalty for selling liquor without license, proof that the sale was made by a person in the defendant's shop in his absence, and without shewing any general or special employment of such person by the defendant in the sale of liquors, is sufficient *prima facie* evidence against him. *Ex parte Parks*, 3 *All.* 237.

The prosecutor need not prove that the defendant had no license. *Ibid.*

The penalty is incurred by the sale of any of the kinds of liquor mentioned in the Act 17 Vic. c. 15. *Ibid.*

4—Form.
A conviction under the Prohibitory Liquor Act 18 Vic. c. 36, must follow the form prescribed in the schedule of the Act, and not the form in the Summary Conviction Act. *Ex parte Breeze*, 3 *All.* 395.

The form of conviction given, stated that in default of payment of the fine and costs of prosecution, the defendant should be imprisoned for three months "unless the said several sums be sooner paid." Held, That a conviction under the Act, which in addition to those sums, required the costs of distress and commitment to be paid, was bad. *Ibid.*

5—Admission of sale—Different Justice—Pleading recovery.
A prosecution for selling liquor without license was instituted before A., a Justice of the Peace who, on the return of the summons, adjourned the trial. The defendant then went before another Justice, and admitted the sale, whereupon such Justice imposed a fine upon him. At the adjourned hearing before A., the defendant pleaded this conviction in bar, but A., notwithstanding, proceeded with the case, and convicted the defendant. Held, That his conviction was good. *Reg.* v. *Roberts, Trin. T.* 1863.

6—Highways.
A conviction for obstructing a highway is bad, unless it appear on the face of it that the place was a public highway. *Reg.* v. *Brittain*, 2 *Kerr* 614.

7—Dedication of a road to the public may be presumed from long user and the expenditure of statute labor on the road, and a party may be convicted under the Stat. 5 Wm. 4, c. 2, s. 16, for encroaching upon such a road, as well as upon highways duly laid out and recorded. *Reg.* v. *Buchannan*, 3 *Kerr* 674.

8—Owner of land not punishable for not removing fence—Duty of Commissioner to do so. See Highways 15.

VI.

GENERALLY.

1—Void for uncertainty.
Where the information in a conviction charged the defendant with measuring or surveying lumber intended for exportation in violation of the Act of Assembly 8 Vic. c. 81, and the evidence referred to three distinct Acts, but it did not appear for which of them the defendant had been convicted. Held, That the conviction was bad for uncertainty. Held also, That the Court had no power to allow costs on the quashing of a conviction. *Regina* v. *Stevens*, 3 *Kerr* 356.

2—A conviction adjudging the defendant to be imprisoned for twenty days or pay £5 and costs, is bad. *Reg.* v. *Wortman*, 4 *All.* 73.

3—A conviction under the 1 Rev. Stat. c. 133, s. 3, for fraudulently taking away lumber, describing it as "the property of another," is defective; it should state the name of the owner. *Ex parte Holder, Hil. T.* 1866.

4—Amending — Improperly including costs.
Where costs had been improperly includ-

ed in a conviction for breach of bye-laws of City of Fredericton, the amount was deducted, and the conviction sustained for the penalty. *Ex parte Mowry*, 3 *All.* 276.

5—A conviction for a penalty, whereby defendant was ordered to pay the fine "forthwith within thirty days," is sufficient under Rev. Stat. c. 138, Form L. *Reg.* v. *McGowan*, *Mich. T.* 1863.

6—Adjudging commitment—Application of forms—Certainty.
A conviction under the Act 33 Vic. c. 33, for selling liquor without license, is bad, if in addition to the costs of prosecution allowed by the Act, the Justices adjudge the defendant in default of payment to be committed to gaol for a certain time unless the penalty and costs, *together with the costs of commitment and conveying him to gaol*, be sooner paid. *Reg.* v. *Harshman*, *East T.* 1873.

The form of conviction (L.) in 1 Rev. Stat. c. 138 specifying the costs of commitment and conveying the defendant to gaol is not applicable to all cases, but only where the Act under which the penalty is imposed, authorizes the Justices to award such costs. *Ibid.*

A conviction for selling liquor without license, stated the sale to have been contrary to the Acts of Assembly, (stating the titles of the Acts.) Held, That it was sufficiently certain, and that the conviction was substantially good under both Acts, the first, (17 Vic. c. 15,) making the sale of liquor without license illegal, and the second, (33 Vic. c. 32,) imposing the penalty for such sale. *Ibid.*

7—Exceeding power—Gaol—Imprisonment.
The Act 34 Vic. c. 12, enacted, That during the erection of a new gaol for King's County, the Sheriff of the County was authorised to imprison any person arrested by him, in either of the gaols of the counties of St. John or Westmorland, as such Sheriff should think fit. Held, That a conviction which adjudged a person to be imprisoned in the common gaol of King's County, at Kingston, was bad—the option of the place of imprisonment being in the Sheriff by the Act. *Reg.* v. *Perkins*, *Trin. T.* 1872.

8—Enlarging Rule for quashing conviction—Application—Excuse for non-service.
A rule *nisi* for quashing a conviction was granted in Easter Term, returnable at the next term. The rule was not served upon the prosecutor or justice, until the day preceding Trinity Term. The Court refused to enlarge the rule,—no satisfactory reason being stated for the delay. *Reg.* v. *Harshman*, *Trin. T.* 1868.

Alien—Liability for tax. See Alien.

Indented Apprentice—Infant—Conviction. See Apprentice.

Removal of proceedings. See Certiorari.

Order of Justices to condemn liquor with packages, etc., is indivisible and if bad in part is bad in toto. See *Ex parte Breese*, 3 *All.* 390.

VII.

COSTS.

1—Costs cannot be given on a conviction for a penalty for breach of a bye-law of the City of Fredericton. The word "costs" in the 81st section means the costs of distress and sale. *Ex parte Mowry*, 3 *All.* 276.

2—Costs not allowed on quashing conviction. See *Reg.* v. *Stevens*, 3 *Kerr* 356.

3—Justices' Summary Conviction Act 12 Vic. c. 31, gives no general powers to award costs on convictions. *Ex parte Clifford*, 3 *All.* 16.

4—Where Justices have power to award costs on a summary conviction, they must specify the amount. *Ex parte Hartt*, 3 *All.* 122.

5—If the prosecutor appears at the trial of a complaint, and the Justice, after hearing, dismisses it, he has no power to award costs against the prosecutor under the Summary Conviction Act, 1 Rev. Stat. c. 138, s. 11. (But see Form P.) *Ex parte Beattie*, *Mich. T.* 1863.

VIII.

NOTICE OF ACTION.

See Action at Law (Notice of Action.)

Quære, As to notice of action where money not paid over. See Supra *Wilson* v. *Boyd*, III. 1.

JUS TERTII.

See Carrier 3.
" Trover 20.

JUSTIFICATION.

Proof of—On cross examination of plaintiff's witness. See Evidence VIII. 6.

Privilege of House of Assembly. See Arrest.

Defamation—General Issue. See Defamation.

Matter not allowed under general issue. See Evidence XIII.

Justifying under third party. See Trespass II. 5, 6, 11.

Under process. See Execution IV. 4.

See Evidence III. 25.

Acts which would have been waste, if done by the tenant, cannot be justified by any person acting under his authority. See Landlord and Tenant VII. 3.

Admissibility of evidence under general issue—Objection not made in time. See Evidence XI. 23.

Breaking and entering close—Defendant acting as servant of constable—General issue answering whole declaration. See Pleading II. 40.

Fences—Defect of—Trespass.
In trespass by cattle, if the defendant justify the entry of the cattle through defect of fences, it must be specially pleaded. *Gurwold* v. *Hollet*, *Mich. T.* 1834.

LAKE.

See Crown Grant I. 19.

LAND DAMAGES.

See Assessment. See Damages.
" Mandamus.

LANDLORD AND TENANT.

I. Leases—Agreements—Construction—Operation.
II. Tenancy—Notice to Quit.
III. Rent.
IV. Rights of Landlord.
V. Defence by Tenant.
VI. Leases.
VII. Miscellaneous.
(See Distress.)

I.

Leases—Agreements—Construction and Operation.

1—Grant of reversion—Tenancy determined.
M. being in possession of premises as tenant from year to year to W., a lease of the same under seal was made by W. to J. for ninety-nine years from the date. Held, That such lease took effect as a grant of the reversion for that term, and entitled J. to put an end to M.'s tenancy by a proper notice to quit. *Doe d. Jarvis* v. *McCarthy*, 3 *Kerr* 63.

2—Refusal to take possession—Liability for rent.
The plaintiff agreed to let a shop to the defendant in the same state that the tenant then in possession had it; the tenant on quitting removed some gas fittings which formed part of the shop, in consequence of which the defendant refused to take possession. Held, That he was not liable for the rent. *Dunn* v. *Howard*, 1 *All.* 615.

3—Agreement for new lease—Conditional.
The lessee of a building lease containing a covenant by the landlord to pay for improvements, being indebted to the landlord at the end of the term, surrendered all his interest in the lease, in order to secure the debt, and the landlord released the arrears of rent and agreed to renew the lease on payment of the debt within a year. Held, on a bill filed for specific performance of this agreement after the expiration of the year, That it was a conditional agreement for a new lease, and not a mortgage. *Purvis* v. *Hume*, 3 *All.* 299.

3 a—Agreement to lease—Condition for purchase.
Defendant agreed to lease ungranted land from the plaintiffs, the rent to be paid on the 1st October, and if before that day she should agree to purchase the plaintiffs' interest in the land, the rent to form part of the purchase money; but if she should determine not to purchase, and notify the plaintiffs thereof, the payment of rent was to be postponed till 1st April, when the lease was to terminate. The defendant gave no notice of intention not to purchase, but continued to pay rent for two years after the 1st April. Held, That the agreement was not absolute, and that the defendant was not liable in an

action for refusing to purchase, nor for land bargained and sold. *McCallmont* v. *Mulhall*, 4 *All.* 200.

After the termination of the plaintiffs' lease, the defendant leased the land from the Crown with the plaintiffs' consent. Held, That the relation of landlord and tenant having ceased, the defendant was liable to the plaintiffs for use and occupation. *Ibid.*

4—Ferry—Season—Termination.
The owner of a ferry leased it to the defendant in May "for the season of 1855." Held, That this was not a lease for a year, but that it terminated either at the closing of the river by ice or on the 31st December 1855. *Fraser* v. *Drynan*, 4 *All.* 74.

Plaintiff managing farm—Tenancy. See No. 8.

Surrender of lease—What amounts to. See Covenant 9.

II.

TENANCY—NOTICE TO QUIT.

5—Where A. went into possession of premises as tenant to B., and had occupied for several years, without any terms of holding being agreed upon, and never paid any rent, but built a barn and made other improvements on the premises, and on being applied to for payment of rent after B.'s death, stated that his improvements were worth more than the rent. Held, That it enured as a tenancy from year to year, and that the tenant could not be ejected without a notice to quit. *Doe d. Macqueen* v. *Hunter*, 1 *Kerr* 518.

6—Agreement to hold on new terms—Evidence.
Plaintiff, in the occupation of property as tenant from year to year of the defendant and two others, who owned the property in equal shares as tenants in common, on being applied to by the defendant shortly before the expiration of his year, stated that he wished to continue in possession another year; defendant then gave him notice that he should expect £100 per annum, for his share of the property, to which the plaintiff made no objection, but continued in possession. Defendant afterwards distrained for a quarter's rent. Held, That there was sufficient evidence for a jury to infer that the plaintiff had agreed to hold as tenant to the defendant upon the new terms. *Sturdee* v. *Merritt*, 3 *Kerr* 641.

7—Sufficiency of Tenancy—Working Farm.
A person working a farm on the shares and occupying part of the house jointly with the owner of the farm, has not such a tenancy as to prevent the owner from maintaining trespass to the land. *West* v. *Atherton*, 2 *All.* 653.

8—Working Farm—Possession—Tenancy.
In trespass for taking hay and grain, it was proved that the land on which they grew belonged to the plaintiff's father, who four years before the trial, gave it up to the plaintiff on condition that he should support his father and family; that the father continued to live on the land, but that the plaintiff took the management of the farm and sowed the grain and cut the grass. Held, That the jury were properly directed that this constituted a tenancy and gave the plaintiff the possession of the crops. *Ferguson* v. *Savoy*, 4 *All.* 263.

9—Tenancy yearly—Admission—Letter.
The plaintiff leased land to A. for two years, from the 1st May, 1848, with an agreement to renew the lease or pay for the improvements. A. assigned to B., who remained in possession till August 1851, and then assigned to the defendant, subject to the payment of the rent due. Before taking the assignment, the defendant wrote to the plaintiff, enquiring about his title to the land, and whether he (defendant) would be safe in paying the rent to B. The plaintiff answered, that he thought he had a right to look to the defendant for the rent; to which the defendant replied, admitting his liability for the rent, and that the plaintiff was the owner of the land. Held, That the letter admitted a tenancy from year to year, at the rent reserved in the lease to A., and that it was properly left to the jury to find whether such a tenancy existed. *Doe* v. *Pelletier*, 4 *All.* 33.

10—Agreement—Letting into possession under.
An Agreement was made between A. and B. in 1824, by which A. agreed to convey land to B. on payment of a certain sum of money on or before the 1st May 1829, together with the interest on the purchase money for the first three years, and eight per cent. for the last two years, as a consideration for the use of the land. B. was let into the possession under the

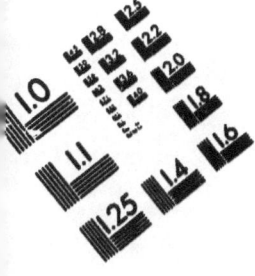

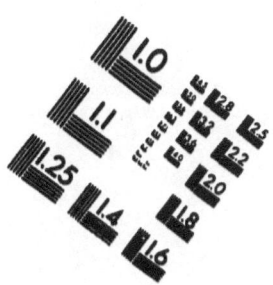

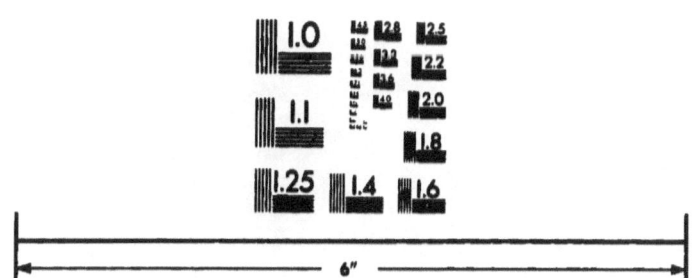

agreement. Held, That this agreement created a tenancy for years, expiring on the 1st May 1829, and not a mere tenancy at will. *Doe d. Cliff* v. *Connaway, Ber.* 382.

11—Agreement to purchase not fulfilled—Tenancy.

A. became tenant from year to year to B., at a certain rent in 1858. In 1860, A. agreed to purchase the land, and gave his note for the price, taking a bond for a deed from B. on payment of the note. The agreement to purchase was never carried out, no payment having been made by A., and by consent of the parties the agreement was destroyed, and A. remained in possession without any new agreement. Held, That the tenancy was not determined by the agreement to purchase, and that B. could distrain for the subsequent rent. Also, that whether the tenancy continued or not was a question of law. *Cronkill* v. *Wortman, Mich. T.* 1863.

12—Holding over—Notice to quit—Ejectment.

Where a tenant, under a parol lease for seven years, holds over after the expiration of the term, no notice to quit is necessary, before bringing an action of ejectment against him. *Doe d. Parkinson* v. *Haubtman, Ber.* 434.

III.

Rent.

13—Payment—Mode—Custom.

In replevin, the defendant proved an occupation by the plaintiff at annual rent from 1st May, and also by several witnesses, that rent was generally paid quarterly, and that on a general letting they thought the custom was to pay quarterly. Held (Chipman, C. J., *dubitante*), That the Judge was right in directing the jury to find for the plaintiff, because there was no sufficient evidence of an agreement to pay the rent quarterly. *Smith* v. *Milliken*, 1 *All.* 210.

Quære, If the evidence of custom was admissible. *Ibid.*

14—Acceptance of rent—Recognition of person.

Quære, Whether the acceptance of ground rent by the lessor from a person in possession, is a sufficient recognition of such person as assignee of a term. *Ansley* v. *Peters*, 1 *All.* 339.

15—Claim by landlord—Sheriff—Execution.

Where a landlord makes a claim for rent to be deducted out of the proceeds of an execution, under the Act 12 Vic. c. 39, the Sheriff is entitled to a reasonable time to inquire into the demand; and where the tenant had denied that any rent was due, and the landlord refused to allow the Sheriff time to make the inquiry, the Court refused the costs of an application to compel the Sheriff to pay the rent. *Nowlin* v. *Anderson*, 1 *All.* 497.

16—Conveyance to third party—Rent payable to—Prima facie case.

The defendant went into possession of property under an agreement with A. for three years; before the expiration of the term, A. conveyed the property in fee to the plaintiff, and told the defendant that the last quarter's rent must be paid to the plaintiff: the defendant paid the rent accordingly, and remained in possession after the expiration of the term, but refused to recognize the plaintiff as landlord. Held, in an action for use and occupation, That the plaintiff had made out a *prima facie* case, and was improperly non-suited, though the defendant had no notice of the conveyance, and though A. admitted he had no title to the land, and went there by permission of P., who was the owner. *Connell* v. *Hammond*, 2 *All.* 120.

Held also, That such evidence of title in P. should not have been received. *Ibid.*

17—Agreement with wife—Agency.

Defendant held land as tenant from year to year under an agreement with the plaintiff's wife and with his consent, by which agreement the rent was to be paid to the wife. Held, That the wife, in making the lease, must be presumed to have been acting as her husband's agent, and that the payment of rent to her would be sufficient unless her husband notified the tenant not to do so. *Doe d. Andrews* v. *Taylor, East. T.* 1861.

18—Disclaimer—What does not amount to.

A refusal to pay rent to the plaintiff, and a denial of his right to the property, but at the same time claiming to hold it under the lease from the wife, does not amount to a disclaimer. *Ibid.*

IV.

Rights of Landlord.

19—Goods seized by Sheriff—Rent not due.

When the goods of a tenant have been seized by the sheriff under a *fi. fa.*, and taken away from the demised premises before any rent became due, the landlord is not entitled to receive any part of the proceeds of such goods from the sheriff, under the Act 7 Wm. 4, c. 14, s. 11. *Street* v. *Glass*, 1 *Kerr* 165.

20—Double rent—Insufficient answer.

It is no answer to an action for the recovery of double the yearly value of premises held over after notice to quit, that subsequent to the notice and while the tenant remained in possession, an agreement was made between him and the landlord to refer to arbitration a claim made by the tenant for improvements on the premises during the tenancy. *Hatheway* v. *McMahon*, 2 *Kerr* 209.

V.

Defence by Tenant.

21—Third person disputing right of Plaintiff.

Where the defendant entered into possession as tenant to F., under a yearly rent, she cannot set up by way of defence to an action brought by the legal assignee of F. for the rent accrued subsequent to the assignment, that a third person disputes the right of the plaintiff, claiming also as assignee of F. *Ansley* v. *Longmire*, 2 *Kerr* 321.

A tenant cannot during his continuance of the possession dispute the title of the landlord under which he came into possession. *Ibid.*

22—Mortgage by Landlord.

A tenant cannot set up as a bar to the demand of his landlord for rent, that the landlord, or one under whom the landlord claimed, had previous to the demise mortgaged the premises in fee to a third person, unless the tenant has been evicted by the mortgagee, or paid the rent to the mortgagee under notice, and to avoid eviction. *Joplin* v. *Johnson*, 2 *Kerr* 541.

23—Disputing title.

The plaintiff being in possession of land, a grant of it was made by the Crown to the rector, church wardens, and vestry of W., of which the rector informed the plainti[illegible] agreed to hold the land from the rec[illegible] at an annual rent, and paid the rent two or three years. Held, That the plaintiff could not dispute the rector's title by shewing a previous grant of the same land to B., through whom he did not profess to claim. *Hughes* v. *Holmes*, 1 *All.* 12.

(See Estoppel I. 3, 20, 21.)

Defence under Mortgagee's title. See Ejectment II. 6.

24—Use and occupation—Tenancy—Evidence.

In an action for use and occupation, where it appeared that the defendant had given the plaintiff notice he would quit the plaintiff's premises at the end of the term; and after the expiration thereof the plaintiff's agent demanded the premises, which the defendant refused to give up; and at a subsequent period, before the end of the first quarter, the defendant tendered the keys to the plaintiff's agent, which he refused to receive, stating he considered the defendant tenant for another year, and liable to pay double rent; the defendant paid the first quarter's rent, after which it did not appear that he was in possession. Held, That the circumstances were not sufficient to create or continue a tenancy after the first quarter, and the verdict for the plaintiff was set aside. *Bowman* v. *Avery*, 3 *Kerr* 206.

25—A tenant having given notice of his intention to quit at the end of his term, afterwards refuse to give up possession, but before the expiration of the first quarter offered the keys to the landlord's agent, which he refused to receive, stating that he should hold the tenant liable for double rent; the tenant then ceased to occupy the premises, and afterwards paid the first quarter's rent, and pending an action for the next half year's rent, paid the last quarter's rent, after judgment by default. Held, These circumstances were not sufficient to constitute a tenancy, and that the landlord could not recover for the intermediate quarters in an action for use and occupation. *Bowman* v. *Avery*, 3 *Kerr* 587.

26—Former recovery—Erection—Claim of reduction of rent. See Action at Law (Former Recovery) *Rourke* v. *McCullough*.

27—Entirety of rent—Conveyance of reversion—Covenant.

The plaintiffs leased land to the defendant for a term of years at the rent of £30, and afterwards during the term, conveyed away the reversion in part of the land. Held, That the rent being entire, the plaintiff could not apportion it, and maintain covenant against the lessee for non-payment. *Rector &c. of Sackville* v. *Bacon*, *Trin. T.* 1864.

28—Sheriff.

Reasonable time allowed for Sheriff to enquire into claim of rent. See No. 15.

VI.

LEASES.

1—Execution of—Possession—Avoidance—Fraud.

To bring a lease within the exception of the Act 26 Geo. 3, c. 3, s. 18, it is not necessary that the execution of the lease and the possession of the land should be exactly concurrent acts. A lease from A. to C. for two years, made at a place 30 miles distant, on the 14th July, and possession taken under it on the 18th or 19th July, and continued thereafter, will not be avoided by a deed of bargain and sale to B., duly acknowledged and registered on the 3rd August; such lease to C., though made in contravention of an agreement for sale to B., will not be void on the ground of fraud, unless C. were cognizant of the agreement; and fraud will not be inferred. *Sutherland* v. *Walter*, 1 *Kerr* 141.

2—Assignee of term—Profert—Recognition—Interest recoverable.

A party suing as assignee of a term, on a covenant contained in the lease, and alleging and making profert of an assignment by deed is bound to prove it; and if several assignments are alleged, a traverse that the plaintiff became entitled *modo et forma*, puts the whole of them in issue. *Ansley* v. *Peters*, 1 *All.* 339.

Quære, Whether, if an assignment by deed had not been alleged, the acceptance of ground rent by the lessor from a person in possession, was a sufficient recognition of such person as assignee. *Ibid.*

In an action by the assignee of a lease against the lessor, on a covenant to pay for improvements according to valuation, the plaintiff is entitled to interest on the amount appraised, from the time it becomes payable. If the lessor refuse to appoint an appraiser, the jury may allow interest on the value of the improvements as part of the damages. *Ansley* v. *Peters*, 1 *All* 339.

3—Lease—Exclusive privilege to search, etc. for Coal—Period—Contingency.

By an instrument under seal, A. agreed to lease to B. the exclusive right to search for, dig, and carry away coal found in and under property thereinafter described; that such exclusive privilege of the right to search should extend over a period of four years from the date, in order that B. should have ample time to complete such search. It then described the land over which the right of search extended; and reserved to the lessor one shilling and three pence per chaldron, in the event of coal being discovered, sufficient to warrant working, and £5 per annum for the right of searching; and it was further agreed that A. did thereby lease to B., his heirs and assigns, for ninety-nine years, such and so many acres, not to exceed four, which might be required in connection with the working of the said mines, and that such privilege should extend to and be made available in entering on the said lands for the purpose of mining, etc., in connection with such mining operations. Held, That the lease for ninety-nine years was contingent upon the discovery of mines; and if none were discovered within the term of four years, the lease for ninety-nine years did not come into existence. *Caledonia Mining Company* v. *Blight*, *East. T.* 1864.

Assignee of Lessee against Lessor—Covenants. See Assignment 3.

Power of Attorney—Authority to execute leases with covenants. See Power of Attorney.

Covenants—Assignee of Lessee against Lessor—Pleading. See Pleading II. 25.

Lessor's title—Actual Entry. See Ejectment I. 2.

Covenants for new lease—Payment of Appraisement—Conditions. See Covenant 8.

Authority to lease—Mode. See Fredericton (City of).

Ejectment by Lessee against Lessor—Surrender by Lessee relied on—Question for jury. See Surrender.

VII.

MISCELLANEOUS.

1—Landlord and Tenant Act—Review of proceedings—Determination of tenancy.

An application to review proceedings under the Landlord and Tenant Act 13 Vic. c. 53, should be made at the first term after the trial, unless some reason is shewn for the delay. *Ex parte Cole*, 2 *All.* 539.

A tenant under a written lease for a year, agreed verbally to give up possession on a week's notice if the landlord could sell the property; he remained in possession after the termination of the lease, and the landlord gave him notice to quit at the termination of the third quarter in the second year. *Semble*, That the verbal agreement formed part of the terms under which he remained in possession, and that the tenancy was properly determined by the notice. *Ibid.*

2—*Semble*, That the Act 13 Vic. c. 53, s. 29, does not apply to a tenancy at will. See *Ex parte Irvin*, 2 *All.* 519.

3—Tenant cutting trees—Clearing wilderness land—Right of property in—Justification by third party.

If a tenant cuts down trees for the purpose of clearing wilderness land, they belong to him, and the cutting is not waste; but the *onus* lies on him to shew that they were cut for that purpose: and per Chipman, C. J., Carter, J. and Parker, J., they should be cut with a present intention of clearing the land. But, per Street, J., if the tenant intended to clear the land at any time during the term, it was not waste. *Rector &c. of Hampton* v *Titus*, 1 *All.* 278.

Acts which would have been waste if done by the tenant, cannot be justified by any person acting under his authority. *Ibid.*

4—Rule *nisi* or summons should issue to allow party to defend as landlord in action of ejectment, when relation of landlord and tenant does not clearly exist. See *Den* v. *Pauls*, 1 *All.* 585, 633.

5—Landlord and tenant—Writ of restitution—Title—Defence—Damages.

The defendant, claiming to be the owner of a house of which the plaintiff was in possession, induced him to attorn, and agree to give up possession on a certain day. The plaintiff, having afterwards discovered that the defendant had no title to the property, refused to give it up, whereupon the defendant took proceedings against him under 1 Rev. Stat. c. 126, s. 27, and obtained judgment, under which he was put in possession of the house. This judgment was reversed on appeal, and a writ of restitution awarded to the plaintiff; but before the writ could be executed by the Sheriff, the defendant pulled down the house, and thereby prevented the plaintiff from getting the benefit of his writ. The plaintiff had recovered a judgment under the 30th section of the Act, for damages and costs, on account of the proceedings against him. Held, In an action on the case for preventing the Sheriff from executing the writ of restitution—1st. That though the defendant might be the owner of the property, having got into possession by process of law, which was afterwards set aside, he could not avail himself of his title, as an answer to the writ of restitution, and that the plaintiff had a right to be put in the same position as he was before the proceedings taken by the defendant to dispossess him; 2nd. That the judgment obtained under the 30th section of the Statute was no bar to the present action; that the plaintiff was, at all events, entitled to nominal damages, and *Semble*, That the amount of damages was dependent upon the plaintiff's interest in the property, and whether the defendant, as owner of the property, could have immediately ejected him, after possession had been given under the writ of restitution. *Allenach* v. *DesBrisay*, *East T.* 1865, *Trin. T.* 1866.

6—Writ of Restitution—Signing and Issue.

A writ of restitution awarded under 1 Rev. Stat. c. 126, s. 30, should be signed and issued by the clerk, under the Seal of the Court, and not by the Judge who awards it. *Ibid.*

Disclaimer—Evidence of. See Disclaimer.

Fire—Alleged negligence of tenant. See Action on the Case I. 2.

Fixtures—Agreement as to. See Fixtures.

Covenant for improvements—New lease. See Covenant 8, 9.

Absconding Debtor—Property seized for rent. See Absconding Debtor 6.

Bailiff—Liability of landlord for Act of. See Distress 3.

Tenant's goods left on farm—Refusal to deliver by succeeding tenant—Conversion. See Trover 17.

Acceptance of lease—Estoppel. See Estoppel I. 3.

Fraudulent removal of goods—Pursuit. See Distress 5, 6.

LARCENY.

See Criminal Law.

LEASE.

See Landlord and Tenant.

LEAVE AND LICENSE.

See Pleading—Trespass.

LEGACY—LEGATEE.

See Will.

Bill for payment of Legacy. See Equity 9.

Action for Legacy. See Action at Law IX. 16.

LEGISLATIVE ACTS.

Ultra Vires.
See British North America Act.
" Supreme Court of Judicature.
" Revenue Act.
" Common School Act.

LETTERS OF ADMINISTRATION.

See Executors and Administrators.

LETTERS PATENT.

See Crown Grant II. 1.
" Corporation 6.
Scire Facias to repeal. See Practice IV. 4.

LEVY.

See Execution.

LIBEL.

See Defamation.

LICENSE.

See Pleading—Trespass.

Operation and Effect.

1–7. To cut Timber.
8. To dig Minerals.
9–14. To sell Land.
15. To sell Liquor.
16. To erect Mill Dam.
17. Fishery.

1—To cut timber.
A license to cut timber and remove it from lands does not enure as a grant of the trees until cut under the license. *Kerr* v. *Connell*, *Ber.* 133.

2—Not assignable.
A license from the Crown to A. to cut and take away a certain quantity of timber on certain land is not assignable. *Sharp* v. *McKeen*, 2 *Kerr* 524.

3—Conveying no interest in land—Assignable.
A deed granting license for five years in consideration of an annual rent, to enter upon lands of the grantor, and the exclusive permission to cut and haul away any quantity of trees growing thereon fit for saw logs and timber, is a mere license, and conveys no interest in the land to the grantee, nor any property in the standing trees. *New Brunswick and Nova Scotia Land Company* v. *Kirk*, 1 *All.* 443.

Such a license is assignable, but the assignee in the absence of any privity of contract with the grantor is not bound to the performance of covenants entered into by the grantee. *Ibid.*

4—A license granted by the Government to cut timber on Crown land, gives the licensee no interest in the land; therefore he cannot maintain trespass under the Rev. Stat. c. 133, against a person for entering on the land, and cutting down and taking away the trees. *Breckenridge* v. *Woolner*, 3 *All.* 303.

5—Rights of licensee.
A license in the name and under the signature of the Governor of the Province, and sealed with the official seal used for public documents, gives the licensee a right to cut and take away timber from Crown lands described in the license: the right of the Governor to issue such licenses being recognized by Acts of Assembly. *Beckwith* v. *McPhelim*, 2 *All.* 501.

Quære, Whether by common law a license affecting Crown lands should not be in the name of the Queen and under the great seal of the Province, or some authority to the Governor shown under the great seal for issuing it. *Ibid.*

A licensee of Crown land, with authority to cut and take away timber therefrom, may maintain an action on the case against a person who wrongfully enters thereon and cuts the timber, in consequence of which the licensee sustains damage. *Beckwith* v. *McPhelim*, 2 *All.* 501.

6—License granted by Government of Canada—Liability of timber to seizure in Province of New Brunswick—Disputed territory. See Crown Timber.

Trespass—Extent of License. See *Prescott* v. *Walton*, 2 *Han.* 230.

7—Usage—Evidence.
Regulations providing that no timber to be cut without license from the Government, first issued.

Quære, Whether evidence could be given of usage to the contrary. See *Coombes* v. *Hatheway*, 3 *Kerr* 592.

8—To dig minerals—Estate—Rights.
A license from the Crown to dig minerals in granted land where the mines are excepted out of the grant, will not justify an injury to the surface soil. *Gesner* v. *Cairns*, 2 *All.* 595.

Quære, Whether such a license, though liable to forfeiture for non-performance of the conditions, is actually forfeited without inquest of office. *Ibid.*

A parol license from the owner of land in which the mines are excepted, to the grantee of the mines to enter and dig them, vests no estate in the licensee, and is revoked by a conveyance of the land to a third person. *Ibid.*

Such a license is no breach of the implied warranty in a deed of bargain and sale, and the grantor is a competent witness for the plaintiff claiming under the grantee, in an action of trespass brought against the licensee. *Ibid.*

A parol assignment of such a license, (though unrevoked) gives no right of entry to the assignee. *Ibid.*

See Crown Grant, *Lesell* v. *Duffy*.

9—To sell land—Probate Court—Conclusiveness.
A license to sell land granted by a Probate Court is not conclusive upon the parties whose rights are affected by it; but it may be shewn, in an action of ejectment for the land, brought by a person claiming title under the license, that it was obtained by fraud, or without complying with the provisions of the Act which authorises the Probate Court to grant such licenses. *Doe* v. *Thompson*, 4 *All.* 483.

Objection to proceedings in Probate Court. See Deed I. 40.

10—Proof of License.
A license by the Governor and Council to an administrator to sell land, made under the Act 26 Geo. 3, c. 11, need not be under seal; and it may be proved by a copy from the records of the Council, certified by the Clerk of the Executive Council under the Act 21 Vic. c. 3. *Caughey* v. *Inman*, *Mich. T.* 1862.

11—Notice—Sale of Land.
A notice by executors to sell land under a license from the Governor in Council under the Act 26 Geo. 3, c. 11, s. 18, must be given thirty days exclusive of the day of sale, both by posting up notices and by publication in the newspapers; but it is not necessary to prove that the notices continued up till the day of sale. *Doe dem. Pike* v. *Tierney*, *Hil. T.* 1831.

12—Administrator's Deed—Purchaser's title under.
Where the petition to the Probate Court for license to sell land, sets out the matters required by law, and due notice of the application has been given, and the administrator's deed is in conformity with the Act, it vests in the purchaser under the license, the title of the intestate; and in ejectment by the purchaser, evidence is not admissible for the purpose of cutting down the deed, to shew that no debts were due from the intestate. *Doe dem. Bowen* v. *Robertson*, *Hil. T.* 1861.

Quære, Whether it could be shewn that no notice was given to the heirs, of the application to the Probate Court for license. *Ibid.*

13—Signature of Judge not necessary.
A license to sell real estate need not be signed by the Judge of Probates: Being a judicial act, it is sufficient if it is signed by the Registrar, as the act of the Court. *Doe dem. Simpson* v. *Falls*, *Trin. T.* 1863.

14—Plaintiff cannot shew license improperly granted because of sufficiency of personal property.
In ejectment by a devisee against a purchaser from the executor, under a license from the Probate Court, the plaintiff cannot shew, for the purpose of defeating the deed, that the license was improperly granted, because the testator left sufficient personal property to pay his debts,

which had been wasted and improperly expended by the executor in unnecessary proceedings in the Probate Court, of which the purchaser (being the attorney of the executor in the Probate Court) was aware: there being no want of jurisdiction shewn on the face of the petition, and such objections to the license being a ground of appeal from the decree of the Probate Court. *Doe dem. Sullivan* v. *Curry*, *Trin. T.* 1872.

15—To sell liquor.
License need not be proved in action on note given for price of liquor. See *McAuley* v. *Lawlor*, 4 *All.* 600.

Prima facie evidence of selling without license—*onus* of proof on defendant. See Evidence III. 23.

16—To erect dam.
Evidence of license. See action on the Case III. 1.

17—Fishery. See.

LIEUTENANT GOVERNOR.

Right to present to Rectory. See Church of England 11.

License granted by, to sell land. See License 10.

LIEN.

I. Principles—Operation.
II. Particular Persons.

I.

Principles—Operation.

1—Where the Court allows one judgment to be set off against another, it must be subject to the attorney's lien generally, and not merely to the extent of the taxed costs in the particular suit. *Rogers* v. *Sedden*, 2 *Kerr* 59.

Set off, of judgment in another Court—Beneficial interest. See Practice XIV. 3

2—Consideration—Parting with lien—Promise.
Parting with property on which the plaintiff has a lien, may be a good consideration for an express promise, but will not support an implied one. *Hartley* v. *Fisher*, 1 *All.* 459.

3—A judgment is not such a lien upon lands, as to prevent the defendant conveying the legal title and seisin to a third person. *Doe d. Peabody* v. *McKnight*, *Ber.* 376.

4—No claim of lien—Offer to deliver logs.
It is no objection to an offer to deliver logs that they are in possession of the owner's agent, a surveyor of lumber, who might have a lien on them, but who had not claimed any lien. *Polley* v. *Waterhouse*, 3 *All.* 291.

5—Memorial.
By the Rev. Stat. c. 113, a registered memorial of a judgment has priority as a charge on the land of the debtor, over a subsequent judgment and execution; and a sale by the Sheriff under such execution is subject to the charge of the prior registered judgment. *Mills* v. *Mills*, 4 *All.* 45.

II.

By Particular Persons.

6—Attorney.
An attorney has a lien on a judgment by him for his costs as between attorney and client. *Linton* v. *Wilson*, 1 *Kerr* 300.

7—Pond-keeper.
The legal obligation of a pond-keeper is the same as that of a warehouse-keeper; and in the absence of an agreement or general usage of trade establishing a general lien, he has only a special lien on timber in his possession, for his reasonable charges for the care of it. *Jack* v. *Eagles*, 2 *All.* 95.

8—Ship-owner—Freight.
A ship-owner's lien for freight extends to every part of the goods belonging to each consignee; and the consignee cannot maintain trover for a part of the goods, which have been landed, on tendering the freight thereon, though the amount due on each package of goods may be ascertained from the bill of lading. *Neill* v. *Reid*, 4 *All.* 246.

Hired men. See Timber.

Parting with possession—lien lost. See Delivery 4.

Agreement giving no lien on partnership property. See Equity 2.

Application to set off judgment against damages in other suit—Power in Court to grant application subject to attorney's lien. See Set off 8.

LIFE ESTATE.

See Will 3, 4, 5.

LIGHTS.

Obstruction of. See Action on the Case IV. 4.

LIMITATION OF ACTIONS—STATUTE OF.

I. GENERAL OPERATION.
II. ACKNOWLEDGMENTS — PART PAYMENT.
III. PERSONAL ACTIONS AND PROCEEDINGS.
IV. REAL ACTIONS—ADVERSE POSSESSION.
A. RIGHT OF ENTRY.
B. TENANCY AT WILL.
C. TENANTS IN COMMON.

I.

GENERAL OPERATION.

1—**Recovery of damages—Nuisance.** To an action on the case for a nuisance, in overflowing the plaintiff's land by a dam, which was erected by the defendant more than six years before bringing the action. Held, That the effect of a plea of the Statute of Limitations was not to bar the action but only to limit the recovery of damages to the last six years. *Connors* v. *McLuggan*, 2 *Kerr* 446.

2—**Tenancy at will.** The 7th section of the Act of Assembly 6 Wm. 4, c. 43, does not apply to a tenancy at will which had actually terminated before the Act passed, although the possession of the tenant continued. *Doe dem Belding* v. *Belding*, 2 *Kerr* 534.

3—**Statute beginning to run—Subsequent disability.** When the Statute of Limitations has once begun to run against a person, no subsequent disability in any one claiming under him will stop it; thus where A. discontinued possession in 1820, and died in 1826, leaving a son under age. Held, That if the Statute began to run against A., his son had not ten years after coming of age in which to bring ejectment. *Doe d. Thompson* v. *Marks*, 3 *Kerr* 659.

4—When Statute has begun to run, no subsequent indorsement to a person whether in or out of the Province, will stop it. *Bradbury* v. *Baillie*, 1 *All.* 690.

5—Coverture ceasing — Action brought within ten years after and within forty years after right accrued, though not within twenty years after coming of age. *Quære*, Whether right barred. See Partition.

6—**Mortgagor and Mortgagee.** The Act 6 Wm. 4, c. 43, s. 2, does not apply to the case of mortgagor and mortgagee; therefore the right of the mortgagee to maintain ejectment is not barred, though the mortgagor has been in possession over twenty years, since the execution of the mortgage. *Doe* v. *De Veber*, 3 *All.* 23.

6 a—The doctrine of Doe v. DeVeber, 3 All. 23, does not apply where the action is brought by the mortgagee against the assignee of the mortgagor, in which case twenty years' possession will bar the right of the mortgagee. *Doe d. Fauls* v. *Jones*, *Hil. T.* 1862.

7—**Assignee of mortgagee in possession.** The assignee of a mortgagee in possession may set up the mortgage as a defence to an action of ejectment by the assignee of an equity of redemption, though the mortgage is more than twenty years old, and the right to recover thereon is barred by the Statute of Limitations. *Doe* v. *Hanson*, 3 *All.* 427.

II.

ACKNOWLEDGMENTS — PART PAYMENT.

See Acknowledgments.

1—**No promise to pay—Acknowledgment insufficient.** A mere acknowledgment of a debt by an administrator is not sufficient to take the case out of the Statute of Limitations; there must be an express promise to pay; and, if there is more than one administrator, *Semble*, That the promise should be by all of them. *Gibbs* v. *Sewell*, *Trin. T.* 1833.

2—**Affirmative evidence of payment necessary.** Where part payment is relied on to take a case out of the Statute of Limitations, it is the duty of the plaintiff to give affirmative evidence of such payment, and if the evidence is doubtful and the jury find against the plaintiff the verdict will not be disturbed. *Charlotte Co. Bank* v. *Berry*, *East. T.* 1863.

3—**Title—Statement in petition.** A statement in a petition by defendant to the Probate Court for letters of administration, that certain land in his possession belonged to the intestate, on which petition letters of administration were granted to the defendant, is a sufficient acknowledgment of title to the heir of the intestate to prevent the operation of the Statute of Limitations. *Doe dem. Spence v. Welling, Trin. T.* 1866.

Acknowledgment of holding land. See No. IV. 19.

4—Before Extinguishment of right.
An acknowledgment under section 13, 6 Wm. 4, c. 43, to prevent the operation of the Statute of Limitations, must be made before the plaintiff's right is extinguished by the 2nd and 27th sections of the Act. *Doe v. De Veber*, 3 *All.* 23.

Payment on account. See Bills and Notes V. 24—27.

5—Verbal offer to Lease—Bidding at sale.
A verbal offer by a person in adverse possession of land to lease it from the owner, or bidding for the land at an auction of it by the owner, is not an acknowledgment of title, within the Statute of Limitations. *Doe v. Hasson*, 3 *All.* 451.

6—Payments by mortgagor—Sale of Equity of Redemption.
S. mortgaged land to the lessor of the plaintiff in 1837 and made payments on account from time to time, the last payment being in October 1843. In 1842 the equity of redemption of S. was sold at Sheriff's sale by a judgment creditor, and the defendant claimed under the purchaser. Held, That notwithstanding the sale of the equity of redemption the payments by S. kept the mortgage alive for twenty years from the time of that payment by 1 Rev. Stat. c. 139, s. 30, and that the mortgagee could recover the possession. [See Chinnery v. Evans, 10 Jur. N. S. 855.] *Doe d. Fox v. Wright, Hil. T.* 1865.

III.

Personal Actions and Proceedings.

Constables—Railway Act—Time in which action must be brought. See Action at Law XI. 11.

Parties abroad. See Pleading II. 21.

Slander—Action for—Allegations. See Pleading I. 7.

Payment on account. See Bills and Notes V. 26, 27.

When right of action accrues—Parties abroad. See Bills and Notes V. 24.

Note payable in instalments. See Bills and Notes V. 25.

1—Issuing writ—Alteration of—Replication.
A replication to a plea of the Statute of Limitations, stating the suing out of a writ on a certain day within six years, is not proved by a writ originally sued out on that day, but afterwards altered and made returnable on a different day—the day of the alteration being considered the issuing of the writ. *Barlow v. O'Donnell*, 1 *All.* 433.

2—Where the plaintiff altered the return day of a writ from the first to the last day of a term, in consequence of which a verdict in his favor was set aside, the Court refused an application to amend the writ by striking out the alteration and restoring it to its original form, though the plaintiff was barred by the Statute of Limitations from bringing a fresh action. *Barlow v. O'Donnell*, 1 *All.* 561.

3—Debt barred by Statute for which process issued, the Sheriff may shew this under general issue. See Sheriff 11.

IV.

Real Actions—Adverse Possession.

Rebuttal of plaintiff's title. See Ejectment I. 4.

1—Question of fact of adverse possession should be left to jury—Previous Act of Assembly.
Where A., a *feme sole* was, previous to her marriage, in the actual occupation, jointly with her brother, of lands which descended to them from their father, and upon her marriage, left the possession in her brother, who occupied more than forty years, paying during that period, all taxes and charges thereon, and receiving all the rents and profits. Held, In ejectment brought by the heirs of A., that under the Act 6 Wm. 4, c. 43, s. 14, which provides—that if at the time of the Act coming into operation, the possession is not adverse, the right of entry should not be barred for five years,—the question of adverse possession should be left to the jury to determine, and that it should be decided according to the law as it stood when the

Act came into operation. *Doe dem. Cole v. Harper, Ber.* 289.

2—**Confined to what?—Evidence of possession—Unimproved land.**

The adverse possession of one entering without colour of title, is confined to the particular part occupied; and the cutting down and carrying away of trees by such person on adjacent wilderness land, will not constitute an adverse possession of such wilderness land, unless the same be inclosed, or the extent of possession defined by a clear demarcation of boundaries. *Doe dem. Des Barres v. White,* 1 *Kerr* 595.

If repeated acts of trespass on wilderness land will constitute a possession of the land, it is necessary in order to make out such adverse possession of twenty years as will bar the right of the owner under the Statute of Limitations, to shew a sufficient number of such acts before the commencement of the twenty years. *Ibid.*

The grantee of the Crown, according to the ordinary mode of granting the wild lands in this Province, being deemed *prima facie* in possession of the land granted when there is no adverse occupant, it is sufficient for a plaintiff in ejectment, who claims under a grant to his lessor more than twenty years old, to shew that the land within that period remained in its natural state and uninclosed. *Ibid.*

3—A. being seized of a lot of land, died intestate in the year 1811, leaving five children. B. his second son, took possession of the land, and exercised acts of ownership over the whole of it until 1824, when he conveyed it to the defendant, who afterwards occupied it. Held, that B.'s possession was not limited to his undivided share, but extended over the whole lot, and that after twenty years the right of the heirs of A.'s eldest son was barred by the Statute of Limitations. *Doe v. Allen,* 2 *All.* 191.

4—**Continuous possession.**

The plaintiff's father conveyed him a farm, on an agreement that fifty acres of it should go to pay a debt of the father. The debt not having been paid, the fifty acres were sold by the Sheriff with the plaintiff's consent in 1824, and purchased by C., who had the boundaries marked with the plaintiff's assistance. C. several years after sold to the defendant, who held up to the same line until 1851, without objection by the plaintiff. Held, That there was a continuous possession of the whole fifty acres for upwards of twenty years in C. and the defendant, which gave the latter title to the land. *Doe v. Baxter,* 2 *All.* 377.

5—**Necessary facts to constitute adverse possession.**

In order to constitute an adverse possession of land, it must be exclusive, continuous, and clearly defined: there must be something to shew the person having the legal title, that a possession has been taken of some definite portion of the land hostile to his title. *Doe dem Mayor &c. of St. John v. Littlehale, Hil. T.* 1861.

Where the land above high water mark was granted to one person, and the beach in front, between high and low water mark, to another, the merely passing over the shore with boats at high water, or the landing boats on the shore at low water by the proprietors of the land above high water mark, and passing to and fro over the beach for a period of twenty years, does not amount to a possession; there being nothing to define a possession of any particular portion of the land, and the acts being consistent with the exercise of a public right of passage when the beach was covered with water, and, with an easement in the proprietor of the adjoining land when the beach was uncovered. *Ibid.*

6—**Possession—Survey.**

An entry or survey of land by the owner is not such a possession as will prevent the operation of the Statute of Limitations, 6 Wm. 4, c. 43, or divest the possession of one holding the land adversely at the time of the entry. *Doe v. Hasson,* 3 *All.* 451.

7—**Extent of possession—Description in deed—Unoccupied remainder.**

A. being indebted, conveyed land (partly wilderness) to the plaintiff in 1822, and two years afterwards, in order to pay the debt, caused fifty acres of the land to be sold at auction by the Sheriff, with the plaintiff's consent, and B. purchased it: the plaintiff bid at the sale, signed the Sheriff's deed as a witness, and assisted B. in running the division line between the fifty acres and the remainder of the land towards the rear of the lot; B. sold to the defendant in 1835, and the plaintiff then continued the division line to the rear; and occupied up to it for several years. Held, That as B.'s entry was not wrongful, his actual possession of a part (there being no other possession of the remainder) extended to the whole of the land described in the deed, and that the plaintiff's right was barred at the expiration of twenty years after B.'s entry. Held also, That the Sheriff's deed was properly received in evidence as part of the *res gestæ*, without proof of any judgment or execution to warrant it. *Doe* v. *Baxter*, 4 *All.* 131.

8—The vendor of part of a tract of land sent a surveyor to lay it off for the purchaser (defendant). The surveyor pointed out a tree to the purchaser as his boundary, up to which he took possession, and occupied upwards of twenty years. Held, That he had acquired a title by possession up to that tree, though it did not correspond with the description in his deed, which deed was prepared from a plan of the survey made by the surveyor after he laid off the land, and the principal part of the land was wilderness, the jury having found that the defendant's possession was up to the tree. *Doe d. Robinson* v. *Chase*, *East. T.* 1864.

9—Acts—Whether of possession or trespass—Question left to jury.

In trespass for taking grass, plaintiff proved that she and her deceased husband had cut the grass on the *locus in quo*, (a wild meadow—the grass being wild and natural,) for upwards of twenty years: there was no fence on the land, or any other act of possession shewn. The defendant had the legal title to the land and lived on the front of the lot,—about four miles from the *locus in quo*,—occasionally cutting lumber on the rear of it near the meadow, and browing his lumber thereon. It was left to the jury to say whether the several acts of cutting the grass by the plaintiff were acts of possession,—claiming it as a right,—or mere acts of trespass; and the jury found in favor of the defendant. Held—No misdirection. *Power* v. *Howie*, *Mich. T.* 1864.

10—Continuance of possession—Character of holding—Original claim—Rebuttal of presumption.

Defendant went into possession of land under an agreement to purchase from his brother. W. the plaintiff's father, paid the purchase money, built a house and occupied the land. After the death of W., the plaintiff, then an infant, 5 years old, went to live with the defendant on the land, and was maintained by him for a number of years. Held, (N. Parker and Wilmot, J. J., *dissentientibus*,) That the presumption was that the defendant continued in possession under his original claim of right, and that the plaintiff's living with him on the land, did not necessarily destroy that right; but that such presumption of right might be rebutted; and, that it was a question for the jury whether certain acts of the defendant after W.'s death, shewed that he was holding the property as his own, or for the benefit of the heirs. Per. N. Parker and Wilmot, J. J.—That the plaintiff's occupation of the land must be presumed to have been in his character as heir of W., and that it was not a question for the jury. *Doe d. Spence* v. *Welling*, *Trin. T.* 1866.

Continuance of possession by widow after death of husband—For whom holding—Adding possession to give title. See Possession 4.

11—Registered deed—Acts of possession necessary—Entry under deed or as trespasser.

There is a distinction in the character of the possession where a person enters on land under a registered deed, and where he enters without any claim of right. It should be left to the jury to say whether the entry was made with the intention of taking possession under his deed, or as a mere trespasser. The mere fact of a party having a registered deed of land, does not operate to give him possession of the land therein described, without shewing acts of possession. *The Madras Board* v. *Ryan*, *Mich. T.* 1864.

12—Defined boundaries—Possession of part—Intention—Title to whole.

If a person enters on land under a registered deed, with defined boundaries, with the intention of taking possession as owner, and not as a mere trespasser, he may be considered as taking possession of the whole lot described in the deed, and not merely of that part actually occupied or enclosed; and such possession, if continued for twenty years, will give a title. It is a question for the jury, with what intention a party enters on land. (Per Parker, Wilmot and Ritchie, J. J., Carter, C. J., and N. Parker, M. R., *dis-*

sen:ientibus.) *Humphreys* v. *Helms*, *Hil. T.* 1861.

Possession of plaintiff—Whether amounting to *disseisin* or not. See Disseisin 5, *Payson* v. *Good*.

Inconsistent evidence as to possession—Verdict of jury for all but improved land. See New Trial III. 49.

A. Right of Entry.

13—Agreement — Tenancy at will—Heirs.

A. the owner of land, put B. in possession in 1799, under an agreement to purchase. In 1820, the heirs of A. demanded possession of the land from B., who refused to give it up. Held, That by entry under the agreement, B. became tenant at will to A.; that under the Statute of Limitations 6 Wm. 4, c. 43, such tenancy terminated at the end of one year after B. went into possession; and that the action not having been brought within twenty years thereafter, the right of the heirs was barred by the Statute. *Doe dem. Purdy* v. *Peters*, *Ber.* 350.

14—Entry of owner with consent of tenant.

Defendant went into possession of land as tenant at will to plaintiff, and remained in possession upwards of twenty years. Held, That such tenancy was not determined by an entry of the owner within twenty years with the consent of the tenant for the purpose of running the line between his possession and the adjoining land, and therefore that the plaintiff's right of entry was barred by the Statute of Limitations. *Doe d. Botsford* v. *Tidd*, *Trin. T.* 1863.

15—Payment on account of mortgage—Purchaser of Equity of Redemption — Action brought within twenty years of payment.

S. mortgaged land to the lessor of the plaintiff in 1837, and made payments to him on account from time to time—the last payment being in October 1843. In 1842, the equity of redemption of S. was sold at Sheriff's sale, and the defendant claimed under the purchaser from the Sheriff. Held, That the mortgagee could maintain ejectment for the land within twenty years after the last payment by S. *Doe d. Fox* v. *Wright*, *Hil. T.* 1865.

16—Female infant—Marriage—Husband bound to bring action within twenty years after right of entry of infant.

A right of entry accrued to a female infant in 1826, and in 1830, a few months before her infancy ceased, she married the plaintiff, who brought an action to recover the land in 1848. Held, That he, being under no disability, was bound to bring his action within twenty years after her right of entry accrued, and therefore that his right was barred. *Starkie* v. *Parks*, 1 *All.* 556.

Semble, That though the husband's right was barred by the Statute of Limitations, that of the wife was only suspended during her disability. *Ibid.*

17—Devise to widow for life—Children's right of entry.

A testator, after directing that so much of his estate as was necessary should be sold for payment of his debts, devised all the residue of his estate to his executors, in trust to hold for the separate use and benefit of his wife during her life or widowhood, and to pay her the income thereof; and after her death or marriage then to be divided among his children. Defendant took possession of the land in 1831, after the testator's death; the widow died in 1856. Held, That the children's right of entry did not accrue until the widow's death, and their title was not barred by the Statute of Limitations. *Doe* v. *Driscoll*, 4 *All.* 176.

18—Unoccupied land—Grantee—Seisin—Possession.

A grant of land from the Crown, under the great seal, with a plan of survey annexed, conveys seisin to the grantee, and his possession will *prima facie* be deemed to continue while the land remains unoccupied and unimproved. Held, therefore, That an adverse possession of ten years in the defendant would not bar the entry of the lessors of the plaintiff, who claimed as heirs of the grantee under a grant made in 1785, the land being shewn to remain unoccupied until the time of the defendant's possession. *Doe dem. Kimpson and Wife* v. *Craft*, 1 *Kerr* 546.

19—Sufficiency of adverse possession—Acknowledgment of holding.

Where land was granted by the Crown to L. S., who let F. into possession over forty years ago, and F. had acknowledged that the land was held by him under L. S. and his heirs, and had paid rent to the widow of L. S., and had also in 1822 agreed with one of the sons of L. S. to hold the land until it was called for by the owners, and had shortly after died in possession. Held, That the defendant who had come in under B., who obtained possession from the widow and family of F., had not such an adverse possession as to bar the entry of the heirs of L. S. *Doe dem. Strange* v. *Thompson*, 1 *Kerr* 564.

Coverture ceasing, action brought within ten years and within forty years after right accrued, though not within twenty years after coming of age. *Quære*, If sufficient. See Partition.

B. TENANCY AT WILL.

20—Determination of tenancy.
In ejectment, the defendant, by virtue of the Act of Limitations 6 Wm. 4, c. 43, s. 7, relied on a tenancy at will, created more than twenty years before the commencement of the action. Held, That cutting down and carrying away wood from the premises in question, and making surveys upon it, and any such entry without the consent of the tenant at will, would operate as a determination of the tenancy. *Doe dem. Lyon* v. *Slavin*, 3 *Kerr* 258.

21—A person taking possession of land under an agreement to purchase, which specified no time for the continuance of the possession in the event of the purchase not being completed, becomes a tenant at will; and such tenancy must be terminated by some act of the parties before he can be ejected on non-completion of the purchase. *Doe* v. *Denny*, 3 *All.* 50.

The Act 6 Wm. 4, c. 43, s. 7, does not apply to such a case; but only to questions arising under the Statute of Limitations. *Ibid.*

22—T. P. put C. in possession of land to hold for him and keep trespassers off, with liberty to cut the grass and fire-wood upon it: C. held it until his death in 1821 (nearly thirty years), but never claimed it as his own; on the death of C., his son D. succeeded to the possession and continued to hold the land as his father had done, till T. P.'s death, and afterwards for W. P., the son, and one of the heirs of T. P., until 1844, when he conveyed it to C. P., a son of W. P., under whom the plaintiff claimed by a deed dated in 1856. The defendant claimed under J. P., a grandson and one of the heirs of T. P., who entered on the land after the conveyance to C. P. in 1844. Held—1st. That C. was not a tenant for years to T. P., subject to a rent service, but at most a tenant at will, and that such a tenancy terminated at his death in 1821; 2nd. That the holding by D. created a new tenancy at will between him and the heirs of T. P., which terminated in 1823, and that at the expiration of twenty years therefrom the right of T. P.'s heirs was barred, and D. had the fee simple—the five years allowed by the 14th section of the Statute of Limitations, 6 Wm. 4, c. 43, having expired on the 1st January 1842; 3rd. That as the plaintiff, being the heir of C. P., might claim by descent, the Judge was right in refusing to leave to the jury, whether at the time C. P. conveyed to the plaintiff, he was not disseised by the entry and possession of J. P. *Doe* v. *McGloyn*, 4 *All.* 180.

See Supra I. 2.

C. TENANTS IN COMMON.

23—As between tenants in common, the right of one tenant to bring ejectment within five years of the Act of Limitations (6 Wm. 4, c. 43) taking effect, is saved by the sixteenth section, where the possession was not adverse according to the law existing at the time when the Act took effect. *Doe dem. Williams* v. *Leavitt*, 2 *Kerr* 83.

24—A., being in possession of land as tenant in common with his brother and sister, went away from the property in 1820, leaving his mother, brother and sister in possession; the defendant married the sister and bought the brother's share in 1824, but the brother remained in possession until 1831, receiving the whole of the profits for the purpose of supporting his mother—to which all the family considered themselves bound to contribute. A. died in 1826, leaving a son, the lessor of the plaintiff, under age, who brought ejectment in 1846. Held, That up to 1831, there was no exclusive possession in any one of the tenants in common to bring the case within the Act 6 Wm. 4, c. 43, s. 12; that the Statute did not begin to run against A. in his lifetime; and that the right of the lessor of the plaintiff was not barred. *Doe d. Thompson* v. *Marks*, 3 *Kerr* 659.

LIMIT BOND.

See Bonds—Bail—Practice.

LIVERY OF SEISIN.

Grant of land conveys seisin. See Crown Grant II. 4.

Allowing party to give evidence of seisin. See Evidence VIII. 12 *a*.

Party in possession—Presumption of livery of seisin. See Deed I. 20.

Fact of Seisin—Circumstances.
In order to shew livery of seisin under an unregistered deed, the grantee shewed that after the deed was delivered he and the grantor were passing by the land, when the latter said to him, "Here is your estate, it don't belong to me—I have deeded it to you," and that the grantee took hold of a part of a building on the land, and said he thought he would repair it, and put tenants in; and that he afterwards exercised ownership over it. The grantee afterwards became insolvent, and in the schedule of his property, filed pursuant to the Act 7 Vic. c. 32, this property was omitted. Held, That the jury were warranted in coming to the conclusion that livery of seisin had been given. *McLardy* v. *Flaherty*, 3 *Kerr* 455.

LOCUS STANDI.

Right to have—Contesting title. See Practice in Equity II. 4.

LOST RECORD.

See Judgment I. 6.

LUNATIC.

Setting aside proceedings against. See Practice VI. 15.

Deed of. See Deed I. 35.

MAGISTRATE.

See Justice of the Peace.

MALICE.

False return of Member—Proof of actual malice necessary to sustain action against Sheriff for making. See Election Law.

Practice of striking out names of persons refusing to take oath admissible in question of malice. See Evidence III. 7.

Registrar refusing to register. See Pleading I. 56.

Proof of—When unnecessary in question of negligence. See Action on the Case II.

Influence of malice. See Criminal Law II. 4.

See Malicious Arrest, etc.

MALICIOUS ARREST AND PROSECUTION.

Reasonable and Probable Cause.

Arrest.
Proof of signature of defendant to affidavit unnecessary, if arrest made by his procurement. See Evidence VII. 5.

Excessive damage—New trial not granted unless damages outrageous. See New Trial III. 11.

Malicious Prosecution.

1—Evidence—Copy of indictment.
A copy of an indictment certified by the proper officer, though improperly obtained, is admissible in evidence in an action for malicious prosecution. *Heany* v. *Lynn*, *Ber.* 27.

2—Prosecutor.
Defendant charged the plaintiff with stealing, on which he was indicted at the Sessions, and acquitted. The prosecution was conducted by the Clerk of the Peace; but the defendant consulted with him, and procured the attendance of the witnesses. Held, Sufficient evidence that the defendant was the prosecutor. *Burgoyne* v. *Moffat*, *Hil. T.* 1861.

3—Motive.
Any motive for a prosecution, other than that of wishing to bring a guilty party to justice, is evidence of malice. Retaining the Clerk of the Peace to prosecute an indictment against the plaintiff, before the Sessions, together with the conduct of the prosecutor before and after, are proper matters to be left to the jury on the question of malice. *Alward* v. *Sharp*, 1 *Han.* 286.

4—Any motive for a prosecution, other than that of bringing a guilty party to justice, is a malicious motive. Malice may be inferred from the want of probable cause;

and the inference is strengthened where the defendant does not come forward as a witness to rebut it. *Burgoyne* v. *Moffatt*, *Hil. T.* 1861.

5—Proceeding against party by summons sufficient without warrant.
It is not essential to the maintenance of an action for malicious prosecution for a crime, that a warrant should have been issued against the plaintiff and that he should have been arrested. It is sufficient that he has been proceeded against by summons on the defendant's complaint. Where the declaration alleged that a warrant had been issued against the plaintiff, and that he had been arrested on the charge, an amendment was allowed, substituting therefor, that a summons had been issued by a Justice of the Peace and served upon the plaintiff, and that he attended before the Justice in obedience thereto. *Vincent* v. *West*, 1 *Han.* 290.

6—Detaining debtor, after payment of debt.
An action will not lie for maliciously, and without probable cause, detaining the plaintiff in prison after payment of the debt for which he was arrested, unless a legal determination of the suit is shewn; or the plaintiff had been ordered to be discharged by the Court. *McPhelim* v. *Weldon*, *Trin. T.* 1862.

See Action at Law.

Reasonable and Probable Cause.

7—Proceeding criminally against party.
Plaintiff was a boarding-house keeper, in whose house defendant had boarded, having the use of a room, and some furniture of his own. He went to England, leaving his furniture in the house, and after being absent several months, applied through his agent, to the plaintiff for the furniture; she gave up a portion of it, but kept the rest, claiming a lien on it for a balance due from defendant for board. Defendant then brought an action of replevin for the furniture, and obtained a verdict, the Judge ruling that a boarding-house keeper had no lien on the goods of his guest. Before and after the trial negotiations for settlement took place between the attorneys, plaintiff offering to give up the goods on being paid a certain sum, which defendant refused, offering a smaller sum. The plaintiff's counsel applied for a new trial in the action of replevin, on the ground of misdirection as to the lien, and the Court, after a few days consideration, refused a rule. While this motion was pending, and while the plaintiff's counsel was absent from the town where she lived, attending the Court, defendant again applied to her for the furniture, offering her a sum of money if she would give it up in the absence of her attorney, and threatening to take proceedings against her and ruin her house if she refused: the plaintiff still claimed a right to hold the furniture, and refused to do anything in the absence of her attorney. Defendant then applied to the Police Magistrate, and obtained a warrant against the plaintiff under the Act 27 Vic. c. 6, for unlawfully, as a bailee, detaining his property and converting it to her own use, under which warrant she was arrested and imprisoned for want of bail, and on examination, the charge was dismissed. In an action for malicious prosecution and false imprisonment, the jury were directed that if the plaintiff was a bailee of the goods, and fraudulently converted them to her own use, the defendant had probable cause for the prosecution, whatever he might have believed on the subject; that if plaintiff had not fraudulently converted the goods, if defendant believed, and had reasonable grounds for believing that she had done so, there was also probable cause; but if he did not believe plaintiff to be guilty of fraudulent conversion, and in his own mind believed and had reasonable grounds for believing her innocent, then there was want of reasonable and probable cause. Held, That the direction was right; that the knowledge and belief of the defendant as to the plaintiff's claim to hold the goods, and his acts in reference thereto, and the inferences to be drawn from the acts of the parties, the negotiations for settlement, the claims by one party and the offers by the other, were proper matters for the consideration of the jury; and that the Judge would not have been justified in directing the jury, that as the plaintiff had no legal right to detain the goods, her refusal to give them up, afforded probable cause for instituting the prosecution against her under the Act. Held also, That under the circumstances, a verdict for £500 damages was not excessive, it not being shown that the jury were actuated by any improper motive, or acted on a wrong principle. *Abell* v. *Light*, 1 *Han.* 240.

8—Inferences from facts—Jury.
Where inferences are to be drawn from the facts proved in an action for malicious prosecution, the case must be left to a jury; and the question of "probable cause" should not be determined by the Judge alone. *Alward* v. *Sharp*, 1 *Han.* 286.

9—Conflicting evidence—Determination of—Reasonable and probable cause.
When the evidence, tending to show whether the plaintiff was or was not guilty of the crime charged against him, is conflicting, the Judge cannot determine the question of "reasonable and probable cause." *Vincent* v. *West*, 1 *Han.* 290.

10—Verdict—Uncertainty as to grounds of finding.
Where the evidence of want of probable cause was such, that it should have been decided by the Judge against the defendant; but he left both that and the question of malice to the jury, who found for the defendant, a new trial was granted; as it could not be known whether the verdict was given on the ground that there was probable cause (which would have been contrary to law) or that there was no malice. *Hughson* v. *Keith*, *Trin. T.* 1863.

Policeman—Acting in *bona fide* belief of duty. See Action at Law XI.

MANDAMUS.

A. When Granted.

To Inferior Courts.
Corporation.
To enforce Contract.
Alternative Mandamus.

B. When Refused.

To Inferior Courts.
Corporation.
General Sessions.
Justice of Peace.

Foundation for Application—Affidavit entitling of—Return to.

Other Remedy—Mandamus Refused.

A. When Granted.

1—To Inferior Courts—To enter Judgment.
A mandamus will issue to compel the Court of Common Pleas to enter up judgment on a verdict, the Court having no power to grant a new trial. *Rex* v. *Justices of Northumberland*, *C. Ms.* 8.

2—To try Cause.
Where the presiding Justices of the Common Pleas, who were also Justices of the Peace, refused to try a cause because from their position and knowledge as Justices of the Peace, they believed that the defendants (who were a committee of the Justices) had contracted with the plaintiff in their public capacity for the performance of public work; the Court granted a mandamus to the Justices of the Common Pleas generally, to try the cause. *Ex parte Leonard*, 1 *All.* 269.

3—To perfect judgment.
The provisions of the Act 35 Geo. 3, c. 2, are imperative as to the time within which a defendant may appear in the Inferior Court in a suit, and if he does not appear within such time, he cannot afterwards be let in to defend, and the plaintiff is entitled to a mandamus to perfect his judgment. *Rex* v. *Justices of York*, *Hil. T.* 1831.

4—Corporation.
A mandamus lies to the Corporation of St. John to compel them to collect a moiety of the amount assessed and apportioned by the Commissioners on the parties benefited by the extension of a street, under the Act 23 Vic. c. 44. *Ex parte Jones*, *Trin. T.* 1861.

5—To enforce contract—Public work.
A mandamus lies to enforce a contract entered into by a person with public officers for the performance of public work, on which he has the legal right to the money, but no legal remedy by action, though a third party was secretly interested with him in the performance of the work, and claims the money under an arbitration to which they had submitted their disputes. *Regina* v. *Justices of York*, 1 *All* 273.

6—To restore pilot.
The right of the Corporation of Saint John to appoint pilots under its Charter has been recognized by Act of Assembly; and the tenure of such appointments being during pleasure, if the Corporation remove a pilot without assigning any cause, a mandamus will not lie to restore him. *Ex parte Langan*, 3 *All.* 135.

6 a—Appraisers of damages—Alternative mandamus.
An application for a mandamus to the appraisers of damages under the Act 19, Vic. c. 17, requiring them to assess the value of land taken for a railroad, was

resisted on the ground that the right of way had been given to, and the track laid out by the European and North American Railway Company under a deed executed by the applicant; that all the right of that Company had been transferred to the Government; and that the land taken by the Government was identical with that laid out by the Company. Held, That as this identity was left doubtful by the affidavits, an alternative mandamus should issue. *Ex parte Gray*, 4 *All.* 118.

B. When Refused.

7—Inferior Court—Entering judgment.
The Court will not grant a mandamus to the Justices of an Inferior Court of Common Pleas, requiring them to enter up judgment for the plaintiff in an action of recognizance of bail in that Court; when such Justices had in the exercise of their discretion set aside the plaintiff's judgment and allowed a render of the principal. *Sedden* v. *Russel*, *Ber.* 217.

8—Inferior Court—To award costs.
A mandamus was refused to compel the Court of Common Pleas to award costs to a plaintiff in an action on a bond after a verdict in his favour—it being a summary action, and the pleadings subsequent to the declaration being special and not according to the summary Act 12 Vic. c. 40. *Ex parte Griffith*, 2 *All.* 93.

Quære, Whether the jury had power to try such an issue. *Ibid.*

9—Corporation—To issue notes.
The Act 18 Vic. c. 6, authorised Commissioners to convey water into the Town of Carleton from certain lakes, and for that purpose to purchase the water rights, a portion of the lands round the lakes, and the land necessary for laying down water pipes, to distribute the water in the town and carry off waste water; and in order to pay for the water rights and lands taken, and for the construction of all necessary works and all incident expenses, the Corporation of Saint John were authorised and required on the requisition of the Commissioners, to issue from time to time, notes or certificates of debt to an amount not exceeding £25,000. The Commissioners entered into a contract for laying down the pipes and conveying the water from the lakes into the Town for £23,000, and required the Corporation to issue notes for that amount, which they refused. Held, That as it was not shewn that the Commissioners had made any arrangements for carrying out the other provisions of the Act, or that the balance of the sum limited would be sufficient for that purpose, the issuing of the notes was discretionary with the Corporation, and that a mandamus would not be granted. *Ex parte Coster*, 3 *All.* 349.

10—General Sessions—To pay for work—Sheriff.
A mandamus was refused to compel the General Sessions of St. John to pay for work done at the gaol by direction of the Sheriff. *Ex parte Thomas*, *Trin. T.* 1862.

10 a—Mandamus refused to compel Magistrate to proceed in a criminal cause at suit of private prosecutor. See *Regina* v. *Duvaney*, 1 *Han.* 571.

See Supra 14.

11—Commissioners of Sewers—Damage—Foundation for application against—Compliance with Act—Powers under—Request—Demand.
The Act 2 Wm. 4, c. 26, incorporating the St. John Water Company, authorised them to draw water from, erect reservoirs on, and carry pipes through private property, provided that no such water should be drawn, etc., without compensation being paid for the use of the same, and for any damage sustained by the operations of the Company, and in case of disagreement between the Company and the owners of the land, the compensation to be determined by arbitration; and if the owner of the property should decline to appoint an arbitrator, the Supreme Court, on application of the Company, should issue a warrant to the Sheriff to summon a jury to assess the amount to be paid. By Act 12 Vic. c. 51, further powers were given to the Company to enter on private property, erect dams, and draw water from any stream, on paying compensation to the owners—the amount to be determined as by the Act 2 Wm. 4, c. 26. After the passing of this Act, the Water Company erected a dam upon a stream flowing through private property, laid down pipes and diverted the water from its natural channel, without the consent of the owners. By Act 18 Vic. c. 38, all the property, rights,

powers and privileges of the Water Company were vested in Commissioners appointed under this Act, saving to all parties all rights, remedies and actions, for any act done, or for any contract theretofore made, and giving the Commissioners power to lay down pipes, etc., for extending a supply of water; and providing that in case of damage done in the execution of the works, the Commissioners should pay the party sustaining the same, such compensation as should be agreed upon, and in case they could not agree, the Commissioners should, on request of such party, apply to a Justice of the Peace for a warrant to the Sheriff to summon a jury to assess the damages. The Commissioners continued the obstruction placed on the stream by the Water Company, and laid down additional pipes, drawing off a much larger quantity of water. A., claiming as one of the heirs of the former owner, then gave notice to the Commissioners that he claimed damages under the Act 2 Wm. 4, c. 26, and the several Acts in amendment and incident thereto, for abstraction of the water by the Commissioners, and requested them to take the necessary steps for summoning a jury to assess such damages. The Commissioners declined to take any steps, and A. gave them a further notice, stating that they had refused to agree upon the amount of compensation for obstructing the stream and diverting the water, and requiring them to take the necessary and legal steps pointed out by the Acts 2 Wm. 4, c. 26, 12 Vic. c. 38, or any of them, for determining the amount of compensation to be paid for all or any damage which he was entitled to receive in his own right, or in behalf of the other heirs, as well for the acts of the St. John Water Company as of said Commissioners. The Commissioners declined to take any proceedings on this application, stating that they were not aware that any damage had been done to A. by their operations. Held, on application by A. for a mandamus—1st That the Commissioners were right in refusing to act on the first notice—the mode of proceeding under the Acts 2 Wm. 4, c. 26 and 12 Vic. c. 51, being by arbitration, and not by a jury; 2nd. That the Commissioners had no power to act under the 2 Wm. 4, c. 26, even if they had been requested to take the proceedings pointed out by that Act; 3rd. That as all rights and remedies against the Water Company were preserved by the 18 Vic. c. 38, the Commissioners were not bound to apply for a jury to assess damages for the acts of the Water Company, as required by the second notice; 4th. That without showing who the other owners of the property were, and how A. was entitled to claim on their behalf, a mandamus could not be issued to assess the damages due to them, but must be confined to A.'s interest in the land; 5th. That it was sufficient for A. to show by his affidavits a *prima facie* case of title to the land, and that he need not produce his deeds; 6th. That the allegation of the withdrawal from its natural course of a large quantity of water from a stream flowing through A.'s land, showed a *prima facie* case of damage to him; 7th. That a demand in the alternative, to do one of two things, and a general refusal, was sufficient to found an application for a mandamus, if the applicant was entitled to part of what he claimed; 8th That a request to a public officer, to take the necessary and legal steps pointed out by an Act of Assembly, to assess damages for the injury done to the applicant's property under the authority of the Act, was sufficiently specific; 9th. That an objection that there had been no sufficient demand could not be taken after the merits of the application had been discussed; 10th. That where an application for a mandamus fails, because there was no demand and refusal, it cannot, as a general rule, be renewed after a demand; though there may be circumstances warranting a departure from this rule. *Regina* v. *Commissioners of Sewers St. John*, 1 *Han*. 3.

12—Affidavit—Entitling of.

Irregular if entitled in a cause in moving for a rule *nisi*—discharged without costs. See *Reg.* v. *Justices of York*, 1 *All.* 90.

13—Return to—Mayor—Reasons for refusing to swear party—Insufficiency of.

The Mayor of Fredericton is merely a ministerial officer, and has no judicial functions to authorise him to refuse to swear in an alderman elect on the ground of disqualification, if properly returned by the presiding officer.

Semble, That an information in nature of a *quo warranto* might lie to try the right of a person to exercise the office; but it would be an insufficient return to a mandamus to the mayor to swear in a person returned as duly elected by the proper officer,—to say that he was not duly elected. *Ex parte Richards*, 2 *Han.* 131.

Trying right to exercise office. See *Quo Warranto.*

Second Application. See Practice V. 17.

14—Other remedy—Mandamus refused —Justice of Peace.

Where a Magistrate commenced the examination of a criminal charge, but refused to proceed because he thought that the only witness offered to prove a material fact, was not competent; the Court refused, on the application of a private prosecutor, to grant a mandamus to compel him to proceed, there being another remedy by bill of indictment before the Grand Jury. *Reg.* v. *Davanny*, 1 *Han.* 571.

15—Remedy on Covenant—Not repairing bridge.

The St. John Water Co., (incorporated by Act 2 Wm. 4, c. 26,) covenanted with C. to build a bridge over certain overflowage on his land, caused by their works, and to keep the same in repair while they continued to overflow his land. All the rights of the Company were afterwards vested in Commissioners, by Act 18 Vic. c. 38, subject to the outstanding liabilities, and saving to every person all rights and remedies by reason of any contract or agreement theretofore made. Held, That C. had a legal remedy by action on the covenant, for not repairing the bridge, and therefore that a mandamus would not lie against the Commissioners to compel them to repair it. *Reg.* v. *Sears*, *East. T.* 1864.

MANSLAUGHTER.

See Criminal Law.

MANURE.

Not incident to land conveyed—Conversion of. See Trover 15.

MARKET.

See Bye-Law 3.
" Power to establish Market.
" See Corporation 14.
" Fredericton (City of.)

MARRIAGE.

Performance of by Commissioner. See Evidence VI. 3.

Averment of—Action for mesne profits. See Ejectment VI. 2.

Proof of marriage. See Evidence VI. 4.

MARRIED WOMAN.

See husband and wife.

Legacy to—Action after decease of. See Action at Law IX. 13.

Coverture ceasing—Infant—Right of entry. See Partition.

MASTER AND SERVANT.

Dismissal from Employment.

1—Justification—Knowingly bearer of challenge.

To have been knowingly the bearer of a challenge to fight a duel, is such an offence as will justify a merchant in the immediate dismissal of a clerk from his employment. *Dolby* v. *Kinnear*, 1 *Kerr* 480.

2—Engaging in other employment.

Plaintiff was engaged by defendant for two years as clerk, and shortly afterwards entered into partnership with other parties for the purpose of carrying on the same kind of business as his employer. Held, That this was such a breach of duty as would justify his dismissal. *Tozer* v. *Hutchinson*, 1 *Han.* 540.

3—If another ground of dismissal existed, the defendant has a right to avail himself of it at the trial, though he was not aware of it at the time of dismissal. *Ibid.*

Dismissal without sufficient cause—Right to immediate action — Damages. See Damages I. 15.

4—Action for wages—Quantum meruit —Previous receipt.

Upon the *quantum meruit* for three years' service as clerk and book keeper, the defence set up was that the plaintiff had taken goods and money from the defendant's store which he had not charged himself with in the books, that the defendant having discovered this, threatened to proceed criminally against the plaintiff, but the matter was arranged by the plaintiff's giving to the defendant a receipt in full of all demands, and the plaintiff's quitting the defendant's service. The plaintiff notwithstanding brought this action, and the case was left to the jury as to the value of the plaintiff's services, and the amount he had

MASTER IN CHANCERY.

MAYOR.

MEDICAL ACT.

MEMORIAL.

MERGER.

MESNE PROFITS.

MERITS.

MILEAGE.

MILITIA.

MILL DAM.

MINES AND MINERALS.

MINISTERIAL OFFICER.

MISDESCRIPTION.

MISNOMER.

MISTAKE.

Revised Statutes.
The power given to correct mistakes in the arrangement of titles, etc., of Revised Statutes, ceases when the text of the Act is printed. See *Reg.* v. *McLaughlin*, 3 *All.* 159.

Mistake in name. See Name.

Mistake in running lines. See Crown Grant I. 11.

MIXTURE OF GOODS.

See Replevin 20; Trover 26.

MONCTON.

See Justice of Peace IV. 10.
" Election 2.

MONEY LENT.

See Assumpsit III. 41.

MONTHS.

A policy of insurance is a mercantile instrument, therefore the term "months" used therein, limiting the time for bringing an action for loss, means calendar months. *Pomares* v. *Provincial Insurance Co.*, *Hil. T.* 1873.

See Insurance 40.

MORTGAGE

See Equitable Mortgage.

1—Extent of Contract—Confined to absolute estate.
A. by deed reciting that he was seised of lands and hereditaments in fee simple, and being indebted to B. had agreed to transfer and convey to him the hereditaments thereinafter mentioned for securing the debt; *granted, bargained, sold, released and confirmed* to B. all the lands &c. and hereditaments situate in the Province of New Brunswick, of which A. was seized in fee, or any other estate of freehold or inheritance. Held, That the deed was confined to absolute estates, and that as there was no assignment of debts, land which A. was entitled to as mortgagee did not pass. *Doe dem. Holderness* v. *Donnelly*, 3 *Kerr* 238.

2—Accessory to debt.
In ejectment, to recover certain premises which had been mortgaged to J. K. and H. G. K. for securing a bond debt, a deed of assigament was put in evidence from J. K. and H. G. K. to the lessors of the plaintiff, creditors of J. K. and H. G. K., and trustees for all the creditors, reciting among other things "that the assignors proposed to assign all their joint and separate estate and effects, real and personal, except as thereinafter excepted," and, after designating certain real and personal estate, assigned all and singular (certain property named in the deed,) and also "debt and debts, sum and sums of money, bonds, bills, notes, securities, vouchers for or affecting the payment of money," and all the estate and effects of whatever nature and kind soever, etc., wearing apparel excepted; upon motion to enter a nonsuit on the ground that the deed of assignment having described other real estate, but omitted to describe or allude to the mortgaged premises, the same were not assigned by the deed. Held, That as the deed expressly mentioned debts, bonds, and securities for money, the bond debt which the mortgage was given to secure passed to the lessors, and carried with it as accessory thereto the land contained in the mortgage. *Doe dem. Burnham* v. *Watts*, 3 *Kerr* 346.

3—Present legal estate—Mortgage debt.
The plaintiff in ejectment claimed under a deed containing the following exception: "subject to an incumbrance of a certain mortgage now in possession and in favor of H." (the defendant.) Held, That these words did not necessarily shew that a present legal estate in possession did not pass to the plaintiff by the deed, or that the mortgage referred to, gave the defendant an immediate estate in possession, which he was entitled to set up to bar the plaintiff's claim. *Doe* v. *Hanson*, 3 *All.* 427.

An executor cannot assign the legal estate in land mortgaged in fee to his testator, unless the land is devised to him. Without such devise, his assignment will only operate as a transfer of the mortgage debt. *Ibid.*

4—Liability of whole land to mortgage—Verbal agreement—Subsequent partition—Privity—Fraud.
A., the father, and B. and C., his sons, being joint owners of two lots of land, mortgaged them to the plaintiff. A. afterwards conveyed to the plaintiff land of which he was sole owner, in payment of half the mortgage debt, and then re-

leased all his interest in the mortgaged lands to B. and C., who occupied the land in common for several years, and made several joint payments to the mortgagee on account of the mortgage debt. B. and C. afterwards divided the land equally between them by deed of partition. In a suit for foreclosure of the mortgage, B. claimed that as between himself and C. his portion of the land had been released by the mortgagee at the time A. conveyed the land to him, and that C.'s lot should be first sold to satisfy the mortgage. Held—1st. That in the absence of any written agreement by the mortgagee, the whole of the land remained equally liable to the mortgage, and should be sold in one lot. 2nd. That if a verbal agreement, and the appropriation of the payment by A., would be sufficient to release a particular part of the mortgaged lands, it would not bind C. who was no party to it. 3rd. That the subsequent partition of the land between B. and C., in ignorance by the latter of the agreement, by which the portion of the land allotted to B. was to be released from the mortgage, was a fraud upon C., and that such agreement would not be carried out for B.'s benefit. *Johnson* v. *McCartney and others*, 1 *Han.* 220.

5—Operation of mortgage—No notice—Rents and profits—Grass.

Where the mortgagee has not given any notice of intention to take the rents and profits of land in possession of the mortgagor, grass growing on the land will be deemed to be the property of the mortgagor, with the assent of the mortgagee. *Baxter* v. *Johnson*, *Trin. T.* 1862.

6—Deed absolute in form—Mortgage.

A deed absolute in form decreed to be only a mortgage on satisfactory evidence that such was the intention, and a subsequent deed from the grantor to a third person with notice of the prior deed, though registered first decreed to stand subordinate thereto, and the grantee in the second deed allowed to redeem the mortgage. In default of doing so, his deed declared fraudulent and void, as against the first deed. *Hillock* v. *Frizzle*, *Mich. T.* 1863.

7—Enrolment of Registry—Proviso for redemption.

The estate of a mortgage in fee of land, cannot pass by deed of bargain and sale without enrolment or registry, nor by feoffment without livery of seisin. *Doe dem. Burnham* v. *Watts*, 2 *Kerr* 441.

The proviso for redemption will not operate as a re-demise to the mortgagor so as to entitle him to the possession of the land until default made, unless there be a stipulation to that effect. *Ibid.*

8—Failure of condition—Ejectment—Notice.

Where a mortgage deed is given to secure the payment of a certain annual sum on a particular day, and the deed contained a clause that until default the mortgagor may continue in possession. Held, That if the annuity is not paid on the day stipulated the mortgagee may eject the mortgagor without notice to quit or demand of possession. *Doe dem. Bryant* v. *Cunard*, 2 *Kerr* 193.

9—Defence—Mortgagee—Assignee—Statute of Limitations.

Assignee of mortgagee in possession may set up the mortgage as a defence to an action of ejectment by the assignee of the equity of redemption, though the mortgage is more than twenty years old, and the right to recover thereon is barred by the Statute of Limitations. See *Doe* v. *Hanson*, 3 *All.* 427.

10—Statute of Limitations—Payment by mortgagor—Sale of Equity of Redemption.

S. mortgaged land to the lessor of the plaintiff in 1837 and made payment on account from time to time, the last payment being in October 1843. In 1842 the equity of redemption of S. was sold at Sheriff's sale by a judgment creditor, and the defendants claimed under the purchaser. Held, That notwithstanding the sale of the equity of redemption the payment by S. kept the mortgage alive for twenty years from the time of that payment, by 1 Rev. Stat. c. 139, s. 30, and that the mortgagee could recover the possession. [See Chinnery v. Evans, 10 Jur. N. S. 855.] *Doe d. Fox* v *Wright*, *Hil. T.* 1865.

11—Possession by verbal permission of mortgagee.

A person who goes into the possession of land by the verbal permission of the mortgagee, cannot be put out of possession by the mortgagor, or any one claiming under him. *Doe dem. Harding* v. *Hanson*, *Hil. T.* 1866.

12—Entry by command of mortgagee—Defence.
A verbal command by a mortgagee to a third person, to enter on land in possession of the mortgagor, and cut and carry away timber, is a defence to an action of trespass by the mortgagor against such person. *Carson* v. *Griffin*, *Hil. T.* 1865.

13—Several mortgages—Power of sale—Assignments—Discharge on records—Claim of payment.
M. gave three several mortgages to A., B. and C. The mortgage to C. contained a power of sale to him and his assigns in default of payment of the amount due on his mortgage; or, in case he or his assigns should pay any part of the moneys payable on the mortgages to A. and B. respectively. C. paid off B.'s mortgage, satisfaction of which was entered on the records,—and the mortgages of A. and C. were afterwards assigned to the defendant. Held, That by the assignment, the power of sale given to C. in the event of his paying B.'s mortgage, vested in the defendants, and was not affected by the discharge on the records; and that in a suit to redeem, the defendants were entitled to claim the amount paid by C. to discharge B.'s mortgage, though that mortgage had not been assigned to them. *Livingston* v. *Bank of New Brunswick*, *Hil. T.* 1865.

14—Excessive claim—Payment—Interest allowed.
In order to prevent the exercise of a power of sale by the mortgagee, the mortgagor paid the amount claimed, under protest: in a suit for redemption of the mortgage, the amount claimed by the mortgagee having been held excessive, the mortgagor was allowed interest on the excess. *Ibid.*

15—Estate of mortgagee—Execution against.
The estate of a mortgagee in fee who has not taken possession of the land, is not seizable in execution on a judgment against him. See Execution I. 3.

16—Mortgagors and Mortgagees.
Non-application of Act 6 Wm. 4, c. 43, s. 2. See Limitation of Actions I. 6 *a*.

17—Extinguishment of debt—Purchase.
If the mortgagee purchases the equity of redemption at Sheriff's sale, the mortgage debt is extinguished. *McPhelim* v. *Weldon*, *Trin. T.* 1862. *In re Beckwith*, *M. Rolls*, *August* 1845.

18—Erection of Mill Dam by Mortgagor—Liability of Mortgagee. See Action on the Case III. 2.

19—Mortgage paid but not cancelled,—mortgagee has no beneficial interest in the property. *Doe* v. *Baxter*, 2 *All.* 377.

20—Evidence—Executor.
An assignment of a mortgage by an executor is not admissible in evidence without proof of probate. *Doe* v. *Hanson*, 3 *All.* 427.

21—Disputing title of mortgagor.
After foreclosure, a stranger to a mortgage may dispute the title with the mortgagor. *Doe* v. *Brown*, 3 *All.* 433.

22—Insurance.
A mortgagor has a right to insure to the value of his property, without disclosing the incumbrance, unless stipulation in policy to the contrary. See Insurance 25.

Mortgage right—Equitable claim. See Equity 3.

Foreclosure. See Equity.

Liability of land mortgaged. See Equity 12.

Surrender by lessee of interest in lease to landlord. See Landlord and Tenant I. 3.

Outstanding mortgage—Answer to plea of property in replevin. See Replevin 5.

Defence by Tenant—Mortgage by Landlord. See Landlord and Tenant V. 22.

Title under Mortgagee. See Ejectment II. 6.

Contesting Mortgage Title of Lessor in Ejectment. See Estoppel I. 22.

Corporation—Validity of Deed to. See Corporation.

Trespass—Disputed Mortgage Title. See Trespass II. 7.

Estoppel—Action against Mortgagor by purchaser of Equity of Redemption. See Estoppel I. 12.

Mortgagee against Mortgagor. See Estoppel I. 13.

Assent of Plaintiffs to mortgage of personal property. See Estoppel I. 16.

Asportavit—Purchaser of Deed from Master in Chancery. See Trespass I. 11.

Registry—Notice.
The registry of a mortgage is not notice of an incumbrance to subsequent purchasers. *Doe* v. *Power*, 1 *All.* 271.

Purchaser of Ship—Notice of prior unregistered mortgage—Injunction to restrain sale. See Shipping Law 3.

MOTHER.

See Heir at Law.

MOTION PAPER.

See Practice V.
" General Rules 67, 68.

MUTUALITY.

Agreement to refer signed by one party, whether bad for want of mutuality. See *Therrian* v. *Therrian* 4 *All.* 48.

Deed bad for want of mutuality. See Deed.

NAME.

See Identity.

False Imprisonment—Not shewn that plaintiff known by one name as well as another. See Pleading II. 20.

Judgment—Averment of same person. See Pleading I. 58.

Identity of person. See Pleading I. 57.

Affidavit—Certainty as to name. See Affidavit III. 5.

Judgment—Nova Scotia.
Whether further evidence than mere identity of name was not necessary to identify the defendant with the defendant in the judgment sued on. See Evidence II. 29.

Corporate name—Sufficiency. See Corporate Name.

Replevin—Claim by wrong name—Assignment of bond in right name. See Replevin 21.

Parties—Same name—Surveyors—Question left to jury to find who was intended. See Identity.

NAVIGABLE RIVER.

Obstructing approach to wharf in navigable river. See Action on the Case IV. 3.

Trespass—Cutting Nets—Damages. See Damages I. 27.

Fishery.
The right of fishing in a public navigable river belongs to the public, and not to the owners of land bounded on the river. *Rose* v. *Belyea*, 1 *Han.* 109.

Common highway—Obstructing navigation of—Damage. See Action on the Case IV. 1, 2.

NAVIGATION.

Injuring plaintiff's nets.

Allegation of cause of injury. See Action on the Case II.

NEGLIGENCE.

See Action on the Case.

Attorney negligently conducting action—Pleading. See Pleading II. 22. See Attorney VII. 3.

Surgeon—Negligence—Declaration. See Action on the Case II. 3. See Evidence III. 10.

Penalty—Negligently kindling fire. See Fires.

Water company—Damage by fire—Duty as to keeping supply of water. See Water Company.

Escape. See Sheriff.

Fire—Negligence of tenant. See Action on the Case I. 2.

Owner and master of steamboat—Collision—Damage. See Principal and Agent 16.

Negligence of servants. See Carrier 7.

Using improper gear. See Carrier 8.

Negligence of master of ship. See Shipping Law.

Municipal corporation liable for negligence in discharge of duty imposed on them by their charter. See Corporation 18.

1—Contributory negligence.
In an action for running down a vessel, if there was negligence on both sides, and the plaintiff, by his own negligence, has contributed to the injury sustained by his vessel, he cannot recover. *Day* v. *Hatheway*, *Mich. T.* 1862.

2—Question not raised at trial.
If in an action for running down a vessel, the defendant did not raise any question of contributory negligence on the part of the plaintiff, and the case went to the jury on the points taken by the defendant's counsel, he cannot object, on a motion for a new trial, that the Judge should have left the question of contributory negligence to the jury. *Marvin* v. *Butterwell*, *Trin. T.* 1867.

3—**Legal right—Obligation.**
The defendants, having authority by law to lay out and open streets in the City of St. John, laid out a street through an unenclosed and hilly piece of ground. Several houses were built on the line of this street, but the land in the vicinity remained unenclosed, and people were accustomed to pass over it as they pleased, in various directions, though there was no right of way, except by the street. The defendants, having determined to level and improve the street, made cuttings through the hill for that purpose—several feet deep in some places. The plaintiff had formerly lived in the neighborhood of the street, and had been in the habit of crossing the open space; and after the street was levelled, she was crossing the open space in the night, and not being aware of the cutting, fell into the street and was injured. Held, per Allen, J. (Fisher, J., *contra*), That the plaintiff had no legal right, as against the defendants, to cross over the land; that there was therefore no legal obligation on the defendants to light the street, or to fence the sides of it against persons using the adjoining lands; and therefore they were not liable for the plaintiff's injury. *Henderson* v. *The Mayor &c. of Saint John, Hil. T.* 1872.

4—**Killing cattle—Railway Train—Evidence.**
In an action against a Railway Company for running over and killing cattle on the track, the evidence of negligence relied on, was that at the time the cattle were killed, the train was being run with the engine behind, which was alleged to be less safe than running in the ordinary way, with the engine at the head of the train: it appeared, however, that the train was not a long one; that a man was stationed on the front car to look out for obstructions on the road, and to signal to the engine driver; that the train was going round a curve at the time, at a slow rate of speed; that every precaution was taken to prevent accidents; and that the train was stopped as soon as it could have been if the engine had been in front. Held, That there was not sufficient evidence of negligence to leave to the jury. *Falconer* v. *European and North American Railway Company, Trin. T.* 1872.

The fact that an accident has occurred, is not of itself evidence of negligence: the plaintiff must give affirmative evidence of negligence on the part of the Railway Company, and if the fact of negligence is left doubtful, the defendants are entitled to a verdict. *Ibid.*

5—**Boom breaking—Obligation.**
By Act 10 Vic. c. 72, amended by 11 Vic. c. 49, and 17 Vic. c. 52, the South Bay Boom Company was authorised to erect piers and a boom between certain points on the River St. John, for the purpose of securing timber and lumber, and was authorized to charge boomage on all timber and lumber brought within the boom or fastened on the outside thereof. Held, that though the Company had the general control and direction of all lumber within the boom, it was under the immediate charge of the owners thereof; and therefore the Company was not liable to a proprietor of land within the limits of the boom, for damage done by lumber in the boom breaking adrift, and floating upon his land—there being no duty imposed upon the Company, by the Acts, to prevent lumber deposited in the boom, from drifting on the adjoining shores: and no evidence of negligence on the part of the Company, or, of their omitting to use all proper precautions in the erection of their piers and booms. *Dever* v. *South Bay Boom Company, East. T.* 1872.

NEW ASSIGNMENT.

Assault. See Pleading I. 12.
License. " " II. 17.
Seisin. " " II. 18.

NEW MATTER.

Leave to file affidavits in answer to. See Affidavit VI. 8.

NEWSPAPER.

Publication in—Presumption. See Joint Stock Company 3.
Publication of notice for three consecutive days. See Costs 34 *b*.
Notice in. See License 11.

NEW TRIAL.

I.

MOTION—AFFIDAVITS—PRACTICE.

1—Issue sent down by equity side of Court.
When an issue is sent down for trial by the equity side of the Court under 17 Vic. c. 18, s. 18, 2 Rev. Stat. page 80, a motion for a new trial must be made before a Judge in equity. *Hodge* v. *Reid*, 1 *Han.* 89.

2—Notice.
Notice of an intended motion for a new trial, must be given to the Judge who tried the cause, though points have been reserved at the trial. *Flaherty* v. *Sayre*, *Ber.* 83.

3—York Sittings.
Under the rule of Court, Mich. 1 Vic., thirty days notice must be given of a motion for a new trial from the York Sittings, although points have been reserved at the trial. *Turner* v. *Hammond*, 2 *Kerr* 536.

See General Rules 72.

4—Affidavits—Jurors—Witnesses—Party.
Affidavits of jurors stating that they have received evidence after retiring from the bar, cannot be received to impeach their verdict and obtain a new trial. *Attorney General* v. *Boyer*, *C. Ms.* 78.

5—On a motion for a new trial, an affidavit stating that one of the jurymen had informed the deponent that the verdict was decided by lot, will not be received. *Hodgson* v. *Carr*, 3 *Kerr* 499.

6—The Court refused to receive affidavits of the jurors stating that they found the defendant was not in a proper state of mind to understand the deed, and intended to assign that as the reason for their verdict. *Babbit* v. *Cowperthwaite*, 3 *All.* 373.

7—Witnesses—Affidavits—Discovery of new evidence.
To support an application for a new trial in consequence of the discovery of new evidence, the affidavits of the witnesses should be produced; or if they refuse to make affidavits, the applicant should state what they can prove. *Coy* v. *Gardiner*, 2 *All.* 91.

8—Discovery of new evidence.
In applying for a new trial in consequence of the discovery of new evidence, it should appear that the evidence was unknown to all the defendants at the former trial. *Smith* v. *Neill*, 4 *All.* 105.

9—Entry on Judge's notes.
Where a new trial is to be moved for on the ground of improper reception of evidence, counsel should take care that the question is correctly entered on the Judge's notes. *Brown* v. *Taylor*, *Ber.* 343.

10—Question not raised at trial.
If in an action for running down a vessel, the defendant did not raise any question of contributory negligence on the part of the plaintiff, and the case went to the jury on the points taken by the defendant's counsel, he cannot object, on a motion for a new trial, that the Judge should have left the question of contributory negligence to the jury. *Marvin* v. *Dutterwell*, *Trin. T.* 1867.

11—Ejectment—Verdict for defendant.
As a general rule, a new trial will not be granted in ejectment where the verdict is for the defendant. *Doe d. Edgett* v. *Downey*, *East. T.* 1873.

12—Defendant's Death—Imposing Terms.
Where the defendant died after a rule *nisi* for a new trial for improper admission of evidence had been granted on his application, the rule was made absolute on the following conditions: 1st. That the defendant's representatives should enter into an agreement that the verdict should stand as security for the result of the new trial, provided the plaintiff obtained the verdict. 2nd. That such verdict should be entered as of the assises, when the cause was previously tried. 3rd. An undertaking that the defendant's death should not be assigned as error. 4th. That notice of trial should be served on the defendant's representatives and on the attorney on the record. (Weldon J., *dissentiente*—that a new trial was grantable *ex debito justiciæ* and therefore no terms could be imposed. *Key* v. *Thomson*, *East. T.* 1871.

Rule nisi—Remodelling of. See Practice VIII. 19.

II.

FOR WHAT CAUSE GRANTED—SUFFICIENCY.

1—Wrong conclusion of jury.
If the Court is satisfied that the jury have come to a wrong conclusion upon

the evidence, a new trial will be granted, though it was a question involving the consideration of fraud, and was left to the jury on that ground, and on the credibility of a witness. *Doe* v. *Hatch*, 1 *All.* 200.

2—Further investigation requisite.
In an action of trespass involving a question of boundary, where the surveys made had not satisfactorily ascertained the bounds of a grant, and the case appeared to require further investigation, the Court granted a new trial on payment of costs. *Scribner* v. *McLaughlin*, 1 *All.* 379.

3—Verdict against law and evidence.
Where a verdict given for the defendant in an action of ejectment was clearly against law and evidence, the Court granted a new trial, the costs to abide the event of the suit. *Doe* v. *Watson*, 1 *All.* 675.

4—The Court is very reluctant to send a cause down to a third trial; but will do so, on payment of costs, when the verdict is clearly against law and evidence. *Hartley* v. *Fisher*, 1 *All.* 694.

5—Improper reception of evidence.
Where evidence has been improperly received, a new trial will be granted, unless the Court is satisfied that the jury were not influenced by the evidence. *McMillan* v. *Fraser*, 2 *All.* 615.

6—Where evidence has been improperly received, a new trial will be granted; and the Court will not enter into an inquiry whether there is proof enough to support the verdict without the objectionable evidence. *Girvan* v. *Mayor of St. John*, *East. T.* 1866. See *Key* v. *Thomson*, 2 *Han.* 224.

7—Improper reception of evidence—Possible influence on jury.
Where a deed offered to show the defendant's title to the land in dispute was improperly received in evidence, a verdict for the defendant was set aside, though it might have been sustained without the deed; it not being clear that the jury were not influenced by it. *Maynes* v. *Dolan*, 3 *All.* 573.

8—Absence of Counsel—Terms of rule.
Where a cause was tried, as undefended in the absence of the defendant's attorney, who was accidentally out of Court in expectation that the case which stood before it would occupy the whole day, the Court granted a rule *nisi* to set aside the verdict on payment of costs, and on condition that the defendant paid the amount of the verdict into Court; the plaintiff to be at liberty to consent to the rule being made absolute and to go trial at the first Circuit. *McLean* v. *McDonald*, *Trin. T.* 1864.

9—Perverse verdict.
Where the verdict is perverse, a new trial will be granted without argument of the questions involved in the case. (See Hawkins *v.* Alder, 18 C. B. 640.) *Allison* v. *Robinson*, *Mich. T.* 1871.

10—Verdict—Point not submitted.
Where the only question left to the jury was the mental capacity of the defendant to execute the deed on which the action was brought, and a verdict was given for the defendant, one of the jurors stating at the time that it was "from the defendant's not being fully acquainted with the contents of the deed," the Court granted a new trial; the defendant's ignorance of the contents not being sufficient to warrant the verdict, if he was competent to execute the deed. *Babbit* v. *Cowperthwaite*, 3 *All.* 373.

11—Mistake of witness.
A new trial may be granted in consequence of a mistake made by a witness in giving his evidence, but the practice must be exercised with much caution. No general rule can be laid down on the subject. *Doe* v. *Albee*, 3 *All.* 375.

12—Mistake of witness—Immaterial as to result.
It is no ground for a new trial, that a witness for the defendant made a mistake in giving his evidence as to the contents of a letter, which mistake he wished to correct; the Court being satisfied that the evidence as corrected together with that given by defendant would be no answer to the plaintiff's case. *McGee* v. *Wetmore*, *Mich. T.* 1861.

13—Discovery of new evidence—Surprise.
Plaintiff in ejectment relied on an adverse possession of fourteen years in A., her father, and possession in herself after his death in 1832, making together twenty years. The defendant held under a lease from the Corporation of Saint John, the grantees of the land. After a verdict for the plaintiff, the defendant's attorney in consequence of the evidence of one of the plaintiff's witnesses, searched the records and found a conveyance from A.

of his interests in the lands to B. dated in 1821, describing it as "corporation ground;" he also upon enquiry of B. (referred to by the plaintiff's witness,) ascertained that B. had held the land under a lease from the Corporation of Saint John, which had since expired, and let A. in as his tenant in 1818, and that he held as such until his death. Held, that this evidence was material, and there being no reason to suppose that the defendant was before aware of its existence, a new trial was granted on payment of costs. *Doe* v. *Baker*, 3 *All.* 591.

14—Verdict inconsistent with evidence—Unless terms assented to, new trial granted.

Where the damages in an action for goods sold and delivered, were inconsistent with any view of the evidence, a new trial was ordered on payment of costs, unless the plaintiff consented to reduce the verdict to conform to the value of the goods as proved by the defendant's witness. *DeMill* v. *Foshay*, 4 *All.* 86.

15—Variance—Description of property—Objection.

Where the *Nisi Prius* record in an action of trespass varied from the declaration delivered, in the description of the property taken, and the plaintiff's counsel, in his opening, claimed for property of which the defendant had no previous knowledge, a verdict for the plaintiff was set aside, though the defendant's counsel had cross-examined the plaintiff in reference to such property—the variance having been objected to at the opening of the case. *Brocheau* v. *Desbrisay*, 4 *All.* 122.

16—Verdict against evidence.

The defendants claimed title to certain premises under a deed sworn to have been made in 1815 or 1816, but never recorded, and alleged to have been destroyed. It was testified by a witness, whose evidence was somewhat shaken, that in 1815 or 1816 he purchased the premises from the grantee for £40, and gave one O. as security for the purchase money; that on paying the purchase money he got a deed of the premises, which was witnessed by A. S., and that afterwards he made a deed of the same premises to G. and C., which deed was copied from the first mentioned deed; and this statement was confirmed by O. as to the bargain for the premises and payment of the purchase

money; and by S., that he had been called on to witness such a deed; and by the deed to G. and C., which referred to the first deed: a verdict against such first deed was set aside as against evidence, and a new trial ordered. *McEachern* v. *Ferguson*, 3 *Kerr* 242.

17—A verdict against the weight of evidence, on a question of boundary, was set aside by the Court, and a new trial granted, on payment of costs, though the cause had been tried by a special jury of view. *Lonchester* v. *Murray*, 3 *Kerr* 335.

18—Verdict against evidence—Statute of Limitations defeating action.

Where the verdict is against evidence in an action of ejectment, and the Statute of Limitations may defeat the plaintiff before he can bring a second action, the Court will grant a new trial. *Doe dem. Estabrooks* v. *Humphrey*, 1 *Han.* 104.

19—Insufficient evidence—Verdict contrary to Judge's charge.

Goods were levied upon under an execution, but not removed by the Sheriff, the defendant having paid the amount. In an action of trespass against the attorney (the execution having been afterwards set aside for irregularity) the plaintiff gave no evidence that the goods were his property or in his possession at the time of the seizure, and the Judge directed the jury to find for the defendant, but they found a verdict for the plaintiff; the Court granted a new trial. *Wilson* v. *Street*, 3 *All.* 80.

20—Misdirection of Judge.

Where the Judge had misdirected the jury, the Court granted the plaintiff a new trial, though they were of opinion that his right was barred by the Statute of Limitations—that objection not having been taken on the trial. *Doe* v. *Baxter*, 3 *All.* 306.

21—Judge's ruling on point of law—Influence on jury.

Where the jury found a question of fact for the plaintiff, although there was a clear preponderance of testimony on defendant's side, and the Court were of opinion that in consequence of the ruling of the Judge on a point of law, under which the plaintiff would recover in any case, the question of fact might have received less consideration than it was entitled to, a new trial was ordered. *Hoyt* v. *Stockton*, 2 *Han.* 60.

22—Insufficient evidence—Credit.

In an action to recover the price of certain pictures and glass sold and delivered to the defendants, the defence set up to the demand for the glass, about £24, was that the purchase had been made on account of one J. W., but the only evidence to prove it, was that a clerk of the plaintiff, but without his privity, had at the defendant's request made out and rendered a bill charging J. W. with the amount; the jury having found a verdict for the plaintiff for £3 12s. 1d., the balance due on the pictures, excluding the price of the glass: the Court on his application granted a new trial on payment of costs. *McDermott* v. *Bell*, 2 *Kerr* 363.

23—Precise point not submitted to jury.

In an action by the assignee of a demand, sued in the name of the assignor, certain receipts and admissions by the assignor were given in evidence to prove payment in full to him by the defendant, which receipts and admissions however were attempted to be impeached as having been made in fraud of the assignee. Held, That the question for the jury was not whether payment had been made before or after the assignment of the demand, nor whether such payment was in fraud of the assignee; but simply, whether the payment had been actually made; and this precise point not having been submitted by the learned Judge to the jury, who found against the receipts and admissions, a new trial was awarded. *Goss* v. *Messinett*, 3 *Kerr* 201.

24—Adverse declarations of juror not objected to.

Where a party, against whom a verdict is rendered, is aware before the trial of a juror expressing a determination to give a verdict against him, and does not object to such juror on his being sworn, the Court will not disturb the verdict. *Scribner* v. *McLaughlin*, 1 *All.* 379.

25—Compromise—Verdict, result of.

Where the verdict for the plaintiff was evidently the result of compromise, and the weight of evidence was in favor of the defendant, the Court set it aside. *Keys* v. *Flynn*, *Ber.* 125.

26—Evidence unsatisfactory.

Where the evidence was multifarious and contradictory, producing no satisfactory result, the Court ordered a new trial on payment of costs. *Merithew* v. *Sisson*, 3 *Kerr* 373.

27—Survey—Line doubtful upon the evidence.

Where in trespass *q. c. fregit*, the case turned upon the true position of a dividing line between two grants, which line had not been ascertained by any proper survey, and was left doubtful upon the evidence; the Court set aside a verdict which had been rendered for the plaintiff, and granted a new trial on payment of costs. *Bull* v. *McCready*, 2 *Kerr* 228.

28—Counsel—Witness.

One of the defendants' counsel, after having been examined as a witness for them, addressed the jury on their behalf, and a verdict was returned for the defendants; on a rule *nisi* for a new trial, Held, That examining a party's counsel as a witness for him, was an improper practice, and accordingly the rule for a new trial was made absolute. *Shields* v. *McGrath et al.*, 3 *Kerr* 398.

29—Jury—Tampering with by defendant.

Where after the jury retired from the bar, the defendant conversed with them respecting the cause, and supplied them with victuals and drink, the verdict was set aside. *Trefethen* v. *Carman*, *Trin. T.* 1831.

30—Jury receiving refreshments from defendant.

The jury after viewing the land in dispute went to the house of one of the defendants and had refreshments; no explanation of the charge was given by the jurors or the officer in charge of them. Held—per Ritchie, C. J., Allen and Weldon, J. J., That a verdict for the defendants ought to be set aside; per Fisher and Wetmore, J. J., That the plaintiff being aware of the fact before the trial, should have applied to the Judge to discharge the jury; and that the objection was too late after verdict. *McNeill* v. *Moore*, *Hil. T.* 1873.

See Infra III. 46. (See Case Mosely v. Simpson—weekly notes, May 31, 1873. V. C. M.)

31—Verdict contrary to evidence as to identity of land.

A new trial was granted in ejectment where the verdict was found for the defendant, contrary to evidence, as to the identity of the land described in a lease to the defendant. *Doe dem. Sands* v. *Philps*, 1 *Kerr* 533.

32—Verdict inconsistent with evidence, and not in accordance with Judge's charge.

The jury having, upon the second trial of an action of trespass against the Sheriff for taking timber, found a verdict for the plaintiff for £200, the value of the timber being over £900, and having been directed to find for the plaintiff for the value of the timber as being his property, or for the defendant, as being D.'s property, under an execution against whom defendant had seized and sold the timber; the Court, on the application of the plaintiff, set aside the verdict and granted a new trial on payment of costs. *Connell* v. *Miller*, 2 *Kerr* 116.

The circumstance that the amount of the verdict was about the same as had been paid by the plaintiff to relieve the timber from the claims of the Crown, etc., and that this sum must have been paid whether the plaintiff or D. was the true owner, was not considered sufficient to sustain the verdict, as this was not stated as the ground of the verdict, and was inconsistent with the position of either party. *Ibid.*

33—Verdict not confined to proper damages.

In trespass, where a boundary was the prominent question in dispute, and the plaintiff, in addition to his evidence of the line which he sought to establish, and the trespasses committed within it, proved a trespass of cutting forty trees on his side of the line, claimed by the defendant. The learned Judge, on the evidence of both sides, left the questions of the lines to the jury, telling them that the line proved by the defendant was the more correct one, but that they might find for the plaintiff for the value of the trees, and the jury, in returning a verdict for the plaintiff, stated that they found the line claimed to by the plaintiff to be the correct line; a new trial was granted, it not appearing to the Court that, on such finding, the jury had confined their damages to the trespass for cutting the trees. *Lyons* v. *Merritt*, 1 *All.* 91.

34—Excessive damage.

In an action against a surgeon for negligence in treating a patient, whereby it was alleged that he lost his hands and feet, a verdict was given for the plaintiff for $25,000. Held, That the damages were excessive, the jury having found, that, without any negligence, the plaintiff would have lost a portion of his hands. In such a case, the Court ordered a new trial, though the plaintiff was willing to assent to reduce the amount of the verdict. *Key* v. *Thomson*, 1 *Han.* 297.

35—Evidence obscure.

A new trial will be granted on payment of costs, where the evidence is obscure, and the case requires further investigation to ascertain whether justice has been done. *Fiddes* v. *Henderson*, *C. Ms.* 47.

36—Ejectment—Evidence conflicting—Preponderance.

A new trial will be granted in an action of ejectment, where the verdict for the plaintiff would change the possession, the evidence being conflicting and preponderating in favor of the defendant. *Doe d. Thompson* v. *Dewar*, *Hil. T.* 1827.

See Supra I. 11.

37—Surprise—Cause unexpectedly called on.

The Judge at *Nisi Prius* stated on Wednesday that he would not continue the Court beyond the following Saturday night, except for the purpose of finishing a cause then on trial, in consequence of which, a material witness for the defendant in one of the causes on the docket left the county on Friday morning by the consent of the attorney (there being then no prospect of the cause in which he was a witness being reached that week); on Saturday evening the Judge stated that he would finish the cause then on trial that night, and call on the next case, being the case in which the witness had left the county, on Monday morning; and the cause was tried accordingly on Monday under a protest by the defendant's counsel, against the cause being tried in the absence of his witness, and a verdict given for the plaintiff. Held, That the defendant was entitled to a new trial on the ground of surprise; and that his right was not waived by his counsel attending at the trial, and making the best defence he could under the circumstances. *Meehan* v. *Sawttier*, *East. T.* 1871.

38—Verdict contrary to Judge's charge—Important principle involved—Though damages small.

Where a verdict is contrary to the Judge's charge, a new trial will be granted, though the amount of damages which the plaintiff would be entitled to recover is small, the principle involved in the case being important. *French* v. *Hodgin*, *Trin T.* 1833.

39—Clear point of law.
On a clear point of law, the Court will set aside the verdict *toties quoties* where there is an improper finding by the jury. *Estabrooks* v. *Orser*, 1 *Kerr* 57.

40—Cause tried as undefended—False statement.
Where a cause was tried out of its order, and in the absence of the defendant's attorney, on the statement of the plaintiff's counsel that it was undefended, the verdict was set aside on an affidavit of merits, and that defendant had intended to defend it. *Sayre* v. *Steves*, *Hil. T.* 1861.

41—Plan used by jury without cognizance of Judge or party—Affidavit of juror refused.
In an action of trespass to try a disputed boundary, one of the witnesses, during the progress of the trial, made a plan of the land and gave it to one of the jurors, explaining to him what the plaintiff claimed: this plan was used by the jurors without the knowledge of the Judge, or of the defendant's counsel, a verdict for the plaintiff was set aside on this ground, without any examination into the merits of the case, the Court refusing to hear affidavits from the jurors that they were not influenced by the plan. *Oulton* v. *Bowser*, *East. T.* 1873.

III.

REFUSAL—INSUFFICIENCY OF REASON.

1—Not taking advantage of available evidence.
Where plaintiff in trespass *q. c. f.* had it in his power to shew definite bounds, but relied on the uncertain lines of another grant, and the jury found against him, the Court refused to disturb the verdict. *Bates* v. *Lyon*, *Ber.* 63.

2—Unconscionable defence—Release.
The Court will not set aside a verdict obtained in an undefended cause, to enable the defendant to set up a release given by the plaintiff before trial, where it appeared that he was living out of the country, separated from his wife, and that the action was brought by her for wages due from the defendant, after her husband had abandoned her. *Clarke* v. *Robinson*, *Ber.* 86.

3—Imaginary damages.
A new trial will not be granted for imaginary damages. *Wilson* v. *Ellis*, *Ber.* 325.

4—Point not raised on trial—Nominal damages.
The Court will not grant a new trial on the grounds that nominal damages should have been given when the point was not raised at the trial. *Rogers* v. *Peck et al.*, *Ber.* 318.

5—Assault—Injury slight.
A new trial was refused in an action for assault and battery, where the verdict was for the defendant; though it was against the Judge's direction; the injury being slight, and the defendant assenting to a *stet processus*. *Moore* v. *Ogden*, 1 *Kerr* 278.

6—Plaintiff's claim not exceeding £5.
The Court will not set aside a verdict for the defendant and grant a new trial in an action of common assumpsit, on the ground of the verdict being against evidence, where it clearly appears that the plaintiff's claim does not exceed £5. *Williston* v. *Walsh*, 2 *Kerr* 181.

7—Cause tried as undefended—Letter not received in time.
An application for a new trial, on the ground that the cause was tried at Woodstock as undefended on the 27th September, the second day of the Court, owing to a letter of the defendant's attorney, giving instructions for the defence, not having been delivered at the post-office in Woodstock, when inquired for on the morning of the 27th, although it had been received at the office on the previous evening, was refused; it appearing that the letter was not dispatched from Saint John, where the attorney resided, until the 25th, and could not reach Woodstock until the evening of the day the Court opened. *Smiley* v. *Winslow*, 2 *Kerr* 349.

8—Due diligence not used—Terms of new trial.
A cause was called on in regular course, and tried in the absence of the defendant and his counsel on the first day of the Court. A new trial was refused, except on the terms of paying money into Court or giving security, it appearing that although the defendant's absence was accidental, he had not used due diligence either in preparing for trial, or getting to the Court. *Gibbs* v. *Steadman*, 2 *Kerr* 406.

9—Discovery of new evidence—Affidavit—Several trials.

The Court refused to set aside a verdict for the plaintiff, and grant a new trial, on the ground of discovery of new evidence, upon the affidavit of G. that he knew of facts which were very material to the defence; that he was present at the last trial, but did not mention the circumstance until after it was concluded. The facts were particularly set out in G.'s affidavit, which was however expressly contradicted by other affidavits; and there were affidavits of six respectable persons, that G. was a man of bad character and utterly unworthy of credit. The cause was of large amount, had been three times tried, and occupied several days each time. *Connell* v. *Miller*, 2 *Kerr* 433.

10—Absence of defendant's counsel from Court.

Where a cause was tried as undefended, in consequence of the defendant's counsel not being in Court when it was called on, the Court refused a new trial, though the amount in dispute was large, and the defendant swore that he had a good defence; but the defence appeared to arise out of partnership transactions between them which remained unsettled. *Doherty* v. *Hogan*, 2 *Kerr* 492.

11—Damages not outrageous.

A new trial will not be granted in an action for a malicious arrest, on the ground of excessive damages, unless the damages are outrageous. *Wentworth* v. *Hallett*, 2 *Kerr* 560.

12—Damages—Question for jury.

In an action of trespass, the amount of damages is entirely for the consideration of the jury, and the Court will not in general disturb the verdict. *Hadden* v. *White*, 2 *Kerr* 635.

13—Damages—Contrary to direction of Judge—Not excessive.

In trespass for taking goods under an execution which was afterwards set aside as illegal, the plaintiff proved that on the levy, and without the goods having been taken from his possession, he paid the Sheriff £10, the amount of the execution; the Judge told the jury that the amount paid by the plaintiff was a fair measure of damages, but they gave a verdict for £29. Held, That the damages were not so excessive as to justify the Court in granting a new trial. *Wilson* v. *Street*, 3 *All.* 251.

14—Damages—Large—Assessed properly.

Where the jury do not appear to have assessed the damages on a wrong principle or acted under the influence of improper motives or bias, the Court will not disturb their finding even if the damages are larger than they might have been disposed to give as jurors. *Godard* v. *the Fredericton Boom Company*, 1 *Han.* 536.

15—Excessive damages—Proper direction of Judge as to measure of.

Where in action to recover insurance, the defendant's witness contradicted the plaintiff as to the value of goods lost by fire, but the jury were properly directed as to the measure of damages, the Court refused to disturb their verdict, even though they might have given less as jurors. *Crozier* v. *the Phœnix Insurance Company*, 2 *Han.* 200.

16—Damages—Left to jury as to question of.

The question of damages having been left open to the jury, and the verdict being for plaintiff, the Court refused a new trial on the ground of excessive damages, although it appeared that the depreciation of the mill property since the date of agreement in question was much greater than the difference between the consideration paid and the amount of the verdict. *Smith* v. *Millidge*, 2 *Kerr* 408.

17—Damages excessive—Conflicting evidence.

Where in trespass there was conflicting evidence as to the quantity and value of trees taken from plaintiff's land, the Court refused to disturb the finding of the jury, even though the damages appeared large. *Prescott* v. *Walton*, 2 *Han.* 230.

Damages when not considered excessive. See Damages 1. 27.—Malicious Arrest, &c. 7.

18—Damages excessive—Assault on public officer.

A new trial on the ground of excessive damages (£230) was refused in an action for assault and battery, defendant being a public officer, and having knocked the plaintiff down in the street and kicked him, in consequence of a dispute between them relative to matters connected with defendant's office. *Wilson* v. *Saunders*, *Hil.* T. 1832.

18 a—Nominal damages.
A new trial refused to the plaintiff in an action against a Justice for false imprisonment, where the verdict was for nominal damages, though the conviction and warrant of commitment were illegal, the case having been fairly left to the jury. *Sewall* v. *Olive*, 4 *All.* 394.

19—Immaterial evidence admitted.
Where the evidence objected to was immaterial and unnecessary a new trial was refused. See *McKenzie*, *Curator*, v. *Scovil*, 2 *Han.* 6.

20—Executors—Administration—Smallness of amount.
In an action against three defendants as executors, two of whom had fully administered, and the amount in the hands of the other defendant was very small, the Court refused to set aside a verdict in favor of all the defendants. *Crookshank* v. *McFarlane*, 2 *All.* 544.

21—Surprise—Defendant's knowledge.
A new trial on the ground of surprise was refused when defendant knew the day before the trial of the evidence the plaintiff was going to give and might have applied for a temporary postponement of the trial in order to answer the evidence. *Gilbert* v. *Stockton*, 1 *Han.* 59.

22—It is no ground for a new trial on the ground of surprise, that the plaintiff if he had been present at the trial, could have contradicted part of the defence set up which he did not expect, he having been voluntarily absent from the trial. *Rankin* v. *Weldon*, *Mich. T.* 1864.

23—Misdirection—Defendant not being called as witness—Inference.
Where defendant knew all the circumstances, and might have been called as a witness. Held, That it was not a misdirection to tell the jury they might infer that if the defendant had been called, his evidence would not have benefited his case. *Tufts* v. *Hatheway*, 4 *All.* 62.

24—Evidence rejected—Tender.
Evidence rejected at a certain stage of cause, but not subsequently tendered, is no ground for a new trial if it has not been absolutely rejected. *Ibid.*

25—Expression of opinion of Judge on effect of evidence—Evidence not tendered.
The expression of a wrong opinion by the Judge on the effect of evidence offered, upon which the counsel withdraws it, is not a ground for a new trial. The evidence should be distinctly tendered *Ruel* v. *McElroy*, 3 *All.* 212.

26—Notice to produce—Generality of—Secondary evidence—No objection at trial.
If secondary evidence of a paper is admitted without objection from the party on whom a notice to produce has been served, he cannot afterwards on motion for a new trial object that the notice to produce was too general. *Rose* v. *Lindsay*, 3 *Kerr* 645.

27—Insufficiency of evidence—Fraud.
In trover for timber seized by the defendant, as Sheriff of Saint John, under a *fi. fa.*, issued against P. at the suit of S. and B., which timber was claimed by the plaintiffs, as trustees under a deed of assignment made by P. to them, expressed to be for the general benefit of the creditors, and executed just before the signing of a judgment in S. and B.'s suit, and the intent of which was to prevent his property being taken under the execution upon such judgment, the case went to the jury upon the question of fraud in the assignment, who found for the defendant. A new trial was granted on payment of costs, it appearing that P. was insolvent at the time of the assignment, that an actual delivery of the timber had been made to the plaintiffs before the issuing of the *fi. fa.*, and the evidence being insufficient in the opinion of the Court to shew that the deed was not intended to be for the benefit of the creditors as expressed on the face of it. *Hayward* v. *White*, 2 *Kerr* 304.

28—Although the *bona fides* of a trust deed, whereby the debtor's property is all assigned to trustees for the benefit, in the first instance, of certain preferred creditors, and afterwards for the benefit of all the creditors generally, is a question for the jury, and has been so left to them by the Judge, yet the Court will set aside the verdict, and grant a new trial, where the evidence does not appear sufficient to warrant the inference of fraud which the jury have drawn. *Burnham* v. *White*, 2 *Kerr* 571.

29—Fraud—Question for jury.
On a question, whether the sale of a horse was fraudulent or not, the jury having decided in the negative, the Court refused to disturb the verdict; the question having been left broadly to the jury

upon evidence which was reconcilable with either view of the case. *Little* v. *Johnson*, 1 *Kerr* 496.

30—Admission of improper evidence under pleadings — Want of objection.

Where a matter of defence, which should have been pleaded specially, and on which the decision of the case mainly depended, was urged to the jury without objection, and the case was fully tried, a new trial was refused on the ground of improper admission of evidence of such defence under the general issue. *Brown* v. *Cunard*, 3 *All.* 316.

31—In trespass for impounding cattle, the defendant pleaded "not guilty," and at the trial his counsel opened a defence, justifying impounding the cattle *damage feasant* and examined several witnesses to prove it, the plaintiff's counsel then objected that the evidence was not admissible under the plea; but further evidence was received, and the defendant obtained a verdict. The Court refused a new trial on the ground of the improper admission of the evidence, the damage if any, being very small.

Quære, whether the plaintiff had not waived the objection, by not taking it before the defendant gave any evidence of justification. *Campbell* v. *Wheeler*, 1 *Han.* 269.

32—Excessive distress—Nominal damages.

Where in an action for excessive distress, the law was correctly stated to the jury, who found a verdict for the defendant, the Court refused a new trial, though they were of opinion that there was excess which might have entitled the plaintiff to a verdict for nominal damages only; a new trial under such circumstances being only grantable on payment of costs. *Ruel* v. *Beer*, 3 *All.* 369.

33—Allegation of custom—Issue taken —Custom invalid.

Where the declaration alleged a custom as the foundation of the cause of action, and the defendant took issue thereon, which was found in favor of the plaintiff, it is no ground for a new trial that the custom proved is invalid. The objection should be taken by demurrer or motion in arrest of judgment. *Breen* v. *Elkin*, 4 *All.* 187.

34—Surprise.

In an action by a surviving partner, a verdict was given for the defendant, on proof of a deed of assignment from him to the plaintiff and M. in trust for the benefit of creditors, which had been executed by the deceased partner, in the name of the firm, and released the debt due from the defendant. A new trial on the ground of surprise was refused, though the plaintiff was absent from the country at the time the deed was executed, and knew nothing of it till it was produced at the trial, and the deceased partner was shown to be in a weak state of mind at the time it was executed. *Tisdale* v. *Hartt*, 4 *All.* 257.

35—Judge receiving evidence after charge to jury.

It is discretionary with the presiding Judge at what time he will receive evidence on a trial; and where he received evidence on the part of the plaintiff, after summing up to the jury, and after the defendant's counsel had consented to a verdict, subject to a motion for a non-suit, a new trial was refused. *Oulton* v. *Reed*, *Hil. T.* 1865.

36—Juror—Relationship.

The fact that a juryman who was open to challenge on the ground of relationship to the defendant has served on the jury is not *per se* a ground for a new trial, there being no evidence of mis-conduct in the juror and the verdict not otherwise objected to, and the defendant and the juror both swearing that they were not aware of the relationship at the time of the trial—even though the plaintiff was not aware of it either. *Bishop* v. *Goff*, *Hil. T.* 1866.

See Infra IV. 5.

37—Replevin—Smallness of recovery.

In an action for replevin for logs the plaintiff was entitled to recover a small portion—about 6,000 feet—but the jury found for the defendant, a new trial was refused as it could only have been granted on payment of costs. *Tompkins* v. *Tibbets*, 1 *Han.* 317.

38—Replevin—Substantial question.

It is no ground for a new trial in Replevin that the jury have not distinctly found on the several issues, it being understood that the substantial question was to whom the property in dispute belonged; and that the Court might enter the verdict on the several issues accordingly. *Fearon* v. *Murray*, *Hil. T.* 1861.

39—Fraud uncontradicted—Suspicious circumstances.

In an action on a policy of insurance, though the circumstances of a loss are suspicious, if there is some evidence of its being accidental, which is uncontradicted, and the question of fraud has been fully left to the jury, who find for the plaintiff, the verdict will not be disturbed. *Dimock v. The New Brunswick Marine Assurance Company*, 1 *All.* 398.

40—Credibility of witness.

Where a case depended upon the testimony of one witness, whose credibility was properly left to the jury and they found a verdict against his evidence, the Court refused a new trial. *Wortman v. Marter*, 3 *All.* 309.

41—No disputed point of law—Fraud—Jury—Credibility of witness—Cumulative evidence.

Where there is no disputed point of law, but the case turns on a question of fraud, and depends upon the credibility of conflicting testimony, the Court is reluctant to grant a third trial on the ground that the verdict is against the weight of evidence. *Smith v. Neill*, 4 *All.* 105.

Neither cumulative evidence, nor evidence merely to discredit a witness, is sufficient to obtain a new trial on the ground of the discovery of new evidence. *Ibid.*

42—Newly discovered evidence—Cumulative.

Where the estate of the plaintiff, claiming under a will, was subject to a condition subsequent, and the defendant endeavored on the trial to shew a request and refusal to perform the condition, in order to defeat the plaintiff's estate; any newly discovered evidence bearing on that point is cumulative, and is no ground for a new trial. *Doe dem. Myers v. Babineau*, *East. T.* 1864.

43—Improper reception of evidence—Immaterial testimony.

Where the question in an action of trespass was the true dividing line between two Crown grants, and a subsequent grant from the Crown was improperly received in evidence, a new trial on the ground of the improper reception of this evidence was refused: it being evident that it had no bearing on the question in dispute, nor any influence on the question left to the jury. *Carter v. Saunders*, *Trin. T.* 1864.

44—Improper admission of evidence—Withdrawal.

Though improper evidence of damage has been given, if it has been expressly withdrawn by the Judge from the consideration of the jury, and by subsequent evidence in the cause, it becomes immaterial, the Court will not disturb the verdict on the ground of its improper admission. *Spurr v. Albert Mining Co.*, *East. T.* 1871.

45—Jury separating after the Judge's charge.

The jury separating after the Judge's charge, and before verdict, will not invalidate the verdict, if there has been no tampering with them. *Lymburn v. DeVeber*, *Hil. T.* 1828.

46—Jury lodging and boarding at plaintiff's house—Necessity—No improper conduct.

Where a jury of view supped and slept at the plaintiff's house after completing the view—Held, No ground for disturbing a verdict for the plaintiff, it appearing that no communication respecting the suit had taken place between the plaintiff and the jury; that there was no inn within ten miles of the place, and no house near except the plaintiff's and his son's, where all the jury could be accommodated; that the jury were taken to the plaintiff's house by the Deputy Sheriff, who attended them, and who objected to their separating; and there was no complaint that the verdict was against evidence. *Spence v. Trenholm*, 1 *Han.* 77.

See Supra II. 30.

47—Plaintiff entitled only to nominal damages.

Where the Judge improperly directed the jury to find for the plaintiff with nominal damages; but they found for defendant—the Court refused a new trial—it being an action against the Sheriff for an escape, in which the plaintiff could, at most, have recovered nominal damages. *Atkinson v. Mitchell*, *Trin. T.* 1865.

48—Rejection of evidence—Immaterial deed.

Where a deed was improperly rejected; but it was clear that it would not have proved title in the defendant—the purpose for which it was offered—a new trial was refused. *Doe d. Sherlock, v. Powers*, *Hil. T.* 1865. (See E. India Co. v. Paul, 7 Moores P. C. 109.)

49—Evidence inconsistent—Possession.

The defendant claimed a lot of land by adverse possession, stating that he had been put in possession by the owner (since deceased) more than twenty years before the action. The land was principally wilderness; and the jury having found a verdict for the plaintiff for all except the improved land, the Court refused a new trial—the defendant's evidence of having been put into possession being inconsistent with other facts in the case. *Doe* v. *Guiggy*, 4 *All.* 602.

50—Nominal damages.
The Court will not send a case down to a new trial to recover merely nominal damages. See *Belyea* v. *Ham*, 2 *Han.* 27.

51—Misconduct of juror—Objection—Challenge.
The proper mode and time for objecting to a juror is by challenge when he is called to be sworn; therefore where an application is made to set aside a verdict for misconduct of a juror, all knowledge of the ground of objection until after the jury were sworn should be positively denied. *Olive* v. *Belyea*, 1 *All.* 463.

An offer to a juror to bet a treat upon the result of a trial, which he accepted, but swore he never afterwards thought of, and did not consider as a bet, is not a ground for setting aside the verdict. *Ibid.*

52—Jurata—Mistake in.
A mistake in the jurata of a *nisi prius* record is not a ground for a new trial. *Palmer* v. *Gilbert*, 1 *All.* 505.

53—Variance—Declaration and record.
A variance between the copy of declaration delivered and the *nisi prius* record, which did not appear to have misled the defendant and could not reasonably do so, is not a ground for a new trial. If discovered before the trial, it might be amended on motion. *Portland Ferry Co.* v. *Pratt*, 2 *All.* 17.

54—Amendment—Lateness of—Consent rule.
A consent rule was entered into by mistake, for more land than the defendant claimed. The day before the Circuit Court he obtained a Judge's order to amend the consent rule by confining it to the land in dispute; the plaintiff entered the cause the first for trial, and a verdict was given for the defendant. Held, That the lateness of the amendment was no ground for disturbing the verdict, and that if it was likely to prejudice the plaintiff it should have been urged before the Judge. *Doe* v. *Baxter*, 2 *All.* 377.

55—Point not distinctly reserved—Mistake in Statute—Correction.
By the accidental omission of the word "not" in the Rev. Stat. c. 126, the action for use and occupation was given on a demise by deed. In assumpsit for use and occupation on a verbal agreement, this Statute was not brought to the Judge's notice, but it was objected generally that the plaintiff could not recover. On a verdict for the plaintiff the Court refused a new trial—the mistake in the Statute having been rectified. *Seery* v. *Brayley*, 3 *All.* 315.

In such a case the defendant should have tendered a bill of exceptions, and not appealed to the discretion of the Court. *Ibid.*

56—Irrelevant testimony—Not submitted to jury.
A new trial will not be granted, though evidence has been improperly received, if such evidence is altogether irrelevant to the issue, and was not submitted to the jury, and their verdict was expressly given on grounds entirely independent of such evidence. *Bryson* v. *Hamilton*, *East. T.* 1873.

IV.

Miscellaneous.

1—Abandoning ground on which rule nisi was granted—Taking different ground.
In an action by a Church Corporation, the defendant obtained a rule *nisi* for entering a non-suit on the ground that the induction of the Rector was not proved. Held, That he could not afterwards abandon that ground, and admit the induction, in order to defeat the action on a different ground. *Doe* v. *Sweeney*, 1 *All.* 416.

2—Allowing verdict to stand for nominal damages.
B. agreed by a note in writing to pay A. £20 in lumber by a certain day, before which time A. assigned the contract to C. Held, That B. was not bound to recognise the assignment, but might deliver the timber to A., which would be a good discharge. *Green* v. *Williston*, 3 *Kerr* 58.

The delivery, however, not having been made until after the commencement of the action, a verdict which had been given for the plaintiff was allowed to stand for nominal damages. *Ibid.*

3—Wrong verdict.
If the jury find a verdict for the defendant in an action of libel, the Court will grant a new trial, if they think the verdict is wrong, though the Judge left the question of libel to the jury without expressing any opinion upon the writing. *Andrews* v. *Wilson*, 3 *Kerr* 86.

4—Trespass against three defendants—Verdict against two.
Quære, Whether, where the two defendants are clearly liable, the evidence of the trespass by the three is ground for a new trial. See *Atkinson* v. *McAuley*, 4 *All.* 243.

5—Juryman—Affinity.
The fact of a juryman, who is open to challenge, having served on the jury, is not, *per se*, a ground for disturbing the verdict; but when a juror was connected by affinity with one of the parties interested (a fact unknown to the opposite side till after the trial), the Court considered this fact in connection with the other circumstances of the case in determining on the propriety of granting a new trial. *Tuck* v. *Harding*, *Trin. T.* 1867.

See Supra III. 36.

6—Court divided—Rule nisi granted.
When the Court is equally divided upon argument, a rule *nisi* falls to the ground and the judgment follows the verdict. *Gaudin* v. *McKilligan*, 2 *All.* 477.

7—Terms—Costs.
It is discretionary with the Court on granting a new trial, to require the payment of costs; but if the verdict was contrary to law or to the Judge's charge, it is usually granted without costs. *The Bank of B. N. A.* v. *Travis*, 2 *All.* 543.

8—Costs—Rule silent as to.
If the rule for a new trial is silent as to costs, the successful party on the new trial is not entitled to the costs of setting aside the first verdict. *Weldon* v. *Weldon*, 3 *All.* 148.

9—Allocatur—Shewing cause.
A new trial having been granted on payment of costs, an *allocatur* allowed for shewing cause was taxed against the party who obtained the new trial. Held, That such taxation was wrong, and the costs accordingly entitled to be deducted. *McEachern* v. *Ferguson*, 3 *Kerr* 355.

10—Costs—Condition—Non-payment.
Where a new trial has been granted on payment of costs, and the costs have been taxed and demanded of the attorney of the party who obtained the rule, who was informed that unless the costs were paid, an application would be made to discharge the rule; the Court granted a rule for that purpose absolute, unless the costs were paid in ten days after service. *Scribner* v. *McLaughlin*, 1 *All.* 440.

Costs to abide event of suit—Same party succeeding — Costs of shewing cause. See Costs 95.

When verdict against Judge's charge, new trial granted without costs. *Doe dem. Blair* v. *Chace*, 3 *All.* 502.

11—Several counts—Verdict sustainable on one—Rejection of witness—Cross examination—Evidence.
In trespass *qu. cl. fregit* and for cutting down a mill dam, the defendants justified the cutting under a license from the plaintiff and as Inspector of Fisheries under the Act 31 Vic. c. 60. Evidence of the alleged license was given on the cross-examination of one of the plaintiff's witnesses, who was afterwards called as a witness by the defendant, and his evidence rejected on the ground that he had been already examined. The jury negatived the license and gave a verdict for the plaintiff for $30 on the count for breaking the close, and $2000 on the count for cutting the dam on the ground that the plaintiff being a tenant was bound to repair it. The verdict not being sustainable on the latter count,—Held, (per Allen and Wetmore, J. J.) That the trespass being entirely unjustified, the plaintiff was entitled to retain his verdict on the first count, the evidence of the license having been fully gone into, and the evidence rejected not affecting this part of the case. Per Weldon and Fisher, J. J., That the evidence having been improperly rejected, the defendant was entitled to a new trial. *Betts* v. *Venning*, *East. T.* 1873.

NEXT OF KIN.

See Heir at Law.

NISI PRIUS—(ORDER OF.)

There must be a motion in Court to make an order of *Nisi Prius* a rule of Court *Underwood* v. *McHenry*, 2 *All.* 94.

Amendment of. See Arbitration V. 6.

Time within which motion to set aside award under submission. See Arbitration IV. 13, 14, 15.

NISI PRIUS RECORD.

Variance — Declaration and Record. See New Trial III. 53. See General Rules 79, 130, 131.

When not evidence. See Set-off 6.

Entry of *Postea* on, where different issues. See Replevin 4.

NOLLE PROSEQUI.

Entering up judgment for costs. See Costs VI. 104.

Failure of evidence.
On the trial of an information for intrusion, a *nolle prosequi* may be entered if the evidence fails to make out the case; and it may be entered by the Solicitor General in the name of the Attorney General. *Reg.* v. *Sturges*, *Trin. T.* 1863.

NON PROS.

Judgment of *Non Pros* cannot be signed in a bailable action, unless the bail piece is on file, pursuant to the rule of Hilary Term, 2 Wm. 4. *Wiggins* v. *Dibblee*, *Trin. T.* 1834.

Cannot be signed until the defendant has filed an appearance; notice of appearance is not sufficient. *Cushing* v. *Gordon*, *Mich. T.* 1872.

Setting aside for irregularity—Delay. See Practice VI. 8, 9.

Evidence of judgment of *Non Pros.* See Evidence II. 29.

NON-RESIDENTS.

Proceedings in Equity. See General Rules 119, 111.

When proceedings cannot be taken against.
The plaintiff remitted bills of exchange from this Province to R. in England. Before the bills became due, R. was declared bankrupt in England, and the defendant, as his official assignee, received the proceeds of the bills. Held, (assuming the defendant to be liable to the plaintiffs for money had and received) That the non-payment of the money was not a breach of "a contract made wholly or in part" within this Province, and therefore that proceedings could not be taken against the defendant under the Act 18 Vic. c. 25. *Crane* v. *Cazenove*, 4 *All.* 578.

NON-SUIT.

1—Objection apparent on record.
Where a plaintiff has no right in law to recover, a non-suit will be ordered, though the objection appears upon the record. See Next Cases 2, 3, 6. *Fisher* v. *Jewett*, *Ber.* 35.

2—If the defendant takes issues upon the facts alleged in the declaration, and they are proved, the plaintiff cannot be non-suited on the ground that these facts do not disclose a cause of action; but the defendant must move in arrest of judgment. *New Brunswick and Nova Scotia Land Co.* v. *Kirk*, 1 *All.* 443.

3—Cause of action proved as alleged.
Where that which is laid as the cause of action, is proved at the trial, the plaintiff cannot be non-suited on the ground that the facts charged do not disclose a cause of action. *Cameron* v. *Beardsley*, 2 *Kerr* 598.

4—Voluntarily becoming non-suit.
Where a party voluntarily becomes non-suit, he cannot afterwards move to set it aside, and obtain a new trial on payment of costs. *Thorne* v. *Bedell*, 3 *Kerr* 339.

5—Discharge of jury—No verdict—Points reserved.
When no verdict has been given, in consequence of the discharge of the jury, a non-suit will not be granted on a point reserved at the trial. *Doe d. Duncan* v. *Christopher*, *Ber.* 83.

6—Material Allegation—Failure in proof.
Though the declaration does not set out a good cause of action, and was therefore demurrable; if the alleged cause of action is not proved, the defendant is entitled to a non-suit. Thus, in an action by overseers of the poor against the defendant, for bringing paupers into the parish, who became chargeable—alleging that the plaintiffs, as overseers of the poor, were compelled to provide for the paupers; if it appears that the plaintiffs were not overseers at the time the paupers were brought into the parish, they fail in proving a material allegation. *Gillespie* v. *Phillips*, *Mich. T.* 1861.

7—Opinion of Judge expressed—Verdict by consent.
Where, at the trial, a non-suit was moved for, and upon hearing the opinion of the Judge, a verdict was taken by consent of counsel, the question cannot afterwards be raised as to whether the case should have been submitted to the jury. *Reed* v. *Weldon*, 1 *Han.* 458.

8—After verdict but before recording.
Quære, Whether a plaintiff can elect to be non-suited after the jury have given a verdict, but before it is recorded. See *Lawton* v. *Chance*, 4 *All.* 411.

9—Subsequent assent after argument.
Where, at the trial, the Judge ruled that the plaintiff could not recover, an application to have a non-suit entered at the close of his argument on a rule *nisi* for a new trial, was held to be too late. See *Travis et al.* v. *Glazier*, 2 *Han.* 215.

10—*Quære*, If a non-suit is moved for on two grounds, the one tenable and the other untenable, and it is granted on the latter, whether the former is available for defendant on argument for setting aside non-suit. See *Doe d. Connel* v. *Dickinson*, 1 *Han.* 456.

(See Noble v. Ward, 1 Ex. 117 L. R.)

11—Nominal damages—Refusal to accede to verdict for.
In trespass for false imprisonment against Justices of the Peace, where the Justices had exceeded their powers in committing the prisoner to an improper place of imprisonment for contempt, but where the plaintiff had received no greater punishment than he was entitled to by law, the Judge offered to direct the jury to find a verdict for the plaintiff with nominal damages. The plaintiff refused to accede and claimed substantial damages, whereupon the Judge non-suited him, and the Court refused to set the non-suit aside. *Armstrong* v. *McCaffrey et al.*, 1 *Han.* 517.

Rule *nisi* to enter a non-suit may be remodelled. See Practice VIII. 19.

NOTICE.

Arbitration—Notice of adjourned meeting of Arbitrators necessary. See Arbitration V. 14.

Bail, notice of 'render—Reasonable time. See Exoneretur.

Corporation—Notice of Meeting. See Joint Stock Company 3.

Instalment—Notice for payment of. See Joint Stock Company 1.

Taxation of Costs—Review—Notice. See Costs.

Official character. See Crown Grant I. 18.

Absconding Debtor's Act—Effect of notice in *Gazette* as to property. See Absconding Debtor 10, 12.

Registry.
Registry of mortgage not notice of incumbrance to a subsequent purchaser. *Doe* v. *Power*, 1 *All.* 271.

Notice to sell land under license—Posting and advertising. See Executors and Administrators V. 2.

1—Parish School Act—Assessors.
Where asscssment is made under the Parish School Act, the Assessors must give notice thereof in the same manner as in cases of assessment for county rates under 1 Rev. Stat. c. 53, s. 12. *Ex parte Street*, 1 *Han.* 107.

2—Insolvent debtor—Order for support.
Where the creditor's attorney was in Court, and heard the order for support made, it is not required to give him other notice. *Ex parte Jardine*, 1 *Han.* 572.

Publication of notice for "three consecutive days" cannot be made in weekly newspaper. See Costs 34 *b*.

NOTICE OF ABANDONMENT.

See Insurance 26.

NOTICE OF ACTION.

See Action at Law.

NOTICE OF APPEAL.

See Practice V. 3.

NOTICE OF DEFENCE.

See Pleading III.

NOTICE OF DISHONOUR.

See Bills and Notes.

NOTICE — HIGHWAYS — ALTERATION.

See Highways 11.

NOTICE OF MOTION.

See New Trial I—Practice V. IX.

Intoxicating Liquors. See Evidence XI. 19, 20.

Proving Property in Replevin. See Pleading II. 29. See Replevin 23, 24.

Importing Goods. See Custom Duties.

Defamation—Supporting Plea. See Defamation 14.

OPINION OF EXPERTS.

See Evidence VIII. 14. Witness.

ORDERS.

See Practice.

Privy Council Orders. See Privy Council.

OVERFLOWING LAND.

See Action on the Case III.

OVERSEERS OF POOR.

Not accounting for money. See Criminal Law.

1—Necessity of shewing the taking oath of office.

Premises in the occupation of a tenant were devised to the Overseers of the Poor of the City of Saint John, for the use of the poor. Held, in an action brought for the rent by the persons who were the duly appointed Overseers at the date of the will and death of the testator, and so continued until the time of bringing the action, That it was not necessary to shew they had taken the oath of office as Overseers. *Matthew* v. *Chittick*, 2 *Kerr* 696.

2—Personal liability.

Where supplies were furnished to the defendant, an Overseer of the Poor, for the use of the poor of the Parish of Saint John, on orders from time to time sent by him as such Overseer to the plaintiff. Held, That he was personally liable for the payment of such supplies. *Gardiner* v. *Matthew*, 3 *Kerr* 601.

3—Bringing paupers into Parish—Action.

The Overseers of the Poor, not having any corporate rights, cannot maintain an action against a person who brings paupers in the Parish, who become chargeable thereon—such act being no injury to the Overseers individually. *Gillespie* v. *Phillips*, *Mich. T.* 1861.

OWNERSHIP OF PROPERTY.

See Property.

PARCHMENT.

Sufficiency of material. See Burns v. Burns, 4 All. 229. See General Rules 83.

PARISH OFFICER.

See Appointment of Officer.

PARISH SCHOOLS.

See Assessment II.

Trustees dividing Parish—Calling meeting—Double purpose.

A majority of the Trustees of Schools have power to divide a Parish into School Districts. *Ex parte Yeats*, 4 *All.* 381.

An application to Trustees to divide a Parish into School districts, and to call a meeting of the inhabitants to determine upon an assessment under the Parish School Act 21 Vic. c. 9, may be made at the same time; and if, on the division of the parish, three or more of the applicants are found to be resident freeholders in the district for which the assessment is required, the trustees may call the meeting without any new application. *Ibid.*

A poll-tax may be levied under the Parish School Act. *Ibid.*

Dismissing Teacher. See School Teacher. See Common School Act.

PAROL EVIDENCE.

See Evidence.

PARTICULARS.

Sufficiency of bill.

A bill of particulars which gives substantial information of the plaintiff's demand and does not confine the claim to any particular count, or mislead the defendant, is sufficient to let in evidence under any count to which the same may be applicable. *Grant* v. *Aiken*, *Ber.* 259.

The plaintiff's bill of particulars was dated at Liverpool, England, and made up in sterling money. Held, That without an affidavit of the defendant, that he was misled by it, it was sufficient to warrant the jury giving a sum sufficient to cover the difference of exchange. *Campbell* v. *Wilson*, *Ber.* 265.

Defect supplied by. See Bills and Notes VI. 14.

Demand of—Not a step in cause. *Johnston* v. *Glazier*, *C. Ms.* 141. *Andrews* v. *Hanson*, 1 *All.* 509.

Signing judgment by default on bill—Practice City Court. See City Court.

Recovery under Common Count—Counsel not claiming under, in opening case. See Trial.

PARTIES.

See Action at Law.
" Husband and Wife.
" Partnership 5.

PARTITION.

A., B. and C. owned lands as tenants in common; A. being under age her father made a partition with B. and C. in 1810; in 1814 A. married, still being under age, and her husband occupied the share allotted to her until his death in 1842, and six years after she objected to the partition, demanded possession of B., and brought ejectment. Held, That the partition having been fair she was bound by it, unless she objected within a reasonable time after her coverture ceased, and that under the circumstances six years was not a reasonable time.

Quære, Whether a demand of possession upon B. without any offer by A. to relinquish any part of what she was in possession of, was a sufficient notice of her dissent to the partition.

Quære also, Whether A.'s right was barred by the Statute of Limitations 6 Wm. 4, c. 43, she having brought her action within ten years after her coverture ceased, and within forty years after her right accrued, though not within twenty years after she became of age. *Doe dem. Estabrooks* v. *Harris*, 2 *All.* 42.

PARTNERSHIP.

Whether contract personal or with firm—Question left to jury. See Contract 15.

1—What constitutes partnership—Proof.

Where J. and N. B., who carried on business as general partners, had certain mill property and transactions relative thereto, the direction and management of which H. appeared to be taking a part, though the nature of his agreement with J. and N. B., or his interest in the mills was not shown; and the plaintiff, who had extensive transactions with the firm of J. and N. B., stated an account with them, whereby they admitted a balance due the plaintiff. Held, That H. was not jointly liable therefor, it not appearing that he was a partner in fact, or held himself out as such, and that his connection with J. and N. B., being at the most a special partnership in regard to the mills, would not make him liable for the general engagements of the firm of J. and N. B., but only for such as related to the special partnership. Circumstances which are equally applicable to a projected company, or security for past advances, are not sufficient of themselves to raise a presumption of partnership so as to create a joint liability in two persons where the credit has been given to one. *McPherson and another* v. *Hoskins and others*, 1 *Kerr* 430.

2—As to the sufficiency of proof of partnership this may vary according to the nature of the demand and residence of the parties. *Pollock* v. *Cunard*, 2 *Kerr* 291.

3—Under law allowing parties to be witnesses, it is not necessary to call plaintiff to prove partnership. See Evidence III. 9.

4—Evidence of a witness who had dealt with all the plaintiffs as partners and purchased goods and settled accounts with the firm for several years held sufficient to prove partnership. *Rankin et al* v. *Hurley*, 1 *Han.* 271.

5—Contract—Parties—Liability.

W. R., one member of a firm entered into a contract under seal, in his own name, with P., for building a vessel, which was, in fact, to be the property of the firm. After the vessel was finished, a settlement in writing of accounts took place between the plaintiff (acting on behalf of P.) and the firm, in which a balance was found due to P., which W. R. requested the plaintiff to pay. Held, in an action against the firm for the money paid to P., That, as it was not founded on the original agreement for the building of the vessel, but under a separate agreement with the firm,—that they were liable. *Harris* v. *Robertson*, *Mich. T.* 1866.

5 a—Actions by and against.

A promise to one member of a firm to pay him for work connected with the partnership business, performed by him for the defendant, enures to the benefit of the firm; and the partner to whom the promise was made cannot sue alone. *Hartley* v. *Fisher*, 1 *All.* 694.

6—Guarantee.
A guarantee by one partner in the name of the firm for a matter not relating to the partnership business, will not bind the firm. *Marks* v. *Wright*, *Hil. T.* 1828.

Pleading—Allegations—Proof—Variance. See Bills and Notes VI. 10, 11.

7—Non-joinder of partner can only be taken advantage of by plea in abatement. *Kelly* v. *Bulloch*, 2 *Kerr* 690.

8—Powers of members.
One partner has power to compound a partnership debt, and may appoint an agent to accept a composition of such debt offered by an insolvent debtor. *Raymond* v. *McMahon*, 4 *All.* 524.

Statute of Limitations—Payment by one partner. See Bills and Notes V. 26.

Execution of deed by partner—Ignorance of co-partner. See New Trial III. 34.

Recognition of Warrant of Attorney. See Warrant of Attorney 8.

PATENT.

If Letters Patent refer to a specification and description of the invention, as being filed in the Provincial Secretary's office, they form part of the Letters Patent, and must be produced in an action for infringement of the patent. *Lusk* v. *Miller*, *Mich. T.* 1872.

Where a Patent is claimed, not for a discovery or invention, but simply for a combination of a number of old and known materials, it is no infringement of the patent to use a part of this combination. *Ibid.*

PAWNEE.

See Bailee—Trover.

PAYMENT.

See Action at Law (Former Recovery.)

Pleading payment—Inference from Receipt.
Debt on a recognizance of bail—judgment against the principal, for £23; the defendant pleaded payment by the principal, and gave in evidence a receipt from the plaintiff to him for £11, "in full discharge" of the judgment. Held, That it could not be inferred from the receipt that this sum was a balance of the judgment after a previous payment, but that it was taken in satisfaction of the whole, and therefore the plea was not proved. *Garcelon* v. *Eaton*, 3 *All.* 411.

Payment by bill—Agent unauthorized to receive. See Principal and Agent 8.

Assignment—Actual payment. See New Trial II. 23.

Payment of rent. See Landlord and Tenant.

Payment taking case out of Statute of Limitations. See Limitation of Actions II.

Rebuttal of presumption of payment. See Evidence VI. 7.

Money paid under mistake. See Assumpsit III. 17.

Appropriation — Want of Privity. See Bills and Notes V. 20.

Application by law—Set-off—Right to shew appropriation on cross-examination. See Evidence VIII. 7.

PAYMENT OF MONEY INTO COURT.

See Evidence X. 9, 10, 11.

PAYMENT—DEMAND OF.

Note payable on demand. See Bills and Notes V. 11, III. 4, 15.

PAYMENT—PRESUMPTION OF.

See Assumpsit III. 44.

PENALTY.

Set off. See Executors and Administrators I. 3. See Justice of the Peace. See Criminal Law.

Negligently kindling fire. See Fires.

PENDENCY OF OTHER SUIT.

See Pleading II. 30.

PEREMPTORY UNDERTAKING.

See Judgment as in Case of Non-suit.

PERJURY.

See Criminal Law.

Jurisdiction to take oath—Prayer Book.
In an action for defamation, in alleging that the plaintiff was guilty of perjury on the trial of a case before two Justices of the Peace, the plaintiff cannot recover if the Justices had no jurisdiction in the case, although the words were spoken in reference to the trial where the plaintiff had given his testimony before the Justices. *McAdam* v. *Weaver*, 2 *Kerr* 176.

Semble, Perjury may be assigned where the oath has been administered on the Common Prayer Book of the Church of England. *Ibid.*

Since the passing of the Act 3 Vic. c. 51, confirming the commissions already issued and authorizing the Judges to issue commissions to take affidavits under the provisions of the Act of Parliament 29 Car. 2, c. 5, wilful false swearing in an affidavit made in a judicial proceeding, and sworn before a commissioner so appointed, is perjury by common law. *Milner* v. *Gilbert*, 3 *Kerr* 617

Completion of. See Pleading I. 51.

PETITION (UNDER INSOLVENT ACT OF 1869.)

See Insolvent Act of 1869.

PILOT.

Appointment of—Removal of. See Mandamus.

PILOTAGE.

Power in Corporation of St. John to make bye-laws respecting. See British North America Act 1867. 5.

PLAN.

See Crown Grant—Evidence II. 1, X. 3, XI. 12.

PLEA.

See Pleading—Practice.

PLEADING.

I. Declaration—Averments—Allegations.

II. Pleas—Subsequent Pleading—Abatement.

III. Notice of Defence.

IV. Miscellaneous.

I.

Declaration.

See Practice.

1—Arguments—Allegations—Money.
In an action to recover in this Province for goods sold and delivered in England, it is not necessary to aver in the declaration that the debt was contracted in sterling money, or the relative value of sterling and currency; and the difference of exchange may be recovered under the common counts. *Campbell* v. *Wilson*, *Ber.* 265.

2—Part Performance—Demand—Averment of surplusage.
In an action of assumpsit the plaintiff averred part performance by the defendant and demand as to the residue, which was not necessary, and failed in proving both. Held, That both averments were surplusage. *Brown* v. *Frink*, *Ber.* 363.

3—Insufficient Allegation—Information.
The allegation that the goods were imported into this Province from the United States, contrary to the Acts of General Assembly, in such case made and provided, is not a sufficient allegation of an offence under 6 Wm. 4, c. 4, s. 4, which imposes a forfeiture of all goods which shall be landed before they are reported at the Treasurer's Office and a permit obtained, etc., and a judgment obtained on an information by the Attorney General was arrested thereon. *Attorney General* v. 250 *barrels of Fish*, *Ber.* 419.

4—Demise.
A demise in a declaration of ejectment, in the name of husband and wife, of the wife's property, laid previous to the marriage, is bad. *Doe d. Thomson and Wife* v. *Barnes*, *Ber.* 426.

5—Special damage.
Allegation of loss and time and expense in regaining property taken under execution, evidence of expenses in proving the plaintiff's right before a Sheriff's jury, is not admissible. *Quære*, If such expenses are recoverable at all. *Wilson* v. *Ells*, *Ber.* 324. (See Damages.)

6—Assumpsit on guarantee—Consideration not sufficiently appearing.
The defendant guaranteed the performance of the following agreement between the plaintiff and D., dated 10th November 1849: "Whereas B. (the plaintiff) has

for some years past been acting as the attorney and agent in this Province for D. of London, in the general management of the Lancaster Mills; and whereas the said D. has seen fit, by letter of attorney bearing date the 19th September last, to appoint G. (the defendant) his attorney and general agent in this Province, and has thereby revoked all power and authority heretofore given to the said B.; and whereas an action of trover has been commenced and is now pending against the said B. at the suit of W. and C. for the value of a quantity of logs which they allege to have been converted at the Lancaster Mills, for the value of which logs (if any) the said B. should not be held personally liable; in consideration of the foregoing premises, it is agreed by the said D. to indemnify and keep harmless the said B. from all damages, costs and charges that may be awarded against him, or that he may be put to in his defence of the said action." Declaration thereon, stating that whereas before making the defendant's promise, to wit, on etc., the plaintiff was the general agent of D. in this Province, in the management of the Lancaster Mills, that an action of trover had been commenced and was pending at the suit of W. and C. for the value of a quantity of logs which had been taken by the plaintiff as the agent, and acting under the directions of D., and in the belief that they were his property, and that D. had requested the plaintiff to defend said action; and whereas D. was desirous of revoking the power of the plaintiff as his agent, and of appointing the defendant, and the defendant was desirous of succeeding the plaintiff in such agency; that the plaintiff agreed with D. to defend said action, and retire from the agency and allow the defendant to succeed him therein, in consideration of receiving the agreement of D. to indemnify the plaintiff against all damages, costs and charges he might be put to in the defence of the action of W. and C.; and also in consideration of receiving the guarantee of the defendant for the due performance by D. of his agreement; that D. did, on the 10th November 1849, agree to give such undertaking, and thereupon in consideration of the premises, and that the plaintiff would accept the agreement of D. and act upon the same, and would defend the said action, and would retire from the said agency and permit the defendant to assume the duties thereof, the defendant undertook and guaranteed to the plaintiff the performance of D.'s agreement. Held, That the consideration did not sufficiently appear by the agreement, to support the declaration. *Beattie* v. *Garbutt*, 3 *All.* 1.

7—Proceedings of record—Slander—Allegation of necessary facts.

Where, to an action of slander, the defendant pleaded the Statute of Limitations, and the plaintiff replied that a previous action was brought within due time for the same slander, in which he had obtained a verdict, and the Court had ordered the judgment to be arrested, (setting out the proceedings of the Court as matters *in pais*, without any *prout patet per recordum*,) and that the same action was brought within a year of such arrest of judgment, concluding with a verification in the ordinary form. Rejoinder, That there is not any record of the several proceedings (setting them out *seriatim*); sur-rejoinder, a mere repetition of the replication; upon demurrer thereto, the Court were of opinion that the proceedings in the former action and arrest of judgment must be entered of record and pleaded as such, with a *prout patet*, and that the replication was therefore bad, but under the circumstances permitted the plaintiff to amend on payment of costs. *Beardsley* v. *Dibblee*, 1 *Kerr* 642.

8—Limit bond—Assignee—Allegation.

Summary action of debt by assignee of a limit bond; on demurrer—Held, 1st. That *nil debet* might be pleaded under the Act of Assembly as the general issue; 2nd. An averment, that the assignee is the plaintiff in the original suit in which the limit bond was given is not essential; 3rd. A breach of the condition of the bond is sufficiently alleged by the words "of which the said J. R." (the principal in the bond) made default. *Maxwell* v. *Roe*, 2 *Kerr* 69.

9—Assignee of limit bond—Plaintiff in original suit—Must be apparent on the record.

In an action by the assignee of a bond for the gaol limits, it is a fatal objection, even on motion for arrest of judgment after verdict, that it does not appear on the record that the assignee was the plaintiff in the suit on which the bond was taken, there being nothing to render proof of that fact necessary on the trial of the issue. *Semble*, The declaration should state the writ on which the defendant is in custody when the limit bond is taken. *Cameron* v. *Beardsley*, 2 *Kerr* 598.

10—Award—Non-fulfilment—Indenture.

Where, by the condition of an arbitration bond the award is directed to be in writing, indented under the hands and seals of the arbitrators; in an action on the bond for non-fulfilment of the award, the declaration not averring that the award was indented; held bad on special demurrer. *Coburn* v. *Taylor*, 2 *Kerr* 120.

11—Deed—Setting out.

In pleading a grant or bargain and sale, the deed should be set out. *Ansley* v. *Peters*, 2 *Kerr* 593.

12—Assault and battery—General replication.

In trespass for assault and battery; the defendants pleaded *molliter manus imposuerunt* in defence of their wharf and close, on which the plaintiff had unlawfully placed a ladder, which he was endeavoring to maintain there by force, whereupon, etc. Held, That an issue, joined on the general replication *de injuria* to this plea, only involved the question as to the defendant's possession of the wharf and close whereon it stood; and the assault being made in defence of such possession against the plaintiff's unlawful entry, etc., and that the Judge was not warranted in directing the jury to find for the plaintiff, if, notwithstanding these facts, it appeared there was another piece of land adjoining the wharf also in dispute, from which the defendants were endeavoring to remove the plaintiff, and that the assault was partly committed with that intent, and that this piece of land was not in the defendants' possession; the plaintiff to have availed himself of this matter should have replied specially or new assigned. *McCulley* v. *Cunard*, 2 *Kerr* 131.

13—Sureties on bond—Clerk—Non-damnificatus.

The bye-laws of a banking company required that the directors should inspect the vaults and take an account of the cash, etc., once a month: in an action against the sureties on a bond given for the good conduct of a clerk in the bank, the defendants pleaded that the bond was executed upon the faith that the plaintiffs would faithfully observe the bye-laws, and averred that they had neglected to do so. Held bad. Held also, that *non damnificatus* was not a good plea to an action on such bond. *Bank of New Brunswick* v. *Wiggins*, 2 *Kerr* 478.

14—Debt for penalty—Uncertainty.

To a declaration in debt for the penalty of a bond entered into by the defendants, K. and W., to the plaintiffs (a company incorporated by the Act of Assembly 5 Wm. 4, 2nd session, c. 10), conditioned for the faithful performance of K's. duty as secretary to the company without embezzling etc., and for due accounting upon notice so to do, or making satisfaction for any loss within three months after proof thereof and notice. The defendant W., after setting out the condition of the bond on oyer pleaded 1st, *non est factum*. 2dly, that if K. did not faithfully perform his duty or failed to account, notice thereof was not duly given three months before the commencement of the suit; 3dly, that if the plaintiffs were damnified it was of their own wrong; 4thly, after setting out a clause in the Act of Incorporation prohibiting the company from trading in gold and silver coins, etc., the plea alleged generally that the company did after the act of incorporation and the execution of the said bond, trade in gold and silver coins, etc., and employ their secretary K. therein, whereby K.'s responsibility was increased. Held, on demurrer, That the 2d, 3d, and 4th pleas were all bad; the 2d, as hypothetical, neither traversing or confessing anything; the 3d, being in the nature of *non damnificatus*, and not alleging performance of the condition, could not be pleaded to a bond of this sort; and the 4th, as not pleaded with sufficient certainty, nor answering all the breaches which might have been assigned, if the defendants had pleaded performance. *Mechanics' Whale Fishing Company* v. *Kirby*, 2 *Kerr* 646.

15—K. and W. entered into a bond to the plaintiffs, conditioned that if K. should at all times faithfully serve the plaintiffs while he continued in their employ as their secretary, without consuming, wasting, embezzling, etc., their moneys, goods, etc.; and should at any time while secretary neglect or refuse to account with the plaintiffs when required by reasonable notice in writing; and if K. and W., or either of them, should within three months after due proof thereof, either by confession of K. or otherwise, and notice thereof in writing given to K. and W. or either of them, make satisfaction and payment to the plaintiffs for the moneys, goods, etc. so wasted, etc., and also for all such loss or damage as the plaintiffs might sustain by reason of K.'s neglect or refusal to account, then the obligation to be void. Held, That the clause providing for proof and notice restrained the preceding clause, and that the defendants were not chargeable on the bond in any case until after proof and notice. Held also, That to make out a breach for not accounting, notice to account should have been given to K. while he was [illegible]. *Mechanics' Whale Fishing Company v. Whitney*, 3 *Kerr* 113.

To an action on this bond, the defendants pleaded a general performance; the plaintiffs replied, assigning as a breach that K. while secretary embezzled and unlawfully made away with large sums of money of the plaintiffs, and that proof was made thereof, and notice given to W.; the defendants rejoined that no due proof of the embezzling, etc. was made, and no due notice given to W. Held bad, as a departure from the plea; and that the want of proof and notice were matters for separate pleas. *Ibid.*

A further breach assigned was, that K. while secretary, made false entries and fraudulent charges in the plaintiffs' books, whereby they sustained loss. Held, That this was not a breach of duty within the terms of the bond, unless in consequence the plaintiffs' moneys were wasted etc., which should have been alleged. *Ibid.*

16—To an action on a surety bond, conditioned *inter alia* for the faithful performance of the principal as secretary to the plaintiffs, and the making of satisfaction for any losses, etc., within three months after due proof thereof and notice—the surety in his fourth plea averred performance up to a certain period, and as an excuse for the subsequent non-performance alleged a dealing by the plaintiffs in gold and silver coins contrary to law, which increased the risk, whereby the surety was discharged; and in his fifth plea alleged that no due proof was made three months before the action; and the plaintiffs in their replication to the fourth plea traversed the dealing in gold and silver, and then assigned several breaches on divers days between periods which embraced not only that time in the pleas covered by the performance, but also that during which the breach was admitted; and in the replication to the fifth plea took issue thereon in the words of the plea. On demurrer to each of these replications and joinders therein, with objections to the adverse pleading in reference to form—Held, That the replication to the fourth plea should not have assigned, but suggested breaches, and confined them to the period for which the surety had pleaded performance, and should have concluded the traverse of the surety's excuse of non-performance with an issue to the country, and that consequently this replication was ill. Held also, That the replication to the fifth plea, taking issue thereon in the words of the plea, was sufficient. Held also, That where one party demurs to any pleading, the only objection which the other party can make to the former pleadings are those which go to the substance, not the form of such pleadings. *Mechanics' Whale Fishing Company v. Whitney*, 3 *Kerr* 312.

17—Contract—Variance—Condition precedent.

Where part of the contract stated in the declaration was in consideration that the plaintiff would sell and deliver to the defendant, certain supplies which he might from time to time require to enable him to get logs, and this was succeeded by an averment that the plaintiff sold and delivered to the defendant such supplies as he from time to time required and demanded of the plaintiff, and it appeared in evidence that the agreement was for supplying only particular articles, which were specified, and that on application by the defendant to the plaintiff for some of the articles, he was unable to furnish them. On motion for a non-suit on the ground of variance, Held, That there was a clear variance between the agreement alleged and the one proved. Held also, That under the agreement it was a condition precedent that the plaintiff should supply to the defendant the articles agreed for, and the defendant having made default in so doing was not entitled to recover. *Read* v. *Ashe*, 3 *Kerr* 327.

18—Assumpsit by administrator—Promises.

In a summary action of assumpsit by an administrator for the work and labour of the intestate, the promise was laid to the plaintiff as administrator only, but no proof thereof given at the trial; on the point reserved for a non-suit, verdict for the plaintiff, and rule *nisi*. Held, That the promise was material and in issue, and not having been proved, a non suit should be entered. *Stephenson* v. *Perley*, 3 *Kerr* 398.

19—Promises by testator—Foreign judgment.

In assumpsit against an administrator *cum testamento annexo*, on promises by the testator, and on a judgment against the executors in Jamaica, the defendant pleaded—first, the general issue; secondly, to the counts on promises by the testator, a judgment recovered against the executors in Jamaica for the same cause of action; thirdly, *plene administravit* before the defendant had notice of the plaintiff's claim. Held, on demurrer, That the first plea was good, as it answered all the promises, express or implied, alleged to have been made by the testator or defendant; that the second plea was bad, because a foreign judgment is not a debt of record, but only evidence of a debt, and the simple contract debt on which it is founded is not merged in it; and that under the Act 7 Vic. c. 41, the third plea was good, without stating that the assets were exhausted after the expiration of eighteen months from the granting of administration. Held also, That it was not necessary for the defendant to plead he had fully administered before notice of the plaintiff's demand, to the executors in Jamaica. *Fergus* v. *Wardlaw*, 3 *Kerr* 665.

20—Bail Bond—Discontinuing Suit.

A plea to an action on a bail bond, that before the return and filing of the writ and entry of the cause, if any such filing and entry was made, the plaintiff discontinued his suit, is bad: 1st. Because the discontinuance should have been alleged as the judgment of the Court, and the manner of making it stated; and 2nd. Because the filing of the writ being stated hypothetically, did not confess and avoid the effect of it. *Bacon* v. *Johns*, 1 *All.* 257.

21—Agreement—Breach—Second agreement—Assent.

The defendant made an agreement to deliver plaintiffs at S. a cargo of deals for a vessel, which he failed in performing; he afterwards agreed to pay the plaintiffs £60 for the loss sustained in not having the cargo of deals ready for the vessel at S. The second agreement was not signed by the plaintiffs, but was in their possession. Held, That the plaintiff's possession of the agreement was *prima facie* evidence of their assent to it, and that upon a count setting out the first agreement and the breach thereof by the defendant, and the agreement to pay £60 sterling in satisfaction of the damage occasioned by such breach, the plaintiffs were entitled to recover the £60. *Holderness* v. *McGhie*, 1 *All.* 429.

22—Trespass—License.

In trespass for breaking the plaintiffs close, subverting the soil, covering the surface with dirt, etc., and digging and carrying away coal; the defendant pleaded, 1st. Not guilty; 2nd. That the Queen being seized in fee of all mines of gold, silver, copper, lead and coals, in the close, *with the appurtenances*, granted a license to defendant to make use of, and dispose of the produce of all the said mines which he might discover and commence the working of: under which grant he justified the acts complained of, as necessary to getting the coal—doing no more damage to the close than was absolutely necessary to the effectual working of the mine. Replication, traversing the Queen's seisin of the mines with the appurtenances, *modo et forma*. Held, 1st. That by the term *appurtenances*, could not be intended such a seisin as would enable the Crown to grant a license to the defendant to use the mine in the manner pleaded, but only such rights as were necessarily incident to the seisin of the mines; but the Queen being seized of the mines, the finding on this issue must be for the defendant. But, 2nd, That as the plea confessed the acts complained of, and contained no legal justification, the plaintiff was entitled to judgment on the whole record, *non obstante veredicto*. *McMahon* v. *Berton*, 2 *All.* 321.

23—Assumpsit—Agreement—Performance—Deviation—Condition precedent.

B. agreed in 1836, to survey at the landings and take delivery of all the spruce and pine logs the plaintiff might cut and haul to the landings at Taxis river, and pay him a certain sum per thousand for all the merchantable logs, as soon as he had driven them past the mouth of Clearwater brook (a tributary of Taxis river). After some of the logs had been driven, B. made an examination of the remainder then lying in the river, sawed some of them into deals, and made an estimate therefrom of the contents of the whole, taking the statements of the parties who cut them as to the quantity, without making any measurement. A partial settlement was made, upon which the plaintiff brought an action against B. on the agreement, and in 1838, while the suit was pending and while a quantity of the logs still remained undriven, the defendants agreed in consideration of the plaintiff's discontinuing the suit, "to pay him the balance that might be due him from B. on account of logs to be furnished by him to B. as per agreement and settlement, when the whole of the spruce and pine logs then remaining in Hovey brook and Taxis river were driven down past the mouth of Clearwater brook." The plaintiff did not drive all the logs, but in a settlement between him and B. in 1843, in which the former estimate of the quantity of logs were taken, B. made a deduction from the plaintiff's account of about 20 M. feet of logs, a supposed quantity still lying in Taxis river, and struck a balance in favour of the plaintiff of £315, including £48 interest; this balance was demanded from the defendants. In an action on the second agreement the declaration averred (*inter alia*) that on the 1st July, 1839, the spruce and pine logs, which at the time of the agreement were remaining on Hovey brook and Taxis river, were driven down past the mouth of Clearwater brook, agreeably to the spirit and effect, true intent and meaning of the agreement; and that afterward by an account stated between the plaintiff and B. there was a balance of £315 due from B. to the plaintiff on account of the logs, of which the defendants afterwards had notice. Held, 1st. That as the settlement referred to was a future one, the agreement between the plaintiff and B. should have been set out in the declaration, in order to show that a settlement was subsequently made between them, and that it was such as to be binding on the defendants according to their agreement with the plaintiff; or if the defendants were liable without such settlement, to shew how they became liable. 2nd. That the driving the whole of the logs past Clearwater brook was a condition precedent to the plaintiff's right to recover, performance of which should have been proved, or a sufficient excuse shewn for the non-performance. 3rd. That the averment of driving the logs according to the spirit and effect, etc. of the agreement, was an averment of performance. 4th. That as the plaintiff and B. had deviated from the mode agreed upon for ascertaining the quantity of logs, the defendants would not be bound by the settlement unless they had notice of the deviation before they entered into the agreement, or subsequently assented to it. 5th. That admitting the quantity of logs to have been properly ascertained, the defendants could not be liable for interest until default made in paying the principal; and they were not liable for the principal because the correct balance was never demanded. *Sutherland* v. *Gilmour*, 2 *All.* 481.

Application of the maxim *de minimis non curat lex.* *Ibid.*

24—Assumpsit—Agreement—Averment —Amendment.

In an action for not delivering deals according to contract, the declaration stated that the defendant was in the possession or occupation of a saw-mill at W. and engaged in the manufacture of lumber at such mill, and had agreed to deliver the plaintiff a quantity of deals as they came from the mill, and that if any accident happened to the said mill so that the deals could not be cut the contract was to be void: averment that no accident happened to the said mill. The contract did not specify any particular mill, and the only mill in the defendant's possession was injured and prevented from sawing. Held, That the averment was material, and that the plaintiff could not shew that another mill, not in the defendant's possession, was the one intended by the contract. *Holderness* v. *Welling*, 2 *All.* 572.

Held also, That if the declaration was amendable as to the description of the mill, the amendment could only be made at the trial. *Ibid.*

25—Debt for legacy—No allegation of receipt of money.

Declaration stated that A. bequeathed to the plaintiff one-fourth of £200, which would be due from B. after A.'s death, according to an obligation held by A. at such time and to such persons as he should appoint by will for payment thereof; that A. by his will directed that B. should pay £50 per annum for four years to A.'s executor, until the £200 was paid; that he appointed the defendan his executor, and that more than four years had elapsed since the death of A. Held, Bad for not averring that the defendant had received the money from B. *Brown* v. *Harding*, 3 *All.* 249.

Quære, Whether, if the defendant had received the money, he would be liable in his representative character. *Ibid.*

26—Assumpsit—Warranty—Payment by note.

In an action for breach of warranty on the sale of goods, the declaration stated that payment was to be made by a note at three months from the plaintiff to one of the defendants, but the evidence did not shew whether the note given was drawn in favor of one or both defendants Held, 1st. That being left doubtful by the evidence, it might be presumed that the note was given in accordance with the agreement as stated in the declaration; 2nd. That if it had appeared that the note was to be given to both defendants, the declaration might have been amended. *Lyman* v. *Cain*, 3 *All.* 259.

27—Covenant—Averment—Readiness—Ability.

In an action on an agreement whereby the plaintiff was to deliver the defendant, on or before the 1st December 1854, at such landing place at Saint John as the defendant might direct, 500 M. feet of deals, to be paid for on delivery, the declaration alleged that on the 30th November 1854, the plaintiff was ready and willing, and offered to deliver the deals at such landing place at Saint John as the defendant might direct; but that the defendant refused to accept the deals or to appoint any landing place where they might be delivered, or to pay the plaintiff for them at the price agreed. Held, That under the averment of readiness and willingness, the plaintiff was bound to prove his ability to deliver the deals, though the defendant had broken the agreement by refusing to take any deals but such as were sawn at a particular mill, and by neglecting to appoint a place for the delivery. *Taylor* v. *Travis*, 3 *All.* 445.

28—Contract and proof—Variance.

Declaration stated that defendant sold plaintiff 500 M. feet of pine logs, to be delivered at such reasonable time thereafter as the plaintiff should require; breach—that though a reasonable time had elapsed, the defendant had refused to deliver the logs to the plaintiff on request. The contract proved was for the sale of 500 M. feet of logs in the defendant's boom at Union Point, marked B., to be selected and scaled by G. when required by plaintiff, and to be delivered in the spring following the date of the agreement. Held, That there was a variance between the contract set out and the proof. *Cushing* v. *Godard*, 3 *All.* 585.

29—Description of plaintiff—Representative character—Surplusage.

Plaintiffs, assignees of L., F. & Co., under a trust deed of assignment, sued on a contract made by the defendant with L., F. & Co., the declaration stated that "J. M. and A. F., assignees of the estate of L. F. & Co., complain," etc. Held—(Parker, J., *dissentiente*) That the declaration did not set out a right of action accruing to the plaintiffs in their representative character, and that the words "assignees," etc., were mere surplusage. *McMillan* v. *Chamberlain*, 4 *All.* 137.

30—Plaintiffs not being clothed with any official character as trustees, should not declare in that capacity, but allege it as matter of description. *Burnham* v. *Watts*, 2 *Kerr* 377.

31—Special counts—Proof.

Holder of bill of exchange, relying on no funds in hands of drawee as an excuse for not presenting bill, and giving notice, such fact should be stated in the declaration; averments must be proved to entitle plaintiff to recover on special counts. See Bills and Notes VI. 12.

32—Obligors—Bond to A. or B. or either.

A bond conditioned for the payment of money to A. and B., or either of them, cannot be sued in the name of one of the obligees, unless the other is dead. *Hazen* v. *Drummond*, 4 *All.* 267.

33—Policy of insurance—Condition precedent — Want of averment.

The following clause in a marine policy of assurance, viz.: "and in case of loss, such loss to be paid in sixty days after proof of loss and adjustment, and proof of interest in the said assured," has the operation of a condition precedent; and the judgment was arrested in an action by the assured against the insurer for the want of any averment in the declaration, that such preliminary proof had been furnished to or dispensed with by the defendant. *Watson* v. *Summers*, 2 *Kerr* 101.

34—Corresponding proof—Description.

Where in replevin the place of taking is described not by name but by abuttals—Held, That it is not necessary on the plea of *non cepit* that the place should be proved to be in one occupation, and that the calling it a "close," where different parts of the land within the abuttals are held by several parties, is not material, the defendants not having been misled by the generality of the description. *Mills* v. *Dewitt*, 1 *Kerr* 486.

35—Administration bond—Necessary statement.

In an action on an administration bond under the Act 3 Vic. c. 61, assigning as a breach a devastavit by the administrator, it must be stated that the estate of the intestate has sustained injury thereby to a certain amount. *Sherlock* v. *McGee*, 1 *All.* 346.

An allegation in the assignment of a breach that goods and chattels came to the hands of the defendant as administrator, necessarily shews that they were the goods of the intestate. *Ibid.*

36—Inferior Court—Claim arising within jurisdiction—Proceedings.

In declaring in the Inferior Court of Common Pleas, it is not necessary to allege that the demand arose within the jurisdiction of the Court. *Stephenson* v. *McLellan*, 1 *All.* 19.

In an action on a judgment obtained in the Court of Common Pleas, it is sufficient to state the recovery of the judgment, without setting forth the prior proceedings. *Ibid.*

37—Policy—Insurance—Conditions—Averments.

In a fire policy, the insurers by an indorsement thereon, consented that the loss should be payable to the order of W. Held, Sufficient in a declaration in covenant on the policy to allege that the loss was not paid to the plaintiff nor to W.; and that as such indorsement gave W. no legal interest in the property, it did not preclude the assured from maintaining an action in his own name; nor was it necessary to aver any order from W. in favor of the assured. *Ketchum* v. *The Protection Insurance Co.*, 1 *All.* 136.

By the tenth condition attached to the policy, it was stipulated "that in the event of a loss the assured should deliver to the insurers a particular account in writing, signed with his own hand, and verified by his oath, and that he should also declare on his oath whether any or what other insurance had been made on the property insured, and in what general manner (as to trade, manufactory, merchandize, or otherwise) the building containing the property insured, and the several parts thereof, were occupied at the time of the loss, who were the occupants of such buildings, and when and how the fire originated, as far as he knew or believed, and that the assured should procure a certificate under the hand and seal of a magistrate or notary public (most contiguous to the place of the fire, and not concerned in the loss as a creditor, or otherwise related to the assured), that he had made due enquiry into the cause and origin of the fire, and also the value of the property destroyed, and was acquainted with the character and circumstances of the assured, and did verily believe that the assured really and by misfortune, and without fraud or evil practice, sustained by such fire loss or damage to the amount specified." The declaration stated the fire to have happened on the 29th July 1845, and that the compliance with this condition, in respect of notice of the fire, took place on the same day; as to the delivery of a particular account in writing, on the 20th August 1845; and in respect to the declaration on oath, the 27th March 1846. Held, Sufficient, the respective times having been laid under a videlicet; the performance of these acts, whether in due season or not, being matter of evidence. Held also, That as W. had no legal interest, it was not necessary to state that he was not related to the notary. *Ibid.*

By the fifteenth condition annexed to the

policy, it was declared "that no suit or action of any kind against the insurers for the recovery of any claim under the policy, should be sustained in any Court of law or Chancery, unless such suit should be commenced within the term of twelve months next after the cause of action accrued," etc. Held, That this was a condition subsequent—the subject of a plea. Held also, That an allegation in a count upon a policy containing this condition, that the insurers had no mayor, president, etc., upon whom process could be served (introduced to anticipate a probable objection that the action was not brought within the twelve months,) was mere surplusage. *Ketchum* v. *The Protection Insurance Co.*, 1 *All.* 136.

The preliminary proof required by the tenth condition may be waived, and being a question of fact, the mode of waiver need not be stated. The fifteenth condition being the subject of a plea, an averment in the declaration that the insurers had waived it, would not be traversable; therefore it might be passed by without notice. Held also, That it could not be waived—that lapse of time extinguished the liability of the insurers, which could not be revived by waiver; but *Semble*, That they might dispense with the condition by deed, and if a deed could avail as a dispensation it should be replied to a plea of the condition. Held also, That the fifteenth condition was valid in law, and operated as an effectual bar everywhere; therefore a plea of the fifteenth condition to a count containing an averment of waiver of this condition is properly pleaded. A replication to such a plea, that the defendants were a foreign corporation, and that no action could have been sustained within the twelve months, unless they had voluntarily appeared, and there was no means of compelling their appearance, although the the plaintiff was willing to prosecute within the twelve months, is bad, as it it neither confesses nor avoids anything material, for the plaintiff might have sued out process within the twelve months, or the defendants might have been sued in the country where they are incorporated, and they are not estopped by voluntarily appearing, from setting up the lapse of time as a defence. *Ibid.*

A plea, embodying the tenth condition, which stated that after the fire, to wit, on the 26th August 1845, the plaintiff was required by the defendants to deliver an account in writing under his hand, verified by his oath and by his books of accounts, etc., and permit extracts, etc., to be taken respecting the loss, etc., and the plaintiff refused, is not double, as they all go to establish one point—the non-performance by the plaintiff of that part of the tenth condition. *Ketchum* v. *The Protection Insurance Co.*, 1 *All.* 136.

A traverse in a plea that the plaintiff was not interested in the goods insured to the whole amount of their value, is too large; for if he was interested in any part, he is entitled to recover *pro tanto*. *Ibid.*

To a declaration, which averred performance by the plaintiff of all the acts required by the tenth condition to be performed by him, a plea traversing the performance of all these acts, is good, according to the rules of pleading at common law. *Ibid.*

A plea which first traverses an allegation in the declaration of the delivering an account of loss according to the tenth condition, and secondly, sets up fraud, is unobjectionable. The refusal to deliver an account in such case is indicatory of fraud, and is consistent with the general charge of fraud subsequently made. *Ibid.*

A plea alleging false swearing in a statement, A. annexed to the declaration of loss made by the plaintiff, is bad, for not averring that any such statement was annexed, and for not shewing when and before whom the oath was made, or in what particular the statement was false. *Ibid.*

38—Claim for total loss—Right to recover for partial loss—Deviation—Right to recover where loss payable to plaintiff. See Insurance 41.

39—The assignee of a policy of insurance and of the property insured, does not by such assignment, acquire any right of action against the insurer on the original contract, though the assignment is made with his consent, and in accordance with one of the conditions of the policy; but a new promise by the insurer, supported by a valid consideration, to give the assignee the benefit of the insurance, will support an action. The declaration in an action by the assignee of a policy of insurance made by the defendant with A., after setting out the policy, the payment of the premium by A., and his assignment to the plaintiff with the defendant's consent according to one of the conditions of the policy, whereby the defendant was released from liability to A., stated, that in consideration that the plaintiff, at the request of the defendant, had undertaken and promised the defendant to perform all things in the policy contained on the plaintiff's part to be performed in pursuance of the consent to assign, and in consideration of the assignment of the property from A. to the plaintiff, and the release thereby of all liability of the defendant to A., and of the assignment of the policy with the defendant's consent, and in consideration of the payment of the premium so received as aforesaid, the defendant promised the plaintiff to be the insurer to him, etc. Held, That there was not a sufficient consideration shewn to support the defendant's promise. *Demill* v. *The Hartford Insurance Company*, 4 *All.* 341.

The receipt of a renewal premium on the policy by the insurer from the assignee, is a sufficient consideration for a new promise by the insurer to the assignee. *Ibid.*

One of the conditions of a policy declared that if the insured should thereafter make any other insurance on the property, and should not, with all reasonable diligence, give notice thereof to the insurer, and have the same endorsed on the policy or otherwise acknowledged in writing, the policy should cease and be of no further effect; and if any subsequent insurance should be made, which, with the sum already insured, should in the opinion of the insurer amount to an over-insurance, he should have the right of cancelling the policy by paying to the insured the unexpired premium *pro rata*. In an action on a policy where there was a subsequent insurance, the declaration averred that notice thereof was forthwith given to the insurer (the defendant), and it thereby became his duty to indorse such subsequent insurance on the policy, or to acknowledge the same in writing, but that he neglected and refused so to do. Held, on demurrer, That the declaration was sufficient, and that a tender of the policy to the insurer for indorsement, or a request to him to indorse or acknowledge it in writing, was not necessary. *Demill* v. *The Hartford Insurance Company*, 4 *All.* 341.

Quære, Whether the defendant could be charged with a breach of duty in not indorsing the subsequent insurance, unless the policy was tendered to him for that purpose; but Held, That the averment that it was the defendant's duty to indorse it, might be treated as surplusage. *Ibid.*

40—Consideration moving from plaintiff.
A declaration in assum[illegible] [illegible]pon an agreement or note, whereby [illegible] defendant "in consideration of value received from the estate of J. & H. K. promise to pay the plaintiffs, trustees of the said estate, £930 in cash or sole leather on or before 1st May, 1843," is not bad on general demurrer, on the ground that the consideration did not move from the plaintiff, or that no demand of payment was averred specially. *Burnham* v. *Watts*, 2 *Kerr* 377.

41—Averment of consideration—Proof.
In an action on a written memorandum, whereby "A. for value received promises to pay B. $750 in current bank bills," it is not sufficient to allege the consideration in the general terms of the [illegible]emorandum, but the plaintiff must s[illegible] [illegible]n what the value consisted as the [illegible]ration for the promise. *Whitney* v. [illegible]*rks*, 1 *Kerr* 137.

42—It is necessary also not only to allege the actual consideration, but the proof must correspond with the allegation. In this case the plaintiff alleged that the consideration consisted of *certain standing trees, goods, wares, and merchandize, and stumpage;* the evidence shewed the consideration to consist of stumpage alone. A verdict having been taken for the plaintiff, subject to a motion for a non-suit, the Court allowed the plaintiff to amend on payment of all costs, and made the rule absolute for a new trial instead of a non-suit, on the condition of the payment of such costs. *Whitney* v. *Marks*, 1 *Kerr* 179.

43—Debt on bond—Award—Breach.
In an action on a bond conditioned for the performance of an award, the particular breach relied on must be stated in the declaration: it is not sufficient to state generally that the defendant refused to comply with the award, and would not

perform the acts on his part to be performed according to the directions of the award. *Burgoyne* v. *Burgoyne*, *C. Ms.* 120.

44—Assumpsit on note—Partnership.
In an action by the payees against the maker of a promissory note payable to A., B., C. and D., the declaration alleged that the defendant promised to pay the plaintiffs, by the name, style and firm of A., B., C. and D. Held, That it was not necessary to prove that the plaintiffs were partners, and that the words "name, style and firm" might have been struck out of the declaration. *Allen* v. *McNaughton*, 4 *All.* 234.

45—Averment of rate of exchange and place. See Bills and Notes I. 4.

46—Consideration—Averment—Aider by verdict.
The declaration stated, that whereas the plaintiff had the custody of certain timber of the defendant, and the defendant had bargained with one J. M. to sell and deliver to him a certain quantity of timber, and thereupon in consideration that the plaintiff at the request of defendant would agree to deliver to J. M. 573 tons of timber, averaging in size 13¾ inches, the defendant promised the plaintiff that his timber in the plaintiff's custody should be of sufficient size to enable the plaintiff thereof to deliver J. M. the said 573 tons of the average size aforesaid; but if the timber should prove of insufficient size, he (the defendant) would pay the plaintiff such loss as he might sustain by reason of the timber being of insufficient size, to enable the plaintiff thereof to comply with his agreement with J. M. The declaration then proceeded to aver that although the plaintiff did on, etc., at etc., *agree* to deliver J. M. 573 tons of timber of the average size of 13¾ inches, and although the defendant's timber in the plaintiff's custody did not average 13¾ inches, but only 13¼ inches, and the plaintiff had by reason thereof sustained great loss, and was forced and obliged to pay J. M. a large sum, viz.: the difference in value between timber of 13¾ and timber of 13¼ inches average; yet the defendant, although requested, had not paid the plaintiff the amount of such loss, etc. Held, on motion in arrest of judgment, That there was a sufficient consideration alleged, and that it was not necessary for the plaintiff to aver that he had performed the contract made by defendant with J. M. by delivering timber of the average size specified, the agreement by plaintiff to deliver and not the delivery itself forming the consideration for the defendant's promise to indemnify. *Cunnard* v. *Plummer*, 2 *Kerr* 418.

Held also, That after verdict neither the mode of alleging the consideration, nor the want of averment of notice to the defendant of J. M.'s demand on the plaintiff, could be objected to. *Ibid.*

47—Insurance policy—Meaning of words by usage of trade. Held, That such usage and construction should be averred in the declaration. See Insurance 21.

48—Libel—Prefatory averments—When necessary.
In a declaration for a libel, prefatory averments are not necessary, where the charge is apparent on the face of the paper without reference to extrinsic facts. The question after verdict is whether enough appears on the record to sustain the action. *Connick* v. *Wilson*, 2 *Kerr* 617.

49—Assignee of term.
A party signing as assignee of a term on a covenant contained in the lease and alleging and making profert of an assignment by deed is bound to prove it, and if several assignments are alleged, a traverse that the plaintiff became entitled *modo et forma*, puts the whole of them in issue. *Ansley* v. *Peters*, 1 *All.* 339.

50—Case—Nuisance—Erecting steam mill—Surplusage.
In an action on the case for a nuisance in erecting a steam mill on land adjacent to the plaintiff's dwelling house, the evidence of persons living in other adjoining premises as to the injurious effect of the steam mill upon them, is admissible in order to shew by necessary inference the damage done to the plaintiff by the erection. No other damage need be shewn than the abridgement of the plaintiff's enjoyment in the occupation of his premises. The judgment will not be arrested because in one or more of the counts annoyance to the plaintiff's tenants as well as to himself and family is alleged. It will be deemed surplusage. *Barlow* v. *Kinnear*, 2 *Kerr* 94.

51—Perjury—Averments.
The introductory averment in a declaration in an action for slander, containing

twenty-three counts, stated that before the committing of the grievances mentioned in certain counts (including the eighteenth) the plaintiff had been duly sworn to a certain affidavit made in the Supreme Court before a commissioner duly authorised, concerning certain proceedings in a suit pending in such Court, and that he had been duly sworn to the truth of the matter in such affidavit contained, and that the defendant intending it to be believed that the plaintiff had been and was guilty of perjury, etc., spoke and published, etc. The eighteenth count stated that in a certain discourse which the defendant had concerning the plaintiff, and of and concerning said affidavit so made by the plaintiff as aforesaid, the defendant further contriving and intending as aforesaid, in the presence and hearing, etc., spoke and published of and concerning the plaintiff, and of and concerning the said affidavit, etc., the false, scandalous and malicious words following, "Mr. M. (the plaintiff) had sworn falsely," whereby the defendant meant to insinuate that the plaintiff had wilfully sworn falsely in the said affidavit, and had thereby been guilty of wilful and corrupt perjury. Held, That the count was not defective, and that it contained proper averments of the facts necessary to shew that perjury was imputed to the plaintiff. Held also, That to constitute perjury at common law it was not necessary to aver that the affidavit had been used, as the crime did not depend on the subsequent use of the affidavit, but was complete on the false swearing. *Milner* v. *Gilbert*, 1 *All.* 51.

52—Trespass—Expulsion.

Expulsion from part of the close is sufficient to sustain the count for expulsion. *Gesner* v. *Cairns*, 2 *All.* 595.

53—Excessive distress—Necessary allegation.

The declaration in an action for excessive distress, alleged that the plaintiff held land as tenant to defendant at a certain rent; that the defendant wrongfully seized goods on the premises as a distress for arrears of rent alleged to be due, viz.: $311, and sold the same for the said alleged arrears, whereas a small part only of the said alleged rent, viz.: $70, was in arrear. There was no allegation that more goods were taken or sold than were necessary to produce the rent actually due. Held, That the declaration disclosed no cause of action; that some rent being due, the distress itself was not a wrong, and that the mere distraining and selling on a claim of more than was due, was not actionable. *Preston* v. *Simonds*, 1 *Han.* 44.

54—Married woman—Living apart—Allegation.

A declaration alleging that the plaintiff was a married woman, living separate and apart from her husband, and compelled to support herself, and that the defendant contracted with her while she was such married woman and compelled to support herself, sufficiently shows the plaintiff's right to sue in her own name under the Act. *Abel* v. *Light*, 1 *Han.* 97.

55—Special assumpsit—Consideration for promise—Allegation—Ambiguity.

The first count of a declaration stated that on the 1st November 1865, in consideration of the assignment of license No. 84, made to defendant by plaintiff, at defendant's request, defendant undertook and promised that F. should deliver to plaintiff whatever quantity, say, not to exceed 165,000 feet of logs by the 10th July then next. Averment, that although the time for the delivery of the logs had elapsed, and the plaintiff was ready and willing to receive them, yet F. did not deliver them, whereby, etc. The fourth count stated that on the day and year aforesaid, in consideration of the assignment by the plaintiff to the defendant of a certain license, then and there agreed upon between them, defendant undertook and promised that F. should deliver plaintiff, whatever quantity of logs said F. had before then agreed to deliver plaintiff in the year 1866, not to exceed 165,000 feet, by the 10th July then next. Averment, that F. had agreed to deliver plaintiff 135,000 feet in 1866. Breach, that F. did not deliver the logs. Held, 1st. That a sufficient consideration for defendant's promise was alleged, but that the promise, as stated in the first count, was uncertain and unintelligible; 2nd. That the words, "on the day and year aforesaid," in the fourth count, did not necessarily refer to the 10th July 1866 (the last day mentioned in the preceding count), but might refer to the 1st November 1865; and being only an ambiguity, the objection could not be taken on general demurrer. *DesBrisay* v. *McLeod*, 1 *Han.* 122

56—Case—Refusing to register under Medical Act.

By the Act 22 Vic. c. 18, s. 11, every person in the Province possessed of a medical degree or diploma to practice medicine or surgery, from any college in Great Britain, Ireland, Canada, France, or the United States, authorized to grant the same, shall on payment, etc., be entitled to be registered under the Act, and by s. 12, no qualification shall be entered on the register, unless the Registrar is satisfied by the proper evidence, that the person is entitled to it. Held, in an action against the Registrar for refusing to register the plaintiff, 1st. That the defendant was not liable unless he acted maliciously; and that an averment in the declaration that he *wrongfully* and *injuriously* refused to register the plaintiff, was insufficient. 2nd. That the mere production of a diploma to the Registrar, was not sufficient evidence of the authority of the college to grant it: the declaration should have averred that proper evidence of the plaintiff's title to registry was tendered to the defendant. *Peterson* v. *Harding*, 4 *All.* 583.

57—Identity in name—Proof.

The plaintiff described himself in the declaration "J. Kerriken, otherwise called J. Carrigan," and in support of the action produced an acknowledgment signed by the defendant, of a balance due from him to J. Kerriken. Held, That it was necessary for the plaintiff to identify himself with the party mentioned in the acknowledgment, and without proof that the J. Kerriken there mentioned was also called J. Carrigan, the action could not be maintained. *Kerriken* v. *Copeland*, 3 *Kerr* 567.

58—Judgment—Name—Averment.

In an action on a judgment signed against J. H. W. by the name of J. W. W., it is sufficient to aver that the defendant and J. W. W. are the same person. *Young* v. *Woodcock*, 3 *Kerr* 554.

59—Defamation.

In an action of defamation for calling a woman a whore, it is sufficient to aver in the declaration that the defendant intended to impute unchastity. *Martindale and Wife* v. *Murphy and Wife*, *Ber.* 85.

60—Assumpsit—Attorney—Negligence.

Declaration stated that in consideration that the plaintiff at the request of the defendant had retained him as an attorney for certain fees, to prosecute an action at the suit of the plaintiff against C. for money owing to him from C., the defendant promised the plaintiff to prosecute the action in a skilful and diligent manner, and accepted the retainer, and afterwards as the plaintiff's attorney, commenced an action against C. at the suit of the plaintiff for the recovery of the money, and it thereby became the duty of the defendant faithfully and diligently to act as the attorney for the plaintiff; yet the defendant not regarding his duty etc. did not faithfully prosecute the action, but on the contrary prosecuted the same to trial in so unskilful and negligent a manner that the plaintiff was non-suited, and was not only prevented from recovering the money from C., but was obliged to pay £17 for the costs of the suit etc. Held, That this was a declaration in *assumpsit* and not in *case*, and that it disclosed a sufficient cause of action. *Carrigan* v. *Andrews*, 1 *All.* 485.

61—Award—Action on—Concurrent Acts.

An award directed that the defendant should pay the plaintiff a sum of money on a certain day, and that on such payment being made the defendant should be entitled to receive, and the plaintiff should deliver him two parcels of sleepers then lying at L. Held, That they were not concurrent acts, and in an action on the award for the money, it was not necessary for the plaintiff to aver a readiness to deliver the sleepers. *Hassell* v. *Wilson*, 1 *All.* 618.

62—Negligence in repairing street—Allegation.

The Corporation of St. John being bound by law to lay out, alter and repair the streets in the city; it is sufficient in an action against them for negligence in repairing a street, to allege that it was the duty of the defendants in so repairing etc., to use due and proper care etc.—without stating any facts to shew their liability—their authority to repair etc. being matter of public law, of which the Court was bound to take notice. *Henderson* v. *The Mayor etc. of St. John*, *Mich. T.* 1872.

63—Allegation of special demand—Necessity of—Readiness to pay.

Where the consideration of an agreement

is an antecedent debt, a demand is not a condition precedent to the right of recovery; but readiness to pay according to the agreement is matter of defence. The declaration alleged, that on the 30th September, 1824, defendant being indebted to plaintiff in £30, as well for money lent and advanced to defendant, as for money had and received, etc., agreed with the plaintiff to pay him the said sum of money sixteen months after date, in hay and grain, to be delivered at W. at the current price; and that the plaintiff, in consideration thereof, agreed to accept payment of the said sum of money at the time and in manner aforesaid; that plaintiff had always been ready and willing to accept and receive the hay and grain at W. in payment of the debt, according to the agreement, but that defendant had not paid the money in hay and grain at W. though often requested etc. Held, on demurrer, That the declaration was sufficient, and that it was not necessary to allege a special demand of the hay and grain at W., but if defendant had the hay and grain ready to deliver according to his agreement, he should have pleaded it. *Stout* v. *Kermott*, *Mich. T.* 1827.

64—Consideration—Sufficiency of—Guarantee.

The declaration stated, that G. was indebted to plaintiff in £50, and that defendant, in consideration thereof, and that plaintiff would give time to G. for three years, promised to pay plaintiff the £50 in three years. Held, That this was not supported by a guarantee by defendant that G. should pay plaintiff the £50 in three years. *Johnston* v *Fraser*, *Mich. T.* 1832.

Counts — Distinct Causes of Action. See Practice I. 4.

Joinder of Actions. See Action at Law.

Material Allegation — Failure in proof — Non-suit although declaration demurrable. See Non-suit.

Replevin Goods not claimed.

If part of the goods mentioned in the writ of Replevin are not found and replevied by the Sheriff, they should not be included in the declaration. *Steeves* v. *Wilson*, *Mich. T.* 1869.

(See Replevin, same case.)

II.

PLEAS—SUBSEQUENT PLEADING, ETC.

1—Rien in arrear is not a good plea in an action for double value. *Strang* v. *Bell*, *Ber.* 287.

2—Debt.

Nil debit is a good plea in a summary action of debt on a record, under the Act 12 Vic. c. 40. *Wetmore* v. *Proven*, 4 *All.* 442.

3—Assumpsit—Discharge of debtor—Order—Fraud—Replication.

Defendant pleaded in assumpsit, that he was discharged from the debt by the order of a Judge under the Insolvent Debtors' Act 21 Vic. c. 17. Replication—that the order was obtained by fraud and concealment, and by giving undue preference to certain creditors. Held, That the plaintiff should have opposed the defendant's discharge before the Judge under section 14, and therefore the replication was bad. *Collins* v. *Boyle*, 4 *All.* 582.

Semble, That fraud in the proceedings before the Judge might vitiate the order. *Ibid.*

4—Covenant—Policy of insurance—Settlement and adjustment of claim—Aider after verdict.

In an action on a policy of insurance for $4000, alleging that the plaintiff had sustained damage to that amount, the defendant pleaded that the loss and damage sustained by the plaintiff, and the amount which he was entitled to receive by virtue of the policy, was settled and adjusted between the plaintiff and defendant at $3,500, and that the defendant paid and satisfied that sum to the plaintiff in full for his loss and damage, and for any claim against the defendant under the policy. Replication—that the defendant did not pay and satisfy to the plaintiff the said sum of $3,500, in manner and form, etc. On a verdict for the defendant on this issue—Held, That even if the plea was bad on demurrer, for not traversing the allegation, that the plaintiff had sustained damage to the amount of $4,000; it was sufficient after verdict, and therefore the plaintiff was not entitled to judgment *non obstante veredicto*; and *Semble*, That the plea would be good on demurrer. *McLean* v. *Phœnix Insurance Company*, 2 *Han.* 179

5—Debt—Policy of guarantee—Non est factum.

In an action of debt on a policy of guarantee under seal, which had been renewed agreeably to its terms by payment of the premium and the giving of a renewal receipt, the defendant pleaded *non est factum*. Held, That this merely traversed the making of the policy, and not the renewal receipt. In an action on a policy of guarantee, the declaration averred general performance, and the defendant in addition to a plea of *non est factum*, gave a notice of defence which set forth that plaintiff did not well and truly perform and fulfil all things contained in the said policy of guarantee and the conditions thereon indorsed, on their part to be performed. Held, That this notice being a traverse of a general averment of performance, was bad. *Commercial Bank* v. *European Assurance Society*, 2 *Han.* 219.

6—Debt—Insurance—Fraud—Lunatic—Deed.

To an action on a policy of insurance against fire, the defendants pleaded that the plaintiff's deed of the premises insured was obtained by fraud and without consideration from one Coll, who was a lunatic, and so continued until his death, and that the plaintiff had no insurable interest. Held, That the plea was bad. The defence that a deed was obtained from a lunatic in fraud, can only be raised by the party defrauded or his representatives. *Hickman* v. *The North British and Mercantile Insurance Company*, 2 *Han.* 235.

7—Award.

To debt on a bond conditioned to perform an award, it is a good plea in bar, that part of one entire sum awarded by the arbitrators, arose out of a matter not included in the submission. *Hill* v. *Coy*, 1 *Kerr* 187.

7 a—Any facts which vitiate an award (except misconduct of the arbitrators) may be pleaded in bar to an action on the arbitration bond or on the award, though such facts do not appear on the face of the award. *Ridcout* v. *Stickney*, 1 *All.* 350.

8—Bail.

Bail cannot plead to an action on the recognizance, a reference of the original suit to arbitration. They should apply to the Court to have an *exoneretur* entered on the bail piece. *Sharp* v. *Connell*, 3 *Kerr* 125.

9—Policy of insurance—Conditions—Breach.

Where by the conditions subjoined and referred to in a policy of insurance upon goods against fire, it is declared "that if there should at any time be more than twenty-five pounds weight of gunpowder on the premises insured, or where any goods are insured, such insurance should be void, and no benefit derived therefrom," the deposit of gunpowder over the above mentioned weight, though for a temporary purpose, will vacate the policy. To a plea alleging such a breach of the conditions of the policy, a replication averring that the powder had been put on the premises without the plaintiff's privity, because a vessel in which it was intended to ship it to Windsor had sailed without it, and the plaintiff had used every exertion to find another conveyance without success, in consequence of which it remained on the premises until a fire broke out, which eventually consumed the plaintiff's premises, but that before it reached those premises, the gunpowder was removed, and thrown into the harbour, and no loss or damage occasioned thereby to the goods insured, was held bad on demurrer. *Faulkner* v. *Central Fire Insurance Company*, 1 *Kerr* 279.

10—Covenant—Breach—Title—Answer.

To an action of covenant upon the words "grant, bargain and sell," in a conveyance of land, assigning as a breach the existence of a prior mortgage, the defendant pleaded that the mortgage was recorded in the public records, and that the plaintiff received the deed subject to such mortgage: an issue thereon having been found for the defendant, judgment was given for the plaintiff, *non obstante veredicto*, the plea being no answer to the action. The covenant is broken immediately, and the plaintiff need not wait until he is evicted before bringing his action *Good* v. *End*, 1 *All.* 603.

11—Covenant—Mutual and independent.

The defendant covenanted with the plaintiff to teach him the trade of a blacksmith, and the plaintiff covenanted to serve the defendant faithfully for five years, and not to absent himself from the defendant's service without leave. Held, That these covenants were mutual and independent, and that the non-performance by the plaintiff was no defence to an action against the defendant for breach of his covenant. *Hunter* v. *Gifford*, 1 *All.* 701.

12—Assumpsit—De injuria.
De injuria may be a good replication in an action of assumpsit, and is not confined to actions of tort. *Bank of British North America* v. *Fisher*, 1 *All.* 606.

In an action by the indorsee against the maker of a promissory note, the defendant pleaded that the note was discounted by the plaintiff on a usurious contract. Replication *de injuria*, held good. *Ibid.*

13—Duplicity.
A plea which averred that a bill of exchange was accepted and received by the plaintiff in full satisfaction and discharge of the sum due, and that afterwards the drawee on sight accepted the said bill of exchange, and became liable to pay the same according to his acceptance, was held bad upon special demurrer for duplicity, as alleging two separate and distinct grounds of defence admitting of different replies. *Boyd* v. *McLauchlan*, 1 *Kerr* 210.

14—Recognizance—Sureties.
The sureties in a recognizance entered into under the Rev. Stat. c. 98, "Of Controverted Elections," cannot plead, that they entered into it by a fraudulent representation of the nature of it, believing it to be the obligation of the principal only. *The Queen* v. *Sparrow and others*, 1 *Han.* 113.

If the recognizance was obtained by fraud, the sureties should apply to the Court to vacate it; but while it stands as a record, they are estopped from denying the truth of it. *Ibid.*

15—False imprisonment—Justification.
In an action for false imprisonment, the defendant justified under a judgment and execution against the plaintiff: replication, that the execution was irregularly issued, and was in consequence ordered by a rule of the Court to be set aside for irregularity. Held—1st. That the replication was not double; 2nd. That the rule of Court was not a record, and could not be pleaded with a *prout patet*, etc.; 3rd. That the nature of the irregularity need not be stated; and that after the execution was set aside it would be no justification for anything previously done under it. *Watson* v. *Roberts*, 1 *All.* 108.

16—To an action of false imprisonment the defendant pleaded in justification a judgment and execution—replication *nul tiel record*. *Quære*, Whether the Court could judicially notice an indorsement on the judgment roll of a rule setting aside the judgment. *Semble*, That the replication was good; but that the more proper course was for the plaintiff to apply to the Court to set aside the plea; or that he might reply the order of the Court for setting aside the judgment, on which issue *in pais* might be taken. *Wilson* v. *Andrews*, 1 *All.* 715.

After a judgment is set aside it cannot afford a justification to the attorney for anything done under it. *Ibid.*

17—Trespass—License covering part.
In trespass for cutting trees, to which the defendant pleads a license to commit the injuries complained of, and the plaintiff replies *de injuria*, evidence of a license which covers some but not all the trespasses proved, will not sustain the justification. It is not necessary to new assign the excess, as the replication traverses the justification to the extent pleaded. *Baxter* v. *Foshay*, 1 *All.* 413.

18—Trespass—Plea not traversing or confessing.
To a declaration in trespass alleging a seisin in fee in the plaintiff, the defendant pleaded that the Queen being seised in fee of all mines etc. granted a license to the defendant, to make use of, work and dispose of all such mines within the *locus in quo* for twenty-five years, by virtue of which he entered for the purpose of working a coal mine: color was then given to the plaintiff by a supposed charter of demise to him for life from the Queen, before the license to the defendant, and the plea stated an entry on the plaintiff's possession for the purpose of working the coal mine under the license. Held, That the plea was bad, as it neither traversed nor confessed the plaintiff's seisin; that if the plaintiff's seisin in the land was admitted, the plea should have shewn how the seisin in the mines was separated from the seisin in the land; and that it should also have shewn how the Queen, or the defendant, acquired a right of entry on the land. Held also, That it was not a case for color. *McMahon* v. *Berton*, 1 *All.* 706.

19—Entry on land to retake timber.
A plea justifying an entry upon plaintiff's land to retake timber carried there by a sudden rise of water, should shew that the defendants were not in fault, by hav-

ing used their best endeavors to prevent the timber coming upon plaintiff's land. *Quære*, Whether an entry and injury to soil and herbage could be justified even under such circumstances. *Read* v. *Smith et al.*, *Ber.* 173.

20—False imprisonment—Name.
In an action for false imprisonment in arresting the plaintiff (R. C.) under a *capias* issued by a Justice of the Peace against W. C., the plea stated that the defendant *duly made oath* before the Justice that the plaintiff, by the name of W. C., was indebted to the defendant in the sum of £5, that the plaintiff was known by the name of W. C., and was the real person against whom the *capais* issued by the name of W. C. Held bad —1st. Because it did not appear that there was any affidavit in writing to warrant the *capais;* 2nd. That it was not sufficiently shewn that the plaintiff was commonly known by the name of W. C. as well as R. C. *Clark* v. *Lawrence*, 3 *Kerr* 152.

21—Limitations—Place—Averment.
Assumpsit. Plea, *actio non accrevit infra sex annos;* replication, that the plaintiff at the time when, etc., was and has ever since continued at Z., in the State of Ohio, one of the United States of America, and out of this Province. Held, on special demurrer, That the replication need not allege the place to be beyond the seas, nor that the plaintiff returned to the Province before bringing his action, to bring him within the exception of the Provincial Statute of Limitations. *Hampson* v. *Abbot*, 1 *Kerr* 490.

22—Negligence—Attorney—Bail Bond.
In an action against an attorney for negligently conducting an action brought by the plaintiff as assignee of a bail bond, in consequence of which the action was discontinued and the defendants therein discharged out of custody; the defendant pleaded that the principal in the original action did appear according to the condition of the bond. Held, That this was no defence to the action. *Crawley* v. *Wilson*, 1 *All.* 704.

23—Nul Tiel Record.
To a plea of appearance in an action in the Court of Common Pleas in September term 12 Vic., the plaintiff replied *nul tiel record*, and on the trial the recognizance of bail appeared to be of that term, but not to have been filed until a year afterwards, and after the term in which the plea was pleaded. Held, That the plea was not proved. *Crawley* v. *Wilson*, 1 *All.* 718.

24—General issue—Notice of tender.
It is irregular to plead the general issue to the whole declaration, and give notice, under the Act 13 Vic. c. 32, of a tender as to part of the demand; and where, on such pleadings, a verdict was found for the defendant, it was set aside and entered for the plaintiff for nominal damages. *Conlan* v. *Campbell*, 3 *All.* 348.

25—Assignee of lessee against lessor—Covenants.
In covenant, by the assignee of lessee against lessor on a lease of land from 1st February 1830, for eleven years, with covenants that at the expiration of the lease the lessee and defendant should each appoint an appraiser to appraise the value of the improvements, etc., and that the defendant should then declare his option to pay for the improvements or continue the lease for a further time, with a clause of forfeiture if the rent should be in arrear. Breach, that at the expiration of the term the plaintiff (assignee) appointed an appraiser, notified the defendant, and requested him to choose one; but he did not, nor pay for the improvements, nor grant a further lease. Second plea, that the defendant was always ready and willing to continue the lease, etc., but the plaintiff never tendered one for his execution. Fourth plea, that before the expiration of the lease a quarter's rent was in arrear, and the defendant demanded it on a day in the following quarter, and took possession as of his former estate. Fifth plea, that the defendant was always ready and willing to continue the lease for a further time, under the like covenants contained in the original one; that the plaintiff continued in possession as tenant from year to year for a long time after the expiration of the lease, when the defendant assigned the reversion to B. and C.; that the plaintiff did not, before such assignment to B. and C., nominate an appraiser, and give notice thereof, etc., nor request the defendant to choose one, nor did he after the assignment request B. and C. to choose an appraiser, etc. On general demurrer to these pleas—Held, That the second plea was bad, the averment of readiness and willingness therein not being sufficient

for the performance of the defendant's covenant, and that he was bound to have made his option, and declared it to the plaintiff. Held also, That the fourth plea was defective, as it shewed no sufficient demand to work a forfeiture. Held also, That the fifth plea was bad for the same reason as the second. *Ansley* v. *Peters*, 3 *Kerr* 543.

25 a—Defence against Rent.
See Former Recovery. See Action at Law VIII.

26—Nuisance—Statute of Limitations.
In an action on the case for a nuisance in overflowing the plaintiff's land by a dam, which was erected by the defendant more than six years before bringing the action. Held, That the effect of a plea of the Statute of Limitations was not to bar the action, but only to limit the recovery of damages to the last six years. *Connors* v. *McLaggan*, 2 *Kerr* 446.

27—Replevin—Non Cepit—Evidence under.
Whatever might formerly have been pleaded to an avowry, may, since the Revised Statutes, cap. 126, be given in evidence at the trial in answer to the defence under the plea of *non cepit*. *Myers* v. *Smith*, 4 *All.* 207.

The defendant in replevin is entitled to damages on a verdict in his favor on the plea of *non cepit*, if he gives such evidence as would have supported an avowry under the former law. *Ibid.*

28—Replevin—Plea—Replication.
In replevin, the defendant pleaded, (2nd) that before the alleged taking, he was master of a ship, and that the goods had been shipped on board at London by D., on which occasion defendant, as master, signed bills of lading to deliver the goods at St. John to the order of D., and that no bill of lading indorsed to the plaintiff by D. was produced by plaintiff to defendant, wherefore he refused to deliver the goods to plaintiff. Replication, That D. had sent the bill of lading to the plaintiff to enable him to receive the goods, and the same was then in plaintiff's possession, with full power from D. to receive the goods from defendant, but D. had not indorsed the bill of lading to the plaintiff; that he requested defendant to deliver the goods; that defendant represented that R. was the owner of the ship, and that he (defendant) would do whatever R. agreed to; that the plaintiff applied to R. for the goods, who informed plaintiff that C. was the agent of D., that his indorsement of the bill of lading would be satisfactory; that the plaintiff then procured C.'s indorsement of the bill of lading as the agent of D., and produced the bill of lading so indorsed to the defendant, who refused to deliver the goods. Rejoinder, That the plaintiff never produced to defendant any proper authority from D. to receive the goods; and that before the bill of lading indorsed by C. was produced to defendant, R. had forbidden the defendant to deliver the goods to plaintiff, under the bill of lading so indorsed. Held, on demurrer, per Allen and Fisher, J. J. (Weldon, J., *dissentiente*), That the plea admitting the property in the goods to be in the plaintiff as alleged in the declaration, was no answer to the action, because the plaintiff was not bound by the bill of lading, and was not deprived of his right to the possession of the goods as owner, by the undertaking of the defendant to deliver them to the order of D.; and though the defendant having received the goods from D. could not voluntarily set up a *jus tertii*, that was no answer to a claim by a third person, who was the real owner. Held, per Weldon, J., That the plea was good; and that the plaintiff should have shewn by replication his right to the goods, and that D. had no title to them, and was wrongfully in possession at the time he shipped them. Held also, That the replication was bad, as the agreement of the defendant to abide by what R. did, was without consideration, and not binding; and it did not allege that C. was the agent of D. That the rejoinder was bad, in stating that the plaintiff produced no "proper authority" from D. to receive the goods, which was a question of law; also, because it both traversed, and confessed and avoided the allegations in the replication. Fourth plea, Alleging the shipment of the goods at London by D., to be carried to St. John, according to the terms of a bill of lading (as in the 2nd plea); that freight was due on the goods, and that defendant retained them for non-payment of the freight. Replication, That the plaintiff tendered to the defendant all money due for freight, according to the bill of lading, and that he refused to receive it, and to deliver the goods to the plaintiff. Rejoinder, That the plaintiff had no authority to receive

the goods, or to make a tender of the freight; wherefore the defendant refused to accept the tender or to deliver the goods to the plaintiff. Held, That the rejoinder was bad, as being a departure from the plea. *Domville* v. *Kevan*, 2 *Han.* 33.

29—Replevin—Onus probandi.
When a defendant in replevin pleads property in himself or a third person, and issue is taken thereon, the *onus* of proving property is on the defendant, and if he fails in doing so, the plaintiff is entitled to recover. *Graham* v. *Wetmore*, 4 *All.* 373.

30—Replevin—Proof of plea.
Defendant in replevin pleaded property in M. and a seizure as Sheriff under execution against M. Replication—property in the plaintiff. On the trial the defendant failed to prove property in M. and a verdict was given for the plaintiff. Held, That the defendant was bound to prove the whole plea, and was not entitled to judgment *non obstante veredicto*, on the ground that the replication had admitted that the property was in custody of the law, and therefore not repleviable. *Graham* v. *Wetmore*, 4 *All.* 377.

31—Puis darrein continuance.
A verdict for the plaintiff was set aside in Easter term, and in May following the defendant obtained a certificate of bankruptcy, but allowed Trinity term to elapse, and omitted to plead his bankruptcy until September, after notice of trial given; the plaintiff took no notice of the plea, and the cause was tried as undefended; the Court in the following term refused to set aside the verdict, and allow the defendant to plead the bankruptcy *puis darrein continuance* as of Trinity term. *Grumble* v. *Perley*, 1 *All.* 512.

32—Pleas *puis darrien continuance* must be pleaded either in term or at the assizes, and are limited to pleading such matters of defence as have arisen since last continuance. *Vittrim* v. *Stevens*, 2 *Han.* 217.

32 *a*—If the defendant omits to plead in due time, a matter of defence arising *puis darrein continuance*, he cannot do so afterwards without leave of the Court: such a plea may be allowed to be pleaded *nunc pro tunc*. *Ibid.*

32 *b*—A plea *puis darrein continuance* regularly pleaded and verified by affidavit, cannot be set aside as false. If the facts stated in the plea are denied, the plaintiff should take issue on it. *Gilbert* v. *Graham*, *Mich. T.* 1872.

When Court will not set aside. See Practice VI. 40.

33—Trespass—Distress for rent.
It is a good plea to a declaration in trespass for taking goods, that the goods were distrained for rent and not being replevied within five days were appraised, and after such appraisement kept and detained in satisfaction of the rent; although the defendant should have proceeded to sell the goods, yet the omission do so will not enable the owner to maintain trespass, the original taking being lawful. The option granted by the Act 50 Geo. 3, c. 21, s. 7, to bring trespass or case, is to be understood according to the subject matter of the grievance, and not the mere election of the party. *Rogers* v. *Buntin*, 2 *Kerr* 230.

(See Action at Law III.)

34—Trespass—Breaking plaintiff's close.
To trespass for breaking the plaintiff's close, cutting down the trees there growing, and carrying away and converting the same: the defendant pleaded in the same plea that the close in which, etc., was his soil and freehold, and that he took and carried away the trees because they were incumbering the close. On special demurrer to the plea—Held, That the plea was not bad either on the ground of not sufficiently answering the declaration or as amounting to the general issue, and that any objection on the ground of duplicity must be specially assigned. *McLachlan* v. *Wilson*, 2 *Kerr* 368.

35—Non Damnificatus—When good. See Bond I. See Supra I. 13.

36—Action against executor—Insolvency.
Where in assumpsit by A. against B., as executor of C., B. pleaded that the estate of C. was insolvent, and only sufficient to pay 1s. 6d. in the pound, and that A.'s rateable proportion thereof was so much, which was acknowledged on the plea to be still due him; on demurrer—Held, That the plea containing no allegation that the defendant had taken proceedings under the Act to have the insolvency ascertained and the assets duly distributed was bad. It is only under the Act of Assembly 26 Geo. 3, c. 11, that such

defence can be made available in a Court of law. *Smith* v. *Eagan*, 1 *Kerr* 43.

37—Bill of Exchange given for debt.

Declaration in assumpsit on the common counts; plea, admitting the sum of £526 12s. 4d. to have been due to the plaintiff, avers that for that sum the defendant, at Saint Andrews in this Province, drew his bill of exchange on one C. M., payable to the plaintiff, which was delivered to plaintiff, and by him received and accepted for and on account of the sum so due; replication, that after the bill of exchange was so received, and before it became due and payable, the plaintiff sent the same by a vessel, of which the said C. M. was master, addressed to the plaintiff's agent in the West Indies, for the purpose of being presented on the said vessel's arrival, but that the vessel foundered at sea on her passage out, whereby the said C. M., the drawee, perished, and the bill of exchange was destroyed and lost, and the plaintiff was unable to present the same, and the same remains wholly unpaid. Special demurrer, assigning for causes that the plaintiff's remedy for the original debt was lost by his taking the bill of exchange, and was not restored by the destruction and consequent non-payment thereof, as set out in the replication; that the facts stated in the replication were immaterial; that after the receipt of the bill the liability for the original debt was only a secondary liability, and the plaintiff's primary remedy was against the personal representative of the drawee; and that the remedy, if any, against the defendant was in equity only. Held, That the replication was not defective for any of the causes assigned, but afforded a sufficient answer to the plea. *Boyd* v. *McLauchlan*, 1 *Kerr* 210.

38—Sheriff—Escape—Justification.

To an action on the case against a Sheriff for an escape, the defendant justified under an order of two Justices, made pursuant to the Insolvent Confined Debtors' Act, directing him to discharge the prisoner in consequence of failure on the part of the plaintiff to pay the weekly support allowed under the Act to the defendant. Held, That the plea was bad as not averring that an order was duly made for payment of a weekly support, and that the plaintiff had failed in payment thereof; the mere recital of these steps in the order of discharge not being sufficient. *Power* v. *Johnson*, 1 *Kerr* 492.

39—Trespass—Cattle.

In trespass by cattle, if the defendant justify the entry of the cattle through defect of fences, it must be specially pleaded. *Griswold* v. *Hallett*, *Mich. T.* 1834.

40—Breaking and entering close—Taking property—Justification—General issue.

In trespass, the first count charged a breaking and entering plaintiff's close, and taking and carrying away 50,000 deals and a horse, and converting and disposing of the same to defendant's use. The defendant pleaded,—as to breaking and entering the close, and seizing the goods in the first count mentioned, and carrying away and disposing of the said horse—*actio non*, because one P. had recovered a judgment in a Justice's Court of the County of K. against the plaintiff for £4 18s. 3d., on which execution was issued, and delivered to D. a constable of said county, to be executed; that D. as such constable, and defendant as his servant, and by his command, seized and took the goods and chattels in the first count mentioned for the cause aforesaid, and entered the plaintiff's close for that purpose; and that after publicly advertising the goods and chattels for five days, the constable sold the horse to satisfy the execution: and, as to all the supposed trespassers in the declaration mentioned, except those stated in the introductory part of the plea,—not guilty. Held, That this plea answered the whole declaration; that defendant, acting as the servant of the constable, was not bound to justify any but his own acts, or to account for what might have been done by the constable in the disposal of any of the goods except the horse; to which other goods, the general issue applied. *Atkinson* v *Desmond*, *Trin. T.* 1863.

41—Former recovery—Verdict—Judgment not signed.

A verdict recovered without judgment signed cannot be pleaded in bar to an action between the same parties. *Gilbert* v. *Graham*, *East. T.* 1873.

42—Abatement—General issue—Also plea in abatement—Latter plea not available.

In an action upon an alleged warranty

of ownership upon the exchange of waggons, the defendant pleaded the general issue, and also in abatement the pendency of another suit for the same cause of action. Held, That he could not avail himself of the latter plea. *Mercer* v. *Cosman*, 2 *Han.* 240.

43—Non-joinder of partner can only be taken advantage of by plea in abatement. See Bills and Notes VI. 10.

44—False plea—Set aside as frivolous.
A plea to an action on a promissory note for £266, alleging "that the defendant had paid the said sum of £266 to the plaintiff, which he had accepted in full discharge, and also that the defendant had given to the plaintiff a new promissory note for the said sum, payable in three months, in full satisfaction and discharge," was set aside by the Court as frivolous, upon motion of the plaintiff, supported by an affidavit that the plea was wholly false, and was pleaded for the purpose of delay. *Gabel* v. *Harding*, 2 *Kerr* 71.

Feigned issue. See Practice XII.

De Injuria. See De Injuria.

Former recovery. See Action at Law. See Former Recovery.

Husband and wife. See.

Filing pleas in abatement. See General Rules 1.

III.

NOTICE OF DEFENCE.

1—A special plea cannot operate as a notice under the Act 13 Vic. c. 32. *Robinson* v. *Palmer*, 2 *All.* 223.

2—Proof of the matter alleged in a notice of defence under the Act 13 Vic. c. 32, will not entitle the defendant to a verdict, unless it amounts to a legal defence. *Whelpley* v. *Riley*, 2 *All.* 275.

3—A notice given under the Act 13 Vic. c. 32, may be set aside with costs, if the matter stated is no defence to the action. *Dowling* v. *Trites*, 2 *All.* 520.

4—A notice of defence under the Act 13 Vic. c. 32, which would have been bad as a special plea, will be set aside with costs. *Wilson* v. *Street*, 2 *All.* 629.

5—Notices under the Act 13 Vic. c. 32 should state the grounds of defence with reasonable certainty, and shew in substance, that the matter alleged would have been pleadable in bar. *Le Gal* v. *Duffy*, 3 *All.* 57.

6—Notice cannot be given of matter not pleadable—Dilatory Plea—Summary Action.
In a summary action the defendant pleaded the general issue, and gave notice of defence under the Act 13 Vic. c. 32, of the pendency of another action for the same promises. Held, bad, because a dilatory plea cannot be pleaded in a summary action, and a defendant cannot give notice of a defence which he cannot plead. *Thomson* v. *Keith*, *Trin. T.* 1864.

7—Pleading and Notice.
If two pleas are pleaded and a notice of other matters of defence given under the Act 13 Vic. c. 32, the plaintiff is not justified in treating them as a nullity, but should apply to a Judge to set them aside. *Oulton* v. *Palmer*, 2 *All.* 364.

8—Libel—Generality of Notice.
A notice of defence in an action of libel stating that the allegations contained in the writing complained of are true; is sufficient under the Act 13 Vic. c. 32, there being no affidavit of the plaintiff that he was misled by the generality of the notice. *Lang* v. *Gilbert*, 4 *All.* 359.

9—Evidence under General Issue—Not confessing and avoiding.
A notice of defence under the Act 13 Vic. c. 32, will not be set aside, because the matter stated might be given in evidence under the general issue; nor because it does not in terms confess and avoid the cause of action alleged in the declaration. *Ladds* v. *Vernon*, *East. T.* 1873.

IV.

MISCELLANEOUS.

Declaration — Copy delivered, presumed true transcript. See Practice I. 5.

Plea in abatement and in bar not allowed. See Supra II. 42

General issue to whole, and tender to part —is bad. See Supra II. 24.

Trial by record—What put in issue.
On a trial by the record, the only thing put in issue by the pleading is the record of the recovery of the judgment described in the declaration; therefore in *scire*

facias assigning breaches on a bond payable by instalments, a variance between the writ of *scire facias* and the declaration in reference to the breaches assigned, and an alleged objection to the form on which execution was prayed for by the writ, were held not to be included in the issue. *Kerr* v. *Kinnear*, 3 *Kerr* 412.

Variance.
On *Nul Tiel Record* pleaded to a judgment of an Inferior Court a variance between the *ca. sa.* and the judgment, or inconsistency between the teste and issue thereof cannot be taken advantage of. *Spence* v. *Stewart*, *Ber.* 113, 219.

Demand of plea before expiry of twenty days, irregular. See Practice VII.

Plea.
Admission on one plea does not qualify the issue joined on another distinct plea. See Evidence X. 2.

Filing Plea—Interlocutory judgment.
It is not necessary that a plea should be filed within twenty four hours after a demand of plea; therefore where a copy of plea was delivered within that time, and the plea sent to Fredericton on the same day, and filed in the clerk's office on the following day, an interlocutory judgment signed in the afternoon of the day on which the plea was delivered, was set aside for irregularity. *McCullough* v. *Collins*, 1 *All.* 499.

Rule to plead several matters.
Though it is not usual to require a rule to plead several matters to be taken out, if insisted on, it must be done. *Wilson* v. *Atkinson*, 3 *Kerr* 474.

Service—Time for pleading.
The day of service of rule to plead is to be computed one of the twenty days allowed for pleading. *Clowes* v. *Scoullar*, 2 *Kerr* 627.

De minimis non curat lex—Application of Maxim. See Supra I. 23.

Estoppel by record must be pleaded, otherwise it is waived. *Miller* v. *Weldon*, 2 *Han.* 188.

Want of necessary averments — Recovery under common counts. See Bills and Notes VI.

Counts of declaration are considered as distinct causes of action. *Crawley* v. *Wilson*, 1 *All.* 764.

Declaration—Entitling—Cause of action—Time.
It is not a ground for arrest of judgment that the declaration is entitled generally of a term, and the cause of action appears to have arisen on a subsequent day in the term. *Williston* v. *Pierce*, 2 *All.* 162.

PLENE ADMINISTRAVIT.

See Executors and Administrators.

POLICE.

See Action at Law. (Notice.)

POLICY OF GUARANTEE.

See Pleading II. 5.

POLICY OF INSURANCE.

See Insurance.

POND-KEEPER.

See Lien—Contract 2.

Liability—Custom.
The defendant, a pond keeper, agreed to receive in charge all the plaintiff's logs, and to provide sufficient warps to secure them, and to deliver them at the plaintiff's mill, at the rate of one shilling per thousand superficial feet; but if he allowed the rafts to be broken up, so they would have to be re-rafted, only nine pence per thousand was to be paid. It was proved that there was no custom in the lumber trade making a pond keeper liable as an insurer. Held, That the defendant was not liable either under the terms of the contract, or construed by the usage of the trade, for logs lost by a storm, and without any want of care on his part. *Brown* v. *Cunard*, 3 *All.* 316.

POOR (OVERSEERS OF.)

See Overseers of Poor.

PORTLAND (TOWN OF.)

Civil Court—Town of Portland.
The proceeding by review according to 1 Rev. Stat. c. 137, does not apply to a judgment of the Civil Court of the Town of Portland, under the Act 34 Vic. c. 11, s. 90. *Ex parte Moore*, *East. T.* 1873.

POSSESSION.

Confinement of Possession. See Limitation of Actions IV. 2, 4. Crown Grant. Ejectment.

Trespass—Sufficient possession to maintain action. See Trespass I. 10.

Trespass—Glebe property. See Trespass I. 8.

Possession enuring to benefit of heirs. See Trespass II. 28.

Prior possession—Wrong doer. See Ejectment I. 7.

Timber — Possession — Seizure by Crown Title against other parties. See Trover 9.

Shewing no right to immediate possession. See Ejectment II. 7.

Wilderness land.
No fixed principle of title by possession of wilderness land to govern all cases. *Coates* v. *McAuley*, 4 *All.* 521.

See Trover 22, same case.

Demand of possession, determining estate. See Tenant at Will 3.

Crops. See Trespass II. 23.

1—Title by prior possession—Disseisin, question for jury.
The lessor of the plaintiff claimed under a deed from P. in 1838, and shewed a documentary title and actual possession in those under whom he claimed, as far back as 1820. The defendant claimed under a deed from S. in 1828, and proved actual possession since that time. S. did not appear to have had any right, and the defendant since the conveyance from S. had applied to P. to purchase the land. Held, That the lessor of the plaintiff had shewn a *prima facie* title by prior possession; and the question of disseisin having been left to the jury, the Court refused to disturb a verdict for the plaintiff. *Doe* v. *Hatheway*, 2 *All.* 69.

2—Grantee of Crown—Nature of possession.
A grantee from the Crown is deemed to be in possession while the land remains unimproved and unoccupied. *Doe* v. *Chace*, 3 *All.* 501.

The possession of one who enters upon land wrongfully is confined to that part of which he has the actual and exclusive occupation. *Ibid.*

3—Plaintiff and defendant occupied adjoining lots for twenty years by a line and fence extending from the front through the cleared land. *Semble*, That in the absence of any actual possession beyond the clearing, it must be considered that the possession from thence to the rear of the lot, was intended to be a continuation of the line in the front. *Belyea* v. *Belyea*, 3 *All.* 588.

4—Possession of widow after death of husband—For whom holding.
A. having been in possession of land fourteen years, died leaving a widow and one child, (the lessor of the plaintiff who was married and not living with her father;) the widow remained in possession about eight years, when the defendant entered. Held, in the absence of evidence for whose benefit the widow was holding, That it could not be presumed that she was holding for the heir, and therefore that her possession could not be added to that of A. to make out title in the lessor of the plaintiff. *Doe* v. *Woodworth*, 3 *All.* 577.

Quære, Whether, if the heir had been an infant, the widow might not be presumed to hold as guardian in socage. *Ibid.*

5—Sufficiency of possession—Crown grant.
Where title is claimed under a Crown grant, which is resisted on the ground that the Crown was out of possession at the time the grant issued, and there is evidence of continuous acts of prior possession of the land, adverse to the Crown, for twenty years, such evidence should be left to the jury; but, in order to prevent a Crown grant from taking effect, on that ground, the possession should be defined, actual, and continuous: mere acts of lumbering on Crown land from year to year, without any apparent bounds, are not sufficient. *Smith* v. *Morrow*, *Mich. T.* 1872.

Sufficiency of possession — Unregistered deed. See Trespass I. 3.

See further—Deed, Ejectment, Limitation of Actions, Trespass.

POSTEA.

See Amendment III. 5. See Replevin 4.

POSTMASTER.

Exemption from highway labor. See Commissioner of Highways *v.* Phair, Ber. 371.

POST OFFICE.

Presumption of letter reaching destination. See Bills and Notes IV. 7.

POUNDAGE.

See Sheriff.

POWER OF ATTORNEY.

Extent of authority.
A power "to make and execute any note, bond or bonds, or other instrument or contract, and to make, execute and acknowledge all contracts, orders, deeds, writings, assurances and instruments which may be requisite or proper to effectuate all or any of the premises," will not *prima facie* authorise the attorney to accept and execute leases of real estate containing burthensome covenants on the part of the lessees. *Mayor of St. John* v. *Lockwood*, 2 *Kerr* 443.

Agent's authority. See Principal and Agent 6, 7.

Execution of — Affidavit. See Attachment 16.

Proof of. See Deed I. 14.

Demand of costs—Power of Attorney. See Attachment.

POWERS OF LEGISLATURE.

See Legislative Acts.
" British North America Act.

PRACTICE.

I. DECLARATION.
II. VENUE.
III. ENTRY DOCKET.
IV. PROCESS — SCIRE FACIAS — SERVICE.
V. MOTIONS AND APPLICATIONS.
VI. STAYING AND SETTING ASIDE PROCEEDINGS, WHEN GRANTED OR REFUSED.
VII. IRREGULARITY.
VIII. RULES.
IX. NOTICES.
X. INQUIRY (WRIT OF).
XI. DEMURRER.
XII. FEIGNED ISSUE.
XIII. ARREST OF JUDGMENT.
XIV. INCIDENTAL PROCEEDINGS.

I.

DECLARATION.

1—**Filing.**
A declaration may be filed *de bene esse*, within thirty days after the last return day of the term at which the writ is returnable. *Pearson* v. *Kierstead*, *Mich. T.* 1865.

2—Under the rule of East T. 25 Geo. 3, a declaration must be filed in all cases; and the time for pleading does not begin to run until it is filed. Therefore, where a copy of the declaration was delivered to the defendant's attorney on the 26th July, but the declaration was not filed till the 30th, a demand of plea cannot be made till after the expiration of twenty days from the day of filing. *Cassmore* v. *Turner*, *U. Ms.* 103.

3—**Entitling.**
Entitling a declaration generally of Trinity term, where the writ is returnable on the last day of the term, and the cause tried in vacation before the next term, is only an irregularity, which is waived by pleading and going to trial, though strictly, the *venire* would not be returnable till Michaelmas term. *Woodward* v. *McRae*, *Mich. T.* 1834.

4—**Counts—Distinct causes.**
The several counts of a declaration are considered as distinct causes of action; and if only one count is demurred to, the Court cannot notice any defects in the other counts. *Crawley* v. *Wilson*, 1 *All.* 704.

5—**Copy delivered—Correctness—Presumption.**
It is presumed that the copy of the declaration delivered is a true transcript of the declaration on file, and the defendant's attorney is not bound to make a comparison. *Brocheau* v. *DesBrisay*, 4 *All.* 122.

II.

VENUE.

1—**Right to lay venue—Change of—Restoring.**
The Court will not change the venue from one county to another, where the cause of action accrued partially out of the Province. *Dempster* v. *Stewart*, 1 *Kerr* 103.

2—The venue i[illegible]ase was laid in the county of [illegible]e was joined and notice of trial [illegible] for that county, [illegible]d afterwards coun[illegible]rmanded: an application on the part of the plaintiff to change the venue from the county of Y. to the county of N., on affidavit that one material witness to prove the plaintiff's case resided in the county of R., and two others in N., was refused with costs, no other special reason being stated. *Commercial Bank* v. *Williston*, 2 *Kerr* 507.

3—The venue may be changed upon the ordinary affidavit, in an action on a written agreement in the nature of a guarantee. *Rowell* v. *Emmerson*, 2 *All.* 455.

Where, after a cause of action has arisen, the county is divided, and an action is brought in a different county, the affidavit to support a motion to change the venue should state in which division of the county the cause of action arose. *Ibid.*

4—The venue in a cause was laid in Northumberland, but the presiding Judge at the Circuit being connected with the plaintiff, declined to try it. The plaintiff then applied to change the venue to Kent, and obtained an order to do so, with leave reserved to the defendant to apply to bring it back to Northumberland. Defendant then obtained an order on the common affidavit to restore the venue to Northumberland. Held, That as this was the first opportunity defendant had of applying to change the venue, the order was properly made. *Rankine* v. *Letson*, 1 *Han.* 29.

5—Though the venue is changed on a false affidavit, the plaintiff cannot bring it back to the county where it was first laid, without the usual undertaking to give material evidence in that county. *Nevers* v. *Travis*, *East. T.* 1834.

6—Where the venue was changed from A. to B., on the usual affidavit that the cause of action arose wholly in B., when in fact part of it arose in another county, the Court refused to bring the venue back to A.,—the plaintiff not being able to give material evidence in that county. But see next case. *Ibid.*

7—Where a cause of action arises in more than one county, or out of the jurisdiction of the Court, the plaintiff may lay his venue where he pleases; and where the venue in such a case had been changed from W. to Y., on the usual affidavit, it was restored on the plaintiff undertaking to give material evidence of some matter arising outside of the county of Y. *Ketchum* v. *New Brunswick Railway Co.*, *Hil. T.* 1873.

See Criminal Law 8, 14, 15.

42

III.

ENTRY DOCKET.

1—Allowing filing of writ.
Where a writ was returnable in Michaelmas term, but the cause was not entered, in consequence, as the plaintiff alleged, of his being unable to obtain the affidavit of the service of the writ, and the defendant appeared within thirty days after the return of the writ, and negotiated with the plaintiff for a settlement, which was not effected, the Court refused, after the lapse of two terms, to allow the plaintiff to file the writ and entry docket. *Wetmore* v. *Briggs*, 4 *All.* 590.

2—Entry of cause—Excuse for non-entry.
A writ was returnable in Trinity Term 1857, but the cause was not entered. The suit was defended and a verdict given for the plaintiff, which was affirmed in Easter Term 1860, after a motion for a new trial. The Court refused in the following term to allow the cause to be entered and the judgment signed, though the plaintiff's attorney swore that the omission to enter the cause was an oversight, and not from any intention of violating the rule of Court. *McAuley* v. *Geddes*, 4 *All.* 591.

3—Insufficient excuse.
The Court refused after trial and verdict for the plaintiffs, to allow a cause to be entered, though the defendant's attorney consented; the only excuse alleged for not entering it at the return of the writ, being that the plaintiffs' attorney expected it would have been settled. *Doherty* v. *McGrath*, *Hil. T.* 1866.

IV.

PROCESS—SCIRE FACIAS—SERVICE.

1—Ac Etiam—Omission.
If a bailable writ states no cause of action in the *ac etiam* clause it is an irregularity for which the bail bond may be set aside, but the irregularity is waived by the party putting in special bail. *Campbell* v. *Lowden*, 1 *All.* 439.

1 a—Summons issued against a corporation under the Act 12 Vic. c. 39, s. 16, should state cause of action truly. See Corporation 20.

2—A *ca. sa.* differing in the amount only from the judgment upon which it is issued, is not void, but only irregular. *Spence* v. *Stewart*, *Ber.* 219.

3—Scire Facias—Suit of Crown.
The writ of *scire facias* issued at the suit of the Crown, is not a prerogative writ; and therefore the Act 2 Wm. 4, c. 20, abolishing the proceedings by two *nihils*, and substituting a service of the writ instead, applies to suits of the Crown. *Reg.* v. *Hammond*, 3 *Kerr* 181.

Semble, That in a writ of *scire facias* issued upon an inquisition taken upon a bond given to the Board of Ordnance, it is sufficient briefly to recite the proceedings on the inquisition, and set out the penalty of the bond, without assigning breaches; also, that the bond being in effect joint and several, each obligor may be proceeded against separately. *Ibid.*

4—Scire Facias—To repeal Letters Patent—Averments.
A *scire facias* at the instance of a private prosecutor, to repeal letters patent, can only issue on the fiat of the Attorney General, who may withhold his assent if no sufficient ground is shewn. A draft of the writ and a statement of the facts on which it is founded should be laid before the Attorney General, and if he is disqualified from acting, the Solicitor General or a Crown lawyer should decide on the application. *Le Gal* v. *Duffy*, 3 *All.* 57.

Letters patent were granted to B. in 1841, subject to forfeiture if he or his assigns did not commence effectual mining operations within two years; in 1852, B. assigned to the plaintiff, who sued out a *scire facias* to repeal a grant of the same rights made to D. in 1850. Held, That the *scire facias* should aver that the conditions of the first grant had been performed, or that the Crown had dispensed with, or waived such performance. Held also, That the defendant might traverse such averments by plea. *Ibid.*

The Act 13 Vic. c. 32, (if applicable to such a case) does not take away the right of pleading. *Ibid.*

5—Scire Facias—Necessary Statements—Joint Debtors—Pleading.
Every writ of *scire facias* should state the particular circumstances which entitle the party to the remedy sought, so that in the case of an ordinary *scire facias* under the Statute of Westminster the party would not be entitled to an execution against a joint debtor not brought into Court in the original action or under the Act of Assembly, 26 Geo. 3, c. 24, and nothing which might have been pleaded to the original action can be pleaded to such ordinary *scire facias*. *Johnston* v. *Tibbetts, et al*, *Ber.* 356.

6—To revive judgment—Joint debtors.
A *scire facias*, in the ordinary form of that writ to revive a judgment against two defendants, where no execution has issued within a year and a day, is a sufficient *scire facias* under the Act 26 Geo. 3, c. 24, to obtain execution against the separate property of one of them, who had not been served with process in the original action. *Berton* v. *Brown*, *Trin. T.* 1831.

7—Execution issued within a year.
A *scire facias* to revive a judgment, is not necessary where an execution has been issued within a year and suspended at the request of the defendant; although such execution has not been returned and filed. *Betts* v. *Johnson*, *Trin. T.* 1832.

8—Scire Facias—Judge's order.
If the service of a writ of *scire facias* is not personal, there must be a Judge's order to perfect it. *Wetmore* v. *Levi*, *Hil. T.* 1861.

9—Scire Facias ad audiendum—Issue—Time of.
It is not necessary that a *scire facias ad audiendum* should issue in the same term in which the writ of error is returnable. *Ibid.*

Altered Writ—Day of alteration considered the issuing of writ. See Limitation of Actions III. 1, 2.

Necessity of Re-sealing. See Alteration 2.

Judge's order for perfecting service—Setting or refusing to set aside. See Practice VI.

SERVICE OF PROCESS.

10—When service not personal, the affidavit should state the name of the person served. *Sandall* v. *Godsoe*, 1 *All.* 441.

11—When not personal—Judge's order.
Where a writ was not served personally, and no Judge's order was obtained to perfect the service according to the Act 7 Wm. 4, c. 14, s. 1, and the defendant denied any knowledge of the suit, a judgment and execution were set aside for irregularity, though the defendant's affidavit of ignorance of the suit was contradicted by his admission since his arrest. *James* v. *Dupres*, 1 *All.* 506.

12—Agent of attorney.
Under the practice of the Court, service cannot be made of papers on the Fredericton agent of an attorney, resident in Saint John, unless the agent be specially authorized to receive such service—the rule of Court requiring attorneys, not resident at Fredericton or Saint John, to have agents at either place, may be considered obsolete. *Hatch* v. *Scoullar*, 1 *Kerr* 571.

13—Service of rule nisi.
Irregularity waived by entering cause on special paper and appearing by counsel. *Barlow* v. *O'Donnell*, 1 *All.* 433.

14—Summons—Service of—Militia.
A summons from a captain of militia in a proceeding to recover a fine for non-attendance, under Act 6 Geo. 4, c. 18, s. 12, is not well served if left at the dwelling house of the party in his absence, and not received by him in time. *Ex parte Ritchie*, 2 *Kerr* 75.

On Foreign Corporation—Affidavit. See Corporation 20.

SERVICE OF NOTICES—RULES—DECLARATIONS.

15—Service on a clerk is insufficient, unless at the office or dwelling house of the attorney. *Moulton* v. *Dibblee*, *Ber.* 128. See General Rules, 106, 108.

Declaration—Ejectment. See Ejectment.

16—Affidavit of service.
Where the affidavit stated service of motion to have been on B. W. H. without stating that he was the party's attorney. Held insufficient. *Brown* v. *Bartlett*, 3 *Kerr* 369.

17—Excuse for not serving.
Where a rule *nisi* has not been served some reason must be shewn for the omission to induce the court to enlarge it—and the application should be made in the term in which it is returnable. *Donoghue* v. *Todd*, 1 *All.* 598.

18—Bill against attorney.
In general the service of copy of bill on an attorney should be personal; service on a clerk at his office, without his authority to receive it, and refusal to accept service, the attorney being absent from county is not good. *Sayre* v. *Gilbert*, 2 *Kerr* 225.

Acceptance by authority—Delay in application to set aside proceedings. See Infra VI. 28.

19—Notice of motion.
In cases of motion requiring 14 days' notice before the term at which the motion is intended to be made, the day of service is considered as one of the days. *Jarvis* v. *Peck*, 3 *Kerr* 507.

Setting aside proceedings for defect or irregularity in service. See Infra VI.

V.

MOTIONS AND APPLICATIONS.

1—Entry on motion paper—Obtaining costs.
Where a notice of motion has been given pursuant to the rule of Hil. T. 6 Wm. 4, and the party giving it does not enter the case on the motion paper; the opposite party, in order to obtain the costs of preparing to resist the motion, must apply to the Court for leave to enter the cause, on the second day of the term for which the notice was given. *Seelye* v. *Williams*, 1 *All.* 442.

2—Where a cause has not been entered on the motion paper according to notice, the party to whom such notice was given may apply to the Court for leave to enter it, in order to obtain costs, immediately after the motion paper is finished. *Jones* v. *Snodgrass*, 1 *All.* 603.

3—Notice of appeal—No entry—Costs.
Where notice of appeal from the judgment of a Judge in Equity is given, and the case is not entered on the appeal paper, the opposite party may move to have it entered and dismissed with costs. *Duncan* v. *Reynolds*, 2 *Han.* 187.

4—Entry—Counsel's duty.
It is the duty of counsel to see that rules obtained by them are properly entered in the minutes of the Court. *Ex parte Glass*, 2 *All.* 88.

5—To rescind Judge's order—Delay.
An application to the Court to rescind a Judge's order the fifth term after it was made, in the interim there having been several proceedings between the parties in relation to the case, was held too late, though the same objection might not apply to an application to amend the consent rule. *Doe d. Hill* v. *Todd*, 3 *Kerr* 295.

5 a—Judge's order granting leave to appeal—Finality of.
The order of a Judge made in vacation, granting leave to appeal to the Queen in Council, and settling the terms on which

the appeal will be granted is final, and cannot be revised or rescinded by the Court. Allen, J., *dubitante*. *Domville* v. *Kevan*, 2 *Han*. 175.

6—Relief—Crown bond—Scire facias. Where the Attorney General had instituted a suit on behalf of the Crown, by *scire facias*, on a treasury bond, conditioned for the payment of duties, the Court refused, upon a summary application on affidavits for relief under the Statute 33 Hen. 8. c. 39, to determine the question as to the defendant's liability, the defendant not having pleaded to the *sci. fa.*, and the Attorney General not assenting to the application. *Regina* v. *Street*, 1 *Kerr* 373.

7—Relief of Insolvent confined debtor, notice and copies of affidavits being served, rule absolute. See *Wilmot* v. *Babino et. al*, *Ber*. 62.

8—Counsel making motion in Court is bound to state on whose behalf he moves. See *Gillespie* v. *Fogarty*, 1 *Kerr* 162.

9—Application for attachment—Time. Attachment against witness for not attending on subpœna must be applied for at the next term after the contempt is committed. See Attachment 9.

10—To enlarge rule—Time. Application to enlarge a rule should be made at the term in which it is returnable. See *Donoghue* v. *Todd*, 1 *All*. 598.

See Enlarging Rule.

11—Motion to enlarge rule *nisi* for attachment against a witness for not obeying a subpœna on the ground that he could not be served with the rule, must be made at the term in which the rule *nisi* is returnable. See *Abbot* v. *French*, 3 *Kerr* 368.

12—For new Trial. See New Trial.
" General Rules 69, 72.

13—Equity side. Where an issue is sent down for trial by the Equity side of the Court, under 17 Vic. c. 18, s. 18, (2 R. S., p. 80,) a motion for a new trial must be made before a Judge in Equity. *Hodge* v. *Reid*, 1 *Han*. 89.

14—Venire de novo. Motion for may be made in the same manner as for a new trial. See *Pelton* v. *Temple*, 1 *Han*. 274.

15—Arrest of judgment—Criminal trial. Objections on motion are confined to the questions in the case stated by the Judge under the Act 1 Rev. Stat. c. 159, s. 22, 23. *Reg*. v. *Fennety*, 3 *All*. 132.

16—Mandamus—Affidavits—Entitling. Affidavits used on motion for a rule *nisi* for a mandamus are irregular if entitled in a cause; but the rule will be discharged without costs. *Reg*. v. *Justices of York*, 1 *All*. 90.

17—Second application for mandamus. Where an application for a mandamus failed because there was no sufficient demand to perform the act, which the applicant claimed to have done, it cannot as a general rule be renewed after a sufficient demand, though there may be circumstances warranting a departure from this rule. *Regina* v. *Commissioners of Sewers St. John*, 1 *Han*. 3.

18—Several causes—Single affidavit. Where the same rule is to be moved for in several causes, the motion may be made on a single affidavit entitled in all the causes. *Brown* v. *Trenholm*, 2 *All*. 515.

19—Attorney. Some reason should be given for striking an attorney off the roll even on his own application. *Ex parte McCully*, 1 *Kerr* 521.

20—Costs—Depriving plaintiff—Default case. Where the defendant suffers damages to be assessed and final judgment signed for a debt over £5, the Court will not entertain a motion to deprive the plaintiff of costs, on the ground that a payment had been made before action brought whereby the debt was reduced below £5. *Bennet* v. *Morse*, 2 *Kerr* 624.

21—Attorney—To pay over proceeds of judgment. The Court will not, on summary application, compel an attorney to pay over the proceeds of a judgment to a person claiming as assignee, unless his right is clear. *Murray* v. *Johnson*, 1 *All*. 697.

22—Bail. Bail cannot plead to an action on recognizance, a reference of the original suit to arbitration,—they should apply to have an exoneretur entered on the bail piece. *Sharp* v. *Connell*, 3 *Kerr* 125.

23—Entitled to have exoneretur entered

when variance between affidavit and cause of action. See Bail 12.

24—Bail—After pleading—Affidavit.
Bail cannot, after pleading that no *ca. sa.* duly issued against the principal, and while that plea stands, apply to the Court to set aside the proceedings for irregularity, on the ground that the execution did not remain in the Sheriff's office four days. *Fulton* v. *Andrews*, 2 *All.* 359.

After failure of such an application, a motion to withdraw the plea and set aside the execution for the same irregularity was refused. *Ibid.*

25—In an application to discharge the bail in a suit, on the ground of delay in the plaintiff's proceedings, it must be sworn that the application is made on behalf of the bail. *Ritchie* v. *Porter*, 2 *All.* 360.

26—*Quære*, Whether it is too late for bail to object to the sufficiency of an affidavit, after the time for putting in bail has expired, if they did not see it before that time. *Simonds* v. *Simonds*, 2 *All.* 468.

27—Equitable jurisdiction—To set aside receipt.
The Court will not entertain an application to its equitable jurisdiction, by an assignee of a chose in action, to set aside as fraudulent a mere matter of evidence, such as a receipt, which has not been pleaded to the action. *Goss* v. *Messinett*, 3 *Kerr* 225.

28—Time—Service of notice.
In cases of motion requiring fourteen days' notice before the term at which the motion is intended to be made, the day of service is considered as one of the days. *Jarvis* v. *Peck*, 3 *Kerr* 507.

Leave to withdraw plea—Discontinuing replevin suit. See Replevin.

29—Attachment for costs in Equity—Application by sureties.
Where action is brought in Supreme Court on a limit bond given by a prisoner in custody on an attachment for costs in Equity, application for relief by the sureties must be made to the Supreme Court. *Bartlett* v. *Glasgow*, *Hil. T.* 1871.

30—Interlocutory Judgment—Motion to set aside—Regularity.
The plaintiff having demurred to the defendant's plea, delivered a copy of his demurrer to the defendant's attorney, received from him a joinder in demurrer with objections, and gave him notice of setting down the case for argument, whereupon the demurrer book of the defendant was made up and delivered; but the plaintiff, discovering that the defendant's papers in the cause were not on file, signed interlocutory judgment; subsequent to which the attorney of the defendant who had been in default for non-payment of Court fees, purged his contempt by paying up the fees, and procured a Judge's order to the clerk to receive his papers. On motion to set aside the interlocutory judgment for irregularity, so signed after the several steps taken. Held, That the signing of the interlocutory judgment was regular, the contempt of the attorney being no excuse for the wrong. Held also, per Street, J., that the subsequent steps did not amount to a waiver of the irregularity, the plaintiff having been in the dark as to the circumstances afterwards discovered. *Partelow* v. *Smith*, 3 *Kerr* 349.

31—Delay.
Where a defendant delayed until the last day of the third term before making application to set aside an interlocutory judgment, and prior to the application the intermediate steps had been taken, of which his attorney had notice respectively, and upon which final judgment was signed. Held, That the application was too late either to set aside the interlocutory judgment and subsequent proceedings for irregularity, or to let the defendant in upon the merits. *Kelly* v. *Wilson*, 3 *Kerr* 471.

See Judgment by Default.

32—To set aside award—Time.
A motion to set aside an award under a submission, with a clause of consent to make it a rule of Court, must be made before the last day of the term next after the award is published. *Nugent* v. *Brown*, 2 *All.* 621.

33—Certiorari.
On application to a Judge at Chambers for a *certiorari*, there should be a summons or rule *nisi* in the first instance. *Ex parte Howell*, 1 *All.* 584.

34—Application to Court pending application to Judge.
Where a defendant has applied to a Judge at Chambers to set aside an arrest on the ground that there is no *ac etiam* clause in the writ, he may afterwards, and while that application is pending, apply to the Court to rescind a Judge's order for bail in the case, on the ground

that the affidavit to hold to bail is defective (Fisher, J., *dissentiente.*) *Nevins* v. *Cole*, *Hil. T.* 1871.

35—Quo Warranto—Application for—Withholding facts.
Where a party applying for a *Quo Warranto* improperly withhold material facts, which ought to have been stated in his affiduvit, the rule was discharged with costs. *Ex parte Gilbert*, *Hil. T.* 1873.

36—Warrant of Attorney—Leave to enter up.
On motion in *banc* for leave to enter up judgment on an old warrant of attorney, it must be shown that the defendant was alive within the term at which the motion is made. *Wiley* v. *Haslip*, 1 *Kerr* 1.

The Court is unwilling to decide questions of importance upon summary application. See Bankrupt 5.

Motions for judgment as in case of non-suit—To enlarge peremptory undertakings. See Judgment as in Case of Non-suit.

VI.

STAYING AND SETTING ASIDE PROCEEDINGS, WHEN GRANTED OR REFUSED.

1—Release.
The Court will not set aside a release given by a surviving plaintiff, on the ground of fraud on the releasor, because that question may be tried between the parties. *Reed* v. *Wilson*, 1 *Kerr* 365.

2—Where a release is pleaded *puis darrein continuance*, the plaintiff cannot apply at the same time to set aside both the plea and the release—the first as being too late, and the latter as being fraudulent. *McLellan* v. *Cougle*, 4 *All.* 237.

Execution—No return of, first issued. See Execution III. 2.

3—Execution—Not warranted by judgment.
An execution requiring the Sheriff to take the defendant, to satisfy the sum of £150, which the plaintiff had recovered against him for his *debt*, which he had sustained as well on the *occasion of the non-performance of certain promises and undertakings* lately made by the defendant to the plaintiff, as for his costs and charges, etc., is not warranted by a judgment in debt on a bond and warrant of attorney, and will be set aside. *Willard* v. *Lodge*, 2 *All.* 160.

4—Bond and warrant of attorney—Absence of attorney.
It is no ground for setting aside a bond and warrant of attorney, that they were executed by the defendant, without the presence of an attorney, in pursuance of a promise and arrangement made while he was under arrest, he having been actually discharged from the arrest before executing them, and not being in the gaol or other place of confinement. *Scoullar* v. *Grass*, 1 *Kerr* 527.

5—Judgment—Fraud.
The plaintiff and defendant referred certain disputes to arbitration, and signed mutual promissory notes for £20, on the same piece of paper, with a condition underwritten that if the award was performed the notes should be void: an award was made in favor of the plaintiff for £1 9s., which the defendant refused to pay, whereupon the plaintiff tore off the lower part of the paper containing his note to the defendant, and the condition, and brought an action against the defendant on the note, in which judgment was signed for the whole amount of the note. The Court set the judgment aside for fraud. *McLoon* v. *Lowell*, *C. Ms.* 67.

6—Judgment—Arrest of.
It is not a good ground for arrest of judgment that the declaration is entitled generally of a term, and the cause of action appears to have accrued on a subsequent day in the term. *Williston* v. *Pierce*, 2 *All.* 162.

7—Insolvent debtor—Order.
If an order of discharge is irregularly obtained it should be set aside before any proceedings are taken against the debtor. *Doe* v. *Holmes*, 4 *All.* 557.

8—Non-pros—Delay in application to set aside.
A judgment of *non pros*, irregularly signed, will not be set aside on summary motion, where there is an unreasonable delay in coming to the Court for that purpose. If the judgment in such case be erroneous, the plaintiff must resort to his writ of error *coram nobis*. *Ledden* v. *Rogers*, 2 *Kerr* 326.

9—The Court refused to set aside a judgment of *non pros*, upon a summary application, for irregularity, where ten months had expired before any application for that purpose was made, and the plaintiff's attorney had shortly after the judgment been served with a copy of the bill of costs, and an execution for the costs had been executed some time before the last Trinity Term, the delay not being satisfactorily accounted for. *Lunchester* v. *Murray*, 2 *Kerr* 334.

10—Two writs for the same cause of action.

Two writs f : the same cause of action were simultaneously issued to different counties, and the defendant arrested on both, and bail entered. The plaintiff's attorney immediately notified the defendant's attorney that there was but one cause of action, and that he intended to discontinue on the second writ: only one declaration was filed. Held, That the defendant could not sign judgment of *non pros* in the other suit. *Johnston* v. *Bransfield*, *Ber.* 78.

11—The Bail piece must be on file before judgment of *non pros* can be signed in a bailable action, pursuant to rule of Hilary Term 2 Wm. 4. *Wiggins* v. *Dibblee*, *Trin. T.* 1872.

12—Judgment of *non pros* cannot be signed until the defendant has filed an appearance ; notice of appearance is not sufficient. *Cushing* v. *Gordon*, *Mich. T.* 1872.

13—Inquisition—Giving verdict for defendant.

On the execution of writ of inquiry the jury gave a verdict for defendant: the Court set aside the inquisition. *Doe* v. *Dobson*, 2 *All.* 456.

14—Delay.

Where the defendant had in Hilary Term obtained a rule for assessing damages before a jury of inquiry, but had neglected to serve the same on the plaintiff until the 14th March ; and in the mean time the plaintiff had, in ignorance of such rule, assessed his damages before a Judge on the 2d March, and proceeded to enter up final judgment thereon in due course on the 29th March; and no application was made to a Judge to stay proceedings until the 5th June : the Court refused to interfere. *Harding* v. *Leddon*, 2 *Kerr* 173.

15—Interlocutory judgment—No personal service—Lunatic.

Where a suit had been commenced and judgment by default signed against a person of unsound mind while he was confined in a lunatic asylum, and the writ had not been served personally on him, and no notice of executing the writ of inquiry given; the Court set aside the interlocutory judgment and subsequent proceedings. *Sandall* v. *Godsoe*, 1 *All.* 441.

16—Where a writ was not served personally, and no Judge's order was obtained to perfect the service according to the Act 7 Wm. 4, c. 14, s. 1, and the defendant denied any knowledge of the suit, a judgment and execution were set aside for irregularity, though the defendant's affidavit of ignorance of the suit was contradicted by his admission since his arrest. *James* v. *Dupres*, 1 *All.* 506.

17—Interlocutory judgment signed for want of a plea, set aside on affidavit of merits and payment of costs; though a demand of plea had been sent to a student in the office of the defendant's attorney, and was admitted to have been received in his office before the judgment was signed. *Estey* v. *Newcomb*, *Ber.* 343.

Ejectment — Setting aside judgment by default. See Ejectment IV. 4.

18—Corporation—Summons—Declaration—Variance.

Where a summons issued against a corporation under the Act 12 Vic. c. 39, s. 16, described the cause of action to be "debt," and the declaration was in covenant, an interlocutory judgment signed thereon was set aside for irregularity. *Gillmore* v. *The Liverpool and London Assurance Co.*, *Hil. T.* 1871.

Setting aside after execution of writ of inquiry. See Judgment by Default.

Other Causes. See do.

19—Verdict—Notice of trial not given—Counsel.

Where no notice of trial was given by plaintiff, and a counsel who had been retained for defendant in a former trial in ignorance of this fact appeared without authority, defendant being absent, and defended, a verdict for the plaintiff was set aside. *Doherty* v. *DesBrisay*, 1 *Han.* 494.

20—Inquiry—Damages—Assessment.

Where on a writ of inquiry before a Sheriff's jury to assess damages for detention of liquor from September 1867 till May following, the plaintiff gave evidence of transactions relative to the liquor prior to September, and the expense of warehousing and insurance on the liquor, and legal expenses, and no rule was laid down by the Sheriff for the guidance of the jury as to the measure of damages, the Court set aside the assessment, being unable to ascertain by the evidence how the jury had arrived at the amount. *Kinnear* v. *Robinson*, 2 *Han.* 73.

21—It is no ground for setting aside the assessment on a writ of inquiry of damages under the Statute 8 and 9 Wm. 3, c. 11, executed at the assizes, that the Sheriff had not returned any panel on the writ, and the damages have been assessed by the jury summoned to try the issues at the assizes. *Wheeler* v. *Gove*, 1 *Kerr* 580.

22—On judgment by default against three defendants jointly, the attendance of one of them at the execution of the writ of inquiry is not a waiver of an irregularity in the previous proceedings against a defendant who did not attend; and the damages being joint, the inquisition was set aside. *McDonald* v. *Upton*, 3 *Kerr* 565.

23—Bail—Proceedings against.
Proceedings against bail were set aside on payment of costs, where notice of trial had been given for the Sittings after Trinity Term 1858, but the cause was not tried in consequence of the defendant's agreement to give a confession, and the confession, though dated 1st June, 1858, was not given till October, 1859, when judgment was signed. *Raymond* v. *McMackin*, 4 *All.* 524.

24—After proceedings taken against the two bail upon a recognizance, to which they have jointly pleaded three several pleas, the Court refused to sustain a summary motion made on behalf of one of the bail for relief on grounds inconsistent with two of the pleas, and involving the same point put in issue by the third. *O'Connor* v. *Mott*, 2 *Kerr* 509.

25—When upon a summary writ returnable in Hilary Term 1842, special bail was regularly put in and notice given, but the cause was not entered by the plaintiff in that or the next succeeding term; but an entry was irregularly made in Michaelmas 1842, and final judgment signed in the April following—the Court stayed proceedings subsequently taken on the recognizance of bail, and ordered an exoneretur to be entered on the bail piece, without costs. *Muldoon* v. *Beveridge*, 2 *Kerr* 532.

26—Exoneretur ordered to be entered on bail last given where defendant arrested in two suits in two counties for same cause of action. *Johnston* v. *Bransfield*, *Ber.* 78.

Affidavit not filed in time—Entry Docket. See Bail 8.

27—Judgment.
A judgment after verdict signed before the expiration of the four day rule is irregular. See Infra VII. 14.

28—It is not sufficient to set aside a judgment for irregularity, that the defendant was not personally served with process, it appearing that the service was accepted by a person who while in the defendant's employ, had authority to accept service of process for him, though at the time of accepting service, he had left the defendant's employ, the defendant not having expressly denied his authority, and not having taken steps to set aside the proceedings promptly, after knowledge of the irregularity. *Farley* v. *Philips*, *Ber.* 347.

29—Judgment—Demurrer books—Merits.
Where the defendant's attorney had by mistake delivered demurrer books to the senior Judges, in consequence of which the plaintiff got judgment without argument, under the rule of Mich. T. 9 Vic.; the Court refused to set aside the judgment without an affidavit of merits, it appearing that there was an issue in fact to be tried, in which substantially the same question was involved as that raised by the demurrer. *Collins* v. *McDonnell*, 2 *All.* 158.

30—Settlement of cause—Trial after.
Where after notice of trial the plaintiff and defendant settled the suit, but the plaintiff neglected to inform his attorney who carried the cause down to trial, and obtained a verdict as in an undefended suit, the Court set aside the judgment with costs. *Mytton* v. *Parlee*, *East. T.* 1864.

31—Service—No Judge's order—Defendant's knowledge.
Although it is an irregularity to proceed in a suit where the service of process is not personal, without having obtained a Judge's order to perfect the service, yet where the defendant was aware that the suit was going on, and after final judgment, gave security for the amount, pay-

able at a future day; the Court refused to set aside the judgment. *O'Regan* v. *Berrymount*, 1 *Kerr* 167.

32—Where process has come to the defendant's knowledge, the Court refused to set aside a judgment for irregularity, though there was no Judge's order to perfect the service of the writ. *O'Leary* v. *Graham*, *Hil. T.* 1860.

33—Judgment and execution.
Plaintiff and defendant referred certain disputes to arbitration, and signed mutual promissory notes for £20, written on the same paper, with a condition underwritten, that if the award was performed the notes should be void; an award was made in favor of the plaintiff for £1 9s. 0d., which the defendant refused to pay; whereupon the plaintiff tore off the lower part of the paper, containing his note in favor of the defendant and the condition, and brought an action against the defendant on the note, and signed judgment by default, and issued execution for the whole amount of the note and costs. After the action was brought, the defendant had offered to pay the amount of the award and the costs of the suit on the note. The Court set aside the judgment and execution with costs. *McLoon* v. *Lowell*, *C. Ms.* 1827.

34—Information—Judgment.
Judgment was arrested on an information where the offence was not sufficiently alleged. *Attorney General* v. 250 *barrels of Fish*, *Ber.* 410.

35—Execution upon judgment—Trial by proviso.
An action of trespass *qu. cl. fr.* was instituted in the name of W. by persons to whom W. had agreed to sell the land. W. did not appear to have expressly authorized the action, but he had received the purchase money, although he had not executed a conveyance, and had delivered the title deeds of the land to the attorney of the vendees, who was also the plaintiff's attorney on the record, before the commencement of the action. The cause had been twice taken down to trial by the plaintiff's attorney, but remained untried, when at a third assizes the defendant gave notice of trial by proviso, and the plaintiff not appearing when the cause was called on was non-suited, and the defendant had since taxed his costs and signed judgment. The plaintiff had seen this bill of costs, and promised it should be paid. Under these circumstances the Court refused to set aside an execution and levy made thereon on W. for the costs. *Wetmore* v. *Reed*, 2 *Kerr* 430.

L. and G. appeared as attorneys of the defendant on the record; the notice of trial by proviso had been by L. alone. Held, That the plaintiff was too late to take advantage of the irregularity, if such, after the taxation of costs, of which due notice had been given, and judgment had been signed. *Ibid.*

36—Nominal plaintiff—Action.
Where application was made by the defendant to set aside proceedings because the action was brought in the name of the plaintiff for the benefit of a third person, without the plaintiff's authority. The Court refused to interfere without an affidavit of the nominal plaintiff. *Glencross* v. *Wark*, *Mich. T.* 1864.

37—Judgment of non-suit—Replevin.
A judgment of non-suit in replevin inadvertently given was set aside, notwithstanding the omission of plaintiff's counsel to take the objection on motion. *McGeehan*, v. *Hall*, 3 *All.* 507.

38—Capias—Debt instead of trespass.
The proceedings in a cause will not be set aside for irregularity because the *capias ad respondendum* was to answer the plaintiff in a plea of debt instead of trespass. *Campbell* v. *Mossop*, *C. Ms.* 154.

39—Second action.
Proceedings will be stayed until costs of prior action paid, where conduct negligent or vexatious. See Second Action.

40—Puis darrein continuance—Release.
Where a new trial has been granted in order that the jury might find whether actual payments had been made, agreeably to certain receipts produced in evidence on a former trial between the parties; if the defendant defeat that object by pleading a release *puis darrein continuance*, the Court will set aside the plea with costs; but has no authority to order the release to be given up to be cancelled. *Goss* v. *Messinett*, 1 *All.* 104.

40 *a*—A plea *puis darrein continuance* regularly pleaded and verified by affidavit, cannot be set aside as false. If the facts stated in the plea are denied, the plaintiff should take issue on it. *Gilbert* v. *Graham*, *Mich. T.* 1872.

41—Bill of Exceptions—Setting aside before return to writ of error. See Bill of Exceptions.

42—Precipe.
Quære, Whether proceedings will be set aside for want of a precipe—Entering an appearance is a waiver of the objection. *Kirlin* v. *Baillie*, 2 *All.* 115.

43—Second Ejectment—Refusal to enter into consent rule.
Where a second ejectment was brought in consequence of the tenant's refusal to enter into a consent rule containing a proper description of the premises, the Court refused to stay the proceedings until the costs of the first suit were paid. *Doe d. Morrice* v. *Roe*, 3 *All.* 84.

44—Several actions—Same cause.
Four actions of trespass for taking goods were brought by the same plaintiff against several defendants, one of which was tried and a rule *nisi* granted to set aside the verdict, the Court refused to stay the proceedings in the other three actions until the determination of the first suit, though it was sworn that the defences were the same in all the cases, and the defendants believed that they were all brought for taking the same goods. *Lawton* v. *Gray*, 3 *All.* 576.

45—Trying cause as undefended—No Plea.
It is irregular to try a cause without a formal plea on which issue can be joined; therefore where a cause was tried as undefended, the Court set aside the verdict on application of the defendant (an attorney) stating that he had not given any plea, and did not consider the cause at issue, for want of particulars which he had demanded, though he had written to the plaintiff's attorney that the plea would be the general issue,—it being doubtful whether he had received notice of trial. *Cameron* v. *Connell*, 3 *All.* 398.

Writ—Misnomer—Affidavit. See Affidavit III. 5.

Levy—Setting aside. See Execution I. 7.

46—Procedendo.
A writ of *procedendo* was issued after a *habeas corpus* to remove the cause was filed, as also common bail, but it appeared that there had been a previous irregularity in the writ of *habeas corpus* by which the cause had been removed, and the writ afterwards was amended by the defendant's attorney, who availed himself of the writ so improperly amended to defeat the plaintiff's right of action, by refusing to receive a declaration; both parties having been guilty of irregularity, the Court set aside the writ of *procedendo* on the condition that the defendant should receive a declaration in the course of the term of which it had been offered to the defendant's attorney. *Wilson* v. *Atkinson*, 3 *Kerr* 343.

47—Suspending proceedings—Amendment.
Pending a writ of error, the Supreme Court may in its discretion allow an application to be made to the Court below to amend formal errors on the record, and may suspend judgment in the mean time. Such proceeding allowed where the award of the *venire* and the day of trial were left blank on the record of the Court below. *Kinnear* v. *Gallagher*, 1 *Kerr* 424.

48—Relief from judgment—Infant—Scire facias.
Where a judgment by default was entered against two defendants, B. and C. (B. alone being served with process) in 1834, upon a joint and several promissory note, purporting to be signed by B., for himself and also for C., and a *scire facias* was now issued whereon to found an execution against C. Held, upon a motion supported by affidavits stating that C. at the date of the note was an infant, did not authorize B. to sign the note for him, and that the note was made wholly without his consent or knowledge, That C. was entitled to be relieved against the judgment; and that neither the fact of the note having been given for a balance due the plaintiff on lumbering transactions in which B. and C. were jointly concerned, nor the fact of C.'s having offered to compromise since coming of age by paying a third of the debt, was sufficient to deprive him of his right to relief. *Mitchell* v. *Astle*, 2 *Kerr* 86.

48 a—Judgment—Non-filing of papers—Estoppel.
After judgment in a case which had been defended, a motion was made to set aside the judgment *fi. fa.*, levy, and all other proceedings, on the grounds that there were no papers or documents on the plaintiff's side of the cause on the files of the Court except the judgment roll, which omission had only very lately came to defendant's knowledge; that he had a good defence on the merits, and that the

fi. fa. differed in amount from the judgment—whereupon a cross application was made to amend the *fi. fa.* that it might correspond with the judgment. Held, That the defendant was estopped, by his proceedings in the action, from taking advantage of the not filing of the plaintiff's papers, etc., and that the latter might amend the *fi. fa.* on payment of costs. Held also, That the plaintiff's attorney, by his neglect, had forfeited his costs of suit. *Lynott* v. *Seelye*, 1 *All.* 35.

49—Non-resident—Judge's order—Necessity of obtaining order.
A writ, issued for service beyond the limits of the Province, under the Act 18 Vic. c. 25, was served on the defendant in Ireland on the 19th September 1870, requiring him to appear within sixty days. On the 17th November following, the plaintiff filed an entry docket in the cause; and on the 12th December obtained a Judge's order authorising him to enter the cause as of Michaelmas Term then last, to enter a rule to plead on filing a declaration, and, in case the defendant did not plead by the first day of Hilary Term, the plaintiff to be at liberty to sign interlocutory judgment, and to proceed according to the ordinary practice, the declaration was filed on the 19th December; interlocutory judgment by default was signed on the 8th February 1871; and final judgment on the 19th May. Held, (Fisher and Wetmore, J. J., *dubitantibus*) That the plaintiff had no right to proceed in the cause after service of the writ without a Judge's order; that the order of 12th December did not relate back to the previous entry of the cause; and that the cause not having been entered in pursuance of the Judge's order, the interlocutory judgment was a nullity. *Mitchell* v. *Lawther*, *Hil. T.* 1872.

50—Necessity of legal proof.
In assessing damages under the Act after judgment by default, the plaintiff must establish the amount of his debt or damages by legal proof. Where the only evidence of the debt was an account shewing several sums of money due from the defendant to the plaintiff on various transactions, with an affidavit of the plaintiff that the "account was just and true,"—it was held insufficient, and the judgment was set aside. *Ibid.*

51—Separate actions—Payment of debt and costs—Judgment roll.
Separate actions having been brought against three joint and several makers of a promissory note, the defendants offered to pay the debt and costs to the plaintiff's attorney, but, there being a dispute about the amount of costs, a Judge's summons was obtained for the plaintiff's attorney to shew cause why the proceedings should not be stayed on payment of the debt and costs. The summons was served on the plaintiff's attorney at Richibucto on the 12th December; the damages were assessed and judgment signed on the following day; the agent of the plaintiff's attorney having no notice of the summons. The Court set aside the judgment, and ordered the proceedings in the three suits to be stayed, on payment of the debt and costs up to the 12th December,—not being satisfied that the judgment rolls had been made up until after the defendant had offered to the plaintiff's attorney to pay the amounts due. *McInerney* v. *Chandler*, *Hil. T.* 1863.

In ordinary cases, the plaintiff's attorney is not justified in making up the judgment roll, in order to charge the defendant with the costs of it, till the damages are assessed. *Ibid.*

VII.

IRREGULARITY.

1—Special jury—Striking—Trial by common jury.
The plaintiff obtained a rule for a special jury, which was struck, and reduced to twenty-four by the defendant at the request of the plaintiff's attorney. The plaintiff's attorney then took the list to examine it, and kept it without making any objection, but afterwards, without notice of his intention to abandon the special jury, tried the cause by the common jury as undefended, the defendant refusing to appear. Held, That the trial was irregular. *Bradbury* v. *Baillie*, 1 *All.* 427.

Quære, Whether a party, after obtaining a rule for a special jury, has a right to abandon it? *Ibid.*

2—Service of rule nisi.
Irregularity waived by entering cause on special paper and appearing by counsel. *Barlow* v. *O'Donnell*, 1 *All.* 433.

3—Taxation of costs on Good Friday not irregular. *Gilmore* v. *Gilbert*, 2 *All.* 50.

4—Affidavit to hold to bail.
Irregularity waived by pleading to the action. *McPhelim* v. *Larson*, 4 *All.* 71.

5—Bail.
Quære, Whether an application for relief under 1 Rev. Stat. c. 124, estops bail from applying to defend on the merits? *Rippey* v. *Austin*, 4 *All.* 77.

Distress—Breaking Door. See Distress.

6—Warrant of attorney—Absence of attorney.
Where a defendant is substantially in custody at the suit of a plaintiff, a bond and warrant of attorney executed to the plaintiff in the absence of an attorney, are irregular. The defendant was within the gaol, and had not actually been discharged therefrom, although he was told he might leave it. *Ledden* v. *Hanson*, 1 *Kerr* 90.

7—Venditioni Exponas.
Irregularity in issuing will not affect a purchaser under Sheriff's deed. See *Doe d. Hazen* v. *Hazen*, 3 *All.* 87.

8—Joint debtors—Service—Venire.
In an action against joint debtors, where all are not served with process, and the plaintiff proceeds under the Act 26 Geo. 3, c. 24, it is irregular in making up the record to allege that the defendants not served *say nothing in bar etc.*, as in a judgment by default; nor should the award of the *venire* be to *assess damages* against such defendants, as well as to try the issue joined between the plaintiff and a defendant who has pleaded. *McLaughlin* v. *Ratchford*, 3 *Kerr* 421.

9—Entry of Cause—Bail. See Supra VI. 25.

10—Interlocutory judgment—Signing.
An interlocutory judgment signed by the plaintiff, after demand of plea, where the defendant had filed the general issue but neglected to give a copy of it to the plaintiff's attorney, was held to be irregular. *Lockwood* v. *Brown*, 2 *Kerr* 82.

11—The plaintiff having demurred to the defendant's plea, delivered a copy of his demurror to the defendant's attorney, received from him a joinder in demurrer with objections, and gave him notice of setting down the case for argument, whereupon the demurrer book of the defendant was made up and delivered; but the plaintiff, discovering that the defendant's papers in the cause were not on file, signed interlocutory judgment; subsequent to which the attorney of the defendant who had been in default for non-payment of Court fees, purged his contempt by paying up the fees, and procured a Judge's order to the clerk to receive his papers. On motion to set aside the interlocutory judgment for irregularity, so signed after the several steps taken—Held, That the signing of the interlocutory judgment was regular, the contempt of the attorney being no excuse for the wrong. Held also, per Street, J., That the subsequent steps did not amount to a waiver of the irregularity, the plaintiff having been in the dark as to the circumstances afterwards discovered. *Partelow* v. *Smith*, 3 *Kerr* 349.

12—Judgment by default—Common bail.
A judgment by default, signed by the plaintiff before common bail is filed, or appearance entered for the defendant, is irregular, and such irregularity will not be considered waived by the mere delivery of a notice of appearance by an attorney for the defendant, if the plaintiff's attorney, after receiving such notice, has neglected to deliver a copy of declaration according to the practice of the Court. *Johnston* v. *Cornwall*, 1 *Kerr* 197.

13—Judgment—Signing—Time.
It is no ground for setting aside a judgment, entered up on a verdict recovered at the assizes, for irregularity, that it was signed on the same day that the rule for judgment is actually entered; more than four days having elapsed since the commencement of the term. This rule is considered as entered on the first day of the term, though not actually done until afterwards. *Frink* v. *Platt*, 1 *Kerr* 656.

14—A judgment having been signed on 16th October, the rule *nisi* being entered on 13th, was set aside as irregular, the four days' rule not having expired. *Hutton* v. *Flaherty*, *Ber.* 129.

15—Demand of plea.
The rules of Easter Term 25 Geo. 3, require, in all cases, a declaration to be filed; therefore, if the plaintiff demands a plea twenty days after delivery of a copy of declaration to the defendant's attorney, but before twenty days after filing the declaration have expired, such demand is irregular. *Passmore* v. *Turner*, *C. Ms.* 103.

16—Recognizance roll—Bail piece.
It is irregular to make up and file a recognisance roll until the special bail piece be on file to warrant it. *O'Connor* v. *Mott*, 2 *Kerr* 509.

Bailable Writ—No cause of action stated in *ac etiam* clause an irregularity. See Supra IV. 1.

Affidavits used in moving for rule *nisi* for mandamus are irregular, if entitled in a cause. See Mandamus. See Affidavit II. 3.

Execution—Part levy—Return—Non-recital. See Execution III. 2.

Service of Process. See Supra IV.

No personal service, nor Judge's order. See Supra VI. 31, 32.

Attorney's name on record.
Irregular for more than one attorney's name to appear on record. See *Gilmore* v. *Bull*, 1 *Kerr* 94.

Trying cause without formal plea on which issue can be joined, is irregular. See Supra VI. 45.

Setting aside proceedings for irregularity. See Supra VI.

VIII.

Rules.

1—Casual ejector.
A rule *nisi* for judgment against the casual ejector need not state the name of the tenant, nor the number of days allowed him to appear. *Doe d. Taylor* v. *Roe*, 1 *All.* 1.

2—Claiming to defend as landlord.
If the relation of landlord and tenant does not clearly exist, there should be a summons or rule *nisi*, before a person claiming as landlord can be allowed to defend an action of ejectment in that character. *Den d. Fauls* v. *Fen*, 1 *All.* 585, 633.

3—Rule for judgment considered as entered on the first day of term, though not actually done until afterwards. *Frink* v. *Platt*, 1 *Kerr* 656.

4—Order of Nisi Prius.
There must be a motion in Court to make an order of *nisi prius* a rule of Court. *Underwood* v. *McHenry*, 2 *All.* 94.

5—Rule for body.
A rule for Sheriff to bring in the body of the defendant, may be taken out in term without motion in Court. *Porter* v. *Burns*, 1 *All.* 106.

Quære, If the usual rule for body be entered in the docket agreeably to the practice, it may not be taken out in vacation. *Ibid.*

6—Costs—Moving Rule with Costs.
A rule dischargeable without costs, if moved with costs will be discharged with costs. *Porter* v. *Burns*, 1 *All.* 106.

7—If a rule for setting aside proceedings with costs, is discharged on shewing cause, the costs of opposing it do not follow as of course. The successful party should apply for costs at the time of discharging the rule. *Kelly* v. *Wilson*, 1 *All.* 199.

8—Where a rule *nisi* for a *certiorai* to remove a conviction is discharged, the successful party is not entitled to the costs of opposing the rule. *Ex parte Daley*, 1 *All.* 435.

9—Where a new trial has been granted on payment of costs, and they have been taxed and demanded of the attorney who obtained the rule who was informed that unless they were paid an application would be made to discharge the rule. The Court granted a rule for that purpose absolute, unless the costs were paid in ten days after service. *Scribner* v. *McLaughlin*, 1 *All.* 440.

See further—Costs.

10—Costs—Attachment—Requisites.
Refusal to pay costs taxed upon an agreement for consent rule—the rule must be drawn up before motion for attachment. *Doe* v. *King*, 3 *Kerr* 178.

11—To enable party to obtain rule for attachment for non-payment of costs, the costs should be taxed after consent rule is taken out. *Doe* v. *King*, 3 *Kerr* 296.

12—Rule for attachment for non-performance of award, the award must be before the Court. *Marks* v. *Marks*, 3 *Kerr* 486.

13—Demanding costs.
Copy of power of attorney should be served on party when costs demanded. *Doe* v. *King*, 3 *Kerr* 492.

14—Affidavit of demand of money must state the day of demand. *Campbell* v. *Todd*, 3 *Kerr* 199.

15—Attachment—Witness.
Clear case of contempt must be shown. Not necessary to shew that witness was called on subpœna if it appears that he did

not attend—the materiality of his testimony not taken into consideration. *Maloney* v. *Morrison*, 3 *Kerr* 240.

16—Mandamus—Rule discharged—Costs not allowed—Affidavits being improperly entitled. See Affidavit II. 3.

Rule for Certiorari. See Certiorari.

17—Rule *nisi* for new trial granted, and on argument, Court equally divided in opinion, judgment follows on the verdict. *Gaudin* v. *McKilligan*, 2 *Kerr* 477.

18—Refusal to amend rule.
Where a rule had been obtained in a former term for setting aside a judgment for irregularity with costs, the Court refused to amend the rule by ordering the plaintiff's attorney to pay the costs. *Hasluck* v. *Watson*, 2 *Kerr* 362.

19—Rule nisi—Remodelling of rule.
Where a rule *nisi* has been granted to enter a non-suit pursuant to leave reserved at the trial the Court may remodel the rule, and order a new trial on payment of costs by the plaintiff. *Doe dem. Bryson* v. *Fleet*, *East. T.* 1873.

Discharging rule for peremptory undertaking. Enlarging rule. See Judgment as in case of Non-suit.

IX.

Notices.

1—Notice of trial—Time of taking effect.
A notice of trial sent to the defendant's attorney through the post office, can only take effect from the time it is received. *Crane* v. *Taylor*, 2 *Kerr* 171.

2—Receipt of notice.
An affidavit of the defendant's attorney that he did not receive any notice of trial, is not sufficiently answered by shewing that a letter containing such notice, directed to the attorney, was put in the post office in due time, it not appearing to have been received by the attorney. *Fraser* v. *Harding*, 2 *Kerr* 375.

3—Requisite notice—Days.
The rule of Hil. T. 9 Geo. 4, requiring "at least fourteen days notice of trial"—means fourteen clear days; therefore a notice served on the 12th for the trial of a cause on the 26th of the same month is insufficient. *Grumble* v. *Perley*, 1 *All.* 376.

4—York sittings.
Under the rule of Court Michaelmas Term 1 Vic., thirty days' notice must be given of a motion for a new trial from the York sittings, although points have been reserved at the trial. *Turner* v. *Hammond*, 2 *Kerr* 536.

5—Term's notice.
Where a year has elapsed after issue joined without any proceedings in a cause, a term's notice must be given of the plaintiff's intention to proceed. *Connell* v. *Sisson*, 4 *All.* 504.

5 a—Term's notice—When not necessary.
A term's notice of intention to proceed is not necessary though four terms have elapsed since issued joined, provided the plaintiff brings the cause to trial at the first circuit when it could be tried after issue joined. *Justices of Northumberland* v. *Russell*, *East. T.* 1873.

6—New notice—When necessary.
There must be a new notice of trial when the cause is made a remanet, or put off by rule of Court or order of *nisi prius*. *Fraser* v. *Harding*, 2 *Kerr* 575.

Notice of trial not given—Setting aside verdict. See Supra VI. 19.

7—Costs—Review of taxation.
As a general rule, notice of an intended motion to review taxation of costs must be given as soon after the taxation as circumstances will permit. *Doe d. McCallum* v. *Roe*, 2 *All.* 143.

8—Bail—Notice of render. See Bail 35.

9—For allowance of interest.
Notice should be given of an application to be allowed interest on the affirmance of a judgment in error. *Mills* v. *Vail*, 4 *All.* 629.

10—Inquiry—Countermand.
Notice of countermand not sufficient to save costs for not proceeding to execute a writ of inquiry, unless given at least ten days before the time appointed for the inquiry. See General Rules 77.

11—Countermand—Inquiry—Sufficiency of notice.
A notice of inquiry is not sufficiently countermanded, unless it is communicated to the Sheriff; therefore where the plaintiff's attorney gave a notice of countermand to the defendant but omitted to inform the Sheriff, who on his way to execute the writ, according to the original notice, told the defendant that it would

be executed on that day—it was held that the defendant was justified in attending and was entitled to his costs of such attendance, notwithstanding the notice of countermand. *Wallace* v. *Scott*, 1 *All.* 261.

12—**Notice—When necessary.**
If four terms have elapsed since signing interlocutory judgment, a term's notice of executing a writ of inquiry is necessary. *McDonald* v. *Upton*, 3 *Kerr* 565.

Notice of meeting of Arbitrators. See Arbitration IV.

Notice of Appeal. See Supra V. 3. See further—Notice, etc.

Demurrer—Setting down cause for argument. See Infra XI. 3.

X.

Inquiry (Writ of).

1—**Defence—Credit—Agent.**
After judgment by default on common counts for work and labour, etc., the defendant may shew on the execution of writ of inquiry that he contracted merely as agent of the person to whom the credit was given. *Falls* v. *Sargent*, 3 *Kerr* 248.

2—**Interlocutory judgment—Revival.**
It is not necessary to issue a *scire facias* to revive an interlocutory judgment more than a year old before issuing a writ of inquiry. *Ibid.*

3—**Term's notice.**
If four terms have elapsed since signing interlocutory judgment, a term's notice of executing a writ of inquiry is necessary. *McDonald* v. *Upton*, 3 *Kerr* 565.

4—**Writ—Direction—Judge—Return.**
Where a writ of inquiry is ordered to be executed before a Judge at *nisi prius* the Judge sits only as an assistant to the Sheriff. The writ should be directed and the inquisition returned as in ordinary cases. A writ directed to the Sheriff and Judge, and an inquisition returned under the seal of the Judge is a nullity and is not waived by the defendant's attending and taking part in the inquisition. *Fowlie* v. *Stronach*, *Ber.* 57.

5—**Setting out declaration in writ.**
Quære, Whether whole declaration should be set out in writ, where, on a special case, the Court held that plaintiff was entitled to recover only on some of the counts. If so, writ may be amended. *Kinnear* v. *Robinson*, 2 *Han.* 73.

6—**Order ex parte—Judge—Vacation.**
An order for executing a writ of inquiry before a Judge at *nisi prius*, obtained *ex parte* from a Judge in vacation, is irregular, and the inquisition will be set aside. *Cunard* v. *Fraser*, *Mich T.* 1834.

7—**No verdict—Second writ.**
If the jury summoned on a writ of inquiry are unable to agree and are discharged, a new writ may be issued without applying to the Court. *Ward* v. *Dow*, *Ber.* 21.

Setting aside proceedings on Writ of Inquiry. See Supra VI. 20–22.

See Judgment by Default.

Countermand of Notice. See Supra IX. 10, 11.

XI.

Demurrer.

See Amendment—Pleading.

1—Court has no power to set aside a demurrer as frivolous. *Petty* v. *Hammond*, 3 *Kerr* 686.

2—Objections of form to a summary writ cannot be taken advantage of on demurrer. *Stephenson* v. *McLean*, 1 *All.* 19.

3—**Setting down cause for argument.**
A party whose pleadings are demurred to, wishing to set the cause down for argument, must give eight days' notice to the opposite party. *Smith* v. *Durnin*, 1 *All.* 263.

4—**Admission from—Plea—Costs.**
Where a cause has been set down for argument on demurrer to a plea, and the defendant obtains leave to amend on payment of costs, he thereby admits that the plea is bad; and he cannot afterwards, by refusing to pay the costs, be allowed to argue in support of it. The plaintiff in such case is entitled to judgment on demurrer. *Howe* v. *Carson*, 3 *Kerr* 111.

5—**Objections—Former pleading.**
Where one party demurs to any pleading, the only objections which the other party can make to the former pleadings are those which go to the substance, not the form of such former pleadings. *Mechanics' Whale Fishing Company* v. *Whitney*, 3 *Kerr* 312.

6—**Conclusion—Sufficiency.**
A demurrer is sufficient in form though it does not conclude with a prayer of judgment. *Tower* v. *Cox*, *East. T.* 1873.

XII.

Feigned Issue.

1—**Doubtful facts.**
Where some of the material facts necessary to be explained in opposing a motion to set aside a judgment on a warrant of attorney, were left doubtful by the affidavits, the Court ordered feigned issues to determine those facts. *Lunt* v. *Estabrooks*, 3 *Kerr* 144.

2—**Evidence under.**
On a feigned issue, directed to try whether by the agreement and intent of the parties a certain judgment had been fully satisfied by a settlement made between them in July 1843, a levy on all the defendant's property on the 9th October, 1843, appeared in evidence. Held, That under the terms of the issue the defendant could not avail himself of such levy as any satisfaction of the judgment. *Lunt* v. *Estabrooks*, 3 *Kerr* 291.

3—**Bond and warrant of attorney—Transactions.**
On a motion to set aside a judgment entered upon a bond and warrant of attorney, where the transaction which led to the giving of the bond and warrant is not satisfactorily explained, and it is questionable whether the debt for which the security was taken, was not satisfied before the entry of judgment, the Court may in its discretion order an issue to be tried, in order that the facts may be ascertained before a jury, and will direct the proceedings on the motion in the mean time to be stayed. *Gilmour* v. *Downes*, 1 *Kerr* 88.

XIII.

Arrest of Judgment.

1—In an action for slander, the defendant pleaded the Statute of Limitations: plaintiff replied, that a previous action was brought for the same slander in due time, in which he had obtained a verdict, and judgment had been arrested (setting out the proceedings in the action as matter in *pais*, without any averment *prout patet per rec.*); and that the present action was brought within a year after such arrest of judgment. Rejoinder, That there is not any record of the several proceedings (setting them out *seriatim*.) Sur-rejoinder, A repetition of the replication. Held, on demurrer, That the arrest of judgment should have been entered of record, and pleaded as such. *Beardsley* v. *Dibblee*, 1 *Kerr* 642.

2—Where the cause of action, as laid in the declaration, is proved, the plaintiff cannot be non-suited on the ground that the facts proved do not make out a cause of action: he must move in arrest of judgment. *Cameron* v. *Beardsley*, 2 *Kerr* 598. (See Non-suit.)

3—If the defendant takes issue upon the facts alleged in the declaration, and they are proved, the plaintiff cannot be nonsuited on the ground that those facts do not disclose a cause of action; but the defendant must move in arrest of judgment. *New Brunswick and Nova Scotia Land Company* v. *Kirk*, 1 *All.* 443.

4—It is not a ground for arrest of judgment that the declaration is entitled generally of a term, and that the cause of action appears to have accrued on a subsequent day in the term. *Williston* v. *Pierce*, 2 *All.* 162.

5—Where the declaration alleged a custom as the foundation of the cause of action, and the defendant took issue thereon, which was found in favor of the plaintiff, it is no ground for a new trial that the custom proved is invalid. The objection should be taken by demurrer or motion in arrest of judgment. *Breen* v. *Elkin*, 4 *All.* 187.

6—It is no ground for arresting the judgment in an action on a replevin bond, that the bond, as stated in the declaration, is not in the form prescribed by the Act, if the bond itself is correct. The variance might be amended even after notice of motion in arrest of judgment. *Steen* v. *Hanson*, 4 *All.* 450.

See Bills and Notes I. 5.

XIV.

Incidental Proceedings.

1—**Review from Justice's Court.**
Court will not receive affidavits to falsify return of Justice. See Justice of the Peace.

2—Party obtaining order for review has the right to begin. *Bustin* v. *Howell*, 1 *All.* 598.

3—**Set-off—Judgments—Lien.**
Where the Court allows one judgment to be set off against another, it must be subject to the attorney's lien generally, and

not merely to the extent of the taxed costs in the particular suit. *Rogers* v. *Leddlen*, 2 *Kerr* 59.

Semble, The Court will allow a judgment of the Inferior Court of Common Pleas to be set off against a judgment obtained in this Court, although the action in the Common Pleas may have been brought in the name of another person; the defendant in this Court having the sole beneficial interest therein. *Ibid.*

4—Verdict—Judge—Power on trial.
At the trial of a cause a Judge has not power, without the consent of parties, to direct a verdict to be given for the plaintiff, subject to be set aside, and verdict entered for the defendant upon points reserved. This can only be effected by the jury finding a special verdict where no consent is given. *Hughes* v. *Sutherland*, 1 *Kerr* 574.

5—Similiter.
By the practice of the Court a cause is at issue though no similiter has been added. *Doe* v. *Smith*, 1 *All.* 580.

6—Pleading and notice of defence.
If two pleas are pleaded and a notice of other matters of defence are given, under the Act 13 Vic. c. 32, the plaintiff is not justified in treating them as a nullity; but should apply to a Judge to set them aside. *Oulton* v. *Palmer*, 2 *All.* 364.

7—Continuances may be entered at any time before final judgment. *McDonald* v. *Upton*, 3 *Kerr* 365.

8—Costs—Acquitted defendant—Certificate of Judge—Granting—Separate judgments. See Costs 97.

9—Concurrent writs—Arrest.
Where two writs for the same cause of action were simultaneously issued to two counties, and the defendant was arrested on both, application should be made to the Court for relief. *Johnston* v. *Bransfield*, *Ber.* 78.

10—Particular practice must be strictly followed—Letting in to defend.
Where any particular practice has been prescribed by Statute, it must be strictly followed. Held therefore, That the Act of Assembly requiring defendants in summary actions to plead within thirty days after the return of the writ is imperative, and that the plaintiff is not bound to receive the plea after the thirty days, although it be tendered before the interlocutory judgment and at the same time with the entry of special bail. The defendant however after interlocutory judgment may under the Act be let in to plead upon the usual terms. *Lingley* v. *Huestis*, 2 *Kerr* 4.

11—Time for pleading—Demand of plea.
Under the practice of the Court a defendant who has appeared, has twenty days to plead from the time of service of a copy of the declaration; and a demand of plea cannot be made before the expiration of such twenty days, although the rule to plead, entered at the time of filing the declaration, may have sooner expired. *Fawcett* v. *Nethery*, 2 *Kerr* 81.

12—Record entitling.
A Record is properly entitled of the term in which issue is joined, though the judgment is not signed until a subsequent term. *McLean* v. *Hubble*, 3 *Kerr* 685.

Assessment—Damages. See Assessment, Damages, Bond.

Particulars—Sufficiency of—Supplying Defects. See Particulars.

Affidavits. See Affidavit.

Leave to file in answer to new matter. See Affidavit VI. 8.

Insolvent Confined Debtor — Payment of weekly allowance. See Insolvent Confined Debtor.

Application for discharge—Costs. See do.

See various titles—Amendments, Attachment, Bail, Certiorari, Execution, Estoppel, Enlarging Rule, Entry of Cause, Execution, Filing Papers, Mandamus, Supersedeas, etc., etc.

PRACTICE AT NISI PRIUS.

See Trial.

PRACTICE IN EQUITY.

I. Practice in General.
II. Injunction.

I.
Practice in General.

1—Reference—Maintenance of children—Extravagant allowance—Further reference.
Where, on a reference as to the amount to be allowed for the maintenance of children, it appeared that the amount recommended for past maintenance was extravagant, considering the ages of the children, and some of the charges were otherwise objectionable; and the sum

recommended for future maintenance appeared to be in excess of their income, and made no distinction in respect to their ages,—one of them being but four years old. The case was sent back to the barrister for further consideration. *Ex parte Gilbert*, *Allen*, *J.*, *January* 1868.

2—Costs—Allowance of—Reference—Party making improper claims.

On a bill filed for an account, the defendant, by his answer, denied any liability. A decree was made for an account, and a reference ordered, and, on taking the accounts, the plaintiff claimed more than he was entitled to, and the defendant improperly resisted what he was clearly liable for. On exceptions to the barrister's report, an amount less than he claimed was decreed to be due to the plaintiff, and the question of costs was reserved. On appeal by the plaintiff this decree was varied, the Court of Appeal deciding that the accounts should have been taken on a different principle from that adopted either by the Judge or by the barrister on the reference. Held, That as the plaintiff was justified in filing the bill, he was entitled to the general costs of the cause up to the time of the decree of reference, and the costs of the hearing on further directions; but that having made improper claims before the barrister, and having thereby unnecessarily increased the expense, he was not entitled to the costs of the reference. *Ryan* v. *Keith*, *Ritchie*, *C. J.*, *January* 1868.

3—Injunction—Application ex parte—Duty as to statement of facts—Dissolution—Use of answer.

It is the duty of a person applying for an injunction *ex parte*, to state not only all the facts in his knowledge which he may believe to be important, but all that might influence the Court in determining the question; and if he omits to do so, the injunction will be dissolved on that ground, without reference to the merits. *Coy* v. *Coy*, *Allen*, *J.*, *April* 1868.

A bill filed for an injunction should contain all the charges intended to be proved against the defendant; and if the facts stated in the bill are answered, or are insufficient to entitle the plaintiff to an injunction, an injunction granted *ex parte* will be dissolved, though the plaintiff, in answering the defendant's affidavits, sets up new facts, which would have entitled him to an injunction if they had been stated in the bill. *Ibid.*

Where an injunction was retained till defendant had answered; after which he moved to dissolve it, and the notice of motion referred to the leave given to defendant to apply to dissolve the injunction after putting in his answer. Held, That the defendant might use his answer as an affidavit on such application, and that the filing a replication did not prevent its being so used. *Coy* v. *Coy*, *Allen*, *J.*, *April* 1868.

4—Injunction—Restraining administrator—Matters of appeal from Probate Court.

Where license to sell land had been granted to an administrator by the Probate Court, an injunction will not be granted to restrain him from selling, on the ground that he had not fully accounted for moneys which came to his hands as administrator; or, that the personal estate was sufficient to pay the debts; or, that the costs were improperly allowed in the Probate Court—these being matters of appeal from the d... of the Probate Court. *Ibid.*

5—Death of one of several defendants—Infant heirs—Service.

Where one of the defendants in a suit for foreclosure, died, after order to take the bill *pro confesso*, leaving infant heirs, an order was made to revive the suit against them, under the Act 17 Vic. c. 18, s. 30, and a copy of the order to revive was directed to be served on each of them and on their father. *Collins* v. *Carmichael*, *Allen*, *J.*, *May* 1868.

6—Examiner's fees—Refusal to proceed.

A cause was set down for hearing, pursuant to Act 26 Vic. c 16, after evidence taken before an Examiner: at the hearing, the defendant's counsel objected to proceed, on the ground that the defendant's evidence had not been completed,—the Examiner having refused to proceed with the examination unless his fees for taking the defendant's evidence up to that time were paid. Held, That if the Examiner was wrong in refusing to proceed, the defendant might have applied to the Court to compel him to do so; or, that he should have applied to set aside the order for hearing. But, under the circumstances, the hearing was postponed on payment of costs by the defendant, and on his undertaking to proceed with the examination within thirty days. *Vernon* v. *Gilbert*, *Allen*, *J.*, *May* 1868.

Semble, That an Examiner may require payment of his fees *de die in diem*. *Ibid.*

7—Costs refused—Delay.

Where an *ex parte* injunction was dissolved because the plaintiff had not fully stated the facts, the defendant was refused costs in consequence of delay in applying to dissolve, he having allowed two applications to be made against him for attachments for breaches of the injunction, and having applied for time to answer both those applications. *Foster* v. *Dowling*, *Allen*, *J.*, *August* 1868.

8—Interrogatories—Service—Pleading to bill.

A plaintiff is not bound to serve a copy of the interrogatories on the defendant, nor can a defendant, who has appeared and been served with a copy of the bill, move to dismiss the bill because no copy of interrogatories has been served on him. Under the orders of July 1853 (No. 7) a defendant may plead, answer or demur to a bill, though no interrogatories have been delivered. *Pitfield* v. *Runney*, *Ritchie*, *C. J.*, *November* 1868.

9—Filing of bill—Time imperative—Dismissal of suit.

The words of the 4th section of the Act 17 Vic. c. 18, requiring the bill to be filed within three months after the defendant's appearance, are imperative; and if the bill is not filed within that time, the suit will be dismissed. This defect cannot be remedied under the 23d section of the Act. *Clementson* v. *Cooper*, *Allen*, *J.*, *December* 1868.

10—Filing demurrer—Defendant's right—Waiver of objection.

A defendant cannot file a demurrer as a matter of right after the expiration of a month after a service of a copy of the bill and interrogatories, as required by Act 17 Vic. c. 18, s. 7; and if so filed, without leave, it may be ordered to be taken off file. The objection is not waived by the plaintiff's solicitor accepting a copy of the demurrer without objection—the application to take the demurrer off file having been made within a few days afterwards. *McCourt* v. *McCarthy*, *Allen*, *J.*, *December* 1868.

11—Defendant filing demurrer with knowledge of bill not filed in time—Plaintiff's right to take advantage of irregularity in it.

Though a suit may be dismissed if the bill is not filed within three months after the defendant's appearance: if defendant, knowing that the bill has not been filed within that time, files a demurrer thereto, the plaintiff may take advantage of any irregularity in it. *McCourt* v. *McCarthy*, *Allen*, *J.*, *December* 1868.

12—Trustees—Authority to appoint—Meaning of term "incapacitated."

A testator by his will appointed seven trustees, and directed that if any of them should die, or refuse to take upon them the execution of the trusts, or become incapacitated to act, the remaining trustees should appoint Held, That the term "incapacitated" meant a personal incapacity to act, and that the insolvency of one of the trustees did not authorize the others to appoint in his place. *In re Smith's Trustees*, *Allen*, *J.*, *April* 1869.

The Court has power to appoint a new trustee in such a case under the 32nd section of "The Trustee Act, 1850," 30 Vic. c. 16. *Ibid.*

13—Cestui que trust—Appointment as trustee.

A *cestui que trust* is not disqualified from being appointed a trustee, though it is generally objectionable; and where such an appointment was asked, notice of the application was ordered to be given to the persons interested under the will. *Ibid.*

14—Foreclosure—Subsequent judgment creditor made defendant—Omission of name in decree—No day given to redeem.

In a suit for foreclosure of a mortgage, a subsequent judgment creditor of the mortgagor, with a registered memorial, was made a defendant; but in the decree of foreclosure *nisi* he was not mentioned, and no day was given him to redeem: a decree of foreclosure absolute was refused, on proof of non-payment of the money by the mortgagor at the day appointed. *Richards* v. *Short*, *Allen*, *J.*, *Nov.* 1870.

15—Memorial of judgment—Proceedings at law first necessary before resort to Equity Court.

A decree will not be made for the sale of land bound by a memorial of judgment, unless the judgment creditor shows some reason why he could not have obtained the fruits of his judgment by an execution. Where a judgment creditor has a legal charge, he must take all necessary proceedings at law to enforce his claim, before he can ask the assistance of a Court of Equity. *Robertson* v. *Armstrong*, *Allen*, *J.*, *November* 1870.

16—Maintenance of infants—Father's duty—Reference for further enquiries.

During the lifetime of a father, maintenance for his children will not, as a general rule, be ordered out of their property—it being his duty to support them, if able. Where children were of the respective ages of five, seven and ten years, with a joint income of $1000 per annum, and the barrister reported that this sum would be sufficient to support and educate them during their minority, and recommended that it should be so appropriated; the case was referred back for further enquiries as to the amount necessary for the maintenance and education of these children—1st, till twelve years of age; 2nd, from twelve to sixteen years; and 3rd, from sixteen till their majority. *Ex parte Stymest, Allen, J., Nov.* 1870.

17—Injunction—Title to sustain—Prima facie right—Conflicting affidavits—Restraint in mean time—Ground for injunction—Continuous injury.

Where the plaintiff is in possession of land, and shews a *prima facie* right to it, and it is not clear that there is any *bona fide* dispute about the boundaries, he has sufficient title to sustain an injunction to prevent the overflowing of the land. *Weeks* v. *Dodds, Allen, J., August* 1869.

Where the affidavits were conflicting as to the effect of a mill-dam in overflowing the plaintiff's land—the defendants affidavits denying that it had ever done so—and an action at law was pending to try the rights of the parties, the defendants were restrained from repairing the dam in such a manner as to overflow the plaintiff's land in the mean time. *Ibid.*

If the fact of overflowing land by means of a mill-dam is established, and it would be a continuous injury to the plaintiff's land, and deprive him of the use of part of it, it is a ground for an injunction. *Ibid.*

18—Objection—Bill not filed—Defendant having answered, too late to object.

It is too late, after the defendant has answered, to object that the bill was not filed within the time required by the Act 17 Vic. c. 18, s. 4. *Hallett* v. *Hodgens, Allen, J., August* 1869.

19—Order pro confesso—Filing bill—Plaintiff when entitled.

Where an order is made for the appearance of an absent defendant, the plaintiff is not entitled to file his bill and obtain an order *pro confesso*, till the expiration of forty days after the time limited by the order for the defendant's appearance, under the Act 17 Vic. c. 18, s. 4. *McLeod* v. *Perry, Allen, J., Aug.* 1869.

20—Costs—Demurrer to part of bill—Pleading to remainder—Setting down demurrer only for argument.

The defendant demurred to part of a bill, and pleaded to and answered the remainder. The plaintiff set the demurrer only down for argument, whereupon the defendant applied for the costs of the plea. Held, That according to the 14th order of August 1842, the plaintiff should have set the plea down for argument at the same time as the demurrer, and was not justified in waiting till the decision of the demurrer. Defendant allowed the costs of the plea, unless the plaintiff replied thereto in seven days. *Buchanan* v. *Peters, Allen, J., March* 1871.

21—Answer not filed in time—Motion to take off file—Time of operation of order—Duty of party applying—Practice of clerk.

A demurrer to part of a bill was overruled on the 8th March, and the defendant allowed seven days to answer. The defendant's solicitor was not aware that the order was made till the 21st March, when he took out the order, served a copy on the plaintiff's solicitor, and filed his answer. On motion by the plaintiff to take this answer off file, as not being filed within the time allowed by the order—the answer was allowed to stand, on payment of the costs of the motion, it not being clear from the minute of the order, whether the time for answering began to run till after service of the order. *Buchanan* v. *Peters, Allen, J., June* 1871.

As a general rule, an order operates from the time it is pronounced, and not from the time it is drawn up. It is the duty of a party applying to the Court, to ascertain the result of his application, and see that the order is properly entered. *Ibid.*

It is not the practice for the Clerk to submit to the solicitors, the minutes of interlocutory orders, before drawing them up. *Ibid.*

22—Injunction standing—Obedience—Legislative Act.

As a general rule, while an injunction stands, it must be obeyed, though it may have been improperly granted, and would be dissolved on application. *Valentine* v. *Hazelton*, *Allen*, *J.*, *December* 1870.

An injunction was granted, directing a Sheriff not to discharge a debtor in his custody on execution, under any Act of the Local Legislature, passed or to be passed. Subsequently, an Act of the Local Legislature (33 Vic. c. 22) was passed, declaring that no person should be held imprisoned in any civil suit longer than two years; and that when any person should be so confined, the Sheriff should forthwith discharge him, and should not be liable for an escape, or in any other suit in consequence thereof. The defendant having been confined in a civil suit upwards of two years, demanded and obtained his discharge from the Sheriff. Held, That the Act released the Sheriff from obeying the injunction; and therefore an attachment against him was refused. *Ibid.*

The Act 33 Vic. c. 22, relating to imprisonment for debt, does not come within the prohibition of the 91st section of "The British North America Act, 1867," par. 21, "*Bankruptcy and Insolvency.*" *Ibid.*

23—Appearance of Defendants—Allowance of—Affidavit for appearance of absent defendant—Necessary statements to obtain order.

An order for the appearance of two of the defendants, residing in England, had been published in the *Gazette*, according to the Act 17 Vic. c. 18, s. 3, and an order made to take the bill *pro confesso* against them at the hearing. Afterwards, before the hearing of the cause, these defendants were allowed to appear on payment of costs, though they were aware, several months before, that the cause was pending, and might have appeared before the order to take the bill *pro confesso*. *Putnam* v. *Casco Bay Copper Co.*, *Allen*, *J.*, *Dec.* 1871.

Where application is made for an order for the appearance of an absent defendant, the affidavit should state (if within the plaintiff's knowledge), whether such defendant has a known place of residence abroad, or, should shew that the plaintiff has no means of ascertaining the defendant's residence. See General Rule, Trin. T. 1856. *Ibid.*

24—Demurrer overruled—Answer allowed—Exceptions—Costs.

A defendant declined to answer part of a bill, and demurred thereto: the demurrer was overruled, and defendant was allowed to answer within a certain time, but having neglected to do so, the plaintiff filed exceptions to the existing answer because it left part of the bill unanswered. A sufficient answer having been afterwards put in,—Held, That the plaintiff was entitled to the costs of the exceptions, as it was the defendant's duty to ascertain the result of his application and to file his answer in time. *Buchanan* v. *Peters*, *Allen*, *J.*, *May* 1872.

25—Costs—Abbreviations—Same counsel—Interrogatories—Irrelevant matter—Part transactions—Answer by defendants concerned in.

Where the same counsel appears at the original hearing and on appeal, two copies of the abbreviation of the pleadings will not be allowed in the costs. *Frye* v. *Prescott*, *Allen*, *J*, *March* 1869.

Where a bill was filed, principally for specific performance of an agreement, by one of the defendants to assign a mortgage, and to redeem the mortgage as against another defendant; but it also embraced other matters relating to partnership, etc., with which some of the defendants had no connection, the plaintiff (though entitled to the general costs in the cause) was not allowed the costs of interrogatories respecting matters entirely irrelevant, or of interrogatories to defendants, upon matters which the plaintiff knew to be entirely within the knowledge of the defendants. *Ibid.*

Where some of the defendants are concerned only in parts of the transactions set forth in the bill, they should only be required to answer such of the interrogatories as relate to those transactions, according to the orders of August 1842. *Ibid.*

26—Bill—Injunction—Application to dissolve—No answer to bill—Sufficiency of statement—Original application granted.

A bill was filed for dissolution of a partnership and for the appointment of a receiver. An injunction was obtained on the statements in the bill, (which was sworn to,) restraining the defendant from interfering with the property, which injunction he applied to dissolve, without success; and afterwards professed to answer the bill, though no answer was, in fact, filed. The facts stated in the bill were sufficient to entitle the plaintiff to a dissolution. A receiver was appointed, on notice, upon the statements in the bill. *Bartlett* v. *Stymest, Allen, J., January* 1868.

27—Filing bill—Time.

The words "within three months therefrom," in the Act 17 Vic. c. 18, s. 4, relate as well to cases where there has been no appearance, as to cases where the defendant has appeared: therefore, in cases of non-appearance, the three months allowed for filing a bill, begin to run at the expiration of forty days after service of the summons. *Godfrey* v. *Reardon, Allen, J, November* 1868.

28—Bill for foreclosure—Parties—Interest.

A bill for foreclosure of a mortgage, against three defendants, stated that one of them was the mortgagor, and that the others claimed a lien on the property; but omitted to state what interest they had, or anything to shew that they were necessary parties: a decree of foreclosure was refused. *Chipman* v. *Tuck, Allen, J., April* 1868.

29—Probate Court—Appeal from—Must be made to Court.

An appeal from the Probate Court must be made to the Supreme Court in term, and not to a Judge sitting in Equity; and where such an appeal is made to a Judge, his proper course is to decline to hear it, (having no jurisdiction,) and not to *dismiss* the appeal. *Ex parte Roach, Allen, J., June* 1871.

30—Disputed handwriting—Comparison by Judge.

If on a *viva voce* hearing before a Judge in Equity, there is conflicting evidence of the handwriting of a witness, the Judge has a right to compare the disputed writing with an admitted signature of the witness, in order to determine whether it is his signature. *Hannington* v. *Harshman, Hil. T.* 1873.

31—Supplemental answer—Allowance of—Omission of statement of facts—Rights of parties interested to be heard against allowance—Adding parties.

Where a defendant omitted to state certain facts in his answer, on the advice of his solicitor that such statement was unnecessary, and that evidence of the facts would be admissible without it, he was allowed to file a supplemental answer on the affidavit of his solicitor stating these circumstances, and on payment of the costs occasioned to the other parties by his application. *McLeod* v. *Firth, Allen, J., January* 1873.

On a bill filed by an executor and trustee for the purpose of obtaining a declaration of the trusts of the will, one of the defendants and devisees claimed that a mortgage given by him for part of the purchase money of property, which he afterwards conveyed to the testator, should be paid out of the estate, on the ground that the purchase was made by him as agent of the testator. On application by this defendant to file a supplemental answer in order to give evidence of this fact,—Held, That other defendants, interested as residuary legatees under the will, were entitled to be heard against filing the supplemental answer, and to their costs occasioned by the application, on the ground that this claim, if sustained, would reduce the residuary estates in which they were interested. *Ibid.*

Semble, That where land is devised to A. for life, in trust to apply the rents and profits for the benefit of his children; and after his decease, the property is devised to his children in fee; they are necessary parties to a suit by the executor for declaring the trusts under the will. *Ibid.*

Where the objection of want of parties was apparent on the bill, which might therefore have been demurred to; but was not taken till the cause had been partly heard, and then, in connexion with the defendant's application for leave to file a supplemental answer, the plaintiff was allowed to amend by adding the necessary parties, without payment of costs. *Ibid.*

32—Answer on file—Bill cannot be taken pro confesso.

If there is an answer on file, the bill cannot be taken *pro confesso*, whether the fact appears by the admission of the plaintiff's counsel or otherwise. *Lockhart* v. *Sancton, Allen, J., January* 1870.

Costs. See further—Costs 57 to 62, 77, 79.

Inherent power in Court to amend pleadings. See Amendment I. 18.

Subsequent alteration of decree—Party not having appeared in suit. See Divorce.

II.

INJUNCTION.

See Supra I. 3, 4, 17, 22, 26.

1 — **Restraining defendant from proceeding on note—Defence at law—Legal rights.**

The plaintiff drew a promissory note in his own favor, which he indorsed and delivered to C., to whom he was indebted. C. assigned all his property to trustees for the benefit of his creditors, and the trustees transferred the note to the defendant, who was a creditor of C. Before the transfer of the note, C. had become bankrupt in England. The defendant having brought an action against the plaintiff on the note,—Held, 1. That if the plaintiff could set up the right of C.'s assignee in bankruptcy to the note, it would be a defence to the action, and therefore the plaintiff had no right to an injunction to restrain the defendant from proceeding on the note; 2. That though the trust deed gave the trustees no power to sell or assign debts, they had a right to pay the creditors of C. with the assets of his estate in kind, if they were willing to receive them; 3. That though a clause in C.'s trust deed, relative to the dividends due to such of his creditors as should not execute the deed within a limited time, might be fraudulent as between the immediate parties, the plaintiff could not take advantage of it as a ground for restraining the action on the note against him. *Gilbert* v. *Campbell, Hil. T.* 1862.

2—**Saint John Water Company—Rights—Private rights affected—Remedy at law—Delay.**

The Act 2 Wm. 4, c. 26, incorporating the St. John Water Company, authorized them to draw water from, erect reservoirs on, and carry pipes through private property, as they might think necessary, on paying compensation to the owners for any damage sustained thereby. The Act 12 Vic. c. 51, authorized the Company, in order to procure a more efficient supply of water, to enter on private property, and "build dams or embankments on any brook, stream, lake or pond, for the purpose of creating artificial ponds or reservoirs, and by such dams or embankments to cause the flowage of such private property, and to continue such flowage as long as they should see fit;" but that no such dams, etc., should be built, or ponds or reservoirs made, or pipes laid down, without compensation to the owner of the land for any damage sustained thereby (pointing out how the damages were to be ascertained in case the parties could not agree). By the Act 18 Vic. c. 28, all the rights and powers of the Company were vested in Commissioners. Sec. 7 declared that it should be the duty of the Commissioners "to extend the present water supply as far as they may deem it practicable or expedient, by carrying a sufficient main or mains to Latimer's Lake and Loch Lomond, or either of them," etc. A dam was erected by the Company over a stream called "Little River," the property of the plaintiff's mother, and a reservoir constructed. After her death, in 1850, the dam was continued, and pipes laid down to convey the water therefrom, of which her husband, the tenant by the courtesy, was aware, but took no proceedings to prevent it. The plaintiff, who was the owner of the fee in remainder, filed a bill in 1863, for an injunction to restrain the Commissioners from continuing the dam. Held, 1st. That the Company had a right to appropriate the water of any stream that could be made available for the purposes contemplated by the Act. 2nd. That the 7th sec. of the Act 18 Vic. c. 35, authorizing the Commissioners to take water from Latimer's Lake, did not abridge any rights previously granted, or impliedly restrict the Commissioners from using the water of Little River. 3rd. That if the making compensation to the owner of the land was a condition precedent to the entry and construction of the works by the Company, or the Commissioners, their entry was illegal, and the person whose right was affected had a remedy at law. 4th. That it did not appear that irreparable injury would be done to the property of the plaintiff by the operations of the Commissioners; and that after so much delay, with knowledge, or the means of knowledge of the works of the Commissioners, it was too late to interfere by injunction. *Botsford* v. *Sears, East. T.* 1864.

3 — **Restraining Administrator from selling assets to pay debts — No sufficient answer—Injunction not dissolved.**

Where an injunction had been granted *ex parte*, to restrain an administrator from selling land under a license granted by the Probate Court, on the ground that he had sold property under a former license under value, and had sufficient property in his hands to pay the debts, an application to dissolve the injunction was refused till the defendant had answered, it not being clearly shewn by his affidavits that he had not a portion of the estate in his possession which belonged to the heirs. *Coy* v. *Coy*, 1 *Han*. 177.

4—Right of judgment creditor to sell under execution — Restraining sale.

A judgment creditor has a right to sell under execution an alleged right that his debtor has in certain land; and a party in possession, and claiming the land, cannot restrain the creditor from selling, and thereby acquiring a *locus standi* to contest the title. *Case* v. *Palmer*, 2 *Han*. 183.

5—Judgment debtor having no interest—Defence at law.

If the judgment debtor has no interest in the land levied on, the Sheriff's deed conveys nothing, and the party in possession will have a good defence at law, and therefore does not require the assistance of a Court of Equity. *Ibid*.

6—Restraining Company from overflowing land until conditions fulfilled.

The St. John Water Company, in con- consideration of being allowed to overflow a part of the plaintiff's land, agreed to build a bridge over the overflowage, for the convenience of the plaintiff, and to keep the same in repair as long as the overflowage continued; in accordance with this agreement, they built the bridge. By Act 18 Vic. c. 38, all the rights and powers of the Company, subject to their outstanding liabilities, were vested in the defendants, who allowed the bridge to get out of repair, though they continued the overflowage; an injunction was granted to restrain them from continuing to overflow the plaintiff's land till the bridge was put in a proper state of repair, and also to restrain them from allowing the bridge to remain out of repair while they continued to overflow the land. *Ryan* v. *Lockhart et al*., *East*. *T*. 1872.

7—Application ex parte—Party applying must state all important facts.

Where a party applies for an *ex parte* injunction, he is bound to state all the facts which are important to be brought before the Court, and which might influence it in determining upon the application; and if important facts, within the knowledge of the party, are omitted, the injunction will be dissolved without regard to the merits. Thus, where an injunction was granted to restrain the defendant from building a wharf beyond the line of high water mark in the harbour of St. John—the plaintiffs claiming by their charter the soil of the harbour, and the space between high and low water mark; but the defendant held, under a prior grant from the Crown, extending to low water mark, and claimed the right to extend his wharf, as the owner of the land, which facts were known to the plaintiffs, but were wholly omitted from their bill—the injunction was dissolved on this ground alone. *Mayor &c. of St. John* v. *Brown*, *East*. *T*. 1872.

Unregistered mortgage of ship—Application refused to restrain purchaser from disposing of ship. See Shipping Law 3.

Erection of dam in public stream—Restraining destruction of dam by persons not obstructed. See Water Course.

PRECIPE.

See Practice VI. 42.

PRESENTMENT.

See Bills and Notes.

PRESIDING OFFICER.

Right to vote—Return by. See Election Law.

PRESUMPTIONS.

See Evidence VI.

Possession of land — Continuance. See Limitation of Actions IV. 18.

Right of way—Lost deed. See Evidence VI. 12.

Payment over of money. See Assumpsit III. 44.

Sheriff's proceedings — Regularity. See Sheriff's Deed 2.

Deed of Master in Chancery. See Deed I. 17.

Newspaper—Publication. See Joint Stock Company 3.

Authority of officer. See Evidence VI. 1, 2, 5.

Surrogate—Oath. " do. 1.

PRINCIPAL AND AGENT.

1—**Credit to whom given.**
Where a purchase is made by an agent, who discloses the name of his principal, it is a question for the jury to determine to whom the credit was given; and where the evidence is conflicting, the Court will not disturb the verdict. *Scott* v. *Curry*, *Hil. T.* 1834.

2—R., a broker, effected insurance with the plaintiff on account of the defendant; the policy was issued in the name of R., on account of "whom it may concern;" but plaintiff knew at the time, that the insurance was for the defendant's benefit, and that R. was only acting as his agent. The premium was not paid, and it did not appear that the plaintiff had charged it either to the defendant or R., though all the entries relating to the transaction in the plaintiff's books were in R.'s name. No claim was made upon the defendant till about a year after the insurance. Held, That the jury were properly directed that if the plaintiff, knowing that R. was only acting as agent for the defendant, gave the credit to R., he could not afterwards look to the defendant for the premium. *Stymest* v. *Soloman et al.*, 2 *Han.* 6.

3—**Subscribers for stock appointing person for specific purpose—Agent—Claim—Commission.**
A person appointed by a number of subscribers for stock in a proposed Joint Stock Company, to receive and remit their subscriptions to the head office of the Company, is not the agent of the latter, and has no claim against the Company for his services. *Quebec and Halifax Steam Navigation Co.* v. *Cunard*, *Ber.* 47.

4—The right of an agent to retain money for agency and commission is exercisable only upon the specific money on account of which the charge is made. *Ibid.*

5—**Agreement—Making of by Agent—Estoppel.**
In trover for timber, plaintiffs claimed under an agreement made between D. of the one part, and S. (under whom defendant claimed) of the other, whereby D. granted license to S. to cut timber on certain land,—the timber to remain the property of D. till the stumpage was paid. The agreement was signed by D. "for the proprietors, by J. B." It was proved by D. that the plaintiffs were the proprietors of the land, for whom he acted as agent when he made the agreement. Held, 1st. That it appeared by the agreement that it was made by D. as agent for the plaintiffs, and that they could take the benefit of it (Ritchie, J., *dubitante*). 2nd. That the defendant, claiming under S., could not dispute that the plaintiffs were the proprietors of the land. *Basey* v. *Hatheway*, *Hil. T.* 1865.

6—**Authority to appear and defend suits.**
Defendant being about to leave the Province, gave a Power of Attorney to an agent, authorizing him to appear to and defend any action that might be brought against the defendant during his absence. A suit was commenced, and a copy of the writ sent to the agent, who declined to appear. Held, That the agent was not bound to appear, and that interlocutory judgment signed for want of appearance, was irregular. *Harris* v. *Mitchell*, 1 *Han.* 2.

7—**Powers and authority.**
Under a power given by the Tobique Mill Company (who were incorporated by Act of Assembly) to their agent, "to manufacture logs into lumber at the mills, and transport them to market, and sell and dispose thereof for the company's benefit." Held, That the agent was not authorized to deliver over the lumber at the mills, without the knowledge of the directors, in payment of securities given by him on behalf of the company, for debts contracted in the course of his agency. Such delivery vests no property in the creditor. *Lombard* v. *Winslow*, 1 *Kerr* 327.

Quære, Whether the Tobique Mill Company could give authority to their agent to make promissory notes, and if he could make them in his own favor. *Ibid.*

8—Where an agent is authorized to receive money only, payment to him by a bill of exchange will not discharge the debtor, although the debtor was ready to have paid his debt in money at the time, and delivered the bill of exchange in lieu of money at the request of the agent. *Crane* v. *Boltenhouse*, 2 *Kerr* 581.

But payment to such agent by the promissory note of a third person, indorsed by the debtor for the purpose of being immediately discounted at a bank, and which is so discounted, and the money therefor received by the agent for his principal, without any liability on the note attaching to the principal, may be considered as a money payment by the debtor. *Crane* v. *Boltenhouse*, 2 *Kerr* 581.

9—The plaintiff entered into a written agreement with B. to supply him with a quantity of logs; B. transferred his right to the logs to the defendants, who entered into the following agreement with the plaintiff: "We agree to pay S. (the plaintiff) the balance that may be due him by B. on account of logs to be furnished by said S. to said B. as per agreement and settlement, when the whole of the logs now remaining on Hovey brook, etc., are driven down past the mouth of Clearwater brook." The plaintiff and B. afterwards made a settlement without the knowledge of the defendants, on which a balance was struck in favor of the plaintiff. Held, That B. was not the agent of the defendant for the purpose of this settlement; and that in an action for the balance, it was necessary for the plaintiff to give in evidence the agreement between himself and B., in order to ascertain whether the settlement was made in accordance therewith. *Sutherland* v. *Gilmour*, 3 *Kerr* 165.

10—The authority of an agent specially authorized to draw a bill of exchange for a particular purpose, ceases on the acceptance, and if the drawer is discharged by want of notice of dishonor, the agent cannot, without further express authority, revive the liability by agreeing to waive the legal discharge. *McGhie* v. *Gilbert*, 1 *All.* 235.

11—Liability of agent.
An agent with power to raise money, whose principal resides abroad, is personally liable to an attorney retained by him to carry on suits for the principal, unless he limits his liability at the time. *Jack* v. *Clewes*, 3 *Kerr* 637.

12—Public agents.
The defendants, under the Act 7 Wm. 4, c. 28, were by the General Sessions of the Peace for the County of York appointed a committee of management for the erection of a new gaol; and in that capacity contracted with the plaintiff, binding themselves and their successors as such, on behalf of the said county, and subscribing their names "a committee on behalf of the county." Held, That they were mere agents for the public, and not personally liable on the contract. *Blair* v. *Robinson*, 3 *Kerr* 487.

13—Referees—When agents of parties.
Plaintiff being lessee of land, assigned one half of it to the defendant, who entered into a bond to pay the plaintiff for half the buildings, such sum as two arbitrators should determine before a certain day: the arbitrators not having been appointed under the bond, the parties afterwards agreed verbally to refer the valuation to arbitrators, who made an award of the value. Held, That the referees were the agents of the parties to settle the value, and that the plaintiff might recover the amount awarded by them, as an account stated. *Coram* v. *Whelen*, 4 *All.* 293.

14—Policy—Issue—Notice.
A policy of insurance is considered as issued when the agent forwards it to the brokers for delivery. (Per Ritchie, J.) *McLaughlan* v. *Ætna Ins. Co.*, 4 *All.* 173.

15—Notice of a prior insurance to an insurance broker, is not notice to the Company. *Ibid.*

16—Liability of principal to indemnify agent—Implied contract.
The defendant being the owner of a steamboat of which the plaintiff was master, sent him to the Bend to tow a ship to Saint John: the ship in launching lost her rudder, and was towed in that state to Saint John, and while going into the harbour in the night came in collision with and sunk a schooner, the owner of which recovered damages against the plaintiff for negligence. In an action by the plaintiff against the defendant for indemnity, the declaration alleged, and it was proved, that towing vessels was a dangerous business, and that the danger was much increased by the loss of the rudder: it was also proved that the plaintiff might have replaced the rudder, and need not have entered the harbour in the night. Held, (Street, J. *dissentiente*), That the plaintiff must be presumed to have known that he was doing an unlawful act, and therefore there was no implied contract by the defendant to indemnify him against loss; and per Parker, J., even if there had been an express contract to indemnify against such risks, it would be void as being contrary to public policy; and per Wilmot, J., that the plaintiff was estopped by the

judgment recovered against him by the owner of the schooner, from disproving his own negligence. *Leavitt* v. *Parks*, 2 *All.* 282.

Held also, That the plaintiff's conduct being unlawful, no subsequent ratification of his acts by the defendant would make him liable. *Ibid.*

Held, per Street J., That to destroy the implied liability of a principal to indemnify, the acts of the agent must be clearly illegal, to his knowledge, and that towing the ship under the circumstances was not so; and therefore if the principal either authorised or approved of the agent's acts, he was liable to indemnify him. *Ibid.*

Semble, That if the action was maintainable, the plaintiff would have been entitled to recover the amount of damages and costs in the judgment against him, though he had not actually paid the costs, having given his note therefor on being discharged from custody; but that he would not have been entitled to damages for his imprisonment, if he had the means of paying. *Ibid.*

17—Accredited agent—Appointment—Seal.

In order to prove that a person acting as the agent of a foreign insurance company, by issuing policies in their name and receiving premiums thereon, is their accredited agent, it is not necessary to shew his appointment under the corporate seal. *Robertson* v. *The Provincial Mutual and General Insurance Company*, 3 *All.* 379.

18—Proof—Writing—Parol.

Semble, That the fact of agency may be proved by parol, though the appointment was in writing. *Wilson* v. *Street*, 3 *All.* 251.

19—Ratification of acts of Agent.

D., a plumber, working on defendant's house, addressed to him a memorandum stating that he would require to send to plaintiffs in Boston for certain articles specified, which defendant gave to T., an expressman, who handed it to plaintiffs. Plaintiffs treated it as an order from D., with whom they had dealings, and sent the goods and invoice to him by T., and D. refused to receive them. T. then delivered them to defendant, who paid T. for them and took his receipt. Plaintiffs remaining ignorant of this transaction demanded payment of D., which he refused. Held, 1st. That by bringing assumpsit for goods sold and delivered against defendant they waived the tort, ratified the sale by T., and treated him as their agent and payment to him discharged defendant. 2nd. That the plaintiff might have maintained trover against defendant for a wrongful conversion. *Dalton et al.* v. *Hamilton*, 1 *Han.* 422.

Signing note — Personal liability. See Bills and Notes II. 15.

Authority—When need not be under seal. See Principal and Surety.

Service of papers.

A person authorized by party to serve, is agent for that purpose. See Action at Law XI. 16, 17.

Lease—Execution by direction. See Evidence IV. 5.

Repairs of ship—Owner. See Assumpsit III. 45.

Negligence of master of ship—Liability of registered owner. See Shipping Law.

Master and Servant, adoption of acts. See Assumpsit III. 15.

Attorney — Presumption of authority to issue execution. See Attorney V. 4.

Husband and wife—Implied authority of wife. See Husband and Wife.

Agent binding attorney. See Costs 64.

Entry on land by permission of agent. See Trespass II. 34.

PRINCIPAL AND SURETY.

Bond for faithful service of officer—Proof and notice. See Pleading I. 13.

Sheriff—Deputy. See Sheriff.

1—Bond—Conduct of clerk—Notice.

By the condition of a bond the obligors agreed to make good to the plaintiffs, a Corporation, any loss sustained by the misconduct of K. as a clerk, within three months after due proof thereof either by confession of K. or otherwise, and notice or warning thereof in writing given to the obligors. Held, That a notice from the solicitor of the company to the obligors, of the general nature of K.'s default, accompanied by an account of [illegible] made by him in the company's [illegible], shewing the moneys received and paid, and a notification that the books were open for the inspection of the obligors,

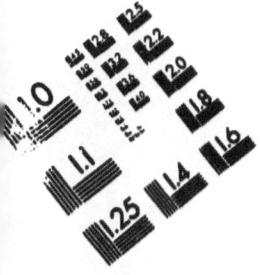

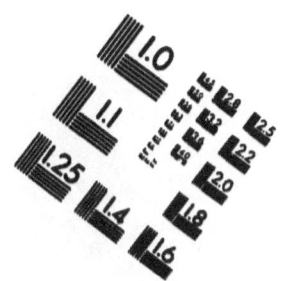

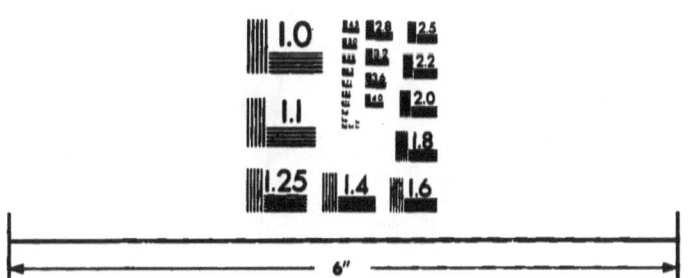

2.8
2.5
3.2
2.2
2.0
1.8
1.0

was sufficient proof, and that an affidavit verifying the accounts was unnecessary. Held also, That neither the notice nor the solicitor's appointment need be under the seal of the company. *Mechanics' Whale Fishing Company* v. *Kirby*, 1 *All.* 223.

2—**Right of surety to recover—Liability of principal.**

A surety who has been damnified, by giving a security for the original debt which was accepted by the creditor in satisfaction thereof, may recover according to his loss from the principal, upon a declaration stating the circumstances specially, though he has not actually paid the money: as, where he had become liable for the principal on a promissory note, and being sued and unable to pay the amount, gave a bond and mortgage, which the creditor accepted in satisfaction of the note. *Trites* v. *Kelly*, *Trin. T.* 1833.

3—The principal is liable for the costs of a suit brought against the surety on his original liability; provided he has not unnecessarily incurred expense in defending the suit. *Ibid.*

4—**Contract under seal—Parol variation.**

B. entered into a contract under seal, to build a house for the plaintiff according to a plan and specification, and the defendant became security for the performance of the contract. The plan of the house was changed in some particulars, by verbal agreement between the plaintiff and B. without the defendant's consent. B. failed to perform the contract in respect to parts of the building in which there had been no alteration. Held, in an action against the surety, That the contract being under seal, he was not discharged at law by the parol variation of it. [See Parker v. Watson, 8 Exch. 404.] *Peters* v. *Bryson*, *Mich. T.* 1866.

5—**Sheriff's bond—Sureties—Defence.**

The sureties in a Sheriff's bond given under 1 Rev. Stat. c. 131, are not liable for a breach of duty committed by the Sheriff after the 31st March in the year for which they became sureties, though the Sheriff is continued in office after that time. *Berton* v. *Tierney*, *Mich. T.* 1864.

6—Where the alleged breach of duty by the Sheriff was the not paying over money levied under an execution, the sureties, in an action against them on their bond, may shew that the money was received by the Sheriff after the 31st March in the year for which they became sureties. *Berton* v. *Tierney*, *Mich. T.* 1864.

7—**Postmaster—Bond to Crown—Relief of sureties.**

One of the conditions of a Bond given to the Crown by a Deputy Postmaster, required him to give three months notice to the Postmaster General of his intention to resign his office, and to pay all sums of money chargeable against him as Postmaster. At the time of his resignation, a Postmaster was a defaulter, and died insolvent, about twenty-one months after. No proceedings were taken against him to enforce payment, though he was applied to several times, and promised payment, and no notice of his indebtedness was given to his sureties till after his death. Held, That his sureties were not entitled to be relieved from the Bond under the 33 Hen. 8, c. 39, s. 79. *The Queen* v. *Hammond and another*, 1 *Han.* 33.

Action against surety—Principal settling demand—Costs not paid by surety—Judgment entered up for nominal damages. See *Blakslee* v. *Nickerson*, 1 *Kerr* 523.

Deputy Treasurer—Term of appointment—Liability. See Deputy Treasurer.

Alteration of position of surety by subsequent agreement. See Surety.

PRIVATE ROAD.

See Highway.

PRIVILEGE FROM ARREST.

See Arrest.

PRIVILEGE OF PARLIAMENT.

See Arrest.

PRIVILEGED COMMUNICATION.

See Defamation 4, 5, 8.

Attorney and Client. See Evidence VIII. 23.

PRIVITY OF ESTATE.

See Covenant.

PRIVY COUNCIL.

Appeal to—Time.

An appeal to the Queen in Council, under

the order of November, 1852, from a judgment of this Court affirming a de cree in equity, may be applied for within fourteen days after the minutes of the decree are settled, though more than fourteen days have elapsed since the judgment was pronounced. *Brookfield* v. *The St. Andrews and Quebec Railway Co.*, 4 *All.* 496.

Judge's order—Leave to appeal.
The order of a Judge made in vacation granting leave to appeal to the Queen in Council, and settling the terms on which the appeal will be granted is final, and cannot be revised or rescinded by the Court (Allen J., *dubitante.*) *Domville* v. *Kevan*, 2 *Han.* 175.

Orders in Council.
See 4 All. page 497, being orders passed 27th November 1852, at the Court at Windsor, and referred to in above case of Brookfield *v.* the St. Andrews and Quebec Railway Co., and appended to said case.

PROBATE (COURT.)

See Executors and Administrators.
" Surrogate Court.

PROCEEDINGS (SETTING ASIDE.)

See Practice VI.

PROCEDENDO.

See Practice VI. 46.

PROCESS.

See Practice IV.

Regular on face, a justification to officer. See Trespass V. 7.

PROHIBITION.

Prohibition to restrain suit.
The Supreme Court will grant a prohibition to restrain the Court of Common Pleas from proceeding in an action brought against the Clerk of the Circuits to recover money paid to him as a fine imposed on the plaintiff by a Judge at *Nisi Prius* for a contempt committed in the *Nisi Prius Court*. *Ex parte Allen*, 2 *All.* 424.

PROMISSORY NOTES.

See Bills and Notes.

PROPERTY.

See Delivery.

Vesting of—Hired men—Claim. See Timber 2.

PROTEST.

See Bills and Notes—Insurance.

PUBLIC AGENTS.

See Principal and Agent.

PUBLIC OFFICERS.

Liability—Commissioners of sewers.
Commissioners of sewers are not liable to actions for work and labor upon the completion of the work, at the suit of persons employed by such commissioners in their public capacity, unless they personally bind themselves to make payment. *Peck* v. *Robinson*, 2 *Kerr* 687.

Prima facie persons doing work under contracts with commissioners of sewers, are presumed to look to the mode of payment provided by the Act of Assembly 10 and 11 Geo. 4, c. 29. *Ibid.*

Quære, Whether commissioners of sewers would be liable to an action if they neglected to make the assessment required by the Act? *Ibid.*

Quære, Whether a supervisor of great roads is personally liable upon contracts made in that capacity? See *Wheeler* v. *Hayward*, 1 *Kerr* 657.

Enforcing contract—With public officers. See Mandamus 5.

Trying right to exercise office. See Quo Warranto.

Clerk of House of Assembly—Liability for contract. See Assumpsit III. 43.

PUIS DARREIN CONTINUANCE.

See Pleading II. 31, 32—Practice VI. 40, 40 *a*.

PURCHASE.

Agreement to purchase land. See Tenant at Will.

For sale and conveyance. See Tenant for Years.

PURCHASER.

See Vendor and Purchaser.
" Sheriff's Sale.

Consideration. See Deed.

Of Equity of Redemption by Mortgagee. See Mortgage 17.

QUANTUM MERUIT.

See Assumpsit III. *d*.

QUARTER MASTER.

See Allen.

QUIET ENJOYMENT.

Breach of Covenant for. See Covenant.

QUO WARRANTO.

See Certiorari.

Right to hold office.
When a person elected a City Councillor has entered upon and is exercising the office, a *quo warranto* is the proper mode of trying his right to it. *Ex parte Cameron*, 1 *Han.* 306.

Withholding material facts.
Where a party applying for a *quo warranto*, improperly withheld material facts, which ought to have been stated in his affidavit, the rule was discharged with costs. *Ex parte Gilbert*, *Hil. T.* 1873.

RAILWAY.

Assessing value of land. See Assessment, Mandamus 6 *a*.

Common Carrier. See Carriers.

RAILWAY COMMISSIONERS.

See Damages—Assessment.
" Joint Stock Company.

RAILWAY COMPANY.

Authority to cut down the level of street—Plaintiff's acquiescence.
The Act 33 Vic. c. 39, incorporating the "Carleton Branch Railway Company," authorised them to locate and construct a railroad from deep water in Carleton to the E. & N. American Railway, investing them with all the powers and privileges necessary for the purpose; among others, the right to purchase, take and hold as much land as might be necessary for the location and construction of the railway; provided, that in all cases they should pay for the land etc. taken and used. The 12th section of the Act authorised the company "to run their line of railway through and upon any of the streets, wharves, places, or squares," as also through all unleased lands belonging to the City of St. John. In making the railway, a contractor under the company, cut down a street in Carleton, on which the plaintiff's house fronted, to a depth of about twelve feet, rendering the approach to his house difficult, and materially injuring the value of his property. The plaintiff had been employed as a laborer by the contractor, and worked on a part of the street so cut down. Held, 1st. That the 12th section of the Act gave the Company no authority to cut down, or alter, the level of the street; 2nd. That the plaintiff, by having worked on the street, was not estopped from maintaining an action for the injury to his property,—the work having been done by the defendants under a claim of right, and not in consequence of any consent or authority given by the plaintiff. *Wood v. The Carleton Branch Railway Company*, *Hil. T.* 1873.

Killing cattle—Liability. See Negligence 4.

RATE.

See Assessment.

RATE PAYER.

See Bastardy—Vote.

RATIFICATION.

See Crown Grant I. 18.
" Principal and Agent.
" Warrant of Attorney.

READINESS AND WILLINGNESS.

Averment—Proof. See Pleading I. 27.

REAL ESTATE.

See Heir at Law.

Execution—Testator. See Execution IV. 18.

REASONABLE AND PROBABLE CAUSE.

See Malicious Prosecution.
" Trespass V. 10.
" Criminal Law I. 8.

REASONABLE TIME.

Dissent—Partition. See Partition.

REBUTTING EVIDENCE.

See Evidence.

RECEIPT.

Application to set aside. See Practice VI. 40.

Written receipt signed by mortgagee is not admissible in evidence to prove payment of rent to him as against the mortgagor. *Joplin* v. *Johnston*, 2 *Kerr* 541.

Attorney proceeding in action after receipt given — Contesting facts.
Where a motion was made to set aside the verdict and proceedings for fraud and irregularity, and requiring the plaintiff's attorney to answer, on the grounds that the action had been proceeded in and the verdict obtained after the plaintiff and defendant had settled, and that the plaintiff had given a receipt in full, and had notified his attorney to discontinue the action; and the motion was resisted by affidavits, controverting those in support of the motion, and among other things stating that the costs remained unpaid, as also £14 19s. of the debt, that the defendant had procured the receipt by fraud in making the plaintiff intoxicated, as appeared by two witnesses; and upon these grounds the attorney of the plaintiff, by his directions, had notified the defendant's attorney he would proceed to trial. Held, That there was no misconduct imputable to the plaintiff's attorney in proceeding in the action, as the plaintiff had a right to contest the disputed facts before a jury. *Moran* v. *Gallagher*, 1 *All*. 24.

RECITAL.

See Registry—Crown Grant.

RECORD.

See Pleading II. 23.

Courts of. See Justice of the Peace I.

Debt of record — Foreign judgment not. See Judgment.

Evidence. See Evidence II. 18.

Variance—Amendment. See Amendment III.

Rule of Court not a record. See Pleading II. 15.

Entitling. See Practice XIV. 12.

Highway—Record of—Necessary statement. See Highway 18, 31.

RECOGNIZANCE.

See Bastardy.

Irregular to make and file a recognizance roll until special bail piece be on file to warrant it. *O'Connor* v. *Mott*, 2 *Kerr* 509.

Recognizance for prosecution of election petition not a record.
A recognizance entered into for the prosecution of an election petition before the House of Assembly, under the Rev. Stat. c. 98, and certified to the Supreme Court by the Speaker as forfeited, is not a record; and in *scire facias* on such a recognizance with an averment *prout patet per recordum*, to which the defendant pleaded *nul tiel record*, the production of the recognizance so certified from the files of the Court does not prove the issue. *The Queen* v. *Sparrow et al.*, 1 *Han*. 239.

RECOGNIZANCE ESTREAT.

Relief. See Supreme Court.

Application for relief—Excuse.
Application to be relieved from a recognizance to appear and give evidence on a prosecution for felony refused—the only excuse for non-attendance being, that the party was in ill health, and expected to be sent for by the Crown officer. *Reg.* v. *Gerow*, *Mich. T.* 1863.

RECTOR.

See Church of England.
" Trespass I. 8.

REFEREES.

Settlement of accounts by—Agents. See Principal and Agent 13.

REFERENCE.

See Arbitration.

REFUSAL TO ADMINISTER OATH.

See Mandamus 13.

REGISTRY.

Non-registry of Nova Scotia grant. See Crown Grant I. 16.

Of deed—Avoidance of lease. See Landlord and Tenant VI. 1.

Unregistered ship. See Shipping Law 6.

Mortgagee in fee.
Estate cannot pass without enrolment or registry. See *Doe d. Burnham* v. *Watts*, 2 *Kerr* 441.

Registry and acknowledgment without delivery. See Evidence II 9.

Certificate of acknowledgment without registry. See Evidence II. 11.

Of mortgage, not notice of incumbrance to subsequent purchaser. See *Doe v. Power*, 1 *All.* 271.

Unregistered conveyance, operating as release. See Deed I. 20.

Memorial of judgment registered evidence of an incumbrance on land. *Scott* v. *Garnett*, 2 *All.* 624.

Registry of deed without previous proof—Operation. See Deed I. 22.

Deeds on same sheet—Registry book admitted in evidence. See Deed I. 23.

Registry of deed before lease—Operation. See Deed V. 12.

Registry Book best evidence of registry. See Deed V. 13.

Subpœna to prove registry. See General Rules 126.

Registry under Medical Act. See Pleading I. 56.

REGISTERED OWNER.

Liability. See Assumpsit III. 45.

REGISTRAR.

See Judicial Notice.

RELATION.

1—Conveyance—Registry—Delivery of deed.
A conveyance of land, registered under the Act 26 Geo. 3, c. 3, conveys the estate, by relation, from the time of the delivery of the deed, unless in the mean time another conveyance has obtained priority. *Doe dem. Bridges* v. *Quint*, *East. T.* 1828.

2—Judgment—Signing—Intermediate Conveyance.
The title conveyed by a Sheriff's deed, to land sold under an execution issued upon a judgment recovered in an action brought on a former judgment in the same Court, does not relate back to the time of signing the first judgment, so as to defeat a conveyance made by the judgment debtor between the times of signing the first and second judgments. *Doe d. Peabody* v. *McKnight*, *Ber.* 376.

3—Registry before proof.
A conveyance of land, appearing by the certificate indorsed, to have been registered before it was proved by the subscribing witness, does not operate as a registered deed by relation from the time of the proof. *Doe dem. Blair* v. *Rideout*, 3 *All.* 502.

4—Grantor and grantee—Delivery of deed—Third party.
As between the grantor and grantee, the registry of the deed transfers the title and possession by relation from the delivery of the deed; but it will not affect the intermediate rights of third parties, not privy to the deed. *Patterson* v. *Tingley*, *Trin. T.* 1863.

5—Possession—Subsequent Registry.
In trespass *qu. cl. fregit*, for cutting grass on the 31st July, the plaintiff proved possession only; the defendant justified as owner of the land, under a deed dated the 15th July, but not registered till the 1st August. Held, That as against the plaintiff, the defendant had not title by relation from the date of the deed. *Ibid.*

6—Execution—Memorial—Registry.
A judgment was recovered against C. and a memorial thereof registered in January 1863; in April 1863, land was conveyed to C., which he conveyed to the defendant on the same day; in 1865, an execution was issued on the judgment against C., under which the land so conveyed to him, was levied on and sold by the Sheriff. Held, That the execution had relation back to the registry of the memorial, and defeated the conveyance to the defendant. *Doe dem. Solomon* v. *Graham*. *Doe dem. Kerr* v. *Jamieson*, *Trin. T.* 1871.

Trespass—Possession — Subsequent deed. See Trespass II. 15.

RELEASE.

Fraud—Setting aside. See Practice VI. 40.

Action by executor—Release by parties beneficially interested—Discharge of debtor. See Discharge 1.

Pleading Puis Darrein Continuance—Setting aside. See Practice VI. 40, 40 *a*.

Release pleaded—Application to set aside plea and release. See Practice VI. 40.

Release by husband. See Husband and Wife.

Release by partner. See New Trial III. 34.

Authority of partner. See Partnership 8.

Latent ambiguity—Evidence—Intention.
In an action on a promissory note for $85, given by the defendant to plaintiff's testator, the defendant relied on a release given to him by the testator, of the same date as the note, and one of the considerations mentioned in the release was a sum of $85. The note had been given for money in the defendant's hands belonging to the testator, after allowing defendant a certain sum for collecting. Held, That the circumstances created a latent ambiguity in the release, and that evidence was therefore admissible to shew whether the note was intended to be released or not. *Caldwell* v. *Keith*, *Trin. T.* 1863.

REMANET.

See Judgment as in Case of Non-suit I. 2, 4, 5.

A cause can only be made a remanet by order of the Judge at *Nisi Prius*. *Shepherd* v. *Hallet*, 1 *Han.* 43.

REMAINDER.

See Deed I. 25. Will 11.
" Half Blood.

Real estate in remainder may be taken in execution. See *Doe* v. *Hazen*, 3 *All.* 87.

Trust—Termination of—Testator's children.
A testator after directing that so much of his estate as was necessary, should be sold for payment of his debts, devised all the residue of his estate to his executors, in trust to hold for the separate use and benefit of his wife during her life or widowhood, and to pay her the income thereof; and after her death or marriage, then to be divided among the testator's children. Held, That the purposes of the trust did not require the estate of the executors to extend beyond the life of the widow; that at her death their estate terminated, and the testator's children took the estate in remainder. *Doe* v. *Driscoll*, 4 *All.* 176.

REMAINDERMAN.

The tenant of a devisee for life may, after the death of such devisee, be ousted by the remainderman without any notice to quit. *Doe d. Fields* v. *McKay*, 2 *Kerr* 435.

Setting up adverse possession against. See Ejectment I. 3.

REMEDY.

See Action at Law.

Suspension of—Taking security. See Judgment I. 2.

RENDER.

See Bail—Exoneretur.

RENEWAL.

See Covenant 8—Landlord and Tenant I. 3.

RENT.

See Landlord and Tenant.

REPAIRS OF VESSEL.

Detention—Deviation. See Insurance 34.

Liability for. See Shipping Law.

REPLEADER.

See Error (Writ of).

REPLEVIN.

1—Action—Owner of land—Timber cut.
Replevin lies by the owner of land, for timber cut upon, and taken away from it; and the proceedings will not be set aside, although the party taking the timber claims title to the land on which it was cut; and, *Semble*, That replevin can be maintained wherever trespass will lie for taking chattels. *Lyons* v. *Goram*, *Mich. T.* 1831.

2—Actual or constructive taker.
If replevin is brought against one, who is not actually or constructively the *taker* of the goods, the writ will be set aside. (But see 1 Rev. Stat. c. 126, s. 9.) *Groves* v. *Griffith*, *Trin. T.* 1833.

3—Possession of goods.
The goods mentioned in a writ of replevin cannot be taken by the Sheriff unless they are in the possession of the defendant named in the writ. *Wiggins* v. *Garrison*, *Ber.* 17.

4—Issues—Separate findings—Postea.
In replevin, where some of the issues are found for the plaintiff, and others for the defendant, each party is entitled to the costs of the issues found in his favor. The *postea* was ordered to be given to

the plaintiff for a certain time to enter the judgment; and in case of his neglecting to do so, then to the defendants for the like purpose. *Dickenson* v. *Ketchum*, *Ber.* 63.

5—**Outstanding mortgage—Answer.**
Though in replevin both parties are actors, the plaintiff is not prevented by 1 Rev. Stat. c. 112, s. 17, from setting up an outstanding mortgage given by the person under whom the defendant claims, in answer to a plea of property in the land on which the grass replevied was cut. *Baxter* v. *Johnston*, *Trin. T.* 1862.

6—**Damages—Counsel fees.**
The plaintiff in replevin cannot recover as part of his damages an amount paid to counsel attending on the execution of a writ *de proprietate probandu*, issued on a claim put in by the defendant: the payment of counsel fees being deemed voluntary. *Davis* v. *Cushing*, *Mich. T.* 1863.

7—**Pleading—Waiver.**
Defendant in replevin pleaded *non cepit*, and gave notice that the goods were the property of A., no objection was made that this defence was not pleaded, as required by the Act 13 Vic. c. 32, and both parties went into evidence of property. On verdict for the defendant—Held, That the plaintiff had a right to waive the pleading of the defence; and not having taken the objection at the trial, the Court refused to set aside the verdict. *Wilbur* v. *Trites*, *Mich. T.* 1863.

8—**Issue of writ de proprietate probanda—Regularity.**
A writ of replevin was returned by the Sheriff to the plaintiff's attorney with a claim of property: the attorney's clerk, in his absence, issued a writ *de proprietate probanda*. The attorney gave notice to the Sheriff that this writ was issued without his authority, and that he should not proceed on it, but the Sheriff, notwithstanding, held the inquisition. Held, on an application to set aside the inquisition, that the writ *de proprietate probanda* was rightly issued, and if the plaintiff was not prepared for the trial of the inquisition, he should have applied to the Sheriff to postpone it. *Jones* v. *Cate*, *Mich. T.* 1863.

9—**Pleading—Special Property.**
In replevin for a pair of oxen, defendant pleaded—1st. Property in himself; 2nd. Property in A. Plaintiff replied that the oxen we : not the property of A., but of himself. Before the taking, the plaintiff had mortgaged the oxen to A., who agreed that he should keep possession of them till the mortgage was due. Held, That the special property of the plaintiff was sufficient to maintain replevin; and that the replication did not necessarily mean that the plaintiff had the absolute property. *Elston* v. *Vance*, *Mich. T.* 1863.

10—In replevin for a vessel, defendant pleaded—1st. Property in himself; 2nd. Property in D.; 3rd. Property in B. The defendant and D. each swore that he was not the owner of the vessel. D. endeavored to shew that it was the defendant's property; and the defendant swore that it belonged to B., who was not called as a witness. The Judge directed the jury that the plaintiff was entitled to recover, unless the defendant had satisfied them that the property was in one of the persons named in the pleas. The jury having found for the plaintiff, the Court refused a new trial, though the plaintiff had no title. *Clarke* v. *Casey*, *Mich. T.* 1864.

11—Defendant in replevin pleaded property in himself. He had assigned all his property to trustees for the benefit of his creditors, but kept possession of the goods in question, and the trustees did not know of their existence. Held, That the general property in the goods passed to the trustees; and, as there was no plea of property in them, the plaintiff was entitled to recover. *McIntosh* v. *Hastings*, *Hil. T.* 1865.

12—**Pleading—Proof.**
In replevin, the defendant pleaded property in himself, and P., (without any plea of *non cepit.*) The property was owned by the plaintiff and P. as tenants in common, and the defendant held under P. Held, That the plea was not proved; that, to entitle the defendant to a verdict, it must be shewn that there was no property in the plaintiff. *Godard* v. *Tuck*, *Hil. T.* 1865.

13—**Damages.**
Substantial damages may be recovered in replevin, though no special damages is alleged in the declaration. Per N. Parker, J., That special damage must be alleged. *Firth* v. *Fitzpatrick*, *Hil. T.* 1866.

14—Pleading—Issue.
Lumber, seized as having been cut without license, was replevied out of the possession of the seizing officer within fourteen days: he appeared to the action, and pleaded—1. Property in the Crown; 2nd. That the lumber was lawfully in his possession by the seizure. Held, That he could not, on the trial of the issues, raise the question whether replevin would lie for lumber so seized; and that unless the pleas were proved, the plaintiff must recover. *DesBrisay* v. *Little*, *Hil. T.* 1866.

If replevin is improperly used, an application should be made to set aside the writ. *Ibid.*

15—Proceedings—Trespasser ab initio.
Defendant, an officer appointed by the Canadian Government for the protection of the fisheries, seized a vessel belonging to the plaintiff in the harbor of Gaspe, in the Province of Quebec, on the 18th August, for an alleged breach of the Act relating to fishing by foreign vessels, (31 Vic. c. 61) and on the 22nd August brought the vessel to the port of Shediac, in the Province of New Brunswick, but did not deliver her to the Collector of Customs there. The Act directed, that vessels seized, should be "forthwith delivered to the Collector, or other principal officer of the Customs at the port nearest the place where seized." There was a Collector of Customs at Gaspe, and at several other ports nearer than Shediac. No proceedings having been taken towards the condemnation of the vessel, the plaintiff replevied her on the 5th September. Held, per Ritchie, C. J., Allen and Weldon, J. J., That by taking the vessel to Shediac, and retaining her there in his own possession, the defendant became a trespasser *ab initio*, and that replevin would lie. Per Fisher and Wetmore, J. J., That by the seizure, the vessel was in the custody of the law, and therefore replevin would not lie. *McGowan* v. *Betts*, *East. T.* 1871.

16—Setting aside writ—Summary motion.
The Court will not set aside a writ of replevin, on a summary motion unless in a clear case. Where there was some proof of property and possession in the plaintiff, and to connect the defendant with the taking, the Court refused to interfere. *Cliff* v. *Gunter*, 2 *Kerr* 493.

17—Termination of suit—Assignment of bond.
Where on a writ *de proprietate probanda*, the finding is for the defendant, the replevin suit is terminated, and the replevin bond cannot be assigned to the defendant. *Pollok* v. *Gardner*, 2 *Kerr* 655.

18—Plea—Non cepit.
In replevin on the plea of *non cepit* proof that the defendant had the goods at the place alleged is sufficient to entitle the plaintiff to recover. *McLeod* v. *McMillan*, 3 *Kerr* 64.

19—Pleading—Mistake—Leave to withdraw plea.
A defendant in replevin, claiming the goods under a sale and delivery from A. an alleged partner of the plaintiff, pleaded by mistake, that at the time of the taking, the plaintiff had no property in the goods except jointly with A.; leave was given to withdraw the plea and plead property in himself, on payment of the costs occasioned by his mistake: the Court rejecting a motion made on behalf of the plaintiff for leave to discontinue the replevin suit without payment of costs, and to order the replevin bond to be cancelled. *Rourke* v. *Keogh*, 1 *All.* 370.

20—Plaintiff's right—Property—Mixture.
The plaintiff being the licensee of Crown land, agreed to allow A. to cut logs thereon to be manufactured into deals, and to furnish him supplies to carry on his lumbering, which were to be paid for in deals of a specified quality, delivered to the plaintiff at Richibucto. Held, (Street, J. *dissentiente*,) That no property in the deals when cut, vested in A. until it was ascertained what portion of them came within the description the plaintiff was to retain, and therefore that the plaintiff might replevy the whole of the deals from the defendant, to whom A. had delivered them before they arrived at Richibucto. Held also, That the defendant having mixed with these deals others belonging to himself, which he refused to point out and which could not otherwise be distinguished, did not deprive the plaintiff of his right to replevy. *DesBrisay* v. *Mooney*, 2 *All.* 53.

Held, per Street, J., That under the agreement, the property in the lumber was in A. until delivered to the plaintiff, and that the Judge ought so to have directed the jury; and that the plaintiff was not entitled under the circumstances to replevy the lumber from the defendant. *DesBrisay* v. *Mooney*, 2 *All.* 53.

21—Breach of bond—Claim of goods—Name.

If a defendant in replevin claims property in part of the goods replevied, and the property is found in him on an inquisition under a writ *de proprietate probanda*, this constitutes a breach of the replevin bond, and entitles the defendant to an assignment of it, in order to recover the costs of the proceeding. *Berry* v. *Mitchell*, 2 *All.* 380.

Quære, as to the disposition by the Sheriff of the goods not claimed by the defendant. *Ibid.*

Property replevied was claimed by the defendant in the name of "Barry" instead of "Berry;" the property was found to be in the claimant, and the bond was assigned to him by his proper name. Held, That the mistake was immaterial. *Ibid.*

22—Pleading—Evidence under plea non cepit.

Whatever might formerly have been pleaded to an avowry, may, since the Rev. Stat. c. 126, be given in evidence at the trial in answer to the defence under the plea of *non cepit*. *Myers* v. *Smith*, 4 *All.* 207.

The defendant in replevin is entitled to damages on a verdict in his favor on the plea of *non cepit*, if he gives such evidence as would have supported an avowry under the former law. *Ibid.*

23—Onus probandi.

When a defendant in replevin pleads property in himself or a third person, and issue is taken thereon, the *onus* of proving property is on the defendant, and if he fails in doing so, the plaintiff is entitled to recover. *Graham* v. *Wetmore*, 4 *All.* 373.

24—Defendant in replevin pleaded property in M., and a seizure as Sheriff under execution against M. Replication—property in the plaintiff. On the trial the defendant failed to prove property in M., and a verdict was given for the plaintiff. Held, That the defendant was bound to prove the whole plea, and was not entitled to judgment *non obstante veredicto*, on the ground that the replication had admitted that the property was in custody of the law and therefore not repleviable. *Graham* v. *Wetmore*, 4 *All.* 377.

Crown cannot maintain replevin under Act 13 Vic. c. 53. See *Reg.* v. *McMahon*, 3 *All.* 125.

25—Damages—Jury not bound to give.

If in an action of replevin, the jury find for the defendant, on the plea of property, they are not bound to give him damages, under 1 Rev. Stat. c. 126, s. 16. *Fearon* v. *Murray*, *Hil. T.* 1861.

26—The Jury not finding on several issues.

It is no ground for a new trial in replevin, that the jury have not distinctly found on the several issues,—it being understood that the substantial question was, to whom the property in dispute belonged; and that the Court might enter the verdict on the several issues, accordingly. *Ibid.*

27—Goods not replevied—Declaration—Evidence—Damages.

A declaration in replevin charged defendant with taking and detaining 500 pieces of deals, 20 futtocks, and 20 ship-knees, on the 1st September 1867. Plea—as to all except 314 pieces of the deals—*non cepit*; and as to them—property in defendant. Under the writ of replevin, the Sheriff took a railway car load of deals, containing 314 pieces. The plaintiff claimed 84 pieces as having been taken from him by the defendant, but only gave evidence of 18 pieces in the load, as being his property. No futtocks or knees were found or replevied—they having been taken by the defendant in 1865. It was doubtful, under the evidence, whether the Sheriff had delivered to the plaintiff the 84 pieces of deals, or only 18 pieces; and also, what had become of the remainder of the load. Verdict for the plaintiff for the value of the futtocks and knees; and for the defendant, on the plea of property, for the value of the load of deals. Held—1st. That the futtocks and knees, not having been replevied, ought not to have been included in the declaration, and that the plaintiff could not recover for them; 2nd. That the defendant had a right to shew at the trial, that the futtocks, etc., had not been replevied; 3rd. That the defendant was only entitled to damages for the value of the deals replevied and delivered by the Sheriff to the plaintiff, and not for the whole load; and that it should have been left to the jury to determine what portion of them was so delivered. *Steeves* v. *Wilson*, *Mich. T.* 1869.

Delivery of Goods—Bill of Lading—Possession—Plea—Replication. See Pleading II. 28.

Pawnee may maintain replevin against pawnor. See Bailee.

Former recovery—Evidence in subsequent action. See Evidence III. 17.

Justice's Court—Removal of proceedings in replevin not by review, but by *certiorari*. See *Bustin* v. *Howell*, 1 *All.* 596.

Cattle impounded—Justice may grant replevin for. See Justice of the Peace II. 11.

Costs. See Costs VI. 101, 102.

Replevin will not lie for liquors seized under a warrant issued by a Justice of the Peace under the prohibitory liquor law 18 Vic. c. 36. *Breeze* v. *Stockford*, 3 *All.* 329.

Judgment as in case of non-suit not grantable in replevin. *McGeehan* v. *Hale*, 3 *All.* 507.

Sheriff—Trial of claim—Sheriff's duty not judicial, and may be performed by Deputy. *Crane* v. *Allison*, 4 *All.* 59.

REPLEVIN BOND.

See Bond I. *C.*

REPRESENTATION.

See Warranty.

RESERVATION.

See Deed—Highway.

RESCINDING CONTRACT.

See Action at Law.

RESIDUARY LEGATEE.

See Will.

RESTITUTION (WRIT OF.)

See Landlord and Tenant VII. 5, 6.

RETAINER.

See Attorney.

RETURN (WRITS—EXECUTIONS.)

See Execution—Practice.
" General Rules 115.

REVENUE.

See Custom House.
" Criminal Law II. 10.

REVENUE ACT.

See Criminal Law I. 9.

Under the Provincial Revenue Act 3 Vic. c. 1, rum not being of the proof of twenty-six by the bubble is not liable to the specific duty thereby imposed; the words of the Act being unambiguous, the known intent of the Legislature to impose the duty cannot be regarded. *Hammond* v. *Robinson*, 2 *Kerr* 295.

By the Act 11 Vic. c. 67, "no spirits shall be imported into the Province in casks of less size than to contain one hundred gallons, or in other than decked vessels of not less than thirty tons register; and all spirits imported contrary to the provisions of the Act, or that may be found on board any vessel of less than thirty tons register, in casks of less size than to contain one hundred gallons, within the limits of any port of entry in the Province, shall be seized and forfeited," etc. Held, That spirits in casks less than one hundred gallons were liable to forfeiture, though the vessel in which they were imported was over thirty tons register. *Attorney General* v. 20 *Casks Spirits*, 2 *All.* 457.

REVENUE OFFICER.

See Criminal Law I. 8.

REVENUE LAWS.

A vessel fraudulently landing goods by means of boats, shall be legally intended to have come into port under the revenue laws. Statutes relating to the revenue are not to be construed as Penal Acts in proceedings against persons for smuggling goods into the Province. *Attorney General* v. *Patterson*, *C. Ms.* 16.

REVERSIONARY INTEREST.

Plaintiff leased cattle to T. for ten years, at the end of which time T. was to give up the cattle, or others in their stead, in as good condition as at the date of the lease. Held, That the plaintiff had no absolute reversionary interest in the cattle, and could not maintain an action on the case against the Sheriff for selling them under an execution against T. during the term. *Good* v. *Winslow*, 4 *All.* 241.

REVESTING PROPERTY.

See Shipping Law 6.

REVIEW.

See Justice of the Peace II.

Replevin.

The proceedings in replevin before a Justice of the Peace under the Act 1 Wm. 4, c. 9, cannot be removed into Supreme Court by an order for review as provided in the Justices' Act 4 Wm. 4, c. 45. The mode of removal is by *certiorari*. The jurisdiction by review cannot be extended to cases not named in the Act 4 Wm. 4, c. 45. *Bastin* v. *Howell*, 1 *All.* 596.

Costs where no jurisdiction. See Costs X., same case.

Party obtaining order for review has the right to begin at the hearing. Same case.

Proceedings by review not applicable to Civil Court of Town of Portland. See Portland (Town of.)

Review of Judge's order. See Practice V. 5 *a*.

Taxation of costs. See Costs.

REVOCATION.

See Executors and Administrators.
" Arbitration.

Of provisions in will. See Contract 14.

RIGHT OF ENTRY.

See Deed I 25—Limitation of Actions

RIGHT OF WAY.

Presumption of—Lost deed. See Evidence VI. 12.

Deed—Construction. See Deed V. 4.

RIGHT TO BEGIN.

Replevin.

Onus of proving property as stated in the pleas is on the defendant and he is bound to begin. *Graham* v. *Wetmore*, 4 *All.* 373.

Proceedings on review from Justices' Court. See Practice XIV. 2.

RIVER.

Highway — Obstructing — Damage. See Action on the Case IV.

Grant bounded by river conveys no title below high water mark. See Crown Grant I. 13.

Wharf built on navigable river. See Action on the Case IV. 3.

Erection of dam—Right to destroy. See Water Course.

ROAD.

See Highway.

ROYAL INSTRUCTIONS.

See Crown Grant III. 2.

RULE FOR BODY.

See Practice VIII. 5.

RULES OF COURT.

See General Rules—Appendix.

Rule of Court not a record. *Watson* v. *Roberts*, 3 *Kerr* 509.

Judge's certificate cannot be made a rule of Court. See Judge IV. 7.

RULES—PRIVY COUNCIL.

See Privy Council.

SAINT JOHN BRIDGE COMPANY.

See Joint Stock Company.

SAINT JOHN (CITY OF).

Under the Charter of the City of Saint John, the fine imposed upon a person carrying on trade within the city without having been admitted a freeman, is recoverable before the Mayor, though the warrant to levy the fine must be under the common seal of the city. *Regina* v. *Small*, 1 *Kerr* 48.

Judgment by default—Particulars—Proof —Practice. See City Court.

Power to make Pilotage Regulations. See Pilotage.

Corporation of Saint John—Limiting power to make bye-laws—No right to do so. See Bye-Law 5.

SALARY.

SALE.

Land—Identity—Evidence.

Defendant, by writing addressed to the plaintiff, stated that he would "take property," and give his notes for a certain sum. Plaintiff wrote on the same paper, that he could not sell "property," but would "re-deed to H." and take notes for a certain sum, specifying the time of payment; to which the defendant agreed. Plaintiff proved that H. had conveyed to him the equity of redemption in a certain property. Held, That this sufficiently identified the property referred to in the agreement; though, if necessary, parol evidence was admissible to shew what property the agreement related to. *Pugsley* v. *Gillespie*, *Mich. T.* 1872.

SATISFACTION.

SCIRE FACIAS.

Every writ of *scire facias* should state the particular circumstances which entitle the party to the remedy sought to be obtained. Any matter which might have been pleaded in the original action cannot be pleaded to an ordinary *scire facias* under the Statute of Westminster. A party can only have judgment prayed for in his *scire facias*, and such judgment will not be available to give him an execution against a joint debtor not brought into Court in the original action, or under the Act of Assembly 26 Geo. 3. s. 24.

Semble, That the pleading to a *scire facias*, under any Act of Assembly, would be governed by the same rules as under the Statute of Westminster. *Johnston* v. *Tibbits*, *Ber.* 355.

SCIENTIFIC WITNESS.

SCHOOLS.

SCHOOL ASSESSMENT.

SCHOOL INSPECTOR.

SCHOOL TEACHER.

Dismissal—Trustees—Inhabitants—Liability.

A licensed school teacher employed by the inhabitants of a school district, with the assent of the trustees, under the provisions of the Parish School Act, (1 Rev. Stat. c. 49) can only be dismissed during his term of engagement, by the trustees; and if the inhabitants exclude him from the school, whereby he is prevented from obtaining the provincial allowance under the Act, they are liable in an action on the case. *Connor* v. *Wiggins*, *Mich. T.* 1861.

If the plaintiff had been guilty of misconduct, but was not legally dismissed by the trustees. *Semble*, That he could only recover nominal damages. *Ibid.*

SCHOOL TRUSTEES.

SEAL.

Solicitor's appointment by Company need not be under seal. See Principal and Surety 1.

Foreign judgment—Seal of Court—Proof. See Judgment III.

Letters of administration need not be under particular seal. See Executors, etc. IV. 2.

License to cut timber—Necessity of seal. See License 5.

Corporate or private seal on acknowledgment of deed in Great Britain. See Deed I. 28.

SEAMAN'S WAGES.

Deviation in voyage — Right to sue — Liability of part owner of vessel for — Jurisdiction of Justice of the Peace. See Shipping Law 9.
" Justice of the Peace II. 3.

SEARCH.

For papers. See Evidence VII. 15, 16, 17.
For witness. " " " 22.

SEARCH WARRANT.

See Justice of the Peace.

SEA WALLS.

Keeping in repair—Liability. See Corporation 23.

SEA WORTHINESS.

See Insurance.

SECONDARY EVIDENCE.

See Evidence VII.

SECOND ACTION.

See Action at Law VIII.
" Former Recovery.

Staying proceedings in.
Proceedings in second action for same cause will be stayed until the costs of the first action are paid, where the plaintiff's conduct has been negligent or vexatious. *Estabrooks* v. *McKenzie*, *C. Ms.* 41.

Staying proceedings until payment of costs of previous action. See Practice VI. 43. Ejectment IV. 5.

SECOND APPLICATION.

Certiorari—Amended Affidavits. See Certiorari III. 13.

Mandamus. See Practice V. 17.

SECURITY.

See principal and surety—Satisfaction—Suspension—Suspension of remedy by taking. See Judgment I. 2.

SECURITY FOR COSTS.

See Costs.

SEDUCTION.

An action cannot be maintained by a father, for the seduction of his daughter while she is hired by the month in the service of another person; though the father received her wages, and was obliged to maintain her in consequence of her pregnancy. (Ritchie, J., *hesitante.*) *Simpson* v. *Reed*, 4 *All.* 52.

SERVICE OF PAPERS.

See Practice IV.

SEPARATE PROPERTY.

See Husband and Wife.

SET-OFF.

Reduction—Payment or set-off. See Costs I. 8.

1—Agreement to set-off—Judgment assigned.
A party taking an assignment of a judgment after notice that the assignor had agreed with the defendant to set-off the amount against a judgment recovered by the defendant against the assignor, is bound by that agreement; and cannot, by issuing execution upon the judgment assigned to him, defeat the defendant's right of set-off. *Coombes* v. *Hatheway*, 3 *Kerr* 632.

2—Right of set-off—Admissibility—Administrator.
In assumpsit upon promises to an intestate, a note of hand made by him, and after his death endorsed to the defendant, cannot be pleaded as a set-off to an action by the administrator. *Curry and Orr, Administrators*, v. *Hibbard*, *Ber.* 183.

3—Penalty—Arbitration bond.
In an action of debt for the penalty of an arbitration bond, in which the plaintiff assigns as the only breach the non-payment of a certain liquidated sum awarded by the arbitrators to be paid to him by the defendant, a set-off may be pleaded; and such set-off is pleadable to the sum so awarded, and not to the

penalty of the bond. *Shaw* v. *Wilson et al.*, *Ber.* 390.

4—In assumpsit for supplies and advances; the defendant, in order to meet the amount proved by the plaintiffs and to claim a balance, gave in evidence a quantity of logs delivered by the defendant in 1846, to B. & Co., with the assent of the plaintiffs, to pay a debt due from the plaintiffs, to B. & Co.; in reply the plaintiffs showed an agreement between the defendant and B. & Co., stipulating that the logs were delivered to B. & Co. by defendant, B. & Co. to give the defendant 20s. per thousand, the defendant to pay the plaintiffs through B. & Co. any amount justly due by defendant to plaintiffs, and stumpage to B. & Co., and any balance due after deducting the amount of such account and stumpage, B. & Co. were to pay defendant. The learned Judge told the jury that the defendant was entitled to be allowed for the logs in this action to the extent of paying the plaintiffs' account, but not to claim a balance in the way of set-off. Held, That the direction was right. *Wigan et al.* v. *Nixon*, 1 *All.* 97.

5—A note for the payment of a certain sum in specific articles, becomes a money debt after the time for delivering the articles has elapsed; and a set-off is admissible in an action upon it, under the Act 4 Vic. c. 4. *Steeves* v. *Hopper*, 1 *All.* 394.

6—Judgment—Commencement of suit.

A judgment recovered by the defendant against the plaintiff after the commencement of the plaintiff's suit, cannot be pleaded as a set-off, even though the verdict on which the judgment is founded was given before the commencement of such suit. *Hammond* v. *Mott*, 3 *All.* 426.

The defendant's original cause of action being merged in the judgment, the Nisi Prius record in the defendant's suit is not evidence of the plaintiff's indebtedness before the commencement of his suit. *Ibid.*

7—Judgment—Execution issued.

It is too late to set off one Judgment against another, after an execution issued upon one of them has been satisfied. *Bradley* v. *Hopley*, *C. Ms.* 147.

8—Judgment not actually signed—Lien.

Defendant had recovered a judgment against the plaintiff in replevin, and issued execution, but nothing w... realized on it; the plaintiff afterwards obtained a verdict against the defendant in assumpsit, and was entitled to sign judgment. Held—1st. That the defendant had a right to set-off his judgment against the damages recovered by the plaintiff, though the plaintiff's judgment was not actually signed. 2nd. That the defendant was not precluded from applying to set-off his judgment, by having pleaded it as a set-off in the action of assumpsit;— his judgment not having been signed at the time the action of assumpsit was commenced, and therefore, not being the subject of set-off. 3rd. That, though the defendant's rule did not, in terms, ask to have his judgment set-off subject to the lien of the plaintiff's attorney for costs, it was in the power of the Court to grant the application subject to such lien. *Abell* v. *Light*, *Trin. T.* 1867.

9—Merger of note in judgment before trial.

Assumpsit with notice of set-off of a promissory note made by the plaintiff and endorsed to the defendant. At the time notice of set-off was given, an action was pending on the note, and before the trial of this action judgment was obtained against the plaintiff on the note; but the judgment was unsatisfied. Held, That the note was merged in the judgment and could not be given in evidence under the notice of set-off. *Atkinson* v. *Keith*, *East. T.* 1862.

The pendency of a suit, or even a verdict does not change the nature of a debt, but a judgment does. *Ibid.*

10—Not endorsed—Time.

A plea of set-off stated—"that before and at the time of exhibiting the bill"—the plaintiff was indebted to the defendant, etc. The declaration was entitled generally of Easter Term, which commenced on the 5th May. Held, That a promissory note made by the plaintiff which was endorsed to the defendant on the same 5th May could not be given in evidence under this plea. *Dingee* v. *Stickney*, *Mich. T.* 1830.

11—Notice—What may be shewn under.

In assumpsit, the defendant may shew, under a notice of set-off for work and labor, and on account stated, that he did work for the plaintiff under a contract under seal; that he did extra work, and that after the completion of the work, he settled with the plaintiff; that mutual accounts were stated between them, and that a balance was found to be due to defendant. *Holmes* v. *Billings*, *Mich. T.* 1861.

12—Set-off—Prima facie evidence of payment, when?

If a defendant gives a notice and particulars of set-off, which are principally made up of goods furnished the plaintiff, it shews *prima facie* that it was not intended as a payment, and the plaintiff is entitled to costs, though the verdict is under £5. *White* v. *Dawson*, 2 *All.* 51.

13—Judgment subject to attorney's lien.

Where the Court allows one judgment to be set off against another, it must be subject to the attorney's lien generally, and not merely to the extent of the taxed costs in the particular suit. *Rogers* v. *Ledden*, 2 *Kerr* 59.

14—Judgment in Inferior Court—Beneficial interest.

Semble, The Court will allow a judgment of the Inferior Court of Common Pleas to be set off against a judgment obtained in this Court; although the action in the Common Pleas may have been brought in the name of another person; the defendant in this Court having the sole beneficial interest therein. *Ibid.*

Corporation—Rent. See Corporation 16.

No appropriation towards payment. See Bills and Notes V. 17.

Defendant cannot prove his set-off in plaintiff's case—Otherwise with payment. See Evidence VIII. 7.

No notice of set-off. See Assumpsit III. 50.

Set-off, after offer to suffer judgment by default—Costs. See Judgment II. 6.

SEVERAL COUNTS.

See Practice I. 4.—Pleading.

SEVERAL ISSUES.

See Costs 74, 101.

Postea on. See Replevin 4.

SHARES.

Assessment on—Note for, may be given. See Bills and Notes II. 9.

SHERIFF.

1—Appointment—Continuance in office.

The plaintiff was appointed Sheriff of W. in May 1849, and received a commission giving him the office until the first Tuesday in April then next, "and from that time till another fit person should be appointed and sworn into said office." Upon his appointment he appointed H. his deputy, taking a bond with sureties to indemnify him against any misconduct of H. during the time he might continue such deputy. The plaintiff was continued in office till March 1856, his appointment being notified annually in the *Royal Gazette* and new bonds given, as required by the Act 6 Wm. 4, c. 1, but no new commission was issued to him. The appointment of H. as deputy was notified in the *Gazette* annually, till January 1856, when he was dismissed for misconduct. Held, That the plaintiff's tenure of office did not expire in April 1850, but that he continued to hold under the commission, notwithstanding the annual notification in the *Gazette*; that the deputation to H., not being limited by his bond to any particular time, also continued till his dismissal; and that his sureties were also liable. *Botsford* v. *Henderson*, 4 *All.* 516.

2—Trial of right of property—Not judicial duty—Deputy.

The duty of the Sheriff on the trial of a claim under a writ *de proprietate probanda*, is a judicial duty, and may therefore be performed by the Deputy Sheriff. The Sheriff may conduct two inquiries at the same time by his deputies. *Crane* v. *Adams*, 4 *All.* 59.

3—Levy—Two executions—Poundage.

Where the Sheriff levies under two executions, but the sale does not produce enough to satisfy both, he is only entitled to poundage on the second execution according to the amount applicable to it after satisfying the first. *Wetmore* v. *DesBrisay*, 4 *All.* 190.

4—Execution creditor purchasing goods.

Where an execution creditor purchases goods at Sheriff's sale, with the knowledge of the Sheriff that the purchase is made in order to satisfy his execution, and the goods are delivered to him by the Sheriff without any demand of payment, the Sheriff cannot recover from him the price of the goods. *Wetmore* v. *DesBrisay*, 4 *All.* 199.

5—Indorsement on writ—Evidence—Costs.

Quære, Whether the indorsement on a writ by the Sheriff of his fees for the service of it, is not conclusive of the amount in the taxation of costs. *Atkinson* v. *McAuley*, 4 *All.* 265.

6—Succeeding Sheriff—Rule.

A *fi. fa.* was put into a Sheriff's hands, under which he levied on real estate, which was sold in April 1859. The Sheriff went out of office a few days before the sale. A rule calling upon him to hand over the *fi. fa.* to the present Sheriff, moved more than six months after his going out of office, was refused *Levy* v. *Lawson*, 4 *All.* 501.

7—Poundage—Right to exact.

The defendant being in gaol on a *ca. sa.* offered bail for the limits to the Sheriff, who refused to take such bail unless the defendant paid or secured, in addition to the usual gaol fees and charges for the limit bond, a certain sum for poundage on the demand for which the defendant was in custody, whereupon one of the bail gave his promissory note to the Sheriff for his poundage. Held, That the Sheriff had no right to exact such a note for poundage, or to claim any poundage on the execution under such circumstances. *Roberts* v. *Watson*, 3 *Kerr* 414.

7 *a*—Two executions for £6000 each, against the same defendant,—one at the suit of the present defendant individually, —the other, at his suit as executor of S. —were delivered to the Sheriff on the same day, with directions that the first-named execution was to be first satisfied. The Sheriff levied under the executions and was afterwards directed by the attorney to abandon the levies, and return the executions *nulla bona;* which he did, indorsing thereon his fees for poundage and expenses. In an action by the Sheriff to recover poundage on £3000, as the amount of a compromise of the second execution made by the judgment creditor with his debtor, there was no distinct evidence of such a compromise; but, on the Sheriff applying for payment of his fees, the defendant (the judgment creditor) stated that he was about making an arrangement with the debtor, and as soon as it was done, he would settle the plaintiff's bill: on another occasion, he stated, that he had received £9000, of what he was contending for against the debtor. Held, in the absence of any evidence by the defendant of what compromise he had made, That the jury were warranted in inferring that the two suits had been compromised for £9000, of which £6000 were applied to satisfy the first execution, leaving £3000 for the latter, and therefore the plaintiff was entitled to recover poundage as on a compromise to that amount; though it was probable, under the evidence, that if the property levied on had been sold by the Sheriff, it would not have produced that sum. *Wetmore* v. *McLeod*, *Trin. T.* 1863.

7 *b*—Defendant tendered the plaintiff the amount due on a judgment, which he refused to take, and issued execution, under which the Sheriff levied on defendant's property: the defendant then obtained a Judge's order, that on payment to the Sheriff of the amount tendered, the execution should be returned "satisfied," and that satisfaction should be entered on the roll: the defendant thereupon paid this amount to the Sheriff, who returned the execution satisfied. Held, That the Sheriff was entitled to retain out of the amount so paid to him, his poundage and execution fees. *Central Bank* v. *McKeen*, *East T.* 1863.

See Infra 16, 17.

8—Liability—Discharge in bankruptcy.

A Sheriff executing a *testatum fi. fa.* on the goods and chattels of the plaintiff,—who had obtained his certificate,—without notice of the proceedings in bankruptcy, was held not liable in trespass, though the debt for which the *testatum fi. fa.* was issued had been proved before the commissioner under the fiat. *Bailey* v. *Hazen*, 3 *Kerr* 413.

9—Sheriff's right to fees—Service of writs by other party.

Where an application was made under the Act of Assembly 6 Wm. 4, c. 1, ss. 11, 12, by a Sheriff against an attorney, to compel him to pay the Sheriff's fees in certain suits in which the writs had not been served by the Sheriff. Held, That the Court could not order money to be paid to the complainant for which he had performed no service. *Drury* v. *Howe*, 3 *Kerr* 588.

10—Misconduct—Sheriff's officer—Inquiry into.
A charge against a Sheriff's officer of misconduct in selling property under execution, cannot be examined in an application to set aside the judgment. *Hardy* v. *Prince*, 3 *All*. 264.

11—Liability—Non-arrest—Damage.
A Sheriff is not liable to an action for neglecting to arrest a party on *mesne* process, unless the plaintiff has sustained some damage by his neglect. *Curran* v. *Beckwith*, 3 *All*. 365.

If the debt for which the process issued is barred by the Statute of Limitations, the Sheriff is not liable for neglecting to execute; and he may give such a defence in evidence under the general issue. *Ibid*.

12—Duty—Return of writ.
A Sheriff is bound to return a writ *de proprietate probanda*, though executed by his deputy without his express authority. *Armstrong* v. *Brown*, 3 *All*. 399.

13—Prisoners—Delivery—New Sheriff—Liability.
If the prisoners be delivered over by the old Sheriff to the new within the gaol, with the writs under which they are detained, and the new Sheriff does not require an indenture, he shall be chargeable in case of an escape after such delivery. *Power* v. *Johnson*, 2 *Kerr* 43.

An execution bearing *teste* on the day it is issued in vacation, upon a judgment entered up as of the preceding term, although irregular, is not, since the Act 5 Wm. 4, c. 37, s 10 and 11, a nullity. Held therefore, That the Sheriff was liable for the escape of a prisoner who had been arrested on a *ca. sa.* so tested (Chipman, C. J., *dubitante*.) *Ibid*.

14—Services—No authority from Sheriff—Recovery of fees.
Under the Act of Assembly 6 Wm. 4, c. 1, s. 11, a person serving processes directed to the Sheriff, but without any authority from him, is precluded from maintaining any action for his services. *Herrington* v. *Lugrin*, 1 *Kerr* 109.

15—Proceedings against—Mode.
Until the general rule of Hil. T. 4 Vic., the mode of proceeding against an ex-Sheriff for not bringing in the body of a defendant, was by *distringas*, and not by attachment, though the practice is otherwise in England. *Henry* v. *Murphy*, 1 *Kerr* 207.

16—Poundage—Attorney's liability.
Where a defendant was arrested on a *ca. sa.*, and discharged under the Insolvent Confined Debtors' Act, without any part of the money being paid, the Sheriff is not entitled to poundage on the amount of the execution, under the ordinance of fees; but he is entitled to his fees for executing the writ, and both the plaintiff and his attorney are liable therefor. *Kavanagh* v. *Phelan*, 1 *Kerr* 472

17—The plaintiff's attorney is not liable to the Sheriff for poundage on an execution, unless he receives the amount from the defendant, though the defendant has escaped from the limits, and his bail have paid the debt and costs to the attorney. *Caldwell* v. *Badger*, 2 *All*. 516.

18—Action—Form—Refusing Debtor the limits.
Case, and not trespass, is the proper remedy against a Sheriff for refusing to give a confined debtor the benefit of the gaol limits. *Caldwell* v. *Winslow*, 2 *All*. 203.

19—Parting with goods—Remedy.
If the Sheriff has parted with goods which he had levied on under an execution, he cannot be called on to sell under a *venditioni exponas*: the remedy against him is by action. *Phillips* v. *Dickenson*, *Trin. T.* 1831.

20—Action of debt does not lie against a Sheriff for an escape. See British Statutes.

21—Special Bailiff—Appointment at request.
If the Sheriff appoints a special bailiff to execute a writ, at the request of the plaintiff, who himself takes charge of the writ and deputation, which do not again come to the Sheriff's hands in the regular course, the plaintiff cannot rule the Sheriff to return the writ. *Kingston* v. *O'Shea*, 1 *All*. 678.

If a side-bar rule to return the writ is taken out under such circumstances, it may be set aside with costs; but if not set aside, no attachment will be granted against the Sheriff for disobeying it. *Ibid*.

22—Defence—Justification—Replevin.
A Sheriff cannot justify the taking of goods mentioned in a writ of replevin if he take them from a third person who is not named in the writ. *Wiggins* v. *Garrison and Wood*, *Ber*. 17.

23—Altered fieri facias.
In an action of trespass against a Sheriff for taking goods, he cannot justify under an altered *fieri facias* re-issued as an *alias*. *Johnston* v. *Winslow*, *Ber.* 53.

24—Remedy against attorney.
A Sheriff who sustains damage by proceeding under an improper writ given to him by an attorney, has his remedy over against such attorney. *Ibid.*

25—Omission to advertise and sell.
If a Sheriff levies on real estate and omits to advertise it, and returns on the execution, that "the lands remain unsold for want of buyers"—this is a breach of his duty, and a false return. It is the Sheriff's duty to advertise and sell under the *fi. fa.* and not to wait for a *venditioni exponas*. *Jarvis* v. *Miller*, *Ber.* 191.

26—Surplus from sale—Proceeds—Appropriation.
A Sheriff has no right to apply any surplus remaining in his hands from a sale under a prior execution to one received after such sale. *Stevenson* v. *Douglas*, *Ber.* 281.

27—The Court will not order a Sheriff to retain in his hands money which he has levied for A. on an execution in order to satisfy an execution in his hands against A. *Bradley* v. *Hopley*, *C. Ms.* 147.

28—Demand for rent.
Sheriff entitled to a reasonable time to make enquiries as to rent demanded. See Landlord and Tenant III. 15

Liability of Attorney General for Sheriff's fees. See Attorney General 3.

Escape—Liability—Damages. See Escape—Damages I. 12.

Remedy of creditor after proceedings taken against Sheriff. See Discharge 2—Escape 1.

Rule for body may be taken out in Term without motion. See Practice VIII. 5.

Coroner—Jury process.
Quære, Whether it is necessary to direct any other but jury process to a Coroner, when the only objection to the Sheriff is, that he is related to defendant. *Stevenson* v. *Douglas*, *Ber.* 281.

Sale—Wrongful conversion by Sheriff. See Trover 29.

SHERIFF'S DEED.

1—Affidavit—Miscalling execution.
The affidavit of the Sheriff under the Act 4 Wm. 4, c. 22, as to the preliminary steps having been duly taken before the the sale of real estate seized in execution, must be made at the same time as the deed of conveyance; and as a deed must in the absence of evidence to the contrary, be presumed to have been executed on the day it bears date, an affidavit purporting to have been sworn on the 2nd February, when the deed bore date the 22nd January previous, and no other proof of the time was offered, was held insufficient. *Doe d. Bustin* v. *Donnelly*, 3 *Kerr* 66.

The miscalling an execution a *testatum fieri facias* in the Sheriff's deed, whereas it was in fact a *fieri facias*, is not a fatal error: the execution being properly set out in the deed. *Ibid.*

2—Regularity of proceedings—Presumption.
A. purchased lands at Sheriff's sale in 1831, and took possession with the assent of the judgment debtor, who never disputed A.'s right or the regularity of the proceedings. Held, in an action of trespass against A. by a person who shewed no title, and had only recently obtained possession, but did not claim under the judgment debtor, that it would be presumed that the Sheriff's proceedings were regular, though there was no evidence of any execution issued or advertisement of the property; and that the Sheriff's deed was therefore properly admitted in evidence. *McLardy* v. *Flaherty*, 3 *Kerr* 455.

Restraining sale—Injunction. See Practice in Equity II. 4.

3—Execution of deed—Parol evidence.
Where a Sheriff's deed and his affidavit of due execution and sale bear different dates, parol evidence is admissible to prove that they were executed on the same day *Doe d. Connell* v. *Dickenson*, 1 *Han.* 456.

Affidavit to be made at same time that deed is executed — Presumption as to time. See Deed I. 37.

Affidavit by Deputy Sheriff on deed—Proof of authority. See Evidence XI. 1.

4—Sale—Former judgment—Relation.
The title conveyed by a Sheriff's deed, to land sold under execution issued upon a judgment recovered in an action brought on a former judgment of this same Court, does not relate back to the time of sign-

ing the first judgment, so as to affect a conveyance made by the judgment debtor between the times of signing the first and second judgments. *Doe dem. Peabody* v. *McKnight, Ber* 376.

5—Judgment—Attaching of—Execution — Relation — Recital not curtailing the granting part.

A Sheriff's deed recited that the Sheriff had seized all the right and title which the judgment debtor had in a certain piece of land (describing it) at the time of registering a memorial of judgment: the granting part of the deed conveyed "all the said lands and tenements." At the time of registering the memorial, the debtor had no title to the land, but it was afterwards granted to him, and he conveyed it to the defendant before the execution issued. Held, 1st. That the judgment attached upon the land when it was granted to the debtor; and that when the execution issued, it related back to the registry of the memorial, and defeated the conveyance to the defendant; 2nd. That the granting part of the deed was not controlled by the recital; but conveyed all the land described in the deed. *Doe dem. Kerr* v. *Jamieson, Trin. T.* 1871.

6 — Variance between execution and judgment — Execution — Alias — Proof of original not necessary.

In ejectment, claiming under a Sheriff's deed, the execution under which the sale took place, recited a judgment for £1105 11s. debt, and £5 11s. costs: the judgment was for £1105 11s. in the whole. Held, That the variance was only an irregularity, which could not be taken advantage of at the trial. Held, also—the sale being under an *alias*, the original execution need not be proved. *Doe d. Walsh* v. *Dalton, Hil. T.* 1860.

SHERIFF'S SALE.

1—What may be taken in execution—Notice—Levy—Advertisement—Evidence—Presumption—Recitals.

Real estate in remainder or reversion may be taken in execution and sold at Sheriff's sale, under the Act 26 Geo. 3, c. 12. *Doe* v. *Hazen*, 3 *All.* 87.

The "six months" notice of sale required by the Act are lunar months. *Ibid.*

The Sheriff need not make an actual entry on the land to levy. The advertisement is proof of a levy. *Ibid.*

An advertisement in which the number of the lot of land to be sold is left blank, is sufficient. *Doe* v. *Hazen*, 3 *All.* 87.

The recital in a Sheriff's deed of other judgments besides that under which the sale took place, does not affect the deed, or render proof of such judgments necessary. *Ibid.*

In making title under a Sheriff's deed more than twenty years old, where the sale was under a *venditioni exponas*, and the land had been advertised in the *Gazette*. Held, (in the absence of evidence to the contrary) that it might be presumed—1st. That a legal levy had been made under a *fi. fa.*; 2nd. That no newspaper was published in the County; 3rd. That the other notices required by the Act had been given; and 4th. That the sale took place during the hours prescribed by law. *Ibid.*

Any irregularity in issuing the *venditioni exponas* will not affect a purchaser under the Sheriff's deed. *Ibid.*

The acquiescence of the judgment debtor in a Sheriff's sale and subsequent possession of the land by the purchaser, short of twenty years, though presumptive evidence that all the necessary proceedings had been taken, will not give a title to the purchaser by estoppel. *Ibid.*

2—Vesting of estate—Purchase—No Conveyance.

A., a judgment creditor, pointed out land to the Sheriff as the property of B. his debtor, which the Sheriff levied upon and sold, and A. became the purchaser, with the knowledge that a third person claimed the title. A. afterwards finding that B. had no title refused to complete the purchase, and no return was made upon the execution. Held, That the mere purchase, without any conveyance from the Sheriff, vested no estate in A., and was no satisfaction of the judgment, and therefore that A. had still a right to issue a *ca. sa* thereon. Held also, That after the sale, B. might have applied to the Court to have satisfaction entered on the record. *Stewart* v. *Brundage*, 1 *All.* 205.

3—Separate lots—Selling—Time.

A Sheriff may sell land under an execution, in separate lots, and at any time between the hours named in the Act 26 Geo. 3, c. 12. *Doe* v. *Watson*, 1 *All.* 675.

4—Advertising—Places.
Lands seized by the Sheriff under execution, must be advertised at the Court House; at the office of the Registrar of Deeds; and in the other places mentioned in the 1 Rev. Stat c. 113, s. 8; as well as in the local newspaper. *Doe dem. Kerr* v. *Jamieson, Mich. T.* 1869.

Purchaser at Sheriff's sale—Operation of Stat. 27 Eliz. c. 4. See Deed II. 2, 3.

Purchase of equity of redemption by mortgagee—Effect. See Mortgage 17.

Judgment creditor—Necessity of sale under execution before contesting title—Locus Standi. See Practice in Equity II. 4.

Person claiming property under Sheriff's sale under execution, not necessary to prove the docketing of judgment. See *Doe dem. Barlow* v. *Hatfield*, 1 *Kerr* 417.

SHIPPING LAW.

1—Registered owner—Repairs—Liability.
The registered owner of a vessel is not liable for the expense of repairs put upon her, unless the work was done upon his credit, and by his authority express or implied. *Thomson* v. *Hughes, Hil. T.* 1834.

2—The defendant having advanced money to D. to build a ship, became the registered owner of three-fourths of the ship as a security for his advances, with an agreement that she should be sold in England, and his debt paid out of the proceeds of the sale. The ship being at St. John, and requiring repairs to enable her to go to England, D. and the master of the ship employed the plaintiff to do the work, directing him to charge it to the owners. The ship was sent to England and sold, and the defendant got the proceeds. Held, That he was liable for the repairs. *Williams* v. *Wood*, 4 *All.* 362.

3—Bona fide purchaser—Legal title—Prior unregistered mortgage—Notice.
The *bona fide* purchaser of a ship, with a legal title according to the provisions of "The Merchant Shipping Act, 1854," is not bound by notice of a prior unregistered mortgage; therefore, an injunction was refused, on the application of an unregistered mortgagee, to restrain the purchaser of a ship at Sheriff's sale, and who, as such purchaser, had become the registered owner, from disposing of the ship until the mortgage was satisfied, though he purchased with notice of the mortgage. (Ritchie, J., *dubitante.*) *De Wolf* v. *Carvill, East. T.* 1865.

4—Negligence of master—Liability of owner of vessel.
The registered owner of a vessel is not liable for goods lost by the fraud or negligence of the master during a voyage, unless the master is employed by or acting for him. Therefore, where defendant made advances to A. to enable him to build a vessel, and took the registry in his own name to secure his debt; but the vessel was sailed by A., and the defendant had no interest in her earnings, and did not employ the master—Held, That he was not liable for goods lost through the negligence of the master. *Newbury* v. *Young, East. T.* 1872.

5—Certificate of registry—Refusal to deliver up.
A person who had been part owner of a ship, and as such had possession of the certificate of registry, and who refuses to deliver it up to a purchaser of the ship at Sheriff's sale, is not liable to the penalty imposed by the 50th section of "The Merchant Shipping Act, 1854," such certificate not being required by the purchaser for "the lawful navigation" of the ship; but, to enable him to perfect his title, by having the change of ownership indorsed upon it, or by delivering it up, and obtaining a new certificate in lieu of it. *Reg.* v. *McAvity, Mich. T.* 1872.

6—Unregistered vessel—Chattel—Transfer—Re-vesting of property—Evidence.
The property in an unregistered ship may be transferred by parol like any other personal chattel. A registry procured by fraud on the true owner, by a person who had obtained possession of the builder's certificate, and made a false declaration of ownership at the Custom House, is null and void, and will be considered at law as well as in equity not to affect the property and right of possession as against the owner and his lawful assignee. The cancelling and giving up of a bill of sale, and at the same time of a bill of exchange given for the consideration money, upon an agreement to annul the sale, is sufficient *prima facie* evidence of re-vesting the property, although there be no actual re-delivery of the possession. *McLean* v. *Grant*, 1 *Kerr* 50.

7—Stranded vessel—Agreement for sale—No property passing.

The owner of a vessel lying stranded on the shore, and abandoned by her crew, agreed with A. by a memorandum in writing, to sell him the vessel for a certain sum, for which promissory notes were given payable at future days, and it was stipulated that a bill of sale and register would be given by B. when the notes were paid. Upon this agreement being made, B. authorized A. to take possession, and A. accordingly took possession of the vessel, repaired and fitted her out for sea, and was employed in navigating her, when B. forcibly resumed the possession. Held, That no property having passed under such agreement, B. still remained the legal owner, and that A. could not maintain trespass against B. for such taking. *Brown* v. *Nickerson*, 1 *Kerr* 467.

8—Seaman's wages—Liability of part owner.

A part owner of a vessel is liable to be sued for seaman's wages under the Act 6 Wm. 4, c. 44. *Ex parte Wood*, 1 *All.* 422.

9—Deviation in voyage—Right to sue for wages.

Where a seaman shipped at Liverpool, England, and signed articles which thus described the voyage: "To come out to Saint John in a ship called the *Portland*, to be under the command of the master of the *Portland* until her arrival in St. John, New Brunswick, there to leave the *Portland*, and to go in a new ship commanded by the master, and to continue by her until her arrival at her port of discharge in the United Kingdom." Held, That an avowed intention to go to Savannah, in Georgia, previous to her return to Great Britain, was an intended departure sufficient to justify the seaman leaving the ship and suing for wages. *Hayward* v. *Maine*, 1 *Kerr* 292.

Deviation—Right in seaman to determine contract—Jurisdiction in Justice to make order for payment. See Justice of the Peace II. 3.

10—Loss by jettison—Contribution—Custom.

Where the owner of a ship is also the owner of part of the cargo, which was thrown overboard for the preservation of the ship in the course of the voyage, on which assurance was effected—Held, That such owner might recover from the insurer on the ship the average proportion which the ship would be liable to contribute to the loss sustained by such jettison of the cargo. Where the goods are laden on deck, according to the custom of a particular trade, the owner thereof is entitled to contribution in general average for a loss by jettison. *Marks* v. *Watson*, 2 *Kerr* 211.

Overloading vessel—Consent of owner of goods—Bill of lading. See Carrier 1, 2.

SHORE.

Grant bounded by. See Crown Grant I. 13.

SIMILITER.

A cause is at issue though no similiter is added. *Doe* v. *Smith*, 1 *All.* 580.

SLANDER.

See Defamation.

SMUGGLING.

See Criminal Law. See Revenue Law.

SOUTH BAY, BOOM COMPANY.

Rights under Statute to receive Boomage. See Boomage.

SPECIAL JURY.

See Jury.

SPECIAL PAPER.

See Practice—Waiver—General Rules 122, 123.

SPECIFIC ARTICLES.

Note for—Damages.

A note for the payment of a certain sum in specific articles, becomes a money debt after the time for delivering the articles has elapsed; and a set-off is admissible in an action upon it, under the Act 4 Vic. c. 4. *Steeves* v. *Hopper*, 1 *All.* 394.

Quære, Whether the plaintiff could declare for special damages for not delivering the articles? If he could, the consideration on which the contract was made should be stated. *Ibid.*

See Bills and Notes I. 12, 13, 14.

SPECIFIC PERFORMANCE.

Delay.

Though in equity, time is not always the

essence of a contract; yet after a delay of four years, specific performance will not in general be decreed. *Purvis* v. *Hume*, 3 *All.* 299.

See Equity—Practice in Equity.
" Landlord and Tenant I. 3.

STAKEHOLDER.

See Action at Law I. 3.

STAMPS.

See Bills and Notes I. 11.

Unstamped Check. See Check 1.

STATUTES.

See British Statutes.

Lumber Act—Expiration of old Act—Liability under new.
The Lumber Act 1 Wm. 4, c. 45, making the first purchaser of the lumber, after the survey, liable to pay the surveyor's fees, having expired before action brought—Held, That the liability of the defendant, depending on such Act, did not continue after the expiration thereof. Held also, That the new Act 7 Wm. 4, c. 10, does not apply to services performed under the old Act. *Cunningham* v. *Pollock*, 1 *Kerr* 324.

Re-inspection of fish. See Evidence III. 6.

Where any particular practice has been prescribed by Statute, it must be strictly followed. See *Lingley* v. *Huestis*, 2 *Kerr* 4.

Known intent disregarded when words of Statute unambiguous. See Revenue Act.

Revised Statutes—Power to amend mistakes in. See Mistakes.

Rights under Statute. See Boomage.

STATUTE OF FRAUDS.

See Contract 14.
" Frauds (Statute of.)

STATUTE OF LIMITATIONS.

See Limitation of Actions.

STATUTE LABOR.

See Postmaster.

Prosecution.
In a prosecution under the Act 5 Wm. 4, c. 2., for non-performance of statute labor, it must be proved that the party has been notified by the overseer, of the time and place of meeting to perform the work; and where the affidavits, in answer to an application for a *certiorari* to remove the proceedings in such a prosecution, stated that the party had been *duly notified*, the Court made the rule absolute, in order to ascertain what the notice really was—the applicant having in his affidavit denied notice. *Ex parte Ferguson*, 1 *All.* 663.

Semble, That is not essential to notify the party to bring any implement to perform the work; and unless he is so notified, he need not bring any. *Ibid.*

STATUTORY FORM.

See Bond (Replevin Bond.)

STAYING PROCEEDINGS.

See Practice VI.

STET PROCESSUS.

See Judgment as in case of Non-suit II. 6.

STEVEDORE.

No implied contract to pay expenses. See Contract 7.

STOCKHOLDER.

See Corporation—Joint Stock Company—Bank—Winding-up Act.

STOLEN GOODS.

See Trover 3.

SUBPŒNA.

See Attachment 6, 7, 8.
" General Rules 125, 126.

SUBSTITUTED AGREEMENT.

See Contract 14. See Agreement 2.

SUMMARY ACTION.

See Judgment by Default.
" Costs 55.

1—Commencement of action.
The day of the issuing of a summary writ, and not the day of the teste, is considered the commencement of the action; therefore a process sued out on a demand which accrued subsequent to the teste but before the issuing, was held sufficient. *Stephenson* v. *McLellan*, 1 *All.* 19.

2—**Plea before appearance—Waiver.**
Under the summary Act 4 Wm. 4, c. 41, (12 Vic. c. 40,) a plea filed before an appearance entered, is a nullity; and it is doubtful whether it can be waived. If it can, a demand of particulars of set-off is not a waiver of it. *Andrews* v. *Hanson*, 1 *All.* 509.

A demand of particulars is not a step in the cause. *Ibid.*

3—**Verdict—Finality—Below £20.**
The rule that the verdict is final in summary actions, will be applied to other actions for mere money demands, where the verdict is for the defendant, and the only amount which the plaintiff could have recovered is less than £20. *McAllister* v. *Day*, 4 *All.* 37.

4—**Several defendants—Death—Suggestion.**
If one of several defendants in a summary action dies before interlocutory judgment, the plaintiff should make a suggestion of the death in the memorandum of judgment and subsequent proceedings, or the judgment will be set aside for irregularity. Where such suggestion was omitted, the plaintiff was allowed to amend on payment of costs. *Crane* v. *Gosline et al.*, 4 *All.* 371.

5—**Plea—Nil debet.**
Nil debet is a good plea in a summary action of debt on a record, under the Act 12 Vic. c. 40. *Wetmore* v. *Provan*, 4 *All.* 442.

6—**Jury.**
The finding of a jury, improperly summoned, in a summary action, is not final under the Act 12 Vic. c. 40. *Wetmore* v. *Levy*, 4 *All.* 510.

7—**Member of Assembly.**
A member of the General Assembly cannot be sued by a summary writ, under the Act 12 Vic. c. 40. *DesBrisay* v. *Steadman*, 4 *All.* 597.

SUMMONS.

Service of. See Practice IV.

Party appearing. See Justice of the Peace IV. 16 a, 17.

Members of House of Assembly must be sued by bill and summons. See Arrest 3.

SUPERSEDEAS.

The issuing of a *fi. fa.*, which is not returned, will not deprive a prisoner of a supersedeas. *Jackson* v. *Black*, 4 *All.* 79.

See Absconding Debtor 1.

Not charging in execution—Settlement pending.
A defendant, rendered by his bail after judgment, wrote to his attorney, requesting him to see the plaintiff's attorney and endeavour to compromise the debt and get time for payment. Within three months after the render of the defendant, this letter was communicated to the plaintiff's attorney, who, after seeing the plaintiff, informed the defendant's attorney of the terms on which the plaintiff was willing to settle. Held, That it was the duty of the defendant's attorney to communicate the offer to his client, and that until he did so, the treaty for settlement was pending, and the defendant was not entitled to a supersedeas for not being charged in execution within three months after the render. *Jones* v. *Steeves*, 1 *Han.* 260.

SUPREME COURT IN EQUITY.

See Practice in Equity—Equity.

1—**Appeal—Time—Decree.**
An appeal from a decree in Equity under the Act 17 Vic. c. 18, s. 32, may be made within twenty days after the minutes of the decree have been settled by the Clerk. *Frost* v. *Nichols*, 3 *All.* 297.

For the purpose of appeal, the decision of the cause is not the pronouncing the decree by the Judge, but the formal entry of it by the Clerk, when perfected. *Ibid.*

2—An appeal to the Queen in Council, under the order of November 1852, from a judgment of this Court affirming a decree in equity, may be applied for within fourteen days after the minutes of the decree are settled, though more than fourteen days have elapsed since the judgment was pronounced. *Brookfield* v. *The St. Andrews and Quebec Railway Company*, 4 *All.* 496.

3—**Costs.**
Costs of interlocutory proceedings being generally in the discretion of the Court before which the proceedings are had, a Court of Appeal will not interfere unless it is evident that injustice has been done. *Allen* v. *Trenholm*, 3 *All.* 421.

As a general rule, appeals are not entertained in questions of costs. *Ibid.*

3 a—Costs—Reversal of order of Judge.
Where an order of a Judge in Equity is reversed on appeal, the Court of Appeal has power to order that the costs of the proceedings in the Court below be allowed to the applicant. *Wiggins* v. *Hendricks, Hil. T.* 1873.

4—Evidence—Discretion as to use of.
On a reference in a suit in equity to take an account, the Barrister received evidence of a claim by the plaintiff in a matter not mentioned in the reference, but made no report upon the validity of the claim. At the hearing of the cause, this evidence was not used, and a decree was made without noticing this claim. Held, on appeal from this decree, That though under the Act 17 Vic. c. 18, it was proper to produce the evidence before the Court of Appeal, the Court was not bound to use it. *Deveber* v. *Andrews*, 4 *All.* 626.

5—Appeal paper. See General Rules 9 *a*.

6—Review by Court—Judge granting leave to appeal. See Practice V. 5 *a*.

7—Entry of cause on appeal paper. See Practice V.

8—Review of taxation of costs. See Costs IV.

9—Supervision of proceedings of trustees.
Semble, That the Court of Equity has power to supervise the proceedings of Trustees of absconding debtors appointed under the 1 Rev. Stat. c. 125, and to open and examine accounts adjusted by them; but it will not interfere where there is no fraud, and the proceedings of the Trustee have been regular and no special ground is stated. *Outhouse* v. *Hickman and others*, 1 *Han.* 38.

Power of Court to amend pleadings in a cause — Ex parte Amendments. See Amendment I. 18.

SUPREME COURT OF JUDICATURE.

1—Jurisdiction.
The Supreme Court of this Province has no power to declare an Act of the Provincial Legislature to be invalid; either on the ground that it interferes with private rights, and is therefore unconstitutional, or, that under the Royal Instructions to the Governor, the Act ought not to have been passed without a suspending clause. [But see Reg. v. Chandler, 1 Han. 548—since the passing of "The British North America Act, 1867."] *Reg.* v. *Kerr, Ber.* 367.

(See British North America Act.)

2—The Supreme Court, by virtue of the Commission under which it was constituted, may exercise the same jurisdiction in regard to the discharge of estreated recognizances in this Province, as the Court of Exchequer does in England under the Stat. 33 Hen. 8, c. 39; and has a general discretionary power, under that Statute to examine into the sufficiency of the reasons alleged in excuse, and to discharge a recognizance forfeited by not appearing for trial at a Court of Oyer and Terminer, and to stay proceedings on such recognizance. *Reg.* v *Appleby, Ber.* 397.

3—The Supreme Court, exercising by the commissions of the Judges, the power of the Barons of the Exchequer in England, has authority to relieve against estreated recognizances, under the Stat. 33 Hen. 8, c. 39. *Rex* v. *Morse, East. T.* 1826.

4—The Supreme Court, being exclusively a Court of Common Law, does not possess the jurisdiction of the equity side of the Court of Exchequer in England, even in revenue cases. *The Attorney General* v. *Baillie*, 1 *Kerr* 443.

5—The Supreme Court has the same jurisdiction as the Court of Exchequer in England, in removing from other Courts, causes affecting the rights of the Crown, or the public revenues. *Wilson* v. *Briscoe*, 2 *All.* 535.

6—Discretionary power.
Pending a writ of error, the Supreme Court may in its discretion allow an application to be made to the Court below to amend formal errors on the record, and may suspend judgment in the mean time. Such proceeding was allowed, where the award of the *venire* and the day of trial were left blank on the record of the Court below. *Kinnear* v. *Gallagher*, 1 *Kerr* 424.

Ordering issue to be tried. See Practice XII.

Power to quash order for support of insolvent debtor.
Where Justices make an order for support under the Insolvent Debtors' Act—

(1 Rev. Stat. c. 124,)—and it appears, by the examination of the debtor that he has given an undue preference to one of his creditors,—this Court has power to quash the order. *McDonald* v. *Watt*, 1 *Han.* 24.

Crown bond—Application for relief—Summary application. See Practice V. 6.

SURETY.

See Consideration 8.
" Principal and Surety.

Alteration of position, by subsequent agreement.
A., with B. as surety, entered into a bond to the plaintiff, conditioned that A. should maintain the plaintiff during his life: by a subsequent agreement under seal, between the plaintiff and A., without B.'s consent, they bound themselves to refer all questions relating to the performance of the condition of the bond to two arbitrators, and to abide by their decision. Held, That the position of the surety was altered by this agreement, and that he was discharged from liability on the bond. *Williamson* v. *Steeves*, 4 *All.* 449.

Relief of. See Principal and Surety 7.

SURGEON.

Negligence. See Action on the Case.

Acting as such. See Evidence VI. 6.

SURPLUSAGE.

See Action on the Case II. 3, III. 5.
" Pleading I. 2, 29, 37, 39, 50.

Reference to Plan. See Trespass II. 19.

SURPRISE.

See New Trial. See Evidence VIII. 3.

SURRENDER.

Of lease—Purpose—New trial.
In ejectment by a lessee against his lessor, a surrender of a lease for twenty-one years was relied on by the latter, who resumed possession at the request of the lessee in a little more than a year after the commencement of the term, paid the lessee for a fence he had erected, and afterwards built upon the land and remained in possession for about fifteen years without any claim made by the lessee; a verdict for the plaintiff on the ground that the possession was only given up for a temporary purpose, was set aside, in order that it might be again submitted to a jury, it appearing that the purpose for which it was alleged to have been given up had ceased in a short time, that the lessor had other property which could have been used therefor, and that between the time of his resuming possession, and the tenant's re-demand of it, the land had much increased in value. *Doe* v. *Jack*, 1 *All.* 476.

See Covenant 9.

SURROGATE COURT.

See Executors and Administrators.

The decision of the Surrogate Court on all matters, properly within its cognizance, under the Act of Assembly 3 Vic. c 61, as relates to the executor's accounts, is final and conclusive, subject to the appeal to the Court of Chancery, except where otherwise provided by the Act; and such decision will be binding on Courts of Law where the amount of assets comes in question, in actions brought by creditors against the executor. *Harrison* v. *Morehouse*, 2 *Kerr* 584.

The principles of equity are not excluded from the proceedings in the Surrogate Court in the settlement of estates. *Ibid.*

Irregularity of proceedings — Remedy by appeal — Objection not allowed on trial. See Deed I. 40.

SURVEY.

See Crown grant.

Return of survey in Surveyor General's office is admissible to explain ambiguity in grant. See Evidence II. 6.

Survey not satisfactorily ascertained. See New Trial II. 2, 27.

SURVEYOR GENERAL.

Notice signed by Surveyor General in official character—Sufficiency. See Crown Grant I. 18.

SUSPENSION—(CLAIM.)

See Satisfaction.

Acceptances given. See Assumpsit III. 11. See Satisfaction. See Action at Law VI.

Taking bill for debt. See Bills and Notes V. 31.

Agreement as to suspension of remedy. See Distress 2.

Persons beyond seas. See Ejectment II. 8.

Note payable at particular place—Necessity of presentment before recovery. See Bills and Notes VI. 12 *a*.

Composition—Note given. See do. V. 9.

See Judgment I. 2.

Bank suspending payment—Winding up—Liability of executors. See Executors and Administrators II. 13.

TAVERN KEEPER.

Selling liquor on credit. See Bills and Notes VI. 3. See Credit.

TAXATION OF COSTS.

See Costs.

TENANTS IN COMMON.

1—Where persons jointly manufacture timber, which is to be divided between them, they are not partners, but tenants in common, and each has a right to dispose only of his own share. *Wiggins* v. *White*, *Ber.* 97.

2—*Quære*, Whether any, and what acts, short of the destruction of the joint property, will enable one tenant in common to sustain trespass against his co-tenant, *Ibid.*

3—If one tenant in common, with the consent of his co-tenant, sells more than his own share of the common property, he will be deemed to have acted as the agent in respect thereof, and an action for money had and received may be maintained against him by his co-tenant. *Shaw* v. *Grant*, *Ber.* 110.

4—Where two persons cut and haul timber, under an agreement that the timber is to be "got on the halves," they are tenants in common. *Kerr* v. *Connell*, *Ber.* 133.

5—One tenant in common cannot recover in assumpsit against his co-tenant, for his share of the common property, unless a sale by the co-tenant be proved. *Doyle* v. *Taylor*, *Ber.* 201.

6—The saws, water-wheel, etc, in a mill, the property of tenants in common, are a part of the inheritance, the damaging or taking away of which, except with intent to repair or replace them, is in the nature of waste, for which one tenant will be answerable to his co-tenant. *Linton* v. *Wilson*, 1 *Kerr* 223.

Action by, money h . and received—Rendering account.

One tenant in common cannot maintain an action for money had and received against his co-tenant, for receiving more than his share of the rents and profits of the joint property, unless there is an account settled and balance agreed upon, even though the defendant may have acted as bailiff of the other co-tenants in receiving the rents. *Frost and another* v. *Disbrow*, 1 *Han.* 73.

Defendant being a tenant in common with the plaintiffs, who were infants, rendered in an account, in which he acknowledged a certain sum to be due from him to the plaintiffs, as their share of the rents of the joint property which he had received; the plaintiffs' guardian disputed the correctness of the account, and claimed a much larger sum from the defendant. Held, in an action for money had and received, That such balance not having been agreed to, the plaintiffs were not entitled to retain a verdict for that amount. *Ibid.*

Limitations — Adverse Possession. See Limitation of Actions IV. 23, 24.

Landlord tenant in common—Holding as tenant on new terms. See Landlord and Tenant II. 6.

Partition. See Partition.

Trespass—Justifying as tenant in common. See Trespass II. 26.

Conveyance to grantor — Operation. See Deed I. 26.

TENANT BY COURTESY.

Possession of husband as tenant—Heir's right of entry. See Ejectment II. 7.

Wife tenant in fee of land—Husband's residence — Crops raised by husband — Liability to seizure. See Execution IV. 16.

TENANT FOR LIFE.

The tenant of a devisee for life may after the death of such devisee, be ousted by the remainderman without any notice to quit. *Doe dem. Fields* v. *McKay*, 2 *Kerr* 435.

TENANT AT WILL.

1—The 29th Section of the Act 13 Vic. c. 53, (Landlord and Tenant) does not apply to a tenancy at will. See *Ex parte Irvin*, 2 *All.* 519.

2—Agreement to purchase—Possession under.
A person let into possession of land by the owner, under an agreement to purchase has only the estate of a tenant at will, unless there is some agreement respecting the occupation of the land before the sale is completed. *Doe dem. Cliff* v. *Connaway, Ber.* 382.

3—Determining tenancy—Notice—Demand.
A. entered into a bond to convey land to B. his heirs or assigns on payment of a certain sum in five years: before the day of payment, A. died, having devised the land to his wife for life, and after her death, to his children, (the lessors of the plaintiff.) B. assigned his interest to the defendant, who paid the purchase money to the widow, and received from her a deed of bargain and sale. After the death of the widow, A.'s children brought ejectment. Held, That the deed from the widow to the defendant terminated any tenancy at will that might have existed, and that no notice to quit, or demand of possession was necessary before bringing the action. *Ibid.*

4—L. having been in possession of land upwards of twenty years, made a written agreement to buy it from the lessor of the plaintiff, but before the time of payment, went away leaving the defendant in possession. Held, That under this agreement L. became tenant at will, and that such tenancy was terminated by a demand of possession made on the defendant who claimed under L., though such demand was not made on the land. *Doe* v. *Little*, 2 *All.* 558.

5—A person taking possession of land under an agreement to purchase, which specified no time for the continuance of the possession in the event of the purchase not being completed, becomes a tenant at will; and such tenancy must be terminated by some act of the parties, before he can be ejected on non-completion of the purchase. *Doe* v. *Denny*, 3 *All.* 50.

The Act 6 Wm. 4. c. 43, s 7, does not apply to such a case; but only to questions arising under the Statute of Limitations. *Doe* v. *Denny*, 3 *All.* 50.

6—Determination of tenancy.
A tenancy at will is determined by the entry of landlord upon the land and cutting down and carrying away wood, and making surveys without the consent of the tenant. *Doe dem. Lyon* v. *Slavin*, 3 *Kerr* 258.

7—Defendant went into possession of land as tenant at will to the lessor of the plaintiff, and remained in upwards of twenty years. Held, That the tenancy was not determined by an entry of the owner within twenty years, with consent of the tenant, to run the line between that and the adjoining land. *Doe dem. Botsford* v. *Tidd, Trin. T.* 1863.

8—Any act upon the land by the landlord for which he would otherwise be liable in trespass at the suit of the tenant amounts to a termination of a tenancy at will. *Ibid.*

9—*Semble*, That a conveyance of the land by the landlord to a third person, duly registered, is a determination of a tenancy at will. *Doe dem. Vernor* v. *McDonald*, *Hil. T.* 1867.

Operation of writing under seal not giving feoffment. See Deed V. 2.

Limitation of action—Application. See Limitation of Actions I. 2.

TENANT FOR YEARS.

What enures as. See Landlord and Tenant II. 5.

Tenancy—Intention.
An agreement was made by A. and B. by mutual bonds for the sale and conveyance of lands by A. to B. on payment of a certain sum on or before the 1st May 1829, together with lawful interest for the first three years, and eight per cent. for the last two years as a consideration for the use of the land. Held, That B. who was let into possession under this agreement was tenant for years until the 1st May 1829. *Doe d. Cliff* v. *Connaway*, *Ber.* 382.

TENANCY.

Working farm on shares. See Trespass I. 19.

TENDER.

Pleading general issue and tender to part of claim. See Pleading II. 24.

Recovery of money without proof of tender of deed. See Condition Precedent 3.

TERMS NOTICE.

Plaintiff's intention to proceed in cause. See Practice IX. 5, 5 *n*.

Executing writ of inquiry. See Practice IX. 12.

TERMINATION OF PROCEEDINGS.

Jury ignoring bill. See Criminal Law.

TESTATUM.

See Execution.

TESTE.

See Execution.

TIDE.

See Crown Grant.

TIMBER.

Liability to seizure.

If timber is cut upon crown lands, over which this Province has exercised and continues to exercise jurisdiction, it is liable to seizure here, though the territory where it is cut is claimed by the Government of Canada as being part of that Province, and license to cut timber has been granted by that Government. *Tibbits* v. *Allan*, 3 *Kerr* 280.

Property in whom.

A. being indebted to plaintiff, and in consideration of further advances that might be made to him, agreed to go upon land, leased by Government to the plaintiff, and manufacture for him a quantity of timber, and raft and deliver it at a certain place in the following spring, at a certain rate per ton—A. to find all necessary supplies and to pay the men's wages; and if there should be any balance due A. on the completion of the agreement, it was to be paid to him by the plaintiff—half in cash and half in goods; and that as A. was only employed to manufacture the timber for the plaintiff at a certain rate per ton, he was not to charge A. with the tonnage or export duty, as was usual where lumberers brought timber to market on their own account. Held, That A. was only the servant of the plaintiff, and had no right in the timber,—the property in which vested in the plaintiff as soon as it was cut; and that the men employed by A. in getting the timber, had no lien for their wages. *Crane* v. *Hutchinson*, 3 *Kerr* 461.

TIMBER LICENSE.

See License—Trover—Replevin.

TIME (COMPUTATION OF.)

The day of service of the rule to plead is to be computed one of the twenty days allowed for pleading. *Clewes* v. *Scoullar*, 2 *Kerr* 627.

Motions when to be made—Days service—Notices. See Practice IV., V.

Words "at least." See Practice IX. 3.

For purposes of justice, Court will take notice of time of day when proceedings had. See Execution I. 7.

The words "Within three months therefrom" relate as well to cases where there has been no appearance, as to cases where defendant has appeared. See Practice in Equity I. 27.

TITLE OF CAUSE.

See Affidavit II.

TITLE TO LAND.

See Limitation of Actions.
" Ejectment—Deed.

Title to land in question. See County Court. See Justice of the Peace.

TOP WHARFAGE.

See Wharf.

TORT.

Waiver of—Assumpsit. See Assumpsit III. 26, 37. See Use and Occupation 4.

TRANSFER.

See Chattel—Delivery.
" Shipping Law 6.

TREASURER.

See Deputy Treasurer.

TREASURY BOND.

Scire Facias—Summary application for relief. See Practice V. 6.

TRESPASS.

I. Real Property—Right to maintain Action — Sufficiency of Title—Party.
II. Defence—Pleading—Evidence.
III. Personal Property.
IV. Damages.
V. Assault and False Imprisonment.
VI. Miscellaneous.

I.

Real Property—Right to maintain Action—Sufficiency of Title—Party.

1—Privilege—Entry necessary.
A grant from the Crown of a privilege to build mills in the bed of a river does not convey any right in the soil; therefore the grantee cannot before actual entry in the exercise of the privilege, maintain trespass against a person for building a mill upon the place where the privilege was granted. *Frink* v. *Hill, East. T.* 1831.

2—Registered deed—Actual adverse possession of defendant.
A deed registered under the Act 26 Geo. 3, c 3 will not enure to give possession to the grantee, so as to enable him to maintain trespass against a person in the actual adverse possession of the land, and who took possession subsequent to the registry of the deed and the entry of the plaintiff under it, and continued such possession for several years before the alleged trespass. *Dunham* v. *King, Trin. T.* 1831.

3—Unregistered deed.
An unregistered deed transfers no property, and gives no right to enter on land. *Patterson* v. *Tingley, Trin. T.* 1863.

4—Entry without title—Third party—Sufficiency of possession—Judge—Jury.
An entry by a person without title, on land in the actual occupation of another does not give him a possession to enable him to maintain trespass even against a third person. *Merritt* v. *Quinton, Ber.* 209.

5—Plaintiff under a claim of right, but without any title, entered on land in the actual possession of B. and—without B.'s authority—surveyed a part of the land and put up a fence thereon; the fence was pulled down and destroyed by the defendant. Held, That the plaintiff had not any possession of the land to enable him to maintain trespass, though no connexion was shown between the defendant and B. *Merritt* v. *Quinton, Ber.* 209.

6—It is a question for the Judge, whether the plaintiff has made out a sufficient possession to entitle him to go to the jury. *Ibid.*

7—Division line—Parol agreement.
Where the respective owners of adjoining lots, agree by parol to a division line, it is binding upon them, though it may differ from the line to which they had previously occupied, and one may maintain trespass against the other for an entry on a part of the land, which before the division had been in the defendant's possession. *Lawrence* v. *McDowall, Ber.* 283.

8—Glebe—Church Corporation—Rector.
Where land is granted to a Church Corporation as a glebe, and a Rector has been duly inducted, he has the possession, and an action of trespass for entering on the land and cutting down trees, must be brought in his name, and not in the name of the Corporation. *Rector &c. of St. Stephen* v. *Tortelott*, 1 *Kerr* 537.

9—Church Corporation.
An action of trespass for damages done to a Parish Church may be brought in the name of the Church Corporation, in the absence of proof of there being any Rector. *Rector &c. of St. George's Church* v. *Cougle*, 1 *Han.* 609.

10—Vacant land—Possession—Wrongdoer—Ouster.
A Crown surveyor in 1831 laid off a lot of land for A. in rear of land granted to the plaintiff, intending that one lot should abut on the other; in 1833, the plaintiff had the side lines of his lot run out, and marked up to A.'s lot, under the belief that it was the rear line of his grant, and exercised acts of possession over the land, but in fact the plaintiff's grant did not extend to A.'s grant, but left a piece of vacant Crown land between them,—defendant afterwards built a camp on this piece of Crown land, which the plaintiff pulled down. In trespass for a second entry on the land and cutting trees—Held, That though the plaintiff had no title to the land where the trees were cut (it being outside the bounds of his grant),

he had sufficient possession to maintain trespass against a wrong doer, and that the erection of the camp by the defendant was not an ouster of the plaintiff's possession. *Morrison* v. *McAlpin*, 1 *Kerr* 650.

11—Master's deed—Mortgagor—De bonis asportatis.

The purchaser of land under a sale by a master in Chancery in a foreclosure suit, whose deed is duly registered, may before entry, maintain trespass *de bonis asportatis* for trees cut on the premises and carried away by a person claiming under the mortgagor. *Jarvis* v. *Edgett*, 1 *All.* 66.

12—Entry—Defined boundaries—Possession.

If a party enters on land, under a registered deed with defined boundaries, with the intention of taking possession as owner, and not as a mere trespasser, he may be considered as taking possession of the whole lot described in the deed, and not merely of that part actually occupied or enclosed; and such possession if continued for twenty years, will give a title. It is a question for the jury with what intention the party entered on the land. (Per Parker, Wilmot and Ritchie, J. J., —Carter, C. J., and N. Parker, M. R., *dissentientibus*.) *Humphreys* v. *Helms*, *Hil. T.* 1861.

13—Continuance of possession.

A lot of wilderness land containing two hundred and forty acres, was granted to H. in 1809, soon after which he left the country. In 1812, H.'s father, without any authority conveyed the land to B., who conveyed to K. in 1825. K. took possession of the land, cut timber upon it, ran out one of the side lines, and in 1828 conveyed it to F. who also entered and lumbered upon it, and conveyed it to the plaintiff in 1834. The several conveyances were registered. The plaintiff cleared about an acre of the land, which was the first improvement, and commenced building a house in 1836, when the defendant, the heir of H., entered and forbade him: the house was not finished, and was burnt soon afterwards, and the land remained unoccupied till 1850, when the plaintiff built another house; after which the defendant again entered, and cut trees upon the land, for which trespass was brought. Held,—per Parker, Wilmot and Ritchie, J. J.,—Carter, C. J., and N. Parker, M. R., *dissentientibus*,—That the jury were properly directed, that if the plaintiff, and those under whom he claimed, entered under registered deeds with defined boundaries, with the intention of taking possession as owners of the land, and not as mere trespassers without any claim of title; they might be considered as having taken possession of the whole lot, and not merely of that part actually occupied; and that such possession, if continued for twenty years, would bar the defendant's right. *Humphreys* v. *Helms*, *Hil. T.* 1861.

14—De bonis Asportatis.

Though plaintiff is not in possession of land, if he has the title he may, since the Act 21 Vic. c. 20, s. 5, maintain trespass *de bonis asportatis* for carrying away trees from it. *Ibid.*

15—Mortgagee—Execution against mortgagor—De bonis asportatis.

A mortgagee in fee of land, who is not in possession cannot maintain trespass *de bonis asportatis* against the Sheriff for seizing, under an execution against the mortgagor, logs cut by him with the mortgagee's permission,—no delivery of the logs having been made to the mortgagee. *DesBrisay* v. *McPhelim*, *Trin. T.* 1862.

16—Joint liability—Common Purpose—Several defendants — Separate trespasses.

In trespass against several defendants if they go upon the land with a common purpose they are jointly liable though the acts of trespass are separate and are committed on different parts of the land. *Ferguson* v. *Savoy*, 4 *All.* 263.

17—Crown right—Escheat—Reasonable use of water—Devise.

A., by will executed in 1824, devised lot No. 11 to his son G., except one hundred acres, which he gave to other children, and he likewise gave to his son D. the privilege of keeping a saw-mill where it then stood, with a log and lumber yard, without molestation or hindrance; but not to dispose of the said mill privilege to any person except his brother G., or his liberty; and all the remainder of said lot No. 11, to remain and be to his son G., with the above exception. G. died in 1840, having devised all his property to his sons, one of whom was the plaintiff. The plaintiff's property was escheated in 1852, and partition made between the Crown and the other heirs of G., by which the saw-mill, with the log and lumber yard adjoining and the privilege of water for the use of the mill, were awarded to D., to hold according to the will of A. The Crown afterwards granted its portion of the land to plaintiff, excepting the saw-mill with the log and lumber yard adjoining, and the use of the water for the mill, as awarded to D. in the partition. D. died in 1861, and devised the saw mill and privilege to the defendant. The plaintiff had a fulling-mill on the land granted to him by the Crown. The fulling-mill and saw-mill were supplied with water from the same aqueduct. Both mills could not be worked at the same time, and when the fulling-mill was in operation, the water was diverted from the saw-mill by an opening in the aqueduct. Held, in trespass for taking possession of the saw-mill, injuring the gates and diverting the water from the fulling-mill—1st. That if the will of A. gave D. only a life estate in the saw-mill, the plaintiff had no right, as any interest he might have had as one of the heirs of A., was escheated to the Crown, and excepted out of the grant to him. 2nd. That in such case the defendant, as one of the heirs of A., would have an undivided interest in the saw-mill with the Crown, and not with the plaintiff. 3rd. That if, in diverting the water from the fulling-mill, the defendant did no more than was necessary for the reasonable use of the water for the saw-mill, the plaintiff could not recover for that act, and that such question should have been left to the jury. *Pickett* v. *Pickett*, 1 *Han.* 156.

18—Expulsion—Part of close.

Expulsion of plaintiff from part of the close is sufficient to sustain the count for expulsion. *Gesner* v. *Cairns*, 2 *All.* 595.

19—Joint occupation—Working farm on shares.

A person working a farm on the shares and occupying part of the house jointly with the owner of the farm, has not such a tenancy as to prevent the owner from maintaining trespass to the land. *West* v. *Atherton*, 2 *All.* 653.

20—Possession—Sufficiency of.

To maintain trespass, the plaintiff's possession should have the characteristics of the possession of a permanent owner, shown by acts done with the apparent object of taking possession as owner,—mere casual acts of a transient or temporary nature few in number and occurring at long intervals, are not sufficient. *Gidney* v. *Bates*, *Mich. T.* 1862.

21—The *locus in quo* was a small uncultivated island and the acts of possession relied on were fastening plaintiff's net to a tree on the island annually for about twenty years; collecting drift wood upon it, and once putting a calf there to pasture,—Held insufficient. *Ibid.*

22—Entry—Intention—Deed—Acts of possession.

There is a distinction in the character of the possession where a person enters on land under a registered deed, and where he goes in without any claim at all. It should be left to the jury to say whether a person entered on land with the intention of taking possession under his deed, or, as a mere trespasser—the mere fact of a person having a registered deed of land, does not give him possession of the land described, without shewing acts of possession. *Governor etc. of the Madras Board* v. *Ryan*, *Mich. T.* 1864.

23—Possession—Sufficiency of.

The *locus in quo* was the rear part of a lot of wilderness land granted to A. in 1799, in a grant containing a number of other lots severally, each described by particular bounds and lines. It was proved that the plaintiff's father was in possession of the front of the lot in 1821, that he built upon and improved it, and that in 1838 he had the dividing line between that and the adjoining lot marked nearly to the rear, that his right was never disputed, and that he died in possession, and devised all his property to the plaintiff, who continued the same possession. No conveyance was shewn from A., or that he had ever been in possession of the lot, or what became of him. Held, per Carter, C. J. and Wilmot, J., That the plaintiff had not shown a sufficient possession, either actual or constructive, of the rear of the lot, to maintain trespass even against a wrong doer, and that a conveyance from A. to the plaintiff's father could not be presumed. *Gaudin* v. *McKilligan*, 2 *All.* 392.

Held, per Parker, J. and Street, J., That in the absence of evidence of a wrongful entry, it might be presumed that the plaintiff's father entered by permission of the grantee, and, there being no adverse possession, his possession would be presumed to extend over the whole lot, as one undivided close. Held also, That as the defendant did not claim the land under any right derived from the grantee, but as being part of another grant in rear, and the question was the boundary line between the two grants, he was not entitled to put the plaintiff to proof of a documentary title. Held also, That the running the line in 1838 was an act of possession of the whole lot. *Gaudin* v. *McKilligan*, 2 *All.* 392.

24—Prior possession—Title.

A person taking possession of land without title, cannot maintain trespass against one who has a prior possession of the land under a Crown grant, and with lines run according to the grant; even though it conveys no title in consequence of the land having been previously granted. *Creamer* v. *Whipple*, 3 *All.* 273.

A defendant in possession under such circumstances, is not bound to prove a title under his grant, as the plaintiff acquires no possession. *Ibid.*

Semble, That a person who takes possession of part of a lot of land without title, does not by running the exterior lines of the lot, acquire such a possession as will enable him to maintain trespass for an entry on the line beyond the bounds of his actual occupation. *Ibid.*

25—Asportavit—Sufficient title to recover upon—Place.

In trespass for breaking and entering a close and cutting the grass, the plaintiff failed to prove any parish in which the *locus in quo* was situated. Held, That being in possession, he had nevertheless sufficient title to the grass to enable him to recover on the *asportavit* count for taking it away, against any person who could not prove a title to the land on which it was cut. *Moran* v. *Laird*, 3 *Kerr* 403.

26—Possession—Absence of proof of better title—Wrong doer.

In trespass for cutting trees, the plaintiff relied on his possession of the land from which they were cut, which was proved to have been called a glebe lot for upwards of twenty years, and had been surveyed by direction of the Church corporation of the parish. Held, That in the absence of proof of any title in the corporation, or any lease from them to the plaintiff, that he was entitled to recover against a mere wrong doer. *Hodgson* v. *Carr*, 3 *Kerr* 499.

27—Owner of land—Life estate—Asportavit.

The owner of land, subject to an estate for life, may maintain trespass *de bonis asportatis* for carrying away trees which have been wrongfully cut upon the land. *Alexander* v. *Hartt*, 1 *Han.* 161.

28—Licensee.

A license granted by the government to cut timber on Crown land, gives the licensee no interest in the land; therefore he cannot maintain trespass under the Rev. Stat. c 133, against a person for entering on the land, and cutting down and taking away the trees. *Breckenridge* v. *Woolner*, 3 *All.* 303.

29—Grantee—Water privilege—Easement.

A deed granting all the right, title, interest, etc. of A. in and to the "water privilege" of a piece of land, conveys only an easement in the land, and no interest in the land itself; therefore the grantee cannot by virtue of the deed maintain trespass for an entry on the land. *Wilson* v. *Sinclair*, 3 *All.* 343.

In trespass by W. being in possession, claiming under the deed, the jury were directed that he was in possession of the land by virtue of the deed. Held, a misdirection. *Ibid.*

Quære, Whether if the case had been left to the jury on the question of possession alone, and they had found for the plaintiff, the Court would have interfered. *Ibid.*

30—Insufficient possession—Evidence.

The plaintiff in trespass claimed under a registered deed from K., who had been in possession of the land, but was not actually so at the time of giving the deed, and it was not shewn how he got possession, or how long he held it: the land had been unfenced for several years before, and the plaintiff had never occupied it, or taken possession. Held, That he had neither the actual or constructive possession, and could not maintain the action. *Creelman* v. *Atkinson*, 3 *All.* 450.

31—Color of title—Possession against wrong doer.

In trespass *quare clausum fregit*, it appeared that the land which was principally wilderness, had been granted to a person who resided out of the country; that one T. or his agent had a charge of the land to prevent trespasses on it, and also had a power of attorney authorising him to sell it, and that, after the death of the grantee, T., believing that the authority continued, conveyed the land to the plaintiff who had the lines of it run out by a surveyor and exercised acts of ownership over the land by cutting timber. Held, That though the plaintiff acquired no title to the land by his deed, he went in under color of title, and had sufficient possession to entitle him to recover against a mere wrong doer who entered on the land and cut timber after the plaintiff took possession and ran out the lines. *Nugent* v. *Parks*, *Hil. T.* 1866.

II.

Defence—Pleading—Evidence.

1—Right of soil—River—Easement.
An easement or privilege granted by deed, to turn the water of a river for the use of mills, and to build mill-dams, does not convey the right of soil, and cannot be given in evidence under the general issue in trespass. *Wallace* v. *Milliken*, *East. T.* 1831.

2—Fence—Breaking—Cattle entering.
Defendant threw down a fence and entered on land in the plaintiff's possession claiming it to be a highway, and in consequence of the fence being thrown down, the defendant's cattle went in upon the plaintiff's field. Held, That this was not a—"breaking into a field under lawful fence"—by the cattle, and therefore that a Justice of the Peace had no jurisdiction to proceed against the defendant in trespass under the Act 1 Wm. 4, c. 9, s. 6. *Colwell* v. *Purdy*, *Trin. T.* 1831.

3—Admission—Killing ox—Consent.
An admission by the defendant that he had killed the plaintiff's ox and ought to pay for it, will not support an action of trespass for taking the ox, there being some evidence that the ox had been worked by the defendant, by consent of the plaintiff's agent. *Bransfield* v. *Bishop*, *Ber.* 89.

4—Entry to remove timber—Necessary evidence.
A man cannot justify an entry on the land of another for the purpose of taking his own property, unless he shews that it was upon the land without any fault or neglect on his part; therefore in trespass *quare cl. fregit*, a plea justifying the entry for the purpose of removing the defendant's timber which had been carried there by a sudden rise of water in the river in which it was being floated to market, is bad, because it does not shew that the defendant was not in fault, by endeavouring to prevent the timber from floating on the plaintiff's land. *Read* v. *Smith*, *Ber.* 173.

5—Entry—Command—License.
A defendant in trespass may justify his entry by the *command* of the owner of the freehold, but not by his mere permission or license; therefore where the plaintiff proves a trespass by the defendant on land in his (plaintiff's) possession, it will be no justification to the defendant to shew that the title was in a third person, from whom he had agreed to purchase it, and under which agreement he went into possession. (See Robinson v. Vaughton, 8 C. and P. 252.) *Parent* v. *Corneilison*, *Ber.* 235.

6—In trespass *quare cl. fregit*, if defendant justifies the entry on the land under a third person he must shew that he entered by the *command* and under the *authority* of such person, not merely that he allowed the defendant to enter. *Keen* v. *Seymour*, *Hil. T.* 1864.

7—Entry on ground opposed to title as mortgagee—Setting up mortgage.
In trespass, where the question in dispute was the dividing line between the plaintiff's and defendant's land the defendant, among other grounds of defence, relied on a mortgage given to him by the plaintiff before the alleged trespass upon the lot occupied by the plaintiff. Held, That as the defendant had entered on the land upon a ground opposed to his title as mortgagee, it afforded no justification of the trespass. *Merrithew* v. *Sisson*, 3 *Kerr* 373.

8—Joint trespassers—Separate trespasses.
Where there are a number of defendants in an action of trespass, and plaintiff proves an act of trespass against some and not against all, and then goes on to prove another act against others of defendants not implicated in the first act proved, he must be taken to have abandoned the first act and be confined to the last act proved. *Maloney* v. *Purden*, 3 *Kerr* 515.

9—Several defendants—Joint liability.
In trespass against several defendants, it

they go upon the land with a common purpose they are jointly liable, though the acts of trespass are separate and are committed on different parts of the land. *Ferguson* v. *Savoy*, 4 *All.* 263.

10—If two persons enter on land wrongfully and cut down trees separately, but unite in taking them away, by removing obstructions in the roads, they are jointly liable for the taking and carrying away, but not for the cutting. *Keen* v. *Seymour*, *Hil. T.* 1864.

11—Verbal command by mortgagee not in possession.
In trespass for cutting and carrying away trees off land in the plaintiff's possession, defendant may justify under a verbal command to enter and cut, given by a mortgagee of the land not in possession. *Carson* v. *Griffin*, *Hil. T.* 1865.

12—Joint trespass—Separate—Abandonment.
In a joint act of trespass, if the plaintiff wishes to rely on a separate act of trespass by one of the defendants, he must abandon the joint trespass; he cannot ask the jury to find in the alternative. *Lawton* v. *Adams*, *East. T.* 1862.

13—Abandonment—Judge—Discretion.
In an action against several defendants, the plaintiff proved acts of trespass on the 6th June, in which all the defendants were concerned, and another act of trespass on the 10th, in which only one of the defendants present on the 6th took part: the plaintiff then elected to proceed for the first trespass proved. Held, That this was a matter in the discretion of the Judge; and that the plaintiff by giving evidence of the trespass on the 10th June, had not abandoned the previous one proved. *Ache* v. *Alexandre*, *East. T.* 1871.

14—Entry to retake cattle wrongfully taken.
In trespass for breaking and entering plaintiff's barn, defendant justified on the ground that his cattle had been wrongfully taken by the plaintiff, who locked them up in his barn, and refused to give them up. Held sufficient, and that defendant had a right to take his cattle from the plaintiff, who was a wrong doer. (See Blades *v.* Higgs, 7 Jur. N. S. 1289.) *Graham* v. *Green*, *Trin. T.* 1862.

15—Deed—Registry—Relation.
In trespass *quare cl. fregit* for cutting grass on the 31st July, the plaintiff proved possession only: the defendant justified as owner of the land under a deed dated the 15th July, but not registered till the 1st August. Held, That as against the plaintiff the defendant had not title by relation from the date of the deed. *Patterson* v. *Tingley*, *Trin. T.* 1863. See Relation 4.

16—Liberum tenementum—Proof—Close.
In trespass *quare cl. fregit* describing the close by abuttals, the defendant pleaded *liberum tenementum*. Held, That under this plea, he was bound to prove that that part of the close described by abuttals on which he entered, was his soil and freehold, and that, having failed to prove title to a small piece of the land so described, on which part of the trespass was committed, the plaintiff was entitled to a verdict. *DesBrisay* v. *Livingstone*, *Trin. T.* 1864.

17—Crown grant—Possession—Question for jury.
Defendant in trespass claimed the *locus in quo* under a grant from the Crown, the plaintiff gave evidence of acts of possession of the land for twenty years prior to the grant, by which he claimed that the Crown was out of possession, and could not grant without office found. Held, That this evidence of possession ought to have been left to the jury. *Smith* v. *Morrow*, *Mich. T.* 1872.

18—Church corporation—Members' rights.
In trespass for boarding up the doors and windows of a parish church, the defendants justified as church wardens, and that they had closed the church for repairs, but the evidence shewed that they had closed it to prevent a clergyman who claimed to be rector, from officiating. Held, in the absence of proof that there was any legally appointed rector, That the defendants had no right to dismantle the church as against the church corporation, even though they were themselves members of it. *Rector etc. of St. George's Church* v. *Cougle*, 1 *Han.* 609.

19—Admission by plea—Plan—Lot.
In trespass the declaration described the premises as four closes in the city of St. John, fronting on Elliott Row, and known and distinguished on the map or plan of the city on file in the Common Clerk's

Office as lots Nos. 294, 295, 296 and 297—plea—not guilty—"so far as relates to the said close No. 295 in the declaration mentioned"—and as to the other closes, payment of money into Court. Held, That the plea admitted the identity of the lot, and therefore evidence of the plan filed in the Common Clerk's Office was unnecessary. *Semble*, That as the number of the lots corresponded with the grant of the lots, which was in evidence, the reference to the plan was surplusage *Merritt* v. *Coxetter*, 2 *Kerr* 385

20—Property delivered to avoid execution.

In trespass for taking hay, which plaintiff claimed to have been delivered to him by defendant in payment of a debt. Held, That evidence was admissible on the part of the defendant, to show that the hay was delivered to plaintiff in order to prevent its being seized on execution against defendant, and that no property was intended to pass to the plaintiff. *Knowles* v. *Adams*, *Hil. T.* 1863.

21—Unregistered deed—Command—Entry.

In trespass defendant pleaded freehold in P. by whose command he entered. Held, That an unregistered deed of release from P. to defendant was not evidence of such command. An unregistered deed transfers no property, and gives no right to enter on land. *Patterson* v. *Tingley*, *Trin. T.* 1863.

22—Distress for rent—Keeping and detaining in satisfaction for rent.

It is a good plea to a declaration in trespass for taking goods, that the goods were distrained for rent and not being replevied within five days were appraised, and after such appraisement kept and detained in satisfaction of the rent; although the defendant should have proceeded to sell the goods, yet the omission to do so will not enable the owner to maintain trespass, the original taking being lawful. The option granted by the Act 50 Geo. 3, c. 21, s. 7, to bring trespass or case, is to be understood according to the subject matter of the grievance, and not the mere election of the party. *Rogers* v. *Buntin*, 2 *Kerr* 230.

23—Tenancy—Right to crops.

In trespass for taking hay and grain, it was proved that the land on which they grew belonged to the plaintiff's father, who, four years before the trial, gave it up to the plaintiff on condition that he should support his father and family: that the father continued to live on the land, but that the plaintiff took the management of the farm and sowed the grain and cut the grass. Held, That the jury were properly directed that this constituted a tenancy and gave the plaintiff the possession of the crops. *Ferguson* v. *Savoy*, 4 *All.* 263.

24—Locus in quo—Highway.

To an action of trespass *quare clausum fregit*, the defendant pleaded that the *locus in quo* had been laid out and recorded as a road three rods wide. Held, That the proof of such laying out and recording would not sustain a justification depending upon the fact of the place being a public highway, the Act of Assembly requiring that no public highway should be laid out of a less width than four rods. *Perley* v. *Dibblee*, 1 *Kerr* 514.

25—Separate trespasses—Evidence—Abandonment—Necessity of.

In trespass against three defendants for taking away logs, which taking occupied several successive days, the plaintiff proved a joint trespass against all the defendants during the first two days, after which one of the defendants went away: a verdict having been found against the other two. Held, That the trespasses were not so separate and distinct as to require the plaintiff to abandon the joint trespass before giving evidence of the trespass by the two defendants. *Atkinson* v. *McAuley*, 4 *All.* 243.

Quære, Whether where the two defendants are clearly liable, the evidence of the trespass by the three, is ground for a new trial. *Ibid.*

26—Denial of title—Claim—Justification—Evidence.

On a verdict in trespass for the plaintiff, claiming title by descent from his father, the Court refused a new trial moved for on the ground that S., one of the defendants, was the plaintiff's brother and therefore justified in entering as a tenant in common with the plaintiff: the defence at the trial being a denial of the father's title, and a claim under a different right. *Sears* v. *Palmer*, 3 *All.* 400.

Quære, Whether if the father's title had not been denied, the verdict would have been good against the other defendants on the plaintiff entering a *nol pros.* as to S., he being a party to all the alleged trespasses. *Sears* v. *Palmer*, 3 *All.* 400.

Defendant in trespass offered as evidence of title a registered deed to himself from one who had neither actual or constructive possession of the land. Held, That this deed was properly rejected. *Ibid.*

27—Possession—Insufficient evidence.
The defendant in an action of trespass justified under A., and in order to show title in him, offered evidence of a conversation between A. and B.,—not made upon the land, but several miles distant from it,—in which A. gave B. permission to build a mill on the land in dispute. B. built the mill more than twenty years before the action, but did not further recognize A.'s right to the land. Held, That this was not sufficient evidence of A.'s possession, and that the justification was not proved. *White* v. *Smith*, 4 *All.* 335.

28—Extent of possession—Unregistered deed—Evidence.
The acts of a near relative and personal representative of a deceased person, done in behalf of his minor children and heirs upon and in regard to land which was claimed by the deceased, but under a defective title, will enure to the benefit of such heirs, to shew possession in them, as against a mere wrong doer, and the title deed, though not sufficient to convey the land for want of due registry or livery of seisin, may be used to shew the extent of the claim of possession. *Hadden* v. *White*, 2 *Kerr* 634.

29—Boundary—Necessary evidence.
In trespass, the plaintiff claimed title under a grant and survey made in 1823; the defendant claimed the same land under a prior grant to D., and conveyances from P. to E., and from E. to himself, made in 1834, under which he entered. Held, That though no conveyance was shewn from D., the original grantee, the defendant was not a mere wilful trespasser, and that the plaintiff could not recover on his possession alone, but was bound to prove that the line contended for by him was the true boundary between his grant and the grant to D., and that the question of boundary should have been submitted to the jury. *Baldwin* v. *Braydon*, 3 *Kerr* 169.

30—Highway—Ploughing soil.
In trespass to land, and ploughing up the soil, the defendant pleaded that there was a public highway over the land, by reason whereof he entered. Held, That if it was a highway the defendant was not justified in ploughing up the soil. *Cole* v. *Maxwell*, 3 *All.* 183.

31—Cattle—Defect of Fences.
In trespass by cattle, if the defendant justify the entry of the cattle through defect of fences, it must be specially pleaded. *Griswold* v. *Hallet*, *Mich. T.* 1834.

32—Adoption of acts—Presumption.
By Act 10 Vic. c. 72, incorporating the South Bay Boom Co., amended by 11 Vic. c. 49, and 17 Vic. c. 52, though timber placed within the Booms is under the general control and direction of the Company, it is under the immediate charge of the owners, to be fastened and secured by them, and at their risk; therefore the Company is not liable in trespass where rafts are fastened to trees on the shore of land within the limits of the Boom, unless the act was done by the Company or their servants, or with their knowledge and consent; or, if done by other persons,—unless the Company has adopted the act. The mere fact that the Company is entitled to boomage on all lumber coming within the boom, does not raise any presumption that the lumber was fastened in a particular place by their direction; nor is the receipt of boomage an adoption of the act of the owners of lumber in fastening it to the land of a riparian proprietor. *Dever* v. *South Bay Boom Co.*, *East. T.* 1872

33—Company—Contractors under—Liability.
The defendants, a Railway Company, being authorized by Act of Assembly to construct a line of railway, entered into a contract with A. and B. for that purpose. The contractors, in order to get ballast to complete the road, laid down a track across the plaintiff's land, leading to a gravel pit, and used it for the transportation of gravel to the railway. Held, That the defendants were not liable for the acts of the contractors, the trespass having been committed without their authority, and being merely collateral to the work which they had agreed with A. and B. to perform. *Payne* v. *Fredericton Railway Co.*, *Mich. T.* 1871.

34—Entry by permission of agent—Cutting lumber.

Defendant had a license from the Crown to cut lumber in rear of land granted to the plaintiffs. The plaintiffs' agent and manager in charge of their land pointed out to the defendant a line as the boundary of the plaintiffs' land, and directed him not to cut over it. The defendant cut lumber up to this line, believing it to be correct; but it was shewn by another survey that the line so pointed out to the defendant was incorrect, and that part of the lumber was cut upon the plaintiffs' land. Held, That the defendant having entered on the plaintiffs' land and cut the lumber by permission of their agent, was not liable in trespass for the cutting, though the agent had no authority to agree to a boundary affecting the plaintiffs' title to the land. *Vernon Mining Co.* v. *Prescott*, *East. T.* 1871.

III.

Personal Property.

1—Tenant in common.

Quære, Whether any and what acts, short of the destruction of the joint property, will enable one tenant in common to sustain trespass against his co-tenant. *Wiggins* v. *White*, *Ber.* 97.

2—Sheriff fi. fa.—Taking goods.

A Sheriff is liable in trespass for taking goods under a *fi. fa.* which had been once returned and re-issued as an alias. *Johnson* v. *Winslow*, *Ber.* 53.

3—Abusing authority—Trespasser ab initio.

Where a person having authority by a Statute, abuses such authority by some positive act contravening the same, he will be liable as a trespasser *ab initio*. *Califf* v. *Wilson*, *Ber.* 79.

4—Agreement—Violation.

Where personal property of the defendant is in the actual possession of the plaintiff under an agreement between them, the latter may sustain trespass against the former for taking it away. *Holmes* v. *Clark*, *Ber.* 87.

5—Satisfaction—Judgment—Sheriff.

Plaintiff brought an action against the Sheriff for taking his goods on an execution against A. and recovered judgment, but not to the full extent of his claim, the jury having found that part of the goods did not belong to the plaintiff and were consequently liable to seizure under the execution. Plaintiff afterwards brought trespass against the defendant who had indemnified the Sheriff for seizing the goods. Held, That the judgment against the Sheriff was a satisfaction for the wrong done to the plaintiff by taking the goods, and that he could not recover. A party cannot split up his claim for damages and proceed for a part of the trespass at one time, and part at another. *Lawton* v. *Adams*, *East. T.* 1862.

6—Master and servant—Relation.

Plaintiff was Chairman of the Board of Agriculture, to superintend the erection of a Provincial Exhibition; plaintiff had contracted to erect the building, but failed to complete it in time, and the committee took possession of it in order to finish it. He left some boards on the ground, which it was necessary to remove before the opening of the Exhibition. Two days before that time one W. sold the boards, and they were taken away. W. informed the defendant that he had sold the boards, who said it was the best thing to do. Held, That the jury were justified in finding that the relation of master and servant existed between the committee and W., and that the sale of the boards was an act done by W. in the course of his employment. *McKay* v. *Botsford*, *Trin. T.* 1863.

IV.

Damages.

1—Special Allegation—Expense of inquiry.

In trespass for taking goods under an execution the declaration alleged as special damage, loss of time and expenditure of money in recovering the possession. Held, That under this allegation, plaintiff could not recover the expense of an inquiry held by the Sheriff for his own information as to the right to the goods, and *quære*, whether such damage could be recovered in any case. *Wilson* v. *Ellis*, *Ber.* 325.

2—Judge directing for small damages for plaintiff—Verdict for defendant—New trial.

In trespass *quare cl. fregit* the main question was the dividing line between the parties, on which the evidence was clearly in favor of the defendant; but he had driven a few stakes on plaintiff's land, for which the Judge directed a verdict for the smallest amount of damages; the jury, however, found for the defendant, and the Court refused a new trial. *O'Flaherty* v. *Devine*, *Hil. T.* 1863.

3—Wilful and malicious trespass—Certificate—Damages.
In trespass against several defendants, the plaintiff had forbidden them from going on his land, and again, after acts of trespass had been committed, notified them to desist, whereupon two of them did so. At the trial plaintiff elected to proceed against all the defendants, and, under the Judge's direction, only recovered for the trespass committed before the two defendants left, amounting to $2. Held, That plaintiff was entitled to the certificate of the Judge; that the trespass was "wilful and malicious." *McMillan* v. *Fairly et al.*, 1 *Han.* 500.

4—Damages when held not excessive.
In trespass for cutting a net with which the plaintiff was fishing in a public navigable river, where the defendant claimed an exclusive right to fish, as owner of the adjoining land, the jury gave a verdict for $40. Held, That the damages were not excessive, though the plaintiff stated the actual damage to the net did not exceed $2. *Rose* v. *Belyea*, 1 *Han.* 109.

5—Conflicting evidence.
Where in trespass there was conflicting evidence as to the quantity and value of trees taken from plaintiff's land, the Court refused to disturb the finding of the jury, even though the damages appeared large. *Prescott* v. *Walton*, 2 *Han.* 230.

6—Distinct lots—Title to one in defendant—No apportionment of damages.
Where in an action for trespass on two distinct lots of land, to one of which the defendant proved title, the jury gave a verdict for the plaintiff without any apportionment of the damages, the Court ordered a new trial, unless the plaintiff consented to accept nominal damages. *White* v. *Smith*, 4 *All.* 335.

7—Splitting claim.
A party cannot split up his claim for damages, and proceed for a part of the trespass at one time, and part at another. See Supra III. 5.

8—Special damage—Claim for—Notice of action. See Action at Law XI. 5 *a*.

Action against Justice of the Peace—Nominal damages. See New Trial III. 18 *a*.

V.

Assault and False Imprisonment.

1—Assault and battery—Felony.
Where, in an action for assault and battery, the plaintiff proves that the injury caused grievous bodily harm, and therefore amounted to a felony under 1 Rev. Stat. c. 149, s. 15, the plaintiff will be non-suited unless it appears that proceedings have been taken against the defendant for the criminal offence. (But see Wells v. Abrahams, 7 L. R. Q B. 554.) *Schohl* v. *Kay*, *Hil. T.* 1862.

See Criminal Law.

Assault on Public Officer—Damages held not excessive. See New Trial III. 18.

2—Justice of the Peace—Proceedings—Jurisdiction.
A Justice of the Peace is liable in an action for false imprisonment if he commits a person for trial who is brought before him on a criminal charge, without taking an examination respecting the charge, as required by law. An examination taken beyond the jurisdiction of the Province is a nullity. *Nury* v. *Owen*, *Ber.* 377.

3—Commitment—Place—Damages.
In trespass for false imprisonment against Justices of the Peace who had exceeded their power in committing the plaintiff for contempt to an improper place of imprisonment, but who otherwise had received no greater punishment than he was liable to by law, the Judge offered to direct a verdict for nominal damages, which the plaintiff refused, claiming substantial damages — whereupon the Judge ordered a non-suit—the Court refused to set the non-suit aside. *Armstrong* v. *McCaffrey*, 1 *Han.* 517.

4—Information—Omission of Christian name—Subsequent insertion.
An information was sworn before the defendant, a Justice of the Peace, of the commission of an alleged offence by —— Garrison (the Christian name being omitted); the defendant afterwards filled in the plaintiff's Christian name, and issued a warrant against him, on which he was arrested. Held, That the warrant was void, and the defendant liable in trespass. *Garrison* v. *Harding*, *Trin. T.* 1872.

5—Damages—Excessive fine—Imprisonment.
In trespass against Justices of the Peace

for false imprisonment, it appeared that the plaintiff, having committed an assault, was convicted by the defendants under the 1 Rev. Stat. c. 159, s. 27, and fined £8, and, in default of payment, sentenced to a month's imprisonment, and that, having refused to pay the fine, he had been imprisoned for a month. Held, That as the imprisonment did not exceed that assigned by the Act for the offence, the plaintiff was only entitled to recover *two pence* damages under 1 Rev. Stat. c. 129, s. 11, though the fine was greater than the Justices had power to impose by the Act. *Davis* v. *Raymond*, *Trin. T.* 1865.

6—Public officer—Execution—Delivery.

A commissioner of highways, who, in the discharge of his duty, procures the conviction of a person for neglecting to perform statute labor, does not make himself a trespasser by delivering an execution, issued by the Justice, to a constable, and telling him that if the defendant was arrested he thought he would pay,—the defendant being afterwards arrested under the execution, which was defective. *Craig* v. *Giberson*, 2 *All.* 207.

7—Party suing out process—Directions—Validity on face—Justification.

A party who merely sues out a process and delivers it to an officer to execute, is not liable as a trespasser, though he may be liable to an action on the case if there are not previous proceedings to warrant the process. *Carter* v. *Purrington*, 2 *All.* 226.

If he gives special direction to the officer or takes part in the arrest, he is liable in trespass unless there is a regular judgment to authorize the execution. *Ibid.*

A process regular on its face, is a justification to the officer. *Ibid.*

8—Justice of the Peace—Second execution.

A Justice of the Peace is not liable to an action of trespass for issuing a second execution for a balance due upon a judgment recovered under the Act 4 Wm. 4, c. 45, before the first execution is returned—the matter being within the Justice's jurisdiction. *Stewart* v. *Hazen*, 2 *All.* 254.

Such an execution may be irregular, but is not void. *Ibid.*

9—Defective conviction and warrant.

Where a Justice of the Peace has jurisdiction to try a complaint, and there has been a regular information, but the conviction and warrant of commitment are defective, he is not liable in trespass for anything done prior to the conviction. *Sewell* v. *Olive*, 4 *All.* 394.

10—Justification—Reasonable and probable cause.

Application having been made to the defendant, a Justice of the Peace, for a warrant to summon a jury to determine on the necessity of a private road through the plaintiff's land, he issued a warrant under which a jury was summoned, but were unable to agree upon the amount of damages to the plaintiff. Another application was made, and another warrant issued by the defendant, under which a second jury was summoned to determine upon the road, but having been resisted by the plaintiff in entering on his land, and threatened with injury if they did so, one of them made oath before the defendant that the plaintiff "had molested the jury" in the discharge of their duty; whereupon the defendant issued a warrant against the plaintiff, on which he was arrested and detained several hours. Held, That though the entry on the plaintiff's land under the warrant might not have been justifiable, in consequence of irregularity in the proceedings, there was no want of *bona fides* in the defendant, and that he had shown reasonable and probable cause for what he did. *Stiles* v. *Brewster*, 4 *All.* 414.

11—Constable—Duty—Execution.

A constable is liable in trespass, if he arrests a debtor under an execution issued out of a Justice's Court, (1 Rev. Stat., c. 137) before he has used reasonable diligence to find goods to levy on. *Hunter* v. *Maddox*, 1 *Han.* 162.

12—Legal adviser—Aiding—Imprisonment illegal.

Procuring, commanding, aiding or assisting in a trespass makes a person a trespasser; and it affords no defence to one who has been instrumental in procuring or promoting the imprisonment of another, under a warrant of a magistrate, that he was merely the legal adviser of the magistrate, the imprisonment itself being illegal. *Thompson* v. *Hatch*, 2 *Kerr* 425.

Misnomer — Plea — Necessary averment. See Pleading II. 20.

Justification—Pleading. See Pleading II. 15, 16.

TRIAL.

Cannot on trial, impeach validity of sale, on ground that execution is irregular. *Doe* v. *Watson*, 1 *All.* 675.

Special counts—Particulars—Recovery under common counts—Counsel opening case.

Where a declaration contains special counts, with a count for money had and received, and the particulars also apply to the latter count, the plaintiff may give evidence under the count for money had and received, though his counsel did not claim to recover on that count in opening the case. *Currick* v. *Atkinson*, *East. T.* 1863.

Power of Judge on trial to direct verdict for plaintiff, subject to be set aside and verdict entered for defendant upon points reserved. This can only be effected by the jury finding a special verdict, when no consent is given. *Hughes* v. *Sutherland*, 1 *Kerr* 374.

TRIAL BY RECORD.

TROVER.

1—Tenant in common—Joint owner.

Quære, Whether any, and what acts of a tenant in common or joint owner of a chattel, other than a destruction of the property will enable his co-tenant to maintain trover against him. *Wiggins* v. *White*, *Ber.* 97.

2—Licensee—Crown land—Wrong doer.

A person having a license from the Crown to cut timber on Crown land, cannot maintain trover against a wrong doer for timber cut and carried away by the latter from off the limits of the licensee. (But see act 13 Vic. c. 7.) *Kerr* v. *Connell*, *Ber.* 133.

3—Hiring horse—Felonious sale.

A. hired the plaintiff's horse to go a certain distance, but went further, and sold the horse under such circumstances as to lead to the presumption that he intended to steal the horse at the time of hiring. Held, That the plaintiff could not maintain trover against the defendant who had afterwards purchased the horse, until he had done everything in his power to prosecute A. for the felony. (See Contra—White *v.* Spottigue 13 M. and W. 602. See further—Judge bound to try issue on the record. Wells *v.* Abraham, 7 L. R., Q. B. 554.) *Pease* v. *McAloon*, 1 *Kerr* 111.

4—Evidence of felony—Judge.

Although the circumstances are not conclusive evidence of felony, but proper for the consideration of a jury, the question of felony cannot be left to them in an action of trover,—it is the duty of the Judge to determine whether there is sufficient *prima facie* evidence of felony to render a prosecution necessary. *Ibid.*

5—Licensee—Timber—Wrongful sale.

Plaintiff having a license from the owner of land to cut timber thereon, contracted with A. to manufacture the timber and raft it for the plaintiff. Held, That the property in the timber vested in the plaintiff as soon as it was cut without any delivery, and that he could maintain trover for it against a person to whom A. had wrongfully sold it. *Seyee* v. *Perley*, 1 *Kerr* 439.

6—Trustees—Absconding debtor—Vesting of property.

The trustees of an absconding debtor duly appointed under the Act 26 Geo. 3, c. 13, may maintain trover for the value of goods of the debtor wrongfully converted by the defendant before proceedings taken under the Act; such right of action being transferred from the debtor to the trustees by operation of the Act. *Ritchie* v. *Boyd*, 1 *Kerr* 264.

7—Shipping timber—Notice—Acquiescence.

A. delivered timber to B. under an agreement that B. should ship as much as he could, and give A. credit for the amount. B. shipped a portion of it, and gave A. notice to take away the remainder; but subsequently shipped a further quantity. Held, in the absence of any proof of acquiescence in the notice by A., That B. was not liable in trover for the timber shipped after the notice. *Hughes* v. *Sutherland*, 1 *Kerr* 574.

8—Seizure by Crown—Proceedings stayed—Property—Subsequent taking by wrong doer.

Timber, cut by plaintiff without license, was seized by an officer for the Crown, and marked; no proceedings were taken towards condemnation; the officer kept no possession of it, and was afterwards ordered by the Government not to proceed to condemnation, but there was no act of the Government by which the constructive possession was revested in the plaintiff, nor any actual possession of the plaintiff subsequent to the seizure. Held, That the plaintiff had no property in the timber to enable him to maintain trover against a person who took it wrongfully, subsequent to the seizure by the Crown. *Tobin* v. *Hutchinson*, 3 *Kerr* 233.

9—Previous seizure—Possession—Title.

The possession of timber which had been previously seized by the Crown for having been cut without license, is a sufficient title against all persons except the Crown, and the person so in possession may maintain trover against a stranger for taking it. *Coombes* v. *Hatheway*, 3 *Kerr* 592.

10—Church Corporation—Trees severed.

The property in trees growing on a glebe is in the Church Corporation, as the owners of the inheritance; and they may maintain trover for them if wrongfully severed, against a tenant of the Rector, or any person acting under the tenant's authority. *Rector etc. of Hampton* v. *Titus*, 1 *All.* 278.

11—Accepted order for timber—Delivery—Usage.

B. drew an order on defendant, a pond keeper, in favor of R. for five hundred tons of pine timber, which the defendant accepted and credited R. with the timber in account. R. afterwards assigned all his property to the plaintiff. Held, in the absence of any proof of title to the timber in B.; or that he had delivered it to the defendant, or of any usage in the timber trade relative to such acceptances, That no property vested in R. by the acceptance in any specific five hundred tons of timber, and that the action could not be maintained. *Pollock* v. *Fisher*, 1 *All.* 515.

12—Assignment by deed—Property passing.
Defendant had in his possession as a pond keeper, timber belonging to H., who while it was in defendant's possession, made a general assignment by deed of his property to the plaintiff. Held, That this was an assignment of the property in the timber, and not merely of a chose in action, and that the plaintiff, after tendering the amount of the plaintiff's lien on the timber, might maintain trover against him. *Jack* v. *Eagles*, 2 *All.* 95.

13—Landlord—Tenant—Gas fittings—Executory agreement.
An agreement by a tenant of a shop that if the landlord would make certain improvements the tenant would put in gas fittings, and leave them there when the lease expired, is executory only, and vests no property in the gas fittings in the landlord unless they are left by the tenant in the shop. If they are removed by the tenant before he leaves, the landlord cannot maintain trover for them. *Dunn* v. *Garret*, 2 *All.* 218.

14—Taking timber—Conversion.
Timber belonging to the plaintiff in this Province, being in the possession of the men who manufactured it and who claimed a lien on it for their wages, was sold by them to the defendant, and taken into Canada at his request, where he caused it to be attached and sold for payment of the wages. Held, That the taking the timber into Canada was a conversion, and that the plaintiff was entitled to recover the value of it, without deducting what the defendant had paid the men. *McMullen* v. *Ritchie*, 2 *All.* 242.

15—Manure—Not incident to land—Conversion.
Manure in heaps on land (not the produce thereof) does not pass to the purchaser of the equity of redemption under a decree of sale, as an incident to the land; and if he uses it, it is a conversion, for which the mortgagor may recover in trover without a demand. *Thomson* v. *Walsh*, 2 *All.* [illegible].

16—Manure—Landlord—Tenant.
Manure lying in heaps in a barn yard is a chattel which may be taken away by the out-going tenant, even after his tenancy has expired, and trover will lie for it, if held or taken away by the landlord. *Fushay* v. *Barnes*, 1 *Han.* 450.

17—Goods of tenant—Refusal by succeeding tenant.
Where goods belonging to the plaintiff were left on a farm of which he had been tenant, and the defendant who succeeded him as tenant, refused to deliver them up without the consent of the landlord; but there was no evidence that the landlord had any claim to the goods or had given the defendant possession, or that he was holding them as the servant of the landlord—the Court refused to set aside a verdict for the plaintiff on the ground that the refusal did not amount to a conversion. *Ruel* v. *McElroy*, 3 *All.* 212.

18—Though a refusal by a servant to give up property in his possession until he can obtain directions from his master, may not amount to a conversion; he has no right to insist on the owner of the property obtaining the master's consent to the delivery. *Ibid.*

19—Holding document for both parties.
A. executed a bill of sale to the plaintiff, and delivered it to the defendant, who agreed to hold it as the agent of both parties. Held, That the defendant's refusal to deliver the bill of sale to the plaintiff, without the consent of A, was not a conversion, and that trover could not be maintained. *Dever* v. *Myshrall*, 3 *All.* 354.

20—Setting up right in third party—Defective claim.
Plaintiff having cut timber without license on Crown land in Canada, brought it into this Province, and put it in possession of the defendants to be rafted for him; the defendants delivered it to M., who claimed it as having been cut on land licensed to him, but in fact his license had expired at the time the timber was cut. Held, in trover for the timber, That the defendants could not set up a right either in M. or in the Canada Government—M. having no legal right to the timber, and the Government not having made any claim to it. *Le Bel* v. *Fredericton Boom Company*, 4 *All.* 198.

21—Allegation of one conversion—Evidence.
In trover for several articles, the plaintiff may give evidence of acts of conversion on several days though there is but one

count in the declaration alleging one conversion. *Ultican* v. *Moffat*, 4 *All.* 298.

22—Sufficiency of possession.
In trover for timber cut by defendant on wilderness land described in a registered deed from B. to the plaintiff, it was proved that for more than twenty years plaintiff had occasionally exercised acts of ownership over the land by cutting timber and wild grass upon it, and that five years before the action, he had made a survey of it and marked the exterior lines; no grant of the land was proved, and no possession shewn in B. Held, That the plaintiff had sufficient possession to entitle him to recover against a person shewing no title. *Coates* v. *McAuley*, 4 *All.* 521.

23—Bill of sale—Condition—Demand —Non-disclosure of title—Conversion.
A. gave B. a bill of sale of a pair of oxen to secure a debt, with a condition that A. should keep possession of the oxen, but if he undertook to sell them, or allow them to be taken in execution the bill of sale was to be absolute. A. afterwards sold the oxen to the defendant, and B. assigned his interest under the bill of sale to the plaintiff, who demanded the oxen of the defendant without informing him of the assignment of the bill of sale Held, That the defendant's refusal to give up the oxen was no conversion as against the plaintiff *Sharp* v. *Lawrence*, *Mich T.* 1865.

24—Joint conversion—Evidence.
Logs were wrongfully cut on the plaintiff's land by P., one of the defendants, who afterwards sold them to T. the other defendant; plaintiff demanded the logs from T., who refused to give them up and denied the plaintiff's right to them. Held, That this was evidence of a joint conversion by the defendants at the time of the sale by P. to T. *Hendricks* v. *Titus*, 2 *Han* 77.

25—Tenant in common—Mixing of property.
Sawing up logs of which the defendant is a tenant in common, and mixing the deals with others so that they cannot be distinguished, is evidence of conversion by one tenant in common against the other. *McKay* v. *Crocker*, *Hil. T.* 1861.

26—Mixing property—Plaintiff's wrong.
Plaintiff cut timber, part on land belonging to the defendant, and part on other land, and wrongfully mixed it with other timber belonging to the defendant, so that it could not be distinguished from the defendant's timber. Held, That as the mixing of the timber was the wrongful act of the plaintiff the defendant had a right to the whole of the timber, and his taking it was not a conversion. *Tucker* v. *Muirhead*, *East. T.* 1866.

27—Appropriation—Assent—Property.
Plaintiff claimed timber under a letter written to him by A., the maker of the timber, stating that part of a quantity of timber in the river (which part was distinguished by a particular mark) was for the plaintiff, and requesting him to send money and provisions to A. to enable him to drive the timber; plaintiff sent the money and provisions to A., and furnished the marks of the timber to the defendants (a company incorporated for the purpose of picking up timber in the river and rafting it, when the marks were furnished), and afterwards obtained a portion of the timber from them. Held, That the letter was an appropriation of the timber by A. to the plaintiff, and that his subsequent acts were an assent to such appropriation, and vested the property in him. *Macpherson* v. *Fredericton Boom Co.*, 1 *Han.* 337.

28—Licensee—Timber cut before license.
A license to cut and carry away lumber from Crown land gives the licensee no property in timber cut on the land before the license issued, though on the land at that time, and the licensee cannot maintain trover for taking away the timber. *Carman* v. *McLeod*, 2 *Han.* 66.

29—Sheriff—Improper sale—Execution —Fees.
A. issued an execution against B. under which a levy was made of B.'s goods but no sale, the execution being withdrawn. A second execution under another judgment was issued by A. against B., and the Sheriff after selling goods to satisfy that execution proceeded to sell other goods of B. to satisfy him for fees on the first execution. Held, That such sale by the Sheriff was a wrongful conversion and that trover would lie. *Miller* v. *Weldon*, 2 *Han.* 188.

Landlord and Tenant — Agreement as to fixtures. See Fixtures.

Principal and Agent. See

Damages — Bill of Exchange See Bills and Notes IV. 2.

Selling Security before time. See Bills and Notes V. 19.

Bankruptcy of party—Property vesting in assignee—Right to maintain Trover, or action for money had and received. See Assumpsit III. 37.

TRUSTS.

Agreement—Undertaking—Conditions—Party—Contract.

The St. Andrews and Quebec Railroad Company and class A. shareholders in the same Company, were incorporated by Act of Assembly 6 Wm. 4, c. 31, and by Act of Parliament, for the purpose of constructing a railroad from St. Andrews to Lower Canada; but being unable to complete the road, they were subsequently empowered by Act 19 Vic. c. 70, to agree with any company authorised to accept the same, for a transfer of the undertaking, and of all their lands, property, etc. Under the authority of this Act, an agreement was entered into between the St. Andrews and Quebec Railway Company, the class A. shareholders, and the defendants, the N. B. and Canada Railway and Land Company, (a company incorporated under the Joint Stock Companies' Act,) whereby the former agreed to convey to the latter (called the Transferee Company,) the undertaking of the St. Andrews & Quebec Railroad Co., and of class A. shareholders, and the control and management thereof, and all the lands, rights and property thereof, subject to certain conditions: (*inter alia*,) that the Transferee Company should complete the railroad, and should forthwith discharge the liabilities of the St. Andrews and Quebec Railroad Company and class A. shareholders, specified in the schedule to the agreement. Among the liabilities specified in the schedule, was the following—"Liability, (if any) to the contractors in New Brunswick." The Act declared that when the agreement of transfer was executed, all the undertaking of the St. Andrews & Quebec Railroad Company and the control and management thereof, and all their lands, property, rights and effects, and all their duties, obligations and liabilities, should be absolutely vested in, and imposed on the Transferee Company. The plaintiff had contracted with the St. Andrews & Quebec Railroad Company to build a portion of their road, and before the agreement of transfer was executed, had commenced a suit against them, which was pending at that time, and a decree was subsequently made in favor of the plaintiff. After the transfer, the St. Stephen's Bank advanced money to the Transferee Company, and obtained judgment against them, and issued execution, under which the lands transferred to them by the agreement, were levied on. Held, That the plaintiff not being a party to the agreement, no trust in his favor for the amount due him, was created thereby, and that he had no lien on the lands which vested in the Transferee Company under the agreement; but that the Transferee Company merely stood in the place of the St. Andrews & Quebec Railroad Company and undertook the discharge of their indebtedness out of the general funds of the Company. Held also, That the word "condition" in the agreement was to be read as a term of the contract, and not as a contingency, which, in case of failure of performance, would work a forfeiture of the estate granted to the Transferee Company. *Brookfield* v. *The N. B. & Canada Railway and Land Company*, *Trin T.* 1871.

Devisee of residue of estate in trust—Construction of will. See Will 5.

Devise in Trust. See Will.

Infant joining in deed with cestui que trust. See Infant.

TRUSTEES.

See Absconding Debtor.

Trustees remaining in office. See Bank.

Conveyance to trustees—Provision for other trustees being nominated and appointed—Legal estate. See Deed III. 3.

Conveyance by.

A person having the legal estate in land may, by conveyance at law, pass such estate, though it was given to him in trust. *Doe* v. *Gilbert*, 1 *All.* 520.

Devise to two persons in trust—Conveyance by one—Effect. See Will 12.

Supervision of proceedings of trustees. See Supreme Court in Equity.

Relation of trustee and cestui que trust created. See Equity 2 *a*.

TRUST DEED.

See Deed.

ULTRA VIRES.

See British North America Act 1867.

UNDERWRITER.

See Insurance.

UNITED STATES CURRENCY.

Note payable in. See Bills and Notes I 15.

USAGE OF TRADE.

See Custom and Usage of Trade.
" Contract.

UNCERTIFICATED ATTORNEY.

See Attorney.

USE AND OCCUPATION.

Defendant marrying widow of tenant—Liability for rent. See Husband and Wife I. 5. See Landlord and Tenant.

Wharf built without authority — Vessel lying. See Action on the Case IV. 8.

1—Agreement to sell—Recission of.
The plaintiff recovered judgment in ejectment against the defendant, but before issuing a writ of possession, agreed to sell him the land, which agreement the defendant afterwards refused to complete. Held, That the defendant was liable in an action for use and occupation, for his holding since the refusal to complete the purchase. *Parker* v. *England*, 3 *All.* 340.

Quære, Whether, without such agreement, the plaintiff could waive the *tort*, and recover for the use and occupation subsequent to the judgment. *Ibid.*

Omission in Statute—Demise by Deed. See New Trial III. 55.

2—Pew—Defence—Joint occupation.
Assumpsit lies for the use and occupation of a pew, and it is no defence under the general issue that others occupied the pew jointly with the defendant. *Trustees of St. Andrews Church* v. *Ferguson*, 1 *Han.* 273.

3—Holding by permission—Necessity of evidence of.
To maintain an action for use and occupation, there must be some evidence of a holding by permission of the plaintiff; therefore, where there is no evidence of any contract or negotiation, and it appears that at an interview between the parties about the property, the defendant refused to make any arrangement, and claimed the title, it was held that the action would not lie. *McCully* v. *Ward*, *East. T.* 1863.

4—The right to waive a *tort*, and bring an action *ex contractu*, applies only to actions for money had and received. *Ibid.*

USES (STATUTE OF.)

The 27 Hen. 8, c 10, Statute of Uses is in force in this Province. *Doe d. Hunnington* v. *McFadden*, *Ber.* 153.

USURY.

See Bills and Notes V. 34.

Mortgage—Broker.
Where a mortgage on real estate was given by A. to B. for the purpose of being sold, and afterwards assigned to C. who took it at a discount of 10 per cent., B., who acted merely as broker in the transaction, receiving one per cent. Held, in a suit for foreclosure against the purchaser of the equity of redemption, That the transaction was usurious, and that even if defendant was only the colorable purchaser it would not affect the case. *Jardine and others* v. *McWilliams*, 1 *Han.* 579.

VARIANCE.

See Amendment—Bail—Bond—Bills and Notes — Conviction — Criminal Law — Pleading—Record.

1—Proof—Allegation.
In an action on a written memorandum, whereby the defendant, for "value received, promised to pay the plaintiff a certain sum in current bank bills," it is necessary not only to allege the actual consideration, but the proof must correspond with the allegations. *Whitney* v. *Marks*, 1 *Kerr* 179.

2—Execution—Judgment—Sale.
A *fi. fa.* was for £47 2s 9d., and the judgment upon which it was founded [illegible] £40 11s. 9d. only. Held, Th[illegible] [illegible]is variance would not defeat the [illegible] made under such execution, on the ground that such execution was not warranted by the judgment, it not being questioned that

the execution had in fact issued upon the judgment. *Linton* v. *Wilson*, 1 *Kerr* 223.

3—**Summary process—Copy—Note.**
A variance between a promissory note proved, and that set out in the copy of a summary process served on the defendant, cannot be taken advantage of on the trial, if the note correspond with the original, which is the record. *Steadman* v. *Holstead*, 3 *Kerr* 356.

4—**Averment—Proof.**
Where the declaration averred that the plaintiff indorsed and delivered a certain order of A. to the defendants, and the evidence was that the plaintiff indorsed and delivered the order to a firm composed of one of the defendants and other individuals, but in which the other defendant had no interest, in part payment of a debt due to such firm. Held, A variance. *Horton* v. *Tibbetts*, 1 *All.* 61.

5—**Words—Transposition of—Description.**
The declaration in an action for false representation in the sale of goods, described the article "Imperial pale yellow Glasgow soap," and set out the price under a videlicet; the evidence was that it was called "Imperial Glasgow pale yellow soap." Held, That the transposition of the words was immaterial, and that the exact price need not be stated. *Magee* v. *Street*, 1 *All.* 242.

6—**Declaration—Proof.**
The declaration stated that J. G. was indebted to the plaintiff in £50, and that the defendants, in consideration that the plaintiff would forbear and give time to J. G. for payment, promised that the defendants would pay. Held, That this declaration was not supported by a guarantee of the defendants that J. G. should pay. *Johnston* v. *Fraser*, *Mich. T.* 1832.

7—The declartion in an action on a judgment of the Court of Common Pleas, stated it to have been recovered for the non-performance of certain promises and undertakings. Held, on *nul tiel record* pleaded, That this declaration was not proved by a copy from the minutes of the Court of Common Pleas, which did not state the cause of action for which judgment was recovered. *Wheeler* v. *Grant*, *Mich. T.* 1832.

8—**Judgment—Execution.**
In an action against bail, in which the judgment set out against the principal was for £596 17s., the defendant pleaded, that no *ca. sa.* was duly sued out against the principal: replication,—that a *ca. sa.* was sued out upon the said judgment (setting out a *ca. sa.* for £81 16s. 10d.) as appears by the record thereof. Rejoinder, That there is not any record of the said writ of *ca. sa.* Held, after judgment for the plaintiff on this issue, That the variance between the amount of the judgment and the execution, was no ground for arresting the judgment. *Spence* v. *Stuart*, *Ber.* 219.

9—**Judgment—Recital.**
In ejectment, claiming under a Sheriff's deed, the execution under which the sale took place recited a judgment for £1105 11s., debt, and £5 11s., costs: the judgment was for £1105 11s., in the whole. Held, That the variance was only an irregularity, which could not be taken advantage of at the trial. *Doe dem Walsh* v. *Dalton*, *Hil. T.* 1866.

Proof of words—Defamation. See Defamation 15.

VENDITIONI EXPONAS.

Irregularity in—Purchaser not affected by. See *Doe* v. *Hazen*, 3 *All.* 87.

VENDOR AND PURCHASER.

See Caveat Emptor. See Sale.

1—**Purchaser's right to good title.**
A purchaser of land has a right to a title free from incumbrances, and if the vendor is unable to give such a title, the purchaser may recover back his deposit. *Scott* v. *Garnett*, 2 *All.* 624.

A notice to the vendor from the purchaser that the land sold does not answer the description, and that he will not complete the sale, is not a waiver of objections to the title. *Ibid.*

2—**Admission of receipt of money.**
Quære, Whether one who has conveyed land, and acknowledged in the deed the receipt of the purchase money, can recover a balance unpaid, on an admission by the purchaser that he owes it. *McAllister* v. *Day*, 4 *All.* 37.

3—**Word "sell"—Meaning—Dependent promise.**
Plaintiff agreed to sell land to the defendant for £40, and the defendant agreed to pay the money on a certain day, for the

consideration above named. Held—1st. That the word "sell" necessarily included an agreement to convey; 2nd. That the defendant's promise to pay the money was a dependent promise, and that the plaintiff could not maintain an action therefor without tendering a conveyance of the land. *Sweeny* v. *Godard*, 4 *All.* 400.

4—Party selling should prepare conveyance—Wife should be a party.
It is the duty of the seller of land to prepare the conveyance, and if he has a wife who would have a right of dower in the land in case she survived him, she should be a party to the conveyance. *Ibid.*

5—Vendor and Vendee—Breach of agreement—Damages.
In an action against the vendee for breach of an [illegible]reement to purchase land, the pla[illegible]nnot recover the amount of the pu[illegible]ey agreed to be paid for the la[illegible]; [illegible] only such damages as he has sustained by the breach of the agreement. *P[illegible]y* v. *Gillespie*, *Mich. T.* 1872.

Agreement · Re[illegible] to purchase. See Landlord and Tenant. I. 3 *a*.

As to recovery of deposit on failure of title. See Assumpsit III. 19, 24.

VENIRE.

See Error (Writ of) 3. See Jury.

Sheriff interested.
Where the Sheriff is interested, the jury process must be directed to the Coroners of the county, if more than one; and though it may be executed by one Coroner, the return must be in the name of the whole of them. *Noble* v. *Temple & Pelton* v. *Temple*, 1 *Han.* 274.

A *venire* directed to one of the Coroners of a county is bad, unless the others are interested. *Ibid.*

Coroner—Interest.
In an action for calls on stock, the Coroner who summoned the jury was a stockholder, but, before receiving the *venire*, transferred his stock, which was not all paid up, to the president of the company. The Act of Incorporation declared that no shareholder should be entitled to transfer his stock, unless all calls were paid. In summoning the jury, the Coroner questioned them as to their views in regard to railways, and was guided in his selection by their answers. Held, That he had not divested himself of his interest, and was not an impartial officer, and there must be a *venire de novo*. *Woodstock Railway Co.* v. *Tupper*, 1 *Han.* 454.

Common Venire, when sufficient—Limit bond.
In an action by the assignee of a limit bond to which *non est factum* is pleaded the common *venire* to try the issue is sufficient; and the plaintiff need not have damages assessed, but may take a verdict for nominal damages, and issue execution for the amount of his debt. *McElroy* v. *Getty*, 1 *Han.* 261.

Motion for *venire de novo* may be made in the same manner as a motion for a new trial. See *Pelton* v. *Noble*, 1 *Han.* 274.

VERDICT.

See Practice—New Trial.

Evidence of amount of original debt. See McIlhaney *v.* Wiswell, Ber. 67.

Postea on. See Replevin 4.

Judgment not signed, verdict cannot be pleaded in bar between same parties. See Pleading II. 41.

VEXATIOUS PROCEEDING.

Staying Proceedings. See Second Action.

VIEW (JURY OF.)

Jury lodging with plaintiff. See New Trial III. 46.

VOLUNTARY CONVEYANCE.

See Deed.

VOTE.

See Election.

VOYAGE.

See Insurance—Shipping Law.

WAGER.

Deposit of money—Horse race. See Action at Law I. 3.

WAGES.

Action for. See Assumpsit—Shipping Law.

WAIVER.

An underwriter may waive the production of preliminary proof of interest in the assured by objecting to pay the loss on a

WAREHOUSEMAN.

WARRANT.

WARRANT OF ATTORNEY.

1—Consideration—Severable—Setting aside.

If part of the consideration for a bond and warrant of attorney is good and severable from the bad; the Court will only destroy the effect of the bad part. *Secord* v. *Green*, 1 *All.* 41.

Where in answer to an application to set aside a warrant of attorney and judgment thereon for fraud, the plaintiff shewed a good consideration for part of the demand, though the remainder was not satisfactorily explained, but no collusion appeared, the Court dismissed the application without costs, the plaintiff consenting to reduce his demand to the sum proved. *Ibid.*

It is not a sufficient ground for setting aside a warrant of attorney founded on a good consideration, that it was executed by the defendant without the privity or request of the plaintiff, if he afterwards accepts it and avails himself of the security. *Ibid.*

2—Judgment—Old warrant—Setting aside.

A judgment signed under a Judge's order upon a warrant of attorney more than a year old, will not be set aside, unless it appears that injustice has been done, though the affidavit, on which the order was made, may not have been strictly sufficient; particularly where the defendant's affidavit supplies the alleged defect *Smith* v. *LeBurgue*, 1 *All.* 266.

3—Application to set aside—Answer. It is no answer to an application by a creditor of the defendant to set aside a judgment on a bond and warrant of attorney given by him to the plaintiff, on the ground of fraud and want of consideration, for the plaintiff to state that the bond was given for the amount of a promissory note given by the defendant, of which the plaintiff was the holder, without stating in what character, under what circumstances, or at what time he became the holder, and what consideration he gave for it. *Bacon* v. *Hoar*, 1 *All.* 664.

4—Continuing security. The defendant owed the plaintiff about £200, and requiring further advances from time to time, applied to the plaintiff, who agreed to make them on receiving sufficient security; the defendant thereupon gave the plaintiff a bond and warrant of attorney for £1855, conditioned for payment of £927 14s., on which judgment was entered up. Held, That the judgment was valid as a continuing security, and could be enforced for the amount really due on a final settlement between the parties, and although, at some period of their dealings, the balance might have been in favor of the defendant, the judgment was not thereby satisfied, if such was not the intention of the parties. Held also, That a want of defeasance did not render the warrant of attorney void. *Lunt* v. *Estabrooks*, 3 *Kerr* 144.

5—Defendant, who, in December 1868, owed plaintiff $1,800 for supplies, gave him a Bond and Warrant of Attorney to confess judgment for $10,000. The defeasance stated it to be given to secure the re-payment of the $1,800 due, and "such further advances in the whole not exceeding $5,000, as the said Eaton may advance to the said Lawrence." Plaintiff having entered up judgment upon the Bond and Warrant of Attorney, in June 1869, issued execution for $3,417. On a motion to set this execution aside, defendant in his affidavit alleged that he shipped lumber to the plaintiff to satisfy the judgment, and had a settlement in 1867, when plaintiff was indebted to him, and that the Bond, etc., was not given as a continuing security. The plaintiff alleged it to be a continuing security, and denied that there had been any settlement. From December 1865 to December 1868, the plaintiff and defendant had transactions to the extent of over $30,000. Held, per Weldon and Fisher, J. J., That it not being clear that there had been any settlement, and there being nothing in the defeasance to prevent it being a continuing security, the plaintiff was entitled to his judgment. *Eaton* v. *Lawrence*, 2 *Han.* 85.

6—Creditor taking for larger sum than due. A Bond and Warrant of Attorney, taken by a creditor for a larger sum than is due to him, are void as against other creditors, under the Stat. 13 Eliz. c. 5, and will, together with the judgment thereon, be set aside on the application of another creditor, whose debt may be defeated thereby. *Biggs* v. *Eagles*, *Trin. T.* 1834.

7—Marking—Initials—Omission. The omission by an attorney who signs a confession under a warrant of attorney, to add the date of signing and to mark the initials of his name upon the warrant of attorney, as required by the rule of Trinity Term 1857, does not render void a judgment signed on such confession. *Levi* v. *Muzeroll*, 3 *All.* 598.

8—Need not be under seal—Recognition—Equities. A warrant of attorney to confess judgment need not be under seal. *Hutchinson* v. *Johnston*, 4 *All.* 40.

A bond and warrant of attorney under seal, were executed by A., in the name of himself and B., with a defeasance stating that the warrant of attorney was given to secure the plaintiff for advances made and to be made to A. and B., in carrying on their shipbuilding operations, and that the plaintiff might sign judgment and issue execution, from time to time, for whatever amount A. and B., or either of them, should then be owing for such advances. Held, That as the warrant of attorney need not be under seal, a judgment signed thereon would bind B. if he recognised it, though A. had no authority to execute it. *Ibid.*

A recognition may be implied from the conduct of a party—as where, knowing of a warrant of attorney and judgment against him, he allows them to stand for three years without objection, and continues to deal with the plaintiff on the security of them. *Hutchinson* v. *Johnston*, 4 *All.* 40.

A party applying to the equitable jurisdiction of the Court, to be relieved from a judgment, must do what is equitable towards the other party. *Ibid.*

Ordering issue to be tried—Doubtful fact. See Practice XII.

Defendant in custody. See Practice VII. 6.

Attorney taking warrant of attorney. See Attorney X. 10.

Suspension of remedy. See Judgment.

Judgment on—Setting aside—Costs. See Costs X. *Hardy* v. *Prince*, 3 *All.* 264.

WARRANTY.

Damages — Evidence in reduction. See Damages II. 2.

Implied warranty—Breach of. See Deed V. 3.

Insurance — Answers to questions. See Insurance 39.

1—Sufficient evidence of.
In an action on the warranty of horses a conversation just before the delivery between the parties, when the plaintiff said, "You say these horses are sound," etc., and the defendant replied, "Yes, they are;" coupled with a subsequent refusal of the defendant to take back the horses, "because they were as he warranted them," are sufficient evidence from which the jury may infer that a warranty was given at the time of the sale, no witness appearing to have been present at the sale. *Libby* v. *Nesbit*, 1 *Kerr* 362.

2—Representation—Question for jury.
Where at the time of a bargain between the parties for the sale of timber, the quantity of which could not be then ascertained, the defendant stated that he "knew the timber to be good, and would make it good—that there had been an opportunity of examining it as it lay on the brow," shortly after which the plaintiff took the timber, which turned out mostly rotten and worthless, and the defendant had afterwards said that he had sold 101 tons for £100, which appeared to be the full price for good timber. Held, That it was a question for the jury, whether the representation amounted to warranty, and that they might infer that a sale took place at the time of such representation. *Irvine* v. *Godard*, 1 *Kerr* 364.

3—Where at the time of making a verbal contract for the sale of 1250 tons of pine timber, then in charge of C., a pond keeper, B., the vendor, represented to A., the vendee, "that the timber was of good quality and uncommon long lengths;" upon which A., who wanted timber of that description for shipment, was induced to give more than the ordinary price; and A. had also seen the timber afloat in the raft, and afterwards received an order from B. upon C. to deliver A. twelve hundred and fifty tons merchantable white pine timber, averaging seventeen inches square, which C. accepted. Held, That it was a proper question for the jury, whether under all the circumstances, the representation amounted to a warranty. *Tisdale* v. *Connell*, 1 *Kerr* 401.

4—Representation—Contract—Pleading—Damages.
In an action upon an alleged warranty of ownership upon the exchange of wagons, the defendant pleaded the general issue, and also in abatement the pendency of another suit for the same cause of action. Held, That he could not avail himself of the latter plea. Where plaintiff exchanged wagons with defendant, the latter representing that he had the wagon he was exchanging built expressly for himself, and subsequently it turned out that the wagon was not his, and it was replevied and taken from the plaintiff by the real owner. Held, That such representation formed part of the contract, and that plaintiff could recover from defendant the value of the wagon, but not the cost of defending his title in a writ *de proprietate probanda*. *Mercer* v. *Cosman*, 2 *Han.* 240.

5—Representation—Quality.
The plaintiff purchased from the defendant, a commission merchant, soap which he had on consignment, and represented to be Glasgow pale yellow soap, a well known and superior article; neither party examined the soap before the sale, but, on examination a few days after, it proved to be useless, of which the plaintiff notified the defendant and requested him to

take it back. Held, That the defendant was liable, though from his information from the consignors he might have believed that the article substantially agreed with his representation, and that the plaintiff was entitled to recover the whole price, though the defendant had remitted the proceeds to the consignors before receiving the notice. *Magee* v. *Street*, 1 *All.* 242.

Article fairly answering description of that agreed to be sold. See Contract 22.

WASTE.

See Action on the Case I. 9.

WATER COMPANY.

Obligation to keep supply of water.
The defendants were incorporated by the Act 2 Wm. 4, c. 26, for the purpose of supplying Saint John with water, and were required to make in every street through which their pipes were laid, vents for supplying water whenever fires should happen in the city. The 9 Vic. c. 64, made all buildings fronting on streets through which pipes were laid, subject to an annual rate for the benefit of the Company, and required them during the continuance of the Act, to establish fire plugs for supplying water whenever fires should happen, and to keep the same in good and sufficient serviceable order. Held, That the duties imposed upon the Company could not be carried beyond the fair import of the terms used by the Legislature; and therefore that they were not bound to keep a supply of water all the time, by day and night, in the pipes, so as to be made liable for the damage sustained by fire catching to a building owned by one of the rate-payers, which might have been saved had the water been immediately available for extinguishing the fire. *Blakslee* v. *Saint John Water Company*, 1 *All* 639.

WEEKLY ALLOWANCE.

See Insolvent Confined Debtor.

WATER COURSE.

See Easement.

Dam—Erection of—Destruction of by persons not obstructed—Injunction.
Though a dam erected in a stream, which is capable of being used as a highway for floating lumber, may be a nuisance as regards the public, and the owner of the dam may consequently be liable to a prosecution for erecting it, no person who has not been thereby obstructed in the exercise of his public right to use the stream, is justified in destroying the dam. Thus, where the plaintiff and defendant owned mills on the opposite sides of such a stream, and the plaintiff had erected a wing-dam, extending from his mill in a diagonal direction to the centre of the stream, for the purpose of increasing the supply of water to his mill, and the defendant also maintained a dam across the stream to supply their mill; they were restrained by injunction from destroying the plaintiff's dam, though they claimed the right to do so, because it obstructed them in floating logs down the stream to their mill. *Davis* v. *Hayden*, *M. Rolls*, *January* 1864.

Agreement to enlarge water course—Evidence. See Evidence II. 24.

WHARF.

Approach to—Obstructing. See Action on the Case IV. 3.

WHARFAGE.

1—Top wharfage—Assumpsit for.
Under the Act 5 Vic. c. 39, s. 6, an action of assumpsit may be maintained to recover top wharfage against the owner of goods landed on a wharf; the words "sue for" and "recover" indicating a proceeding *in personam*. The remedy by distress given by section 7 is only cumulative. (See Vestry of St. Pancras *v.* Buttersbury, 2 C. B., N. S. 477, Mayor of Blackburn *v.* Parkinson, 1 E. and E. 71.) *McLeod* v. *Yeats*, *East. T.* 1861.

2—Averment and proof concerning wharf.
In order to recover top wharfage, the plaintiff must aver and prove affirmatively that the wharf was "properly planked or timbered on the surface," and this is not proved by evidence that the wharf was in good order. *Ibid.*

3—Wharf below low water mark.
Plaintiff and defendant, owners of lots which extended side by side from St. John street to low water mark, in the harbor of St. John, by deed made a common passage way twelve feet wide along

the length of each lot, on which each was bound to build and keep in repair a wharf, and each conveying to the other the right of way over the wharf, the plaintiff's right of wharfage on the north side of the street being reserved. Afterwards the plaintiff obtained from the Corporation of St. John the right to erect a wharf beyond low water mark, extending from the end of said passage way for the public use, in the same manner as the part already built. Subsequently an Act was passed allowing the owners of wharves to collect top wharfage on goods landed on them. Held, That defendants were entitled to pay plaintiff top wharfage on goods landed by them on the wharf built by plaintiff below low water mark. *Collins* v. *Hall & Fairweather*, 2 *Han.* 90.

Liability to pay wharfage. See Easement 8.

WHARFINGER.

Vessels subject to order of. See Fredericton (City of) 9.

WIDOW.

Holding possession. See Possession 4.

Restraint of marriage. See Will 8.

Dower—Right—Action. See Dower.

WIFE.

See Husband and Wife.

Wife of one prisoner offered as witness for another. See Witness.

Dower barred by adultery. See Divorce 2.

WILDERNESS LAND.

See Ejectment—Limitation of Actions—Possession—Trespass.

WILFUL INJURIES.

Injuring fence—Summary conviction. See Justice of the Peace IV. 11.

WILL.

1—Proof of—Witness—Signature.
Where the defendant made title to the land in question under a deed from one of the devisees in trust under the will of J. H., to which will the defendant's name appeared as the last of three attesting witnesses, and one of the other witnesses when called to prove the will could not remember the defendant's having been present at the execution—but swore that it was executed in presence of himself and one C., the other attesting witness, who was out of the Province. Held, That proof of the defendant's signature was admissible and sufficient to raise the presumption that the will was duly proved under the Statute of Frauds — (Parker, J., *dissentiente*). *Hamilton* v. *Love*, 2 *Kerr* 223.

2—Construction—Term grandson.
The testator devised property to his wife for life, and at her death to his grandson Rufus; he also gave property to his son and daughters, describing each of them by their christian and surnames. At the date of the will the testator had a legitimate grandson named Rufus living in a foreign country, who, it appeared, he had only seen once when a child, about six years before making the will, and was never heard to speak of afterwards; he also had an illegitimate grandson living with him, brought up and educated by him, recognized as his grandson, and called Rufus. Held, (Street J., *dissentiente*,) That there was nothing on the face of the will to shew that the testator intended the illegitimate grandson as his devisee. *Doe* v. *Taylor*, 1 *All.* 525.

Held, per Street, J., 1st. That from the whole context of the will, the words "grandson Rufus," taken in their strict primary sense as applicable only to the legitimate grandson, were not sensible with reference to the extrinsic circumstances proved, and that the Court might look to those circumstances to see if the words were sensible if applied to the illegitimate grandson. 2nd. That the words were ambiguous, and that evidence of the instructions given for the will was admissible to shew which of the grandsons was intended; and that the intention was a question for the jury. *Ibid.*

3—Estate for life.
A testator, after bequeathing to his wife all his personal property, gave to her all the rents and profits that should be derived from the lands at G. or elsewhere, that he should be possessed of at the time of his death. He then gave to his brother J. all the lands that should belong to him at his death, situated at G. or elsewhere, and in the event of surviving his brother J. he gave all the

lands that should belong to him to his nieces. Held, That the words of the devise gave J. only an estate for life, and that no intention could be gathered from the will to extend it to an estate in fee. *Doe* v. *Green*, 2 *All.* 314.

4—Testator being seized in fee of the land after mentioned, devised (before the Act 1 Vic. c. 9) as follows: "I give and bequeath to my wife the income of all my real estate during her life, and after her decease I give and bequeath to my son Benjamin F., my son James G., and my son Isaac P. my two lots of land and the buildings thereon in Dock Street, to be equally divided between them." Held, That the sons only took life estates in the two lots after the death of the wife. *Doe* v. *Stan on*, 2 *All.* 632.

5—Devise in trust for wife—Conditions —Remainder.

A testator after directing that so much of his estate as was necessary, should be sold for payment of his debts, devised all the residue of his estate to his executors, in trust to hold for the separate use and benefit of his wife during her life or widowhood, and pay to her the income thereof; and after her death or marriage, then to be divided among the testator's children. Held, That the purposes of the trust did not require the estate of the executors to extend beyond the life of the widow; that at her death their estate terminated, and the testator's children took the estate in remainder. *Doe* v. *Driscoll*, 4 *All.* 176.

6—Estate for life—Children.

A testator devised as follows: "Also, I give to my son S. H. G. the use of my farm (describing it), also to his lawful children, and in case of his death without children, then to be equally divided between my five daughters (naming them) and their heirs for ever." When the testator died, S. H. G. had no child born; but his wife was then *enciente*, and a son was born shortly afterwards. S. H. G., at his death, left this son and four younger children surviving him. Held, That S. H. G., by this devise, took an estate for life, and at his death, all his children then living, an estate in fee. *Gourley et al.* v. *Gilbert et al.*, 1 *Han.* 80.

7—Implication—Deed.

A., by deed dated 2nd April 1853, conveyed to his daughter a farm, described as the property purchased by him from B., except a part that he had before leased, to hold the same during his life; and after his decease, he thereby gave, granted, bargained and sold, to his said daughter, her heirs and assigns, "all the above mentioned premises, and every part thereof." The part excepted had been leased by A. to T. in 1851, for five years, with a covenant to renew or pay for improvements. In January, A. made his will, stating (*inter alia*) as fo[illegible] "I having already conveyed to my [illegible]ter E. S., her heirs and assigns, by way of advancement, subject as in the deed thereof is mentioned, all that farm or tract of land situate, etc., formerly purchased by me from B., with all buildings, etc., to hold to her, my said daughter, her heirs and assigns, I do not make further mention of her, my said daughter, in this, my will." Held—1st. That the testator's daughter took no estate under the will by implication; 2nd. That under the deed, she took the whole farm after the death of A. *Miles* v. *Coy and Fraser, Executors &c. of John Harding*, 1 *Han.* 174.

8—Condition—Restraint of marriage—Widow's estate—Remainderman.

A testator devised all his real [illegible]nd personal estate to his wife durin[illegible] life or widowhood; but, in case [illegible]rried again, he willed that she should [illegible]e only his personal property with his farm at Q., which she might sell at her discretion; he then devised to certain of his relatives the whole of his real property, of whatever nature and wherever situated, except the farm in Q. Held, That this condition was not void as being in restraint of matrimony, and that the widow's estate in the land therefore ceased on her marriage. *Doe d. Livingstone* v. *Currie*, 3 *Kerr* 450.

Held also, That ejectment might be maintained by the remaindermen against the person who married the widow without any demand of possession. *Ibid.*

The will contained a clause that any two of the devisees in remainder (some of whom were under age) should have a right to purchase the land at a valuation to be made by the executors. Held, That this did not prevent those devisees who were of age from disposing of their shares to a stranger, who might thereupon maintain ejectment against a person wrongfully in possession. *Ibid.*

9—Stock—Meaning of word.

A testator devised a farm to his son, and

by a codicil to his will, directed that the horses, stock, and farming utensils on the farm, should remain thereon for the benefit of the farm; adding the words "which I do give and bequeath with the said farm." Held, That the word "stock" was not confined to live stock, but included the hay and crop grown on the farm, and which had been severed at the time of the testator's death. *Wetmore* v. *Ketchum*, *Mich. T.* 1862.

10—Devise in trust—Charge—Payment of debts.

A testator directed that the residue of his real and personal estate should be divided into nine equal parts, and gave one-ninth to his executors, in trust to apply the rents and income thereof, for the support and education of his grandson, M. B., till he came of age, and then to convey the same to him absolutely; but in case his grandson died before he came of age, then such ninth part to be divided among the testator's children, share and share alike. By a codicil to his will, the testator declared that such devise in trust for his grandson, was to be held subject to the payment of a mortgage given to the testator by his deceased son W. H. B. (the father of M. B.), and to the other debts due from the estate of W. H. B. After the mortgage was given to the testator, W. H. B. conveyed the land on which it was secured to a trustee in trust to sell, and, in the first place, pay all his debts, and apply the balance to the use of his wife and son. M. B., the testator's grandson, died before coming of age. Held, That the testator's children, to whom the ninth was devised in case of the death of M. B., took it subject to the payment of the debts of W. H. B., and not merely as an auxiliary fund in case the property conveyed by W. H. B., in trust for payment of his debts, should prove insufficient. *Botsford* v. *Bostford*, *Trin. T.* 1866.

11—Devise—Vested estate—Limitation over.

A testator devised to P., his second wife, one-half of his real and personal estate, and directed that the children of his second wife should remain with her and enjoy all his real and personal estate till they were of age; after which, the other half of his estate should be equally divided between the children of his first wife; that the children of his first wife should assist his wife P., and her children, in all the work necessary to be done on his real and personal estate, till the children of his wife P. should be able to do the work themselves; and if the children of his first wife would not assist his wife P. and her children, they should have no part in his estate; but it should be given to those that would assist his wife P. and her children in the work which should be necessary to be done on his real and personal estate. Held—1st. That the children of the first wife took a vested estate in remainder in half the testator's land, after P.'s children came of age, dependent on the performance of the condition; 2nd. That the condition to assist P. and her children was a condition subsequent, and that before the estate of the children by the first wife could be forfeited by non-performance of this condition, it was necessary to shew a request for assistance by P. and her children. *Doe d. Myers* v. *Babineau*, *East. T.* 1864.

Quære, Whether the limitation over, in case of non-performance of the condition, was not void for uncertainty. *Ibid.*

12—Devise to two persons in trust to sell—Conveyance by one.

Where the devise was to two persons in trust to sell, and only one conveyed to the defendant, the other refusing to act, that conveyance passes at least an undivided moiety of the estate, so as to justify the entry of the vendee.

Quære, Whether the oral disclaimer of a devised estate is sufficient. *Hamilton* v. *Love*, 2 *Kerr* 243.

13—Estate—Mortgage in fee.

By the devise of an estate, which the testator has previously mortgaged in fee, nothing passes at law. *De Veber* v. *Andrews*, 2 *Kerr* 604.

14—Undue influence—Incapacity—Intention—Evidence.

Where a will was contested by the heir-at-law, on the ground of undue influence by the devisee with the testator, but no evidence thereof was given, the Judge should not leave such a question to the jury. *Doe ex dem. Levi* v. *Samuel*, 1 *Han.* 265.

Letters written by a testator to his relatives before making his will, stating his intention to leave his property to them, are not admissible in evidence to defeat a will disposing of his property to another person; though the will is attacked on the ground of the testator's incapacity, as being *in extremis* at the time of its execution. *Doe ex dem Levi* v. *Samuel*, 1 *Han*. 265.

Trespass—Life estate in saw mill. See Trespass I. 17.

15—**Evidence—Certified copy of will.** *Semble*, That a certified copy of a will cannot be given in evidence under the 1 Rev. Stat. c. 112. *Connell* v. *Haley*, 4 *All*. 636.

Will—Revocation—Previous contract. See Contract 14.

16—Executors—Liability as contributories—Bank Stock undisposed of—Payment of legacies under Will not allowed against their contingent liability to calls. See Winding-up Act.

17—**Legatee—Action—Certain legacy.** A legatee may maintain an action of debt against an executor for a certain legacy given by his testator. *Livingstone* v. *Powell*, *Ber*. 225.

18—**Devise subject to payment—Action.** Where a devise of land is made to B., subject to the payment of a sum of money to A., and B. accepts the devise. *Quære*, Whether an action at law will lie under the Act of Assembly or at common law for recovery of the money? *De Veber* v. *Andrews*, 2 *Kerr* 604.

19—**Legacy—Married woman—Representative—Action.** If a legacy is bequeathed to a married woman, who dies before any act done by husband to reduce it into possession, he can only maintain an action for it as the representative of his wife, though he may be beneficially entitled to it. *Collins* v. *Cahir*, 2 *All*. 103.

Profits of Bank Stock—Payment to executor—Action. See Assumpsit III. 14.

Pleading—No averment of receipt of money. See Pleading I. 25.

20—**Reference—Inquiry into receipts.** The plaintiff and defendant were executors of A., who bequeathed a legacy of £50 to the plaintiff's wife, charged upon land devised by the will to the defendant. On a bill filed for payment of this legacy, it appeared that the plaintiff, as executor, had received assets belonging to A.'s estate, which he had not accounted for, and that the defendant had in consequence been obliged to charge the real estate devised to him, to raise money to pay the testator's debt. At the hearing a reference was directed to inquire what moneys belonging to the estate had been received by the plaintiff, and how he had applied them. On appeal by the plaintiff from this order—Held, That the inquiry was proper; and that if the plaintiff had caused the fund from which the legacy was to be paid, to be used for the payment of the testator's debts, the defendant should hold that fund discharged from the legacy, or so much thereof as the plaintiff had virtually received from the assets in his hands. *De Veber* v. *Andrews*, 3 *All*. 383.

21—**Creditor—Bequest to—Action.** A bequest by a debtor to his creditor of a legacy to the amount of the debt, payable out of the proceeds of certain property which remains unsold, is no defence to an action by the creditor for his debt. *Bishop* v. *Robinson*, 1 *Han*. 68.

22—**Legacy—Bill to recover—Personal estate—Insufficiency.** *Quære*, Whether, if in a suit to obtain payment of a legacy, the bill shews the personal estate insufficient for payment of the debts, it must not also shew that the legacy was charged on the land, if the plaintiff seeks payment therefrom. *Wallace* v. *Woods*, 1 *Han*. 230.

WINDING-UP ACT.

1—**Judge's order—Authorizing calls, evidence—Judge's signature.** In an action against a stockholder for calls under the Winding-up Act, the order of a Judge of the Supreme Court, authorising such calls, is *prima facie* evidence of the defendant's liability. *McKenzie, Curator etc.* v. *Scovil*, 2 *Han*. 6.

2—A Judge at *nisi prius* is bound to take judicial notice of the signature of another Judge of the Court, in an order made under the Winding-up Act. *Ibid*.

3—**Stockholders—Liability.** The stockholders of the Westmorland Bank, by their charter, in addition to the liability in respect of the stock held by them for payment of the debts of the bank, are liable in their private and individual capacity for an amount equal to the sum of their stock. *McKenzie, Curator of Westmorland Bank* v. *Wiswell*, 1 *Han*. 503.

4—**Executors—Liability—Register.** The executors of the estate of C. invested a portion of its funds in bank stock in their own names, but for the benefit of the estate, by which the dividends were received. After their death their representatives, by writing, agreed to transfer the stock to the widow of C., who had taken out letters of administration *cum testamento annexo de bonis non*. The stock certificates were handed over to her, and she afterwards received the dividends, but no transfer was made on the books of the bank as required by its charter and bye-laws. The bank suspended, and the estates of the executors were placed by the Judge on the list of contributories for the stock standing in their names on the register. Held, That they being *prima facie* legally liable, the Judge was right in not altering the register by substituting the name of the party equitably entitled to the stock. *In re President &c. Westmorland Bank ex parte Allison*, 1 *Han.* 506.

5—**Executors—Liability.**
A testator died possessed of Bank Stock, which his executors allowed to remain undisposed of, and received the dividends. By the terms of the Bank Charter the stockholders were individually liable for the payment of the debts of the Bank, in proportion to the stock they held. About two years after the death of the testator, the Bank suspended payment, and was wound up under the Act 27 Vic. c. 44, and a call made on the executors as contributories. Held, That they were liable therefor in their representative capacity, and that the payment of legacies under the will could not be allowed against their contingent liability to calls under the charter. *McKenzie, Curator &c.* v. *King*, *Mich. T.* 1871.

WINDOWS.

See Lights.

WITNESS.

1—**Scientific Witness—Questions.**
A scientific witness cannot be asked questions, the answers to which are based upon previous evidence given by other witnesses, and upon which conclusions are drawn which are for the jury to determine. *Key* v *Thomson*, 2 *Han.* 224.

2—**Joint indictment—Wife of one prisoner offered as witness for another.**
A and B were tried together on a joint indictment for assault on a peace officer and the wife of A was offered as a witness to disprove the charge against B. Held that her evidence was properly rejected, but had the husband not been on his trial, she would have been a competent witness. *The Queen* v *Thomson and Conroy*, 2 *Han.* 71.

(See also the Queen *v.* James Thomson et al. L. R. C. C. vol. 1, page 377.)

3—**Deceased witness—Evidence on former trial.**
Where the evidence of a witness taken on a former trial in the same cause and since deceased, was read from the Judge's notes, the defendant's counsel offered evidence to shew a statement made by the witness while giving his evidence in the presence of the plaintiff. Held, That the evidence was properly rejected. *Prescott* v. *Walton*, 2 *Han.* 230.

4—**Credibility of—Cause left to jury upon.**
Where the maker of a promissory note set up infancy as a defence against the indorsee, and the only witness to prove the infancy was the payee of the note, who was a brother of the maker, and who had himself indorsed it to the plaintiff: the Court refused to disturb a verdict in favor of the indorsee, although the witness was not contradicted or otherwise discredited than by the above circumstances, the Judge having left the case to the jury upon the credit of the witness. *Bugbee* v. *McDonald*, 2 *Kerr* 61.

5—Where a cause depended on the testimony of one witness, whose credibility was properly left to the jury, and they found a verdict against his evidence, the Court refused to grant a new trial. *Wortman* v. *Marter*, 3 *All.* 309.

6—**Holding communication with party in suit.**
Where a witness under examination *de bene esse* before a Judge had held communication relative to the suit with one of the parties during an adjournment of the examination, notwithstanding a caution to the contrary given him by the Judge, it was held not a sufficient ground for suppressing the examination. *Doe dem Beatty* v. *Keillor*, 2 *Kerr* 643.

7—**Contempt—Attendance—Subsequent Absence.**
A subpœna to attend on the 10th September, and so from day to day until the cause was tried, was served on the 11th September, and the witness attended for several days, and knew the cause was

not tried: Held, that he was guilty of a contempt in subsequently absenting himself. *Johnston* v. *Wiliston*. 2 *All.* 171.

Where a witness accepted the conduct money, and went with the person who served him with the subpœna, and remained at the Court several days, an attachment was granted against him for subsequently absenting himself, though he and another person swore, in contradiction to the party who served the subpœna, that the original writ was not shewn to him, and he also swore that he attended the Court as a juror, and left in consequence of ill health, with the intention of returning,—his absence appearing to be wilful. *Ibid.*

8—Counsel—Witness.
A counsel in a case will not be allowed to be a witness for his client, unless there is other counsel to examine him and comment on his testimony. *Hamilton* v. *McLean*, *Hil. T.* 1828.

9—Prosecution for Solemnizing Marriage—Criminal proceedings.
A prosecution to recover a fine under 1 Rev. Stat. c. 146, for solemnizing marriage between minors without consent of their parents is a "criminal proceeding," and therefore the defendant is not a competent witness under the Act 19 Vic. c. 45. *Ex parte Jarvis*, *Hil. T.* 1861.

10—Bastardy.
Bastardy not a criminal proceeding—party charged, a competent witness. *Ex parte Cook*, 4 *All.* 506.

Recalling witness. See Evidence VIII.

11—Diligence in discovering.
Whether due diligence has been used to discover an attesting witness must depend on the circumstances of the case. *Crane* v. *Cyr*, 2 *All.* 577.

Privilege. See Arrest.

Expenses.
Witness attending trial as a juror or too much intoxicated to be examined, cannot recover his fees. See Costs II. 37.

Taxable expenses—Cause put off on payment. See Costs II. 35.

Mileage. See Costs II.

Materiality of witness. See Costs II.

Affidavits of attendance—sufficiency. See Costs II. 30. General Rules 31 32.

Examination—Cross-examination. See Evidence VIII.

Subscribing witness—Assignment of judgment.
Affidavit of subscribing witness necessary before attorney compelled to pay over the proceeds of a judgment at the instance of the assignee. *Murray* v. *Johnston*, 1 *All.* 667.

Cases as to competency or incompetency of witness from interest, before Act allowing all parties to be examined in civil causes:

Turner *v.* Elliot,	Ber. 117.
Beard *v.* Venning,	1 Kerr 77.
Robinson *v.* Taylor,	2 Kerr 198.
Yeoman *v.* McManus,	3 Kerr 61.
Fraser *v.* Harding,	3 Kerr 94.
Hughes *v.* Holmes,	3 Kerr 141.
Reg. *v.* McCoubray,	3 Kerr 384.
McLardy *v.* Flaherty,	3 Kerr 455.
Vanwart *v.* Roberts,	3 Kerr 572.
Harkins *v.* Johnston,	1 All. 70.
Kerr *v.* Morrison,	1 All. 378.
Doe *v.* Gilbert,	1 All. 520.
Whelpley *v.* Riley,	2 All. 275.
Doe *v.* Baxter,	2 All. 377.
Lawton *v.* Wilder,	2 All. 416.
Doe *v.* McCoskery,	2 All. 461.
Doe *v.* Harris,	2 All. 42.
Hazen *v.* Bryson,	3 All. 101.

WORDS (MEANING, CONSTRUCTION.)

"Adjacent and adjoining"—Distinction. See Deed I. 18.

"At least" day's service. See Practice IX. 3.

"Bank or edge." See Crown Grant I. 19.

"Bail" in County Court Acts includes sureties on a limit bond. See Bail 18.

"Breaking into field under lawful fence"—What does not constitute. See Trespass II. 2.

Covenant "To keep up" a mill-dam. See Covenant 2.

"Contiguous small islands"—"Low water mark." See Crown Grant I. 20.

"Costs"—The costs mentioned in condition of replevin bond mean taxable costs. See *Steen* v. *Hanson*, 4 *All.* 589.

"Costs" in 81st section in charter of Fredericton mean costs of distress and sale. See *Ex parte Mowry*, 3 *All.* 270.

"Criminal proceeding," what so considered. See Witness 9, 10.

WORK AND LABOUR.

WOUNDING.

WRIT.

Altered fi. fa.

A returned *fi. fa.* having been altered and reissued by the attorney, as an alias, was held void and not receivable in evidence in an action of trespass against the Sheriff for taking goods under it. *Johnson* v. *Winslow*, *Ber.* 53.

Mistake in indorsement by Sheriff may be amended. *Ibid.*

Return by Sheriff "*cepi corpus*" on *capias* issued against two defendants, applicable to both. *Rex* v. *Sheriff of Gloucester*, *Ber.* 187.

Issue of.

In the absence of evidence of the actual time of issuing a writ of *mesne* process, it will be presumed to have been issued on the day it bears date. *Pomares* v. *Provincial Insurance Co.*, *Hil. T.* 1873.

Alteration made in the return day of writ, though before it is returnable, vitiates it, unless it is resealed. *Andrews* v. *McKenzie*, 1 *All.* 264.

When writ not served personally, the affidavit should state the name of the person upon whom it is served. *Sandall* v. *Godsoe*, 1 *All.* 44.

Writ not served personally—No Judge's order to perfect service. See Practice VI. 16—General Rules 90–98.

Return of. See General Rules 96–98.

WRIT OF ERROR.

WRIT DE PROPRIETATE PROBANDA.

WRIT OF INQUIRY.

WRIT OF RESTITUTION.

Account st
count
On a sett
plaintiff
partners,
note in h
the defen
the defen
owed the
1st. That
ted by t
without p
the amou
ered as a
was no p
2 *All.* 64

Assessmen
A New
rolled un
ment of
exemption
rates and
vincial A
Chamber

Criminal I
Not a
An overs
liable und
3, c. 28
an indict
first Gene
year, for
support of
year. It i
ment sho
nor that
neglected
fendant a
money fo
Reg. v. *M*

Contract—
ledgm
By an ag
defendant
Treasurer
the plain
coined in
defendant
coin for t
Crown ha
coining, t

ADDENDA.

CASES INADVERTENTLY OMITTED IN DIGEST.

Account stated—Settlement of Accounts—Evidence—Recovery.
On a settlement of accounts between the plaintiff and defendant who had been partners, the plaintiff wrote a promissory note in his own favor, which he read to the defendant and requested him to sign; the defendant refused; but admitted he owed the plaintiff the amount. Held, 1st. That evidence of the amount admitted by the defendant, was receivable without producing the note. 2nd. That the amount acknowledged could be recovered as an amount stated, though there was no promise to pay. *Hea* v. *Jones*, 2 *All.* 646.

Assessment—Volunteer taxes.
A New Brunswick volunteer, who enrolled under 31 Vic. c. 4, of the Parliament of Canada, is not entitled to the exemption from City, County and Parish rates and taxes, provided for by the Provincial Act 28 Vic. c. 1, s. 17. *Ruel, Chamberlain &c.* v. *Hunter*, 1 *Han.* 606.

Criminal Law—Overseers of poor—Not accounting—Indictment.
An overseer of the poor of a parish is liable under the Acts of Assembly 26 Geo. 3, c. 28 and 43, and 33 Geo. 3, c. 6, to an indictment for not accounting at the first General Sessions of the Peace in the year, for moneys received by him for the support of the poor during the preceding year. It is not necessary that the indictment should be against all the overseers nor that it should allege that they all neglected to account, if it charge the defendant specifically with the receipt of money for which he did not account. *Reg.* v. *Matthew*, 2 *Kerr* 543.

Contract—Representation—Acknowledgment by acts.
By an agreement between plaintiff and defendant, therein described as Province Treasurer, for and on behalf of the Queen, the plaintiff agreed to procure—to be coined in England and delivered to the defendant—a certain amount of copper coin for the use of the Province. The Crown having refused to authorize the coining, the plaintiff made application to the Legislature for compensation, and a grant of money was made to him "to reimburse him expenses incurred in endeavouring to execute a contract entered into with the Provincial Government for a supply of copper coin—the same to be in full." Held, in an action against the defendant for falsely representing that he had the authority of the Queen to make the contract—1st. That the defendant, having acted under the direction of the Provincial Government which represented the Crown, had the authority of the Queen; 2nd. That by accepting the grant of money from the Legislature, the plaintiff had acknowledged that the contract was made with the Provincial Government, and therefore that the defendant was not liable. *Sears* v. *Robinson*, 4 *All.* 366.
Quære, Whether the words of the agreement amounted to a representation that the defendant had the Queen's authority to make the contract. *Ibid.*

Executors and administrators—Assets—Real estate.
On an issue of *plene administravit* real estate of an intestate unsold is not assets in the hands of his administrator for payment of debts.
Quære, Whether under a different issue an administrator might be made liable for the value of real estate which he had neglected to make available. *Crawford* v. *Wilcox et al.*, 1 *All.* 634.

Mortgage—Fraudulent or not—Sufficiency of—Consideration.
The plaintiff claimed title under a mortgage from P., stating as consideration a debt of £300—but there was no proof of any debt beyond £25; the defendant claimed under a Sheriff's deed founded on a judgment recovered against P. since the mortgage, and gave evidence to shew that the mortgage was fraudulent. The Jury were directed that if there was a debt due from P. and the mortgage was given *bona fide* for the purpose of securing it, it would be valid. Held, That this direction was right, and that it was not enough to shew a consideration to the

extent of £25. *Doe* v. *Gilbert*, 1 *All.* 520.

Information—Liquor Act—Search Warrant.

A warrant cannot issue under the Act 18 Vic. c. 36, to search for liquors in a dwelling-house, in which a family resides, without the information of three persons, though there may be a shop or place in the house for the sale of liquors. An information stating that intoxicating liquors are kept for illegal sale by A. "in his house or shop or on the premises where he now dwells, in the County of C.," is not sufficiently certain to authorize the search of a dwelling-house under the said Act. Such an information will not justify a search warrant, stating that there was a place in the dwelling-house for the sale of liquors. *Ex parte Caldwell*, 3 *All.* 393.

Judge—Nisi Prius—Order for trial of causes — Authority to make—Counsel's Duty.

A Judge at *Nisi Prius* has authority to make such order at the time of trial of the causes as to him may seem requisite for the effectual despatch of the business of the Court, and it is the duty of the Attorney and Counsel in a cause to attend until the cause is disposed of. It is no ground for setting aside a verdict on the score of irregularity, that a cause has been tried out of its order in consequence of several causes standing on the docket before it having been put off by consent to a future day. *Bowes* v. *Sutherland*, 2 *Kerr* 1.

Judgment as in case of non-suit—Cause made a remanet.

Where a cause has been taken down to trial and made a remanet, either by special order of the Judge or for want of time to try all the causes on the docket, the defendant cannot obtain judgment as in case of a non-suit for a subsequent default. *Mills* v. *Leach*, 4 *All.* 355.

Motion—Entry.

A motion for judgment absolute as in case of a non-suit, for not proceeding to trial pursuant to a peremptory undertaking, should not be entered on the motion paper; and if this course be adopted, the costs occasioned thereby will not be allowed. *O'Regan* v. *Robinson*, 3 *Kerr* 224.

Leave to amend—Duty of party.

It is the duty of a party who has obtained leave to amend his pleadings to take out the rule and serve it on the opposite party, and if he omits to do so, he cannot set up his ignorance of the terms of the rule as an answer to a proceeding taken by the opposite party in consequence of the conditions of the rule not having been complied with. A party who obtains leave to amend his pleadings on payment of costs, is bound to pay the costs within a reasonable time after taxation. *Patterson* v. *Patterson*, 1 *All.* 400.

Mortgage — Foreclosure — Plaintiff's right to costs of defending suit for redemption.

In a suit for foreclosure of a mortgage, by which the mortgagor, in addition to other property conveyed, assigned a mortgage given to him by M., the plaintiff is not entitled to recover the costs incurred by him in defending a suit for redemption brought against him by the assignee of the redemption of M., in which suit each party was ordered to pay his own costs. *Bank of New Brunswick* v. *Cronk et al.*, 1 *Han.* 228.

Partnership—Liability of partners.

F. & S. D. and B. entered into a partnership for the buying and selling of shingles; F. & S. D. to furnish the capital and B. to purchase shingles; profits to be equally divided. The shingles to be shipped to F. & S. at Boston and money provided by drafts drawn by D. upon them; the business in New Brunswick being done under the name of M. & D. Plaintiffs sold goods to D. on the credit of the partnership and took his notes in payment. Held, That the goods being proper for the business of the firm and sold on the credit of the firm, the other partners were liable, and that as regards contracts with third parties it was of no consequence whether D. had advanced his proper share of the capital or not. *Jones* v. *Foster et al. impleaded with Dowling*, 1 *Han.* 596.

Pleading—False representation—Insufficient averment.

In an action for deceit, the declaration stated that the plaintiff bargained with the defendant to buy and take an assignment from him for the sum of five shillings, of certain judgments in the defendant's hands, *inter alia* a judgment in favor of the defendant recovered in the Supreme Court of Nova Scotia against J. C. for £129, and that the defendant then and there falsely, fraudulently and deceitfully represented to the plaintiff that the said judgment had been recorded in the Book of Registry of Deeds, whereby J. C.'s lands were bound, and that an execution could issue thereon under which his lands could be sold, and that the judgment had priority over a mortgage on the land given to A. Averment, That the judgment had not been recorded, and that J. C.'s lands were not bound thereby, and that no execution could issue on the judgment under which J. C.'s land could be sold, and that the judgment had not priority over A.'s mortgage, as the defendant, at the time of making the said false and deceitful representation, well knew, whereby the defendant falsely deceived the plaintiff, and thereby the judgment against J. C. became of no value to the plaintiff, and he had sustained damage to the amount of £500 in not being able to issue execution and sell the land, and in consequence of the judgment not having priority over A.'s mortgage. It was proved that the defendant was the attorney on the judgment, that it was not recorded, and that by the law of Nova Scotia, land could not be sold under execution unless the judgment was recorded. Verdict for the plaintiff for £126. Held, That as the declaration did not shew that the false representation was the inducement to the plaintiff to enter into the contract, but that the contract was only for the assignment of the judgment (which the defendant had given the plaintiff), and as the injury to the plaintiff depended on the consideration paid, and there was no allegation of the value of the judgment, or of J. C.'s land, the verdict could not be sustained. *Knapp et al.* v. *McFarlan and Dixon*, 4 *All.* 284.

Probate Court—Granting Administration—Jurisdiction.

The Probate Court has jurisdiction to grant administration without a citation on an estate of a person dying in the Province, on the petition of a person alleging himself to be a creditor of the deceased, and that he died without leaving any next of kin. If administration is irregularly granted, application should be made to the Probate Court to revoke it. *Doe dem Shore* v. *Gearon*, 1 *Han.* 144.

Representation—Title to land—Word "purchase."

An agreement by which the defendant agreed to sell to the plaintiff—"all his right, title and interest to the timber growing on a certain block of land, being the same tract which he (defendant) purchased from the Crown"—does not amount to a representation that the defendant has a title to the land. The term "purchase" does not necessarily imply a conveyance of land, but may be understood to signify a bargain or agreement for it. *Ash and another* v. *Clarke*, 3 *Kerr* 187.

Service of notice on student—Requisite statement.

Affidavit of service of a notice of motion "on a student in the office of plaintiff's attorney" not sufficient, it not stating that the service was at the office. *Ber.* 342.

Student at law—Graduate.

To entitle a student at law to the benefit of the reduction of the term of study allowed to graduates by the Act 26 Vic. c. 23, he must be a graduate at the time of commencing his study. *Ex parte Travis*, 1 *Han.* 30.

Term's notice—When necessary.

If four terms have elapsed after issue joined, without any proceeding being taken in a cause, a term's notice of the plaintiff's intention to proceed must be given, though a year may not have elapsed. *Collins* v. *Kerlin*, 4 *All.* 505.

Venue—Application to change—Convenience—Expense.

Where, on an application to change the venue, it appeared that the change would be a convenience to the defendant, whose witnesses all resided in the County to which the venue was proposed to be changed, but that it would be less expensive to the plaintiff to try the cause in the County where he had laid the venue, the Court refused to interfere. *Carvill* v. *St. John Insurance Co.*, 3 *All.* 431.

See Levy *v.* Rice, 5 C. P. 119, L. R. See Church *v.* Barnett, 6 C. P. 116, L. R.

THE FOLLOWING CASES SHOULD HAVE APPEARED UNDER THEIR RESPECTIVE HEADS.

Affidavit to hold to bail—Filing—Time—Waiver.

It is in general sufficient that affidavits to hold to bail be filed within thirty days after the term in which the writ is returnable, and as the defendant cannot object to the want of the affidavit being on file until he has entered special bail, such entry is not a waiver of the omission to file the affidavit. But pleading to the action after a term has intervened is a waiver, as the defendant might have searched the office and informed himself of the irregularity. If a defendant, being aware that the plaintiff has not filed his entry docket or declaration in the cause, appears at the trial and defends the action, he thereby waives the previous irregularity in the plaintiff's proceedings. *Read* v. *McLellan*, 1 *All.* 3.

Judgment as in case of Non-suit—Insufficient excuse.

An affidavit of the plaintiff's attorney that the reason for not proceeding to trial after notice was that the plaintiff resided in a distant part of the Province and did not appear nor send his witnesses, is not a sufficient answer to a motion for judgment as in case of a non-suit, there being nothing to shew why the plaintiff was not ready or that he intended to proceed in the cause. *Katham* v. *Hawkes*, 1 *Kerr* 525.

Jury—Elisors summoning—Impartiality.

It is not a sufficient objection to elisors named to summon the jury in an action against the Sheriff for a false return to a writ of election that one of them had voted for the plaintiff at the election, and that the other had always been opposed to the defendant and to the returned candidate. *Stiles v. Gilbert*, 3 *All.* 503.

Malicious prosecution—Termination of proceedings.

Defendant made complaint before a magistrate that the plaintiff had threatened to shoot him, whereupon a warrant was issued and the plaintiff arrested and brought before the magistrate, who, after hearing the parties, dismissed the complaint. Held, in an action for malicious prosecution, That there was evidence of the termination of the proceedings before the magistrate. Malice is not a question for the Judge to determine. *Wasson* v. *Taylor*, 1 *Han.* 102.

Pleading—Declaration—Common breach.

The declaration contained a special count setting out an agreement made by the defendant to pay the plaintiff £18 15s., which was due by A. to the plaintiff on the 1st May then next, in consideration of his giving time to A. until the said 1st May; or that A. should then deliver to the plaintiff a yoke of oxen and a colt in good working condition: and averring that A. did not pay or deliver etc., of which the defendant had notice; to this were subjoined the common counts: Held, That the usual breach at the conclusion of the declaration sufficiently alleged the non-payment by the defendant of the sum mentioned in the special counts. *Marks* v. *Scott*, 2 *Kerr* 379.

ERRATA ET CORRIGENDA.

Page 1—On head title, "Hilary" Term inclusive, should be "Easter."
" "—Under title Abandonment, trespass "25," should be "II. 8, 12, 13, 25."
" "—Under title Abatement, Bills and Notes VI. "9" should be "10."
" 2—Under Acceptance, Contract "12," read "8."
" 3—Second line from top, left column, for Contract "6," read "2."
" "—Under Account, Attorney VIII. "32," read "4."
" "—Under Ac Etiam, Practice "VI." 1, read "IV."
" 7—Under No. 11, for Assumpsit III. "47," read "43."
" "—Under No. 13, Legacy, for Assumpsit III. "19," read "14."
" 8—Under No. 18, for Assumpsit III. "20," read "15."
" "—Under 21, for Assumpsit III. "34," read "29."
" "—Under 27, for Assumpsit III. "24," read "19."
" "—On seventh line from top, left column, for Assumpsit III. "38," read "5." On ninth line, for Assumpsit III. "8," read "33."
" 9—Third line from top, right column, for Assumpsit III. "56," read "52."
" 14—Under No. 4, Principal and Agent "22," read "16."
" 15—Under No. 4, Crown Grant "21," read "II. 2."
" 18—Under No. 4, left column, "sufficient" should be "insufficient."
" 19—Under No. 6, right column, Ejectment "VI." 2, read "IV."
" 20—Under Agreement, To Lease, Landlord and Tenant "4," read "I. 3."
" 28—Under Appraisers, "14" read "VI. 2."
" 39—Under No. 14, Bills and Notes "I." 9 read "II."
" "—Under Assignment, fifth line, Landlord and Tenant "VI. 2," read "14."
" 60—Under No. 25, for "pleading," read "practice."
" 62—Under Bankrupt, sixth line, for Non-suit II. "22," read "11."
" 64—Under No. 8, for 33 Vic. cap. "33," read "32."
" 80—Under Bill of Lading, for Pleading II. "5," read "28."
Under ditto, for Contract "21," read "17."
" 88—Under Calls, Bills and Notes "I." 9, read "II."
" 99—Under Contract, ninth line, for Action at Law "15," read "IX. 15."
Under ditto, twentieth line, for "contract," read "corporation."
" 117—Title "Supreme Court," should be "County Court."
" 154—Under Disseisin, first line, Limitation of Actions "22," read "IV. 22."
" 157—Under Dower, No. 5, Non-suit III. "13," read "12."
" 168—Second line from bottom, right column, New Trial II. "16," read "18."
" 173—Under Escape, No. 1, for 2 All. "4," read "475."
" 177—Under No. 6, Corporation "7," read "6."
" 178—Second line from top, left column, for Evidence VII. "3," read "23."
" 193—Under No. 23, Evidence "III." 5, read "IV."
" 214—Title "Farms," should be "Forms."
" 226—Under Indemnity, Principal and Agent "22," read "16."
" 246—Under No. 18, insert name of case, "Laney v. Siddal, 3 Kerr 223."
" 275—On seventh line from top, right column, for "influence," read "inference."
" 278—Under No. 10, for see "Supra," read "Infra."
" 302—Under Overseers of Poor, insert "See Addenda, Reg. v. Mathew."
" 304—Under Pendency of other Suit, for II. "39," read "41."
" 305—Under No. 1, "arguments" should be "averments."
" 338—Under 45, Levy, Execution, I. "7," read "8."
" 342—Third line from top, left column, Maloney v. Morrison, "3 Kerr," should be "1 All."
" 345—Under No. 5, 1 All. "580," read "508."
" 373—Under No. 28, third line "II." 15, read "III."
" 412—Title Witness, under No. 8, insert "See also Shields v. McGrath, New Trial II. 28."

" 23—DesBrisay v. Livingstone. Insert at end of paragraph, "Defendant refusing to swear that he would be prejudiced thereby."
" 201—Under Use and Occupation, eighth line from top, left column, for "defendant was liable," should be "defendant was *not* liable."

TA

TABLE OF NAMES IN THE DIGEST OF UNREPORTED CASES.

A.

B.

C.

M.

N.

O.

P.

Q.

R.

TABLE OF CASES IN PUBLISHED REPORTS.

A.

B.

C.

D.

G.

J.

K.

L.

56

S.

W.

Y.

APPENDIX.

CONTENTS

OF

RULES OF COURT.

FROM E

Al

Michae

1—*Orde*
shall b
rule to

GENERAL RULES

OF

THE SUPREME COURT,

FROM EASTER TERM 25 GEO. III. 1785, TO MICHAELMAS TERM 36 VIC. A. D. 1872,

COLLATED AND ALPHABETICALLY ARRANGED.

ABATEMENT (PLEAS IN.)

Michaelmas Term, 7 Victoria, 1843.

1—*Ordered*, That no plea in abatement shall be filed after the expiration of the rule to plead.

AFFIDAVITS.

Hilary Term, 11 Victoria, 1848.

2—**Illiterate persons.**
It is ordered, That from and after the first day of Easter Term next, where any affidavit is taken by any Commissioner of this Court, made by any person unable to write or appearing to be illiterate, the Commissioner taking such affidavit shall himself read over, and, if necessary, explain the affidavit to the party making the same; and shall certify or state in the jurat, that the affidavit was read by him to the deponent, who seemed perfectly to understand the same, and also that the said deponent wrote his or her signature, or made his or her mark, in the presence of the Commissioner taking the said affidavit.

3—**Where more than one deponent.**
It is further Ordered, That after the time aforesaid, where there are two or more deponents in the same affidavit, the names of the deponents who are sworn thereto shall be specified in the jurat.

Michaelmas Term, 11 Victoria, 1847.

4—**Papers annexed to affidavits.**
It is Ordered, That from and after the last day of Hilary Term next, the Judge, Commissioner, or Officer taking any affidavit to which any other paper or papers may be annexed, do at the time of taking such affidavit, mark every such annexed paper with his name, or the initial letters of his name.

Easter Term, 11 Victoria, 1848.

5—*It is further Ordered*, That the General Rule of Michaelmas Term last, in regard to marking papers annexed to any affidavit, shall not extend to affidavits of service of writs returned by the Sheriff, or other officer, to whom the writs are respectively directed.

Hilary Term, 23 Victoria, 1860.

5 a—**Serving affidavits in equity suits.**
It is Ordered, That it shall not be necessary in any case where a defendant has not appeared, except in applications on notice for an injunction, to serve a copy of any affidavit to be used on any motion, or the hearing of any petition on such defendant, unless service shall be specially directed by any Judge; and it shall in no case be necessary to serve the opposite party with a copy of any affidavit of service of process, or of service of any notice, or other paper, unless specially ordered.

AGENTS.

Michaelmas Term, 31 George 3, 1791.

6—*Ordered by the Court*, That all attorneys practising in this Court, who are non-residents of Fredericton, or the City o Saint John, do appoint an agent at one or other of the said places, and give notice to the Clerk or his Deputy of the name of such Agent, and at which of said places he resides; which notice shall

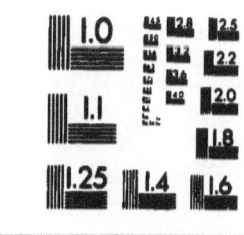

be put up in the Clerk's Office; and that all notices, served on such Agents, respectively, shall be deemed as proper and legal a service as if served upon such attorney.

Hilary Term, 7 William 4, 1837.

7—*Whereas*, It is deemed improper that any clerk in the Office of the Clerk of the Pleas of this Court should act as an agent of any attorney with or without any remuneration or gratuity, *It is Ordered*, That henceforth no attorney of this Court do employ any such clerk as his agent in any suit or matter pending in this Court, or in the transaction of any business in the office either of the Clerk of the Crown, or Clerk of the Pleas; and that the Clerk of the Pleas do not allow or suffer any clerk or other person employed in his office to act as such agent under any pretence whatsoever.

Trinity Term, 3 Victoria, 1840.

8—*It is further Ordered*, That henceforth no attorney of this Court do employ any student in the office of a Barrister of this Court, as his Agent in any suit or matter pending in this Court, or in the transaction of any business before a Judge or in the Office either of the Clerk of the Crown or the Clerk of the Pleas; and that no Barrister of this Court do suffer any one of his students to act as the Agent of any other attorney. Provided that this rule shall not extend to prevent the employment by a Barrister, who may himself be the Agent of any attorney, of any student in his office in the professional business of such attorney.

8—The Judges will in future expect, that in the assessment of damages in vacation, as well as in other matters brought before them out of Court, where the parties do not appear in person, they be attended by a Barrister or Attorney of the Court; or where this cannot conveniently be done, that the clerk or student employed to attend on behalf of any attorney, be of competent experience, skill and knowledge of the business entrusted to him.

APPEAL PAPER.

Hilary Term, 32 Victoria, 1869.

9 *A*—It is ordered that hereafter there shall be but one appeal paper and that the Clerk of the Pleas shall enter causes thereon in the following order:—

1st. Appeals from the decision of a Judge in Equity.

2nd. Appeals from the Court of Divorce and matrimonial causes.

3rd. Appeals from Court of Probate.

4th. Appeals under the Act 27 Vic., c. 44, for winding-up the affairs of incorporated companies.

5th. Appeals from the County Courts—and, in case of any other appeals not hereinafter provided for, they shall be entered after the County Court Appeals in the order of time in which they may be allowed by law.

All appeals shall be heard in their order, and at the time prescribed by the rules of Court.

Trinity Term, 31 Victoria, 1868.

9 *B*—1st. When the minutes of any decree shall not be settled under the Act 17 Vic., c. 18, s. 32, more than fourteen days before the first of any term, a party intending to appeal therefrom shall enter the cause on the Equity Appeal Paper of the term next after the settling of such minutes, but may obtain the order of a Judge to postpone the hearing of such appeal until the second term thereafter, which order shall be made unless good cause be shown to the contrary, and such order shall direct the time of serving the grounds of appeal on the opposite party.

2nd—Where an appeal is intended to be made from any order of a Judge in Equity in a cause where no decree is made, and such order shall have been made within fourteen days before the first day of any term, a like order may be made as is provided for in the preceding rule.

3rd—Whenever an appeal is made from a decree or order of the Court or of a Judge in Equity, or from the Court of Divorce and matrimonial causes or from a Probate Court, the Court may order the whole or any part of the pleadings, evidence, judgment or other proceedings to be printed, and such number of printed copies thereof to be furnished for the use of the Appellate Court as may be deemed necessary, and may make order for the payment of the expenses thereof in the costs of the suit.

4th—**Hearing Causes.**
All causes intended for hearing at the Sittings in Equity, shall be set down with the Clerk in Equity six days before the first day of the sitting of the Court, and shall be entered by him on a docket to be kept for that purpose; and no cause, not so entered, shall be heard without the order of the Judge sitting in such Court.

APPEARANCE.

Easter Term, 25 George 3, 1785.

10—*Ordered*, That where an attorney appears for the defendant, a copy of the declaration, with notice of the rule to plead, shall be served on him, he paying for such copy at the rate of sixpence per sheet, and on default of pleading in twenty days, judgment to be entered, and a writ of inquiry may be executed as aforesaid, a plea being first demanded after the said twenty days.

ASSESSMENT OF DAMAGES.

Trinity Term, 26 George 3, 1786.

11—*Ordered*, That in causes where interlocutory judgments have been signed, and the causes of action appear to be upon complicated accounts, the same shall be referred to a jury of inquiry, and judgment shall be considered to be entered as of the precedent term.

Michaelmas Term, 6 William 4, 1835.

12—*It is Ordered*, That in all cases, where application shall be made to a Judge in vacation after judgment by default, to make inquiry or assessment, under the Act of Assembly 5 Wm. 4, c. 37, s. 9, there shall be produced to the Judge a certificate or memorandum, of the day on which interlocutory judgment was signed, or judgment by default entered, signed by the Clerk of the Pleas or his deputy; and that no such inquiry or assessment shall be made, unless such certificate or memorandum be so produced.

ATTACHMENT.

Hilary Term, 15 Victoria, 1852.

13—*It is Ordered*, That in future no attachment do issue unless taken out in the term during which the same may have been granted, or in the vacation next succeeding the same, without the order of the Court, or a Judge.

See No. 136.

ATTORNEYS.

Hilary Term, 60 George 3, 1820.

14—*It is ordered*, That in future, no attorney of the Court not being an established resident within the Province, be permitted to act as an attorney of this Court.

ATTORNEYS, BARRISTERS AND STUDENTS—(ADMISSION OF.)

Hilary Term, 4 George 4, 1823.

15—1st. *It is Ordered*, That hereafter, no person, who shall study the Law in this Province for the purpose of being admitted an Attorney of this Court, shall be so admitted unless he shall have so studied with some Barrister of this Court for the term of four years, if he be a Graduate of any College, or if not such Graduate, for the term of five years: *Provided*, That this Rule shall not extend to any person who shall have commenced his studies under any Barrister of this Court before the commencement of the present Term.

2nd. That no person producing a Certificate of admission as an Attorney of the Supreme Court of any other Province, Colony, or Island, in His Majesty's dominions, in order to obtain admission and enrollment as an Attorney of this Court, shall be so admitted and enrolled, unless he shall have served a regular Apprenticeship in such Province, Colony, or Island, agreeably to the terms prescribed in the foregoing rule for Students at Law in this Province, nor unless he shall produce an authenticated copy of the Certificate of such service, by virtue of which he may have obtained admission as an Attorney of the Supreme Court of such Province, Colony, or Island, nor unless such Certificate shall include the qualifications as to age and moral character requisite in that behalf to be included in Certificates of service as Apprentices to the Law in this Province.

3rd. That after the expiration of two years from the time of admission as Attorneys, such Attorneys may be called to the Bar, provided there appears no just cause to prevent such call.

4th. That no person, admitted as an Attorney of this Court, shall, until he be called to the degree of a Barrister, be permitted to wear a Gown, or to make any motion as Counsel in any cause in this Court.

5th. That notice of every application, for admission as an Attorney of this Court, be filed with the Clerk of the Pleas on the first day of the Term at which such application may be made.

6th. That no person, under the degree of a Barrister, be hereafter entitled to take a Student for admission as an Attorney.

7th. That every Barrister taking a Student for admission as an Attorney, shall enter the name of such Student forthwith, with the Clerk of the Pleas of this Court, to be enrolled by him in a Roll to be kept for that purpose, with the date of the commencement of such Student's term of study.

8th. That no Student in any Barrister's office, shall be permitted hereafter to practice in the name of any Attorney, or otherwise, in any Inferior Court of Common Pleas in this Province.

Hilary Term, 6 George 4, 1825.

16—*Ordered*, That whenever any Attorney of this Court shall be desirous of being called to the Bar as Barrister, he shall make known his wishes, by petition to the Court, on the first day of the Term—which Petition shall be delivered to the Clerk, and be open for the inspection of Gentlemen of the Bar, until the sitting of the Court on Thursday following in the same Term, when the Court will determine upon the said Petition.

Michaelmas Term, 6 William 4, 1835.

17—*It is Ordered*, That any Attorney, who, on his being admitted an Attorney, was a Graduate of any College, may be called to the Bar after the expiration of one year from the time of his admission as an Attorney.

Michaelmas Term, 1 Victoria, 1837.

18—1st. *Whereas* it is expedient, That every person desirous of being admitted as an Attorney of this Court, should, before such admission, be examined as to his fitness and capacity to act as such Attorney. *It is Ordered*, That the Judges of this Court, together with four Barristers of not less than five years standing, to be for that purpose appointed by rule of Court in Hilary Term in every year, or any two of them, whereof a Judge to be one, shall be competent to conduct the examination of any person who may have made application for admission as an Attorney of this Court in the form hereafter mentioned; and that from and after the last day of next Hilary Term, subject to such appeal as hereafter mentioned, no person shall be admitted to be sworn as an Attorney of this Court without the production of a certificate signed by such examiners, testifying his fitness and capacity to act as an Attorney.

2nd. *It is Ordered*, That the said examination shall be held at such times and places respectively, and under such regulations as the Judges, or any three of them, may from time to time appoint.

3rd. That in case any person shall be dissatisfied with the refusal of the examiners to grant such certificate, he shall be at liberty to apply for admission, by petition in writing to the Judges: which application shall be heard by not less than three of the Judges, at such time and place as they may appoint.

4th. That every person who may desire to be admitted an Attorney, shall, on or before the Thursday in the first week of the term immediately preceding that at which he shall propose to be admitted, make application by Petition to the Court, in the form hereunto annexed, or to the like effect, which petition shall be accompanied by the requisite certificates of the age, moral character, and service of the applicant; and the certificate of moral character shall be full, positive and explicit, and shall contain particular testimonials to the sober and temperate habits of the applicant, and the Court, if satisfied with the certificates, will, during such term, make order for the examination of such applicant.

5th. That the foregoing rules touching examination, shall extend to persons who may apply for admission upon certificates from any other part of Her Majesty's dominions, as well as to persons who may have pursued their studies in this Province; and any person coming from any other part of Her Majesty's dominions shall produce a certificate from the Court in which he may have become a practitioner, or one of the Judges thereof, that he has conducted himself with credit and reputation since his admission there.

6th. That no Attorney of this Court who shall have been absent from the Province, or have discontinued the practice of the Law for the space of five years together, shall hereafter be permitted to commence or resume practice as an Attorney until he be re-admitted and re-sworn.

7th. That every attorney who may desire to be re-admitted, shall apply by petition to the Court, stating therein the place or places in which he may have resided, and the business, profession or employment in which he may have been engaged or concerned since his first admission; which petition shall be verified by the affidavit of the petitioner, and shall be presented to the Court on or before the Thursday in the first week of the term, immediately preceding that at which he may desire to be re-admitted.

8th. That every applicant for re-admission shall be examined as to his fitness and capacity to act as an Attorney, in the same manner as if applying for a first admission, unless the Court shall see fit in any case to dispense with such examination, and shall make order accordingly.

9th. That from and after the present Michaelmas Term, no Attorney of any other part of Her Majesty's dominions shall be admitted as an Attorney of this Court, unless he shall have entered as a Student with one of the Attorneys of this Court, having the rank of Barrister, and resident and practising in the Province, and shall have continued as such Student for one year; the entry of every such Student to be registered with the Clerk, as in the case of other Students; and a certificate of such year's study from the Barrister with whom the same may have been performed shall be one of the testimonials necessary for the admission of such applicant.

Form of Petition for Admission as an Attorney.

To the Honorable the Chief Justice, and Justices of the Supreme Court.

The Petition of A. B. Humbly Sheweth, That your petitioner was born in on [*state the place and day of birth*], as by the accompanying certificate (or affidavit) will appear. That on he entered as a Student in the office of C. D., Esquire, a Barrister of this Court, at in this Province, and has continued as such from that time hitherto; during which time he has not absented himself without the permission of the said C. D., nor been engaged in any other profession, business or employment.

[If the applicant have studied part of the time with any other Barrister, or been absent without permission, or engaged in any other profession, business or employment, since commencing his studies, he must state fully the reasons therefor, the particular time and length of such other study, or absence, or engagements in other pursuits, together with such other particulars as he may think advisable, explanatory of his conduct. If the applicant have not studied in this Province, he must state the particular grounds on which he applies for admission, the place or places in which he may have resided and practiced since his admission by any other Court; and, if he have been engaged in any other profession, business or employment, he must state the particulars of the same, with any other matters explanatory of his conduct and pursuits as he may deem necessary or advisable. *]

That your petitioner is at present resident at and is desirous of being admitted an Attorney of this Honorable Court at the ensuing Term, and prays that your Honors will make such order touching his examination or admission as by the rules of the Court are required, or as to your Honors may seem meet. Dated the day of 18 .

Michaelmas Term, 4 Victoria, 1840.

19—*It is Ordered*, That any Attorney who may before his admission have been an Attorney of some other part of Her Majesty's Dominions, and who shall have been a Student in this Province for one year pursuant to the ninth Rule of Michaelmas Term, 1st Victoria, may be called to the Bar after the expiration of one year from the time of his admission as an Attorney of this Court.

20—*It is Ordered*, That the admission and enrollment of Attorneys may take place on the Thursday in the first week of the Term, if there is no sufficient objection to the applicant.

---

* If the petitioner's full time of study has not expired at the time of application, he must further state his intention to continue a Student in the Barrister's office until such time expires, and will be required to produce an additional certificate to that effect at the ensuing term.

Trinity Term, 5 Victoria, 1842.

21—*It is Ordered*, That Students, applying for examination after four years' study, on the ground of being Graduates of some College, do, in addition to the certificates now required, produce certificates from the President, Vice-President, or some resident Professor of the College, stating the particular period during which their Collegiate studies have been pursued.

Trinity Term, 6 Victoria, 1843.

22—1st. *Whereas* it is expedient that there should be an examination of persons who may hereafter desire to enter upon the study of the Law, in order to their admission as Attorneys of this Court, *It is Ordered*, That such and so many Barristers as may for that purpose from time to time be appointed by rule of Court, or any two of them shall be competent to conduct the examination of any person who may have made application to be admitted a Student; and in order to such examination, application shall be made by petition to this Court by such person, stating his age, place of birth, and present residence; the name and place of residence of his father or guardian, and the several branches of education in which he may have been instructed; and that proper certificates as to character and habits shall accompany every such petition; and this Court will thereupon make such order for the examination or otherwise, as may appear necessary and proper.

2nd. That no entry shall be made in the Clerk's book of any Student, nor shall he be deemed to have commenced his study of the Law with any Barrister, until he produce the certificate of the examiners before whom his examination may be had, testifying his fitness and capacity.

3rd. That in case any person shall be dissatisfied with the refusal of the examiners to grant such certificate, he shall be at liberty to apply, by petition, to the Judges, who will make such order thereupon as the case may in their opinion require.

4th. That every Student who may be transferred from one Barrister to another, during the progress of his studies, shall forthwith deliver to the Clerk a memorandum of such transfer, accompanied by a certificate of the Barrister whose office he may be desirous of leaving; or in case of his death, absence, or refusal to grant such certificate, the certificate of the Barrister to whose office he is transferred, of the cause and reason of such transfer.

5th. That the aforegoing rules shall not extend to persons who may already have been admitted as Attorneys in any other part of Her Majesty's Dominions; but that such persons before being registered as Students under the ninth rule of Michaelmas Term, 1 Vic., shall apply, by petition, to the Court, accompanied by the requisite certificates; and the Court will make order thereupon.

6th. That if any person, who may, after his commencing to study the Law, have discontinued the same, shall be desirous of resuming his studies, he shall apply, by petition, to the Court for that purpose, who will make such order thereupon in regard to the time of his previous study, as may appear meet; otherwise the time of such former study shall not be allowed to such Student.

Michaelmas Term, 11 Victoria, 1847.

23—*Whereas* certain rules and regulations, touching the examination of persons as Students at Law, and Attorneys, and the admission of Attorneys and Barristers of the Supreme Court, were duly made by the Barristers' Society in Hilary Term last, at a meeting of the said Society holden at Fredericton, pursuant to the Act of Assembly, 9th Vic. c. 49, which said rules and regulations have been sanctioned by the Judges of this Court, in conformity to the said Act, and are as follows:—

"At a meeting of the Barristers' Society of New Brunswick, holden in the Supreme Court Room, at Fredericton, this eighth day of February, A. D. 1847, the following rules were adopted:—

Rules touching the Examination of persons as Students at Law and Attorneys, and regulating the admission of Attorneys and Barristers of the Supreme Court.

"I. That before any person is presented to the Barristers' Society for the purpose of being examined, in order to his being entered as a Student in the Office of any Barrister of this Society, he shall present a Petition to the Benchers, setting forth his age, place of birth, residence, place of education, the branches in which he is prepared to undergo an examination, and the name of the Barrister with whom he purposes studying; which Petition shall be subscribed by the applicant, and certified by such Barrister, as to his character and habits, and that he verily believes him to be a proper person to be admitted as a Student at Law; and upon such applicant being approved of by the Benchers, he shall be fully and strictly examined in the English and Latin Languages, Mathematics, Geography and History, by the said Benchers, or any three of them, at Fredericton.

"II. That upon the applicant passing such examination, and the Benchers being satisfied as to his moral character, good habits, and fitness to enter upon the study of the Law, he shall receive a certificate to that effect.

"III. That every Student making application for admission as an Attorney, shall give a Term's notice thereof to this Society, and shall undergo a full and strict examination before the Benchers, or any three of them, in the Elementary principles of the Law of Real and Personal Property, Forms of Action, Pleading, Evidence, and Practice.

"IV. That upon the Student passing such examination, and the Benchers being fully satisfied as to his moral character, habits and conduct during the term of his study, he shall be recommended for admission as an Attorney; provided always, that in case any Student shall not pass his examination before three of the Benchers as aforesaid, such Benchers shall report the fact to the whole body of Benchers, and he may be heard before them against the refusal of his certificate.

"V. That every Attorney applying to be called to the Bar, shall give to this Society a Term's notice of such his intention; and if, during the period since his admission as an Attorney, his practice and conduct have been professional and honorable, and no objections are made to his moral character and habits, he shall be recommended accordingly; but if objections be made, an enquiry therein shall be instituted by the Benchers, or a Committee of them; and upon such inquiry, the said Benchers, or a Committee as aforesaid, shall either grant or withhold a certificate of recommendation for such Attorney's admission as a Barrister, as to them may appear just and right in the premises."

Further Regulations by Barristers' Society, passed 8th February, 1867.

Before any person is presented to the Barristers' Society, for the purpose of being examined, in order to his being entered as a Student in the office of any Barrister, he shall give a Term's previous notice in writing put up in the Library Room, on or before the first Friday of the Term, and shall present a Petition to the Council of the said Society, setting forth his age, place of birth, residence, place of education, the branches in which he is prepared to undergo an examination, and the name of the Barrister with whom he proposes to study, which petition shall be subscribed by the applicant, and certified by such Barrister, after a careful enquiry and personal examination, as to the character, habits and education of the applicant, and that upon such enquiry and examination, the Barrister verily believes the applicant to be a proper person and properly qualified to be admitted as a Student-at-Law, and upon his being approved by the Council, he shall be fully examined at Fredericton, at such time as may be appointed, by questions in writing, in such branches as two members of the Council (one being an examiner) may determine, subject to the approval of a Judge, and who shall certify accordingly.

Upon the applicant passing such examination, and the Council being satisfied as to his moral character, good habits, and fitness to enter on the study of the Law, he shall receive a certificate to that effect.

Every Student making application for admission, as an Attorney, shall give a Term's notice, by a writing for that purpose put up in the Law Library on or before the first Friday of the Term, and shall undergo an examination at such time and place as the Council or any two members thereof, (an examiner being one), may appoint, by written questions previously prepared, under the authority of the Council, who may alter, add to or amend the same, for such Student or Students to answer, who shall put the answers to such questions in writing, and during such examination shall not be permitted to refer to any book, or person, or other source of information, to assist him in such answers, and shall write the same in a legible hand, in the presence of one of the said Council, or the Secretary of the said Society, which written answers shall be submitted to the aforesaid two members of Council for their opinion upon the same, who, after examination, shall submit them for the approval of one of the Judges, such answers to be so submitted and decided on, without the said members or Judge knowing the name of the respective parties who gave in the same, such answers being designated by letters or numbers only; and if such Student shall be deemed qualified, he shall receive a first, second or third class certificate, according to the merits of his written answers.

That upon a Student passing such examination, and the Council being fully satisfied as to his moral character, habits and conduct during the term of his study, he shall be recommended for admission as an Attorney.

And whereas it is highly necessary, as well for the interest of every person entering upon the study of the Law, as for "securing to the Province and the Profession, a learned and honorable body," especially in the late curtailed period of study, that Students of the Law, during their Studentship, should confine themselves exclusively to the study of their profession, and not receive any emolument or reward for their services, or engage in any other profession, business, or employment: No Student, therefore, shall receive any salary or remuneration whatever for his services from the Barrister with whom he studies, nor from any other person, nor shall he be allowed to practice or try causes in any Court, on pain of being refused admission.

Every Attorney applying to be called to the Bar shall give to this Society, a Term's notice of such his intention, and if during the period since his admission as an Attorney, his practice and conduct have been professional and honorable, and no objections are made to his moral character and habits, he shall be recommended accordingly, but, if objections be made, an enquiry therein shall be instituted by the Council, and upon such enquiry the said Council shall either grant or withhold a certificate of recommendation for such Attorney's admission, as Barrister, as to them may appear just and right in the premises, subject to appeal as aforesaid.

Easter Term, 19 Victoria, 1856.

24—*It is Ordered*, That any Barrister of the Supreme or Superior Court or Courts of any of Her Majesty's Colonies or Possessions in North America, Bermuda, or the West Indies, and entitled to practice as such in all the Supreme Courts of that Colony or Possession in which he may have been originally admitted a Barrister, may, upon the recommendation of the Barristers' Society, be called, sworn, and enrolled a Barrister of this Court, and entitled to the rights and privileges as such so long as he shall be a member of the said Barristers' Society; provided always, that no such Barrister of any other British Colony or Possession shall be entitled to be admitted a Barrister of this Court, unless it be proved to the satisfaction of this Court, that a Barrister of this Court would be entitled to like rights and privileges in all the Superior Courts of that Colony or Possession in which the applicant may have been originally admitted a Barrister.

Hilary Term, 21 Victoria, 1858.

25—*It is Ordered*, That the privilege granted by the Rule of Court to Students applying for admission as Attorneys, and to Attorneys applying for admission as Barristers, when such Students and Attorneys are Graduates of some College or University, be confined to Graduates of some University situate within the British Dominions; but that such order shall not apply to any Student already entered.

Examination. See No. 124.

See Acts of Assembly 26 Vic. (1866), cap. 23, limiting term of study.

AWARDS AND WARRANTS OF ATTORNEY.

Michaelmas Term, 6 William 4, 1835.

26—*It is Ordered*, That when a rule to show cause is obtained to set aside an Award or Warrant of Attorney, or a judgment entered upon an Award or Warrant of Attorney, the several objections, intended to be insisted upon at the time of making such rule absolute, shall be stated in the rule to show cause.

Hilary Term, 7 William 4, 1837.

27—*It is Ordered*, That no judgment be signed upon any Warrant authorizing any Attorney to confess judgment without such Warrant being delivered to, and filed by the Clerk.

It is Ordered, That every Attorney of this Court who shall prepare any Warrant of Attorney to confess any judgment which is to be subject to any defeazance, do cause such defeazance to be written on the same paper or parchment on which the Warrant of Attorney shall be written, or cause a memorandum in writing to be made on such Warrant, containing the substance and effect of such defeazance.

It is Ordered, That no Sheriff, Bailiff, or Sheriff's Officer, shall presume to exact or take from any person or persons being in his custody by arrest, any Warrant to confess judgment, but in the presence of an Attorney for the Defendant, which Attorney shall then subscribe his name thereto; and that no Attorney do acknowledge or enter any judgment by color of any Warrant given by any Defendant being under arrest, otherwise than is as aforesaid.

Easter Term, 11 Victoria, 1848.

28—No Judgment to be signed on a Warrant of Attorney after one year from its date without the order of the Court, or of a Judge.

Trinity Term, 20 Victoria, 1857.

29—I. *It is Ordered*, That in no case where the Warrant of Attorney to confess judgment appears to have been executed, not personally, but by an Attorney or Agent in the name of the Principal, shall any confession be signed thereon by an Attorney of this Court, unless the deed or other power conveying the authority to execute the Warrant, together with an affidavit of the due execution thereof by the principal, be produced to, and read and examined by the Attorney who is applied to to sign the confession, before signing the same; nor shall judgment be entered upon any such confession unless such deed or other power, and affidavit of execution, be produced to the Clerk, and filed with the Warrant of Attorney and confession.

II. *It is further Ordered*, That if such deed or other power bear date or appear to have been given more than a year and a day before the application to sign judgment, no judgment be entered thereupon without the order of a Judge, nor after ten years without a rule of Court founded on a previous rule *nisi*, as is now the practice in regard to Warrants of Attorney of those respective dates.

III. *It is further Ordered*, That every Warrant of Attorney to confess judgment; and every deed or other power by which authority is granted to execute the Warrant, bear date of the day upon which the same are respectively executed; and if it should happen that such Warrant of Attorney, deed, or other power, is to be given by two or more persons who cannot conveniently execute the same on the same day, then the warrant, deed, or power, shall bear date of the day on which it shall be first executed; and the day on which any subsequent execution shall take place shall be specified in the attestation of the subscribing witness or witnesses to such execution.

IV. *It is further Ordered*, That every Attorney signing a confession of judgment upon a Warrant of Attorney, do annex to his signature the date of signing, and do mark with his name, or initial letters of his name, the said Warrant of Attorney, and also any deed or power under which the Warrant is executed, where the execution is not personal.

Barristers. See Attorneys, etc.

Bail. See Special Bail.

BILL OF PARTICULARS.

Hilary Term, 6 William 4, 1836.

30—*It is Ordered*, That a copy of the Bill of Particulars of the Plaintiff's demand, and also of the Defendant's set-off (if any) shall be filed by the Plaintiff's Attorney, with every record of *Nisi Prius*, at the time of entering the same.

BILL AND TAXATION OF COSTS.

Michaelmas Term, 40 George 3, 1800.

31—*Ordered*, That every Attorney of this Court deliver a regular bill of costs to his Client, or to the Client of the adverse

Attorney, as the case may be, before he demands the expenses of the suit; and all receipts by Attorneys from their Clients, without this previous step, will be considered as a breach of this Rule.

Easter Term, 12 Victoria, 1849.

32—*It is Ordered*, That the following Regulations be observed in the Office of the Clerk of the Pleas:—

1st. Every affidavit used before the Clerk, on the taxation of costs, to be retained and filed on a file to be kept for this purpose.

2nd. The names of witnesses, the days attendance and mileage of each witness, to be specified in every Bill of Costs, brought for taxation.

BLANK WRITS.

See Records, etc.

CALCULATING INTEREST.

Hilary Term, 2 George 4, 1821.

33—Interest upon Bonds, Debts, and other Securities for money, payable with interest, should be ascertained by adding the Interest to the principal at the time of each payment, and deducting the payment, which is the same thing as first deducting the Interest from the payment, and then giving credit for the balance on account of principal; and not by charging Interest upon the whole Bond to the time of the last payment, and Interest for the Debtor on the several payments from their respective dates, thereby inverting the principle of compound Interest, and charging Interest on his own debts, when a payment is made of less than the Interest due at the time. Nothing should be credited until a sum is paid equal to the Interest then due, except by endorsing it specially as a sum paid in part of the Interest then due.

CLERK OF PLEAS.

Regulation to be observed in office of. See Nos. 28, 32, 34, 49, 61, 82 *a*, 89.

CONFESSION OF JUDGMENT.

Easter Term, 11 Victoria, 1848.

34—No Judgment to be signed upon any confession, cognovit, or retraxit, after one year from the date thereof, or from the Term whereof the same is granted, without the order of the Court, or of a Judge.

CONSENT RULE.

See Rule (Consent.)

COSTS—TAXATION.

See Bill and Taxation—Security for Costs.

CROWN OFFICE.

Regulations to be observed. See 98, 136.

CROWN PAPER.

See Special Paper.

DAMAGES (ASSESSMENT OF.)

See No. 11.

Damages—Interest on—Form of entry of Judgment. See No. 51.

DEED — PROOF OF EXECUTION.

See Subpœna.

DECLARATIONS.

Easter Term, 25 George 3, 1785.

35—That all Attorneys file their Declarations on or before the last day of the Term next ensuing the return and filing the Writ, or be *non prossed*.

Easter Term, 26 George 3, 1786.

36—*It is Ordered*, That upon all Process where no Affidavit is made or filed of the cause of action, the Plaintiff may file or deliver the Declaration *De Bene Esse* at the return of such Process, with notice to plead in twenty days; and if Defendant doth not enter an appearance or file common Bail, and plead within the said twenty days, Plaintiff having first filed common Bail for Defendant, may sign Judgment for want of a Plea, provided that such Declaration be delivered or filed in the Clerk's Office with notice thereon, within *twenty* days after the return of such Process, and a rule to plead be duly entered.

Michaelmas Term, 6 George 4, 1825

37—*It is Ordered*, That the time for delivering or filing Declarations *De Bene Esse*, agreeably to the rule made in Easter Term in the 26th George 3, be enlarged to thirty days.

DEFAULT—NON PROS—JUDGMENT.

Hilary Term, 6 William 4, 1836.

38—*It is Ordered*, That no Judgment of *Non Pros* shall be signed for want of a declaration, replication, or other subsequent pleading, until ten days next after a demand thereof shall have been made in writing upon the Plaintiff, his Attorney, or Agent, as the case may be.

Hilary Term, 2 Victoria, 1839.

39—*Ordered*, That in future where the Defendant in any action shall plead one or more special pleas, and serve copies on the Plaintiff's Attorney, with rule to reply in twenty days, the Plaintiff shall file and deliver his replication in twenty days from the time of such service of plea and rule, and in default thereof the Defendant shall be entitled to judgment of *non pros*, a replication being first demanded after the said twenty days; and in like manner twenty days shall be allowed for every subsequent pleading, and the opposite party shall be entitled to judgment by default or *non pros*, as the case may be, for not rejoining, surrejoining, etc., a rule to rejoin, surrejoin, etc., being served and demand made as aforesaid, unless the Court or a Judge shall think proper to allow further time. Provided that no such judgment of *non pros* or default shall be signed until ten days after demand of replication, rejoinder, etc.

That all such rules to reply, rejoin, surrejoin, etc., may be taken out in vacation and entered as of the preceding term, the Attorney delivering to the Clerk a præcipe for such rule.

DELIVERY OF PLEAS.

See Pleas.

DEMAND OF PLEAS.

See Pleas.

DEMURRER AND SPECIAL CASES.

Trinity Term, 3 Victoria, 1840.

40—*It is further Ordered*, That where a general Demurrer shall hereafter be put in to any Declaration or other pleading, the party putting in the same shall deliver at the same time to the opposite party a statement or minute of the grounds of such Demurrer; and if the opposite party intend to rely on any defects in the previous pleading, he shall deliver with the joinder in demurrer a statement or minute of such alleged defects; and such particulars shall be entered in the margin of the books delivered to the Judges. This regulation to extend also to cases of Special Demurrer where other grounds are intended to be relied on, than those specifically set out.

Hilary Term, 9 Victoria, 1846.

41—*Ordered*, That twenty days from the delivery of a copy of any demurrer, shall be allowed to the opposite party to join in demurrer, and furnish a note of objections to the previous pleading, (if any) agreeably to the rule of Trinity Term, 3 Vic.; on failure of which, the joinder in demurrer may be added by the party demurring, in making up the demurrer book; and no copy of such demurrer book need be served on the opposite Attorney, nor shall any motion or rule for a concilium be required; but demurrers, as well as special cases and special verdicts, shall be entered for argument at the request of either party, of which notice shall be given to the opposite Attorney eight days before the term at which such entry is made.

Trinity Term, 31 Victoria, 1868.

41 *A*—All special cases submitted for the opinion of the Supreme Court,—either on the Equity or Pleas side,—shall be printed at the joint expense of both parties, and copies thereof furnished for the use of the Judges and for the Clerk of the Court, and the cost thereof shall be taxed and allowed after the decision of the case according to the rights of the parties.

DEMURRER BOOKS.

Trinity Term, 2 William 4, 1831.

42—*Whereas* expense is often unnecessarily incurred in making up Demurrer Books, from setting forth those parts of the pleadings to which the Demurrers do not apply. *It is therefore Ordered*, That from and after the end of this Term, when there shall be a demurrer to part only of the declaration or other subsequent pleadings, those parts only of the declaration and pleadings to which such demurrer relates shall be copied into the Demurrer Books; and, if any other parts shall be copied, the Clerk shall not allow the costs thereof on taxation, either as between party and party, or as between Attorney and Client.

Hilary Term, 6 William 4. 1836.

43—*It is Ordered*, That Demurrer Books be delivered to the Judges on or before the first day of the term at which the Demurrer is to be argued, the books for the Chief Justice and senior Puisne Judge to be prepared and delivered by the Plaintiff's Attorney, and the books for the two junior Judges by the Defendant's Attorney: and that the same rule do also apply to other cases in which paper books are required by the practice of the Court to be delivered to the Judges.

Michaelmas Term, 9 Victoria, 1845.

44—*Ordered*, That if either party make default in the delivery of the demurrer books, as required by the rule of Hilary Term, 6 Wm. 4, the other party who has complied with the rule, may move for judgment without having delivered books to all the Judges.

DIVORCE AND MATRIMONIAL CAUSES.

See Appeal Paper 9 *A B*.

Hilary Term, 26 Victoria, 1863.

45—*It is Ordered*, That the Clerk of the Pleas do keep a Paper, to be called the Divorce and Matrimonial Appeal Paper, in which shall be entered all Appeals from decisions of the Court of Divorce and Matrimonial Causes; such entries to be made on or before the first day of the Term next after the decisions in the said Court; such appeals to be heard next after the Equity appeal paper.

46—*It is Ordered*, That upon hearing of an appeal from the Court of Divorce and Matrimonial Causes, pursuant to the Act of Assembly, 23rd Victoria, cap. 37, it shall be the duty of the appellant to procure and file with the Clerk of the Pleas in this Court, certified copies of the libel and answer and Decree; and that on hearing the appeal, the evidence be received from the Report of the Judge of the Court of Divorce and Matrimonial Causes.

DOCKETS.

See Records, etc.

EJECTMENT.

Michaelmas Term, 6 William 4, 1835.

47—*It is Ordered*, That in all actions of ejectment, the notice to appear may be for any return day specifically, but when the notice to appear is for the term generally, the day of appearance shall be the first day of the term.

It is Ordered, That in all actions of ejectment, there shall be fourteen days exclusive between the day of serving the declaration and the day of appearance, whether the person served with the declaration lives within the County where the Court sits or not, any former Rule to the contrary notwithstanding.

Trinity Term, 6 William 4, 1836.

48—*It is Ordered*, That the notice to appear in Ejectment, shall not be made in future for the return day in the second week of the term; but for the term generally, or the Tuesday or Saturday in the first week.

Consent Rules. (See Nos. 102, 103.)

ENTRY OF CAUSE IN CLERK'S OFFICE.

See Appeal Paper 9 *A* and *B*. See Rules 40, 41.

Easter Term, 11 Victoria, 1848.

Entry of Cause. See 9 *A* and *B*.

49—No Judgment, interlocutory or final, to be signed in any cause until it is ascertained, upon search, that the cause has been duly entered; provided, that where there is an interlocutory judgment, the search need not be repeated when final judgment is signed; and provided also, that entries may be made as heretofore accustomed in cases of Warrants of Attorney to confess judgment.

ENTRY FOR HEARING AT SITTINGS IN EQUITY.

Trinity Term, 31 Victoria, 1868.

49 *A*—All causes intended for hearing at the Sittings in Equity, shall be set down with the Clerk in Equity six days before the first day of the Sitting of the Court,

and shall be entered by him on a Docket to be kept for that purpose, and no cause not so entered shall be heard without the order of the Judge sitting in such Court.

Entry of cause for argument. See Appeal Paper—Motion Paper.

Entry of Cause—Equity Appeal Paper. See Appeal Paper 9 *A* and *B*.

Michaelmas Term, 19 Victoria, 1855.

50—*It is Ordered*, That a Paper be prepared by the Clerk of the Court on the Equity side, and delivered to the Court on the first day of each Term, containing a List of the Causes in Equity in which appeals are to be heard, which shall be called the Equity Appeal Paper, and the Causes therein shall come on to be heard in order next after the Special Paper of the same Term.

ENTRY ON JUDGMENT ROLL—INTEREST ON DAMAGES.

Michaelmas Term, 20 Victoria, 1856.

51—*It is Ordered*, That where interest is awarded under the Act of Assembly 12th Victoria, cap. 39, sec. 29, the entry on the Judgment roll shall be in the form following, or to the like effect:—

"Therefore it is considered that the said plaintiff do recover against the said defendant, etc. etc. etc., together with —— now adjudged by the Court here to the said plaintiff for interest upon the damages (*or* debt) pursuant to the Act of Assembly in such case made and provided, because the final judgment has been delayed by the act of the defendant; and also —— for his costs and charges, etc. etc. etc., which said damages, interest, costs, and charges, amount in the whole to ——."

Equity Appeal Paper. See Appeal Paper 9 *A* and *B*.

Equity—Service on Non-residents. See Practice in Equity.

EXAMINING WITNESSES UPON INTERROGATORIES.

Hilary Term, 7 William 4, 1837.

52—*It is Ordered*, That the party applying for the examination of a witness or witnesses *de bene esse*, under the Act 26 Geo. 3, c. 20, or for an order for such examination, or for the issuing a commission, under the Act 5 Wm. 4, c. 34, do state in the affidavit or affidavits upon which such application is founded, the nature of the action, the venue, and the state of the pleadings or proceedings at the time of such application; also the name of the opposite Attorney or agent: and do also, whenever time will permit, give notice of such application, together with a copy of the affidavit or affidavits, to such attorney or agent.

FOREIGN JUDGMENT—HOLDING TO BAIL UPON.

Hilary Term, 26 Victoria, 1863.

53—*It is Ordered*, That no person shall be held to bail upon the Judgment of the Court of any Foreign Country, or of any British Colony, without a Judge's order.

GRADUATE'S CERTIFICATE.

See Attorneys, Barristers, etc.

HEARING CAUSES—ENTRY.

See Appeal Paper 9 *B* 4.

INFANTS—PROCEEDINGS AGAINST.

Trinity Term, 31 Victoria, 1868.

53 *A*—When any person residing out of the Province, against whom a suit is commenced, is an infant, and does not appear within the time limited by the order made for that purpose, under the Act 17 Vic. c. 18, s. 3, the Court may make the like order for the appearance of the infant, as is provided by the 12th rule of the 5th July 1856 (See Botsford Rules 23), and at the expiration of the time so limited, the plaintiff may proceed to prove his case against the infant in the manner provided by the said rule.

Interest—Calculation of—Mode. See No. 33.

Interest on Damages—Judgment form of. See No. 51.

Interrogatories—Examination on. See No. 52.

INTERLOCUTORY JUDGMENT.

Easter Term, 25 George 3, 1785.

54—That on filing a Declaration in any action, the plaintiff be entitled to Judgment, if the defendant doth not plead in twenty days after notice of Declaration being filed in the Clerk's Office, the Rule to plead being first entered; and if the defendant hath not entered his appearance in such action, the plaintiff may file a common appearance, and enter an Interlocutory Judgment for want of a Plea as of the preceding term, without any imparlance, and proceed to a Writ of Inquiry as if the same Interlocutory Judgment had been rendered and entered the same preceding Term; and the like proceeding to entry of Judgment and executing Writ of Inquiry, where a defendant in custody neglects to plead, pursuant to a rule served on himself, or the Sheriff as aforesaid.

Trinity Term, 3 Victoria, 1840.

55—*It is Ordered*, That Interlocutory Judgment shall not be signed in any case for want of appearance until the process with the requisite affidavit of service, and (where the case requires) the order of the Court or Judge for perfecting such service, shall be filed.

Trinity Term, 20 Victoria, 1857.

56—*It is Ordered*, That from and after the present Term, in every Memorandum of Interlocutory Judgment, the Term at which the writ has been made returnable be specified on the margin or at the foot of the Memorandum, and that it be also stated whether the action is summary or not summary.

JUDGMENT AS IN CASE OF NON-SUIT.

Hilary Term, 6 William 4, 1836.

57—*It is Ordered*, That no motion shall be made for Judgment, as in case of a non-suit, pursuant to the Statute 14 Geo. 2, c. 17, without notice having been first given thereof to the plaintiff, his attorney or agent, as the case may be, together with a copy of the affidavit on which the same is grounded, at least fourteen days before the term at which such motion is intended to be made, and without entering the same on the Motion Paper.

It is Ordered, That on motion made in open Court pursuant to the said entry, and on due proof of the service of notice and copy of affidavit as directed by the preceding rule, the defendant shall be entitled to a rule absolute for Judgment as in case of a non-suit, unless the Court on just cause and reasonable terms shall allow a further time for the trial of the issue, or unless the Court should think fit to enlarge the time for showing cause to the next term.

Trinity Term, 12 Victoria, 1849.

58—*It is Ordered*, That in the notice of motion for judgment, as in case of a non-suit, the copy of affidavit, as required by Rule 3, Hilary Term, 6 Wm. 4, shall be deemed sufficient if served on Tuesday the fourteenth day preceding the Term, so as to make the notice of motion in this case conform to the other notices of motion upon the Motion Paper.

Michaelmas Term, 23 Victoria, 1859.

59—*It is Ordered*, That in future the affidavit on which motion is made for Judgment as in case of a non-suit for not proceeding to trial according to the practice of the Court, (where notice of trial has not been given,) do state the particular Term in or before which issue has been joined, or do state some particular day in vacation on or before which issue has been joined.

JUDGMENT IN DEBT.

Trinity Term, 1 Victoria, 1838.

60—*It is Ordered*, That the entry of the judgment on the record, in actions of debt, where the amount to be recovered is ascertained and assessed by the Court, under the Act of Assembly, 7 Wm. 4, c. 14, s. 6, shall be in the following form, or of the like tenor and effect, viz.:

"And the said A. B. (*the Plaintiff*) prays that the amount to be recovered in this action, may be ascertained and assessed by the Court here, according to the form of the Act of Assembly, in such case made and provided; and thereupon it is suggested and proved, and manifestly appears to the Court here, that the said A. B. ought to recover for his debt in this action, the sum of £——; therefore it is considered that the said A. B. do recover against the said C. D. (*the Defendant*) the said sum of £——, for his debt, so ascertained and assessed by the Court here, and also, etc., (*proceed with the entry in regard to costs, in the usual form*,) and the said C. D. in mercy, etc.

JUDGMENT—DEFAULT—NON PROS.

See Nos. 38, 39.

JUDGMENT ROLLS.

See Records, Writs, etc.

Easter Term, 11 Victoria, 1848.

61—All Judgment Rolls to be endorsed with the title of the Term wherein final judgment is awarded; and when judgment is entered in vacation, then to be endorsed of the Term next preceding, and the Rolls are to be numbered consecutively as they are brought in and filed of such Term, and to be referred to in pleading as the Rolls of such Term.

Judgment Roll on offer to suffer Judgment by default.

Trinity Term, 22 Victoria, 1859.

62—*It is Ordered*, That in any case (not summary) where, under the provisions of the Act of Assembly, 18th Victoria, cap. 9, an offer and consent in writing has been filed by the defendant, to suffer judgment by default, for a certain specified sum as debt or damages, (as the case may be) and the plaintiff has not, after due notice thereof, filed his acceptance of such offer, but has taken the case down to trial, and has recovered a verdict, but not for a greater sum than the sum so offered, the entry or suggestion on the Judgment Roll shall be as follows:—

"And now, pursuant to the Act of Assembly passed in the eighteenth year of the Reign of Queen Victoria, entitled, 'An Act concerning Tender in Actions at Law and Suits in Equity,' on the —— day of —— in the year of our Lord —— the said defendant C. D., files in the Office of the Clerk of the Pleas of this Court, an offer or consent in writing in the words following:—[*insert the offer*]—which offer and consent the said plaintiff A. B., has not accepted; therefore the issue joined between the parties remains to be tried: Therefore let a jury thereupon come, etc." [*as in ordinary cases, to the conclusion of the postea*,] and then proceed as follows:—

"And inasmuch as it appears by the said return, that the debt [*or damages*] was not greater in amount than the sum for which the said C. D. offered to suffer judgment by default, it is considered that the said A. B. do recover his said debt [*or damages*] so assessed at the sum of ——, together with his costs and charges by him about his suit in this behalf expended, up to the said —— day of ——, and for these costs and charges to ——, which said debt, [*or damages*] costs and charges in the whole, amount to ——, and that the said A. B. have execution thereof. And it is further considered that the said C. D. do recover against the said A. B. —— for his costs and charges by him incurred after the said —— day of ——, and that he have execution thereof."

(On interest on Damages. See 51.)

JUDGE'S SUMMONS.

Hilary Term, 6 William 4, 1836.

63—*It is Ordered*, That it shall not be necessary to issue more than one summons for attendance before a Judge upon the same matter, and the party taking out such summons, shall, if the Judge see fit, be entitled to an order on the return of the summons, unless cause is shown to the contrary.

JURY RETIRING TO CONSIDER VERDICT—ENTERING TIME.

Easter Term, 18 Victoria, 1855.

64—1st. The Clerk at any Circuit Court or Sittings, shall enter on the Minutes the time when the Jury retire to consider of their verdict, and also the time when the Jury return into Court to deliver their verdict.

2nd. If they return within two hours, the verdict shall be taken and entered in manner heretofore accustomed.

3rd. If they return after the lapse of two hours, after they are called over by their names and answer thereto, they shall be asked thus—Gentlemen of the Jury, are you all agreed on your verdict, or how many and which of you are agreed thereupon?

If they shall answer that they are all agreed, the verdict shall be taken and entered in the usual manner. If they shall answer that they are not all agreed, but that five (or six) are agreed, the names of the Jurors by whom the verdict is so returned shall be taken and entered in the Minutes, and the verdict shall be recorded as follows:—

The Jury having considered of their verdict, and not being able all to agree within two hours, five (*or six*) of their number, namely, A. B., [*the names to be here specified*,] do say that they do find [*the finding to be here stated*.]

This entry shall then be read over to the Jury distinctly, and shall be returned on the Postea as follows:—

POSTEA.

[*Commencing in the ordinary form.*]

And the Jurors of that Jury being summoned also come, who to speak the truth of the matters within contained, are chosen, tried, and sworn, and having retired to consider of their verdict, and not being able to agree within two hours, five (*or six*) of their number, namely, [*here set forth the names*,] pursuant to the Act of Assembly relating to Jurors, say upon their oath, [*here state the verdict*.]

Constable's Oath. See No. 82.

MESNE PROCESS.

Michaelmas Term, 6 William 4, 1835.

65—*It is Ordered*, That every mesne process, in any action, shall contain the names of all the Defendants, if more than one, in the action.

MONEYS PAID INTO COURT.

Statement of—Rules respecting. See Rules 140, 141.

MOTION DAY.

Michaelmas Term, 29 Victoria, 1865.

66—*It is Ordered*, That Tuesday in the second week of each Term shall be the regular day for motions, instead of Saturday of that week; on which day, motions shall have the precedence of the ordinary business, which however shall be proceeded with after the motions are concluded;—

Provided, however, that one or more of the Judges will sit in Court on the second Saturday, whenever occasion may require

MOTION PAPER.

Hilary Term, 6 William 4, 1836.

67—1st. *It is Ordered*, That in future the Clerk of the Pleas do keep a paper, to be called the Motion Paper, in which shall be entered all motions of which notice may have been given, such entries to be made on or before the first day of each term, and to stand in the said paper in the order in which they may be made, and the matters contained in such Motion Paper shall come on to be heard on the second day of the term, before the Special Paper is gone into.

2nd. *It is Ordered*, That if notice of any motion, and a copy of the affidavit or affidavits, on which it is intended to be grounded, shall be served on the opposite party, his Attorney or Agent, as the case may be, fourteen days before the term at which the motion is intended to be made, a rule absolute may be made in the first instance, if the Court shall see fit, and in all such cases the cause shall be entered on the Motion Paper.

Michaelmas Term, 30 Victoria, 1866.

68—*It is Ordered*, That hereafter causes for argument may be entered on the respective papers on the Monday preceding each Term, and shall not be entered after the opening of the Court, without leave given therefor.

The causes entered on the motion paper, shall come on to be heard immediately after the conclusion of the Common motions at the beginning of each Term; and the causes upon the other papers respectively shall be taken up in their order, as now provided, immediately after the motion paper is concluded.

NEW TRIALS.

Michaelmas Term, 5 William 4, 1834.

69—*It is Ordered*, That in future, the Attorney for the party intending to move for a new trial, or for setting aside a verdict, shall cause to be delivered to the Judge before whom the cause was tried, a note in writing specifying the name of the cause, the time and place of the trial, and the general grounds of the intended motion; such note in writing to be delivered to the Judge in causes tried in vacation, on or before the first day of the next ensuing term.

Michaelmas Term, 6 William 4, 1835.

70—*It is Ordered*, That no motion for a new trial shall be made after the first Saturday in any term.

Michaelmas Term, 1 Victoria, 1837.

71—*Whereas* it is desirable, that arguments on rules for new trials or the like, made in causes tried at the Sittings for the County of York, should be heard and disposed of more speedily than can be done under the present practice of the Court: *It is Ordered*, That in future any party intending, after trial had at the said Sittings, to move the Court for a rule to show cause why a new trial should not be granted, or for any rule of a like description, do give notice to the opposite party of such his intention, together with a note in writing, specifying the general grounds of the intended motion, thirty days before the ensuing term, and that rules *nisi* granted on such motions be made returnable in the same term, unless the Court should see fit, with the consent of parties, or for other good reason, to extend the time for shewing cause to the ensuing term.

Hilary Term, 30 Victoria, 1867.

72—*Ordered*, That in future the notices of motions for new trials, or to set aside verdicts, required to be given by the Rules of Michaelmas Term, 5 Wm. 4, and Michaelmas Term, 1 Victoria, shall state particularly the grounds of the intended motion.

For example:—If the motion is to be made on the grounds of misdirection, or the improper admission or rejection of evidence, the notice shall set forth the particular part or parts of the Judge's direction objected to, and the particular portion or portions of evidence alleged to have been improperly admitted or rejected; and in like manner on all other grounds, specifying the same separately and distinctly, and as particularly as the circumstances of the case will admit of, and the party shall on the motion be confined to the grounds so specified.

New Trial from York Sittings.

Easter Term, 18 Victoria, 1855.

73—*It is Ordered*, That when a Rule *nisi* for a new trial—or of the like kind—has been granted in a cause tried at the Sittings for the County of York, the case shall be entered by the Clerk on the special paper for the Term at which the Rule is granted, without its being necessary to serve the Rule *nisi* as in other cases, unless the Court shall order the same to be served; and the cause shall be called on for argument in the order in which it is entered.

Hilary Term, 23 Victoria, 1860.

74—*It is Ordered*, That the Rule of Court of Michaelmas Term 1st Victoria, No. 10, relating to motions for new trials in causes tried at the Sittings for the County of York, shall not apply to causes tried at the Sittings holden in January in each year, but that motions for new trials in causes tried at the said last mentioned Sittings, shall be made as in causes tried at any of the Circuit Courts.

NISI PRIUS RECORD.

See Trials at Nisi Prius.

NISI PRIUS SITTINGS.

Michaelmas Term, 6 William 4, 1835.

75—*It is Ordered*, That there shall be sittings of Nisi Prius for the County of York, after the respective terms of this Court, on the following days in each and every year, that is to say: Sittings after Hilary Term, on the third Tuesday in February; Sittings after Trinity Term, on the fourth Tuesday in June; Sittings after Michaelmas Term, on the fourth Tuesday in October. The said respective Sittings to continue for so long a time, as in the opinion of the Judge holding the same, may be necessary for the dispatch of the business depending.

Ordered, That the Sheriff of the County of York do summon and return Grand Jurors and Petit Jurors, to attend at the several Sittings in that County, now appointed or hereafter to be appointed, in like manner as has been heretofore accustomed with regard to the terms of this Court; and that hereafter no Jurors be summoned to attend at the Terms, without special order.

It is Ordered, That all general rules of this Court, which relate to the entering of causes, the filing of Nisi Prius Records, or other proceedings at Nisi Prius, shall apply to, and be in force at, the Nisi Prius Sittings in the County of York.

It is Ordered, That in all actions, in which the issue is made up and the *Venire Facias Juratores* is awarded, as of the last return day, that is to say, the second

Saturday after the first Tuesday, in any term, such Writ of *Venire Facias Juratores* may be awarded, and made returnable forthwith.

Michaelmas Term, 11 Victoria, 1847.

76—*It is Ordered*, That after the present year there shall be Sittings of Nisi Prius for the County of York after the Hilary and Trinity Terms of this Court only, that is to say: Sittings after Hilary Term on the third Tuesday in February in each and every year; and Sittings after Trinity Term on the fourth Tuesday in June in each and every year; the said respective Sittings to continue for so long a time, as in the opinion of the Judge holding the same, may be necessary for the dispatch of the business depending. *And it is further Ordered*, That all the parts of the General Rule of Michaelmas Term in the sixth year of the Reign of King William the Fourth, which relate to Nisi Prius Sittings for the County of York, shall remain in force, excepting the appointment of such Sittings after the Michaelmas Term of this Court.

NON PROS.

See 38, 39.

NOTICE OF COUNTERMAND.

Hilary Term, 9 George 4, 1828.

77—*It is Ordered*, That no notice of countermand shall be deemed sufficient to save the costs for not proceeding to trial pursuant to notice, unless it be given at least ten days before the time of the intended trial.

Michaelmas Term, 12 Victoria, 1848.

78—*It is Ordered*, That no notice of countermand shall be deemed sufficient to save costs, if any there be, for not proceeding to the execution of a Writ of Inquiry of damages pursuant to notice, unless it be given at least ten days before the time appointed for such Inquiry.

NOTICE OF GROUNDS OF DEFENCE—COPY TO BE FILED WITH NISI PRIUS RECORD.

Trinity Term, 13 Victoria, 1850.

79—*It is Ordered*, That a copy of the notice of any matter of defence delivered with the plea, pursuant to the Act 13th Victoria, cap. 32, and a copy of any order of the Court or a Judge which shall have been made touching such notice, shall be filed with the Nisi Prius record at the Court of Nisi Prius, and be annexed to such record.

See Rules 130, 131.

NOTICE OF GROUNDS FOR NEW TRIAL, ETC.

See New Trial 72.

NOTICE OF DEFENCE—NUMBERING GROUNDS—OBJECTIONS—WHEN TAKEN.

Easter Term, 22 Victoria, 1859.

80—*It is. Ordered*, That when a notice delivered under the Act of Assembly, 13th Victoria, cap. 32, includes several distinct grounds of defence, which would, before such Act, have required separate pleas, such separate grounds of defence be numbered consecutively and placed in several clauses; but any objection to the form of the notice, on the ground of duplicity, must be made to a Judge within fourteen days after the same is delivered, who will upon summons, make such order for allowance or disallowance of the notice, or amendment of the same, and on such terms as the case may require; and no objection to the notice on the ground of duplicity will be allowed at the trial of the cause.

NOTICE OF TRIAL AND INQUIRY.

Hilary Term, 9 George 4, 1828.

81—*It is Ordered*, That from henceforth there be *at least* fourteen days' notice of trial, and for Writs of Inquiry, in all cases, whether the defendant lives within the County where the Court sits or not; any former rule of this Court to the contrary notwithstanding.

NOTICE OF GROUNDS FOR NEW TRIAL.

See No. 72.

NOTICE OF JUDGMENT AS IN CASE OF NON-SUIT.

See Judgment as in Case of Non-suit.

OATH OF CONSTABLE—RETIRING OF JURY.

Easter Term, 18 Victoria, 1855.

82—The oath of the Constable who shall

have charge of the Jury, shall be as follows:—

You shall keep this Jury together in one of the Jury Rooms of this Court House [*or as the place may be*] until their verdict is agreed on, or the Court shall otherwise order; you shall not suffer any person to speak to them, or any of them, neither shall you yourself speak to them, unless it be to ask if they are agreed on their verdict, except by direction of the Court. —So help your God.

PAPERS ANNEXED TO AFFIDAVITS (MARKING OF).

See Nos. 4, 5.

PAPERS TAKEN OFF THE FILES OF COURT.

Hilary Term, 31 Victoria, 1868.

82 *A—Ordered*, That all papers which may have been taken off the files of this Court, either on the Equity or Common Law side, under the order of the Court or any Judge thereof, by any Attorney or other person, be forthwith returned to the Clerk of this Court and restored to their respective files.

No record, paper or document on file in the Office of the Clerk of this Court shall hereafter be removed therefrom, except under the especial order of the Court or one of the Judges thereof, to be obtained only on it being made clearly to appear by affidavit to the Court or Judge, that the original record, paper or document is indispensably necessary to be used in some Court of this Province, or before a Judge thereof, and that a copy of such record, paper or document cannot be used in lieu thereof.

The Clerk of the Pleas or the Clerk in Equity, as the case may be, shall enter in a Book the title of the cause, the description of the record or papers, the date of removal, and the name of the Attorney on whose application any such order shall have been granted; and shall enclose the record or papers permitted to be removed, in a sealed envelope, indorsing thereon a description of the record or papers enclosed, and direct the same to the Clerk of the Circuits or the Clerk of the Court in which the same are to be used to be delivered to the presiding Judge at the Circuit or Court where it is intended to use them, and shall himself place the same in the possession of the said Clerk, or remit the same to him by Mail if necessary; and if such records or papers are required to be used on the trial, the presiding Judge shall break the seal of the envelope, and deliver the said records or papers to the Custody of the Clerk of the Court during the progress of the trial, and such Clerk shall, at the conclusion of the trial, again enclose and seal up the said records or papers, and after being identified by the signature or initials of the presiding Judge, shall forthwith return the same to the proper custodian.

PARCHMENT—PATENT (USE OF PROHIBITED.)

Hilary Term, 25 Victoria, 1862.

83—*It is Ordered*, That from and after the first day of Easter Term next, the article called and known as *patent parchment*, be not used for the Writs and Records of this Court.

PERSONS OTHER THAN ATTORNEYS CONDUCTING SUITS—FEES ON FILING PAPERS.

Easter Term, 12 Victoria, 1849.

84—*It is Ordered*, That where parties who are not Attorneys of this Court, prosecute or defend any action in person, no papers, writs or records be received or filed in the Clerk's Office, or entries made, without the fees being paid thereon at the time of such filing or entering.

PAYMENT OF MONEY INTO COURT.

Trinity Term, 2 Victoria, 1839.

85—*Whereas* by an Act passed in the first year of Her Majesty's reign, intituled "An Act for the further amendment of the Law," it is enacted "that it shall and may be lawful for the defendant in all personal actions pending or to be brought in the Supreme Court of this Province, (except actions for assault and battery, false imprisonment, libel, slander, malicious arrest or prosecution, criminal conversation or debauching of the plaintiff's daughter or servant,) by leave of the said Court or a Judge of such Court, to pay into the said Court a sum of money by way of compensation or amends, in such manner and under such regulations as to the payment of costs, and the form of pleading, as the said Court, or any three of the Judges thereof, shall, by any rules or orders by them to be from time to time made, order and direct."

Ordered, That when money is paid into Court under the said Act, such payment shall be pleaded, and as near as may be in the following form, *mutatis mutandis:*

"C. D. ats. A. B. } And the said defendant comes by E. F., his Attorney," (*or* "in person, etc.") and says (*or in case it be pleaded as to part only, add* "as to —— being part of the sum in the Declaration, or —— Count of the Declaration mentioned," *or* as to the residue of the sum of ——) that the plaintiff ought not further to maintain his action, because the defendant now brings into Court the sum of —— ready to be paid to the plaintiff, and the defendant further says that the plaintiff has not sustained damages (*or in actions of debt* "that he is not indebted to the plaintiff") to a greater amount than the said sum of etc., in respect to the cause of action in the Declaration mentioned," (*or* "in the introductory part of the plea mentioned) and this he, the defendant, is ready to verify, wherefore he prays judgment, if the plaintiff ought further to maintain his action thereof against him;" and no other plea shall be pleaded to the said action, or to so much thereof as the said plea of payment into Court is applicable.

It is Ordered, That upon a rule or Judge's order being made for paying money into Court under the said Act, the money shall be paid to the Clerk at the time of filing the plea, together with his poundage thereon, and the Clerk shall make a minute of such payment in the margin of the plea, and shall also give a memorandum of such payment to be delivered with the copy of the plea to the plaintiff's attorney; which sum shall be paid out to the plaintiff's attorney on demand.

It is Ordered, That the plaintiff, after delivery of a plea of payment of money into Court, shall be at liberty to reply to the same, by accepting the sum so paid into Court in full satisfaction and discharge of the cause of action, in respect of which it has been paid in, and he shall be at liberty in that case to tax his costs of suit, and in case of non-payment thereof within ten days, to sign judgment for his costs of suit; or the plaintiff may reply "that he has sustained damages" (*or* "that the defendant was and is indebted to him" *as the case may be*) to a greater amount than the said sum; and in the event of an issue thereon being found for the defendant, the defendant shall be entitled to judgment and his cost of suit: Provided that if the sum of money paid into Court in any action not summary would have been recoverable under the summary form, the plaintiff, if he take the money out of Court in discharge of the action, shall not be entitled to more than summary costs, unless he obtain the order of the Court or a Judge for the larger costs, upon good cause shewn therefor.

PLEA (ABATEMENT.)

See No. 1.

PLEAS (DELIVERY OF.)

Hilary Term, 6 Victoria, 1843.

86—*Ordered*, That in future copies of all pleas shall be delivered to the Plaintiff's Attorney within the time allowed for pleading; otherwise the Plaintiff shall be at liberty [illegible] demand of plea being duly made) to sign interlocutory judgment: and that it shall not be necessary to search for a plea before such signing, after the expiration of the rule to plead.

PLEAS (DEMAND OF.)

Trinity Term, 5 Victoria, 1842.

87—*Ordered*, That where the Attorneys for the respective parties reside in different counties, the Defendant's Attorney shall be allowed seven days after demand of plea, wherein to file the plea, and serve the opposite Attorney with a copy thereof, unless the demand be accompanied by a direction to deliver a copy of the plea to some person resident in the same place in which the Defendant's Attorney resides; in which case such copy of plea [illegible] be delivered within twenty-four hours, according to the present practice, [illegible] the plea forthwith transmitted to the Clerk for filing.

PRACTICE IN EQUITY—SERVICE ON NON-RESIDENTS.

Trinity Term, 19 Victoria, 1856.

87 *A*—Upon any suit being commenced against any defendant, if it shall be

made to appear upon affidavit that such defendant doth not reside within the Province, but has a known place of residence without the limits thereof, an order may be made for the appearance of such defendant at a certain day therein named, and a copy of such order shall within one year be served upon such defendant either personally or by delivering the same at the residence of said defendant to some adult person belonging to his family; and if such defendant do not appear within the time limited by such order or such further time as the Court may appoint, the plaintiff shall be entitled to the like decree, as in case of non-appearance, when the defendant is served with process within the Province—provided, that in case the defendant reside in any part of Europe or the West Indies, such service be made three calendar months before the day of appearance, and if such defendant reside in any part of the United States of America or in any of the British North American Colonies, such service shall be made two calendar months before the day of appearance; and if in any other part of the world, such service shall be made six calendar months before the day of appearance.

2nd. The proof of such service may be made by affidavit sworn before any Judge of any Superior Court in the Country where the same is made, or the Mayor or other Chief Magistrate of any City, Borough or Town corporate in any part of Her Majesty's Dominions—provided always, that where the same is sworn in any country, not part of Her Majesty's Dominions, it shall be authenticated by a certificate under the hand and seal of the British Ambassador, Envoy, Minister, Consul or Vice-Consul; and if in any part of the British Dominions, by a certificate under the hand and seal of a Public Notary

3rd. The provisions contained in the fourteenth section of the second chapter of the Act relating to the administration of justice in Equity are hereby rescinded.

4th. The order for hearing the cause in the manner provided for by the fifteenth section of the last named chapter of the said Act, instead of the time therein appointed, may be made within one calendar month after the cause shall be at issue, on service of notice and of a copy of the affidavit on which the application is to be made, on the opposite party, ten days before such application, the time for hearing which shall have been previously appointed by the Judge to whom the same is to be made; provided, that in cases which are already at issue, the order may be made within one calendar month from the Saturday next after the second Tuesday in the present term.

PRISONERS—PROCEEDINGS AGAINST.

Hilary Term, 2 Victoria, 1839.

88—1st. *It is Ordered*, That from and after the last day of this term, in all cases where a prisoner is or shall be taken, detained or charged in custody by mesne process thereafter returnable, issuing out of this Court, and the plaintiff shall not cause a declaration against such prisoner to be delivered to such prisoner, or to the Sheriff in whose custody such prisoner is or shall be detained or charged, within three calendar months after the return of the process by virtue whereof such prisoner is or shall be taken, detained, or charged in custody; and cause an affidavit to be made and filed with the Clerk of this Court, of the delivery of such declaration, and of the time when, and the person to whom the same was delivered, before the last day of the term next after the delivery of such declaration, the prisoner shall be discharged out of custody by writ of *supersedeas* to be granted by this Court, or one of the Judges thereof, upon filing common bail; unless upon notice given to the plaintiff's attorney, good cause shall be shewn to the contrary; and in case of a commitment or render in discharge of bail, after the return of process, and before a declaration delivered, unless the plaintiff shall cause a declaration to be delivered, and an affidavit thereof made and filed; before the end of the term next after such commitment or render shall be made, and due notice of such render given, the prisoner shall be discharged out of custody by writ of *supersedeas* to be granted as aforesaid, upon filing common bail, unless upon notice given to the plaintiff's attorney good cause shall be shewn to the contrary.

2nd. That on every declaration so to be delivered against a prisoner as aforesaid, a rule to appear and plead shall be indorsed according to the form following, that is to say, "The defendant, C. D., is to appear and plead hereto at the suit of the plaintiff, A. B., within twenty days after service of this declaration; otherwise judgment will be entered against him by default."

G. H., Plaintiff's Attorney.

——— 184 .

And that judgment shall not be entered against such defendant by default until the expiration of the said rule.

3rd. That the Sheriff who shall have received a copy of a declaration against any prisoner in his custody, shall indorse thereon the time of his so receiving the same, and shall forthwith deliver the same to the said prisoner, and shall also enter in a book to be by him kept for that purpose, the time of receiving such declaration, and of delivering the same to the prisoner.

4th. That where the plaintiff declares against the prisoner, it shall not be necessary to make more than two copies of the declaration, of which one shall be served, and the other filed with an affidavit of service, and a copy of the Rule to appear and plead indorsed thereon.

5th. That upon application made by the plaintiff, before the time at which the defendant may be supersedable, and good and sufficient cause shewn by affidavit, further time to declare may be given by rule of Court or order of a Judge.

6th. That upon every application for a *supersedeas* for want of declaring in due time, in addition to the certificate of the Sheriff that no declaration has been delivered to him for the prisoner, there shall be an affidavit of the defendant, that he has not been served with such declaration.

7th. That unless the plaintiff shall proceed to trial or final judgment within three terms next after the delivery or filing of declaration, if by the course of this Court the plaintiff can so proceed; of which three terms, the term wherein such declaration shall be delivered shall be taken to be one; or if by the course of the Court the plaintiff cannot so proceed to trial or final judgment within the time above limited; then unless the plaintiff shall proceed to trial or final judgment as soon after as by the course of this Court he may so proceed, the prisoner shall be discharged out of custody by writ of *supersedeas* to be granted as aforesaid, upon filing common bail, unless upon notice given to the plaintiff's attorney good cause shall be shewn to the contrary.

8th. That in all cases after final judgment obtained against a prisoner, unless the Plaintiff shall cause such prisoner to be charged in execution, within three calendar months next after the day on which such final judgment shall be signed—in case no writ of error shall be depending, nor injunction be obtained for stay of proceedings; and if any writ of error shall be depending or injunction be obtained, then within three calendar months next after judgment shall be affirmed, the writ of error be non-prossed or discontinued, or the injunction dissolved; the prisoner shall be discharged out of custody by *supersedeas* to be granted as aforesaid, unless upon notice given to the Plaintiff's Attorney, good cause shall be shewn to the contrary.

9th. That after trial had, unless the Plaintiff do proceed to have his judgment entered up and signed as soon as by the course and practice of this Court he may so do, or within one calendar month thereafter, in case no such injunction shall be obtained or order made for stay of proceedings; and if any such injunction shall be obtained, or order made, then within one calendar month after such injunction shall be dissolved or order discharged, the prisoner shall be discharged out of custody, in like manner as in the last preceding rule is provided.

10th. That in case of a render in discharge of bail after final judgment obtained, unless the Plaintiff shall cause the Defendant to be charged in execution within three calendar months next after such render and due notice thereof given; and in case of render after trial and before judgment, unless the Plaintiff do proceed to have his judgment entered up and signed within the time limited by the last preceding rule, or within one calendar month after such render and due notice thereof, the prisoner shall be entitled to his discharge in manner aforesaid, unless good cause be shewn to the contrary.

11th. That no treaty or agreement shall be

sufficient cause to prevent any prisoner's having the benefit of a *supersedeas*, unless the same be in writing, signed by the prisoner or his attorney, or some person duly authorized by such prisoner.

RECOGNIZANCE ROLL.

Easter Term, 11 Victoria, 1848.

89—No Recognizance Roll or a Recognizance of Bail to be received or filed until it is ascertained, upon search, that the Recognizance or Bail-piece is on file.

RECORDS — WRITS — DOCKETS — JUDGMENT ROLLS.

Easter Term, 25 George 3, 1785.

90—*It is Ordered*, That all the Processes, Records, Rolls, and Judgments of this Court, be made on parchment, according to the usage of the Court of King's Bench in England.

91—That the Bill issued out of the Court of King's Bench in England, commonly called the Bill of Middlesex, be the first process *ad Respondendum*, where it is to be executed by the Sheriff of the County where the Court sits; and that the first process, going into other Counties, shall be a common *Capias*, in form of the *alias* or *Latitat*, leaving out the words "as before we have commanded you," except where it is actually the *Alias Capias*; the recital of the issuing and returning a Bill being now supposed unnecessary.

92—That every Attorney of this Court enter the return, and file the Writ or Process, in all actions which have not been agreed, and in which they intend to proceed; and shall make a docket of all such returns and rules, and on the last day of the term shall deliver the same to the Clerk of the Court; and shall pay to the Clerk his own fees, as well as those of the Judges and Crier, in such actions.

Hilary Term, 45 George 3, 1805.

93—*It is Ordered*, That the Clerk of this Court be in future authorized to deliver blank Writs, signed and sealed, to the several and respective Attorneys of this Court, to be by them filled up as occasion may require; they accounting to the said Clerk therefor, and forthwith forwarding to him proper Præcipes for such of the said Writs as they may from time to time fill up and issue, in the same manner as is practised by the Filacers in England.

Hilary Term, 50 George 3, 1810.

94—*It is Ordered*, That the Rolls of all Judgments entered at the several Terms, be brought in and filed on or before the first day of the Term next after the Term in which they shall be respectively entered.

That in all cases where blank Writs shall be filled up by the Attorneys, the Præcipes and Affidavits for Bail, in cases of Bailable process, be transmitted to the Clerk's Office by the very first opportunity, after issuing the Process; and that no Attorney do, on any account, suffer any blank Writ to go out of his hands to be filled up and issued by any other than an Attorney of this Court—and that no Rule to plead or other proceeding in the cause be had, unless the Præcipe and the Affidavit, in cases where an Affidavit is made, be duly filed.

That all Judgment Rolls be engrossed upon Parchment in a fair legible hand, with a margin of not less than an inch in breadth, and a sufficient space at the top for binding up the same, and at the bottom for numbering the Roll; and that no Roll be received or filed by the Clerk that is not made up in the manner herein directed.

That no Processes be signed or filed by the Clerk which are not engrossed upon Parchment agreeably to the former Rule of this Court in that behalf made.

That the Rule respecting the filing of Dockets and payment of Fees be strictly enforced, and that the Clerk report to the Court any delinquency in this respect without delay.

Hilary Term, 60 George 3, 1820.

95—*Whereas*, by a standing Rule of this Court, made and entered of Easter Term, in the twenty-fifth year of His Majesty's reign, *It is Ordered*, "That every Attorney of this Court enter the return and file the Writs or Process in all actions which have not been agreed, and in which they intend to proceed, and shall make a Docket of all such Returns and Rules, and on the last day of the Term shall deliver the same, with the Writs and Processes in such actions to the Clerk of the Court, and shall pay to the

Clerk of the Court his own fees, as well as those of the Judges and Crier in such actions;" *and whereas*, notwithstanding the repeated orders of this Court, enjoining a strict and punctual compliance with the said Rule, the same has been in various instances violated and neglected: *It is hereby Ordered*, That in future, if any Attorney of this Court shall neglect a compliance with the said Rule, in every respect, agreeable to the true intent and meaning thereof, on or before the first day of the Term next after the Term in which such Rule ought to have been complied with, every such Attorney shall be considered as in contempt of the Court, on account of such neglect of, and disobedience to the said Rule. And the Clerk of this Court is hereby enjoined not to receive or file from, or for, any such Attorney, at any time afterwards, any Writ, Præcipe, Process, or any other paper or proceedings whatever, of a date subsequent to the Term in which such Rule ought to have been complied with, until such contempt shall have been purged by a compliance with the said Rule. And the Clerk is further enjoined, on the second day of the Term next after the Term in which the said Rule ought to have been complied with, to prepare, and deliver to the Court, the name or names of all such Attorneys as shall be so in contempt as aforesaid.

Michaelmas Term, 6 George 4, 1825.

96—Upon reference to the Rule of Hilary Term, 45 George 3, relating to the delivery of blank Writs to the Attorneys of this Court.

It is Ordered, That from and after Hilary Term next, no Attorney of this Court do presume to issue any Writ or Process whatever, unless the same be actually signed and sealed by the proper Officer of this Court; and that the Clerk of the Pleas do forthwith furnish a copy of this Rule to every Attorney of this Court.

Hilary Term, 7 William 4, 1837.

97—*It is Ordered*, That from and after this present Hilary Term, every Attorney of this Court enter the return and file the Writ or Process in all actions which have not at or before such return been settled or discontinued, and make and file with the Clerk a docket of all such returns and rules, on or before the last return day of the term at which such Writs are returnable, or within thirty days thereafter; and that the Clerk do not in future receive or file any docket, or enter any such rule after the said thirty days, without the special order of the Court or a Judge, to be made on affidavit or affidavits, properly accounting for the delay.

Trinity Term, 23 Victoria, 1860.

98—*It is Ordered*, That the following Regulations be observed in the Office of the Clerk of the Crown in this Court:—

Blank Writs issued by Clerk.

1st. Blank Writs of Habeas Corpus, and any others which require the fiat of a Judge to be endorsed thereon before they can be issued for the purpose of being executed, and Blank Writs of Subpœna, may be delivered to the respective Attorneys of this Court signed and sealed, to be by them filled up as occasion may require; they accounting to the Clerk therefor, and forwarding to his office proper Præcipes for such of the said Writs as they may from time to time fill up and issue, stating in the Præcipes the name of the Judge whose fiat has been indorsed, where a fiat is necessary.

2nd. No other Blank Writs than those above specified, to be signed and sealed; nor shall any mere blank pieces of parchment be signed and sealed by the Clerk of the Crown.

REPLEVIN.

Easter Term, 50 George 3, 1810.

99—*It is Ordered*, That the Writ of Replevin, under the Act of Assembly 50 Geo. 3, c. 21, be in the form following, viz:—

"George the Third, by the Grace of God, of the United Kingdom of (L. S.) Great Britain and Ireland, King, Defender of the Faith, etc., etc., etc.

To the Sheriff of GREETING.

"We command you if A. B. shall make you secure of prosecuting his complaint, and also of returning the Goods and Chattels, to wit: which C. D. hath taken and unjustly detained as it is alleged, if a return thereof shall be adjudged, that then the Goods and Chattels aforesaid, to him, the said A. B. without delay you cause to be replevied and delivered; and put by sureties and safe pledges, the aforesaid C. D., that he be before us at Fredericton on the Tuesday in next, to answer to the said A. B. of a Plea, wherefore he took the said Goods and Chattels of the said A. B., and them unjustly detained against gages and pledges, as he saith, and have there then the names of the pledges and this Writ. Witness at Fredericton, the day of in the year of our Reign." And if the Defendant shall not appear at the return of such Writ, or within twenty days after the return thereof, then the Plaintiff shall be at liberty to issue a Process against such Defendant, returnable at the next ensuing Term, in the following form, viz:

"George the Third, by the Grace of God, of the United Kingdom of (L. S.) Great Britain and Ireland, King, Defender of the Faith, etc., etc., etc.

To the Sheriff of GREETING.

"We command you that you take C. D., if he shall be found in your Bailiwick, and him safely keep, so that you may have his body before us, at Fredericton, on the Tuesday in next, to answer A. B. of a Plea, wherefore he took the Goods and Chattels of the said A. B., and them unjustly detained against gages and pledges, as he saith, and have you there then this Writ. Witness at Fredericton, the day of in the year of our Reign." And shall serve such Defendant personally with a copy of such Process, upon which copy shall be written an English notice to such Defendant, of the intent and meaning of such service; which notice shall be in the form used in the service of Processes in actions in which no affidavit shall be made and filed of the cause of action; and if such Defendant shall not appear at the return of such process, or within twenty days after such return, the Plaintiff shall be at liberty, upon the usual Affidavit being made and filed of the personal service of such Process, to enter a common appearance, or file common Bail for such Defendant, and to proceed thereon as if such Defendant had entered his or her appearance or filed common bail.

And it is further Ordered, That in all cases in which the Sheriff shall be a party, the foregoing Processes shall be directed to the Coroner, as in other cases in which the Sheriff is a party.

Michaelmas Term, 22 Victoria, 1858.

100—*It is Ordered*, That when upon the trial of any action of replevin, the defence arises under the 15th and 16th Sections of Chapter 126 of the Revised Statutes, and upon the plea of *non cepit* a verdict is found for the defendant, the *postea* be in the form following, with such variations as the case may require:—

"Afterwards, etc. [*in the usual form*] say upon their oaths, that the said defendant did take and detain the said goods and chattels mentioned in the said declaration, as a distress for rent upon certain premises enjoyed by the said plaintiff under a grant or demise at a certain rent, and that there was due to the defendant for such rent at the time of making the distress, and still is due the sum of——, and they assess the damages of the said defendant by reason of the premises for the said rent, and the costs and charges of making the said distress, at the sum of——, pursuant to Chapter 126 of the Revised Statutes, besides his costs and charges, etc."

If the Bailiff of the landlord, or any one acting in aid of the landlord, be made a defendant, the *postea* may be varied, as follows:—

"And that there was due to the defendant, C. D., etc. [*as before*] and that the said defendant, E. F., was, at the time of making the said distress, the Bailiff of the said C. D.," *or* "that the said E. F. was then and there present, aiding and assisting the said C. D. in making the said distress, etc."

And that the entry of judgment on the said *postea* be in the form following, with the requisite variations as before, according to the circumstances of the case:—

"Therefore it is considered that the said plaintiff take nothing by his suit, but that the said defendant do go thereof without day, etc.; and it is further considered, that the said defendant (*or* that the said defendant C. D.) do recover against the said plaintiff the said sum of ——, for his damages so assessed as aforesaid, and also —— for his costs and charges, by the Court of our said Lady the Queen now here adjudged to the said defendant, according to the said Revised Statutes; which said damages, costs and ch[illegible]s in the whole amount to ——, and that the said defendant have execution thereof."

NOTE.—See form of Writ, 1 Rev. Stat., Title xxxiv. cap. 126.

REPLEVIN BONDS.

NOTE.—See 1 Rev. Statutes, cap. 126.

Michaelmas Term, 4 Victoria, 1840.

101—*Whereas* the Justices of the Supreme Court, or any three of them, are authorised and required by the Act of Assembly 3 Victoria, c. 63, intituled "An Act further to regulate proceedings in Replevin by allowing damages in certain cases to the Defendant," to frame and prescribe suitable and proper forms for the Replevin Bonds hereafter to be taken, and for the entering of any verdict or judgment pursuant to the said Act, such forms from the time of the said Act taking effect, to be observed and complied with in the same manner as if the same were in the Act specified and contained, and such forms to be applicable to the Inferior Court of Common Pleas as well as the Supreme Court. Provided that nothing in the said Act contained, shall extend or be construed to extend to affect any proceedings in any action of Replevin commenced before the said Act goes into operation: *It is Ordered*, That upon and after the first day of January 1841, being the time appointed for the said Act to commence and take effect, the following forms framed pursuant to the said Act shall be used, with such alterations as the description of the Court, the Officer to whom the Writ is directed, the number and character of the parties or the circumstances of the case may render necessary; but that any variance not being matter of substance shall not affect the validity of the Bonds or entries.

No. 1.—Replevin Bond.

KNOW ALL MEN BY THESE PRESENTS, That we (*name and additions of Plaintiff and his sureties*) are jointly and severally held and firmly bound unto Esquire, Sheriff of the County of (*or City and County as the case may be*) in the sum of (*double the value of the goods to be replevied*) of lawful money of New Brunswick, to be paid to the said , his certain Attorney, Executors, Administrators or Assigns; for which payment to be well and truly made, we bind ourselves and each of us, our and each and every of our Heirs, Executors and Administrators, firmly by these Presents, sealed with our Seals. Dated the day of in the year of the reign of our Sovereign Lady Victoria, by the Grace of God of the United Kingdom of Great Britain and Ireland, Queen, Defender of the Faith, etc., and in the year of our Lord one thousand eight hundred and .

The Condition of this Obligation is such, That if the above bounden (*Plaintiff*) do appear before our said Lady the Queen, at Fredericton, on (*the return day of the Writ of Replevin*) and do then and there prosecute his suit with effect and without delay against (*the Defendant*) for taking and unjustly detaining his goods and chattels, to wit: (*here specify the goods to be replevied*) and do make a return of the said goods and chattels, if a return of the same shall be adjudged, and do pay all such damages as may be awarded to the said (*Defendant*) pursuant to the Act of Assembly, made and passed in the third year of Her Majesty's reign, intituled "An Act further to regulate proceedings in Replevin, by allowing damages in certain cases to the Defendant; then this Obligation to be void, otherwise to remain in full force and virtue.

Sealed and delivered in the presence of }

If the Writ be issued out of any Inferior Court of Common Pleas, the condition of the Bond will be as follows:—

"The condition of this Obligation is such, that if the above bounden (*the Plaintiff*) do appear before the Justices of the Inferior Court of Common Pleas for the said County of at on (*as specified in the Writ, or* before the Recorder of the said City of Saint John at the next Inferior Court of Common Pleas, to be holden for the said City and County at the said City on, etc.,) then (*conclude as in the foregoing form.*)

No. 2.—Verdict on Postea where Damages are awarded to the Defendant.

(*Commence in the usual form*). Say upon their oaths, that (*stating the negative or affirmative of the pleading which concludes to the Country, according as it makes for the Defendant*) in manner and form as the said hath "complained against him" *or* "in pleading alleged," and they assess the damages of the said Defendant by reason of the premises to pursuant to the Act of Assembly in such case made and provided, besides his costs and charges, etc., (*as in the usual form.*)

No. 3.—Entry of Judgment on the above.

Therefore it is considered, that the said Plaintiff take nothing by his suit, but that the said Defendant do go thereof without day, etc., and that he have a return of the said goods and chattels, to hold to him irreplevisable for ever. And it is further considered, that the said Defendant do recover against the said Plaintiff his said damages, costs and charges, by the Jurors aforesaid in form aforesaid assessed, and also for his said costs and charges by the Court of our said Lady the Queen, now here (*or in the Inferior Court* "by the Justices here") adjudged of increase to the Defendant, according to the form of the Statute in such case made and provided; which said damages, costs and charges, in the whole amount to , and that the said Defendant have execution thereof.

No. 4.—Entry of Verdict on Postea where the value of the goods is assessed by the Jury.

(*Commence as in form No. 2.*) In manner and form as the said hath complained against him, (*or* in pleading alleged,) and at the prayer of the said Defendant they further say upon their oaths aforesaid, that the said goods and chattels at the time of the replevying thereof, were worth according to the true value thereof, which they award to the said Defendant in damages according to the form of the Act of Assembly in such case made and provided; and they assess the Defendant's other damages by reason of the premises to pursuant to the said Act, besides his costs and charges, etc., (*as in the usual form.*)

No. 5.—Entry of Judgment on the above.

Therefore it is considered, that the said Plaintiff take nothing by his suit, but that the said Defendant do go thereof without day, etc. And it is further considered, that the said Defendant do recover against the said Plaintiff the said sum of being the value of the goods and chattels aforesaid by the Jury in form aforesaid assessed; and also for his said other damages, costs and charges, by the Court of our said Lady the Queen, now here (*or in* " *Inferior Court* "by the Justices here") adjudged of increase to the said Defendant, according to the form of the Statute in such case made and provided; which said damages, costs and charges, in the whole amount to and that the said Defendant have execution thereof.

RULE (CONSENT).

Trinity Term, 7 George 4, 1826.

102—*Whereas* by the common Consent Rule in actions of ejectment, the defendant is required to confess Lease, Entry, and Ouster, and insist upon his title only; and whereas in many instances of late years, Defendants in ejectment, have put the Plaintiff, after the title of the Lessor of the Plaintiff has been established, to give evidence that such Defendant was in possession, at the time the Ejectment was brought, of the premises mentioned in the Ejectment, and for want of such proof, have caused such Plaintiffs to be non-suited;

And whereas such practice is contrary to the true intent and meaning of such Consent Rule, and of the provisions therein contained, for the Defendant's insisting upon the title only: *It is therefore Ordered*, That from henceforth in every action of Ejectment, the Defendant shall specify in the Consent Rule for what premises he intends to defend, and shall consent in such Rule, to confess upon the trial, that the Defendant (if he defends as Tenant, or in case he defends as Landlord, that his Tenant) was, at the time of the service of the declaration, in the possession of such premises; and that if upon the trial the Defendant shall not confess such possession, as well as Lease, Entry, and Ouster, whereby the Plaintiff shall not be able further to prosecute his suit against the said Defendant, then no costs shall be allowed for not further prosecuting the same, but the said Defendant shall pay costs to the Plaintiff in that case to be taxed.

Trinity Term, 8 Victoria, 1845.

103—*Ordered*, That in every action of

ejectment, when any person or persons shall apply to be made Defendant or Defendants in such action, and be allowed to enter into a special consent rule to admit lease and entry, but not ouster, unless an actual ouster of the lessor of the Plaintiff by him or them should be proved, on the ground that the defence to the action will involve a question of joint tenancy or tenancy in common; the affidavit on which such application is founded shall state the person or persons with whom the party so applying, claims to be joint tenant or tenant in common, and that he is advised and believes that he is joint tenant or tenant in common, with such person or persons.

RETURN OF WRIT.

See Side-Bar Rule.

RULES TO PLEAD.

Easter Term, 25 George 3, 1785.

104—That all Defendants have twenty days to plead from the day of the notice in writing delivered of the filing such Declaration, except where the Defendant is returned in custody; in which case the Defendant shall have twenty days to plead, from the time of serving a copy of the Declaration, and of the rule to plead, to be served on the Sheriff or Defendant.

SCIRE FACIAS.

See Writ of.

SECURITY FOR COSTS.

Michaelmas Term, 8 Victoria, 1844.

105—*Ordered*, That the rule of Trinity Term, 30 George 3, be rescinded, and that in future where security for costs is ordered, such security shall be given in the sum of forty pounds in all cases, except in summary; and that in summary cases, security shall be given in the sum of twenty pounds.

SERVICE OF NOTICES.

Easter Term, 25 George 3, 1785.

106—That all notices to be served on Defendants, or the Attorneys of either party, shall be deemed well served if left at the dwelling house, or last, or most usual place of his or their lodgings.

107—That all notices be served on the Attorneys for the parties, except notices of exception to Bail, which may be served on the Defendant or his Attorney, or on the person who serves the notice of Bail.

Hilary Term, 28 Victoria, 1865.

108—*Ordered*, That no service of any paper on an Attorney in any cause, shall be deemed good service by leaving such paper at his dwelling house or last place of abode, unless it shall appear by the affidavit of service that the Attorney has no Office, or if having an Office, that the same was closed, or if open, that there was no person in such Office upon whom service could be made; in any of which cases, leaving the same at the dwelling house or last place of residence of the Attorney, shall be deemed sufficient service thereof.

SERVICE OF PROCESS.

Trinity Term, 3 Victoria, 1840.

109—*It is Ordered*, That from and after the first day of Michaelmas term next, when service of Process is effected at the usual place of abode of the Defendant, pursuant to the Act 7 Wm. 4, c. 14, s. 1, the Affidavit of such service shall be in the following form, or to that effect, in order to entitle the Plaintiff to an order for perfecting such service.

Form of Affidavit.

A. B. (*name, residence and addition of Deponent*) maketh oath and saith, that he, this deponent, did on the day of deliver a true copy of the annexed Writ or Process, at the house of C. D., the Defendant, named in such Writ or Process. (*or the house of any other person as the case may be*,) situate in the Parish of in the County of , unto E. F., the wife of such Defendant, (*or* to G. H. an adult person residing in the said house, and known to this deponent as a member or inmate of the family of such Defendant) and this deponent further saith, that the said house was at the time of such delivery the usual place of abode of such Defendant, and that the said copy of the said Process was accompanied with an English notice in writing to the Defendant, of the intent and meaning of the service of such Process, pursuant to the Statute in such case made and provided; and this deponent further saith, that at the time of making such service of the said Process, the said Defendant was not, as this deponent verily believes, without the limits of the said County.

Easter Term, 13 Victoria, 1850.

110—1st. *Whereas* by the Act of Assembly 12th Victoria, cap. 39, sec. 44, the Act of Assembly 7th William 4, cap. 14, allowing service of Process to be made at the usual place of abode of the defendants, is repealed; and the said Act of 12th Victoria limits and restricts service of Process at the dwelling to cases where the defendant shall be within the jurisdiction of the Court, at the time of such service; and the Rule No. 2 of this Court of Trinity Term, 3rd Victoria, is thereby virtually superseded: *It is Ordered*, That such Rule be rescinded, and that the affidavit of such service shall be in the following form, or to that effect, in order to entitle the plaintiff to an order for perfecting such service:—

"A. B., Sheriff of ——, (*or* A. B., of ——, a Deputy of the Sheriff of ——,) maketh oath and saith, that he, this deponent, did, on the —— day of ——, deliver a true copy of the annexed writ or process at the house of C. D., the defendant named in such writ or process, (*or* the house of any other person, *as the case may be*,) situate in the Parish of ——, in the County of ——, unto E. F., the wife of such defendant, (*or* to G. H., an adult person residing in the said house, and known to this deponent as a member or inmate of the family of such defendant); and this deponent further saith, that the said house was at the time of such delivery the usual place of abode of such defendant, [and that the said copy of the said process was accompanied with an English notice in writing to the defendant, of the intent and meaning of the service of such process, pursuant to the Statute in such case made and provided]; * and this deponent further saith, that the said defendant was at the time of such service within the limits of this Province, as this deponent knows, for the following reasons, (*here state the particular means of knowledge the deponent has of the defendant's being within the Province; if this fact is not known to the serving officer it may be proved by the affidavit of another person; and the affidavit of the serving officer may omit the words after the * and conclude as follows:*—) and this deponent further saith, that he verily believes that at the time of such service the defendant was within this Province."

(The clause between brackets may be omitted in the service of Summary Writs.)

2nd. *It is further Ordered*, That in order to entitle the plaintiff to an order for making a service at the dwelling good service, the Writ or Process shall be delivered to the Sheriff of the County into which it is issued for service, and that such service be effected, and the affidavit thereof made by the Sheriff, or his general or special Deputy.

3rd. *It is further Ordered*, That these Rules shall apply *mutatis mutandis* to Writs directed to the Coroner.

4th. *It is further Ordered*, That these Rules apply to every Writ or Process issued after the end of the present Term.

Trinity Term, 20 Victoria, 1857.

Service of Process on Non-Residents.

111—*It is Ordered*, That where service of process is made on persons resident out of the Province, under the Act of Assembly 14 Victoria, cap 2, the nature and place of the business carried on by the defendant in the Province, and the particular nature of the agency or employment of the person with whom the copy of Process may have been left for the defendant, be stated in the affidavit of the Sheriff or Deputy Sheriff making such service, or otherwise proved by affidavit to the satisfaction of the Judge, before any order is made for perfecting such service.

See Practice in Equity, Rule 87 *a*.

SHERIFFS—FEES.

Easter Term, 25 George 3, 1785.

112—That the Sheriffs indorse their returns on all Processes delivered to them by the day of their returns respectively, and deliver them to the Attorneys who issued the same. That they attend the Court every Term, by themselves or their under-Sheriffs, and that they appoint Deputies, respectively, who shall always reside in the district in which the Court sits, and as near as convenient to the Court House; who shall always attend the Court in the absence of the High Sheriff; and that all Writs, Rules, and Orders delivered to such Deputy, shall be of like effect as if served upon the High Sheriff.

Michaelmas Term, 5 William 4, 1834.

113—In order to secure to Sheriffs the proper emoluments of their office, *It is Ordered*, That, after the first day of Hilary Term next, no costs for the service or return of any Writ or Process, be taxed or allowed in any bill of costs, without the production of such Writ or Process, with the return thereof, signed by the Sheriff or his Deputy, and the fees for the service and return, marked thereupon by such Sheriff or Deputy.

Hilary Term, 4 Victoria, 1841.

114—*Ordered*, That from and after the last day of this term, when any Sheriff, before his going out of office, shall arrest any Defendant, and a *Cepi Corpus* shall be returned, he shall and may within the time allowed by Law, be called upon to bring in the body by a rule for that purpose, notwithstanding he may be out of office, before any such rule shall be granted.

SIDE-BAR RULES—RETURN OF WRIT.

Michaelmas Term, 8 Victoria, 1844.

115—*It is Ordered*, That no side-bar rule shall be taken out for the return of any writ after six months from the day on which such writ is made returnable; and that after such six months, motion be made in open Court, or the order of a Judge obtained, before any such rule do issue.

SPECIAL BAIL.

Easter Term, 25 George 3, 1785.

116—That there be allowed *twenty* days to all Defendants to put in Special Bail; and the like number to all Plaintiffs to except against such Bail, from the time of due notice of Bail put in.

Hilary Term, 26 George 3, 1786.

117—*Ordered*, That in all Process where an Affidavit is made and filed of the cause of Action, the Sheriffs of the different Counties, at the time of taking the Bail Bond, shall serve the sureties therein with a copy of such process, subscribed with the following notice:

"A. B.

"Take notice, that unless Special Bail is put in above by the Defendant in this cause within *twenty* days after the return of this Process, the condition of the Bail Bond you have entered into will be forfeited;" and upon affidavit made and filed, together with a return of the Process by the Sheriff, of the service of such copies as aforesaid, the Declaration may be filed *De Bene Esse*, at the return of the Process, with notice to plead in *twenty* days; and if Defendant puts in Special Bail, and doth not plead within time, Judgment may be signed: provided such Declaration be filed in the Clerk's Office with notice thereon within *twenty* days after the return of the Process.

Michaelmas Term, 59 George 3, 1819.

118—*Ordered*, That the time for putting in Special Bail, agreeably to the rule made in Easter Term, in the twenty-fifth year of His present Majesty's Reign, be enlarged to thirty days.

Michaelmas Term, 6 George 4, 1825.

119—*Ordered*, That if any person or persons, who are, or who hereafter shall become Bail in this Court for any Defendant, in any action whatever, shall be impleaded by action of debt upon the recognizance in such suit acknowledged, such person or persons shall have liberty to surrender such Defendant by the space of twenty entire days next after the return of the Writ of Capias *ad respondendum* or other Process sued out against such Bail; and upon notice thereof given to the Plaintiff or his Attorney, in the suit aforesaid, all further proceedings against such Bail upon the Recognizance aforesaid, shall cease.

Hilary Term, 2 William 4, 1832.

120—*It is Ordered*, That in all cases, where Bail is put in before a Commissioner, the Bail-piece, together with the affidavit of the due taking thereof, shall be forthwith transmitted, by the Attorney who puts in the Bail, to one of the Judges of this Court; and the notice of Bail, in such cases, shall specify the Judge to whom the Bail-piece has been so transmitted, as well as the Commissioner, before whom the Bail was put in, and the names and additions of the Bail.

2nd. That Plaintiffs shall be allowed twenty days, after service of the notice of Bail, to except against such Bail: and such exception shall be entered with the Judge before whom Bail was put in, or to whom the Bail-piece has been transmitted, as the case may be.

3rd. That Defendants shall be allowed twenty days, after service of notice of exception, to procure their Bail to justify, or to add other Bail, who shall justify within the said twenty days, unless in either case, upon application made before the said twenty days expire, the Court, or a Judge, shall see fit to extend the time.

4th. That Bail shall justify in open Court, or before the Judge with whom the exception is entered, notice of justifying being first duly given: and that in all cases, when the Bail reside more than ten miles from the place where they are to justify, they may justify by affidavit without personal attendance.

5th. That Bail must be Housekeepers or Freeholders; and, in cases where the sum sworn to does not exceed three hundred pounds, must be worth double the sum sworn to; and in cases above three hundred pounds, must be worth three hundred pounds more than the sum sworn to, over and above their just debts, and every other sum for which they are Bail.

6th. That the affidavit of justification shall be according to the following form; and may be made before a Judge or a Commissioner of this Court for taking affidavits.

Form of Affidavit.

In the Supreme Court,
Between, etc.

A. B. and C. D., Bail for the Defendant in this cause, severally make oath and say, and first this Deponent, A. B., for himself saith, that he is a Housekeeper, (*or Freeholder, as the case may be*) residing at (*describing particularly the place of residence*,) that he is possessed of property to the amount of £—— (*double the amount of the sum sworn to, if under £300, and if above £300, the amount of the sum sworn to, and £300 added thereto*) over and above all his just debts, (*if Bail in any other action add*) and every other sum for which he is now Bail—(*if not Bail in any other action, add*) that he is not Bail for any Defendant except in this action; that this Deponent's property to the amount of the said sum of £ ——, (*and if Bail in any other action*, "and of all other sums for which he is now Bail as aforesaid") consists of real property of the value of £ ——, and of personal property of the value of £ ——, (*as the case may be*) and this Deponent, C. D., for himself saith (*as before*.)

Sworn, etc.

7th. That if the Notice of Bail shall be accompanied by such an affidavit of justification, and the Plaintiff afterwards except to such Bail, he shall, if such Bail are allowed, pay the costs of justification; and, if such Bail are rejected, the Defendant shall pay the costs of opposition, unless the Court, or a Judge, shall otherwise order.

8th. That, in cases of exception, when Bail have duly justified and been allowed, and a Rule for an allowance has been entered in Court, or an order therefor made by a Judge, and a copy of such rule or order has been served on the Plaintiff's Attorney, the Bail shall be deemed perfected; and the Attorney who puts in the Bail shall forthwith obtain the Bail-piece from the Judge, with whom it lies, and file the same with the Clerk.

9th. That if the Plaintiff does not except against the Bail, within twenty days after service of notice of Bail, the Bail shall, in like manner, be deemed perfected; and the Attorney who puts in the Bail, shall forthwith, after the expiration of the said twenty days, obtain the Bail-piece from the Judge, and file the same with the Clerk.

10th. That, in cases of render in discharge of Bail, the Clerk, upon production of a certificate of the Sheriff, to whose custody the Defendant has been committed, that such Defendant is in his custody, together with an affidavit of the service of notice of render upon the Plaintiff's Attorney, shall indorse upon the Bail-piece an EXONERETUR, in the words following: "The Bail within named are exonerated;" and shall set down the day of the month and year of his so doing, and sign his name thereto; and such certificate and affidavit shall thereupon be filed with the Bail-piece.

11th. That hereafter proceedings against Bail, in an action upon the recognizance, shall not cease, as provided for in the rule of this Court of Michaelmas Term, one thousand eight hundred and twenty-five, without the costs incurred in such action up to the time of notice of render being first paid.

12th. That any former Rules of this Court, inconsistent with any of these present Rules, relating to Bail, shall be hereafter of no effect.

13th. That any Attorney, who shall neglect to transmit, or to file the Bail-piece, as the case may be, according to the foregoing Rules, shall be deemed to be in contempt of the Court for disobedience to its rules.

Michaelmas Term, 5 William 4, 1834.

121—*Ordered*, That it shall be deemed irregular to put in Bail before a Commissioner, in any parish or city in the Province, in which one or more of the Judges of this Court may reside, unless at times when such Judge or Judges may be absent from their place of residence; and further, that always, during the sitting of the Court in Term time, it shall be irregular to put in Bail before a Commissioner, in the Parish of Fredericton, in the County of York; and that no Judge do receive any Bail-piece, transmitted to him, in which the Bail may have been entered contrary to this Rule.

SPECIAL CASES.

See Demurrers and Special Cases, No. 41.

SPECIAL CONSENT RULE.

See No. 103.

SPECIAL AND CROWN PAPER.

Hilary Term, 7 George 4, 1826.

122—*Ordered*, That the Clerk of the Crown do keep a paper to be called the Crown paper, in which shall be entered demurrers, and other special matters for argument on the Crown side; and that the Clerk of the Pleas do in like manner keep a paper, to be called the Special paper, in which shall be entered all demurrers, and other special matters, for argument on the Plea side: such entries to stand on such papers respectively, in the order in which they may be made, with the said respective Clerks; and that all the matters contained in the said papers shall come on to be argued on the *Monday in the second week* in each term, in the order in which they are entered, always beginning with the Crown paper.

Michaelmas Term, 6 William 4, 1835.

123—*It is Ordered*, That the matters contained in the Crown Paper and Special Paper, respectively, shall come on to be argued on the *second day* in each term, any former rule to the contrary notwithstanding.

See Nos. 66, 67, 68.

STUDENTS AND ATTORNEYS—EXAMINATION OF—BY WHOM.

Michaelmas Term, 11 Victoria, 1847.

124—*It is Ordered*, That the Examination of persons desirous of becoming Students, or being admitted as Attorneys of this Court, shall be conducted by the Benchers of the Barristers' Society, as provided for by the said Rules and Regulations; and that no person be entered as a Student, or sworn and enrolled as an Attorney of this Court, or admitted as a Barrister, unless he produce a certificate to be granted pursuant to the said Rules: Provided that this order do not extend to Barristers from other parts of Her Majesty's Dominions, applying to be admitted Barristers here; and provided also, that nothing herein contained shall extend or be construed to impair or interfere with the general superintending power and authority of this Court over all or any of the matters aforesaid.

It is further Ordered, That such of the Rules and Orders of this Court as are inconsistent with the said Rules and Regulations of the Barristers' Society, or so far as they regulate matters therein provided for, (excepting as aforesaid,) be suspended until the further order of the Court in the premises.

See Attorneys, Barristers, etc.

SUBPŒNA.

Michaelmas Term, 6 William 4, 183[illegible]

125—*It is Ordered*, That the names of any number of Witnesses may be put in one Writ of Subpœna.

Trinity Term, 12 Victoria, 1849.

Subpœna to prove Execution of Deeds in order to be Registered.

126—*Whereas* by the Act of Assembly 10th Victoria, cap. 42, it is enacted, "that process of Subpœna may be issued out of the Supreme Court of Judicature as in ordinary cases, (and in such form as the said Court may by general rule or order prescribe,) to compel the attendance of any witness, or the production of any conveyance or instrument for the due proof thereof, in order to be registered agreeably to the provisions of this Act; and such Court shall have the like power to punish disobedience to any such Subpœna, in the same manner and to the same extent as in other cases; provided that no such witness shall be compelled to produce, under such Subpœna, any writing or other document that he would not be compelled to produce on a trial:" *It is Ordered*, That the several processes of Subpœna to be used under and in pursuance of the above recited Act, shall be in the form or to the effect following:—

No. 1.—Subpœna ad Testificandum.

Victoria, by the Grace of God, of the United Kingdom of Great Britain and Ireland, Queen, Defender of the Faith.

To A. B., [*names of the witness or witnesses*] Greeting:—

We command you that, laying aside all and singular business and excuses, you and every of you be and appear in your proper persons before [*name and description of the Court, Judge, or other Officer before whom proof is to be made,*] at [*the place or office where proof is to be made,*] on —— the —— day of ——, at —— of the clock in the ——noon of the same day, to testify all and singular those things which you or either of you know concerning the execution of a certain [*describe the conveyance or instrument to be proved,*] purporting to be made between [*the parties to the deed or instrument,*] and bearing date the —— day of ——, A. D. 18 , to which [*deed or instrument*] you and each of you were severally a subscribing witness or witnesses; and further to prove the execution of the said —— *, in order that the same may be duly registered according to the provisions of the Act of Assembly in such case made and provided; and this you or any of you shall in no wise omit, under the penalty upon each of you of one hundred pounds.—Witness —— Esquire, at Fredericton, the —— day of ——, in the —— year of our Reign.

No. 2.—Subpœna duces tecum.

[*The same as the above to the asterisk* *, *then thus*]—and also that you bring with you, and produce at the time and place aforesaid, the said [*describe the deed or instrument*] hereinbefore mentioned and described, in order that the same may be duly registered, etc. [*conclude as in the preceding form.*]

SUMMARY ACTION.

Trinity Term, 5 William 4, 1834.

127—1st. *It is Ordered*, That the Writ in Summary Actions shall be on Parchment, according to the usage in this Court in other actions.

2nd. That in every action which has not been agreed, and in which it is intended to proceed, the Plaintiff's Attorney shall file the Writ, and enter the cause at the term in which the Writ is returnable, and shall make a Docket of such causes, and deliver the same to the Clerk, and pay the fees in like manner as in other actions.

3rd. That in actions to be tried at Nisi Prius, the Writ and Plea shall be delivered from the files of this Court to the Plaintiff's Attorney, and shall form the record, and be filed as such, at the Court of Nisi Prius.

4th. That the result of trials at Nisi Prius shall be entered in a brief and summary form, according to the circumstances of each case, and endorsed on the Writ, or annexed thereto, in the nature of a Postea, and returned by the Clerk of the Circuits accordingly.

5th. That the Clerk of this Court shall not, in any case, sign final Judgment, unless the Writ be on file in his office; and in every Memorandum of Judgment, there shall be reference made to such Writ so on file.

Michaelmas Term, 2 Victoria, 1838.

128—*Ordered*, That in future, in Summary Actions tried at Nisi Prius, a copy of the plea, instead of the original plea, may be filed in the Court of Nisi Prius as a part of the record.

SURVIVING PARTIES.

Trinity Term, 22 Victoria, 1859.

129—In summary causes, when one of the several plaintiffs or defendants shall happen to die after the commencement of the action, the subsequent proceedings shall be in the name of or against the surviving plaintiff or plaintiffs, or defendant or defendants, as the case may be; describing him or them respectively, as survivor or survivors of A. B., who hath died since the commencement of this suit, and who was a joint plaintiff or defendant therein.

TAXATION OF COSTS.

See Bill and Taxation.

TRIAL.

See New Trial.

TRIALS AT NISI PRIUS.

Hilary Term, 7 George 4, 1826.

130—In order to prevent inconvenience and delay in the trial of causes at Nisi Prius.

1st. *It is Ordered*, That no record of Nisi Prius shall be received at any Circuit Court in any County in this Province, unless the same shall be delivered, to be entered with the Clerk of the Circuits, at or before the opening of the Court, on the first day of the sittings, unless the Judge, in his discretion, under special circumstances, shall allow the Clerk to receive a Record, and enter the cause for trial after the time above limited; and that every cause shall be tried in the order in which it shall be so entered, beginning with *Remanets*, unless it shall be made out to the satisfaction of the Judge, in open Court, that there is reasonable cause to the contrary, who thereupon may make such order for the trial of the cause so to be put off, as to him shall seem just.

2nd. *Ordered*, That a list of all the causes, entered as aforesaid, shall be made by the Clerk of the Circuits, and by him delivered to the Judge as soon as practicable after the entry so made.

Michaelmas Term, 36 Victoria, 1872.

131—*It is Ordered*, That the Clerks of the Circuits shall not hereafter enter any cause on the Docket at Nisi Prius, unless the Nisi Prius Record is regularly and properly made up, and duly filed with the Clerk at the time of the entry, and that after being so filed, no such Record shall be altered or taken off the files during the Circuit without leave of the Court.

See Rule 79.

TRIAL BY RECORD.

Trinity Term, 3 Victoria, 1840.

132—*It is Ordered*, That in any case of trial by the Record, it shall be sufficient for the party to make up and deliver to the Chief Justice one paper book, instead of delivering books to all the Judges, unless the Court should otherwise order in any particular case.

Trinity Term, 9 Victoria, 1846.

133—*Ordered*, That in future all cases of trial by the record be entered upon a separate paper, to be called the "Record Trial Docket," which shall be taken up immediately after the motion paper is concluded; the entries to be made in open Court on the first day of each term, and to stand in the Docket in the order in which they may be made, unless the Court should otherwise direct; and that eight days' notice be given of all such trials by the record.

Hilary Term, 13 Victoria, 1850.

134—*It is Ordered*, That if the party who may have given the Notice of Trial by the Record, pursuant to the Rule of Trinity Term, 9th Victoria, shall not enter the same for Trial on the first day of Term, as required by such Rule, the other party may move to enter the same for Trial on the second day of Term, and proceed to trial at such time as the Court may thereupon appoint, on delivering to the Chief Justice a Paper Book, in case such Book should not already have been delivered.

It is further Ordered, That either party may give Notice of Trial by the Record, and enter the same pursuant to the Rule of Trinity Term, 9th Victoria—but that if Notice be given by both parties, the Notice of the party seeking to perfect the Record shall have precedence, provided he duly enter the case, and deliver the Paper Book to the Chief Justice.

WARRANTS OF ATTORNEY.

See Awards and Warrants.

WARRANT OF ATTORNEY TO CONFESS JUDGMENT.

See No. 29.

WITNESSES — EXAMINATION OF.

See No. 52.

WRITS.

See Records, etc.

WRITS OF ASSISTANCE.

Hilary Term, 59 George 3, 1819.

135—*It is Ordered*, That the Writs of assistance to the Officers of His Majesty's Customs in this Province, do issue out of this Court, from time to time, according to the practice of the Exchequer in England.

WRITS OF ATTACHMENT.

Trinity Term, 23 Victoria, 1860.

136—Where Writs of Attachment or other Writs are issued out of the Crown Office upon a Rule of Court therefor, or by order of a Judge, the Clerk shall at the time of signing and sealing the Writ, put at the foot thereof, or indorse thereon, a memorandum in the form following, or to that effect, as the case may be:—

"By Rule of Court of ——— Term, A. D. 18—," *or* "By Order of the Chief Justice or Mr. Justice ——, dated ——, filed in the Crown Office.

See No. 13.

WRITS OF ERROR.

Trinity Term, 8 George 4, 1827.

137—*It is Ordered*, That henceforth no Writ of Error *Coram Nobis* shall be allowed but in open Court; and then on affidavit of the Error to be assigned.

WRITS OF SCIRE FACIAS.

Hilary Term, 9 George 4, 1828.

138—*It is Ordered*, That from henceforth all Defendants in Scire Facias have twenty days to appear from the return day of the Scire Facias; and that, where a Defendant appears in Scire Facias, there shall be the like time for pleading as in other actions in this Court.

Hilary Term, 2 Victoria, 1839.

139—*Ordered*, That the Writ of *Scire Facias* to be issued under the Act of Assembly, 26 Geo. 3, c. 24, shall be in the form following, or to that effect; adding in the body of the same any special matter which in particular cases may be deemed requisite.

Victoria, etc. To the Sheriff of Greeting:

Whereas A. B., lately in our Court before us at Fredericton, impleaded C. D. and E. F. in a plea of , (the said C. D. having been duly taken and brought into Court by virtue of process issued in the said suit against the said C. D. and E. F., and the said E. F. not having been taken and brought into Court by virtue of such process) and did afterwards by the judgment of the same Court recover as well against the said E. F. as the said C. D., [*state the recovery*] in the same manner as if they had both been taken and brought into Court, pursuant to the Act of Assembly in such case made and provided, whereof the said C. D. and E. F. are convicted as by the record and proceedings thereof still remaining in our same Court manifestly appear.

And now on behalf of the said A. B. in our same Court, we are informed that although judgment be thereupon given, yet satisfaction of the [debt and] damages aforesaid still remains to be made to him; and he is desirous of executing an Execution for such [debt and] damages against the body, or the lands or goods, the sole property of the said E. F., whereof the said A. B. hath humbly besought us to provide him a proper remedy in this behalf: And we being willing that what is just in this behalf should be done, command you that by honest and lawful men of your Bailiwick, you make known to the said E. F., that he be before us at Fredericton, on to shew if he has or knows of any thing to say for himself, why the said A. B. ought not to have execution for the [debt and] damages aforesaid, to be executed against the body or the lands or goods, the sole property of him, the said E. F., according to the force, form and effect of the said recovery, and pursuant to the said Act of Assembly in such case made and provided, if it shall seem expedient for him so to do; and further to do and receive what our said Court before us shall then and there consider of him in this behalf; and have you there the names of those by whom you shall so make known to him, and this Writ. Witness, etc.

Easter Term, 34 Victoria, 1870.

Return of Moneys Paid.

140—*Ordered*, That the Clerk in Equity do, on the first day of each Term, furnish for the information of the Judges and any parties interested, a detailed return of all moneys in the Bank of New Brunswick, or elsewhere, paid in in this Court, or in the Court in Equity, or by direction of either, with the name of the cause, the amount paid in each cause, whether paid in in every case to the credit of the specific cause, or how otherwise; the date of payment and the amount of increase or interest (if any) in each case, and the amount (if any) drawn out in each cause, with the date or respective dates thereof, and by what authority drawn: a copy of which return shall be entered at length in the Minutes of the Term.

Michaelmas Term, 35 Victoria, 1871.

Moneys—Deposit Place.

141—1st. *It is Ordered*, That hereafter all moneys paid into the Supreme Court, or the Supreme Court in Equity, shall, unless otherwise specially ordered, be paid into the Bank of New Brunswick to the credit of the Supreme Court, or the Supreme Court in Equity, and to the credit of the particular cause or matter in which the same shall be paid in; and a deposit receipt thereof shall be forthwith delivered to the Clerk of the Pleas or Clerk in Equity, as the case may be; and no money shall be considered as properly paid in till such deposit receipt is so filed.

2nd. No moneys paid into Court shall be drawn out except by order of the Court, or of a Judge thereof, to be signed by the Clerk and countersigned by the presiding Judge of the Court, or the Judge who make the same; and no such order shall be made unless it be first certified to the Court or Judge, by the Clerk, that such money has been duly deposited and the deposit receipt filed and entered.

3rd. The Clerk of the Pleas and Clerk in Equity shall keep Books, in which such receipts shall be entered immediately on the same being filed with him; and such Books shall be open to public inspection at all reasonable times.

www.ingramcontent.com/pod-product-compliance
Lightning Source LLC
Chambersburg PA
CBHW032004110726
47901CB00004B/968
* 9 7 8 3 7 4 1 1 9 4 6 4 1 *